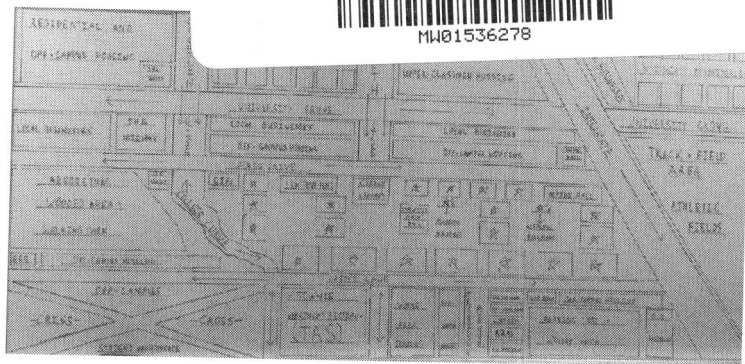

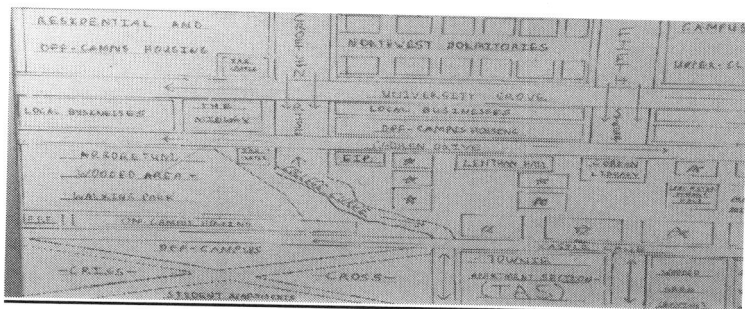

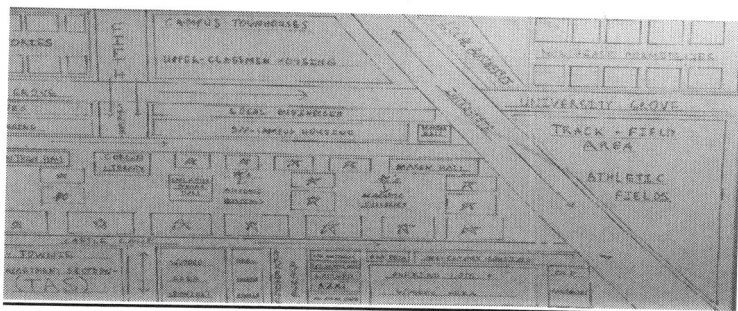

Prologue: One More Night

One car ride later and everything had changed for Jake Raley. The landscape hurtled by as he stared gloomily out the window.

He hadn't been relishing today's events. The more he thought it over, the more he realized just how terrified he was.

His saving grace, and perhaps the only thing keeping him from a breakdown, was that when they finally got to their destination, he wouldn't be alone. But even that was little comfort now with the future so close.

Jake looked away from the window to face his father at the wheel. His dad seemed to be entirely indifferent on today's events. That only fueled Jake's already palpable anxiety.

But there was no fighting it now. The day was here.

Jake would never live it down if he backed out. He doubted he even *could* back down now. Today the die was cast...and he was completely fucked.

Reaching over from his comfortable position in the passenger's seat, Jake turned up the radio dial in an attempt to lose himself in the music pouring out. Thankfully, his dad had the same taste in music for the most part. It was much better than with his mom who opted for the boring, slow shit.

Letting the music envelop him, Jake leaned back in his seat to get the full force of the heat now blasting at him. It always drove him crazy that he couldn't get warm when he was so tense.

The winter in upstate Ohio was no help in that regard. Fortunately, Jake had had nineteen years to acquire a taste for it. And he still hated it. Thankfully, that was a matter on which his dad was not indifferent.

"Snow is such a pain in the ass," Jake announced, talking to no one in particular.

"Can't really argue with that" his dad responded.

"Refresh my memory D, why exactly do we live in Ohio?"

"Trust me, you don't want to live anywhere below sea level. And you definitely don't want your ass to be anywhere near a place that gets any form of natural disaster." Jake's dad rattled it off as if he'd practiced that response in particular a thousand times on the off chance his son would ask that question. That probably wasn't far from the truth.

A major snowstorm had hit a few days earlier. Since it was still so damn cold, none of the snow had melted but fortunately the snowplows had done their job and cleared the roads. *This time.*

After all the fussing around and last minute packing, which had probably still resulted in him leaving *something* important behind at home, he was finally on his way…to college. Or rather, he was finally transferring *into* college.

Being a transfer student meant two things to Jake. First, instead of coming to school in the fall like most every other undergraduate out there, he was starting during the winter. Second, making friends was going to be even more difficult because as he'd heard from many sources, college students tended to make most of their friends during those precious first few weeks of the fall. With that on his mind, now fresher than ever, the anxiety took hold again.

He'd also heard that college was going to encompass the best times in his life more than once. It got increasingly annoying the more he heard it.

Jake had never seen a need for the abrupt change of scenery that was college. He was already having the time of his life with his friends back home. That was due partially to the parties he'd been throwing at his house. The place that everybody now called 'Raley's Ring'. The memories he had of those days and nights tried their hardest to get him to smile but it was no use. The anxiety he felt won out, as it always did.

Now he was leaving practically everything and everyone he'd ever known behind, all in the name of some distant unknown.

Jake didn't even know what he wanted his major to be yet.

What am I gonna do?

Chapter 1

It was like any other Bids night in his memory.

Jeff Chester was staring at the night sky feeling a firm buzz. He slowly took another drag of his cigarette before prying his eyes away from the stars to look at the new fuck across the way. He wasn't much to look at. *I can't believe this is the group of pledges I got fucked with.*

'New fucks' were how the brothers of Alpha Zeta Xi (AZXi) referred to their pledges after bids were extended and handed out on the Saturday of 'Bids'. That day always fell on a Saturday of the school's choosing just so everything was uniform and they could regulate the timeline of pledging for everyone simultaneously. *It's all just more bullshit.*

In the middle of every Bids celebration the brothers of AZXi went to the Rho Beta house (Betas) to drink and celebrate with them. The parking lot of the Beta sorority house looped in a 'U' formation around the building itself. Calling it a house didn't exactly feel right but they were in Gladen Hills, not the fucking suburbs. Most of the 'houses' around here were anything but. Jeff supposed the proper term for most of the structures would've been slums. Of course the Beta house was actually an old hotel from back when Gladen Hills was a more respectable town. The thing had been converted to student housing like so many other buildings on the outskirts of campus.

God this place sucks. If the National wasn't right here I'd condemn this whole fucking corner and be better off.

Overall the town wasn't much to look at, but it was home.

The National was by far the most important piece of the puzzle that was Gladen Hills. It was the place where all the Alpha Zeta Xis went to drink. And that kind of thing happened every night of the week. *Might as well be home.*

The two Jeff was staring at were at the end of the Beta driveway. And they both had a lot to learn. One was excused because he wasn't a brother yet, just another new fuck. The other was Jared McAlpin. Maturity and seriousness in general escaped him.

Jeff didn't consider the majority of his brothers to be all that impressive, and Jared was no exception. But that was only because most of them hadn't sacrificed the way he had. What was worse, most of them didn't even give a fuck about what he'd done. More often than not the whole idea just made him angry.

Thinking about that now would only banish the buzz he was just starting to enjoy. He shrugged it off and took one final drag off his cigarette before tossing it to the ground, making sure to step on it. The last thing he needed was some Beta chick complaining about it when he was trying to get hammered. He'd heard enough bitching tonight from Dana because he was booked up for the weekend.

What the fuck does she expect me to do? This is Bids weekend for Christ's sake. During Bids every Greek in town was interested in one thing and one thing only: getting wasted. That wasn't the material the school's administration was looking to advertise either. *Fuck them.*

Jeff continued staring at the two guys, one ⸸
brother. Now they were standing behind one of the c⸸
new fuck hunched over vomiting. *Poor bastard is alread⸸*
struggling. He has no idea what he's in for.

Shaking his head, Jeff finished drinking his beer before
moving to the end of the parking lot to get a good look at Arkridge
Avenue. If things held to pattern, there wouldn't be that many
people out tonight, at least not right now. Most in the Greek
Circle were smart enough to know that getting hammered behind
closed doors was preferable to getting another fuckin' open
container ticket from bastard cops who had nothing better to do.
And non-Greeks knew better than to go out on Bids altogether
because it was fucking chaos at the bars between the members
and their pledges who actually made it there.

Tonight was no different. There wasn't a soul on Arkridge
Avenue in either direction. Now was the time where new fucks all
across campus were being initiated into the Greek Circle with a
night of binge drinking and whatever other illegal substance could
be consumed within reason…most of the time.

Looking both ways again, mostly just because he was
getting drunker than he realized, Jeff turned around to walk inside.
He stopped mid-turn to see the two guys heading toward the same
door. Jared and the new fuck didn't pay much attention to him,
maybe because they didn't see him, probably because they were
more hammered than he was. The pair hobbled toward the
entrance of the Beta house and walked in. Jeff just shook his head.
Not everyone can drink like I can.

Up until now Jeff had become accustomed to the silence
of the night since he'd been outside alone. But as he neared the
doorway he was drawn in by the loud music and screams coming
from within.

Now feeling very good, he walked through the doors. He
strutted through the entrance hallway like he was the king of
Gladen Hills.

Jeff immediately spotted a drunken Calvin Gretman being
led upstairs by his impossibly hot girlfriend Jennifer. *Good.*
Gretman doesn't get laid enough; why not let his porn-star girl ride
him like the world's about to end.

Not that he was jealous. He had Dana. She was also
insanely hot by his standards, of which he actually had some.
That was more than he could say for half his brothers. *It's not their*
fault. Hot girls who knew they were tended to skew more in the

nt. Thankfully, he hadn't run into that
loved her, and that was good enough for

ward the hallway, he realized the new
where to be seen. In fact, no brother was
on now, only random Rho Beta sisters
s conversations. Jeff shook his head in
disgust. *I wish I could bitch-slap the brother who thought it was a
good idea to make these girls our sister sorority.*

If it were up to Jeff the Alpha Zeta Xis would never party
with the Rho Betas. Changing their sister sorority would've been
first on the list if he was social chair like Guapo, but there was no
fixing it now. It was just another of the accepted rules of the
Greek Circle. Every single organization was already matched up
with a sibling and that's where Bids was spent, every single
semester. Most of their 'rules' and choices were relics of an era
Jeff didn't particularly care about, mostly because that was before
AZXi's time, back when the Kappa Nus and Alpha Kappas were
the only games in town.

AZXi was a relatively young frat, which was what had
drawn Jeff when he went through the Rush process a few years
ago. Whereas some of the frats on campus were littered with high
standing traditions and rules, AZXi was young enough where Jeff's
era would be making their traditions and rules. Hopefully what
his era did would far outlast any of their own time at the school.
Unless you called yourself 'Guapo' and never planned on
graduating.

Just then Jeff heard something interesting. He moved as
close to the sounds as possible without drawing attention from the
myriad girls standing around. He knew if the Betas saw what he
thought was going on, things may or may not end well. He
wanted to help what he thought was happening with Jared and the
new fuck but couldn't risk it with how many eyes were on him.
Maybe there's hope for those two dumbasses yet.

Jeff knew the new fuck was hammered and having a great
time even if he didn't realize the significance of what he was
doing behind one of the closed doors in that long hallway. *If I'd
followed them in here I could be helping instead of stuck out here
with my dick in my hand.* Disappointed as he was, Jeff hoped
Jared was keeping a close eye on the new fuck. Every brother
knew that girls' chapter rooms were off limits and the last thing
AZXi needed was trouble from one of the bigger sororities on

campus. Still, that didn't make Jeff stop what he guessed was taking place in the Rho Beta chapter room, whichever one it was. He had standards after all.

Snapping himself out of the hazy memory was more effort than it should've been. Four weeks ago on Bids he was standing around the same chicks thinking the same thing: *why the fuck is Rho Beta our sister sorority?*

Having ninety or so sisters in your organization did two things outright. First, it made the parties extremely crowded *when* everybody showed up. Second, it tended to fray the relationships and inner-workings of the entire group.

Jeff couldn't fathom how AZXi would even function if they had that many actives. They had twenty-five brothers right now, not counting the four miserable pledges. It was ideal because it kept cliques from forming within the frat. There weren't enough people to have everyone divided into sub-groups. *Who would join an organization when you can't even remember everyone's fucking name?*

That wasn't the point of brotherhood. Every one of the ill-conceived bastards in AZXi was someone Jeff cared about. Granted he spent more time with some than with others but there was a respect level for every one despite his misgivings. They lived together. They drank together. They pledged together.

That was what the school administration could never understand. A difficult pledge process bonded people. Not only did it allow the pledges to become closer with each other, it gave them the opportunity to earn the respect of every member. Rather than allowing for that personal growth, the administration branded it hazing. According to them, having the pledges walk in a straight line was illegal. The penalties for such things were extreme.

"Come on bro, line 'em up! Flip cup baby!" Jared shouted to no one in particular. Although it could've qualified as speaking to Jeff, he could never tell with the kid. Jared tended to get over-excited about most things, no matter how insignificant.

Before following along with the others surrounding the table Jeff looked around the AZXi basement. The fog machine they sometimes used wasn't in action tonight yet a thin layer of mist or in this case smoke and humidity filled the air. It made it somewhat difficult to make out the smaller things on the opposite side of the one room basement. Girls were debating pop stars' talents or texting on their phones while the guys were mostly surrounding the various drinking game tables, eagerly awaiting the next round of their specific event.

Jeff quickly got his game face on as he lined up his full cup to the girl across the table that would be his direct opponent. The entire opposing team was made up of Betas…and then Calvin standing at the far end next to Jennifer, as usual. Not surprisingly, Jeff's opponent didn't have a full cup. In fact hers barely had enough to fill a shot glass. *Fuckin' typical.*

In flip cup, the lower the amount of alcohol a person had in their cup the quicker they could drink it and get to flipping their cup to get to the next person in line. That might suggest that only filling each cup a little would be the way to go but Jeff never saw it that way. He played these kinds of games to get fucked up, not necessarily win although that was preferred. That's why he always filled his beer, to ensure he had a good time regardless.

Jeff's team got its ass kicked but he at least got to slam his entire beer before it ended. That was victory enough for him. *At least I'm still drinking, fuck the win.*

As everyone at the table refilled their cups Jeff's mind wandered yet again. It began looking more and more like he'd need something a little stronger than alcohol to get through the night. Tonight was important. It was a big night for the pledges and that meant it was a big night for him. He was the pledge-master in charge of that motley crew of four.

He surveyed the basement that always doubled as the AZXi party area and found both parts of the equation he was looking for: Eric Saren at the beer pong table and Dylan Edwards stumbling in, likely having just pissed. *That'll work.*

Looking from one to the other, he checked his phone for the time. Like most things in the AZXi house, the clock on the wall wasn't functional. It was just another of the many things on a long list needing repair in their house. The time read half past eleven, which meant the Betas would be leaving soon and they could get the night going. But not before Jeff and Dylan got down to some business first.

****

Again Jake's mind stumbled onto the memory of being dropped off at school. A lot had changed since that day a year ago.

Not all the changes were for the better but at least some were. One of the best things was sitting right beside him on the couch in his suite's common room. And she went by the name of Kelly Frazer. Jake had been fortunate enough to meet her shortly after coming to Gladen Hills last spring. He'd instantly been attracted to everything about her. She could do no wrong in his eyes.

Unfortunately, Kelly also had a boyfriend at the time that felt much the same way. That situation had thrown some instant turmoil into his college experience. But Jake was her boyfriend now, and he was extremely happy. She was the one thing holding him together during these last few weeks.

He'd been naïve enough to accept a bid to pledge a frat not even knowing the full extent of what that acceptance meant. His cousins had strong feelings on the matter as the rest of his family likely would've had he had the balls to actually tell any of them.

When it came to an important choice, Jake said fuck everyone else and made an uninformed decision…as usual.

In retrospect, Jake was constantly kicking himself for not listening to the people he was closest to. They tended to see things rationally, which usually made the right choices easier to see. Jake's main problem was that he couldn't see the right choice beyond his passion and strong emotions.

Such was the case back when he was having issues with his high school girlfriend Alison. They'd been dating on and off for two years while his cousins, who doubled as the siblings he didn't have, consistently told him to end it before things got *really* bad. Jake would routinely ignore their rationales, however much sense they made, because in his mind he was in love. And what a spectacular idiot he was. She cheated on him repeatedly. He ended it the moment he found out and swore it wouldn't happen again.

Now it was two years later and he was happier than ever. He was absolutely sure that he was never really in love with Alison because now he knew what love really felt like. Jake had never felt that way before Kelly. They'd only been together for roughly a year but he was sure it was real.

While Kelly worked on her calculus homework in Jake's lap he stared out the window at the snow-covered ground, wondering exactly how cold it was out there. He knew he'd soon have to be outside and wondered if he was wearing enough warm clothing. Of course at these times, the clothing had to be more functional than anything else. Not functional for insulation's sake either, more so for physical strain. *God knows I'll be doing a lot of that tonight.*

Except for his mostly white sneakers, which he always preferred, Jake was dressed in all black. It was at least comfortable which helped. He'd learned too late in the pledge process that he'd need to have some form of comfort during those lengthier sessions the brothers insisted on putting him through.

Jake wasn't even supposed to be with Kelly right now. He should've been sitting in the basement quad area of the dorm with his pledge brothers waiting for the inevitable call that would send them to Hell. But after barely seeing her all week, he'd decided to say 'fuck it'.

Just sitting here with her while she did her math was enough to calm his nerves. Those same nerves he remembered becoming so frayed the day his dad had driven him to Gladen Hills a year ago. He couldn't fault anyone but himself. Nobody had made him accept the bid to pledge a frat, and certainly no one had kept him from quitting. *This is all on you dumbass.*

He took one more look down at Kelly. Even in her sweats and tank top she was still the sexiest girl on campus. If he weren't pledging, his night would consist of watching a movie with her and following that up with some incredible sex. That was one thing leaps and bounds better here than in high school.

Given that most of the guys in Gladen Hills who joined frats did so to get laid, Jake wondered again why he wanted to enter the Greek Circle in the first place. He was already getting that much from an extremely hot girl… and regularly.

How the fuck did you get into this?

Jake stumbled into the Blue Hold dining hall on the Northeast end of the campus, still feeling the dizzying effects of last night. He practically forgot why he was going into the building at the ridiculously early hour of half past eleven in the morning. God knew he should still be sleeping, but as happened frequently with a drunken college student, plans were made the previous night that couldn't be undone. Actually they could be, but the earlier food was taken in, the earlier recovery could begin. And that was a necessity.

Last night he'd convinced one of his good friends they should have breakfast to talk about some things. His buddy Dan Scribner was a salt of the earth type. He didn't have much time to hang around and bullshit because he was constantly working on his family's farm twenty minutes outside Gladen Hills. Jake considered that an inconvenience because Scribner was one of those friends that he could talk to about anything, much like his cousins. However, for today's particular topic, Scribner would be a better authority.

Jake felt his phone vibrating in his pocket after about ten seconds of it going off. Talking was tough right now. "Yo" was the sole word he could speak.

He listened intently to what his friend said before hanging up.

Scribner was right where he said he'd be, sitting at a table on the far end by himself looking exactly as Jake felt. A slight smile crept across Jake's face at the notion that someone he knew was suffering as much as he was.

Quickly, Jake grabbed a tray and got some plain pancakes, but only a few. Eating hung-over wasn't enjoyable for him, just necessary.

Despite the fact that they lived in the same suite together, they hadn't walked to the Blue Hold at the same time because as usual, Scribner had to work on the farm this morning even after partying hard the night before. *How the fuck does he do it?*

Once Jake got his food, such as it was, he finally sat down across from his friend.

"Not again, you know this is what I do" Jake said before any criticism came out.

"You know, I wish I did everything so ass-backwards and maybe I wouldn't be fat," Scribner said casually. His high-pitched voice was grating with so extreme a hangover.

He'd never considered Scribner fat. In fact, the most obvious thing about him was his fire colored red hair and beard. Those made him stand out far more than any weight gain ever would. "I'm not even going to comment on that. Talking to a guy about their weight is just weird" Jake replied.

After a few minutes of pointless eating, his friend asked why Jake wanted to talk to him. True to form, Scribner was a down-to-business kind of guy. A hung-over Scribner was even more to the point.

"I wanna join a frat Scribbs" Jake blurted out after finishing a mouthful of pancakes.

"Why the fuck would you do that?" Scribner asked once the initial surprise faded.

"SIMS was the one I was thinking about man" Jake replied, ignoring the question.

After watching Scribner take a large gulp of water that was now running desperately low, he came back with his trademark sarcasm. "Well that settles it. You're clearly still drunk from last night."

"Of course I am Scribbs, but that's not the point" Jake replied with a grin.

"I think it's absolutely the point. Why SIMS though Raley? They're real sketchy and they make their pledges drink...like a lot."

"I was hoping you'd be with me on this. I don't want to do this alone."

"Look man, we've had some great ideas. I mean just look at the Raley's Ring shit for fuck's sake. But frats around here are sketchy, plain and simple. And SIMS is fuckin' bat-shit. There's no chance I'll ever do that." Scribner had a real firm opinion on the matter so it was clear he'd given it at least some thought.

Jake was undeterred and that showed on his face.

"Are you gonna go to Rush anyways?"

"Yeah I think I am" Jake replied tentatively. He never much cared for trying new things alone…or at all really, but Rush was important. It was the doorway into the Greek Circle. It was the time when he could wade into the uncertainty of it all.

"Well keep me posted then."

"Yeah I will…how bad could it be anyway?"

That was it. That was the moment you fucking moron.

If only he could smack the complacent dumbass he had been upside the head, then maybe he wouldn't be feeling so depressed these days.

As if on cue, a knock came on the suite's door. No doubt it was his pledge brother J-Hood, signaling that it was time for them to get to that fucking house. And those were probably their pledge-master's words exactly.

He looked down at Kelly who'd also heard the loud knocking. By the look in her eyes, she also knew just what it meant.

"Sorry babe, I gotta go."

"OK, I'll see you in a few hours" Kelly replied in an appropriately sad fashion.

"Let's hope it's only a few hours."

Another round of knocking hit the door while Jake grabbed his backpack off the floor. He leaned down to give Kelly as deep a kiss as he could on his limited schedule.

Reaching the door, he opened it to find J-Hood standing there, also looking solemn. They didn't speak. There was no need. They both knew what to do. Jake nodded at his pledge brother before leaving his basement suite and closing the door behind him, letting Kelly know he'd left. He only imagined she was as upset about the night's events as him.

The two of them moved past the common area of the north end of the dorm toward the nearest exit. Since they were located on the ground floor, it wasn't terribly far from where they were. Some days that was a good thing. Today, Jake would've gladly taken the extra minute to head out a different exit, if only to piss off the bastards waiting for them at the frat house.

They reached the exit where their other two pledge brothers were waiting for them. William Anthony and Matthew Summers were the final two pieces of the Alpha Epsilon pledge class puzzle. And they looked just as happy as he and J-Hood did.

****

Daniel Scribner always believed that he and his roommate Dukes had a similar sense of humor. That was readily apparent again now with the finding of what they could only describe as the Holy Grail. Dukes had somehow stumbled across an online video of David Hasselhoff eating a cheeseburger.

Admittedly when Scribner first heard about it he wasn't all that impressed with the concept. However, upon seeing the execution he'd had to admit he was wrong. And that gave no shortage of ammunition for Dukes.

They were just walking back from the main floor's computer lounge. Scribner wanted to swing by the RA's desk to tell their other suitemate Derek about the video but he wasn't there. *He must be doing a lap around the building or something.*

"Hey, remember that time you weren't going to watch that awesome video I told you about because you're a pussy?" Dukes blurted it out to the thankfully empty hallway.

There were a number of ways to respond when Dukes was on a sarcasm binge, a few of which Scribner kept on hand for these increasingly common situations. Given that he was relatively tired from the day's activities, he opted for the silent treatment, which was easy and useful.

Dukes had allegedly made it to all of his classes for the first time in a long time that day, which had likely taken a lot out of him. Scribner could guess as much given that when he failed to respond, Dukes didn't press the issue like he would have if he were on top of his game with his usual twelve hours of sleep.

They reached their suite's door and Scribner punched in the code near the handle to release the lock. It didn't matter how tired Dukes was, if Scribner couldn't accomplish even the easiest of tasks like a door code on the first try, he might as well hang a sign out advertising that he wanted to be targeted relentlessly. Unfortunately for Dukes, whatever colorful names the guy was no doubt letting bubble near the surface would have to sit a little longer.

They walked through the door and were greeted by a girl who was lying on the couch with a notebook out. Scribner didn't need to be introduced; he'd met Kelly on a number of occasions through Jake. The girl was hard at work over some awful looking math problems, which Dukes had no problem interrupting. "Good you're here, where's Raley? I've gotta show him this sweet video."

"He already left guys" Kelly responded, sounding sullen as usual.

"Pledging shit again?" Scribner asked.

"You think he'd leave so late for anything else?"

"Other girls maybe?" Dukes blurted out before Scribner could even shake his head. He cracked a grin completely by reaction alone.

"Very funny Simon" Kelly retorted with her usual amount of disdain.

What took him most by surprise about the exchange was her using of Dukes' real name. It *always* did. They'd all grown accustomed to their nicknames by now. These days it was just courtesy.

"Who the fuck is Simon?" Scribner responded, feigning confusion. Kelly simply flashed her usual half-smile, half-grin back at them. It always seemed to give her some kind of sick pleasure when using their real names, like a parent disciplining children.

"I don't suppose you know when he'll be back right?"

Kelly frowned at Scribner. "I don't think he even knows" she bit out with sarcasm and contempt. It likely wasn't directed at him, just the situation.

"Well aren't you just a useless ball of sunshine" Scribner replied without thinking. *All this time with Dukes is starting to fuck with me.* That wasn't to say he thought it wasn't funny, but tact was still a form of art.

"Why don't you try going without sex for weeks when you're actually dating someone and see how that goes Dan."

"After you've made it sound so good...done" Dukes interrupted with all the tact of a freight train.

Well at least now we know she isn't pissed at us...yet. That didn't mean much since Dukes had a way of pushing buttons no matter who the person was.

"Always great talking to you guys," Kelly replied, contempt practically dripping from her mouth.

She walked into Jake's empty dorm room. Lucky for her, and by extension, Scribner and Dukes, Jake's roommate Wayne was *never* in the suite. Usually he was in class, the library, lacrosse practice or his girlfriend's across campus. That meant for all intents and purposes that

Jake had a single…and a hot girlfriend. Despite that, he was basically being ass-raped every night by some frat he was joining. *It's all a wash really.*

    Scribner looked outside the open window to the night-covered campus and remembered that breakfast he'd had with Raley a semester earlier. Had he been a weaker kid, he might've been sucked into the lifestyle his friend was pitching. And he might've rushed and pledged a frat too; likely the one Jake went with. *But I'm not and I didn't.* Knowing as much felt good. And here he stood; inside the dormitory he shared with his friends, wondering what he'd do with the night ahead of him. That was freedom he was in no way ready to give up.

****

    The night was entirely too brisk for Jake's liking, but of all the things to be unhappy about tonight, the cold was a distant fourth. *First has to be pledging, second has to be not getting laid right now, third has to be class tomorrow.* Fourth was right on.

    Jake was running in a line behind his three pledge brothers over the snow-encrusted sidewalk. The house was about a mile away from his dorm, which is why they all usually gathered there. It was the quickest route into Hell.

    In all fairness, it tended not to matter much because when they were called and ordered to the house, it was usually to the tune of a minute or maybe ninety seconds. Even if they were in a car already, they'd be hard pressed to get it started and get to the house *that* quick. *And there's no fucking way I'm going to wait in a car in the winter, heat or no heat.* Thankfully his pledge brothers had agreed with him.

    The problem was that there was no set time they'd be called out at. It could've been at any point between eleven at night and two in the morning. A three-hour window when the frat guys could mind-fuck them into oblivion. And there was never a guarantee of getting called out, although they usually were. *Why pass up a night to fuck with us?*

    Jake had come to Gladen Hills with the hope that these would be the most insane times of his life. It was hard not to after all the shit he'd been spoon-fed from the people he'd talked to before leaving home, not to mention his cousins. In a way, things had been pretty insane but that was because he was so tightly wound now with pledging.

    For twelve thousand a year, the party isn't even close to being worth the cover charge. Jake had been to wilder parties in high school. He'd *thrown* wilder parties in high school so clearly something needed a change.

Papers, tests, and school in general were so far removed from his train of thought that he was going crazy. For him, college to an extent was about learning, but it was also about seeing if he could handle being away from the only home he'd ever known.

Jake wanted to make sure he was doing everything he could to make his college experience memorable. When else would he be surrounded by so many like-minded people in so small a space? Pledging was supposed to help with that. The Greek Circle along with the sports teams led the wildest lives in Gladen Hills.

Jake was athletic and had played soccer in high school but he wasn't willing to put forth that amount of dedication to play at the college level. And sororities obviously weren't an option so that left the frats.

He'd heard all the stigmas before. Frats were all full of stupid people going nowhere; they were only interested in getting fucked up and making idiots of themselves. That was all Jake knew before Gladen Hills. Even he had to admit, based on what he'd seen before Rush, he couldn't find fault in those claims. Yet here he was, running to a house full of those types of people.

Once again, he wondered if he'd made the right choice.

Chapter 2

"That Beta party was kinda weak" Eric blurted out.

"In terms of what exactly Eric?" Calvin countered.

He was slightly taken aback by the use of his actual name as opposed to the nickname 'Biz'. It was a name he'd grown fond of since everyone here had dubbed it on him. "We've had much better parties son," he clarified as Calvin gave him an icy stare.

"You know I'm dating one of them right?" Calvin finally responded normally.

"Yeah but there's at least one hot girl in every sorority. Unless you're talking about the AG's."

"Didn't you fuck some of them?"

"We aren't talking about me Gretman" he responded with a smirk, identifying Calvin by his last name. He looked back at his friend and fraternity brother as a grin started piercing through. "OK OK, there were some low points in my past" he relented. He didn't really care what his brothers thought of the girls he'd slept with. For him at least, it needed to be done at the time it happened, usually due to being blackout drunk.

"Low points huh…as in multiple times? Yikes Biz."

"Just chill son" Eric replied in his usual semi-high-pitched voice he sometimes pulled out if he was drunk enough.

"So you're saying that I'm with *the one* hot Beta then?"

"This is what I'm saying" Eric agreed, happy to switch the conversation.

Calvin smiled back at him, looking particularly proud.

Why not? He probably just finished fucking his amazingly hot girlfriend twenty feet from where we're standing, all in the name of getting to the callout on time. Damn.

Eric trudged his way up the disgustingly steep stairs toward the private bathroom he and his pledge brother Jerry shared. Unfortunately, nobody respected the term 'private' during parties. He was willing to bet that his got more use than the one next to Calvin's room downstairs, which was actually designated as the 'party' bathroom. *God forbid anybody in this house follow the damn rules.* He supposed he'd mention again it at the next meeting this weekend.

Reaching the top of the stairs, he found the bathroom door shut, meaning somebody was inside. That took him by a complete lack of surprise. To be fair it could've been Jerry in there, which would've been fine. But more likely it was either another brother, which would only be semi-fine, *or* it was a Beta sister who had no problem using it because she didn't live here. And that would be *far* from fine.

Given that Eric was a gambling man to the core, he silently gave it even odds that it was a Beta sister or an AZXi brother though he was leaning toward Beta. He figured he might as well hang out in his room while he waited for the unknown culprit.

As he went to open his own bedroom door, he realized he hadn't locked it, or at least it wasn't locked now. *I thought I locked this thing for sure…*

Sure enough, he found his brothers Jeff and Dylan occupying *his* room as if they owned the place. This also didn't surprise Eric because Jeff was the only person he knew that could successfully card his door to get in. Dylan and Kevin were fast approaching that skill level too, which worried him.

Mostly though, Eric knew they'd be in here because Jeff had pulled the same stunt before. Apparently he didn't want any trace of these activities in *his own* room where his girlfriend Dana might catch on. *It takes real skill to keep your drug use from your girlfriend. That's love for sure.*

Eric just stood there in the doorway shaking his head.

Jeff was sitting on Eric's couch watching and waiting for Dylan to finish slicing up the lines of cocaine on Eric's desk.

Just another night at the AZXi house.

"Really guys?" Eric said into the otherwise silent room.

"What? Never seen coke before Biz?"

Dylan didn't even shift in his seat. He was too focused on the task at hand to be bothered by the bullshit conversation. *Can't really blame him for that.*

"I don't know what's worse about this: the fact that this isn't the first time *this week* that there's been coke in my room, or the fact that *I'm* not doing any of it."

Eric realized his mistake as soon as he said it.

Sure enough, Jeff's face lit up like a Christmas tree. "You want any?" he practically stammered with enthusiasm.

Every time. Every damn time.

"No Buttons, you know I don't touch that shit" Eric responded with the same fervor he always had in these situations. Thankfully they were decreasing in frequency.

Eric Saren wasn't into drugs. He didn't smoke cigarettes or pot. And he sure as hell wasn't snorting cocaine off desks. Although a thorough search of his room would now lend itself to the idea that he was an addict.

Jeff's happy face evaporated as quickly as it had appeared, and again, his normal face took shape. The one designed to say not to fuck with him.

Dylan looked up to Eric with dazed yet locked eyes. "This is straight right?"

"Yeah it's fine, just not in my room next time Dills" he replied. He felt like he'd just cancelled Christmas for his younger, drunker brother.

"Nobody comes up here during parties Biz" Jeff added.

"Yeah, except drunken people looking to use the bathroom…you know, like I just did." He said it with such confidence that he could practically picture the chuckles it would've elicited had there been a bigger audience. "Seriously though, we could all get real fucked for doing this."

Eric didn't really think much harm would come from such a minor amount of coke, but alcohol tended to accentuate his nervous tendencies. It didn't help that his name was on the lease for the house, but so was Jeff's...and Calvin's. *And they don't care at all.*

"It's Gladen Hills Biz, far from the real world." The same conviction he'd heard in his own voice seconds before was the same kind he heard in Jeff's now.

"Oh and people don't get in trouble here?" Eric asked rhetorically.

Dylan paused after snorting a line to look at him with the same puzzled face now coming from Jeff.

Eric had to concede. In his nearly three years at school, he'd yet to see *anyone* get fucked for drug or alcohol abuse. *It's actually kinda ridiculous.* He always just chalked it up to the fact that Gladen Hills was a college town and as such, the economy was built on the college. And to be frank, college kids spent a lot more money when they were hammered in some fashion. It was probably naïve to think in such basic terms, but he didn't care enough to invest more thought into it.

After conceding it, Jeff went back to doing his half, which amounted to two lines altogether, the same as Dylan. Eric silently hoped they hadn't done any more before he'd arrived. Again he laid even odds.

"The Betas are gonna be bouncing soon, we gotta get ready to call the pledges."

"Given that I'm the pledge-master, I can't picture myself not knowing that, or you know, anything related to the pledge program," Jeff said sarcastically. "Plus they can't start without me."

"OK then where's Jerry?"

Having finished his half, Dylan was now watching the conversation intently as if it was a heated tennis match. His eyes darted back and forth like the pendulum in a clock.

"How the fuck should I know?" Jeff responded.

"Since he's the assistant pledge-master, I just figured you'd know since like, you know *everything* about the pledge program."

"He's my *assistant*" Jeff replied quickly, really relishing the term. "Meaning he should report to me about *my* program."

Eric shook his head. He'd let Jeff have this one. But that was mostly because he still had to piss really badly.

He turned to head back out toward the bathroom. To his dismay the bathroom was now empty. Now he'd never know who was in there.

His cousins had often warned him about the amount of time he spent gambling but he didn't consider it a problem. Mostly because he was really good at it and he won more often than not.

Upon entering the bathroom he happily noted he would've been right; there was a distinct essence of perfume emanating from the sink. *A Rho Beta chick.*

Re-entering his bedroom afterward, he found Jeff and Dylan largely unmoved. "How do I look?" Jeff asked Dylan after clearing his nose of any excess coke.

"Ugly as ever" Eric interrupted with a grin.

"This coming from the guy that's dry as fuck" Jeff retorted.

Jeff calling him dry was his way of stating that Eric hadn't gotten laid in a while.

Way too long. "Like I told Gretman, we all can't have girlfriends to bang on a regular basis" Eric conceded. It was a flimsy excuse but it worked.

He noted that Dylan was silently nodding his head in agreement. *Like you have trouble getting laid around here Dills. You probably banged out last night.*

Mostly, he figured Dylan was simply lamenting the fact that he wasn't fucking anyone as gorgeous as Jennifer at the moment. It was hard for *anyone* to not be jealous.

"Rumor has it that actually talking to girls helps with getting some" Jeff replied. "Speaking of which, how's your cousin these days?"

Eric frowned. "Why don't you find out yourself Buttons? Although I doubt Dana would appreciate that…or even allow it."

"That's the price you pay for guaranteed pussy Biz" Jeff said, apparently not sensing the cool nature of his comment.

"It might be your price."

"You got a better one? I mean, besides your hand."

Eric had to admit, even a semi-controlling girlfriend like Dana was better than that. "Well played Buttons," he conceded.

Once the upcoming callout ended they could all get to the bars where his dry streak would hopefully end. At least that was his plan. It was always the plan.

Eric rarely went out on Thursday nights because of his Friday class. But his only class tomorrow had been earmarked as a fun one since it was the day before a break. It meant the experiments and problem sets would be easier. Eric could find no fault in going out tonight with that on the docket tomorrow. Productivity was definitely going to be at an all-time low with a nine-day break looming, and apparently his professor was smart enough to pick up on that. *Thank God.*

Calvin and Jennifer entered the room as Eric was about to leave.

"Good thing nobody comes up here though right?" Eric said triumphantly.

"Like *they* count Biz."

"Meaning what exactly Jeff?" Jennifer interrupted.

Calvin didn't seem to even register the semi-insult. Eric noticed he looked like he was completely in his own world, but that didn't stop him from phoning in a question. "Yo Buttons, you calling them out soon or do we have time?"

"For what?"

Eric already had an idea and he was betting that Jeff already knew too. They weren't lucky enough to get confirmation from the source as he was now firmly on the defensive with Jennifer staring daggers straight through him.

"What?" Calvin asked innocently.

"Now your brothers know."

Eric felt it was his brotherly duty to step in. "Um, it's not exactly as if you guys are quiet about it." That got a huge grin from Calvin while Jennifer looked utterly mortified.

Eric reached his hand up in a fist-bumping motion so that Calvin could reciprocate on a job well done. Jennifer forcibly lowered Calvin's hand as he was about to humor Eric with the same gesture. *At least Gretman thought it was funny.*

"You know Eric, Cal told me about your problem. And I don't know that I feel like helping you out with it right about now" Jennifer stated with enough of a smirk to get Eric's full attention. Jennifer was in a huge sorority after all, albeit one that Eric wasn't crazy about. *Just keep those thoughts to yourself.*

"Didn't realize I was that much of a charity case," Eric said with a little self-loathing thrown in for good measure, even if he didn't fully believe it. It would've taken an idiot not to notice Jeff and Calvin stirring from Eric's comment. Ordinarily they would've had a field day with Eric's pity party, helping it along any way they could but tonight neither of them did. Maybe Jeff's mind was on something else but Calvin surely wanted to speed things along so he and Jennifer could get back to his bedroom. Either way, Eric was grateful for the oversight.

"I'll see what I can do," Jennifer said before trailing off.

"I wouldn't worry about it anyways Jen; see Eric's not much of a fan of the Beta..."

"Son!" Eric hastily interrupted. "Just chill and let the girl speak." Calvin's words were admittedly true and he'd heard them countless times from Eric in the past. He'd been thinking it all through the party tonight although he hadn't said anything...yet.

"Just find me at the Midway later. We'll see what's going on," Jennifer offered.

"You've got twenty minutes Gretman!" Jeff shouted to them as the couple walked down the stairs to the main floor.

"I only need ten" Calvin shouted back.

"I wouldn't brag about that!"

Eric shook his head. *Jeff's always gotta have the last word.*

In any event, Calvin was getting laid in a few short minutes and the three of them would be going about their normal evenings. He wondered which one was really having the last word.

"I can't believe he gets to fuck her regularly," Dylan said abruptly.

Eric noticed that Jeff looked somewhat jealous although he'd never admit it.

Eric suddenly snapped out of the daze he'd entered a second ago. And he now remembered why he knew Calvin had just gotten laid. His mind had gone into overdrive about the moments leading up to that revelation. It happened sometimes.

He then mentally slapped himself for mentioning the Beta party wasn't that fun to the guy dating the girl who'd just offered to set him up not twenty minutes ago. His alcohol-addled brain couldn't be trusted. *Why can't I just chill and let it be?*

Eric looked across the Alpha Zeta Xi basement at the cause of his abrupt jump out of the memory.

"I called them a minute ago. They'll be here soon so everybody shut the fuck up and get ready. And get on the music Guapo" Jeff ordered everyone.

He noticed Guapo was already at the DJ booth in the corner of the room even before Jeff had spoken. He wouldn't have been surprised if his brother had grown roots back there. *Damn Guapo.* As usual, he was sipping a beer casually. The guy simply enjoyed a drink as opposed to pounding it quickly like Eric usually did.

Thankfully, there was still plenty of time to slam a beer before the pledges arrived. *I just have to find somebody willing to slam one real quick.*

Eric surveyed the basement and quickly made the obvious assessment that any one of the people standing around him would be down. *Why not get everyone involved?*

****

Jake never liked being the first one in line. It was entirely too much pressure to be the first idiot to enter into the brother's line of sight. It was like being first was some kind of death wish because it earned the first looks of hatred and disdain from the assholes at the house. The back of the line was better by the smallest margin.

The Gladen Hills campus was exceedingly quiet during the weeknights, at least where they were. The dormitories on Northeast were lit up against the night sky by the various lights from the sidewalks and parking lots. The ones that always stood out to Jake, and to everyone else, were the safety lights littering every area of the college. They were bright red and ten feet off the ground, raised by a lean black tower no more than a foot across. Jake never had occasion to press one of the buttons that accompanied the red lights. Apparently doing so would transport campus security to that location, or so he'd been told.

As far as towns went, Gladen Hills was relatively safe. There were more security cars around than the college knew what to do with, and they all seemed to be biding their time. It was as if they were waiting for the next inevitable stupid act from an undergrad that would signal an end to the monotony of a typical day. The only things that went wrong were those caused by students fueled by alcohol, drugs or some combination.

He had to snap himself out of those thoughts as he came across some ice on the sidewalk. He thought he'd heard Will say something about it but he wasn't paying attention. It almost cost him. Thankfully he was able to spot it on his own and only had to slightly stutter step over it.

Will was in the lead, J-Hood right behind him and Matt was right in front of Jake.

They were nearing the end of the fourth week of pledging, which meant they were all knee-deep in shit. But at least they were in it together, for whatever that was worth.

Jake's initial impressions of his pledge brothers had been remarkably spot on. The first time he'd seen Will was at a Rush event. Jake would never forget the visual as long as he lived. Will was standing right near the keg, a spot where he was always very comfortable. He had two full cups of beer in his hands and at the time, Jake thought he was grabbing one for somebody else. Without warning or any nudges from a bystander Will lifted both cups to his face and began pouring the gold liquid to his mouth a couple inches away. While some spilled, he'd been thoroughly amazed that most of the beer had gotten to its destination in Will's stomach. That had been proof enough that it wasn't Will's first time doing that. After finishing both cups at virtually the same time, he crumpled the plastic, threw it on the floor and screamed like a banshee.

He didn't remember exactly what Will was screaming or if it was even English because by that point, Jake was laughing hysterically. He didn't officially meet him until one of the following Rush events and his personality matched the act Jake witnessed prior. He was wild, crazy, sort of full of himself, but hysterical through and through. At least he had been back then.

It was just a shame that Jake hadn't been able to enjoy that aspect of Will at all recently. Not that Will was becoming less entertaining, it was just that Jake was in an entirely different mindset these days than he was when they'd met.

J-Hood on the other hand was of a different variety entirely. Jake had first seen him talking to a girl at the same Rush event as the one he saw Will at for the first time. Except J-Hood was only 'Justin' back then since the nickname hadn't been assigned yet.

The guy was casually drinking a beer, looking around like he couldn't give a fuck. Originally he thought J-Hood was dating the girl nearby because of the way she looked to be just giving it away to him. He instantly pegged J-Hood as somebody that was awesome strictly based on the level of hotness his girlfriend came in at. Of course, he wasn't dating her, because as Jake learned later, he'd just met the damn girl. His initial thoughts that she looked very into him were right on though, as they ended up fucking later that night.

J-Hood wasn't the type to brag about the girls he hooked up with though. He was very subtle about it. If asked, he'd tell you, all while keeping the details to a minimum. That was the polar opposite of Will who'd give you exponentially more detail than you'd ever want or need, essentially providing a play-by-play. There was an interesting balance between the two that Jake believed he fit into.

That left only Matt Summers, whom Jake had seen around a few times prior to ever going to the AZXi house. Jake didn't remember the details of the instances in which he saw the guy because Summers always seemed to be in the background, nothing more than a hazy memory. Jake could've sworn he saw him at multiple places only to find out he wasn't there. Other times he wouldn't see him at all before finding out days later that Summers saw him but didn't say anything. Jake found it all extremely sketchy but he was still a good guy. He didn't cause any trouble with anyone.

His nickname of 'Woodworks' wasn't nearly as popular as J-Hood's was, but it was infinitely more appropriate. He always seemed to appear from out of nowhere when least expected. Jake had always wondered if he did it on purpose because of the way it worked out so often, although he never asked. He doubted he would've gotten a straight answer anyways.

Jake nearly slipped on another patch of ice that only he managed to stumble upon. True to form, Summers kept him propped up as he wobbled and fell forward toward him. The kid didn't respond. He simply stopped to make sure Jake was OK before turning to keep moving with the others.

They rounded the corner of Castle Lane, which led over to Arkridge Avenue on the outskirts of Gladen Hills. The irony wasn't lost on Jake that the furthest away from the bright center of the town was where the seedy elements had taken hold. And those seedy elements were exactly where Jake's pledge class was heading. Arkridge was the place where the laws of society went to die.

There, finally, the frat house came into view.

Much like every other house on the miserable street, the particular frat house was far from a hospitable environment. Everything about these buildings screamed for people like him to run in the opposite direction. *I can't believe there are idiots that actually choose to live in these houses.*

Their destination in particular looked from the outside to be enough like a regular house, albeit one that needed repairs. In truth it was actually divided by a center wall separating the place into two distinct sides. There were three brothers in small rooms on the right side, and then four brothers in even smaller rooms on the left.

The original architects probably had the house mapped out for no more than three bedrooms but in the interest of generating more cash, landlords had split perfectly adequate sized bedrooms into doubles, thereby going from three rooms to seven.

Simply walking onto Arkridge Avenue was enough to make Jake hate his life even more than he did when he'd left Kelly back in his dorm. They ran closer to the two-story house, making their way past the sorority house where Jake's last good memory with the brothers had taken place. But that was shortly before blacking out and ending up back at the frat house the day pledging officially started.

Then they ran past the Lambda frat house, which was right next door to the Hell they'd all become accustomed to.

The house being as sketchy as it was had a gravel parking lot in the back that was accessible by way of two driveways, one on either side of the house. The two-driveway setup allowed people to come and go without worrying about blocking people in on one side. It was one of the few good architectural ideas around here.

The backyard of the house doubled as the parking lot, and it was already full of cars, as it usually was on callout nights with multiple brothers driving to the house to join in on the hazing. *Even the fuckers in this fraternity didn't want to go out in this cold tonight. Good thing they don't fucking mind making us run through it.*

The pledges arrived in the backyard, which was lit up solely by the lone floodlight coming off the houses' rear. All four of them faced the house and the two guys standing in front of them. One of them was standing on top of the lone picnic table to make his presence and words somehow more dramatic.

Pledge-master Jeff Chester always seemed to enjoy these little talks.

****

Jeff never cared for theatrics much. Still, even he had to admit they did make sense in certain cases, and since tonight was special, he decided to run with it.

It had been affectionately deemed 'Hell Night' by past brothers, even before Jeff's time, and that title was designated for the worst pledging night so far. *These poor bastard pledges don't have a clue what's gonna happen.*

"You fucks are late" Jeff deadpanned to the four pledges, now standing in a straight line before him. As ridiculous a statement it was, he and Jerry had no trouble keeping a straight face. Most pledges, including these ones, were usually as on time as they could be. Of course they were never actually told that since doing anything 'right' was outrageously rare, if not altogether non-existent.

Jeff looked down from his perch on the picnic table to his assistant Jerry, who picked up the call right away. "Get down on the fucking ground and pound out thirty."

They'd all been here before; it was as much a routine now at the end of week four as the mandatory daily seven AM breakfasts.

Like a well-oiled unit, they all went down onto the snowy ground and began counting out the thirty push-ups.

"Down one, down two, down three…" Will led the other three.

I can't fucking believe these idiots elected Will Anthony to be the pledge class president. Granted he wasn't their original choice, but since the original choice had since de-pledged, there weren't many options left. *Maybe J-Hood?* He shook his head at the thought. For the life of him Jeff couldn't see why everyone else in the frat was all over that kid. *It makes absolutely no sense.* That just left Raley and Summers. Jake Raley seemed to be a little bitch at times, and fuck if he'd ever heard or seen Summers do anything worth noting.

"Listen up gentlemen, if you can even be called that. A chain is only as strong as its weakest link. And right now…your chain is broken…it's rusted…it's so fucked up it might as well be at the bottom of the goddamn ocean" he yelled. Jeff continued looking down at the pledges still counting out push-ups. Noticing that they weren't paying attention to his face, even he had to smirk.

The pledges finished and began to stand up. Jeff quickly shot a look to Jerry to stop the outright display of idiocy. "I don't recall telling you fucks to get up, so do us a favor and stay the fuck on the ground!" Jerry yelled.

They appeared to get the message since they practically became statues.

"As I was saying, you are a pledge class of one. When you are together you are a singular unit. Therefore one can assume, if one of you fucks up and say, watches '*24*' during your scheduled suite hours, you all fuck up. Even if you weren't the one watching Jack Bauer kick some ass. So with that said, we'll need another thirty pushups."

The pledges began their second set of push-ups with Will again leading the count. It was hard for Jeff not to notice all the pledges flinching before three of them looked at the fourth over his '*24*' comment.

It still amazed Jeff that Summers had been fucking stupid enough to watch TV in a suite he shared with Aaron who was already an active brother in Alpha Zeta Xi. *As if it wouldn't come back to haunt you. Kinda like right now asshole.* Still, he doubted Summers minded. One thing he could say about that kid was that push-ups didn't seem to bother him at all.

After they finished their second set, Jeff instructed them to stand up. "Put your fucking blindfolds on" he angrily ordered.

The pledges were mandated to have blindfolds on for each callout so they couldn't see what was happening. It carried the added bonus of allowing the brothers to have more fun with the situation than would otherwise be permitted. Jeff always thought it was in place for an extra mind-fuck, but it was all the same after Crossing.

Jerry grabbed Will's hand and placed it on his shoulder so he could lead the pledges downstairs without incident. Jeff watched intently. The rest of the pledges placed their right hands on the shoulder of the person in front of them to begin moving down into the house.

After arriving inside the music was cued up perfectly to coincide with the first pledge entering the room. The opening song was the same every time, as it had been for Jeff's pledge class and every one before him. '*Bombtrack*' from Rage Against the Machines. It always set the tone perfectly.

****

Once again Jake was the last pledge in the line as they entered the basement. Once inside Jeff slammed the door. The music was already in full swing. It was always heavy metal music that blasted throughout the entire callout. The further into the play-list they got, the weirder the music became. Jake was never a fan of heavy metal, so the fact that it was always playing made the callouts even more unpleasant.

As usual without warning, someone grabbed his hand to place in their own to start the customary handshake greeting. This was the main test of the callouts. The pledges were meant to greet the brothers with no more clues than a handshake and sometimes their voice if the brother in question was feeling charitable.

"Greet me," the brother ordered in his usual up-beat voice that made it seem like he was always happy. Jake knew better.

"Greetings Brother Aiden Multayza. Twenty-two, Chi class, communications, the Bronx, senior" he rattled off without a breath under the six second limit. Of course that didn't matter in most cases, and it certainly didn't with Aiden, or as he was called around here: Guapo.

"Great job Raley, but that was way too fuckin' long. Give me fifty now!" Guapo yelled without hesitation, again brandishing his upbeat and now supremely annoying voice. Jake got down on the cold cement floor and began doing his assigned pushups.

As he went up and down, he listened through the blaring music to hear other brothers yelling at his fellow pledge brothers for making various mistakes. Of course it was more likely they were being yelled at for no better reason other than proximity. *We're here and we're pledges...why not haze us?*

After finishing, Jake got back to his feet, now feeling winded from the hundred or so pushups he'd already done inside of ten minutes. He reached out his hand again to give Guapo the same greeting he'd already received.

"Raley, I'd be fucking surprised to see you doing pushups if you weren't part of the worst pledge class I've ever seen" Jerry yelled into Jake's ear, just to make sure he was heard over the music. Jake stood his ground and said nothing, mostly because he had no response. He knew Jerry was full of shit. *They all are.* Jake greeted a few more of the ass-hats all while only standing roughly five feet from the door they came through.

After a few more minutes of no greetings from the brothers, Jake became acclimated to the noise level. He heard one of the other brothers yelling at Summers, who was roughly a foot from him. Apparently Summers had legitimately fucked up a greeting, which wasn't entirely out of the question for him. Jake could never tell if the kid gave a fuck or not. *At least J-Hood and Will are actually trying...most of the time.*

"Are you fucking serious!? Does the guy in front of you look like me?" the brother yelled at Summers.

For the moment, Jake just stood there. *How the fuck is he gonna know that when he's blindfolded you bastard?*

That moment didn't last long, as his hand was again fashioned to greet another brother. "Greetings Brother Calvin Gretman. Twenty-two, Psi class, business administration, Akron, senior."

Calvin was unique in that he never hazed the pledges without good reason. Whatever reasoning passed for 'good' around these parts though was another matter entirely. Since Jake at least tried his best where success was possible, Calvin and him never had much friction.

"Good job Raley" Calvin reaffirmed Jake's previous thoughts "but unfortunately you are a pledge class of one are you not?"

"Yes sir."

"Your pledge brother is over there on the ground for fucking up my pledge brother's greeting. Does that seem fair to you?"

"No sir!" Jake yelled back, feeling a needless batch of push-ups approaching.

"Then get on the fucking floor and count out twenty" Calvin bellowed.

For a second, Jake thought Calvin saw how tired he was getting and went to take pity on him. *Are you out of your fucking mind? They'll never stop. You've been tired down here plenty of times before tonight.*

"Hold on a second, lets try something different, give me a wall-sit and give me my pledge brother's greeting instead of mine."

Jake reversed his backpack to his front before blindly reaching out behind him to find the wall. He located it in short order and assumed the position of sitting in a chair with his knees bent and arms outstretched. It was a difficult task because his legs were being used to prop up his body against the wall at roughly a ninety-degree angle.

"You better be at ninety fucking degrees Raley" Calvin yelled at him as he continued the pose and rattled out his pledge brother Petey's greeting flawlessly.

Jake really didn't have much trouble with the information half of the greeting process. It was guessing who was in front of him with the blindfold on that usually sucked, although he was improving with that too. *After four damn weeks I better be good at this shit.*

After Calvin released him from his wall-sit, he didn't long for the next visitor.

He felt a momentary wave of relief. Jared was Jake's big brother in AZXi. That meant he was the one brother that *didn't* haze him at callouts. Each pledge was assigned a Big on Bids, which was when they really met for the first time and apparently they'd been inseparable the entire night, even at the Rho Beta house.

Jake reached out his hand to Jared even though he never made Jake greet him.

"Hey bro, how're you doing?" Jared asked in a very happy manner.

"Is this shit almost over? I'm losing my fucking mind down here."

"Sorry bro, there's still a little more to go through tonight. You can text me later if you want after it's done."

"No thanks man. I just want to get back and get the fuck into bed...with Kelly" Jake replied, trying to keep his frustration in check. After all, it wasn't Jared's fault he was in this situation. *It's all on you.*

"You want to grab lunch tomorrow then?"

"Sounds good" Jake said before Jared patted him on the shoulder and walked away. *At least he's perceptive on top of being goofy...*

He was again extremely thankful for having Jared as his Big. Jake had always noted that he was extremely hard on the rest of his pledge class. That was no more apparent now as he listened to the guy yell at J-Hood for some perceived injustice.

A familiar voice broke through the loud music. "How we doing son?"

"How does it look like its going?"

"Yeah I know...not well."

"Well Eric, you always could tell when I was pissed off."

"It was never really that hard to see" Eric responded with what Jake assumed was a smile on his face.

His cousin Eric Saren always did know when Jake was upset, and he usually knew how to keep him from going off the deep end with his anger but even Eric's skills were being taxed these days. Jake didn't know for sure but he had a feeling his cousin was keeping the rest of the brothers at bay while they talked.

"Jared said the night wasn't over yet, how much more is there Biz?" Jake practically begged his cousin for an answer.

"Gotta quiz you guys on the history in your books as usual. Then Jeff's got something else for you guys...I'm sorry man."

"That why you're here? Thought you'd try some positive reinforcement?"

"Something like that. Just hang in there, you've got this man."

Jake felt himself grow calmer. Mostly just having Eric around was a good thing, especially now, but his words helped immensely too.

As soon as Jake began getting comfortable, the voice of the last person he wanted to hear came up to him. The one person even Eric couldn't hold at bay.

"Get out your fucking pledge book Raley" Jeff ordered.

****

By the way Raley tightened up and froze at the sound of his voice, Jeff could tell he wasn't having a good night. *Oh well, he signed up to pledge AZXi.* Jeff would be damned if he wasn't going to give him the full experience that acceptance entailed.

Of course Eric had tried waving Jeff off as he drew closer to his cousin but he ignored that. *Just trying to baby him a little longer. Fuck that.*

Jeff never saw what good that did. It only made it that much worse when he did get yelled at again. Eric may have been able to keep Jerry under control when it came to his cousin because they were pledge brothers. Jeff however had no such affiliation with Eric other than wearing the same fraternity letters as him. There was respect, but they weren't all that close. *Maybe we could've been...*

He shook the thoughts from his head. *This is my program. It's always my call.*

The books that every single pledge had to make were comprised of a hundred lined pages in a composite notebook. A long time ago some pledge-master thought it'd be funny to have the pledges go to the store and actually count out the pages in the notebooks before buying them. That could've strictly been another mind-fuck but Jeff and Jerry kept it going strictly because some of the notebooks had ninety-eight or one hundred-two pages. The notebooks had to have a specific amount of pages because there was a very particular setup for each one.

The first half of the book had interview information the pledges got from each of the twenty-five active brothers in AZXi. The second half was reserved for the history of the frat. That meant it was filled with pledge classes, names, family trees, Bids parties, Executive Boards, the credo, the crest and a bunch of side notes. Once everything was transcribed the books became akin to sorority gold because the AZXi history was only contained in these books outside the original copy. The original was kept in the Historian's Binder locked down within a hidden spot in the house. Every brother and pledge had a book they were responsible for protecting.

The history had never fallen into sorority hands but that wasn't for a lack of trying. There'd been many attempts over the years that he'd heard about or been a direct part of.

After another half hour or so of quizzing the pledges on the frat's history it was clear they didn't know or give a fuck about it.

Something has to be done with these miserable fucks...

Jeff figured he'd give it more thought later on tonight or in the morning.

Either way it was time for the theatrics again. He motioned for Jerry and the others to line the pledges up against the back wall where Jeff instructed them to take their blindfolds off.

It took a few seconds for their eyes to get accustomed to actually being used. It was always entertaining to watch.

"It all really comes down to willpower boys. It's all about who wants it more. If you want to just be handed letters at the end of six weeks, the Tau Chi house is right across the street. They take any bitch that says hey to them at the bars" Jeff said sternly.

Jerry stepped forward. "We can't teach you how to have balls. You should've walked in with those."

"I hope for your guys' sake that none of you have forgotten some basic knowledge because tonight we're going re-test you on the Greek alphabet. If any of you mess this up, then we head to the track and run until you learn some respect for this fraternity and the brothers in it" Jeff finished.

Of course it didn't really matter, they'd be heading to the track regardless.

On top of that, he'd already seen them butcher the history they should've had a good grasp on by now. Even if it hadn't been an AZXi rite of passage to go to the track on Hell Night Jeff might've still taken them but he wouldn't fuck with tradition.

Sure enough, the pledges fucked up the alphabet even worse than they had the first time during week one. It wasn't surprising. All it did was give Jeff the authority to do whatever the fuck he wanted to do.

Thankfully, the track wasn't all that far from where they were on Arkridge Avenue so leading the pledges through the night wasn't difficult.

If the campus police saw them it would've required an explanation Jeff hadn't dreamt up yet. Although he was sure he could come up with one if he had to.

Most of the campus cops didn't travel down here much, especially so late at night. Given that it was well after one in the morning, he wasn't overly concerned.

The pledges looked like shit as they followed along.

Jeff hoped tonight would raise some kind of motivation in them to work harder so they could cross earlier than the six week barrier the school placed over the Greek Circle.

"Do any of you fucks know why we're out here?" Jeff asked.

Without warning, one of them spoke. "You're going to whack us right sir?"

Jeff stifled a smirk that rose in him as soon as he heard the comment. *Raley's definitely a smart-ass. He didn't get the 'shudder' nickname for nothing.*

Funny or not it was grating for a pledge-master to have to deal with so he covered his amusement as best he could. "Very fucking funny Raley, I *wish* that was the case. But we're out here to hopefully teach you some respect for Alpha Zeta Xi." He glared back at Jake who clearly didn't buy that by the look in his eye.

Jeff sent them out on a warm-up lap at first to get them accustomed to running in the cold. After they returned he instructed them to begin Indian runs for a few laps.

As they began, Jeff and Jerry watched the last person in line sprint to the front and so on as they completed lap after lap.

Exhaustion began showing on their faces after the fourth lap but Jeff wasn't finished yet, not even close. The night was still young.

Chapter 3

The downright annoying sound that was Jake's alarm clock was going off furiously on the windowsill next to his bed. Maybe it wasn't going off furiously as much as Jake was just furious that it was going off. *Seriously, fuck that sound.* As a matter of fact as of now, the only sound worse than the alarm was the ring-tone he had set during pledging. That chime could literally drive fear into his heart. It didn't even matter if it was pledging related or not. When the damn thing went off that's all it reminded him of.

Without even opening his eyes, Jake reached up as steadily as he could so as not to move Kelly who was resting her head on his chest. He hit the snooze button with one attempt before letting his hand rest back on the bed.

Jake thought he'd been successful not disturbing Kelly, but she began to shift after a few seconds. He begrudgingly opened his eyes. *Now I'll have to wake up too.*

Kelly's face couldn't have been more than an inch or two away from his when their eyes locked and they both began smiling. *She's so beautiful.*

"What time is it baby?"

"A little past eight."

He couldn't even speak without yawning. That didn't go unnoticed.

"What time did you get back last night?"

"Not too late, just a little after three" Jake answered, trying to infuse nonchalance into the comment. Getting himself worked up would only do the same to her.

"Didn't you leave at midnight?"

She knows I did. "What can I say Kel, I'm just living the dream."

Kelly's eyes continued staring into Jake's with a look of sadness coupled with pity. He was grateful for that much at least. "Tell you what…" she began as she shifted her body on top of his. "Why don't you just take all your frustrations out on me before class" she finished with a seductive smile on her make-up-free face. Even without all the trimmings of a girl ready to hit the bars, she had him turned on.

Jake was powerless. Their lips touched and found a groove instantly. After a few seconds his hands were moving up and down Kelly's warm body. Without warning, the alarm clock began ringing...again. *You just had to be an idiot and hit the snooze button instead of turning the fucking thing off.* His left arm found the off switch even with his eyes closed against Kelly's.

Their kiss broke off and she smiled.

"Just so you know, this could get a little rough."

"Just how I like my days to start."

****

It was more of a miracle than any he'd ever claimed to see before. His roommate Dukes was actually going to class...in the morning. *I don't even remember a time that this guy was functional so early, let alone ready for class. Something's up.* Dukes apparently went to all his classes yesterday but none of those had been morning classes so his attendance wasn't *that* surprising. He fully intended to get to the bottom of it while they walked. Scribner knew it'd drive him fuckin' crazy all day otherwise. Letting things go was never his strong suit.

Within a couple minutes they were ready to go. Unfortunately within that short time he heard the door to Derek's room shut as he headed off to class. Scribner was hoping to catch him so they could walk together.

Dukes didn't say one word as they left their room. *He has no idea what to say or how to act in the morning. Lucky bastard.*

As they entered the common area of the suite, their mutual silence paid off...in spades. The unmistakable sounds of sex were coming straight out of Jake and Wayne's shared dorm room.

Scribner smiled widely. *I love living here.*

Dukes may not have known how to handle a typical morning conversation but he was born for situations like these. Sure enough, the grin on his face was as unmistakable as the sounds they were hearing.

"Who do you think it is this time?"

"No question, that's Raley and Kelly."

Dukes didn't look convinced.

"Wayne doesn't fuck girls like that and Amanda sure as hell doesn't make those sounds." At almost that exact moment a gigantic moan of ecstasy came through the door. Scribner grinned even wider. *That couldn't have happened more perfectly.*

"Could go either way I think."

"That's because you're a dumbass."

Scribner's own conviction wasn't shaken. He'd known Jake Raley for a very long time and he was sorry to say, he actually had a pretty good idea of how he and Kelly sounded when they were fucking. *This is textbook.*

"Oh yes Jake, harder...harder" Kelly's distinct voice came through. *I dare you to say anything now pal.* Scribner simply extended his already large grin a little more and focused all of its radiance in Dukes' direction. It almost hurt to smile so much.

"Yeah OK...I still can't believe Raley has sex with girls though" Dukes admitted.

"I've known that kid for five years, I know what I'm talking about."

"It's a little weird that you know what they sound like" Dukes retorted. "Still, I thought it'd be different. Like there'd be a lot of 'no, please don't' and 'shut up bitch'...and then whatever Raley would say."

Scribner couldn't help but laugh. *Good thing Raley didn't hear that.* He didn't really believe he would've been offended...too much. *With how pissed he is these days, who the fuck knows?*

"Wait 'til you see a real Raley's Ring party. Then you'll have a little more faith in the kid" Scribner commented after his laugh. *We'll fix that next week when we get home and throw it down like old times.* He just had to get Raley on board, but he was fairly certain he could.

Knowing they'd have to get to class soon, Scribner took off his backpack, headed over to the Jake's door and began humping it. After a few seconds of pounding his waist against the door, he began making the fakest sounding sex noises he could come up with to mimic Kelly. Interestingly, Kelly began to get louder. *Either she's close to finishing or just trying to drown me out. That's a shame for her.*

"Kelly, we all know Raley's terrible in bed, so those noises aren't fooling anybody...except maybe Raley" Dukes added from his right.

"I'm going to kill both of you when this is over" Jake's panting; angry voice came back from the other side of the door.

"Frankly, I'm surprised it's still going. Aren't you usually two minutes and done? I mean, shouldn't you be napping while Kelly lies there unsatisfied?" Dukes continued, unfazed by the threat.

Scribner continued humping the door in a rhythmic motion timed to allow Dukes his verbal jabs.

"Just leave it alone babe" Kelly's muffled voice came through. *Oops. Well this was fun...*

That was all they needed to hear. They grabbed their backpacks quickly and made for the door.

Scribner wasn't convinced Jake would've gotten violent but also wasn't willing to risk it. *Did he really expect us to pass that up? Oh well, now we're gone and Raley can think he forced us to leave and we can enjoy the joke. Everybody wins.*

"Did you talk to Daryl about rushing at all?" Scribner asked once they were far enough away from their dorm. It caught him off guard that he was so invested in the answer. He'd said time and again that he didn't want to rush or pledge a frat. Yet here he was, actually considering it with the right circumstances. And they were rapidly piling up as he got deeper into freshman year.

"Yeah he wants to check out a couple places, I'm really only interested in AZXi if I do go. But he's down with looking there too."

They continued to walk through the cool morning past the Blue Hold dining hall. It was pretty busy. *I can't believe people like eating breakfast around here.*

"Where else does he want to go?"

"Alpha Kappa (AK) mostly, and maybe that other place on Fifth Street. Phi Psi?"

Scribner didn't know Dukes' friend Daryl all that well, having only met him twice, but he seemed like a cool dude. Now that assessment was seriously being called into question. "Dude, Phi Psi is so damn sketchy. All they do is drugs. Maybe it's not a problem for Daryl, but you know him better than I do."

"High school has that affect on people" Dukes said with victory in his voice.

So Daryl is clearly a huge drug addict.

As they continued walking toward campus the incline of the ground got steeper. *Of course walking to class is all uphill from Northeast.* It made the prospect of going to class a little more daunting, especially in the morning when getting out of bed was a real pain in the ass. There were more than a few times he'd fallen prey to that way of thinking and simply given in. *It would've been so easy to just shut off the alarm and go back to sleep. Classes aren't even that hard right now. That'll change when I get into the business school.* As long as he kept going to class he shouldn't have any problem keeping the GPA required to get in.

"Wait a sec, don't you just have English today? What the fuck are you even doing out of bed? Weren't you up 'til like three last night?" Scribner asked, suddenly realizing he'd forgotten to bring it up.

"Yeah, right about the time Raley got back from being raped at the frat house. He looked terrible by the way. That's why I was surprised by how Kelly got confused into fucking him."

"Nah, that girl would fuck anything. I just don't think Raley sees it and I sure as hell don't have the heart to tell him. She did some fucked up shit when they first started going out. But he let it all go because he's in love...or some other bullshit."

Scribner's feelings on the subject were not a secret. He didn't believe Jake and Kelly were good together. Moreover, he believed she was a raving bitch when they started hooking up, at least based on everything Raley had told him. *Getting those phone calls from him about her sucked balls.* That underlying impression wasn't going away.

"You're so gay Scribbs. You need to get laid."

"My left hand doesn't count?"

"Not when you name it Steve."

Scribner knew he'd been beaten on that count so he switched topics. "So what the hell were you doing up 'til three anyways?"

"Apparently some professors actually require you to write papers and then make you go to class to hand them in. I mean, what the fuck is up with that?" Dukes asked incredulously, like some great injustice had been done.

"That's what you get for choosing a bullshit major like English."

"Yeah you're right. When you get that business degree, you're looking at a shift manager position at McDonald's by your mid-thirties. You'll be all set."

Scribner smirked before going quiet. *My roommate is such an ass.*

After walking a few more minutes they reached the incredibly steep stairs that led into the heart of campus. The campus core was located on a huge plateau that overlooked the rest of Gladen Hills. Scribner didn't know but he was pretty sure Dukes had his class in the one lone building not up in the core.

"Yo, you want to grab lunch at Lance after? Maybe like eleven thirty?"

"If I'm still on campus, yeah" Dukes said before heading over toward Grantel Hall, which was only a few hundred feet from the interstate. That was about as close to a sure answer as he was likely to get from his roommate, and they both knew it.

Resigning himself to the fact that he'd come so far and there was no turning back; Scribner tightened the straps on his backpack and grabbed the nearest railing on the stairs before making his way up.

****

Riley Nichol shifted into consciousness from a very deep sleep. Her body hadn't yet caught up to her mind. No limbs were moving and her eyes didn't open. Almost frantically, she tried to remember what day it was. *What the hell happened last night? Oww my head...*

Finally she forced herself to open her eyes and what she saw was sure to make her best friend Tory absolutely giddy. Lying beside Riley, in her own bed of all places, was one of the Alpha Zeta Xi brothers.

How did Jerry get here? How did I even get here? Fuck...Tory is gonna have a field day with this one.

She started looking over Jerry who was still sleeping. She again reprimanded herself for having an after-hours party last night. *Why do you constantly do this to yourself? Nothing good happens at after-hours.* Thankfully, she noticed Jerry still had his clothes on. *At least we didn't have sex...or did we? Fuck...*

Jerry began to stir before opening his eyes very slowly. He looked at Riley as soon as he got his bearings. It took about a minute longer than she would've expected from a seasoned drinker like him.

"You came over pretty late last night" she blurted out as soon as she believed he was capable of responding. The jagged memories of last night were cascading in.

"Had to get the pledges in line."

"I hope you're not being too hard on them."

Jerry grinned. *Of course he's not going easy on them; he's the assistant pledge-master.* Under the circumstances, he had every right to be amused.

"They aren't getting anything worse than Biz and I got when we pledged" he finally responded after getting a good yawn out. *Right...because you two had it so easy.*

"I don't think we did anything since we're both still dressed" she answered his unspoken question. *It'd be great if I remembered for sure though.* She swore the look of disappointment came and went very quickly across his face.

"We haven't been here since freshman year," she thought out loud. *Why the hell would you say that?*

"Now that was a good time," Jerry said happily.

"I seem to remember you being the one who messed that up."

"Yeah, I do that from time to time" he responded, looking devilish.

Just as the silence was reaching an uncomfortable level, the door to her bedroom opened without a knock and in walked her best friend Tory, followed closely by her EIPi niece, Danielle.

"Oh hey Riles, didn't know you were entertaining in here" Tory said without a second thought. *Saved again by the madness that is Tory Brye.* As if that statement wasn't enough, she went on with yet another attempt at her version of an icebreaker. "Haven't seen you two together in a while."

"We're not together" Riley quickly jumped.

"Well that's my cue" Jerry commented before getting his socks on and grabbing his shoes with an appropriate amount of haste.

If there was one thing that made a frat guy squirm, it was the appearance of multiple sorority girls in the morning the night after a party. They loved hanging out when the alcohol was flowing, but in the cold sober light of day, frat boys wanted out before dealing with three girls on the verge of a laughing spree.

Riley watched Jerry get his shoes on from the corner of her bed while carefully noting that Tory had the largest grin on her face, even though Danielle was giving her a run for her money. It was just a shame her headache was hitting its stride. *Why did I do shots at after-hours?*

Jerry didn't even wait to tie his shoes before standing up and simply nodding in Riley's direction. Then he b-lined it for the door. Riley half-expected to hear the sound of a dead sprint when he cleared the doorframe.

"Went back to the well on that one didn't you Riles?"

Leave it to T to turn sex into a joke as fast as possible. No wonder she laughs off so many flings.

"I thought you hated him." Danielle was half-asking, half-stating.

"I don't hate him" Riley responded, "it's usually just a passionate dislike."

Tory stepped in the middle to ask how it was.

Riley couldn't help but smile. It sounded like she was a kid asking for a bedtime story. "Nothing happened, unless you can tell me something I don't know."

"I woke up with a Tau Chi so I doubt I'll be much help" Tory answered quickly.

"Who was it?"

"One of their newer guys, he just crossed last semester" Tory responded without fully answering her question.

"And you say I go back to the well? You drain yours with the same frats every weekend" Riley stated, louder than she'd wanted to. *My head...*

She looked over at Dani to get her view of the evening.

"Somebody had to look after the house last night, so thankfully I woke up alone" she said almost haughtily.

Quite the pair Tory and her make. One's happy she got some last night and the other's utterly indifferent to sex. Guess that puts me somewhere in the middle?

"Ah, my head hurts so fucking bad" she blurted out, trying to convey as much agony as possible. *They might as well suffer with me.*

"Riles, week four is basically done. When are we looking at for Crossing?

Always keeping things focused right Dani?

"I just woke up, give me a second" she answered before collapsing against her pillow and pulling the covers up to a comfortable position. After getting them over her head, she didn't hear any movement from her friends.

"How long are you going to need?"

Riley cracked a grin behind her blanket and turned away from the sound of the voice toward the wall. "At least 'til lunch."

Another few seconds of precious nothing came and went. Then a sarcastic voice broke the tender silence. "Don't you worry Riles, I'll take notes for you today" Tory added with what sounded like a huge smile on her lips.

"Thanks T...please shut the door behind you!" Riley spit out the words quickly as she tried getting comfortable. She wasn't making any progress because she was still wearing her jeans from the previous night. As the door closed behind her friends Riley struggled under the covers. *Is it really worth getting up to get these jeans off?* In the end, her laziness won out as she settled in for what was likely to be a long nap.

****

Panting from the morning's events, Jake lay there. He was basically dead after losing a good chunk of bodily fluids to his girlfriend. "You always know just how to handle me when I'm tense babe" he announced between stunted breaths.

"It's not exactly difficult."

Both of them were completely naked. Normally, that'd mean they'd be insanely cold but given they'd essentially just exercised; Jake in particular was feeling quite toasty. *If I could just feel like this all the time.*

"I won't have you selling yourself short Kel, you have talents your parents would be ashamed of...I don't deserve you at all" he said with a smile as he rolled over to fully face her. Staring at her amazing, curved body, he mentally battled over whether he could actually do her again now. Given the proper recovery time of ten minutes he bet he could, but that'd mean missing class. *Good, an added bonus.*

"That's a lot of pressure baby."

"Yeah but I think we just found out definitively that you can handle a lot of pressure" he replied. Jake raised his eyebrows in a knowing fashion, making the moment as cheesy as possible, and not giving a damn.

Kelly smiled back with her luscious lips.

Now She was saying something about hurrying to class. Jake wasn't paying much attention to her actual words because he'd already made up his mind to skip.

"You just destroyed any chance I may have had of getting to class babe. The only movement I'll be doing is some tossing and turning before going back to sleep."

Kelly was standing up now, putting her jeans on over her pink thong, she looked back down at him while topless. Jake pried his eyes away from her chest before seeing her disapproving look. There was also a hint of jealousy behind her dark blue eyes.

Sadly she kept getting dressed as he lay there, now finishing up with her tank top and sweatshirt.

"So how much do you love me?" Jake asked, trying to sound innocent.

"Enough I guess. You want me to take notes for you today right?"

"What would I do without you Kel?" Jake asked rhetorically as he slid his shorts back on. Sleeping naked always just felt weird. He always felt self-conscious, at least after the sex was over. During it he couldn't give a fuck, but afterward clothing was required, at least for him. *Kelly could stay like that all day.*

"OK, I'll see you later. Text me if you want to grab lunch at Lancaster."

"I would but I've got plans with Jared...and I have to kill Scribbs and Dukes before that. Class aside, I'm booked up all morning."

Kelly walked back over to his bed and he half-expected her to playfully hit him because of his smart-ass comment. Instead she leaned down and kissed him again. *I don't want you to go.*

Jake watched helplessly as the door closed behind his girlfriend once she broke off their sensual kiss.

For a few moments he simply laid in bed.

With pledging kicking into high gear and two weeks to go, the idea of having somebody he could get close to and connect with was paramount. Jake could've sworn in the past couple weeks that Kelly was pulling away somehow but he kept the thoughts at bay. *You're just being an idiot. She loves you.*

Being depressed full time because of school and frat commitments wasn't exactly the dream life he'd pictured after graduating high school. *Quit being a moron and relax.* For now his bed was insanely warm and there was silence all around him. On top of that, they were coming up on spring break. *I get to spend a week away from all those jackasses at the AZXi house.* The excitement from that thought alone nearly kept Jake from falling asleep. Yet somehow he still managed to drift off.

****

Jeff hated the library, mostly because it was a stark contrast to the life he was leading off campus. By far, that was the life he preferred to be in tune with. Unfortunately, reality had a way of biting him in the ass.

Here it was, the Friday before spring break and instead of being able to half-ass it all day like he could back in high school, he was being forced to study for a fucking exam. Forced was probably the wrong word, because no one forced him to do anything. It was just one of those unwritten things a student had to do if they wanted to remain a student. *All this studying for what? Some bullshit diploma at graduation?* The ceremony came every year. And every year they lost more brothers. Soon it'd be his turn. *Quit being a pussy and read the fucking textbook.*

His computer science test was in an hour.

"Who the fuck gives a test the Friday before spring break?"

Thankfully, he was in the 'non-quiet' section of the Cordan library and there was enough low chatter in the vicinity that no one really took notice of his outburst. Save for one guy that chuckled and nodded in agreement before going back to his own textbook.

"Did you expect an answer?"

He looked to his side at his girlfriend Dana, who was also studying, albeit for a different class. *Damn her boobs look so good in that shirt.* It was as low-cut as anything she owned and Jeff was thankful it was on her today. Since Dana was a petite girl, she had curves that were compacted into a shorter package, which just accentuated everything more. It was a rare package: a girl with a nice ass *and* a good rack. He'd definitely hit the jackpot when they met sophomore year.

"It was rhetorical…but it still doesn't make any goddamn sense" he responded finally. He was doing his best to stare at his textbook instead of her chest.

"Shouldn't have stayed out so late last night, maybe you wouldn't be so cranky today," Dana said with as much diplomacy as she could.

"I wasn't out having a good time" Jeff defended himself.

"I thought you said you liked hazing the pledges?"

"I do…but that's not the point" he said, trying to find a clever deflection. "The point is we shouldn't be taking a test this close to a long break."

"Can't avoid it now" she said, returning her eyes to her book. *She's awfully cheerful today.* Considering the current circumstances of being fucked by their professors with a test, it was surprising.

Just get through today so you can focus on tonight.

Jeff made a decision at the track last night that'd likely turn some heads in the frat. *It's my program so they can fuck themselves.*

Dana didn't need to hear anything about that though. She wasn't affiliated with anything in the Greek Circle so she didn't know or care to know about their issues.

Realizing that Dana was done playing along with Jeff's admittedly over the top anger for something he couldn't change, he turned his attention back to the textbook.

It was a good thing he already knew most of the shit he'd need otherwise he'd be real pissed. Once again, he turned his eyes away, this time toward the entrance of the main room. Calvin Gretman was coming toward them with his girlfriend Jennifer in tow.

Jeff couldn't decide if they'd spotted him and were coming to their area because of that, or if it was just a coincidence. *Calvin Gretman, savior of Alpha Zeta Xi and the curer of cancer, thank God he's here. No chance this is a coincidence.* He'd only told Jerry about his plan for the pledges since that's the only brother he felt obligated to include. *Of course he didn't keep his fucking mouth shut, the bastard.* The timeline of his plan becoming known was just shorter than Jeff planned. That annoyed him.

Calvin and Jennifer reached their table and exchanged the usual greetings before the business end came up. "Buttons, can I talk to you for a sec?" Calvin asked with more innocence than expected. In fact, the use of his nickname meant that Calvin didn't think the situation was as important as Jeff predicted. *Or it might just be a show he's putting on for the girls.*

Calvin was the president of AZXi that much was true. But Jeff was the pledge-master and that meant he could make certain decisions without having a fucking committee meeting every time. *Chop off my balls next time instead of running to Gretman why don't you Jerry...*

Jeff and Calvin had always had a tense relationship, which reached back to their earlier AZXi years. The issues had never fully healed and no one saw that changing anytime soon. *He better not try to get on my nerves. Today is the last day he should be fucking with me.*

****

Calvin followed Jeff's lead as they walked away from their girlfriends. He liked to appease his frat brother whenever he could. It tended to make things go easier.

Today was more or less routine. He knew when Jeff was elected pledge-master that there were bound to be days like today. Of course being diplomatic, he'd kept that to himself during the elections. Their relationship had always been strained since the earlier days. Recently though, with his own graduation coming up, Jeff seemed more tense than usual. *I didn't even think that was possible two years ago.* What happened between them had in fact been a long time ago. *It might as well have been yesterday for him.*

As they reached what Calvin considered a safe distance from wandering eyes and ears, specifically from their girlfriends, he slowed his walk. They were about fifteen feet from the table they'd left the girls at. It wasn't that Calvin didn't want Jennifer to know what was going on with AZXi, it was just one of those unspoken things. He was sure he could find out all about Rho Beta if he wanted to, because Jen would likely spill the details if he asked. *You'd do the same if she asked you but why mess with that?* That could very well piss off certain people in their respective organizations. The ones that didn't have relationships to bank on would be the likely candidates.

Most of Calvin's brothers didn't have girlfriends. The ones that did certainly hadn't been dating as long as he and Jennifer had. The only one close was Jeff, and even he was a year behind them. He always considered that people outside of relationships couldn't really fathom trusting someone completely like he did with Jen. In fact, he may very well trust her more than most, if not all of his brothers. Oddly enough, Jeff might be the one who'd get the most pissed about

Calvin sharing state secrets about their frat with an outsider, and a Beta girl no less. *I can't really blame him.*

Jeff tended to take everything in Gladen Hills pretty seriously, especially when it came to AZXi. Of course, it all dated back to their unfortunate experience years ago. That made days like today harder. *Oh well, might as well get down business.*

"I hear you're calling the pledges out tonight?" Calvin began with the most important question.

"Jerry tell you that?"

"No, Eric told me. But I'm guessing Jerry told him."

Jeff looked surprised for a millisecond but then the answer sunk in. "Of course he did. I didn't think he'd have the balls to go to you directly."

"So you knew this would come back around to me. Why not just tell me yourself and spare us the trouble?"

"Because there's no trouble. It's *my* program and I don't need permission to make a decision like this."

Great, he's already pissed off. And we have a new record.

Calvin tried refocusing his energy on staying collected so they didn't get into an argument in the middle of Cordan. *Behind closed doors at the frat house, fine, not here in public.* The last thing they needed were two members of the AZXi Executive Board fighting in the library. *That'd do wonders at next semester's Rush.*

"You don't need permission Buttons, but I'd like a reason."

"So no permission, I just need to explain myself to you, is that it?"

"It's not a requirement but I'd appreciate it."

Seriously, is it too much to ask for the president of the frat to get a reason for something like this?

"I think they could use a good lesson before break" Jeff finally bit out.

Oh good...that makes no sense.

"How do you know they'll all still be around? The whole reason Thursdays are Hell Nights is because the pledges usually go home early."

"I know for a fact they'll all still be around."

Relax; don't let him see anything's bothering you.

"Why didn't you post this on the forums then?"

"Because I don't need the whole frat there, especially since some of the brothers are heading home early. All I'm gonna need is Jerry. That's the only reason I told him."

Calvin realized that unless he wanted to pull rank, there'd be no real victory in their situation. Jeff was being as stubborn now as he was on most things, especially things he was passionate about. *It's not even my place. Vice president oversees the pledge program, not the president.* Even with that in mind, Calvin still couldn't shake the feeling that he wasn't being given his due respect. *There's no way I'll ever get that much from him...*

The AZXi founding fathers clearly had a lack of ideas about just what kind of authority to give to the vice president when they drafted their charter and constitution. That was the only reason Calvin could think of for why the VP got such authority, because he sure as hell wouldn't have done it that way. *This should be my call, not his.*

The whole thing was at a dead end because Kevin was the VP and he and Jeff were pledge brothers. Moreover, Kevin hated arguing and avoided it as much as possible. He was the polar opposite of Jeff, who basically thrived on it.

"Just take it easier on them. We can fuck them up when we're *all* back from break" he said with more defeat than he cared to show. Showing that to someone like Jeff Chester was like displaying blood to a shark.

"Relax, it'll be quick."

Jeff turned back to his table where Dana and Jennifer were still talking.

Frustration was stirring in Calvin but it was fading.

One day I might need to use authority to step over Jeff. But not today. Today was more about procedure than anything else. And it didn't really matter if Jeff didn't want to follow it to the letter under these circumstances.

How bad could it go anyways?

****

All-in-all, the torture that was his Friday physics lab could've gone worse, but not by much. *Thank god that was my only class today.*

Eric always felt like that was all he could handle after three hours of lab trials and experiments. He'd always enjoyed science but he preferred learning and doing the work on his own time. That was why studying was never overly agitating.

Truthfully, he could probably afford to do some studying right now, but his lazier side was winning that battle. *I'm about to go on break, there's no point in doing any more work now when I'll forget it all by the end.* It was far from true but that reason would work.

As usual Jerry met him near the entrance to the physics labs where his own class finished at roughly the same time. *And I thought I looked terrible today.* Somehow even in these situations, Jerry always found a way to make it to class. Eric never really understood how he did it. Being hung-over for the kinds of classes they were taking was always a nightmarish scenario. That was the primary reason he didn't go out much on Thursdays. Once again, he thanked God that his professor had been wise enough to make today a more laid-back class.

He noticed that Jerry was putting away his phone as he approached. *He was probably texting one of his self-proclaimed 'slam-pieces'.* Most other people called them one-night stands but not his pledge brother. *Insensitive as sin but still funny.* Eric shrugged it off because they'd originally heard it from a girl who referred to Jerry by that very term, which made it funnier.

"You tell Gretman about the callout tonight?"

Eric nodded. "I figured it was better he found out ahead of time rather than when he walks in the house later with Jennifer ready to bang out, only to be interrupted by Buttons screaming at them." He knew Jerry was on the same page, like he was ninety-eight percent of the time.

"Yeah but the party tonight is with the DXA's at their place. So nobody was gonna be at the house anyways" Jerry said, trying to maintain his stance as the one who was betrayed. Eric knew better, Jerry wasn't even fully on board with Jeff's idea of a non-sanctioned callout to begin with, even if it was his intention to play it otherwise.

"Yeah but he's the president. He should know what's going down with the pledges" Eric responded calmly. "It's not like he really wanted to stop it, he just wants to be kept in the loop. And I don't have a problem with giving him that much."

"Kevin said it was straight and he's the check for pledge-master so we're good" Jerry said, making sure to have the last word.

Eric wasn't an idiot. The only reason Jerry even ran the idea by Kevin in the first place was to make entirely sure he was in fact, OK with it. Given Kevin's stance on most issues that didn't directly affect him, he was likely to let it slide. It was even likelier when taking into account how close he was with Buttons. Moreover, the only reason Jerry let Eric know was because he knew he'd tell Calvin, who'd confront Jeff. *So basically, everything went the way you wanted Jer.*

Jerry never did like deliberately stepping on people's toes, and he hated being on anyone's bad side. *Even if you deserve it on occasion son.*

"So, I saw you leaving the EIPi house this morning when I drove through campus…you banging Riley again?"

"Weak son" he paused. "Nah, we didn't bang, just made out and went to sleep."

It was a hundred to one shot that something like that actually happened in Gladen Hills, especially between two people who'd already banged. He didn't think Jerry was lying, more likely he guessed they were just too drunk to function.

"OK...how'd it go with the pledges last night?"

Jerry grimaced. "I swear Raley hasn't been trying at all since he got his ass handed to him at Bids."

"Dude, everybody gets their ass handed to them at Bids" Eric quickly retorted, defending his younger cousin.

"True, but Jared and him aren't allowed back in the Beta house."

Eric smirked. *Seriously, what the hell did they even do?* It was definitely a source of pride that Jake had already made an impression with one sorority before Crossing. Even if it was an outright negative one, it was still impressive.

"I'll have to ask Jennifer what went down, see if she knows anything."

"When you talked to the DXA treasurer, did she say enough of them would be around tonight to make the party worth it?" Jerry asked.

"I didn't ask." *I should've though.* "Talk to Guapo, God knows he's got nothing better to do other than check on that shit. You got something better to do tonight?"

Of course Jerry had nothing else to do. *As long as he's still in town, he'll be there...and he'll be getting hammered, same as always.*

"I suppose I could pencil in two or three drinks," Jerry answered while smirking as though he was making some great sacrifice.

"Trying to get laid tonight son?"

"I'm on a perpetual quest Biz."

"You and me both" Eric said with a hint of depression.

"Jen didn't hook you up last night?"

"She was trying, but she got too drunk before anything could be done."

"What can she do" Jerry stated instead of asking.

If it mattered as much to her as it does to me then she could've done a lot more but it's not her problem.

After a few more minutes of walking down the hill toward Arkridge Avenue and some more idle chitchat his thoughts swung back to his cousin. *Last night definitely kicked his ass. That was easy to see even before they went to the track. I should probably call him later.*

His cousin tended to take certain things harder than most. *Tonight is gonna be more of the same.*

Chapter 4

Even Jake had to admit it. When the sun was shining and the weather cooperated by melting some of the damn snow, Gladen Hills actually looked pretty nice.

Today the dining hall venue was the central location of Lancaster. That meant Jake's choices were wider than normal. Grilled cheese, hamburgers, and chicken tenders were all things that made his mouth water, and Lancaster had them all. Not only that, it had them in vast quantities. And what was churned out didn't suffer in quality because of it. That couldn't be said for the other two dining halls. *Lance beats out Hanoran and the Blue Hold every time.*

As he neared the entrance Jake spotted a familiar sight: his two suitemates.

I could tackle both of them right now and they'd never see it coming.

Throwing them into the snow would definitely feel good after the bullshit they put him through earlier when he was with Kelly. But given the restful sleep he'd gotten afterward and the phenomenal session his girlfriend had continued on with after they'd left, he tossed the idea aside. *I'll get them later.*

"What's up boys?" Jake asked cheerily.

"Other than doing what I want whenever I want? Not a thing" Dukes said with a straight face.

I'll let that slide. As of today, with pledging now officially on hold, Jake could say the exact same thing.

"You wanna grab something to eat?" Jake asked, looking past Dukes to Scribner.

"You came down here to eat by yourself?"

"Nah, but I figure I got some time to kill while I wait for Jared."

"That's cute, even when you aren't pledging, you still get to suck their dicks" Dukes added without prompting.

"You always know just what to say to make me wanna kill you."

"Well I'm here with fifteen hundred acres and a back hoe if you ever do go through with it" Scribner added with a smirk.

Anytime Scribner mentioned anything about being a farmer it made Jake smile. It made his bright red appearance stand out even more when Jake imagined him driving a tractor around a farm.

Maybe I'll take you up on that one day Scribbs.

Jake led the way through the middle section of doors behind a group of laughing sorority girls. *The girl in front is real hot.* Jake looked around at his friends to see if they'd noticed too. Scribner definitely had because he was doing enough staring for all three of them. Jake noticed the lettering on the girl's sweatshirt as 'ABI'. *Eric said they were one of the hottest sororities. Good call Biz.*

It didn't take long for his friends to get their food. Sitting there watching Scribner and Dukes eat was nothing short of pure torture. *You can't eat before Jared gets here.*

"Why come in here at all if you're not eating?" Dukes asked.

"No point in eating twice. And since we live together, I think you should be more supportive of anything that keeps me sane" Jake replied without looking up.

"I think that time has come and gone."

"Still think pledging was a good idea?" Scribner asked between bites.

"Maybe I did, I can't really remember anymore…but this place was getting really old. Then again, pledging is giving me the same fuckin' feeling" he responded, getting annoyed just thinking about it.

"It seems like a lot of bullshit just to party Raley" Scribner answered honestly.

You're absolutely right Scribbs. Truthfully, if it were all about partying, then it probably would've been too much to deal with, but there was another reason. At the moment however, Jake couldn't fathom what his past self had seen in a frat lifestyle to make any of the shit in the past four weeks worth it.

"It's not about partying…" he began. The completely baffled looks that were already appearing on his friends' faces caused him to stop short. "It's not *just* about partying" he relented, putting emphasis on the change. That seemed to settle their stances but they still looked confused. *Yeah, I wouldn't believe me either.* "I want something more out of college than just a degree," he practically blurted out.

Thankfully with Dukes on point, the situation didn't detour into a melodramatic festival. "I love it when you bear your soul like that Raley; it turns me on."

"It's not my fault you can't get laid in this town" Jake replied with a grin.

Dukes responded with his best 'wounded' impression while Scribner laughed.

"That's it! Where's my chloroform? I'm going out tonight!" Dukes announced in triumph.

Without another word, he grabbed his backpack and nodded at Scribner as if saying goodbye without actually saying it. Then he moved to the nearest exit with not nearly as much speed as Jake would've expected. *He really doesn't move fast for anyone or anything.*

With his overly dramatic exit, Scribner and Jake were alone at the table. For a few moments, the two simply stared at each other and smirked. They knew Dukes' forced show of being hurt was all just an act.

"So listen, you sure you're really alright man? You've been looking really out of it lately" Scribner asked with more concern than usual. *Hard to believe this is the same guy that was humping my bedroom door a few hours ago.*

"I appreciate the concern Scribbs, but I'm good. Trust me, I'd tell you if I wasn't" Jake answered, half-lying. He was struggling. *But not today. Today I'm free.* "Plus we have a week off from school, and that means no pledging. It might as well be a national holiday." That was good enough for his friend. Thankfully, he was finishing up his meal as Jake's phone rang with Jared's name on the caller ID.

"Alright, Jared's calling me, I'm heading upstairs" Jake said with enough volume behind his words to make it to Scribner a few feet away at the garbage can.

"Sounds good man, I'll catch you back at the dorm."

As Jake made his way up the stairs he noticed Jared coming through the doors. He raised his arm to show Jake he noticed him. His Big had a goofy smile on his face, much like the same one he had whenever Jake saw him, no matter the circumstances. *I'll bet he never gets pissed.*

"You ready to eat bro?"

"Definitely, let's head to the grill" Jake said, practically salivating.

"I'm gonna get Subway and meet you down there. Grab a table" he responded. Jared then walked over to the franchise located on the upper level of Lancaster. Jake was actually a huge fan of their subs but for today he had his mind set on the grill's food.

"Alright, I'll meet you down there" Jake said before b-lining it back down the stairs and into the grill area to wait in line for a couple burgers and fries.

"So how'd the rest of the night go?" Jared asked once they sat down at the table Jake had chosen. Jake didn't know his Big that well, having only met him a few weeks prior during Rush but he didn't believe there was any maliciousness in his question.

He knows how fuckin' terrible the rest of the night was. "How the fuck do you think it went? After Summers fucked up the alphabet, we went to the track and ran 'til Jeff was satisfied. And I feel pretty comfortable saying that that bastard is never satisfied" Jake belted out. He'd used enough volume that even in the crowded dining hall, people caught on. Jared didn't seem to mind, which was one of the things to like about his Big: he took everything in stride. That made him ideal since Jake was known for a freak-out more often than most. *Biz is eligible for sainthood for putting up with me.*

"At least it's only another two weeks 'til week six" Jared announced giddily.

"I don't know" Jake began. *"If* we ever cross, I just can't see myself being friends with that jackass. I fucking hate him."

Jared must've known I'd be pissed after last night. He began to relax a little; partially from embarrassment at being so mad at someone he barely knew. "Sorry" was all Jake could say in response, ashamed at his frustration.

"It's straight bro, I thought the same thing. There were nine of us and I thought Kevin went out of his way just to fuck with me."

"What's your point?"

Jared chuckled while taking another bite from his meatball sub. "Trust me bro, you aren't getting singled out."

There's no goddamn way I'm not being singled out. Jeff Chester is the Antichrist.

"Look, pledging is the most fun you'll never wanna have again. Yeah it's miserable, but you'll have some sick memories."

Jake sat there in contemplation. There were already some stupidly funny things that had happened during the opening weeks that he found entertaining now. But that still didn't change the fact that what was happening now was anything but fun.

"You get out of pledging what you put into it. Like Jeff and Jerry are always telling you guys, you can let this whole process fuck with you. *Or* you can man up, finish it and get down to living the dream with your best friends" he finished with an air of triumph, as if there was no possible argument against him.

"My best friends aren't even in the frat."

Once again, Jared looked anything but shaken. "It's straight, I get it bro. But this is what makes the Greek Circle different from other clubs…you have to earn it. Trust me…when it's over, it'll make sense."

Jake wouldn't get anywhere by yelling at Jared or arguing with him about whether he thought the guy was full of shit. *Just relax and eat your damn food.*

The thought of pledging continuing after spring break started souring his mood the longer it stayed in his head, almost to the point where he didn't want to eat.

This better be a long fucking break.

****

Leave it to Riley to have some kind of crisis before she could get down to partying. It was sadly becoming a recurring theme. *Last year, January fifteenth. That's when it all fell apart.* That winter was the first full semester she'd been a member of EIPi. She loved pretty much everything her sorority had done for her life at Gladen Hills. Nowhere was that more apparent than with the person standing right next to her as they walked across campus with the sun setting in the distance.

Tory was going on about something that happened last night that she'd forgotten during her blackout. Riley wasn't paying that much attention because it was a common occurrence, albeit a funnier one.

"…And then I left and walked home" Tory finished.

It was at these moments that Riley usually chimed in with a general response to keep Tory appeased, which usually worked when her mind was wandering. "I love it when you keep things classy T."

"I know Riles. It might as well be my middle name."

The campus looked particularly beautiful tonight, even more so when she took into account having a week off with no schoolwork. The sun had a bright orange glow and it was just hitting the horizon past the buildings and farmland to the west. Even though it was growing colder, the effects were stunning.

"So again, why aren't you just coming straight with me to the Gamma house?"

"I told you, I gotta deal with this before I go. It shouldn't be any longer than ten or twenty minutes so I said I'd talk to him now."

Danielle had understood just fine but then again Tory and her were very different. Dani decided to just wait and head down with a larger group of their sisters later. *Not Tory. If there's a party she's always the first one through the door ready to get crazy.*

As they walked past the Blue Hold, they approached the destination dorm. Riley knew her friend would wait if asked but there was no reason to delay a clearly eager Tory Brye from a party so she kept quiet.

"Alright, I'll be over soon" Riley said to her as they reached the entrance. Thankfully, it was before nine so her student ID would work to get her into the building even though she didn't live there. She lifted the card out of her jacket pocket and swiped it at the scanner on the left side of the alcove. The door clicked loudly as it unlocked.

"OK...I'll have beers ready" Tory said with a grin as she continued her walk to Arkridge Avenue. From Northeast it was pretty much a straight shot down the Interstate to hit the outskirts of campus where most of the frat houses were. That didn't change the fact that Northeast was still out of the way from EIPi when heading to Arkridge but Tory had come along anyway.

Once inside, Riley walked left into the main common area. There was only one person sitting in the room and there was no sound coming from the rest of the dorm, almost like it was completely empty. *Most underclassmen probably cleared out already for break. The only ones left around here are the ones ready to drink before going home.* Those types of people were sure as hell not going to be in here with this guy, who was clearly brooding in his typical fashion.

"OK Jake, what the hell is so important it couldn't wait 'til break?"

Her younger cousin looked pensive. "I need your help with something," he said, finally looking up from the floor to face her.

Yeah but what else is new?

It was probably a testament to growing up together that Riley could read Jake Raley like a picture book. It definitely had its advantages. "Yes, you should break up with Kelly" she stated quickly.

Jake didn't flinch. *Yeah, he definitely expected that one.*

"I know where you stand on that subject...this is something else," he replied coolly. *What could be more important than ending it with that whore you're dating?*

Shaking off the thought, Riley moved to sit on the couch with her cousin. She made a point to sit near, but not too near him. Generally it was better to give him space, because he usually flailed around when he was upset. It could either be an annoying tick, or an extremely funny one depending on the situation's severity.

"OK, what's going on?" she asked, trying to inject as much care into her voice as she could without it sounding forced. It wasn't as easy as it should've been.

For another long stretch, Jake appeared lost in his own thoughts.

"OK, what would happen if I de-pledged and walked away?" *Oh Jesus here we go. One mistake after another.* "You can't Jake," she answered quickly, matching his somber tone without trying.

As expected, Jake abruptly stood up. "Why the fuck can't I? I'm done with this bullshit," he practically yelled at her. Any other normal person outside their family would've taken Jake's yelling as offensive. She'd known him long enough to realize his anger and frustration was in no way aimed at her though. She was simply the one who'd answered his texts about needing to talk. *That makes this my problem now too.*

"Have you talked to Eric?"

"I'm talking to you because I *can't* talk to him!"

Riley shook her head. Her cousin was the kind of person who'd let things simmer inside for a long time before finally letting it boil over and exploding along with it. *Just like when we were kids.* Riley wasn't offended by his comments about talking to her because Eric was unavailable for whatever new reason Jake had cooked up. She always knew they were closer. *Just because they're boys.*

"You know, he was your cousin long before he was your frat brother Jake, and that's still more important."

"I don't think that's true Rye."

"That's because you're being dramatic," she said, starting to feel frustrated.

"You know me. You know I hate being told what to do, even more so being told what I can't do."

Great, he's getting mad again. "You've only got two weeks left, not to mention a full week off right now." *Come on Jake, just suck it up.*

"Full week off my ass, I'll be studying that damn pledge book all break learning family trees and pledge classes. We're supposed to have it fully memorized by week five," he lamented. "It hit me today after lunch, this break isn't really a break. I've basically got homework in the form of that fucking pledge book. And for those of you keeping score at home, that's more homework than I have from my actual classes!"

Riley smirked. "Any chance I could see that pledge book?"

For the first time since walking in she saw a side of Jake she enjoyed. He actually smirked back at her knowingly. "Even if I de-pledge, you aren't getting that book. Eric would get real pissed if I let a sorority girl look at it, even if it is you."

Now we're getting somewhere. "You guys are so weird" she said disapprovingly.

Jake took to it like a bee to honey. "Right, because sororities don't keep secrets."

Riley grinned in spite of herself. "So what brought this whole thing on exactly?"

"It might be the fact that this is killing me and Kelly. It could be the fact that I've done more physical activity in the past four weeks than I have during my whole life before now. But I think the deal was sealed when I realized last night how much I fucking hate Jeff" he ranted, all without stopping to take a breath.

"Yeah, he is an ass..." Riley agreed, recalling her memories of the guy.

"I can't fucking stand him...or Jerry, they're driving me out of my fucking mind" he bit out. Commiserating about Jerry was something she was far more qualified for, but she wasn't even close to being comfortable enough with everything to start down that road. Luckily Jake didn't seem to notice how uncomfortable she looked for those precious few seconds while Jerry flashed through her mind.

"So what'll happen if I walk away?"

"Well for starters, knowing you, you'll regret it instantly. Then you'll want to try again, but no other frat is gonna take you seriously because de-pledges don't get second chances...anywhere." Her cousin didn't look convinced. "I'm serious Jake; Gladen isn't *that* big of a school. People talk, especially the ones that drink, and that includes the entire Greek Circle." *He must've noticed that, serving beer at the AZXi parties.*

"Most importantly though...Eric is gonna be disappointed" she said solemnly. Despite what Jake was saying about not being able to talk to him, she knew how he felt about his older cousin.

"I doubt he'll even notice" Jake said with enough self-pity to fill the room.

OK...that's it. "Get the fuck over it Jake."

Everything in the room froze as Riley let her frustration rush out. "This is something *you* wanted remember? You signed up for a reason, so my advice is try remembering what exactly that reason was and get on with it." It might as well have been a direct order. Clearly Jake wasn't expecting her to be so tough and blunt because the look on his face went from stubborn to ashamed in milliseconds. *You asked for it.*

"I just don't think I can do this for another two weeks Rye."

As much as she wanted to hug her cousin, she knew she had to stay strong.

"I don't care where you're trying to earn letters, pledging is always ninety percent mental. It might not seem that way, but the whole thing is a mind fuck. If Eric and I can get through it, so can you. Don't let it get to you. Keep your temper in check." Riley kept her voice as stern as she could but some genuine concern crept in anyway.

"I'll think about it...but that's all I can promise" Jake finally answered.

Before all her progress was undone, she figured she should leave Jake to his thoughts now that she'd made her point. "Fine...if you'll excuse me, I have to go stop Tory from making poor life choices" she announced while standing up.

"Who's your party with tonight?"

"The Gammas."

The look on Jake's face told her all she needed to know. He looked disgusted, but in a fun way. "Yikes, you girls can do better than that."

Yeah, he's one of them for sure. "You definitely have more in common with the AZXis than you think," she said with a knowing smirk. *That'll drive him crazy.*

Riley gave him a quick hug before practically jogging to the exit. She didn't like gambling as much as Eric, but if she did she'd bet heavily on Jake finishing out pledging.

****

Standing outside the DXA house in the winter temperatures reiterated to Jeff what he already knew. *This sorority is just not fun, no fucking way.* There was just no getting around it. The thought came to him once he saw his pack of cigarettes was empty, save for a final pair. That his half pack was now down to two plus the one he was currently finishing was a direct commentary on the nature of the party. Not that it was a shock, given that it was the Friday before spring break and more than half the town was gone. *It's still a poor showing.*

The more cigarettes he went through at a party usually correlated with how much fun he was having. If he were having a good time, he usually left the party less to go outside and smoke. Likewise, if there wasn't much keeping him from leaving, he usually went through a pack each time. Adding to the awful nature of the night was his fucking assistant pledge-master as Jerry saw fit to consistently voice his disapproval. The incessant bitching was putting a full stop on any buzz Jeff was attempting to build.

"I don't know about this son, it seems mad weird," he said, for about the thousandth time. He tended to repeat himself while drunk. *At least I let you get drunk in peace tonight asshole.*

"I'm telling you, these pledges are half-assing it, especially Summers and Raley. This will get things straight before break" Jeff practically lashed out. *You're lucky I'm not drunk because I'd probably beat the shit out of you. You clearly don't understand how the chain of command works.* In the old days, Jeff would've never questioned an older brother that'd pledged and crossed before him. *And that was a pain in the ass when I knew they were doing shit wrong...but I still kept my mouth shut. But not you new guys, you all think you know exactly what the fuck is up.*

"Yeah, but what if they all just walk out and we don't cross any pledges this semester? That'll straight kill our numbers" Jerry responded.

If they end up walking out then you might have a point...but they won't. No chance. "J-Hood will never quit anything and Will is too close with you and Biz for that to be an issue."

"Raley is Biz's cousin; you think that'll stop him?" Jerry asked, actually posing an interesting question for the first time tonight.

True, if any of them are gonna quit, it'll definitely be Raley. Guess we'll find out in the morning. "We'll see" was all Jeff could respond with, making sure not to let any doubt creep into his voice.

"And if I don't go with you?" Jerry asked in defiance. It was drunken defiance but it was still there, clear as day. Fortunately, Jeff was prepared for it. While Jerry could stop himself, he sure as hell couldn't stop Jeff. Not on his best day, and especially not while drunk.

"Then I'll do it anyway and the pledges will see we're not united and that'll be great for our image as a frat that we can't even agree on how to haze" Jeff retorted. *Chew on that one, dumbass.* He placed as much of a threatening tone into his words as he could. Jerry's love of the frat and its need for a good image were among the easiest of strings to pull on, especially when he'd had a few beers. There could be problems behind the scenes, and there no doubt would be, but the pledges wouldn't and couldn't ever know a thing about them until *after* Crossing. Jerry not going along with him for a callout would shatter that image of solidarity the pledges had of the active brothers.

"Look, I know they'll finish strong because of this...because of what we do tonight" Jeff said confidently.

"*If* they finish," Jerry said, resigned.

He could've just as easily thrown out the fact that Jerry's title was that of *assistant* pledge-master and it was built-in that he should follow the *actual* pledge-master. He didn't want to throw out his title

though. *It's enough of a joke when Gretman says he's president.*
"When you have pledges, you can do whatever the fuck you want with them and I won't say shit because it won't be my place, but this is my time."

"I'd love to get that in writing."

At least he's on board. It took long enough. "For now all you get is my word."

As he walked away, he listened intently for the sounds of Jerry's following footsteps. They came right on cue.

****

No matter what the trouble was in his life, there was always one thing that could get Jake back to a good place, and that was Nintendo. He'd been a huge fan of the company ever since he was a little kid playing the original Mario Brothers with his dad and cousins. And that devotion stayed with him throughout all their subsequent system releases right up to now.

If there was one game that he always loved playing regardless of the circumstances, it had to be Goldeneye. His ability in this game was one of the few things he'd actually go out of his way to brag about since there weren't many other skills worth noting. At least he didn't think so.

As he finished playing another round on the hardest difficulty, he looked over to his pledge brother J-Hood who was in no way enjoying himself. *Why does he have his pledge book out?* "Come on son, run a mission, you don't need to look at that damn book for at least a couple days."

J-Hood simply raised his head from the page and looked back at him. "Just memorized the credo, what the fuck is up?!" he stated in his usual monotone voice.

Jake smirked. The credo was basically a five-paragraph amalgamation of shit the founding fathers had tossed in to make themselves sound better to the school. Jake was willing to bet that most, if not every other organization had something just like it. Just another necessity set by a school administration disgusted by every facet of the Greek Circle. That didn't make the memorization of such a tedious and bullshit section of their books any less impressive. He himself hadn't even looked at the thing after reading it the first time through while copying it down three weeks ago.

"Why the fuck are you still looking at that shit?"

"I'm telling you…I bet there's a callout tonight."

The very thought was enough to make Jake cringe. After that came extreme anger. "Buttons is a complete psycho, but even he's not that crazy. He said pledging would be on hold 'til next Sunday."

J-Hood didn't look convinced but he didn't argue any further either.

The original plan had been to hang out in Jake's suite before heading out to see if there were any Open parties on Arkridge Avenue. More likely, for Jake at least, the night would begin and end in his suite. He didn't have any further aspirations past playing videogames. Heading to Arkridge would just provide a chance to run into the brothers of a frat he'd sooner avoid for the next week…if not forever.

"Finally finished studying then?"

"Yeah, for now at least" J-Hood replied.

Jake looked at the pledge book the guy was putting away into his backpack. Just seeing it made him angry but he couldn't explain why.

Their pledge books encompassed about sixty or so pages of AZXi history inside a one hundred-page composition notebook they all got from a local store on University Grove. They had to copy all the information in by hand from pages taken from the Historian's Binder that Jeff gave them during their first week.

The most fucked up thing about the books was they all had to be written in pen and if there was *any* mistake, the book would have to be scrapped. But not just simply thrown away, it'd have to be burned because the history was supposed to stay within the brotherhood of AZXi. No outsider was ever supposed to have access to it. Jake didn't even want to recollect how many failed attempts each of the four of them went through before they'd all come out with a perfect book. The flames of the many bonfires they'd seen with their failed notebooks were readily visible in his mind.

After the history had been transcribed, the bookends had to be covered in laminate with black on the front and yellow on the back, signifying the fraternity colors. On the front were the frat letters in yellow type, on the back were the pledge class letters in black type. Their letters were an 'Alpha' and an 'Epsilon' back-to-back. It was supposed to signify pride they all had in their pledge class. *Pride went right out the fuckin' window after ten minutes of hearing how awful we are. And that was the first callout.*

Jake was getting lost in his own head when he was abruptly jolted out by two separate things: J-Hood's phone rang its usual rap song and his suitemates walked in.

"Thought you guys were going out?"

"We are, just finished eating at the Hold" Scribner responded.

Jake instantly missed the days when could eat with his friends at the dining hall. *It's probably been over four weeks since I've had dinner with them. Thanks again brother Jeff.* Once pledging started dinner was mandated at five PM everyday, and it had to be with his pledge brothers. He didn't particularly mind eating with them, but having dinner with the same people every weeknight for four weeks straight was sickening. *I wouldn't be able to eat with Eric and Riley that many nights without killing someone.*

"It was filling, yet in no way satisfying" Dukes chimed in.

"Yo Justin, you get a chance to look at that econ shit?" Scribner asked J-Hood.

"Nah not yet" J-Hood replied casually. "Raley we gotta get to the house. That was Will, Jeff wants us there now."

Jake immediately felt his heart sink, but his depression gave way to anger just as quickly. Rage began bubbling. "You've got to be fucking kidding me."

"We gotta go man," he repeated, betraying no emotion. Never had the notion of quitting been as close for Jake as it was at that moment.

This was supposed to be our free time. Those fucks at the house told us we'd have tonight off. And now they want to fuck with us like it's no big deal.

Jake felt his body start shaking involuntarily. *This is all on you. You could've gotten a ride home with Kelly earlier today but no, you wanted to chill with your friends. And now look where you are.* Jake was now staring down a one-way ticket to AZXi.

With the most begrudging movement he could muster, Jake went to his room for his backpack, which housed his own pledge book. He re-entered the common room to find Dukes already screwing around on his Goldeneye game.

J-Hood was already heading out the door. Jake hurried to strap on his backpack and follow him. *Why are you even going? Just tell those bastards to go fuck themselves.*

As he left, he turned toward Scribner who gave him a solemn nod. *Well at least somebody gives a fuck about how I'm feeling right now.* Jake doubted he'd find anybody else like that at the frat house.

****

"I'd like to think Jerry and I have been fair during this whole process. I'd like to think that that should've been good enough to make you guys a great pledge class, if not a halfway decent one. Yet here we are at the end of week four and you guys still don't have a fucking clue about what makes a good AZXi" Jeff yelled at the four dumbfounded pledges standing before him. His words echoed throughout the empty basement with great effect. *And Gretman wanted to stop me.*

"Do any of you have the slightest idea what to say now?" Jerry asked in his gruff tone reserved solely for the pledges.

True to form, not a single one even moved.

"You can talk one at a time if need be" Jeff said, hoping to finally get a response.

"What more is there to do?" Jake asked.

Jeff hid a smirk. *Thank you for being an asshole Raley.*

"I want you to grow a pair of balls and finish this program! I want you to earn the letters you signed up for! The letters we wear!" Jeff screamed back. It was mostly directed at Raley, but he kept his stance so that all of them bore the brunt in some way.

Raley looked like he was squaring his shoulders for a fight. *Relax kid, you don't have the balls to do anything.*

"And before you say anything else Raley no, you haven't earned shit. All you do is show us one disappointment after another, and it's fucking disgusting" Jerry yelled, now at the whole pledge class. That seemed to shut Raley down, as he recoiled slightly.

Just like I thought kid.

There was one reason why tonight was deemed a callout and yet no blindfolds were being worn by the pledges. Tonight was primarily a visual experience, and Jeff didn't want any of these poor excuses for pledges to miss a damn thing.

This is it. No turning back from this moment. More than likely, his action tonight would cause the frat to question his authority and choices for the rest of the semester. *At least that won't be much different from how it is now.*

"Pledge Raley give me your pledge book now!"

The look of fear on the kid's face was priceless. Unfortunately Jeff couldn't allow himself to show amusement. *We're a long way from the night we named you 'shudder' kid.*

Finally Raley handed over his pledge book, very hesitantly. *This is it.*

****

Jeff basically ripped the book from Jake's shaking hands. *What the fuck is gonna happen now?*

Here they were at a callout by all accounts, and yet there was no music blasting from the speakers. There were no other brothers in the basement except for the two pledge-masters. They weren't wearing blindfolds and they didn't have to greet either brother when they came down.

Without warning Jeff ripped out a handful of pages from Jake's pledge book. There was no mistaking the reactions that came inadvertently from himself and the rest of his pledge class. They were wincing at the pages being torn as if skin was being ripped from their own bodies. *Are you fucking kidding me?*

Jerry moved to J-Hood and asked for his book. He then proceeded to read through a few pages before ripping out a handful from that one.

The anger bubbling inside was reaching a boil. *That's it. I'm done.* Jake prepared himself to lunge at Jeff the next time he paced by. He was almost in range of Jake's arm when the weirdest thing happened.

"Please list the Iota pledge class," Jeff repeated in a normal voice.

Jake's confusion overcame his deep desire to punch Jeff, if only for the moment.

Jeff knew none of them memorized the pledge classes that far back. They hadn't known it last night and they damn sure hadn't gotten to it since then. All Jake could do was stare back at Jeff in pure hatred.

Once again, it looked like Jeff was hiding a smile behind that stonewalled face.

You're loving this aren't you? You fuckin' bastard.

"I only ask because I know you don't know. That's why this page isn't in the book anymore. If you don't know it then it must not be that important right?"

I can't. I won't redo that book one more time...

"Pledge J-Hood, who was Final Bids with for the Delta class?" Jerry asked.

When J-Hood returned his question with nothing, more pages were ripped out.

That sick form of torment continued on with the rest of Jake's book before they moved on to Will and Summers' books too.

When it was over there was paper littering the AZXi basement floor. The sight of it all did a strange thing to Jake, his anger was still present, but now a different sensation was creeping up: pure sadness. He didn't think it was possible to care so much about a book but he'd put too much work into it to not care.

"Seeing how you guys have a week off, you're going to re-do your books from scratch all over again. Hopefully you'll use that time to memorize everything in them or we'll just go through it all over again. If you want these letters" Jeff started yelling and grabbing his own AZXi jersey, "then it's time to step the fuck up and show us! Now get the fuck out of our sight!"

It wasn't the first callout Jake had considered quitting after, but it was definitely the first time he felt that it was his only way out. He tried remembering his talk with Riley but even that was little comfort now as they walked over the ruins of their pledge books. *Well at least I have all of spring break to tell Eric I'm done.*

Chapter 5

The harsh light of day was creeping through the clouds when they arrived in the driveway. It had been another early wake-up call that morning. *At least this time I didn't have to sit through breakfast at Lancaster.*

There was something about going home to Reesewood that brought on the oddest feeling. It was an entirely different life he was entering into...and a much more peaceful one at that. Still, even though it was good to see the house he grew up in, there was still something nagging at him.

He waved at the car now backing down his driveway.

Jake took a deep breath before raising the garage door that would allow him entrance. It felt lighter than it did the last time he raised it two months ago. *Well at least all those push-ups are good for something.*

Passing through the car-less garage, he lowered his guard, almost without noticing. No cars in the garage meant his mother wasn't home, which meant no one could bother him about his classes. The house and its surroundings suddenly became that much more relaxing. Jake smiled to the empty space before making his way toward the door on the far left side.

There's still so much shit Mom keeps in here for no damn reason. It was technically a two-car garage but since the divorce years ago only one car was ever parked inside. *None of this would change even if I had a car.* There were so many assorted trinkets on the right side that it'd take days to sort it all out. *I couldn't be paid enough to go through it all...*

The only thing Jake and his mother seemed to have in common was their last name. He had an almost compulsive need to keep everything straight and in its place. His mother was clearly was indifferent on the subject, if not altogether against it.

Feeling his blood pressure rise at the mere thought of dealing with it all Jake hurriedly got out his keys, unlocked the door and moved inside. Thankfully the temperature indoors was incredibly warm compared to the garage. Within seconds of arriving inside, the first greeting came in the form of his cat Shelby. He'd had his cat for a little over ten years by now and thankfully she hadn't lost a step. Jake knelt down and dropped his bags full of clothes so he could pet his cat unhindered. She was purring loudly enough to put a smile on his face. *I missed you too.*

Strangely, Jake noticed a lone piece of paper sitting on the kitchen counter in the next room. The kitchen counter was usually full of papers and assorted nonsense his mother failed to organize. That could only mean one thing: it was a note intended for him. *Yaps needed help dealing with Paps. He needed to have some more tests done at the hospital so I'll be over there for a day or two. Call if you need anything.*

Jake set the paper down. *Well that worked out nicely.*

If I had a car then I'd definitely go visit. Yaps and Paps always want company. Since most of their grandkids were in college, their visits usually meant they wanted food or money...or both. *That never stops them from humoring us anyway.*

His thoughts strayed away from his family to settle on the fact that he was home alone. Re-reading the note, Jake focused on one detail of it. The part stating his mother would be gone for a *few days,* meaning plural. *Dear God I have the house to myself...I'm free.* He could do whatever he wanted...and there was one thing he desperately wanted.

He all but sprinted toward the stairs and up to his bedroom. He found it much the same way he'd left it in January when he'd left for school. His room was his bubble, a shield from the rest of the world. Today it held the glorious promise of uninterrupted sleep in a place by himself. He wasn't going to pass that up.

After about five hours of blissful sleep, Jake had woken up with a new lease on life, not to mention a freshly cemented sex drive he was keen on dealing with immediately. After putting on a pair of sweatpants and a t-shirt the first order of business was calling Kelly.

Just as he was hanging up the phone and telling Kelly he loved her he saw a car pull into the driveway. *So much for being alone for the day.*

Realizing who it was almost immediately; Jake moved to open the front door. With the sunlight now fully streaming through the outer glass, the car's occupant strolled inside gleefully. "What the hell are you doing here?"

"Read your wall post to Eric, your mom's gone 'til Monday. That means we're partying tonight," Scribner answered matter-of-factly.

Of course that's why he's here. Jake was ashamed for not realizing it sooner. His friend had a nose for when to throw a party and better yet, when not to.

"First, quit stalking me online and second…I don't know man, Kelly's coming over in a couple hours. I just wanted to chill for the day."

His friend clearly hadn't been prepared for Jake's lack of desire to socialize with anyone other than Kelly until at least tomorrow. "Dude, you haven't drank since your Bids, and you bitched out last night. Now put your big boy pants on, and get ready to get fuckin' stupid."

Jake didn't really believe he'd win the argument and the more he thought about it the more he didn't want to. *Well-played Scribbs.* "What'd you have in mind?"

"Raley's Ring, we're bringing it back man. Most of the gang is on break this week too, we could make a killing."

"Fine. Set it up. Nine tonight then?"

"Done. I'll be here around eight to help set up."

Am I really that easy to talk into shit like this? Jake waved it off. *I want to drink tonight so who cares?* Given how much fun he'd had the last time he'd gone out drinking he was sure it would be a good time. *And it's Raley's Ring.* There was really only one thing left to do before Kelly got there: inspect the damage his mother had done to their party area in the basement.

Jake walked down the wooden, creaky steps in apprehension of what insanity could've been wrought on the area.

Thankfully, the basement looked mostly undisturbed; the posters of models and drinking games still plastered the walls. The chalkboard for beer pong sign up was still nailed to wall and the thirty pack box covers still wallpapered the top and bottom of the main room. The table in the center was remarkably not covered with papers or any other shit. *This might as well be a Christmas-day miracle.*

Every time Jake looked around the basement he'd molded from a storage space into a party center, he felt incredibly proud. It was intoxicating to feel that way again after so long. *It's good to be home.*

Jake looked up from the beer soaked ground back over to the wall with the beer pong list taped up. He always thought it'd be nice to have some kind of white board or something in place of a piece of printer paper so people could sign up for beer pong in an organized fashion. Of course, that was probably just because he was drunk. His mind wasn't finished brainstorming though. It went further and began thinking of ways to decorate the area with symbols of drinking. *Posters and maybe a wallpaper design with beers we've drank...that'd look pretty sweet.*

The voice of his friend Scribner suddenly shot out from the couch behind him. His words were tough to make out since he'd also been heavily drinking.

"How'd you do tonight?" Scribner repeated.

Only then did he remember he was counting the money he'd collected. Below him at his fingertips was a small stack of cash sitting on the lone table in the television nook section of the basement. He hadn't gotten very far into counting it before he went off on his brainstorm.

"Taking into account that I fronted the money for the drinks...a little under even" he finally responded with an edge of disappointment. *Nothing new there.*

"Yeah but we drank for free" Scribner pointed out.

"True but that's part of the problem isn't it?"

"For our livers maybe."

"Well you and Eric drink...a lot." He tried sounding as delicate as possible, even though he knew it wasn't offensive.

"Thanks pal."

Jake smiled. *He's got a point. It's a good time down here. But between Eric and his new best friend Jerry, the drinks are disappearing quicker every night. There's gotta be a better way.*

As soon as his cousin flashed into his mind, he came stumbling in from the main party area with Jerry. *Probably just finished another round of beer pong.*

"You ever thought about running this place like a legit bar?" Eric exclaimed.

"Exhibit A" Jake motioned to Eric, referencing his earlier comment.

"No he's got a point Raley" Scribner said, waving off his sarcasm.

"No...I'm pretty sure I was kidding" Eric drunkenly slurred while shifting in his newfound position on the couch. *I'll need a forklift to get him up.*

Scribner wouldn't listen, even though the owner of the idea had since disowned it.

"Well let's run a test," he proclaimed before practically running out of the TV nook.

I'm too fucked up for this right now...

All Jake could do to process the situation was stare back at the now absent-minded look on his cousin's face.

"On that note, I'm outta here Biz" Jerry announced before moving over toward him for a handshake. Eric reciprocated as best he could, although it looked like he too was still processing the confusion from Scribner's exit.

Jerry moved over toward Jake and shook his hand. "Good to meet you man."

"Why you leaving son?" Eric finally asked.

"Gotta wake up early tomorrow."

"That is so weeeaaaak" his cousin responded, elongating the final word for effect.

Jake smiled. *Classic drunken Biz.* Having found a very comfortable position on the old couch he wasn't likely to press the issue. *The couch does look real nice right now.* He thought about taking a seat next to Eric before he realized Jerry was already halfway out of the basement and Scribner was still missing.

"What'd you think son?" Eric asked of Jerry once he left.

Jake shrugged. "He seems cool but a little full of himself."

"That's fair."

"Yo Scribbs! What the fuck are you doing?" Jake called out to the other side of the wall in front of him that his friend had disappeared behind.

Within seconds, Scribner came back from the laundry room with a full plastic bottle of vodka.

"OK, I'm not that drunk so that can't be vodka" Jake stated hesitantly.

"Nah, it's just water. I filled it up at the sink," Scribner answered. He still looked like he was on a mission. "Grab the shot glasses."

Jake complied, if only to see what exactly the guy was up to. Handing him the five that were in the immediate area, Scribner got to work. He began filling the shot glasses and then dumping their contents into the used plastic cups within reach.

"OK, accounting for spilling and shit, let's call it forty."

"What the hell are you talking about?" Eric asked, beating Jake to it.

"Charge a dollar a shot and you're golden man" Scribner said, now with a huge smile Jake would've seen fit to put on someone who'd just cured cancer. *Could I really charge people to drink that disgusting piss? I don't even like doing it for free.*

"Don't charge your close friends, just the non-regulars. The rest of us can drink for the normal five bucks total."

Jake had to admit the idea had merit. *There are a lot of people coming down here that aren't really close friends...more like acquaintances.* Still, the concept of actually making money and running a semi-legitimate operation had its benefits, not to mention amazing social implications. *You could definitely get popular doing something like this...*

"Yeah OK but who the fuck would want to man the bar all night and serve drinks and keep everything straight?"

"Yeah, fuck that" Eric answered before shooting a look back at Scribner, almost daring him to come up with an answer for that one too.

"I'll straight volunteer for that Raley. This could be a blast."

He wants in. Scribbs could definitely run this place for me, he doesn't get hammered that much and he's kinda responsible. The benefits of boosting Jake's own popularity weighed heavily on his mind. *This makes too much sense not to do.*

"Scribbs you've got yourself a deal" Jake stated, now sporting a smile to match the one on his friend's face. "I've gotta clean this place up a little."

"What for?" Eric asked, now lying on the couch with his eyes closed.

"Think about it Biz, when people pay outrageous amounts for drinks at a bar, you're essentially paying for the atmosphere as much as the alcohol...maybe even more so. And if we can make the atmosphere sick, no one will complain about the price."

"What the fuck are you gonna do to brighten this place?" Scribner asked.

Jake smiled. *Wait and see Scribbs.*

Jake looked around the basement, marveling at the designs he'd mapped out two years ago. He noted the way the beer pong rules were displayed in particular. As long as they'd been partying down here there were never any problems with the central drinking game.

That was in no small part thanks to the sixteen rules Jake had laminated and plastered on both walls on opposite sides of the table. Those sixteen rules covered every possible scenario of a game. They were so ironclad that most of the regular people memorized them.

Gladen isn't even close to this much fun. Jake shook his head. *Jeff can't control me down here. This is my place. Jerry is never coming back down here.*

Partying at school had become a lost art with the dry pledge process he was involved in. Or rather, the dry process he'd *been* involved in. Jake was now fully confident in his decision to quit AZXi. Being home was just the fuel he needed to resolve to tell Eric he was done.

For now, he shoved those thoughts aside. He had to focus on cleaning up to make the basement ready for the people that'd be flooding it in a couple hours.

After Kelly comes over.

"So if your mom's gone, does that mean you're actually gonna relax tonight?" Kelly asked him as they walked down into the fully lit basement.

Having just finished with some extremely satisfying and actually slightly rougher sex than usual, Jake was feeling on top of the world. All he could focus on was how good Kelly's ass looked in her jeans. Not that it mattered, his girlfriend liked when he was checking her out and being noticeable about it.

"Hey, I'm always relaxed. She just knows how to make other people as paranoid as she is and it drives me crazy."

"Just like everyone else's mother?"

Fine...fine. "Yes, I'll be able to relax tonight babe" he answered with a smile as they reached the bottom of the stairs.

She stopped short of entering the TV nook that doubled as the bar serving space. "If you don't, I'll make sure you do" she promised before leaning in to kiss him.

"Sounds like I might get tense on purpose" he shot back with a grin before leaning in and kissing her again. It felt like an addiction. He very much couldn't keep his hands off her when they were alone, or with others for that matter.

As they continued kissing in the empty basement, the sound of footsteps became louder and louder as someone approached from upstairs.

"You left the door unlocked when you came in earlier, didn't you?" Jake asked, knowing full well who was coming down the stairs. There wasn't a single person on the guest list that would actually show up on time, much less early other than his cousin.

"Let me help you" Kelly offered as she broke away from Jake's firm grasp to help with one of the bags of ice Eric was holding as he rounded the corner from the stairway.

She definitely left it unlocked.

Eric and Kelly walked over behind the bar counter and dumped the bags of ice into the large cooler Jake had bought a few summers ago when Raley's Ring started heating up. After emptying the ice, Eric looked back to Jake who was clearly in no hurry to help at the moment having zoned in again on Kelly's figure.

"Yo Jerry told me about your pledge books, that's really messed up man" Eric said sincerely.

Too bad that makes no difference. It still happened.

"Yeah and the rest of the shit is just in good fun right?" Jake shot back. It sounded much harsher in reality than it had in his head.

"You know what I mean son."

"Yeah but it still doesn't make it any less of a pain in the ass. And no, I haven't started re-writing the fuckin' thing yet."

"It's so cute that you have your little pledge books to write in," Kelly said in her soothing voice as Eric went back up stairs for the thirty-packs of beer.

"Yeah if by cute you mean agonizing."

"Only two more weeks right?"

"If I don't quit," he blurted out while staring into her eyes.

"You're not serious are you?"

She doesn't think I'll actually go through with it either. Just like Riley.

Jake had been threatening to quit in one form or another to anyone who would listen since pledging started. *This time is different.* "Usually a safe bet" he agreed, "but this time…I don't know…"

"You obviously haven't told Eric yet."

Jake looked away. "No…because I don't know how."

"Yo Jake! I need help with the beer!" Eric's voice traveled down the steps.

Jake looked deep into Kelly's eyes before moving away to help his cousin. "Don't say anything. I've gotta be the one to tell him."

****

Scribner looked around the basement. It'd only been about an hour since he'd gotten there and the place was already packed. *Good thing Raley still listens to me.* The one thing that usually told him the party was full was the beer pong sign-up board. Raley still hadn't wised up to the idea of allowing for more than one drinking game during a party so beer pong was always front and center. The chalkboard that he'd helped nail to the wall two summers ago was completely full of names. Half were crossed out, which was no real shock given who the reigning champs were.

A ping pong ball flew right past his view of the board before splashing down into a cup on the opposing side. That was followed by the customary chant by Raley's pledge brother Will. *That guy is always yelling about being the best.* It was such a common occurrence that Scribner just considered it white noise. *Will's definitely got skills...just not as much as Eric...now that fucker can flat out play.*

Scribner had no objection to them running the table all night as it kept things going smoothly. The more games they won, the more competitors they played. The more people that played meant more beer sold. And more alcohol being sold equated to money in Raley's pocket, which equated to money in Scribner's. *It's a thing of beauty.*

The kid was generous when it came time to give Scribner a cut at the end of the night. That was usually due to the fact that Raley was hammered by then. Tonight was shaping up to be no different, although there was something a little off about his friend. For one, he was helping out behind the bar, which was a rarity on a night when Eric was around. Not only that, the two cousins weren't interacting much.

Eric Saren was the only person in the basement of fifty plus people that could ever be considered closer to Raley than he was. Yet here they were, on opposite sides of the party, acting like they didn't know each other. He'd known Raley long enough to know that this was likely due to some form of drama, forced or otherwise.

Scribner was at least thankful for the kid's help tonight given how packed it was. People were happily shelling out money for shots, mixed drinks, and cans of beer. All he could do was smile as Eric and Will sent another team packing and a fresh pair of faces up to the bar to buy beer for their upcoming match. The fact that it was his concept based on Eric's idea made the whole operation more thrilling.

After handing the two new players their beers, he put two over to the side so they were in easy reach for when either Eric or Will inevitably came over. The difference was that neither of them would pay. Raley was very particular on which of his 'friends' would be charged per beer and which ones would be charged just one amount for the entire night. As it stood, there were about twelve people that fell into the latter category of being special enough to simply throw a five on the table and have that square everything. They were all guys except for Raley's chick Kelly. Her, Scribner could take or leave. She didn't seem all that interested in talking to him and he sure as fuck wasn't interested in chatting with her. Still his friend said he was in love so she drank for free.

Within seconds of collecting money from the new opponents, Will strolled over to the bar and made a motion to get beers for the next game. *Son of a bitch hasn't been down here more than three times and he thinks he runs the place.* It was a little funny if not slightly annoying. Realizing there was no one else in line for drinks at the moment, Scribner took the rare downtime to mix up his own drink. It would be his second of the night. He figured he might as well do a shot too while he mixed a rum and coke.

After slamming the first shot and topping off his plastic cup with coke, Jake sauntered over from his end of the bar. "I think I'm starting to realize why I hate pledging so much," he blurted out.

I don't think I asked but OK. Before Jake went on, Scribner poured another shot and ripped it immediately. *If Raley's gonna bitch I better be buzzed.*

"OK shoot" he finally said after getting the second shot down and taking a sip of his mixed drink to ensure he made it correctly. *Perfect...strong as Hell.*

"Down here...in this place, me and you are the center of everything...and it feels fuckin' amazing. Back at school I'm the bottom of the fuckin' pile...again."

Scribner took another sip. *OK, maybe that's true.* Between the two of them, they ran an underage-drinking ring in a suburban town. *And we've never been caught.*

Raley was *the* center of attention down here. Everyone knew him or at least knew *of* him. *The whole thing is named after him for Christ's sake. It must've been a huge fuckin' shock going from this back to the bottom in Gladen.*

"It can only get better kid" he responded with sincerity.

"I don't know Scribbs" he responded while looking out past the bar to the party.

"This is a little above my pay-grade pal" he confessed. "Have you talked to Biz about it?"

Raley snapped out of the daze immediately to look directly at his cousin. Depression snuck in and out of the kid's eyes so quick Scribner almost missed it.

"He doesn't get it" Jake finally said before taking a large sip of his own drink.

He wasn't a fan of Raley making his own drinks because at least when he made them he could slowly dial back the liquor as the kid got drunker. That tended to not only allow him to maintain a level head, but also enjoy himself more. Problem was, when he was mixing his own drinks, he tended to add more and more as the night wore on.

"What makes you say that?" Scribner asked while shrugging off his negativity.

"Because ever since we were kids, he's always been the center of everything. And the worst part is it's not like he fuckin' he asks for it, he just...*is*. Jake turned away from the party so nobody would see his face. Thankfully Kelly was off talking to a couple other girls she'd met through Raley so she didn't notice her boyfriend's rant.

Lucky me, I get to baby-sit tonight.

"I think you're stretching it a little there Raley."

"Try growing up with someone like that Scribbs. I didn't even care but it starts to wear you down" he responded with unmistakable agony. *He's on the edge...fuck.* Scribner was the only thing standing in the way. Then a funny thing happened, which unfortunately was a rare event. Raley pulled himself out of his downward spiral and started talking rationally. "The point is I like being in charge like this. I like feeling this good Scribbs...and I don't get that at school."

"It is nice being on top," Scribner agreed.

"It's that only child thing. I grew up with my cousins around all the time but I'm still used to at least two people, namely my parents, being all about me. Ironically, that's what makes my mom so damn annoying, because she is *all* about me" Jake continued.

What the fuck is he talking about?

"You're such a buzz-kill. We aren't at school. Stop thinking about that shit."

"You're right...we aren't at school" Raley responded with a smile of his own.

"Fuck all that man. We'll deal with it later."

No point in dealing with that shit now. If he wants to talk about it then tomorrow's the time. Tonight we run shit.

****

As usual, the thing that shot Jake into consciousness was the raging headache currently surging in him. Unfortunately, that usually caused him to move slightly, which caused his headache to get worse. It was an awful sequence of events, one that was followed by the sight of seeing his girlfriend's jeans being pulled up over her black thong. Jake smirked because he'd been positive he ripped that underwear last night. Of course it was good he hadn't. His track record on such things wasn't something Kelly was happy about. Thankfully, the sight of her in a bra was enough to momentarily take his mind off the pain. It was even enough to get him talking. "Now that was a good night" he choked out.

The comment had the desired effect at least. Kelly turned around to face Jake's sprawled out body. He opened his eyes widely to a sight he'd seen hundreds of times before but was still incredibly satisfying. *God bless Victoria's Secret...those damn push-up bra's really make magic happen.*

Kelly clearly relished her boyfriend again gawking at her for the latest in a series numbering in the thousands.

"You actually remember it?"

"I remember what I need to."

"Glad I struck a nerve baby."

"Oh you struck one alright, and I hope you have trouble walking today."

"I think you're good there," she said before putting on her top. Although the sight of her rack was now covered she still looked beautiful.

"I've gotta go babe."

"Absolutely not" he shot back with the best puppy-dog look he could achieve. In his current state, that didn't amount to much.

"Not for nothing, but you wore me out Jake" she said with a hint of regret.

"Well believe me, that was not at all part of the plan."

"I figured it wasn't," she said before leaning in for a light kiss.

He watched her stand back up straight and grab her jacket even though it pained him to keep his eyes open.

"What time is it Kel?" He was in no position to turn his head to look at the clock.

"A little past eleven" she answered with a look that basically said 'it's time to get the fuck up'. *I can always tell what she's thinking when she gives me a look.* It was one of the things he'd found incredibly sexy when they started seeing each other.

"Fine, fine" he yielded. "I'll call you later."

Jake realized something after Kelly left and the memories from the previous night came back in hazy pieces. He'd barely interacted with his cousin, and that was something Eric wasn't likely to let go. *If he noticed, I'll know soon.*

Given his current state, he hoped Eric wouldn't be evil enough to call or text any time today. *I might as well get up on the off chance Eric calls me.*

With all his current strength, he tried pushing himself up off the mattress only to be rewarded by an intense stabbing pain in his head. "Oh, way too soon" he said to the empty room. *So much for that plan…*

Some four hours after passing out Jake still found himself in a state of utter pain.

Now it was exacerbated by the fact that he was up and walking around. He took the stairs one at a time just to make sure he didn't collapse and roll down them. It had only happened once in his life but no repeats were needed.

He reached the bottom and headed toward his backpack. It was still parked in the same spot he'd left it when he'd gotten home. It was on one of the dining room chairs situated around the large dark oak table they used for holiday dinners. He'd figured it was a prime spot to use for work.

His backpack held some of his schoolbooks he'd likely never open over break. There was also a complete copy of the AZXi history along with a spare notebook.

Jake looked into the bag before slightly losing his balance to the throbbing headache. He used a chair to steady himself before taking out the AZXi history. They'd been specifically told *not* to make a copy by Jeff. *Just another thing that makes zero fucking sense.* Having more than one copy of the history made it possible for them to not all have to pour over the same sheets at the same times. It made even more sense now that none of them were even in the same zip code. *How the fuck could we redo our books without copies of the history…fuckin' bastards.*

Silently he flipped through the pages in his hands, glancing at the names of pledge classes that came before his. He stopped when he reached the Alpha Beta class. Eric and Jerry's names were written underneath. It took him a while to pry his eyes away. Jake knew Eric had gone through a similar Hell when he pledged. *Eric's stronger than I am, he can handle it…I just can't…*

Finally his eyes moved off the history.
Why'd you think you could do it? You aren't the same.

Feelings of anguish and turmoil swept through him without warning. Ever since they'd stepped out of the car those feelings were pummeling him fast and often. Still, there was solace to be had since his cousin was with him now, along with his dad. *It's only for a little while. Don't get used to it.*

Jake was the last of the three to enter through the open doorway into the dorm room he'd be occupying for the spring semester ahead.

"Well this isn't too bad" Jake's dad said thoughtfully.

"They're all like this Uncle Jeremy."

Even though there was still a flood of emotions hurtling through him, Jake found the energy to speak. "He never went to college so he's got no real comparison Biz."

"Yeah but you aren't making my mistakes. I can be proud of that at least."

Dropping the boxes he was carrying on the untouched side of the room, Jake's dad moved toward the door. "I'll start grabbing the rest from the car," he announced before heading back out.

Jake surveyed the room he'd be living in for the next few months. *So this is it, this is the beginning of college.* The left side of the room was already full since his roommate had been living there the previous semester.

How did I get paired up with this other guy? What happened to his previous roommate? Did he just bounce because he couldn't stand living here? Why couldn't I live with Biz for a while? Negative emotions started swirling.

"I think Rye got real lucky not having to help you move in" Eric grinned.

For a moment Jake forgot where he was and what he was doing to just focus on bantering with his cousin. "Where's she at anyways?"

"Her sorority is having a random party today I guess."

Riley's in a sorority. Jake still couldn't wrap his mind around it.

As if reading Jake's thoughts, Eric added his own. "Hey at least it stopped her from complaining about being bored around here."

"Well that's fair" Jake replied. He had never heard Riley complain in such a way so it was all news to him. *What else don't I know?*

"Look on the bright side son" Eric began, "at least it's a co-ed dorm. Although you'll probably get a girlfriend real quick."

"Oh I will?"

"You'd rather be dating than single, am I right?"

Alison was out of her mind but it still felt good being with her.

"It's straight man. I'm the same way" Eric responded to Jake's unvoiced thoughts.

Jake's dad marched into the room with determination and planted another two boxes on the ground in triumph. "Where's your roommate then?"

"Transfer students get here earlier than everyone else so he won't be around for another couple days. Unless they're dedicated partiers like Biz" Jake grinned.

"Didn't I see a bunch of kids walking around when we drove in?"

"Those kids live off campus. They get here whenever they want" Eric explained.

Jake's dad nodded. "There's a couple more boxes left in the car, any chance you could run down and grab them while Jake starts unpacking?" his dad asked Eric.

"No problem" Eric replied before walking out of the room.

"Nervous?" his dad asked, as if sensing Jake's anxiety.

Jake shuffled slightly to the boxes to check their contents without saying a word.

"You're gonna be fine. I'm not worried about you at all."

"You don't have to live here Dad." Jake blurted it out so quickly his voice cracked.

I've never lived away from home before. The bubble he'd been living in for eighteen years was gone.

"Listen Jake, all you have to do is be yourself...its gotten you this far right?"

Jake turned away from the boxes to look at his dad. "Yeah" he agreed.

His dad shrugged. "I get lucky every now and then."

Eric re-entered the room with what looked to be the last of his things.

"You want any help unpacking?"

Jake considered his dad's offer before saying he was fine. *I still have Eric here.*

His dad moved to the doorway before stopping short, as if realizing he forgot something important. He turned around to hug Jake, more forcefully than he had in years. After pulling away, he looked Jake square in the eyes. "Be careful alright?"

Jake smiled back. *So Dad really is as paranoid as Mom. He just hides it better.*

"Don't worry Uncle Jeremy, I've got him" Eric added casually.

"Yeah but you two got in enough trouble when you were still home so just behave yourselves."

Jake smirked at the memories. *What could possibly go wrong Dad?*

He looked over his son again before smiling and turning to leave. His footsteps echoed down the hall more loudly than anything Jake had ever heard.

"Alright I should head out too, Jerry just texted me about a party tonight. I'm trying to shower first though."

"I still can't believe you pledged a frat Biz" Jake said, almost disgusted by the thought of it for reasons he didn't understand.

Eric shrugged. "I know J, it's hard to explain."

"I appreciate the invite and everything but I should unpack my room first" Jake said sarcastically. He was still hoping for the very invite he was turning down.

"Son, you know I'd take you but I'm still new to the frat. I can't just bring someone along this soon. It'd be mad sketchy. You hated when people did that to you at Raley's Ring" Eric answered diplomatically. *That pissed me off every time it happened...*

Jake smirked, only because he didn't know what else to do. "Hey, I was talking to Riley about us maybe doing a weekly cousins dinner or something?"

Eric was literally walking out the door when he heard the question. "I don't know if I'll be able to swing that with my classes and shit, but let me know."

"Sounds good" was all Jake could say as Eric walked out of the room.

Eric's footsteps echoed even louder in Jake's head than his father's. It made the situation all the more intimidating. He turned from the open doorway after all but slamming the thing shut by accident.

Walking back to the window at the opposite side of the room past all the un-touched boxes, one thing became painfully clear to Jake. *I actually thought I'd be able to hang out with them all the time? They have their own lives here. What the hell is wrong with me?*

Jake couldn't blame his cousins. They'd had to endure his plentiful outbursts when they were all younger. It made sense that they'd want to do their own thing here. *Do they even care that I'm going to school here now?* Even as he fought it, that shred of doubt was lingering in his head.

Riley couldn't even help me move in and Eric is already gone and I've only been here twenty minutes.
The landscape outside his window had looked almost welcoming when he'd driven in. Now it only looked cold and forbidding.
Jesus...what the hell am I gonna do?

Jake looked back down at the frat's history in his hands. He focused on the spot in the books where his pledge class would be marked down after Crossing. It was blank...just waiting for the day.

The most immediate challenge to finishing was staring him dead in the face. The composite notebook was sitting on the table, just awaiting the AZXi history. Without warning and no thought, Jake moved his backpack out of the way to sit in the now vacant chair. He flipped to the notebook's front page. It would likely take him the better part of the remaining day and another one afterward to finish.

Remembering how utterly helpless he felt on that first day at Gladen Hills, it all became clear as his pen hit the paper. He'd felt it then, he was remembering it now.

Jake was pledging because at the end of it all, he'd be given something worthwhile, something he'd always wanted: the privilege to never feel that alone again.

Chapter 6

Looking at her cousin asleep in the back seat, Riley realized it was the most content she'd seen him in weeks. It was quiet and relaxing. *For both of us.*

Once she made sure he was actually asleep, she turned her attention to her other cousin who was driving the car back to Gladen Hills. Eric hadn't yet noticed Jake was passed out.

Riley thought about how different the two boys were. Eric was calm, cool and collected in almost every instance she'd ever seen. That made him invaluable any time she needed advice. Jake on the other hand was an extremely passionate person. He could rarely take emotion out of *any* situation. That made the fact that Jake idolized Eric all the more interesting since they rarely looked at life in the same way. And yet Jake was following Eric by joining the same frat when there were plenty of other options.

She checked the exit numbers on the signs outside her window and realized they still had about ten minutes before they got back to school. *Now is as good a time as any.* "OK Eric let's go, tell me how much longer it'll be 'til they cross" she ordered.

A slight grin pierced Eric's face. It quickly vanished as if he didn't mean for it to happen. *Typical.*

"Two things Rye: you aren't his mom and on the off chance he can hear us, I won't say anything. Besides, no one is supposed to know. I wouldn't expect you to tell me when your girls are crossing." *He knew I'd ask.*

The last time she'd spoken to her younger cousin, he was dead-set on quitting AZXi. She hadn't been able to let go of that all through spring break. She'd still been able to enjoy herself but that thought had always been there, simmering.

"But for real though" Eric interrupted, "when are you crossing the girls because you have some good looking ones in this pledge class."

"Really? After you just said I wouldn't tell you?"

"I said I didn't expect you to, not that you wouldn't. I figured it was worth a shot" he responded, another grin coming into view.

"Which ones did you have an eye on?"

"The one that's a little shorter than you, darker hair. Brynn I think?"

Now it was Riley who couldn't keep her feelings hidden. "Of the six pledges we have this semester, my Little is the one you're after?!"

"Well to be fair, she is pretty hot" a new voice entered the conversation.

Jake had just woken up from what looked to be a thoroughly refreshing nap. He could clearly read the surprise on Riley's face as she looked back at him. Eric's shaken eyes were also visible in the rear-view mirror. "What? I have a girlfriend. It doesn't mean I lost my eyes" he retorted to their unspoken jabs.

"No, just your balls" Eric quickly shot out. Riley smirked. He wasn't usually quick-witted, especially when it came to sparring matches with their younger cousin, but every now and again he surprised Riley.

"How's that going by the way Jake?" she asked, showing concern. She'd never done much to hide her feelings about Kelly, having been there at the beginning of their affair. After seeing that first hand, she knew all too well what the girl was capable of. Jake either didn't know or didn't care to know. *Probably both.*

"Everything's great, unless you know something I don't."

"Well we know a ton you don't but I think you got this one son."

"Gee, thanks for the compliment Biz."

"OK I have some questions now that you're up Jake. What's the deal with your pledge brother Matt, and other one, Justin?"

Jake clearly didn't want to talk about that, but it looked like he was in the mood to humor her anyway. "Well J-Hood is a beast, so good luck being noticed in the sea of girls he's currently dealing with. The guys got some sick multi-tasking skills."

"So true" Eric agreed immediately. She could only guess that was Justin's nickname although she'd never heard it before. *That wasn't even close to a full response.*

"And Matt…well let's just say I'd prefer if you stayed away from my friends and god-willing, future brothers. I'll also attempt to stay away from your sisters," he added, as if reading that she was unhappy. *At least he decided over break to stick with pledging.*

The main concern she had now lay with his views for the future within the frat. "I didn't ask you to do that and we definitely aren't going to start this protective shit now," she ordered sternly. She was more irritated than she sounded. *That's probably a good thing.* Jake looked confused. The 'protective shit' she'd described usually went in the reverse direction for them. "When Eric and I were freshman we made a deal. Now that you're here you'll need to go along with this" she continued, trying to clear things up.

"Along with what?"

It felt insanely good to be back in her roommate-less room with a guy as hot as Jerry in her bed. *Finally.*

Realizing she was losing focus on Jerry for even the tiniest amount of time, she again poured all her attention toward kissing him. *We drank so much tonight. He better not have a hard time getting it up…*

It was one thing that guys never seemed to understand. Girls enjoyed sex too, as much as guys…maybe even more. That meant when a bad case of performance issues came around they got just as pissed. If Jerry couldn't pull it together she'd likely contemplate killing someone…probably Jerry since it'd been so long. By now in her career of *not* having sex, she had fully left behind any doubts she might've had about the fact that Jerry was her cousin's best friend. *Eric is just gonna have to get over this. If he ever finds out.* Riley was more than content to let the situation remain hidden.

"Is your roommate coming back?" he asked when they finally broke from their kiss.

Well he's clearly confident...he better not have any trouble. "I'm pretty sure she hooked up with some guy from the Lambdas so I doubt it." *She better not come back.* Her roommate hadn't seemed like the type for random hookups, at least not in the three months she'd known her. On top of that Riley doubted they'd be friends once the school year ended. *She did seem really into that Lambda guy.* For all she knew her roommate could have a sex drive the same as everybody else. *I doubt it...but why am I even thinking about that right now?!*

"So you're planning on keeping me here all night then? I would love to know how you plan on accomplishing that," Jerry said with a goofy grin. *He's clearly drunk. Might as well see how hammered he really is.*

"Step one is making sure my door is closed and locked because we can't have any one walking in during step two" she answered with a seductive smile. *Why are you talking like this? It sounds so weird.* Although she had discovered she was talking like that more and more since she got to Gladen Hills. It wasn't that she disliked being so open with her sexuality, she just wasn't used to it yet. But she definitely liked being so confident. She liked feeling wanted.

Jerry leaned in to kiss her again. *He wants me.*

"Out of curiosity for what step two is I guess I'll get the door" he said after breaking off the kiss earlier than she would've liked. *It's fine, it's fine. As soon as the door is shut I can get his shirt off. His chest is always so ripped.* The anticipation was growing in her.

Jerry got off the bed and began sauntering over to the door, a little too slowly for her liking. Finally he reached it just in time to see a person fly by on a scooter. From the sound she heard, it wasn't motorized. *It was going so fast.*

For some odd reason Jerry stopped short of closing the door and simply looked out into the well-lit hallway to the right where the figure disappeared from her view.

"Son?" Jerry asked. He seemed unsure of what he was doing, which she could definitely join him in feeling. *I'm practically drooling at getting your clothes off and you're trying to have a conversation with somebody else? What the hell is going on?*

After a few seconds of no response from the figure in the hallway, she heard a crash as if someone had just keeled over. To Riley's utter horror, Jerry actually took a few steps out of her warm inviting room. *You've gotta be kidding me right now.* She shook her head. *All guys are idiots.*

Riley began to hear what she thought was an actual conversation taking place between Jerry and the mysterious scooter maniac in the hall. She straightened herself out and fixed her bra which wasn't fitting too well since she'd been rolling around in bed. After composing herself she walked to the open doorway.

"You don't live in this dorm right? Wait...which dorm am I in?" the kid asked.

Suddenly it all became clear to her. She stepped to the side of Jerry to get a full look at the kid lying on the floor with the scooter under him. There laid her cousin Eric. *And he's clearly wasted. Perfect.*

"You are so ugly right now Biz. You're in Randall Hall. Our dorm is just two buildings over so you're close," Jerry answered, not noticing Riley standing there.

"So if this isn't our dorm like you claim, then why are you here? Did you get lost too?!" Eric asked, sounding more and more like a confused child. Neither of them was paying much attention to her. *So typical. Lost in their own world just like usual.*

"Don't worry one bit about that son" Jerry responded in his usual high and mighty tone as he turned and finally noticed Riley. *Oh good, you remembered I exist.* Riley loved her cousin. And in any other situation it would probably be extremely funny. *But not now. Definitely not tonight.*

Eric clearly just noticed her presence too, because he became as serious as he could under the circumstances. "Son, please tell me you aren't hooking up with my cousin?" *Well at least he's not drunk enough to miss the obvious. Too bad.*

"Nah, just dropped in to say hey." He then threw Riley a smirk somehow without letting Eric catch on.

Eric bought the excuse completely. "Well let me chill too. I haven't seen Riley in a hot minute...well maybe a lukewarm minute" he corrected himself. "I didn't know you two were friends."

"Well we don't hang out that often Eric...just sometimes." She tried to infuse as much bitterness into her wording as she could, mostly for Jerry's benefit. He was now fixated on watching

her drunken cousin stumble over to her roommate's vacant bed.
He forgot I'm here again.

Once Eric reached the bed he tried taking off his shoes.
That wouldn't have been an issue if he wasn't completely fucked
up. It was fun watching him squirm trying to get them off without
untying them first. She almost forgot what he was interrupting.
"Oh no you don't. Get the hell up!" But she was already
too late. Eric had collapsed onto the mattress.

"I can't. I'm too tired to make it back. It's way too far."
Your dorm is two buildings over! That didn't matter now. Her
cousin was dug in. *Great. It's gonna be bad enough getting him
to go the bathroom now, let alone back to his dorm. I can't
believe it.*

"It's OK, I got this" Jerry announced to her, clearly not
caring or else not believing Eric could hear him.

"No way, this one is mine." She all but marched to her
cousin's side and began talking as sternly as her buzz would
allow. "Eric, this is not cool, Jerry and I were hoping to hang out
alone."

It took a few seconds for the words to sink in to Eric's
alcohol soaked brain.

"I knew it!" he announced while simultaneously sitting
up. His stance made it seem as if he'd just made a huge discovery
all on his own.

"The only reason you know is because I told you so relax.
He's not my boyfriend, we're just having fun." It wasn't everyday
she got to tell her insanely smart cousin that he was wrong. She
was relishing every second of it. Something about those words
stuck with her though. It wasn't like she'd never thought about
dating Jerry; it had just never come up when they hung out. She
almost hoped that her statement might trigger something in Jerry to
make him want to broach the subject at some point. If it had, he
wasn't showing it.

"Oh come on. Of the three thousand guys at this school
my best friend is the one you have to hook up with?"
If only Jerry had just shut the door earlier...

"Look...when I'm done pledging in the spring and you
want to hook up with one of my sisters, I promise not to stop you."
It worked like a charm.

"Where are you tryin' to pledge?" He blurted out the
question almost immediately, clearly interested in the new topic.

"Epsilon Iota Pi if I get in, but that's not important right now. How about we make a deal Eric?" Her cousin was obviously intrigued because she had all of his limited focus. "How about you never give me any shit for who I hook up with, whoever they may be..." she trailed off to look at Jerry. "And not only will I not care about who you fuck; I will help whenever I can." She watched it marinate in Eric's head. It was fun to watch as he clearly ran through all the possible benefits in his mind, albeit slower than normal.

"Son, that's as good a deal as I'm getting right now" Jerry interrupted before shooting a grin at Riley. She followed it up with a seductive smile. *Damn Eric for stumbling in here.*

"That's mad weird since she's practically my sisterrrrr" Eric slurred. "But yeah that deal sounds rrrrreal fresh. I...am...down" he concluded.

"Good. Now get out," Riley quickly ordered.

Clearly the surge of adrenaline he'd just gotten from signing up for the deal was hitting full stride since he was now standing straight up. It hit fever pitch as he actually tried jumping into his shoes instead of sliding them on. Once again drunken Eric made her laugh along with Jerry. He was recording the whole thing on his phone as his friend tried and failed repeatedly at the extremely simple action. Eric didn't notice.

"This was working a lot better in my head" he said, sounding confused that his plan wasn't working. Finally he slid them on in utter defeat. "OK I'm out. By the way son, the party at the AZXi house was sick. I was there 'til after midnight...you know if I was going to pledge that would definitely be the place" he rambled as he walked to the door. He seemed to be talking to himself as he walked out, closing the door behind him.

Riley then sat on her own bed next to Jerry. She leaned in to kiss him as the door opened. It was Eric...again. "But I don't think I'll pledge" he said, picking up right where he left off. "It's just not for me."

As soon as he finished Riley reflexively threw one of her two pillows in his direction. It hit him square in the face. It would've made her laugh if she wasn't frustrated. Eric took the hint. He closed the door and exited for the second and hopefully last time. It seemed likely as they listened to his dying footsteps running down the hall toward the nearest exit. In his current state, it was entirely possible that he was scared of follow-up pillow hits. *Finally...he's gone.*

Jerry all but sprinted to the door to bolt it shut. The sound was music to her ears. *"I bet he won't remember any of that."* *"That's why it's recorded. Just in case"* he replied before joining her in bed. They didn't waste any time. She kissed him immediately. *This better be worth the wait.* They continued kissing as Riley reached out to switch off the lamp on her nightstand.

Riley finished her story, taking no chances as to how much her point would come across to her younger cousin. *He better understand.* She didn't need protection in the form of a younger cousin at all, least of all at school. The concept annoyed her to no end. It wasn't Jake's fault though; the concept of *anyone* telling her that would make her skin crawl. As a matter of fact, it had on multiple occasions when her older brother had done just that. They both meant well but Riley didn't need protection in any form. *Eric's the only one of the three that gets it.*

"To be fair I didn't remember anything from that night" Eric announced casually.

"I'm completely shocked by that" Jake replied sarcastically.

Riley's thoughts strayed to the memory of that night. *At least Jerry brought his A-game.* Despite how drunk they were he got the job done quite well. She smiled to herself. "Good thing Jerry recorded it then" she added.

"Yeah he tends to notice when I've hit the blackout point" Eric agreed.

"Um it isn't exactly a challenge to tell when you've hit that level Biz" Jake interrupted haughtily.

"I think you just don't want to give Jerry any credit."

Riley smiled. *That's exactly it.*

Jake looked somewhat disheartened. "First of all, you're damn right I don't. Second I've known you longer and I bet I could tell just as well when you've reached the point of no return."

She could tell he was getting anxious about their destination, which was now very close. "Come on Jake. You slept practically the whole ride here. Didn't you relax enough on break?"

"Of course I relaxed…and I napped a lot too. But I'm trying to soak up every bit of freedom I have before I set foot back in that town because then pledging is back on."

"It's definitely not easy," she agreed, trying to comfort him as best she could while recalling her own difficulty pledging. "But it's definitely worth it."

Jake frowned slightly. "That's what I keep telling myself. But I don't know how much more of this shit I can handle."

"You know what you signed up for and there's no backing out now J" Eric said, almost sternly.

He's right Jake. Anyone that de-pledged in Gladen Hills would be better off transferring to a different school if they wanted to maintain a social life. It was all downhill for someone after de-pledging although it was far worse for girls. Sadly not even she was above shunning someone like that given the right set of circumstances.

"I'm not de-pledging so just chill" Jake responded, clearly agitated.

What made him change his mind?

"By the way Rye, I didn't know you hooked up with Jerry."

Shame swept over her. *You just had to open your mouth and tell him the whole story didn't you?* "It was during freshman year on and off. Then we started pledging." *And he just let it end without saying a thing. Typical frat guy.*

"And pledging killed another relationship, or whatever it was, sounds about right. Kelly isn't very happy with the arrangement."

"You're breaking my heart. You've got two weeks left, get it together and get it done. This is all on you if you want to cross."

Jake shifted uncomfortably in his seat. "I'm curious Eric; do you and Jeff and the rest of those fucks actually believe the shit you say to us?"

Now he's getting pissed. Please not now. Riley looked at Eric to discern if he was also noticing that being stern wasn't helping.

"Completely. Just get it done. I'd like to be able to drink with you again."

For a millisecond, she thought that might actually calm Jake down.

"Oh damn Biz! Why didn't you say *you* were upset about all this shit and also not being able to drink with me? How the fuck have you survived this long?!" Jake practically shouted.

Riley felt a twinge of guilt. *What can I do? Pledging is just hard.*

"Just calm down Jake, we're almost back. Besides, you don't have anything pledging related to do tonight do you?" She was trying to sound as motherly as possible without wanting to vomit as a result.

"Just the weekly pledge meeting. That'll equate to about forty push-ups and then getting the week's tasks. I for one can't wait," he answered bitterly.

The car was now rounding the corner onto the far side of University Grove where the Northeast dorms were located. Eric made a left hand turn into the loading dock so Jake could get out and get his things without blocking traffic.

"Thanks for the ride Biz. I'll see you later tonight. Rye, I'm sure I'll see you soon too. Hopefully at least" he added somberly.

It was as if he once again received the crushing realization that his time wasn't his own. He closed the door and gathered his things out of the trunk. As he did so Riley's eyes started boring into Eric's head. She wondered how long it'd take him to notice her death stare. His eyes were firmly fixed on their cousin who was now trudging toward the dorm entrance.

Jake finally entered the building and disappeared. Only then did Eric turn to her.

"I hope you're planning on crossing them soon because I don't know how much more Jake can handle. And I don't know how much more I can handle of Jake. You know he's not like us," she concluded, feeling emotionally spent just saying the words.

Casually, Eric put the car in reverse and looked behind them as he started backing out of the loading dock. For a second she almost thought he hadn't heard her.

"You're right. He isn't like us. But that doesn't mean he can't handle it."

****

Going shopping for groceries had never been fun for her, especially when doing it alone. But it had to be done…and by herself as it turned out since she'd gotten back to school before everybody else. That was a first since she was usually the last one to get back after a break. Today she'd been very eager to leave since she could only take so much more shit from her mother before losing her mind.

It's always the same shit every time I'm home. It never fucking ends.

Anytime she was forced to deal with her parents things got annoying. Her dad was much easier to deal with although that wasn't saying much. She loved bother her parents but it didn't make living with them any easier.

That was why she enjoyed living in Gladen Hills so much: the freedom of it all. She'd heard stories from her friends about dealing with their own parents but they just didn't compare. *Everyone probably feels like this.* Still, her break was more grating than usual and she couldn't pinpoint why. Maybe it was her mom's constant analyzing of her clothes. Maybe it was her dad's indifference to it altogether. Either way it felt really good to get the fuck out and back to school where she belonged.

She finished putting the last of her vitamin waters in the fridge and looked around the kitchenette of the second floor. *This is clearly the smallest one in the house. It makes no sense.* It was something she'd never been able to understand. As she continued surveying, she noticed the entire area was bare and somewhat eerie. It was weird seeing no signs of activity in the house. No dishes in the sink, no messy countertops.

She started feeling sad at the emptiness around her. Being alone had never felt right. Being an only child with no close family had essentially given her the sour taste of being lonely from an early age. She'd never gotten used to it and never wanted to go back. *I never have to feel that again, not if I don't want to.*

When high school had hit and her body started developing, the idea of being chased by guys was like a drug. That addiction followed her to college. To some people, like a few of her own sisters, that made her seem like a slut, but she didn't care. The girls she was closest to didn't mind, and she took confidence from that. *Who cares what they all think anyway?*

Before long, she heard the sounds of approaching footsteps. *Thank God someone's home.* Hopefully this would be exactly who she was waiting for. Without any delay she left the kitchenette and entered the hallway just as the person entered a bedroom on the left and disappeared from the hall. As usual she didn't need an invitation and simply followed them inside.

Happiness flooded her without warning. Even though she knew it was her best friend already because of which room she'd entered, seeing her was a different sensation. The other girl turned to examine who had followed her and the expression on her face told her she was feeling the exact same way. They all but rushed in to hug each other. *Nine days is too long to be separated from my soul mate.*

They broke their hug and looked at each other, still smiling.

"Well Riles, how was your break?"

"I was mostly working at the mall. So long, boring and generally depressing."

Tory grinned. *She must've been with her cute cousins.* Riley was fairly sarcastic in her own right but Tory found that after spending time with the two of them, mostly the younger one, that Riley's abilities increased.

"No it was good actually. And I definitely needed some money" Riley continued. "How about yours T?"

"Outside of my mom constantly yelling at me about my clothes, it was a dream."

"So basically you were just wearing tank-tops around the house again right?"

Was I? Huh, I guess that's all I was wearing actually. That probably hadn't helped but whatever. That's what I like wearing. "I can't help it if she doesn't like the way they apparently make my boobs fall out."

Riley wrinkled her face slightly. "There's nothing apparent about it T. It's a fact. If she saw you at school on a Friday night she'd probably kill you…and me."

My mom would have a heart attack if she saw what I wore on the weekends. The thought made her smile. It was completely fine since she never planned on living at home again after college.

"Did you drink at all over break?"

"Not really. Jake asked me to go over to his place for a party but I was too tired after work so I skipped it. What about you?"

Tory recollected the previous week and came up with an answer. "Just wine…a lot of wine," she answered, *almost* feeling ashamed.

As if sensing a chance to enter into the conversation, Danielle strolled in from the hall through the open doorway. "No shock there huh Riles?"

Tory shrugged. *So what if I love my wine?!*

"Didn't know you were back Dani. You finish having cute quality time with your Little?" Tory chided her sister slightly.

Danielle smirked back at her. "Yes I did. You should try it sometime…when you get one." After getting in her jab at Tory, she hugged both of them in turn, Riley first.

"I look at it like having kids or graduating. I'm not ready for it yet" she remarked, feeling proud.

"If you aren't ready for kids then you might want to try using condoms a little more" Riley said, with just the right amount of levity.

"You know, you make *one*…." Tory trailed off mid-sentence because of the shocked looks she was now getting for saying 'one'. "OK OK" she relented, "*five* mistakes and you guys just can't let it go."

"Kinda hard when one of those 'mistakes' happened like a week before break" Riley chuckled. "Seems more like a trend."

"Sex is so much better without them and I'm on the pill so whatever."

"How's Angela holding up?" Riley asked Danielle, switching the topic.

"Well nothing bad has happened to her in the week since pledging stopped so as of now she's good."

"Good, we don't need anyone else crying at a callout" Tory quipped.

"You may want to stop channeling Satan at them and it wouldn't be a problem."

"Sorry but that's the name of the game Dani."

As the assistant pledge mom Tory's job was quite literally to make the pledges lives hell, *especially* during the callouts. Riley was supposed to motivate them and keep them focused as the head pledge mom. On the flip side, Tory was supposed to be the bitch and tear them down constantly. *It's gotta suck for the pledges that I'm awesome at the job.* Tory had been trying to make a good impression all year hoping that her dedication would show the rest of the sisters she was good enough to get an E-board position at the end of the semester. *That's a still long way away. Stop trying to plan ahead. It never works.*

"T is right Dani" Riley added.

"Oh I know," she quickly agreed. "She's really good at it too."

Tory stood there, confused. *Why'd she say it like that?*

"Angie really hates you right now…but she's OK with you Riles."

"Good, that's the way it should be."

Tory didn't say anything. It wasn't like she hadn't been hearing something similar throughout her entire life. Girls had constantly not liked her for one reason or another all along. *At least here I got away from all those bitches in high school.* Joining EIPi had helped with putting all that shit in the past. *Thank God I have Riles here. I guess all I can do is not graduate and stay here forever…*

****

Calvin never procrastinated and yet here he sat. Sunday night at the end of spring break and he was just now completing a paper due Monday morning. *At least I don't do this shit that often.* That was more than he could say for the rest of his brothers, save for Jerry and Eric. But those two were more the exception than the rule.

Eric suddenly appeared in Calvin's open doorway.

"What up son?" he greeted him warmly.

"Hey Biz, how'd your break go? Wait don't tell me…I bet all you did was play online poker or hit up the casino."

Eric smirked. "Gotta make that cash," he responded in his usual playful tone.

"Guess you're buying the first round tonight since I'm assuming it went well?"

"I'm not drinking tonight man. It's Sunday and we just got back."

"Biz isn't drinking tonight? What the fuck else is new?" a new voice entered the conversation. Even if Calvin had been blindfolded he would've recognized that tone anywhere. And it belonged to Jeff Chester.

"Some of us actually have work to do in class Buttons" Eric countered.

"I do work pal, just don't have nearly as much as you. And that's not being lazy, that's called picking the right major."

Funnily enough Calvin actually agreed with his brazen brother for once. *That's the last time that'll happen this month.* Eric's choice of major *was* kind of crazy considering the lifestyle he was leading on the weekends. *If Biz can make a bio-chem class schedule work with the amount of drinking he does then well done.*

Calvin doubted their favorite bar was even open tonight. The National had weird hours in general. And Sundays were weirder still. Plus they were coming off a weeklong break so it could go either way. Still, with the beer Jeff was currently slugging back, he assumed the guy had already gotten confirmation that it would be open.

Jeff must've already talked to Debbie. He probably stayed here over the break too. He never goes home. While Eric had been home with Raley and their family and he'd been at home with a visiting Jennifer, Jeff had been here, likely very alone. Calvin knew better than to touch that subject though. It was weird enough to even think about.

"Come on Biz, this is my last semester here. That means every day is another day pissed away where we could all be drinking."

"I have a quiz and a lab tomorrow, there's no way man."

They both returned Eric's solid reasoning with looks of extreme disgust.

"I went to a lab hung-over once...I couldn't even figure out how to use a calculator I was so fucked up."

"I don't see the problem, sounds memorable" Jeff replied casually.

"Hey Buttons, how many have you had?" Calvin asked.

"This is my fourth."

No wonder you came into my room freely, you're feeling pretty good. "Good, then we have time before you black out," Calvin replied with a hollow grin.

Eric let his anxiousness show instantly. "You want me to bounce?"

"Nah, definitely stay. I wish Kevin had come back tonight so he could be part of this but whatever," Calvin lamented.

Jeff already seemed to be taking up a defensive stance. *He always thinks he's being attacked...every time.* He'd learned a long time ago to not pussyfoot around with Jeff. It was better to just dive in and let things fall as they may.

"We think ripping up their pledge books was a mistake."

Jeff turned away to stare directly at Eric. At the moment he was clearly the less resolute of the two facing him. *Classic Jeff.* "Did Raley redo his book or not?"

"Yeah he finished it, wasn't happy about it though." Eric already looked defeated. *Sorry Biz but we all agreed before break this needed to be done.*

"They're supposed to leave pledging here when they go home. End of story" Calvin added sharply. *But I shouldn't have to tell you that.*

"The Nu and Tau classes both had shit to do over their breaks so it's not like this is new. And I figured if they were gonna do anything they might as well redo their books which already had mistakes in them. At least my way allows them to learn the shit they should've already fucking known by now. Win-win, case closed."

"I bet the pledges would have a different view."

"I imagine they do but this is *my* program, it's *my* call. And it worked because I bet they'll actually know their shit now that they've rewritten it all...again. It's done."

"The bottom line is that this was a risky move...and it wasn't necessary. We've had plenty of pledges that didn't know their shit in the past" Calvin said. "And if we have any more de-pledges this semester, we're fucked."

Calvin noticed an abrupt change in Jeff's stance at the mention of the previous de-pledges. "They won't de-pledge," he promised. It could've actually been considered more of a threat though.

"Guess we'll know at the next callout" Calvin replied, shooting an icy glare back.

"When it turns out I'm right are you gonna finally admit it?"

"Even if you are it still doesn't mean I like this."

Calvin never liked the side of himself that came out when he argued with Jeff. He became more irrational, all in the name of one-upping his brother. *Just keep it together.*

Jeff had never gotten past losing to him in the presidential election the year before. But he couldn't change how Jeff felt. *I was the better fit for the job. Why can't he just let that go?*

"Jesus, just let it go Gretman" Jeff responded before finishing his beer and exiting the room in the span of a few seconds.

Well that could've gone better.

"He already knows what I think. I texted him over break to let him know how pissed Will and Jake were," Eric said defensively.

Oh sure now you don't have a problem talking. "And?"

"What do you think? He didn't give a fuck. But he's right. It's done now."

They were both right and he knew it. *It is done; nothing I say will change that.*

"As much of a pain in the ass as he is, he's still our brother at the end of the day" Calvin admitted, to himself as much as to Eric.

"If it makes you feel any better, Jerry didn't like it either. And he's the one who's supposed to be the bigger ass of the two."

"You'd think that would help" Calvin smiled slightly. *But it doesn't.*

"Well in a few months it's not gonna be your problem anymore son" Eric added with a touch of regret.

"You're right. Then it'll be *your* problem."

Eric winced at the concept.

Calvin had always assumed Eric would be the one to follow in his footsteps to become president but he never seemed sold on the idea. *There's still time to turn that around. One problem at a time.*

"Graduation. The worst best thing to happen to us."

"At least anyone who actually enjoys college" Eric agreed.

"I'd like to think we're enjoying it enough for everyone."

"True but I think by next year I'll be ready to leave."

He couldn't tell if Eric believed what he was saying. Ironically that had once been Calvin's stance on the issue of graduation not so many months ago. Now he was staring down the barrel of that fateful ceremony in two months and he wasn't even close to being ready to leave it all behind. He'd almost considered failing all his classes and getting stuck here for another semester or two like their brother Guapo had been doing for years. But he couldn't actually go through with it. He didn't have it in himself to fail.

After a few seconds of pensive silence, a new third party entered the room, this one a warmer presence than the previous entry. "What's up boys?" Brent all but exclaimed as he entered Calvin's bedroom.

"Just prepping for the pledge meeting Segs" Eric answered. 'Segs' had a better ring to it than plain old 'Brent' or 'Segcand'. *Another solid nickname for AZXi.*

Brent's pledge brother Aaron walked in right after and greeted them in the same warm fashion. "Wouldn't miss a pledge meeting" Aaron chimed in.

"Pretty sure you missed one of your own last semester though" Calvin said with a smirk. Aaron shrugged at being reminded of the mistake.

"You clearly just like fucking with the pledges" Eric interrupted.

"I would if I could" Brent remarked somewhat sadly.

"Sorry, first semester brothers can't haze pledges," Eric said with fervor.

"A little part of me dies any time you say that Biz" Brent replied.

Eric checked his phone for the time while attempting to get up from his spot on Calvin's bed. He passed by Brent and Aaron, quickening his pace. The other two followed suit but the doorway was in no way big enough to support all three leaving at once. Calvin watched the situation unfold with complete attention. As soon as anyone admitted what they were doing, chaos would erupt.

Might as well help this along. "Who's trying to get a good spot on the couch?"

All three quickly looked at each other and sprinted for the door. As usual Eric was ahead of the curve and made it out first, giving him the best chance for a coveted seat on a couch.

The common area on his side of the house where the pledge meetings took place was relatively small, much like the rest of the building. That meant that there was no way to fit the twenty or so brothers who showed up for the meetings. In the scramble to say hello to everyone who hadn't been seen over break, these three had clearly forgotten that. *Priceless.*

Calvin didn't mind standing off to the side during those meetings. It tended to make his presence more intimidating. At least he thought so. He smiled again, for what felt like the millionth time since he'd gotten back to school. He certainly would have no trouble soaking up every inch of the place before he'd be forced to leave at the end of the semester. *Don't think about that now.*

Hopefully he'd have a memorable final stretch in Gladen Hills. Glancing at his fraternity's composite picture as he left his bedroom for the common area, he looked at all the faces on it. *With a gang like that, how could it not be wild?*

Chapter 7

The only sound outside of the television was the hitting of fingers against controller buttons. It was a noise Jake was both extremely familiar and comfortable with. But there wasn't any time to think about that; he had to beat Scribner and Dukes in Super Smash Bros. That was the only thing that mattered.

Smash Brothers was the national pastime in their suite. It was a great way to procrastinate the more important things in life and it was used accordingly. It even made their otherwise unsocial suitemates Wayne and Derek come out of their shells on the odd occasions when they were actually around.

Wayne was barely around since he had classes, lacrosse practice and a girlfriend living on Northwest. All of that contributed to the fact that for all intents and purposes, Jake had a single dorm room. That certainly helped as far as Kelly was concerned because they could be together without interruptions most of the time.

Realizing his thoughts were straying from the game, he came back around to notice his suitemates were actually coming close to turning the match around on him. *Not today.* It took a minute or so of admittedly deep focus, but he quickly dispatched Scribner and then Dukes shortly thereafter. They put their controllers down almost simultaneously as the match ended. *A thing of beauty.*

Jake looked up from his spot on the floor to where his roommates were sitting on the couch behind him. He was between them and the TV so it didn't take long for their eyes to meet and notice his pleased look.

"I only let you win because this is the happiest I've seen you in the past month" Dukes said, trying to soften the loss.

"Yeah well we know the reason for that" Scribner added with a smirk.

"Yeah...because Raley is a bitch."

"I would love to see you pledge and keep it together," Jake countered.

"Yeah except that'll never happen."

"I wonder which of us is the bitch now" Jake said thoughtfully to Scribner.

"Pretty sure it's still you" Dukes replied.

"There's clearly no winning with you...unless we're playing Smash...bitch." Clearly sensing a verbal battle on the horizon Scribner shot for a different topic. "You missed a solid Raley's Ring party over break."

Jake rolled his eyes. *Like he'll believe that Scribbs.*

"I'll never go to that circle jerk so stop asking" came Dukes' quick response.

"I'd think that too if all I did was stay home and play online poker."

"Hmm, winning money over spending it? Always a tough call but I think I made the right one."

"How much?"

"Just a couple hundred this time."

"That's low for you" Jake replied while Scribner nodded.

"Yeah well...I wasn't really paying attention."

In general most of what Dukes said was designed to make himself look better, or at least less bad. Jake had learned a long time ago that picking his battles was insanely important. Of course, knowing it one minute didn't mean it would be followed the next.

"God I hate you" he responded with a grin.

"I would too...but rematch?"

"I can't. Gotta leave for the pledge meeting. J-Hood will be here soon."

"Wow, just got back to school and already you've gotta go get fucked" Scribner said with a depressingly accurate tone.

"Come on Scribbs. Jealousy doesn't look good on you."

The only responses were a smirk from Scribner and a headshake from Dukes. Jake turned away from the warm inviting glow of the television, which was begging for a rematch. *I should be back early enough; maybe we can play later.*

He entered his dorm room, which also had the comforting sight of his bed that hadn't been slept in for over a week. That would have to wait too. He reached down by the desk chair for his backpack. That was a less than comfortable sight because of what it meant. *Good old AZXi.* He slung it over his shoulder and left his room, closing the door behind him. Jake didn't even have the drive to look at his suitemates on the way out since they were already knee-deep in a rematch. *Enjoy victory while I'm gone boys.*

Trudging toward the suite entrance, Jake's mind once again landed on just saying fuck it and quitting. He snapped out of it just in time to see his pledge brother walk into view of the building's entrance as he reached the quad outside his suite. It was a straight-shot hallway from that quad to the nearest exit.

At least I'm not gonna be suffering alone.

****

The common area of the house was filled with laughs, smoke and the smell of beer, stale or otherwise. There was no cigarette smoking actually allowed inside since not everybody who lived there was on board with it. So the only scent of it came from the clothing of those who smoked outside, and there were plenty of them. That was why it was so potent so often, especially for Jeff since he smoked roughly a pack a day.

Today the smell of beer wasn't stale for the most part, at least for now. Someone had bought a thirty rack on the way back to school and decided to share it with everyone. *Wasn't it Petey? Fuck, now I don't remember.* It was basically gone; with five of those consumed by him in an hour. Jeff usually hazed better with a few in him so it worked out. *I could probably use a few more now that Gretman tried fucking me fifteen minutes ago...bastard.*

He quickly glanced around the room. There were eighteen brothers there, which wasn't bad for the Sunday after spring break. He'd never admit as much but it was good to have actual people in the house again after spending most of last week alone.

Eric had managed to grab a spot on the couch as usual. He must've beaten Aaron and Brent to it since they were sitting on the two stools in the corner. Calvin was always in the same spot: standing in the doorway that connected the kitchen to the common room. *He probably thinks he's looks more badass that way...what a fuckin' tool.*

It certainly made sense on paper, but Calvin could never intimidate Jeff in any situation, regardless of his stance.

As he turned his gaze away from Calvin who was talking to Brent about some other shit, he noticed the time on the cable box beneath the TV in the corner opposite him. He'd told the pledges to be there by seven and it was now three minutes to. *Almost game time.*

Thankfully everyone seemed to be following the protocols today. If anyone attended the pledge meetings on Sunday they had to wear AZXi letters. *Now that makes shit intimidating.* Unlike the active meetings that never included pledges, wearing letters was absolutely required during these times. It was a solid reminder to the pledges that they *didn't* have the right yet, plus it was also a good display of solidarity among the brothers, not to mention a show of pride.

Jeff stood up. "Guys shut the fuck up, they'll be here soon," he announced. The brothers were usually pretty good about keeping quiet. It was getting them to that point that required effort.

Tonight they responded quickly, with the exception of a few sarcastic comments about Jeff's awkward display of power. They usually originated from Guapo, and that was the case tonight. He shot his pledge brother a death stare as he waited for him to stop chuckling at his own joke.

After staring him down, he noticed the rest of the brothers had actually quieted down too. It was downright surprising. That was until he noticed that Calvin and Eric had actually helped out. He didn't fully understand why one minute they were trying to undermine him and the next they were trying to help.

He looked at the cable box again; it was one minute 'til seven. As he continued to stare, it literally changed to exactly seven as the front door opened. *That couldn't have been more perfect.* Whether it was planned or not was irrelevant, it was still beautiful. Of course the fact that it was incredibly well timed was equally irrelevant as the pledges couldn't be given a pat on the back for it, or even be told they were on time. The opposite was actually true. They were going to be fucked with over being late, like they were for every pledge meeting. Jeff maintained his stern face and did his best to get pissed so his words wouldn't ring hollow.

He had approximately five minutes until he had to speak.

Every time they entered a room or saw an AZXi on campus, they had to greet them. The greetings here involved the exact same parts they were supposed to give at callouts. It was all designed to make the pledges show respect. It also had the added bonus of making them memorize everything quicker by doing it more often.

A brother could always turn down a greeting, especially if they were on campus. In some cases it became more annoying than respectful. If someone was rushing to class or talking to a chick and a pledge tried to get in the way to simply greet them with information that they'd already heard a hundred times it was definitely annoying. He and Jerry didn't have that luxury to turn them away though, as the pledge-masters, they had to be greeted at every turn.

As the pledges finished their greetings one by one, they stood in a line in front of the main couch that Jeff and Jerry always sat on. They stood so that they would all be facing the two of them. By now his stern, angry persona was front and center. These days it was never a problem for Jeff to get to that point.

"You're late. Brother Jerry take them in the kitchen and give them forty push-ups for fucking this up. Make sure they count them out *together* this time." He glared at each of the four as he spoke.

As his assistant led the pledges out of the room, he *almost* allowed himself to smirk at punishing them for being flawless in their punctuality. A pledge doing anything right during pledging was like having Eric successfully hit on some chick at a bar. It just didn't happen.

The pledges started chanting out the numbers of their push-ups in damn near perfect unison as Jeff once again surveyed the brothers in the common room. Not a whole lot happening on anyone's faces as usual, but the look of concern was unmistakable on Eric's.

They re-entered the room after completing their push-up punishment. Jake and Will were panting slightly while J-Hood and Summers looked like they couldn't get more comfortable. *Typical.* It was one of the sad truths he'd learned early on as pledge-master. Summers could literally bang out a hundred push-ups without breaking a sweat. It made the task of hazing him harder than it should've been. But it did require creativity during the callouts, and that was never a bad thing. It usually yielded pretty funny shit.

"OK Alpha Epsilons, it's week five and this is where the fun begins" he began. The fun for the brothers had already commenced on Bids. It hadn't ceased yet. But week five always allowed the pledges to at least have a monochrome of entertainment.

"Get out your notebooks" Jerry ordered.

The pledges took out their notebooks on cue. These were not to be confused with their AZXi pledge books. These books were literally for notes they took down at pledge meetings. They dealt with the week's tasks.

"This week we begin house hours. That means anytime from eight in the morning until five in the afternoon, if you don't have class or something class-related, you are here at the house. When you're here your job is to keep this entire place spotless. When that task is done you will be studying your pledge books or for an actual class…in that order. Of course this week if you aren't here or in class, there is one other acceptable thing you can be doing; and that's working on this list."

Jeff motioned for Jerry to hand over the scavenger hunt list to the pledges.

The list was four pages long, back and front. It consisted of two hundred eighty seven items that the pledges would need to get done within the next week. It was an impossible task as always, just like everything else but there was some insanely entertaining stuff on there. *If these kids put some actual effort and creativity into it they might actually cross early. Maybe.*

No pledge class *ever* finished their list. It was always an unrealistic amount of things based on the number of pledges in the class for that semester. The things on the actual list consisted of letters from brothers and sorority girls to pictures of pledges doing various things to outrageous tasks like getting a cure for AIDS. It was all in the presentation. Eric and Jerry actually came up with a ridiculous three-point plan on how to cure cancer when they pledged. The general rule of thumb was that if it made the brothers laugh, it counted. But that was never said out loud. *They should be able to figure that out on their own...*

"That list is due in full by Friday at five. At that point you will be giving a presentation to myself, Jerry and the brothers. So get it organized. Any questions?"

As usual the pledges were dumbfounded and had nothing to contribute so Jeff didn't wait all that long for a response. "Good, then get the fuck out of my house."

No more than a second passed before the brothers started yelling at them to hurry and get out. It was just another reminder that they couldn't do anything right. As they hurriedly exited and shut the door behind them, Jeff actually allowed himself to hope that they would actually make an effort on that list. It would make his program look good. But there was something else too. Maybe he just wanted them to succeed at something...anything. *Time will tell.*

Everything was blurry so early in the morning.

Jeff Chester had to physically remind himself that it was Wednesday.

It was still tough, even at the late stage in his college career to actually focus so soon each day. The only thing currently registering for Jeff was the sound of running water while he brushed his teeth. His computer science classes unfortunately required him to be up early because most of them were only offered at eight AM.

Jeff slowly had the revelation that he was in fact dawdling in the bathroom like a chick. He finished rinsing his toothbrush before switching off the light and heading back to his room down the hall.

The brothers on his side of the house shared that bathroom. Two of which were his pledge brothers: Kevin and Guapo. The fourth was Petey, Gretman's pledge brother. Thankfully none of them were up around now so he could shower and get ready without any traffic problems.

He reached his room and started essentially throwing the necessary notebooks and textbooks into his backpack. Since it was Wednesday that meant he'd have three classes in a row. *How the fuck can it already be Wednesday?* That meant he'd assigned the pledges the scavenger hunt three days ago. That was a crazy thought. From what he'd heard from the various brothers that *hadn't* been contacted about contributing to the list, he wasn't overly optimistic about their progress.

He grabbed his backpack and walked out of the room, nearly slamming the door behind him on reflex. Jeff always made sure to lock it for whatever good it did. There was just no telling how much damage unsupervised frat guys could cause in the time he'd be away, so he always did whatever he could to stop potential problems. That wasn't to say he wouldn't also contribute to such destruction if he were in fact part of the unsupervised crowd.

He reached the bottom of the stairs and noticed a weird sight on the lone couch on his side's common area. One of the pledges was passed out in the fetal position. *This fucker should be at breakfast right now, and why does he have his callout shit on?* That did nothing to stop his thoughts from moving to the worst possible conclusion.

"What the fuck are you doing here?" Jeff asked as loudly as he could in the pledge's direction without waking up the rest of the house.

Raley started shifting from his obviously uncomfortable position to look up at him. He looked terrible. That could probably be attributed to the fact that he'd slept on an AZXi house couch without a blanket or pillow. Not that such a thing was uncommon; it was just that most people that did that were usually blackout drunk. And there was no way Jake Raley had gone on a bender on a Tuesday night while he was pledging. *He doesn't have the balls for that.* Within a matter of seconds the look on his face went from exhausted to ashamed to scared. *Great. What the fuck has this kid done now?*

"It's a long story" was all the pledge could say.

Jeff took a deep breath while trying to remain calm. *Why can't this pledge class just stop being a pain in my ass?*

"My class doesn't start for another twenty minutes. Humor me."

****

Jake never much liked the idea of taking his laptop outside his room for fear of it somehow breaking and or getting lost. Yet here he was on the ragged edge of sleeplessness and depression with his computer out in the middle of the Cordan library. He barely noticed that his three pledge brothers were pouring over their AZXi pledge books studying family trees and Bids parties. *Like any of that matters now...*

Technically they weren't supposed to have those books out at any point outside of the house or their dorms but these were desperate times. The brothers would probably be less pissed about a lapse in judgment regarding book guidelines than they would be about them not knowing the frat's history mid-way through week five. Either way Jake wasn't concerning himself with memorizing worthless facts about AZXi right now. He had a bigger agenda.

"What are you doing Raley?" J-Hood asked.

Jake shrugged absently. "Well after going through three days of house hours and the shit we went through last night...I can say with great authority that I'm ready to kill someone. Probably Jeff."

"You're way too dramatic Raley" Will chimed in. "But yeah, I'm with you on that" he admitted, to Jake's surprise.

"After what happened to me and Summers last night, I think I'm entitled to be dramatic pal" he said bitterly, not really caring that Will just agreed with him.

"I still can't believe you two did all that...fucking crazy."

"Enough man. I've already heard it from Jeff and Jerry all morning. I can't take any more" Jake stated sternly. Summers was sitting on the other side of the table simply nodding in solemn agreement. "The only way to get out of house hours is to be working on the list or being in office hours. So to answer you J-Hood, I'm typing up fake syllabuses to make it look like there's office hours at every conceivable time of day."

"OK but why?" Summers asked.

"Instead of being at office hours which don't exist, I'll be sleeping" he finished with a satisfied smirk. It was as though he just remembered how clever it was. *Fuck Jeff.*

"Seems like a lot of work just to avoid house hours" J-Hood said, all but shooting down Jake's hopes for a compliment.

"Maybe," he conceded "but to me house hours are far worse than making a fake syllabus...or four."

"Yo you want to make me a couple?" Will asked with a grin.

Ah yes, the sweet taste of victory...

"Me too" Summers added.

The focus of the group then shifted from Jake to J-Hood to see if he'd join their latest ill-advised scheme. As usual, he showed no emotion with no facial expression to go along with it. It was like looking at a blank page, although something was going on beneath the surface. There always was.

"Yeah...word. Sign me up" J-Hood relented.

"Good, we are a pledge class of one after all" Jake joked. "Just email me your schedules so I can make magic happen." *Three for three. Sweet sweet validation.*

Summers and Will both left their seats at the table, presumably to find an open computer to email him their information. J-Hood however stayed firmly where he was.

"You aren't going to get it done now?"

"Nah. I want to get more memorized before the next callout. It might make the whole thing better."

Jake shook his head. "Wishful thinking Hood. Nothing would make a callout tolerable. I'd personally settle for them simply being *not* awful but that'll never happen either. Eric says they're necessary but I haven't figured out why the fuck that is."

Quicker than expected, Will returned to their table with a smile on his face. That faded quickly though. "I bet we get called out tonight" he began somberly. "Third night back after spring break...they've gotta keep fucking us for all that time off."

"Especially since we didn't get the call last night" J-Hood agreed casually.

"I think Monday night's callout was rough enough to allow for a day off. Or a couple weeks" Jake added.

"I doubt the brothers will see it that way."

"Quit acting like pussies. It'll be worth it" J-Hood said, holding back a hint of aggravation. *Is J-Hood starting to crack?*

"Summers isn't back yet?"

"Probably disappeared back into the woodworks," Jake answered Will while returning focus to his laptop.

Summers was constantly around but never in the spotlight. "Bastard probably went somewhere to download the latest '24' episode," Jake murmured.

"At least this time he isn't doing something stupid like watching it in front of Aaron" J-Hood added.

Thank God for that. The last time Summers had that big a lapse in judgment was the night before spring break. *And that went oh so well for us...*

"I know they were friends before pledging but how could you think Aaron wouldn't tell Jerry and Jeff about it? I just don't fucking get it" Jake said, frustrated. *I wouldn't even do something that fucking stupid in front of Biz and he's family.*

Summers re-entered the area.

Jake could've sworn he was coming back from a different direction than the one he originally left. After he sat back down with a smug look on his face Jake asked the question he was sure was on his two pledge brother's minds. "So how was the episode?"

"It's downloading right now. I left my bag by the computer over in the corner. I did send that email though" he replied without a care in the world.

Wow...just wow.

"Now that's brotherhood. You don't even attempt to lie about what you're doing anymore," Will said with the appropriate amount of bitterness.

"Hey we're stuck in this building for another two hours. Might as well do something fun before we get fucked" Summers replied casually.

"I hate it when he makes perfect sense" Jake said to the other two. "I'm gonna call Kelly."

"I don't get it" J-Hood began. "You have a constant source of pussy during all this... why are you always such a bitch?"

"What can I say? I just don't like being told what to do." His three pledge brothers looked back at him with looks of pure confusion. "I never said it made sense."

****

Calvin finished sending a text message to Jennifer before setting his phone back down on the desk. For the first time since he'd gotten back to Gladen Hills, it was clean and clear. His desk had been piled on with papers and shit that needed attention since before break. It only took him three days to sort through everything to make it look pristine. *That's what happens when you put everything off for a week...*

It was a good thing his visit had been so relaxing. Thankfully, Jennifer got along very well with his family. Seeing how she fit in with them like she completely belonged just made him love her more. It was the kind of thing he wanted to talk to his brothers about but just didn't. There was far too much testosterone around to ever let that kind of thing off his chest. Calvin wasn't ashamed of his feelings, he just didn't feel that these were the kind of guys he could talk to about that sort of thing, except for maybe Eric...or Petey. Jeff was in a relationship too but they tended to look at thing so much differently that he didn't think that conversation was worth the trouble.

He plugged his phone into the charger before surveying the room for his AZXi jersey. It was right where he'd left it, at the foot of his bed. He reached for it, once again smiling at his nickname stitched on the back of the black cloth. 'Guitarded' was the name given to him by his frat brothers because he loved playing the guitar. He was actually about seventy percent sure that was why Jennifer slept with him the first time. Not that it mattered much these days. Why the relationship began was a moot point as of now since they'd been together almost three years.

Calvin slid the jersey over his head like he'd done a thousand times before and silently wondered how many more times he'd actually be going through that same motion. Before his thoughts could stray too far into a depressing spiral, in walked Jeff Chester to give him a big push in that same direction.

"I just got an email from the Dean" he announced, clearly not wasting any time on small talk. Calvin took a deep breath. He'd been waiting for the news since word had reached him about just how stupid the pledges had been on the scav list last night.

"Well he didn't waste time."

Jeff grimaced. "From everything we've gone through with that fucker are you really that surprised?"

Good point Buttons.

The Dean and the AZXis didn't have a cherished history together. In fact, he wouldn't have been surprised if in the deep recesses of that bastard's head was some private crusade to revoke their charter. He'd certainly made it a priority to discipline their fraternity whenever he could. Whether there was a real need or not was entirely unimportant. For all intents and purposes Dean Standor was the bane of AZXi's existence. Unfortunately that meant that as president, it was Calvin's job to keep him from coming down on them.

"What'd he say exactly?" He figured he might as well hear it from Jeff before jumping to conclusions. Even if those facts were twisted by the messenger. Jeff had much more reason to hate the Dean than even Calvin did.

"Me and you in his office on Monday" he replied, holding back his anger.

"Monday? I don't get it…that's four days away. He never passes up a chance to fuck with us and take the moral high ground."

"Rumor is that he's not actually in Gladen this week."

"So word of our pledge's nightly activities reached him even outside this town? Good to know" Calvin said, almost getting angrier than Jeff.

"He's probably got us all fucking low-jacked. Fuckin' prick" Jeff fumed.

"Well this'll be just the thing to get us through the weekend. At least we won't have to deal with the pledges though."

"I hate that fucking guy" Jeff seethed. This was one hot-button topic that Calvin wanted nothing to do with. *Come Monday it's gonna be my problem…*

"Look I know how much you hate him but we don't need any more shit between us and him. Let me do the talking this time" Calvin offered.

"Fuck that. He can go fuck himself!"

"I agree Buttons but we tried it your way and look where it got us. We have pledges getting into it with the school administration for the first time in years."

"There's no way you can pin this one on me."

"Why not?" Calvin countered.

"Because we put most of the same shit on the scav list each fucking semester and they got in trouble for doing a *traditional* thing" he answered angrily.

Calvin didn't really believe that this particular case was Jeff's fault but given how he'd been riding rough shot on the pledges all semester it stood to reason that they were reacting in kind, if even on a subconscious level. *Who the hell knows anymore?*

"So this was just bad luck then?"

For a second, he almost thought he saw Jeff smirk before it evaporated just as quickly. "Welcome to my world Gretman" he said with a foreboding tone.

"Glad to be here. All I know is this time, we do things *my* way."

"Sure thing boss" Jeff said before turning his back and storming out of the room. Calvin felt frustration rising. *Son of a bitch...*

The only person on the planet that Jeff hated more than Calvin was Dean Standor.

He didn't want to leave Gladen Hills with any kind of bad blood or regrets. Not being able to have a legitimate conversation with one of the brothers would likely be one such regret. It would certainly make things awkward during alumni events in the future. It was entirely likely that Calvin had been fooling himself into thinking that the rift between them started at the presidential election last year. *All this started before that...back when AZXi first hit the Dean's radar.*

It was much easier to think about Jeff's feelings toward Calvin as being purely of the jealous variety than to get into why it was Jeff hated the Dean so much. Maybe even more into why it was that Jeff was so pissed all the time and why he was so hard on the pledges. *I can't deal with any of this right now.*

Maybe he'd chat with Jennifer or Eric about it soon. Not tonight though. Tonight there was a callout. He hadn't missed one since he'd accepted a bid two and a half years ago. And he wouldn't start tonight.

Chapter 8

By that point in the night they were already deep into the callout play-list that Guapo had set up. As usual the Alpha Epsilons were making fools of themselves. It wasn't unexpected but it didn't make Jeff any less frustrated because he was the one most directly responsible for their fuck-ups. And the fuck-ups were becoming more and more common. Being the one in charge was a fact that was frequently brought up by Gretman, among others. The sight in the corner showed he wasn't the only one to blame at least.

Jared was standing off in the corner with his Little, Raley. *Like Raley isn't already dogging it on his own terms, Jared's gotta baby the fucking kid too?* The drinks he'd had at the National were helping accelerate his frustration.

As he approached, Jared got the look in his eye like he'd been caught banging a professor's daughter. First came shame at being caught, next came his fuckin' signature giddy enjoyment at having done something he shouldn't have. Since Raley was blindfolded he couldn't see Jeff standing next to him so he continued talking.

"I know I know...I'm fucked" Raley stated with shame and regret.

"Nah, Summers and Bill-Butt are way more fucked than you bro."

Jeff all but grabbed Jared by the shoulder and walked him away from earshot of the pledge. That amounted to only being a foot or two away since the music was always blaringly loud at callouts.

"Quit holding his fucking hand at every callout."

"I told the kid I'd never give him push-ups Buttons. He's my Little."

Jeff stood there for a moment, trying to figure out why the underclassman wasn't more upset at being reprimanded. *How the fuck could anyone be so happy ALL the time?*

All Jeff could do was stare back with a look of pure loathing at being essentially told 'fuck that' from a kid who crossed only two semesters ago. Sadly that wasn't unheard of. The new generation of AZXis had a lot to learn about respect. The worst part was he doubted they even knew they were doing it to the upperclassmen. If only he'd been allowed to graduate on time he wouldn't have to deal with that shit for long.

"He's right on the edge man. What do you want me to do?"

"I want *him* to learn his shit" Jeff responded while motioning toward the pledge.

Something happened then that Jeff didn't expect.

"So then why'd you rip up their pledge books?" Jared asked. It didn't even sound like he was trying to be a smartass...and he probably wasn't. That pissed Jeff off even more. *Who the fuck are you to ask me that? You're not even on the fucking E-Board.*

"I got enough shit from Gretman. It's done. And by the way they clearly know more now than they did. It just still isn't good enough."

Jared just gave him a nod before walking away toward Summers.

The pledges know more...but that's probably because they had a week off to look over everything. He'd be damned if he ever said that out loud. It was bad enough that everyone was probably thinking the same thing.

Special treatment is sure as hell not going to do these pledges any favors. Apparently Jeff was the only one who saw that. Jared was far from the only big brother that was all but carrying their Little's across the finish line. Eric, Kevin and Petey were all doing the same thing but he wouldn't confront his closest friends with that accusation. And arguing about anything with Eric was pointless. The kid barely hazed *anyone*, let alone someone in his family tree, AZXi or otherwise.

That made only four brothers who had Littles to protect. He was fairly certain the rest of the frat could pick up their slack *if* they chose to step up and do what he was asking. Every semester was the same though. The pledge program started strong and then by about week three, nobody gave a fuck. Not the pledges, not the actives, not the Executive Board. It was a goddamn mess every time. And now it was Jeff's mess.

****

"So you're telling me it's week fucking five and you still don't know all the pledge classes? What the fuck are you waiting for?" Calvin yelled into Jake's blindfolded face. He tended to swear more at callouts than he did normally. He used it as another form of intimidation since it made everything seem more serious than it was.

"I don't know sir" was all Raley said.

"Well at least you know you have no good answer."

"Yes sir."

He seemed more assured now that he'd gotten a semi-compliment. That feeling wasn't likely to last so he let the kid have it, if only for a few seconds. He remembered what a pain in the ass these things were for pledges. *Jesus that was so damn long ago.*

"Give me all the pledge classes starting with the most recent," he ordered.

The kid did a decent enough job going back about halfway. *Still not great...but OK for this class.*

AZXi had been around twelve years, and each semester in that time housed a different pledge class. Each class was designated by a different Greek letter or letters. With twenty-three singular letters already used, they were now into the lettered combination classes. After the Psi class hadn't amounted to much the frat went into the Alpha classes. They'd skipped over the 'omega' letter for fear of it generating bad luck.

The change had been done a year after he'd crossed and in that time he'd essentially gone balls deep in drinking and partying. That was all the more reason to bring it back down to a manageable level when he got older and more involved in the frat. It didn't look good for the president of an organization to be a blackout mess *all* the time. That was probably one of the reasons he never had any good stories like the other guys, because he never got *that* drunk anymore.

In any event, twenty-seven pledge classes full of names in alphabetical order was a lot to stomach for anyone. The most recent class that actually memorized them all had been the Alpha Beta class with Eric and Jerry. *Those two were absolutely ridiculous.* Every time he thought about them it made complete sense that one was a bio-chem major and the other a physics major. They clearly had the intelligence for such insane academic concepts. *Economics is complicated too if you don't understand it but who the hell really gets biochemistry?*

The pledge started faltering the further in he went. Raley didn't fuck up really badly until he hit the Mu class. That made it all the sweeter. The Mu class was special given that his older brother pledged that semester. Adam and Calvin were extremely close before his brother left for college. It was entirely fair to say that Calvin joined AZXi on the basis of all of Adam's stories. That was a different time though. They'd mellowed slightly, or so Adam claimed.

Having just witnessed an indirect insult to Adam, Calvin let Raley have it. "Wrong! How the hell could you make this many mistakes on the recently graduated alumni? You met some of these fucking guys at your own goddamn Rush."

Raley stood as stoic as ever and took it all in.

"I'm not even gonna ask if you know your own family tree because I can't take any more disappointment tonight. Let me ask you a question pledge: you think I like being down here with you when I could be out drinking or hanging with my girlfriend?" Calvin allowed himself to smile since it was hidden from the blindfolded kid. Even though he couldn't see his eyes, his facial expression had the look of 'you really don't want me to answer that question'.

"No sir" the pledge replied through ground teeth.

"You know if you knew your history, you'd be back in your dorm room fucking your girlfriend right now" Calvin added, just to pour salt in the wound.

Again Raley's facial expression left nothing to be assumed, he clearly didn't buy a word of that. But that was normal, and no less fun.

"Sorry sir."

"Don't be sorry. Just fucking fix it!"

He let that sink in before closing his pledge book and putting it in his backpack. "If you can't deal with this then the Lambdas are right next door. So I'll ask again: can you handle this?"

"Yes sir!" Raley shouted.

"Good. Then you won't mind doing a wall-sit for me while you prove it."

Raley simply nodded before adjusting his backpack across his stomach. Then he reached backward to find the wall and leaned up against it with his back while pointing his arms out directly in front of him, assuming the ninety-degree position required.

The exercise was a different method for fucking with the pledges, and it was a personal favorite of Calvin's. He didn't have any trouble doing them when he was pledging so he liked assigning them now. In a weird way it showed him that he could do something better than someone else. Generally when the pledges did that exercise it was for the purpose of reciting frat history at the same time to really drive the point home. Tonight though, Calvin wanted Raley to just sit there with his own thoughts.

****

After what had seemed like a full ten hours of torture, they'd finally been screamed at to leave the frat house. Not a moment too soon either since Jake had literally been one more condescending comment away from punching brother James Brock in the face. That fucker's idea of hazing had been to make any pledge that messed up his greeting memorize a bible passage from 'Pulp Fiction'. Of course he'd messed up sometime during week four but he hadn't memorized the passage. *And now I'm paying the price for not giving a fuck about that guy.*

Interestingly, James Brock or J-Bro as the AZXis called him, was the semester's Rush Chair. That meant that at the beginning of all this he was the go-between for the pledges, or then rushes and the active brothers. Jake's initial thoughts of the guy were that he seemed nice enough and generally levelheaded but pledging had warped those thoughts. What had seemed nice and levelheaded before Bids had turned into condescension and hypocrisy.

During Rush, J-Bro almost seemed to not give a damn about the frat at all. It was almost like it shouldn't be taken too seriously. It was a selling point for someone like Jake who wasn't sure about the whole thing. *That bastard hazes us just like everyone else. Fuck 'em all.* That wasn't even to mention the fact that Gretman had made him do a wall-sit with no damn purpose behind it. Or that Jeff was targeting his Big to get him to stop being tolerable at callouts. *Can't have that can you, Jeff?*

Jeff had probably thought he was talking far enough away from Jake so he couldn't hear a thing but Jake had extremely good hearing. *And Jared says he doesn't single me out? Yeah right. Maybe I should give him the name of a good psychiatrist because that Jeff bastard is not all there.*

They'd been so overworked with sit-ups, push-ups and wall-sits at the callout that by the time they left, their clothes were all soaking with sweat. It tended not to be noticeable in most cases since their clothes were always black for callouts. He'd assumed that was so they wouldn't stand out to any passers-by when they sprinted to the house at all hours of the night. However, an added bonus was that no one could see how hard they were actually working.

Now that they were a good distance from the house Jake actually began to notice the cold air and temperature that was now seeping into his wet clothes. He was heavily anticipating that warm bed in his dorm room with Kelly next to him.

"Well that's another one down," said J-Hood's now frustratingly cool voice as it pierced the frigid air around them. *Seriously, does this guy just have no fucking emotion on anything? Good, bad or whatever?*

Jake actually liked his pledge brother for just that reason most of the time. But he was in no mood to be positive tonight. "That might mean something if we knew how many were left" Jake answered abruptly.

"Relax Raley. This is the best time in pledging. The time when the next callout is furthest away" J-Hood replied calmly.

"You may have a point there," Jake conceded.

"I know."

"So we're coming up on the end of week five. So God willing and this thing actually goes according to plan we should be done with this shit next week."

J-Hood nodded. "Yeah, it'll be nice to straight chill again."

Jake had often wondered what the hell J-Hood did in his spare time and now he had an answer. *Apparently he just 'straight chills'...whatever the fuck that means.*

"I never even want to look at Cordan again. I hate that damn place so much. Such miserable memories."

"Word."

"The worst part is that I'm not even tired after all that shit. There's no way I can pass out now."

"That's because we're wired to be up late now."

Jake frowned. *It's the gift that just keeps on giving isn't it?*

Despite the fact that it was still cold out, the landscape was comforting to Jake as they walked back to Northeast. Will and Summers both lived on Northwest so they usually took separate paths back after callouts.

"This part I don't mind actually. Being out at night like this when it's quiet. It's a good reminder that this place isn't the Hell the brothers want us to think it is."

Now it actually looked like J-Hood was giving a sincere nod back.

"God knows at least Dukes will be awake when I get back. The son of a bitch is *always* up late. I guess barely making it to class helps."

J-Hood seemed interested. "Didn't you say that he was thinking about pledging next semester?"

"Nah not him. Scribner more than Dukes, and even he's a long shot," Jake answered. He almost felt sad about it.

"Yeah me and Scribner got a few classes together. I've been trying to work on getting him to pledge."

Jake had to chuckle. That got J-Hood's attention.

"I doubt the words of someone like you or me who haven't even experienced being on the other side of all this is going to sway him much...except in the wrong direction." *Or the right one, depending.* Given the mess he was currently sifting through with pledging, he wasn't relishing the thought of talking someone else *into* that lifestyle.

"Yeah you're probably right. But how 'bout him talking with some of the older guys like Eric or Calvin, even Guapo might work."

Jake shook his head. "I think that's something I'd want to worry about later. We have enough to deal with without adding next semester's Rush."

"It's never too early Raley."

He dug in. "It's definitely too early to start selling a frat having only seen one party from a brother's perspective." *Bids...at least I think I had fun that night...*

"Ah Bids" J-Hood thought aloud "anything that night tops the physical shit during pledging for pure madness."

While that was undoubtedly true it didn't really make sense to Jake to exchange six weeks of Hell for one night of blacking out hard. That payoff would hopefully happen *after* Crossing.

They said their goodbyes as Jake reached his dormitory entrance. He heard J-Hood's footsteps recede through the shallow snow as he got out his Gladen Hills ID to open the door. The fun would start again tomorrow with breakfast at Lance at seven thirty AM like it did every weekday.

Entering the dorm after a callout was always a surreal experience. It was almost like an oasis after dealing with the harsh desert of AZXi. The best part about the oasis was Kelly. *And thank fucking God.* As he neared his suite room door the faint sounds of the TV were readily identifiable. That wasn't a shock since it was only a little past two in the morning. *Might as well be the afternoon for Dukes.*

Upon entering it became clear he was watching 'The OC'. It was something of a guilty pleasure for the two of them...although neither of them felt that guilty about it. It was something Scribner definitely didn't understand and also mocked them for whenever he could.

Jake trudged inside and sat on the couch opposite Dukes. His suitemate didn't even bother tearing his gaze away from the TV. That was most likely because he knew it couldn't be anyone other than Jake coming back so late.

After all but collapsing on the uncomfortable college issued furniture, Dukes finally spoke up. "Well Jacob, how was your evening?" He was using a very proper voice that he clearly wasn't being sincere with. *Might as well play the game with him.*

"Well Simon, I strongly considered going to buy beer only to remember we live in Gladen Hills and buying alcohol after two-thirty is considered a sin" he responded in kind. It was sad but true. Living in Ohio meant all alcohol sales stopped at the stroke of two thirty AM. *Just not down at Raley's Ring...*

"Well I'm jealous. Thinking about drinking? Now that's a great night."

Jake smiled. He might as well just enjoy the company for once. "I'm jealous of you chilling here, watching The OC."

Dukes nodded. "I'm on a marathon run right now, heading through season one."

Jake's jealousy increased. Season one was almost unanimously considered to be the show's best. It was a fact that they'd talked about at great length. It was also one of the few things they could agree on.

"I just finished up season three with Kelly. She loves the show. I don't know...I guess I find it kind of weird since that season is full of garbage" Jake mused.

Dukes pressed the pause button immediately. "She liked season three?! It might be time to let that one go Raley...she's clearly no good."

"Oh really?" Kelly's voice hit the room like a comet. She clearly wasn't in the mood for Dukes' comedy tonight. *She's probably getting pissed about her homework again.* That was both good and bad. It meant she'd want to get her frustrations out...probably with Jake.

His face lit up when she entered the room, the same as it did every time. Even in sweats and a tank top, she looked unbelievably sexy. "Hey babe, I didn't think you'd still be awake." That was a blatant lie, he'd hoped for nothing more.

"I'm working on my comp-sci project since my group is fucking worthless."

"In that case, get over here gorgeous."

She actually cracked a smile to match Jake's before joining him. She hit the couch and dropped on top of him resting her head on his chest for support to face the TV. It was a dance they'd perfected over the course of the ten months they'd been dating. They liked being close. That particular position of him on the bottom with his back to the cushions while she lay on top of him was their specialty.

He felt content in the moment.

"So Kelly, what I was saying was that maybe you'd be happier with someone other than Raley. I'm pretty sure there's a special dorm for people who enjoy season three and other forms of bad TV" Dukes interrupted their moment of happiness.

"I'm sure there's a special dorm for people that like this show altogether man. There aren't a lot of guys that watch this. You, me and your friend Daryl are the only ones I can actually name."

"I like to chalk that up to being everyone else's loss."

"At least we can agree on that Simon" Kelly chimed in.

"I told you babe, it really freaks me out when you call him by his first name."

"You mean his *real* name?"

Without warning, Dukes got up from his seat on the far couch and moved toward the room he shared with Scribner. He reached the door and walked inside, all without turning to look at them or saying a word. *Classic Dukes.*

"Now look what you've done Kel" Jake said as seriously as he could.

"You're not serious?" she only half stated.

He held his serious stance for a few seconds before grinning. "You're right. He was probably just tired and went to bed. That was as a good a time as any to leave. Not a whole lot actually offends him. He usually just drives other people to that point."

"You two are ridiculous."

"Yeah but we're Facebook friends, so it's legit."

They just looked back at each other, smiling, feeling completely content.

"So did you just get back a little while ago baby?"

He'd almost forgotten why he was up and active so late. *I'm still pledging a frat.* It felt like getting hit with a sack of anvils any time he came crashing back into reality. Any moment of happiness away from that house caused him to forget it all. Most of the time it was being with Kelly that did the trick. He loved her for that.

"Yes ma'am. Another fun-filled night at the AZXi house, which was our third one this week if you're keeping score. Seriously, you should come along next time."

"If I saw those guys doing any of that shit to you, they wouldn't like what I have to say" she stated with that stubborn streak he'd found so attractive when they met.

"I doubt they'd like what either of us has to say on that subject Kel."

She sat up to look into his eyes. "Tell me again sweetie: why'd you think this was a good idea?"

Please don't make me go through this Kel. Not tonight.

The times when he was in the mood for such talks were becoming increasingly rare. Being serious was enough of a challenge during class and callouts. He'd be damned if that started bleeding over into whatever precious free time he still had.

"Isn't it obvious? I wanted to go to the gym but I never could get motivated. I figured pledging would help make me exercise" he paused to think. "Except now I'm being forced to all the time so I guess I didn't plan that too well."

Judging by Kelly's face, she wasn't amused. "You know Jake, just one time I'd like to have a real conversation with you."

"We definitely have before…that one time," he said while he thought about the last time they talked without kidding around. *I know its been a while babe.*

She sighed before getting up from the couch and moving toward Jake's room.

"What do you want me to say Kel? That I'm not exactly happy with the way things turned out? That I can't even see myself with these assholes if I cross? Because I don't know what to fucking do. I just know that if I quit now…at the minimum my relationship with Eric is fucked because he vouched for me to get in."

Kelly looked at him curiously.

"He never said it and I doubt he will…but I know it's the truth."

Kelly dropped the dissatisfied look and walked back to the couch that Jake was now sitting up on. He was panting from the flood of emotion. *Why couldn't you just leave it alone Kel?*

She put her arm around him before leaning her head on his shoulder. It felt warm. "Baby, do you really think quitting all this will mess things up with Eric? He's your family." Kelly sounded almost motherly. *Why can't anyone else see how much she cares about me?* Jake paused to stare into her eyes. *Maybe she's right.* Jake knew in his heart that his relationship with Eric would transcend all the frat bullshit.

"Not permanently. But this kind of mistake…I mean…half the reason I joined the frat was to stay close to Eric. He's been my brother since we were kids." *Don't cry. Not in front of her.* Jake had sworn up and down before he left for college that he wouldn't cry here and so far he hadn't.

"If that's true, then what's the other half of the reason?"

"I don't know Kel…I guess I just wanted college to be…different."

He couldn't believe he'd said it out loud. He'd always thought as much but never said it. As he'd feared, they sat in silence as the time on the wall clock ticked by.

"Jake…pledging a frat might be the most stereotypical thing anyone does when they want to do something different" Kelly finally said into the crushing silence.

The irony hadn't been lost on him. He was well aware of the stereotypes. The point was that it was different for someone like him.

The sadness was creeping up from all sides now. "I should be so lucky as to have a stereotypical experience," he replied sullenly. His eyes were locked at a spot on the far wall halfway between the floor and ceiling. He could feel Kelly's worried eyes piercing him, trying to find a way to help.

"Why? So you can become a typical frat guy? That's not who the guy I love is Jake" she said. It almost sounded like a warning.

"You know that's not what I want Kel. I just can't help seeing the people having the most fun around here are the ones affiliated with *something*. I mean *anything*. Those are the people going through college the way I want to…and it's killing me that I'm not getting that."

"There are worse ways to go through life than what you're doing" she said, again finding that comforting tone he'd gotten so accustomed to since Bids. For a moment, the two of them just sat there holding each other, trying to find some way to move forward.

"Is it so wrong to want something more?" Jake was ashamed. He didn't even mean for the words to slip out.

"Do you really think that *these* guys in *this* frat are going to give you that?" she asked, sounding legitimately curious.

Even before Bids. When his dad first dropped him off in Gladen Hills last year, the thoughts of getting more from college were on the forefront of his mind.

"I think so…" he responded in as hopeful a tone as he could. His eyes felt heavy from water forming at their base.

"Alright then finish it. Quitting now…Eric *will* forgive you but you're the one who might not get past it. I don't get how making you feel like this will make you a better member when you get in but everyone has traditions I guess. I'd just like to see you more."

He looked away from the wall where his eyes had been locked since the middle of their talk to meet Kelly's gaze. She looked like she was going to cry and he wasn't sure why. Instinctively he wrapped her up in his arms and kissed her forehead. She hugged him tightly. "You know me too well I guess."

She looked at him with loving eyes, not a tear in sight. "Count your blessings."

"And I suppose you're included in that list?"

"If you can't answer that then you're in more trouble than you think."

He leaned in to kiss her like he'd been dying to since she walked into the room. Every time their lips touched, the rest of the world could wait. He loved every minute.

They started to kiss more passionately as she leaned back on the couch, taking him with her. Now with Dukes out of the picture so late, there wasn't likely to be any traffic in the common room. Kelly knew that as much as he did. She pulled his right hand down to her waistline. It was inviting. He loved feeling it. She moaned as he ran his fingers along her waist and into her pants. Jake grew warm as their tongues danced and he let his fingers do the initial work for the road ahead.

Chapter 9

It was like clockwork. Annoying clockwork. It took roughly fifteen or twenty minutes for her hair to get dry every single time she showered. By now it was just something she had to build in to her plans of getting ready. She really did get jealous of Riley's ability to get ready in a half hour. Showered, make-up, clothes... everything.

Tonight was a little different. She wanted to look better because they were having a party with the Tau Chis. She and Brian hadn't really talked in a couple weeks after the last time they'd hooked up. Naturally she wanted to get his attention, not necessarily just so they could fuck again though. Tory just wanted to be noticed. Getting checked out was how she had fun most nights. It didn't hurt that sometimes looking good got her free drinks at the Midway either. *Unless I count what it does to my liver.*

She stood there staring into the mirror after putting on her favorite black bra. It was comfortable and it made her boobs look bigger than they were. Not that they were small, she just preferred them looking as pronounced as possible. That also tended to help with free drinks. Her auburn hair was still glistening from the shower and the hair dryer had already been running for a solid ten minutes. Tonight she'd decided she'd curl it. *It'll make everything look better with what I'm wearing.*

The Tau Chis lived right across the street from the AZXis and if she ran into any of them tonight, she wouldn't mind catching their attention too. After what happened with them last semester the more they saw of her looking her best, the better. That wasn't the main plan but any possible benefits were fine by her.

Riley would see right through her admittedly obvious strategy and call her on it in some way. It wasn't like her best friend got particularly jealous about all the attention she got from frat guys, Riley just didn't really comprehend why she acted the way she did. Tory could look sexy once she worked at it but Riley was naturally beautiful. The crazy thing was that she never really used her gifts to get guys. Sure she'd had flings in the past but one-night stands were rare. For Tory they were her bread and butter.

After another couple minutes with the blow dryer, Tory turned it off. It tended to overheat after fifteen minutes if it was in constant use since it was so old. She'd had it since she was fourteen. Part of the reason she was going to a state school instead of a private one was because her parents weren't exactly wealthy. Tory wasn't ashamed of it. She just didn't want it broadcast. She'd have to let it sit and cool for a few minutes before turning it back on. *Just like any guy after a few drinks at Thirst Point. Some guys just can't hold their liquor like they think they can...so annoying.*

Leaving her personal bathroom, Tory moved into the outer bedroom. She didn't have to look far to find her favorite jeans. They were the ones that accentuated her ass. Tonight she'd gladly sacrifice being a little less comfortable while having her second best asset shown off. *No question there.* She slipped them on over her matching black underwear and wiped away a few more drops of water coming off her hair.

Tory went through a mental checklist about everything she had to do tomorrow. After a little deliberation she decided that going to the mall would trump her classes. *Perfect.* They'd just be getting their tests back in History and she was sure she aced it. Spanish was always a joke so she skipped it more often than not. And that did it for her Friday classes. *Tomorrow's gonna be a good day.*

Tory wasn't sure but she thought Danielle was done with classes tomorrow after eleven. That just left Riley. She was sure with a little convincing she could get her to skip class too. Going to the mall with Riley was always welcome because she kept her focused. Riley always said that she got that prioritizing mindset from her mother who always had itineraries. Having met her mother before, she knew it wasn't a lie.

Maybe I can finally grab some hair dye tomorrow and then I can go blonde.

She liked her hair but she loved changing things more. It certainly helped that whenever she dyed her hair in the past it would piss off her mom. *That's always a bonus.* That was part of the reason she loved Riley's mom since her own mom was too judgmental to be around. It seemed like she did her best to get on Tory's nerves at every turn. That was how she'd ended up at Gladen Hills. It was one of the three colleges that she'd been accepted to and it was the least favorite of her mom's. For all she knew she might have ended up here anyway but that certainly helped.

There was a knock on the door and Danielle's voice came through. Tory let her in after slipping on the only clean tube top she had. Danielle immediately noticed her boobs but didn't say a word. *That wouldn't happen if she was Riley.*

"Can I borrow your black heels?"

The two of them wore about the same size so they tended to swap shoes most of the time. Plus Dani was shorter so she raided her heel collection frequently. Tory pointed her in the direction of her shoe rack. Dani walked over and said thanks.

Riley popped in a few seconds later.

"I'm not sure if your boobs are big enough T."

Tory smiled. *Five whole seconds.* "You guys ready to go?"

Of course Riles is ready. She probably only started prepping like ten minutes ago. Tory shook her head, both to the question as well as her thoughts. She might as well hurry up. *There's no point in keeping Brian and any other boys waiting...*

****

It was a little much having four consecutive callouts the week they got back from spring break but Jeff didn't care. *After what I've been putting up with it's the least these kids can do to show they give a fuck.*

Tonight really didn't even count as a callout anyways. They were doing something pledging related past eleven at night but it wasn't like usual. They'd gotten the pledges to the house around midnight after the party with Phi Theta ended. The girls hadn't even gotten to their house until around half past ten. *Those girls think they're hot shit so they can do whatever the fuck they want.*

Jeff never liked them because of their condescending attitude. That made his raids on their apartments freshman year so damn satisfying, especially now. That was a long time ago though. He didn't do much sorority raiding these days with the college atmosphere changing so much but it was definitely missed.

The real trick of the evening, aside from having to put up with those girls was finding four sober brothers to drive. Tonight's particular pledging activity required driving to an undisclosed location. Fortunately since it was a Thursday night, the requisite brothers were standing by. Had it been a Friday, there would've been zero chance of finding even *one* sober AZXi.

Eric barely went out on Thursdays so he was down. Jerry was essentially ordered not to drink by Jeff so that he *could* drive so that left two open slots. Kevin and Dylan had both been fortunate catches. Dylan had an organic chemistry test tomorrow that he was too happy to take a study break from. Kevin had just gotten back from a visit home about a half hour ago so he didn't really have much time to slam beers. Actually he did, Jeff just talked him out of it.

That had left the night wide open for him since he didn't have to drive. He drank at the party to his heart's content. After he was done with the idiot pledges he was going to Dana's place. Although it was more likely that he'd have to get her to come back to his room at the house while he waited.

Jeff was sitting in Dylan's black Jetta, driving down some sketchy looking farm road with no streetlights. There were only a handful of streets in Gladen Hills that even had lights and theirs wasn't one.

Each pledge-master was told by the previous semester's pledge-master where to go for tonight's activity. That way the pledges couldn't get any inside information on where they were going. It wasn't foolproof as some previous classes had proven, but it worked more often than not.

Judging by the happy look on Dylan's face, he was clearly soaking up every instant before going back to study. *Can't really blame you Dills.*

Jeff motioned for Dylan to take a left at the next intersection.

The pavement abruptly changed over to dirt as he made the turn. They were almost at their destination, which was perfect considering their car's pledge wasn't entertaining them all like he was supposed to.

Dylan pulled over on the right side of the road before turning off the car.

Jeff motioned to the backseat for Brent to get Summers outside.

After a few minutes they had all four pledges out of their respective cars on the side of the road. They lined them up with their backs facing the farmland. There wasn't a light or person within sight of any direction not that the pledges could tell as they were all still blindfolded.

"Alright pledges, after we get back in the cars you'll count out five minutes and remove your blindfolds. Then you can start walking back to the house. It's your job to get back before two in the morning. That gives you a little under two hours. Plenty of time if you ask me."

Raley stirred at the comment. *Yeah, yeah, I know where you stand on all of this kid.* "If you aren't back in time it will not end well so don't fuck up."

With that, Jeff motioned for the brothers still outside to get back in their cars. Dylan and Brent were already sitting in the car quietly by the time Jeff sat in the passenger's seat.

Jeff took one final look at the pledges as Dylan peeled away, clearly going for dramatic effect. He was leaving them stranded in the middle of nowhere and it was doubtful the pledges had any idea where they were.

****

"Well…this is real fucked."

Jake didn't even wait until the fifth 'minute' had passed. He ripped off the blindfold in three. He was at least glad to see his pledge brothers had similar bouts of impatience as they had or were doing the same. They all blinked quickly a few times to get their eyes acclimated to actually being used without the blindfolds that had become commonplace since Bids. All four looked in every direction, trying to get a bearing.

"Which way do you think we should head?" J-Hood asked.

It wasn't a good sign that the most levelheaded of them was at a loss for a plan.

"This is so fucking pointless" Jake complained.

"Calm down Raley. This is better than push-ups all night" Will said.

"Is it? At least then we know where the fuck we are. I see no improvement here…I'm so sick of this shit." *Come on just relax. Quit acting like a little bitch.*

"Speaking of being tired of this, help or shut the fuck up."

Jake stood there shocked. There was no mistaking J-Hood's annoyance.

"I'm thinking since there's a ton of lights in that direction, that's our best bet." It'd been so long since Summers had spoken that Jake had forgotten he had a voice.

"That's good enough for me" Will answered.

"Word" was all J-Hood added.

The three of them started off in that direction. Will was the only one who looked at Jake to make sure he was following.

They walked in silence for the first couple minutes. Since being dropped off Jake's mood had gone from bad to unbearable. It was one thing pissing off the brothers. It was another thing to piss off his pledge brothers. *And yet you couldn't keep your mouth shut to stop bitching.*

"How long do you think it'll take to get back?" Will asked no one in particular.

"I'm not even sure where we are yet" J-Hood replied casually.

Summers remained quiet. Jake took a few seconds as he continued walking slightly behind his pledge class to look around. The only thing he could make out through the darkness was the farmland on all sides. Normally that might've been a clue of some kind but the entire college was surrounded by farmland in every direction. *I've lived here a year and I still have no goddamn idea where we are.* There must've been at least a dozen different roads leading out of town that led to similar areas.

"I think I recognize this farm," Summers announced, louder than usual.

"Gladen Hills is surrounded by farms. You do know that right?"

"I'm not so sure he does" Jake interrupted.

Summers looked extremely confused but it was always hard to tell. *He's harder to read than J-Hood.* For all they knew, Summers could've recognized the farm because he was a field hand or maybe he even lived there. Neither would've surprised Jake.

"There's no way Summers is that fucked" J-Hood offered.

Jake wasn't entirely convinced of that either but didn't say anything as they continued soldiering on.

Last night's temperatures had been low after the callout but they hadn't really noticed since they'd been sweating so much after the two hours spent at the AZXi house. Tonight was worse and the wind was gusting. Fortunately Jeff and the others demanded they all bring jackets, gloves and hats with them on their latest mind-fuck. It would've pained Jake to give Jeff any credit so he chalked it up to covering their own asses. There wasn't a doubt in his mind that Jeff was every inch the hard bastard inside and out. What's more, he doubted the guy had ever done anything for anyone other than himself. After a little while it became clear that J-Hood was walking quicker than Will and Summers so Jake strode past them to catch up.

"Since when do you get pissed...like at anything?"

"The right circumstances can fuck with anybody" J-Hood replied gruffly.

Good point. Jake had always assumed that J-Hood was a new kind of emotionless robot set to bring about the apocalypse...while fucking hot chicks as he went.

"So I don't think I ever actually asked but you're straight with being called J-Hood right?"

"It'd be kind of fucked up if I wasn't."

"True, but the brothers call you that and there's no stopping that."

"It's fine with me" he said, putting the matter to rest. "There's two 'J' names in the mix, gotta split it up somehow."

"Maybe but nicknames definitely seem to be a part of the game around here. I mean barely anyone gets called by the name on their birth certificate. We've got 'Guapo', 'Biz', 'Jer-Bear', 'Petey', 'Segs', 'Dills', 'Bill-Butt', 'J-Bro' and then the last names. 'Raley', 'Summers', 'Gretman'…it just goes on and on."

"OK I get the point."

Jake grinned. *I rest my case pal.*

"Do you think when you spend so much time with people that, depending on the group, you might change who you are?" Jake asked.

"Isn't that what pledging? You learn about your pledge brothers and the brothers? We spend too much time together not to."

"That might've been the initial thought but I still think the physical shit is crazy," Jake lamented. Even now, his joints were sore from last night.

"What we're doing now is just that. Drop us off in the middle of nowhere, get home together."

This is the longest conversation I've ever had with J-Hood…because we were abandoned like kidnap victims miles outside of town.

"I know…shit's real," J-Hood offered to the silence. "But I'm the same person who started at Bids, just a little more tired."

A little!? This guy's only a 'little' more tired? I'd sell one of you into prostitution if it got me a full eight hours of sleep and you're only a 'little' tired?

"There are ways of getting around exhaustion," he continued, as if sensing Jake's awe through the darkness.

"Well by all means, share it with the class."

"I don't do it that much but coke gets the job done."

Jake had heard stories from his cousins about drugs in Gladen Hills but he never paid any attention to it. Jake had always assumed, apparently incorrectly, that it was too far removed from his own circle. It was like being slapped across the face by reality and then getting laughed at for being such a fucking idiot. *You're pledging a frat for Christ sakes. Of course people are doing drugs.* Jake knew Eric wasn't doing anything like that but Riley was a question mark. She'd come to a few Raley's Ring parties but their time actually partying together was low. For all he knew she could be the biggest drug dealer in town. *God I'm a dumbass.*

"I'm sorry could you please say that again…?"

"Relax. It's not a big deal" was the best rendition of comfort he got from J-Hood.

"Hey if you're good, I'm good" Jake managed to say in a believable fashion even if he couldn't fool himself.

"I'm sure you're good. I've seen your chick. How's that going?"

"It's kind of like having your own personal cheerleader during an intense game. Except you know…you get to sleep with her afterward," Jake said with a confidence he hadn't felt in a while.

"That wasn't a thing? Fucking cheerleaders?" He asked with such nonchalance that Jake doubted he'd ever heard the word 'no' from any girl…ever.

"I'm guessing that was common?"

All he got was a smirk and a shrug. A blind man could've read that. *No shock there. Why the fuck couldn't we have been friends earlier? It definitely would've made things more interesting in high school.*

"It is what it is."

"Only you would think that Hood."

"Sex isn't hard to get," he said, as if it was the most obvious conclusion.

"The only reason I agree is because my sex life boils down to my relationships. The one I had and the one I'm in." That left Jake's overall number low but he didn't care…too much.

"Yeah I dated one chick in high school. I tried to make it work but long distance fuckin' sucks." Jake thought there was a hint of sadness but it could've been the result of his inflection changing. "Then the resentment comes, shit got annoying, so that ended."

"Is that why you pledged?"

"I probably would've done it anyways. This just sped it up."

Jake didn't even want to think of how many girls he'd fucked in the little amount of time J-Hood had been single. *He's probably fucked more girls this past semester than I have in my entire life…*

"What are you two sexy dudes talking about?" Will asked as he and Summers finally caught up with them.

"You don't find it even a little weird saying shit?"

It certainly wasn't the first time he'd questioned his pledge brother's homoerotic tendencies, even if they were becoming more frequent.

Will spanked him and started grinning. *That answers that.*

"You better hope we're close to civilization because another move like that, I'll kill you and pay Hood and Summers to say it was an accident" Jake said with fervor. While it wasn't true now, another week of pledging might make it so.

"Oh come on Raley, learn how to take a joke" Will said happily. *Either Summers just blew him while we weren't watching or something else is going on.*

"It's frigid and I want to get back so forgive my fuckin' lack of patience," he said with as much of a threatening tone as he could.

"Is Raley freaking out again?!" Summers' voice chimed in.

"What gave it away?" J-Hood asked calmly.

"It's usually a safe bet when Raley and Bill-Butt are chilling."

"That should make it real interesting when they live together next semester."

Fuck my life. Jake hated being reminded of his dumbass decision to sign a lease with Will when pledging started. It seemed to make sense at the time and he hadn't gotten *really* fed up with the guy until week three. Now he was staring down the barrel of another school year trapped in a house with the guy and things never looked bleaker. *I'd almost rather live with Jeff over this bastard. Almost.*

"I'm just praying Bill Butt fails out before then," he announced bitterly, not caring about anyone else.

"I hope you're not serious?"

"No I'm not" he lied. "You just annoy the shit out of me sometimes."

"Well you do get pissed really easily Raley…it's not all Bill-Butt" J-Hood added.

That wasn't news to him. His whole life he'd heard that. His dad had a short temper and he'd passed it along to his son. There wasn't a lot he could do about it. "I know. I'm working on it" was all he could say. *I just wish I knew how.*

****

Even at one in the morning, the line at the Midway was too long. Just like her hair-dryer though, it was something Tory had to get used to since there was no fixing it.

The party at Tau Chi had been a definite success. Not only had she gotten the immediate attention from Brian, but his Little was also checking her out the entire time they were playing beer pong. She'd never been a fan of the game since flip cup was more her speed. However, Tory found she could interact with the guys more freely in beer pong. That and she could do things like showing off her boobs to distract them from making the shot all in the name of winning…even if it wasn't the *only* reason.

After the party ended she'd had a quick conversation with Brian and his Little. She'd confirmed that he still had her number, which was good *and* bad. It was definitely good because he could text her tonight. On the flip side it was awful since he'd had it the whole time and they hadn't talked in weeks. *Whatever…tonight is tonight.*

She definitely had the feeling she'd be getting a text soon. The sex with him had been good the few times they'd done it and she was sure with a little more practice on his part that it could get really good. Even still, Tory sure as hell wasn't going to text him first and look like the desperate one. That was partially because she didn't get that drunk at Tau Chi. There was nothing to do now except take shots and dance her ass off in the Midway and wait for him.

Despite trying all night, Riley still wouldn't budge on going to the mall tomorrow. It was driving her crazy. "Seriously quit being lame and come to the mall with us," Tory said for what felt like the thousandth time. Danielle had said yes quickly.

"I'm not sure which part of 'I have class tomorrow' you don't understand T."

"It's probably a little confusing since you are kinda sloppy right now" Danielle chimed in with a smile.

"She's right Riles. For someone with class tomorrow you drank a lot."

"And? You've never gotten drunk the night before class?"

"Please…going to class sober fuckin' sucks" Tory replied with a smirk.

"I had to go out tonight because I wanted to see what the Tau Chi pledges looked like. You talk about them so damn much" Riley tried convincing them. *Not my fault they look that good.* Tory had noticed them when she fucked Brian on Bids. *Definitely a couple cute ones in that class.*

"And you guys call me a whore."

"Well neither of us have fucked any of them," Riley slurred the words.

"Neither have I" Tory answered with proud confidence.

"And you wouldn't?" Danielle asked.

"Didn't say that. I just haven't."

"You should really seek help," Riley joked.

"Don't tell me you wouldn't hook up with any of their new guys Riles."

She'd known her friend long enough to see when she'd noticed a hot guy. *The signs were there. She wants to sleep with one of them for sure.*

By Tory's recollection, Riley hadn't had sex in at least a month, maybe longer. *My girl needs to get some ASAP.* For some reason she kept relatively quiet about her sex life and didn't like to admit when she wanted some. *I'll never understand it.*

"They were all pretty cute" Riley finally conceded.

"Your guy Sam was looking pretty good tonight too."

"Yeah but Riles doesn't go back to her flings" Danielle interjected.

Tory smirked. *Yeah...unless his name is Jerry Culson.*

"He definitely looked hot" Riley answered absently.

Good for you Riles. Get it.

"Does that mean I could try and get him?" Tory asked innocently.

"You'd hook up with a sister's ex?" Dani asked. She sounded completely blown away by the mere concept of it.

As if EIPi doesn't have a track record with that sort of thing. Come on Dani. Frats sure as hell don't have a problem doing it so why should we feel ashamed? It was something that always bothered her.

"They never actually dated and yeah...if she was cool with it." Tory didn't even know why she was saying it but it was already out before she could think.

They both looked at Riley, waiting for her to respond in some way, *any* way.

"It's too weird T. I'd appreciate it if you didn't" she finally ruled. There was no denying it; there was an edge to her voice.

Fair enough Riles. "Fine, problem solved."

"Just like that?" Danielle sounded confused, as if she didn't believe Tory possessed that kind of self-control.

"I could never do that to Riles...at least I wouldn't enjoy it." That gained her two curious looks from her sisters. "Oh I'd enjoy it; I'd just hate myself after."

That got her two nods of agreement. *It's at least closer to the truth.*

"So basically the same feeling you get when we down an entire Masterson pizza after the bars?"

"It tastes so good but you hate yourself in the morning" Danielle agreed.

Tory smiled and nodded. *Yeah...that's pretty similar actually.*

"That's actually how Tory feels after every night of drinking" Riley added.

"Bitch I knew that was coming" Tory smiled again.

"It had to be said."

"I'll let it go only if you buy me a shot when we get inside."

"Oh you're saying you wouldn't let it go otherwise?" Dani asked.

"No point in risking it. SoCo-limes it is" Riley announced.

Not exactly what I was thinking but it'll work.

Finally they reached the front door. Even with two bouncers it had still taken forever. Since they were all seasoned veterans they had their ID's ready. Not one of them was legal but they all had fakes and they all looked good even with jackets on so they were sure to get inside for over twenty-one.

With little deliberation, they all got wrist-banded and let through. *And I almost wasn't gonna wear this top.* Tory had unzipped her jacket the closer they got to the door so her outfit was easier to see.

I need to hang up my jacket and get to the Tau Chi corner. That ought to get Brian's attention. The rest should be easy. Tory grinned and walked through the door into the haze of undergrads, loud music and alcohol.

****

After another half hour of walking they'd decided to take their chances in cutting through one of the million fields between them and what was hopefully the campus. When they'd walked another ten minutes they'd figured out that it wasn't a smart idea after all. In their borderline delirious state they'd deduced that they could've potentially been shot at for trespassing. Who knew what the fuck would happen then? The farmers out here were probably decent shots but they'd convinced themselves that they were practically marksmen for the CIA. *Just keep it together and you won't get killed.* With that scenario in their minds they'd turned around and followed the road. All that shit had set them back. And what's more, they *still* didn't have that good of an idea where the hell they were.

Jake wasn't in a happy place by the time they'd gotten a small confirmation they were going the right way. J-Hood had noticed an area with a ton of lights in the hills off to their left. It looked enough like the Gladen Hills campus. The closer they got to the hills the surer they became. Not a moment too soon either as Jake was losing his mind.

"It's a beautiful sight boys!" Will announced. "Who's trying to swing by the National and grab a drink before we get back to the house? We got time."

Jake looked at him sourly. "Says the only twenty-one year old in the group."

Will shrugged it off. "You guys need to grow the fuck up already."

"Now that I know it's an inconvenience for you, I'll speed that right the fuck up."

Without warning, Will jumped on his back as if expecting to get a ride back to campus. Jake swayed at the added weight but didn't fall.

"You're playing with fire," Jake warned him.

"Chill chill chill."

"I just want to get back early enough so I can get laid. I'm going fuckin' nuts."

"She's not gonna wait up for you?" J-Hood asked. He sounded confused at the idea that a girl wouldn't do whatever her boyfriend wanted.

"I'm sure she would if I asked but I can't expect that while I deal with all this."

"Sounds fuckin' stupid to me" Will added even though Jake was in no way looking for his opinion.

Out of the corner of his eye he saw Will reach into his pocket only to come away with nothing. *Did he really forget the brothers took our cells away? Come on.* "Looking for your phone?"

"Yeah, I was trying to text that Trip-E to see what she's up to."

How on God's green earth does Will find willing girls to fuck? It doesn't make sense. "I can't believe she hasn't gotten sick of you yet" Jake said bitterly.

"It's because I'm cuddly" Will responded immediately.

"Get the fuck out of here."

"Hey Raley, I have no problem being a little bigger. With that and my game, I'm golden" Will said confidently.

Could it really be that simple? No way…it can't be. "It's such a sick world."

"When someone like Guapo can get laid regularly then you know this town is something special" Summers chimed in.

So true Summers. Guapo was another Jake couldn't fathom a reason on why he got as much action as he did. Just the concept of these fuckers getting laid so much got him pissed and he wasn't even sure why.

After a few more miles they finally reached the outskirts of campus. *Of course the bastards were kind enough to drive us out in a direction away from the corner of campus the house is in.* It didn't take long once they got back into town to reach the AZXi house. There were a few lights on within the first floor but other than that the place looked deserted. That was natural; it was a little under two in the morning. *Everyone's still at the bars.*

They reached the door and walked inside.

Sadly they found Jerry and Jeff along with Jeff's chick in the main common room. Jeff had a cigarette in his hand and his girl on his lap. Jerry was holding a full beer that he clearly didn't need judging by his hammered face. Jeff didn't meet their eyes until they were all inside. He flicked his cigarette twice to get the ashes off and finally set it in the plastic cup being used as an ashtray before looking at them.

The clock on the cable box was easy to see. Its glowing green numbering showed it was before two AM. In any normal world it would've been great for them to be back early...just not in the AZXi house.

His girlfriend shifted off his lap before Jeff started yelling. "I told you fucks to get back by two in the morning. This isn't the time to show-off! This is the time to follow fucking instructions. Get your shit and get the fuck out of my sight!"

Thankfully all their backpacks had been neatly laid out on the adjacent couch for quick access. They all grabbed their stuff as if it were an emergency evacuation, exiting out the front door within seconds.

Once they were outside Jake felt a huge smile on his face that his pledge brothers quickly noticed.

"What're you so happy about?" Will asked as they ran down Arkridge Avenue.

"No push-ups!? What a great fuckin' night!"

Chapter 10

It got colder in the EIPi house than Riley preferred. That coupled with the fact that winter seemed to last longer in Gladen Hills didn't make for comfortable times. Fortunately having just gotten out of the shower, she felt warm and toasty, even if it was only for the moment.

She turned off her hair-dryer and unplugged it like she always did, just to be safe. She'd only started getting ready about fifteen minutes ago but she was about done. Granted she didn't do nearly as much prep work as Tory but she was more than satisfied with her appearance.

Riley was wearing her Capri pants as well as her favorite sweater that wasn't a full hoodie. Wearing a sweater to a party might have bordered on sacrilegious for her best friend but Riley wasn't trying to impress anyone. Not when the party in question was with AZXi where her two cousins were going to be. The less they saw of her looking hotter than usual, the less she'd have to worry about it getting back to her immediate family. Not that Jake or Eric would say anything necessarily but flirting with guys around them just felt...wrong. But that could change depending on her BAC.

Not that she didn't enjoy being the moral center with her friends and family but sometimes Riley needed some counsel too. Without even thinking, she found herself walking over to the corner of her room where she kept her sorority composite pictures. She found her big sister's picture quickly given she'd looked at it a hundred times. Felicia Crystal was located on the top row signifying her important position within the sorority. She'd been president during her final year at school, the same as she'd wanted for Riley.

Riley had a younger sister and they drove each other crazy. When she'd joined EIPi, getting Felicia as her Big was a miracle. Felicia loved talking to her at all times. Whether it was two in the afternoon and they were texting during class or they were drunkenly downing pizza at Masterson's at three in the morning, it didn't matter. She was always there for Riley...until she graduated.

They still talked on the phone but it wasn't the same. *It'll never be the same...* Riley had been on the verge of tears the day she left Gladen Hills. Felicia hadn't had that kind of self-control. She'd been crying all throughout their Senior Day. *She was leaving all this behind. What am I gonna do when it's my turn?*

Riley tried thinking of something else. It was too early to destroy a buzz she didn't have. She scanned the pictures on the composite for anything that'd make her happier. She loved EIPi but there were only a few other pictures that made her smile like Felicia's. They'd lost a good chunk of their actives when the last batch of seniors graduated. Fortunately they still had the requisite twenty-six actives to fill the house.

She glanced over Rachel Hager's picture. She'd gotten elected president after Felicia when Riley hadn't run. She wasn't convinced she was old enough to be taken seriously. She wasn't even sure she wanted it. Riley was only a junior, as she would've been during her entire presidency, not that that stopped Rachel who was graduating early.

An impatient knock on the door snapped Riley out of her daze. "It's open" she called out. It was rare to lock her door at EIPi. Home was a different story. Sometimes she wished she could bar that door to keep her family out.

Tory strolled in like she owned the place. She was in there enough that it would've made sense. Her friend dropped to the bed as if in a trance. Riley immediately noticed her outfit. It looked like she was in the mood for attention...again.

"I always find parties with AZXi to be a little...not fun."

Riley frowned. "OK I'll go with that" she started in before changing her tone to sarcastic concern. "Why is that Tory?"

It looked as if she was going to start on a long-winded answer so Riley beat her to it. "Wait, don't tell me, it's because you're not good at beer pong and that's all they want to do there right?"

Tory smiled and shook her head.

"Is it because you don't think any of their actives are cute?"

"Seriously? Are you even trying to guess right?"

"It took you this long to figure out I wasn't? I know it's because you think it'll be awkward with Eric, even though it won't be."

"I don't know what you mean by that Riles."

Riley rolled her eyes. "You were screwing my cousin and then it ended, it's not that crazy...especially in this town."

"We haven't even talked since...and that as the beginning of this semester when things got all fucked up."

It's not even a real problem. Riley didn't understand how the two of them got together in the first place plus Tory wasn't known for being upset over guys moving on. *She's usually the one that moves on first...*

"Weren't you all hung up on Brian last night?" Riley asked, trying to get the topic changed. She was in no hurry to deal with her cousin's love life.

"He never texted me so whatever."

Well...she doesn't sound bitter. "There's over three thousand guys at this school T. I doubt you'll have trouble."

"You're right. And normally I'd skip a social if I didn't want to see somebody."

"A good rebound usually helps...but usually it's you telling me that."

"It's just how I deal with things."

"Yeah, because that's *real* healthy."

"You sound like Eric you know that?"

Clearly you want Eric more than you're letting on. She still didn't want to get involved, mostly because she didn't want her friend to get hurt. To the best of her knowledge, Eric didn't want a girlfriend. And with Tory's track record, she severely doubted he'd be interested in anything serious with her. She was sorry to say but as of now, Tory wasn't girlfriend material.

"You think we're alike? You should see him and Jake together."

"Your younger cousin you had to talk off a ledge before break?"

"Yeah. I actually think Jake came to Gladen was because of Eric." *He'll never admit that to me though.*

"Wow, and you say I'm unhealthy?"

"At least I can understand that. We're his family. We've literally never spent more than a week apart since birth. It kinda makes sense I guess."

"He better be cute because that's a little weird."

"He's got a girlfriend." *I don't know why he has that girlfriend but whatever...*

"So you're saying there's no chance?" Tory asked sarcastically.

"I doubt they're breaking up any time soon T."

"Sadly?"

"They aren't good together but he doesn't see it."

"Seems like a common thing with your family" Tory responded with a shrug.

"What does that mean?"

"That DXA Eric replaced me with...she's like not pretty...at all."

"Well at least you aren't biased. But you're still coming tonight" she said with a tone that left no room for argument. Tory didn't look convinced. *Maybe she really was looking for a relationship but just doesn't know how anymore. What do I say to that?*

"I don't know. I could just drink at the National with the townies and wait for the AZXi party to end. They are right next to each other."

Oh absolutely not. No way that's happening to one of my sisters. "There's no way I'm letting you drink alone with townies on a Friday night. Come on. Let's get Dani and go...right now." *My God I sound like my mother.*

"It's before nine, isn't it a little early?"

Riley shook her head. "They have pledges. One of which is my cousin and they'll be serving so there's no such thing as too early."

"That seems a little mean Riles."

"After what you do to our pledges I can't believe you just said that."

"None of them are my family."

"It's their job to serve and if we don't take advantage, someone else will. So it might as well be his family." *Yeah...that kinda makes sense.*

Tory grinned. "OK then. Let's get Dani."

****

"Serving at parties is a privilege so if you fuck it up then you won't be doing it anymore" Jeff stated as sternly as ever. He wasn't yelling at Jake and the others like normal. That type of behavior was saved for callouts and tonight was just a regular party. At least he hoped it was.

Their scavenger hunt presentation hadn't gone well at all. *Maybe if we didn't have a callout every fucking night we could've done a little more.* Jake wasn't fooled. Not even when they were yelled at for the presentation. *There's no way anyone's ever finished the scav list. No fucking way.* That made their punishment of only fifty push-ups much easier to bear. *When success isn't an option, failure is easier to take. Might as well be the Alpha Epsilon slogan.*

Jeff stared each one of them down before walking away, leaving them to their work. *How is standing here and serving you fuckers beer a privilege? On what planet is that even remotely true?* Still, serving was much better than cleaning the house daily or getting left in the middle of nowhere. *It's all the same at the end of the day. We just get to be the active's bitches for a couple hours.*

On top of filling *any* empty cup of the brothers and subsequently the sorority girls, they had to be dressed up in the same attire they'd worn to Formal Rush. Tuesdays and Thursdays they had to dress up but also whenever they served. Button down shirts with ties and khakis were required.

Jeff returned to their spot near the keg almost immediately with an empty cup and promptly made Summers fill it. *I'm surprised he just didn't make Summers walk the five feet toward him for that. He must not be drunk enough yet.*

"You think it'd be in poor taste to piss in these pitchers before pouring beers?" Summers asked once Jeff walked away.

"I'd be down...if this wasn't a party with two of my cousins" Jake answered quickly. Clearly his pledge brother noticed he was the wrong person to ask so he went over to J-Hood to try another angle.

"Did you tell Summers it was a good idea to piss in the pitchers?" J-Hood asked.

"Come on Hood. Does that sound like me?" he asked. "OK OK maybe it does but I definitely didn't."

"I told him I'd beat his ass," he said while flashing a look at Summers. *I sure as hell wouldn't want to be on the receiving end of one of those punches.*

"Maybe when we get out of here we won't have to drive these drunken idiots all over town like usual" Jake said hopefully.

It was a sad truth that while there weren't any callouts on the weekend they still had to be available for the brothers to make sure they got rides all over town. Gladen Hills had a pretty reliable bus system that took students wherever, especially on the weekends. But the brothers preferred having their own personal servants drive them from place to place. *Just another pain in the ass like everything else around here.*

After a few more minutes of making sure every brother was topped off, a group of girls entered through the back door. Jake recognized Riley immediately. She came in with three others. Two of which he recognized as her good friends. He didn't know either of their names but he knew the one in the tight jeans was extremely slutty.

Riley greeted Jeff before she took off her jacket and left it on the lone couch. *They know each other? That sucks for her.* She came up to him afterward but instead of saying hello and giving him a hug, she simply smiled and asked for her cup to be filled.

"You know, it's bad enough becoming the little bitch of AZXi but now this?"

"You're my cousin and I love you...but my cup still isn't full" she grinned back at him. *Fuck my life. Thanks a lot Rye.* She hung around next to him for a few seconds while he went ahead and filled her friend's cups too.

"Hey Rye, did you meet J-Hood yet?" Jake asked as his pledge brother returned to the keg for a pitcher refill.

Riley played it cool. "I just hope he doesn't hit on me immediately like Will did when I met him."

Jake did a double take. *Is she checking him out?*

"What up?" J-Hood gave a quick smile while pumping the keg.

"J-Hood isn't your real name I'm guessing" she played coy.

"Nah. It's Justin but that seems to be the new hotness right now" he smiled again.

I didn't even know he could smile...

"It's definitely memorable" she smiled back before looking over at the beer pong table where Biz was. "Alright I'm up on the table…nice meeting you. And thanks for the beer Jake" she said to him, almost as an afterthought.

"Try not to choke!"

J-Hood's eyes watched her intently as she walked away. "Damn Raley, how many cousins do you have?"

Jake shrugged. "You wouldn't believe me if I told you. My family is Greek."

J-Hood barely heard the answer since his eyes were still locked on Riley. "How many of them look like *that*?" he asked, finally prying his stare away to notice his pitcher was overflowing.

Jake remembered the pact he'd been shoehorned into by his cousins. *Fine, maybe I can't stop anything from happening but I'll be damned if I actively help.* "She's like my sister Hood."

"My bad man, she's just mad hot."

"Biz and I have been hearing it since we got here but if it's info you want on that subject I got nothing for you."

"Alright, word" he responded before walking toward the beer pong table and dropping the pitcher off for the game.

"Since four of you are more than enough to serve tonight, one of you needs to go over to the beer pong table and retrieve any loose balls that fly by…and yes I know how that sounds" Jeff ordered suddenly from behind them.

Jake needed to blink twice. *Did that bastard just make a joke?*

"I'll do it" he responded after letting the shock settle.

"What a surprise. Raley wants to get balls" Jerry chimed in.

Jeff nodded and sent him away to the table.

At least I'll get to chill next to Biz and Rye. That's a step up from normal.

****

Eric always loved beer pong and it certainly didn't hurt that he was good at it either. He watched his cousin come over and stand next to the table to wait for any stray shots. Jake didn't look all that happy but that was pretty much his default setting these days. *It's almost over J, just a little more time.*

One of his favorite things to do was run the table all night. Unfortunately two out of his three top choices for teammates were currently pledging so they couldn't play. Will was just damn entertaining, on top of being very talented. Jake was extremely competitive and always ready for a full-night run but he also kept Eric focused. Usually their relationship worked in the opposite direction but he wasn't ashamed to admit he could get sidetracked during a good party.

With them out of commission and Jerry essentially playing the role of assistant pledge-master he'd had to recruit his other cousin Riley. He'd texted her before the party even started asking if she wanted to play. They didn't get a lot of opportunities to hang out so she jumped at the chance. Eric did regret not finding more time to see his family but his classes kept him from seeing most people in any given week.

Their competition was Gretman and Segs. *Both solid but Segs is clearly hammered, as he should be now that he knows he isn't going to be kicked out of AZXi. That should help.* Segs had started drinking earlier than everyone else in celebration for the E-Board's decision of keeping him active. As it stood, they weren't beating Riley and him by as much as they should've been as it was currently four cups to three.

Riley was a streaky player. Some nights she'd be sickeningly good and other nights she might miss the table altogether. Tonight she was landing somewhere in between. Mostly she was getting rim shots but she did manage to hit one. Eric didn't have to see Jake's eyes to know he was disappointed in *both* their performances. At least Jake's retrieval skills were entertaining to watch. Eric had to admit his cousin's reflexes were pretty amazing. It didn't go unnoticed by others at the table either but that wasn't necessarily a good thing.

"Your cousin has a way with balls," Segs slurred out. *So unoriginal but somebody had to say it. It might as well be the drunkest dude here.*

"Come on Segs, give the kid a break. God knows you wouldn't be able to get any shots and the game would end without us winning" Eric chimed in.

"It's cool Raley. Segs clearly thought that was the funniest thing ever. Don't worry about it" Calvin added while patting Brent on the back hinting that he should take it easy on the pledges. *Hopefully he's learned something after what happened.*

Jake was clearly confused by another brother being nice to him because he tensed up and looked back at Segcand. Eric did the same. The guy was laughing at nothing while also being oblivious to their entire conversation. A conversation he'd started no less. *Brent Segcand is so ugly sometimes...*

Eric stepped forward to line up his shot first. Riley didn't care at what point she shot during any of their turns. *If she cared more maybe she'd be better.*

He launched the ping pong ball in the usual high-arced method and it splashed down in the front cup in one fluid motion. *Perfect.* Eric stared back at Calvin since Brent hadn't noticed. That was even more amusing since it was his beer to drink.

Come on Rye, hit that same cup and it'll be game.

It was a wild yet completely justified rule. If a team couldn't pay enough attention to not take away a previously hit cup then they deserved to lose. As Riley stepped forward it was clear she wasn't thinking the same thing. *That proves it. She's not mentally here. Not as bad as Segs but still.*

Her ball missed the table completely. At that point Segs was finally handed the front beer by Calvin. *Either Gretman didn't think she'd hit it or didn't notice. Terrific...*

"I have yet to meet a girl who could play beer pong well," Jake blurted out. It was extremely sexist but slightly true. Calvin and Eric both nodded in agreement without thinking while Brent steadied himself.

"That's a little fucked up Raley...and to one of our guests no less."

Riley obviously hadn't taken offense so he had for her. *Well Segs is obviously blackout...as if anyone could miss that.* Brent Segcand had classic good looks and was pre-med. Like so many others in AZXi, that meant he had no trouble getting laid...no matter how he acted. All that added up to the fact that he couldn't care less about sorority girls for the most part...even if they were related to his brothers.

"Alright man, let's take this down. I hit it. You quit it," Calvin announced to his drunken teammate.

Before any shots were thrown Jerry walked over.

"What are you ugly dudes about to do?" he asked gleefully. *He's not taking his APM role too seriously tonight.*

"About to take this game down real quick," Brent slurred back absently.

"OK Segs, let's see it then."

Calvin fired his laser-beam, zero arc shot to hit the front most of the two cups.

Eric immediately felt fear. There was nothing worse in beer pong than losing with no chance of rebuttal shots. And that fate was approaching as Segs stepped up to hit the final cup. The look on Riley's face screamed utter indifference. *How can she not see what's happening?* Eric looked over to the side where he saw Jake looking back at him. He shook his head and gave a comforting look. *He doesn't think Brent will hit the last cup. That makes one of us J.*

Segs fired the ball and just like that…it hit the final cup and fell off the table marking the first loss of the evening on Eric and Riley's end. *I knew it…*

"What the fuck is up Biz?" was all Segs could say while using the wall to remain upright. After Eric gave him a nod back Brent just slapped the remaining three cups off the table on his end and strolled out of the basement like he'd won the lottery. Eric laughed at the ridiculousness of it all. *Somehow he just finds a way…*

"OK I guess that means he's done for the night" Calvin said, almost like he was unsure. It was clear to Eric as well as everyone else that he was right. "Biz, you trying to be my partner next game?"

It wasn't his preferred method for staying on the table but it'd work. He looked over to Riley who didn't seem as disturbed as she should've been for losing like that. "You OK with that or did you want to sign us up again?"

"No it's fine. Tory wants me to play flip cup anyways" she motioned past Eric to the table in the far corner. He got a quick glance at Tory as he checked that direction. *She looks good tonight. Too bad she's pissed at me…for something.* They hadn't really talked in months and she didn't seem eager to now. *Better leave it.*

Eric was almost positive that she saw him making out with Diane the DXA at the Midway when this semester started. He'd messed it up with Diane that night too and didn't even get further than making out before she bounced with the rest of her sisters. It had been a ridiculous sequence of events that had gotten him nowhere. He'd lost the ability to continue hooking up with Tory because of that. She was the only other girl he'd hooked up with this year besides that AG sister. *That's so awful but what can I do?*

"Alllllright, I'm in" he said to Calvin.

"Why is Segcand so damn ugly all the time?" Jerry asked no one. "I motion to de-brother immediately" Jerry grinned as if Segs hadn't just avoided that same fate.

"It's definitely the age-old question Jer. And as president I'm definitely going to consider that" Calvin answered with a grin. *Well I'm glad we can all joke about it now…*

As Eric set up the cups again on the other side of the table he noticed Jared walk up to Jake. Their conversation was very short and it ended with them heading outside. He quickly checked the basement and almost immediately found Jeff staring at them leaving. He had an incredibly sour look on his face but he wasn't moving to stop it. *Interesting. Jeff respects all AZXi traditions. Even the ones that go against what he's doing. Good.*

Even if Eric wasn't there directly, he hoped his cousin would relax. Before a feeling that felt strangely like jealousy crept into his system he realized he should find his Little. *After this game.* All four pledges couldn't be missing at once. There were definitely limits to Jeff's patience, that was clear to everybody. J-Hood and Jake were already gone so he couldn't take Summers out now. Nothing left to do but wait and play another round. *Hopefully this game will go better.*

Will came over after Eric reset the six-cup rack and grinned at him while filling the cups. Will was obviously disappointed by the outcome of the previous game too. He took a huge gulp of beer from his side cup. *Got a lot to prove with this game...*

****

There's gotta be a better way to do this.

The party room was massive but it was still filled to the brim with no space to move. It had taken the better part of ten minutes just to get their pitcher filled a quarter of the way at one of the three open kegs. Music was blasting from the various speakers but with all the people around it was hard to make out what the fuck was playing. That was how things worked in Gladen Hills on a Friday night.

If an underage kid wanted to go out without a fake, the options were limited. Undergrads would walk up and down Arkridge Avenue looking for an open party at one of the frats. Kappa Nu or K-Nu was the biggest contender. They had Opens all the time, sometimes several in one weekend. Thirsty Thursdays, Fall-Over Fridays and Sloppy Saturdays were the banners to which hundreds of freshman and sophomores flocked every weekend. These were the kids that had come to school looking for a good time and they'd found it by chugging keg beer at a frat house. Not so long ago Scribner had been one of these kids. He'd reveled in it too. But that was then and he wasn't the same kid he was a semester ago. Even then, the problems with such a party could've been overlooked but not now. *Has it always been this much of a pain in the ass?*

The 'Opens' novelty had since run its course for both himself and Dukes. He stood there at the keg, practically fighting for the tap, trying to get their pitcher good enough to play the beer pong game they'd waited a half hour to get on the list for. It probably wouldn't have been as big of a problem if not for one simple fact: neither of them was that drunk. Getting bumped into by a hundred drunken freshmen was enough to get anyone pissed.

Must be nice being a K-Nu brother and have your own keg behind the bar. They're fucking kings down here.

Dukes finally deemed their pitcher acceptable so they moved away from the cluster-fuck near the keg. *Not a second too soon.* Getting run into by hot girls was one thing but it seemed like there were exponentially more guys than girls. That was another problem with Opens. They knew less people since most of their circle from last semester had stopped going out *as* much. It seemed like the novelty of getting hammered was wearing off... just not for the two of them.

"You better not fuck this up tonight," Dukes said as they headed through the near impassable crowd toward one of the two tables at the back wall.

"What do you mean?" Scribner asked as they reached the table and began filling the cups. *It's a miracle no one took our spot.* Dukes nodded in the direction of their opponents and suddenly it became very clear. "You don't want to lose to girls."

"Especially hot girls."

Scribner smirked. "The blonde is alright but the redhead is what I'm talking about." Dukes shot him a look like he should be committed immediately. "What can I say? Redheads are beautiful."

"Or hideous" Dukes pointed at Scribner. *I walked right into that.*

"I could just go back to the dorms I guess," he threatened.

"Yeah man, just leave. This party sucks anyways" he was practically oozing sarcasm as he motioned to the girls across the table. *They are really hot...might as well stay.*

"Fuck that, I'm not leaving" Scribner said proudly.

Dukes nodded before waving him to follow. His teammate walked up to the two opposing girls who'd just finished filling their own cups. *Where the fuck did they get their beers from? And so quick?*

"I just wanted to apologize in advance for what's about to happen to you. You had a great run. But everybody has that time in their life where they have to realize that people are better than them. This is your time. We are better. I'll see you out there!"

Nothing surprising about that. He probably just made that shit up.

The blonde girl smiled back at Dukes. Then both she and the redhead looked toward Scribner as if he was going to say something equally as asinine. "I'd like to apologize in advance for him being an asshole. My name is Dan. I'm six foot one and a buck seventy-five. I lift weights. I like long walks on the beach. I have a cat. Her name's Cleo, I adopted her. And it's nice to meet you." He extended his arm to shake their hands. He didn't want to assume too much but the redhead looked interested.

They walked back over to their side and had to clear away some of the crowd that slipped into their designated shooting area. "I can't believe you said that...pussy" Dukes chided him, almost sounding offended.

"Me? Does basically saying 'fuck you' to girls actually work?" He was almost afraid to hear the answer. Dukes just shrugged absently.

The girls both took their opening shots but only the blonde made it.

Dukes took his first shot, which went in without a problem. *How does he always hit cups?* He'd arched his arm up full length and released the ball midway. It looked like he was throwing the ball away without a care in the world. *Unbelievable.*

Scribner went to take his shot knowing full well Dukes expected him to make it so they could have the balls back for another turn. He shot and leaned over the extra long table...and missed completely. *There's always a learning curve.* Dukes looked at him in complete disgust. "Oh bite me" Scribner replied to the unspoken jab.

It took a few seconds with all the white noise from the party to realize the blonde was saying something. "There are lean rules here," she said, sounding frustrated.

Scribner just shrugged and looked at the redhead.

"Elbows can't go past the end of the table," she agreed.

Some houses had lean rules, others didn't. Dukes of course had leaned too but Scribner's shot was much more obvious. "He missed anyways so it's fine. Just don't fuck up next time."

"Who the hell plays lean rules on a table this size?" he asked his partner. *This fuckin' thing is easily over seven feet long for Christ sake.*

"Your mother."

"Actually she's more of a flip cup player."

The game went on and they started to pull ahead thanks to Dukes. Scribner's attention wandered when he realized they'd probably win with or without his help. He again noticed all the freshmen acting like the party was best time ever. Scribner shook his head. *A hand job is the best thing on the planet for a virgin.*

He saw their rack was down to two cups while the girls had four left to hit. *Might as well try and accomplish something now.* Scribner actually focused before taking his shot, making sure to keep his elbow back. He hit the first cup with sick precision. *That's what's up.*

After he saw it go in he knew the game was over.

Sure enough Dukes hit the final cup within seconds, ending the game. His partner's final cup hitting record was disgusting. He tended to rise to the challenge whenever it was presented. And if his teammate hit the first of the final two cups it was almost a guaranteed game-over.

OK...at least that felt good.

****

It was like being part of some weird ass-backwards callout. Kevin and Jared had J-Hood and him out in the back driveway of the house with no one else around. It was also similar in that they didn't have jackets on even though it was still pretty cold and their dress shirts were definitely not doing the trick.

"You sure we shouldn't have gotten their jackets Kev?" Jared asked, seeing how uncomfortable Jake looked. J-Hood of course showed no hint that he was anything other than comfortable.

"Their jackets are right here son," Kevin said while holding up a pitcher of beer. "Alright boys, get a bite of this. Come on Hood" he said, motioning the pitcher toward his Little. "You and Raley are about to take this thing down." The pitcher was a little over half full but it was wide and held more beer than Jake pictured he could drink in one night, let alone one sitting.

"I don't know if I can handle that much." *Why would you ever say that out loud?*

Kevin's face held the look of utter horror. *Oh great, here come the push-ups.* "Jesus Jared is this kid serious?"

"You'll be fine" Jared said while patting him on the back. "Just relax."

J-Hood started chugging the pitcher and the gold liquid disappeared at an alarmingly fast rate.

"Where are Will and Matt?" Jake asked.

"Petey and Eric are gonna chill with them later. There's no point in pulling you all out at once" Kevin answered.

"What happens if Jeff sees this?"

"Nothing would happen to *us*," Kevin said haughtily. "But you two would probably get yelled at some more at the next callout." *Now that's comforting. As if we aren't getting yelled at enough. Thanks a lot.*

"OK and when is the next callout again?" Jake asked innocently. *Maybe they're drunk enough to actually answer.*

"Even if I knew I wouldn't tell you guys. It's part of what makes the whole process work. When the pledges don't know a damn thing it's sick."

You aren't wrong about that pal.

After J-Hood had taken down more than his fair share he handed the pitcher over. He wiped a small amount of excess beer from his mouth and let out a long burp.

Fuck. There was nothing left to do except start. It felt so cold. *Just keep going...*

"We know not being able to drink for six weeks blows so take in some while you can boys. This place can be real fun with the right touches" he heard Kevin say.

It was apparent to everyone standing there that Jake was taking a lot longer to finish a smaller amount than his pledge brother had. *Just keep going...*

He finished the final few sips and let out a sigh of satisfaction as he handed the empty pitcher over to Jared who was still grinning. His Big handed the pitcher over to Kevin who looked as though he was about to throw it against the ground and smash it to pieces. He stopped and shook his head at Jared. "Damn it Biz" was all he said to justify the confusing event.

"What's up?" Jake asked.

"Your damn cousin told us Enderel pitcher slams were out of the question on any night that isn't Bids or Crossing. We apparently don't have the money to be buying new ones all the time. I think it's fucked up but I'm not the treasurer."

"I find ignoring him helps sometimes" Jake responded, suddenly feeling brazen in front of the actives.

"Nah it's straight. We'll break a few when you guys get your letters" Jared said happily. Kevin nodded back at him while putting his hand on J-Hood's shoulder.

"Hopefully soon."

"Raley! Hood! Get the fuck over here!" Jeff yelled in their direction from the back door's steps. *Thank God you're here...now I can kill you.*

Jake hadn't even noticed that they'd been standing about twenty feet back from the house to avoid being nearby anyone else. But now Jeff was walking toward them as he and J-Hood trudged over the graveled driveway to meet him.

"You guys are done for the night but be here at eight AM tomorrow to clean the house like usual." Jeff wasn't yelling for once. "Now get the fuck out of here!" he exclaimed, raising his voice again to its usual level.

That's weird. Why are we being freed for the night when it's only half past eleven? Something's not right…

****

Jeff watched with morbid fascination as the two pledges moved quickly back inside the house to get their jackets and leave. Jerry appeared from the side of the house once the pledges were indoors. Jared and Kevin were still far enough back in driveway talking so thankfully they weren't involved.

When they'd pre-gamed at the National earlier Jared's ex had been there. That in and of itself shouldn't have been a problem minus the fact that she should've known that the AZXis always went there and now didn't really care for her ass. *Why the fuck would she come downtown at all?*

Aaron had struck up a chat with her near the end of the bar, away from everyone. He doubted the bastard even knew what he was doing. Segs and Aaron had gotten obliterated at some breakfast with their non-AZXi friends earlier after the decision regarding Segs came down, so now they were both sloppy as hell.

Jeff hadn't had the chance to say anything to Aaron yet. He knew Jared never would. *The kid's just too nice. Jared would be fucked up if one of us banged his ex…* He doubted it'd be a problem though. Aaron wouldn't make it past eleven with the way he kept drinking. *He'll black out all this and not remember a damn thing.*

"I don't think anyone said a thing to the pledges," Jerry announced with obvious happiness. He was right but Jeff didn't say anything, just lit up a cigarette from the nearly full pack in his pocket. Jerry instinctively took a couple steps back since he wasn't keen on inhaling. "Isn't it a little early for them to be going?"

"It is but there's no way of really stopping their Bigs if they want to continue force feeding alcohol to these kids by the pitcher" he finally answered. "There'll be plenty of time for them to drink tomorrow."

Jerry nodded and smiled widely before walking back into the party.

The pledges were in for a surprise tonight and by all accounts they were completely blind to what was in store. *This is gonna be priceless. And these kids thought being dropped off on a farm five miles from the school was wild…*

****

After a few games on the table, somehow the party had gotten *more* crowded. And thanks to the beer pong they'd been playing, Scribner was kind of drunk despite winning all their games. Or maybe he was just on the higher end of being buzzed. It was hard to tell.

Unfortunately the night couldn't continue since the kegs had all run out a little before midnight. That meant there was a huge exodus of kids leaving Arkridge Avenue at the same time. *It wouldn't take a genius to figure out an Open with booze just let out. Good thing the cops here only care some of the time.*

They were walking in the middle of several different groups that had left the same time as them. Scribner was zoning in and out of the various conversations going on.

"I'm just tired of carrying you on the table Scribbs" Dukes said. He thought it was Dukes at least. He didn't know for sure since he was trying to walk straight and staring at the ground to do it.

"I don't give a fuck."

"Scribbs you care so much it's almost sad."

"We played a bunch of girls and some terrible dudes. It'd be weird if we hadn't run the table."

"Hey we weren't that bad" said the blonde chick from earlier in the night. *Yeah, she would be standing right there. Damn she's got a nice rack.*

"No no no, he said the guys we played were worthless" Dukes corrected her with a straight face. *That might be what I said but not what I meant.*

"Ohhh OK" she replied before turning back to her friends. The redhead she was with earlier wasn't nearby. *That blows…*

"Dude those chicks were awful too" Scribner said in hushed tones.

"I know but there's no point in pissing them off."

"Really? You don't think it'd be funny? Because there's nothing quite like pissing off people you don't know."

"Wow that was really deep shit Scribbs."

"You know what I mean…not like nice people…but the bastards that you know are just like assholes" he clarified. "Me and my friends used to do it all the time back in high school."

"Yeah and was Raley involved in any of that?"

"Not really. He didn't really start drinking 'til senior year, and we were usually drunk when we did shit like that." *Still can't believe Raley didn't have his first real beer until the end of his senior year. But then he went nuts and made Raley's Ring with me and Eric so it's all good.*

"He doesn't even really drink now," Dukes countered.

"True but just imagine less than that. He's doing maddddd work now" he slurred.

As he was steadying himself on the incline of the hill leading to Northeast, two guys walked past them through the crowd. They were clearly oblivious to everyone else. "I can't believe I had to miss the bus uptown just so you could finish getting that girl's number," the taller one said.

"Just doing work bro," the shorter one replied. "Said she might be heading uptown too. I'm tryin' to make moves on that."

"Like you don't say that every weekend. Or every night."

I recognize one of them...

Then it hit him. Neither of them was wearing any frat letters but that's how he knew them. "Yo I think that kid was Raley's Big or something."

Dukes said nothing, as expected.

"I recognize him, saw him with Raley before. The other guy is in AZXi too, Gretman I think his name is."

"Jesus you learning frat history with Raley, Scribbs?" Dukes asked sarcastically.

He just shrugged it off and continued watching the two guys walk farther and farther away. *I wonder where they're headed.*

Dukes struck up a conversation with the blonde chick out of nowhere. As soon as Scribner heard the words 'The OC' he tuned out the conversation. *What kind of a pussy watches that show?*

He watched as the frat guys turned left and headed toward the nearest bus stop to go uptown. The frats let out around the same time as the Opens most of the time. But whereas the freshman would have to go back to their dorms and either sleep it off or just chill, the Greeks went up to the bars and kept partying 'til they closed. Sometimes 'til way after based on what Scribner had heard.

Damn it. Why can't I have a fake ID? He felt himself getting jealous, which he immediately shook off. *Fuck that. Look how fuckin' miserable Raley is...all the time.*

A few groups they'd left Arkridge Avenue with were nearby as they hit the boundaries of Northeast. *Almost home.*

Scribner turned down the loading dock pavement to head toward the door to his dorm with Dukes close behind. Then he heard the blonde chick's voice again. *Her voice is kind of annoying. She seems like a bitch...*

"Aren't you coming over to watch...?" her voice trailed off. It took Scribner a second to realize she was talking to his roommate.

"Wouldn't miss it" was the casual response Dukes gave as he turned and shot Scribner a look of pure victory. The girl turned and headed toward the dorm next to theirs. Dukes went to catch up to her but stopped and turned toward him. "And *that's* why you don't piss girls off" he said triumphantly before turning away again. Like clockwork he turned back to Scribner. *"And* why you watch The OC." Scribner had to grin in spite of himself. *Damn him.*

Chapter 11

It makes no sense. Dukes doesn't get laid...ever. How the fuck did he go back with that chick. He couldn't have said more than ten things to her. And one of them was about the fucking 'OC'. I just don't get it.

It had only been fifteen minutes since he'd seen them head back to her place and it still hadn't sunk in. *At least I'll have the room to myself tonight.*

Scribner trudged back into the dorms and into his suite on the bottom floor. He started punching in the key code but almost forgot what he was doing. *Two-Four-Three-One-Five.* He heard the satisfying click as the mechanical lock released. *Not so hard.*

He walked inside and noticed the last idiot out of the room left the lights on. It must've been the alcohol settling in because Scribner felt overwhelmed and couldn't make it to his room five feet away. He all but collapsed on the nearest couch.

"Scribbs?"

The word jostled him upright. *What the fuck?* Scribner pulled his head up from the cushion, which was easier said than done. He looked over in the direction of the voice. "Damn Raley, how the fuck did you get there?"

"You do realize you walked right by me."

Scribner shrugged. "Man chill. I'm a little drunk here."

"I'd expect so on a Friday night. But why're you back so early?"

"Wasn't feeling it tonight *and* the beer ran out," he said sullenly. "But more importantly, why are you here? Shouldn't you still be somebody's bitch?"

"I don't like to question good things Scribbs. They let us out early and I wasn't about to ask why. It's a good thing though because I'm buzzed myself."

He doesn't look drunk but he'd know better than me. And his tolerance is probably way down...and it wasn't all that high to begin with.

"And here I thought you weren't allowed to drink during pledging."

"We're not but our Bigs can give us beer to ease the pain."

"Well now that we've covered that shit, let's get down to business. I couldn't help but overhear you and Kelly talking the other night."

Raley looked back at him with surprise.

"It's not exactly like you were being quiet plus Dukes woke me up when he came in the room."

"You 'overhear' a lot you know that?"

"We've been friends way too long Raley. Is everything straight?"

His friend took a deep breath. "I guess...I mean I don't think Kelly likes me pledging and I know she doesn't like never seeing me."

"Yeah but that's because she's got the sex drive of a pornstar" Scribner blurted out. *Oops.*

"I know, it's awesome isn't it?" he answered with a big ass goofy smile.

Clearly he doesn't mind at all. It does sound great...in theory.

"Well where is she tonight? I imagine she'd want to know you're free."

"She probably would but I know she went out with her friends. She hasn't done that in a while so I'm not interrupting" he responded with a hint of regret.

"Well I'd like to weigh in here Raley if you don't mind."

"Since when do you need permission?"

"True. So here's what I got. You aren't happy. At least not as happy as you should be. This is college. Only class should make you this pissed and at least that you can skip."

Raley nodded. "I just look at pledging as an investment...just like class. So yeah it's terrible but I look back on shit that happened the first week and I think, damn that sucked but it's kind of funny. And I'm sure the shit I've done this week, which definitely blows right now, will be the same. At least it better be. I'm getting to the end here and I'd appreciate a little support."

Good for you Raley. "Then you got it man."

"Good, so J-Hood said he's been talking to you about pledging next semester?"

Scribner winced. "I'm not gonna lie and say I haven't considered it. But I see how terrible you look and how miserable he looks during class and I just can't justify it to myself that it'll be worth all that shit."

"That's the question right? Are you willing to sacrifice those six weeks?"

"Well I guess we know where you stand huh?"

"Doing this shit for five weeks didn't already give it away Scribbs?"

Well at least he's still the same guy behind all this shit.

"I think you need to get laid again pal" he fired back with a grin.

"You're goddamn I do" Raley replied before looking around the room. "Where's Dukes at?"

Scribner grimaced at the mention of his name. *Great now I have to say this shit out loud.* "You won't believe this...he went back with some bitchy blonde with big tits."

He'd rather have thrown up everything he drank tonight than see Dukes win. Raley had the same look of loathing and confusion on his face that Scribner would've seen in the mirror. *And that's why we're friends.*

"Well at least with him out of the suite and the brothers leaving me alone I might actually relax."

As if on cue, Raley's phone started ringing and his smile changed to a look of complete horror. Scribner wished he could've taken a picture to save as his caller ID. *Shit would be priceless. And he wants me to sign up for this same shit? Fuck that.*

Raley answered the phone but didn't say more than three words. After hanging up the look of horror changed to anger. "FUCK!" he screamed.

"What's up?"

"I forgot the cardinal rule of pledging...again. FUCK!" he yelled again. "Expect the worst and you'll never be surprised. I knew it too. I knew something was fucked when they sent us home early. Son of a bitch!"

"Sooooo does that mean you won't be relaxing tonight?" Scribner couldn't help himself and grinned after he asked.

"Very funny you bastard."

Scribner watched as Raley got his shoes and backpack, which was always in an easy to reach spot. Once he was ready to go he looked back at Scribner as if expecting him to somehow get him out of it.

He shrugged. "I could kidnap you I guess. Maybe hide you out on the farm for the night" he said, hoping to get to Raley to crack a smile that never came. *Well that was a miserable failure.*

Jake looked solemn. The only emotion on display now was depression.

Poor bastard.

He turned and left the suite, slamming the door behind him. *At least he's actually doing something tonight...even if it does suck balls.* That was more than Scribner could say for himself as he looked around the now empty room.

****

How could you be so fucking stupid? Of course they were gonna call us back out tonight. They wouldn't let us go that early. Zero fucking chance. Anger flooded his body as he met up with his pledge class. *I should beat Jeff's ass for being such a fuck...but I don't have the balls.* Never had his lack of a backbone been more apparent.

Jake was now running in a line with his three pledge brothers heading back to the house on Arkridge...on the same night they were told they wouldn't have to go back until the next morning. *You knew it was coming and I just sat there to let it happen.*

"What do you think this is about?" Will asked.

"Does it really matter?" Jake asked angrily between breaths as they ran.

"I don't know. It didn't seem normal" Summers replied, ignoring Jake.

"They said callout hours didn't extend to the weekends," J-Hood added from the front of the line.

"Right because we've never been lied to by these bastards. They're a trustworthy bunch for sure," Jake said bitterly.

"Either way I doubt this'll be fun," Summers added while exhaling.

"When exactly was the last time you went to the house for a fun visit?" Will asked, sounding annoyed.

"Bids" all three of the others said in unison immediately. *At least we're on the same page with that much.*

"I bet it would've been better if any of us actually remembered what the fuck happened" Will lamented.

"We can thank our Bigs for a great night I think" Summers said hesitantly.

Jake wasn't sure about that. He was almost ninety percent certain that Jared had gotten him *into* trouble, not the other way around. *Maybe one day I'll actually get the full story about that goddamn night.*

"I can't imagine you did anything too crazy with Biz being your Big."

"I don't know Raley. I've known Biz a while" Will chimed in without prompting, just like usual. *He doesn't know Eric better than me. Who the fuck does he think he is? He's my family.*

"I'm going to pretend like you didn't just tell me you knew my cousin better than me." Jake tried keeping his frustration in check with minimal effect.

"Alright everybody chill...we're getting close" J-Hood interrupted.

They'd been talking so much during the run that Jake had lost track of how close they were as they made the turn onto Arkridge. They slowed their pace as they neared the house.

Right at the end of the driveway where it met the street was Jerry, standing like a statue. *What an asshole.* He put up his hand to stop them. "Let's go. Into the back" he said quietly.

He always yells when we get here. And he's never at the front of the driveway.

Nevertheless, they did as instructed and walked back in a single file line with Jerry at the front. The only difference between how it looked earlier when he'd been back here with Jared and Kevin was that there wasn't a soul around except for Jeff.

Their pledge-master was putting out a cigarette under his shoe when they rounded the corner. Jake was so busy trying to stare down Jeff with contempt that he didn't notice the ground change. He fell right to his knees, nearly losing his backpack in the process. Fortunately he was the last in line so he didn't cause anyone else to fall.

Summers turned and helped him up when he heard the noise.

Jeff and Jerry didn't even bat an eye at Jake's fall. *Fuckin' figures.*

"Tonight we have something special planned" Jeff began. "Since you dumbasses fucked up a very easy scavenger hunt to the point where I'm ashamed to call you my pledges, we thought we'd try a different approach to possibly gain us some favor with the rest of the brothers. Because right now they think Jerry and I are incompetent."

Jake tried to hide his amusement. *If any of that shit is even remotely true then it's awesome. Who would've thought I'd agree with any of the actives?*

"We're sending you to Canada for the weekend. While you're there you will complete another scavenger hunt list unique to that area."

They're so fucked up they don't even want us in the country anymore. Great.

Jerry walked over to Will and handed him their new list.

"You will complete all eighty-seven items before getting back here by eight AM on Sunday. If you actually complete everything then you won't have to clean the house."

Jake was near to seething. *Yeah, that'll be the fuckin' day.*

"What the fuck are you waiting for? Canada isn't driving to you! Get going!"

Suddenly they were off again, running through the night. Once they hit the pavement they sped up. They were sprinting until they hit the corner of Arkridge and Castle. Once there they stopped.

"OK, get everything you need for the weekend and meet in the far lot behind the National in twenty minutes. That's where I'm parked" Will ordered.

As they all took off in their various directions a feeling of horror swept over Jake when he checked his backpack. *Where the hell did I put my cell phone? Shit...it must've fallen out back at the house when I wiped out. That's fucking lovely.*

Jake turned around and started making his way back. His three pledge brothers hadn't looked back on their way to the dorms. *Three times to the house in one night... just fuckin' great. And now I won't even have the rest of my pledge class with me...*

****

"Did we really have to call the pledges out tonight?" Tory asked.

No...probably not...but now we're drunk and it'll be fun.

It was messed up but Riley enjoyed hazing the pledges more when she'd had a few drinks. It wasn't going to be a mandatory callout anyways. It was more or less just to entertain whatever sisters wanted to come. For her and Tory it was obviously mandatory, just like every other time.

"I mean the party was great and the bars weren't too crowded," Tory continued.

"That's why it's perfect. The pledges won't be expecting it. Besides you're the assistant pledge mom. You should be happy to haze them since Crossing's next week."

Tory smiled back at her. "You just get me Riles. Oh by the way, your cousins were looking good tonight."

Well that's a little awkward. Riley had hesitated to even point Jake out to Tory because she was sure she'd think he was cute just like Eric. *And yet I did it anyways.*

"Oh come on, not again T. Not after what happened with Eric." She'd responded so quickly she'd forgotten Dani was right next to them. She wasn't really talking so it was an easy oversight. Dani obviously knew Tory and Eric had a thing but wasn't well versed on the details. *Lucky her.*

"You know Riles...is it so wrong to want a guy that knows what he's doing?" Tory asked playfully.

Riley cringed. *The funny thing is you're still being serious.*

"You're saying that Eric knew what he was doing?" *Why the hell would you even ask that question? Don't answer T, please don't answer.*

She quickly stepped in to fill the void the answer would've gone into. "Listen, I have a pact with the two of them, they don't care what I do if I don't care who they do."

"You needed an agreement for that?" Danielle asked.

"It's just a precaution. My family is...close, and I wanted to make sure neither of them would go crazy. I know it's weird."

"Whatever. Expecting to keep hooking up with the same person for more than a month in this town? I must be new here," Tory said, mostly talking to herself.

"Did he end it or something?" Dani asked, clearly curious.

"I'd say it was more mutual" Riley replied.

"You'd say it was mutual?" Tory asked.

Riley frowned. "I do a lap around the Midway and I see you both making out with different people whereas that time the previous week, it was you two going at it. So who the fuck knows who went where first?" *Probably Eric but who really cares now?*

"I saw him making out with a DXA so I found another guy...makes perfect sense to me" Tory answered with passion.

"T, making out is the hug of the twenty-first century" Riley began. "Here watch." Without thinking, Riley turned to Danielle and kissed her. She was trying to prove a point although she wasn't ashamed to say with alcohol she became adventurous. She pulled back from Danielle's priceless face and looked at Tory to see the look of defeat mirrored with her own look of triumph. *And there it is.*

"I really wish you wouldn't do that" Dani responded as she wiped her lips clean.

"Maybe if you stopped looking so hot it wouldn't be a problem," she countered.

"OK then. Maybe after these girls cross then we won't be forced to watch the awkward moments where Riles has to yell at her Little" Tory changed gears.

Danielle looked dismissive. "I'm still surprised you took a Little this semester."

"I didn't wanna wait another semester. And the frats have no problem doing it this way and if they can so can we." *Done and done.*

Danielle and Tory both chuckled.

Yeah, yeah. I know the frats get away with a ton of shit that we can't and it's not even close to fair but this is the world we live in.

After another minute they reached the EIPi house. Fortunately they weren't the first ones there, as there were multiple lights lit-up on the upper two floors. *Good. I won't have to make any calls to fill the callout.*

They walked inside after Tory hit the code on the outer metal door.

Riley moved ahead to see if there was anyone in the party common room. Rachel was there along with Jessie, Brianna and Amy. *Not a bad start. And no boys...good.*

She turned back to Danielle and Tory. "Go change if you want. I'm gonna call the pledges in ten minutes."

****

Jake's mind was still reeling. He couldn't even begin to wrap his head around what he'd seen. It went against everything he'd built up in his head. It didn't help that he was cold and miserable even though the heat was blasting in Will's car. *It doesn't matter. It doesn't change anything.*

Will had thankfully listened when he'd asked to have the heat turned up. After all, they were heading north and the temperature was likely to drop, which would be another thing adding to his misery. Jake had never liked the cold. *At least Will did the nice thing for once and actually listened to me. That's a start. It'd be better if I were in the front seat but whatever.* J-Hood was sitting next to Will and he sure as hell wasn't going to argue with that guy over a seat he'd gotten fairly. *If I hadn't had to run back to AZXi for my damn phone I would've been at the car first.*

Jake continued staring out the window into the black landscape beyond. He tried to shove the thoughts of his uncomfortably cold body aside so he could think. He was trying to piece everything together when J-Hood spoke up. "You guys taken a look at this list?"

"I haven't," Jake answered absently. Summers nodded at him as if he was supposed to relay that information to J-Hood as well.

"It's not too bad actually."

Bad was a relative term of course. The Alpha Epsilons had discovered many different levels of it throughout pledging and it wasn't over yet.

"I know my way around up there. I chilled with Biz and Jer-Bear in Canada all the time last summer" Will announced triumphantly. *OK we get it, you're friends with both of them. Just shut the fuck up already.*

"Word?" was the response from J-Hood. Except now it sounded like a question.

"Yeah I looked it over. We shouldn't have any problem finishing it."

"Why'd you take so long to get packed Raley? We were waiting in that lot for like ten minutes" Will chided him.

"My bad, I didn't realize the Canadian border was closing at a specific time."

"What happened anyway?" J-Hood asked, ignoring the sarcasm. He obviously wanted an answer that wasn't laced with it.

"I had to run back to the house to get my phone. I dropped it when we ran to the house to get the list." He hoped his response to J-Hood got under Will's skin since they'd both asked the same question.

"You found it right?" Summers asked. It didn't sound like he cared one way or the other but Jake answered regardless.

"I definitely wouldn't be sitting here if I hadn't."

"Not having a cell phone? That's an America I don't want to live in" Will added with a chuckle.

Jake smirked in the darkness where Will wouldn't notice.

I'm trapped with these guys for God knows how long...just like suite hours. And out of the fucking country no less. He realized he needed to get his head right before they got to their destination. For that he needed to rethink what went down back at AZXi.

Jake sat there in silence, drowning out whatever Will had playing on the radio while continuing to look out the window into the black.

It doesn't fucking matter.
It...can't matter.

I've only got twenty minutes to get my damn phone, get packed and get to the National. It'd be difficult but not impossible. Fortunately there didn't seem to be anyone outside the AZXi house when Jake got back. *About time my luck changed.*

Jake headed into the backyard area. Right off to the side of that god-forsaken pothole he'd stumbled on was his phone. He picked it up from the ground and gave it a quick once over to make sure there was no damage. It was on and he had two text messages. *It's still working. Thank God.*

He flipped it open and checked the messages. The first one was from Jared. 'Bro just have fun this weekend. The list isn't that bad. Have a few drinks and chill. The drinking age in Canada is nineteen so giddy up'. Jake smiled. *He's got a way with words.*

The second was from Eric. 'J have a good time. Chill with your pledge bros, do some work on the list, and since there's no brothers around, feel free to get a little crazy...one time'. *The only one who still calls me 'J'.*

He closed up his phone and put it in his backpack. He made sure to actually zip up the pocket he put it into so there wouldn't be any more mistakes. Jake started jogging down the left side driveway so that he could make a quick getaway. As he made his way around the side of the house he heard a familiar voice coming down the street. He'd recognize that voice anywhere since it had been a regular part of his world the past few weeks. *Brother Aaron Ajersul.* Fortunately that particular bastard wasn't too mean to Jake's pledge class since he and Brent Segcand had just crossed last semester. *But Segcand can go fuck himself after what happened with Will last week.*

Aaron was walking down Arkridge Avenue away from Castle Lane and campus. It was clear he was going to be calling it an early night since it was only a little before one. *Not surprising considering how fucked up he is. He may have been worse than Segcand.*

Jake stood there, confused because Aaron wasn't alone. He was walking back toward the Orchard Apartments with a chick. A decent looking one too from what Jake could tell from the shadows he was currently staying hidden in. He wasn't about to show himself. *They don't need to know I'm here.*

"So...where...do you live again?"

"Right down next to the AZXi house" the girl answered.

"So we...are...close."

Jake shook his head in awe. *She clearly wants to get laid and Aaron was in the right place at the right time.*

A harsh voice suddenly cut through the night. It was aimed at the couple Jake was watching. "Yo Aaron! Come here for a second." There was no mistaking it. That voice belonged to Jeff Chester. Jake was so busy paying attention to the two in the street he hadn't noticed Jeff come outside to have another cigarette. *That bastard should really cut down on his smoking. If I gave a fuck about his health I'd tell him.*

Aaron jogged unsteadily over to Jeff. The look of glee was clear as day even from Jake's position in the bushes ten feet to their right. Fortunately, the floodlights on the front steps didn't go right, they were aimed left. The line of unkempt hedges that separated their house from the Lambdas was thick enough that without light, he couldn't be seen. That left him with a front row seat. *Is Jeff gonna haze an active for a change? Now that'll be entertaining.* Jake kneeled down to get more concealed.

"Jesus Aaron do you know who that is?" Jeff asked angrily. He was motioning to the girl waiting impatiently in the street.

"Uhhhhh…the girl I'm about to…fuuuuuck?" Aaron answered hesitantly as if he didn't really understand the question.

Calvin suddenly entered the conversation from the left side house door.

And I thought the house was empty.

"Besides that" Calvin interrupted.

"I don't know mannnnn. I just met her…at the…National earlier."

"Dude, that's Jared's ex" Jeff responded solemnly but still with a hint of anger.

Aaron looked to sober up almost on the spot. It was incredible to watch.

"Get the fuck out" was all he could say.

Jared was never one to talk about *anything* serious so Jake had never pressed it. He'd forgotten how he'd heard it but he knew Jared's chick had ended things earlier that semester. His Big always seemed perfectly fine so Jake just assumed he was coping well.

"Yeah it is. And knowing her, she's probably just using you to piss off Jared."

"Man, Jared didn't say a word and he was at the National with all of us tonight" Aaron tried explaining.

"Yeah but he'd never say a word. It's just how he is. But dude…this is real fucked up" Calvin added in the most reasonable tone Jake had ever heard from him.

I guess these fucks don't have to yell about every little thing.

"Look, you're borderline blackout. You should just walk away from this and act like it never happened. That shouldn't be too much of a stretch for you" Jeff finished.

"That's your brother's ex. Just walk away," Calvin agreed.

Even from the trees Jake could see the look of disappointment on Aaron's face, but he still nodded in agreement.

"Just find another girl to fuck. There's plenty at this school" Jeff went on.

"You don't have to be an ass about it Buttons" Aaron fired back.

"I would say don't get this fucked up again but we all know that'd do about as much good as you telling me not to be an ass."

Jake smirked. *Might as well tell Jeff to stop breathing while we're at it.*

"Alright fine...I'm out. See you guys tomorrow" Aaron said in a depressed tone before turning and heading away from the girl in the street. She'd apparently gotten a phone call at some point during the guys' conversation because she was no longer looking in their direction to notice Aaron leaving.

"Night man" Calvin said with an upbeat tone.

"Later" was all Jeff said.

They both watched intently as he walked away from her and out of sight toward Castle Lane and the dorms on the other side of the campus. *That's gonna be a long walk...*

Calvin turned to look at Jeff after Aaron was gone and gave him a look that Jake couldn't quite read.

"Dude they only broke up like three months ago. That's way too soon," Jeff said without being spoken to.

"I hear ya man."

"If me and Dana ever broke up..." he paused for a second. "I don't want any brother near her for at least double that" he said, trying to keep himself in check. *Who knew Jeff Chester actually cared for...anyone?* Jake shuddered at the thought.

"If ever" Calvin added.

I must be dreaming. Is someone actually getting along with Jeff right now?

"You wouldn't want any of us touching Jen would you?"

"I might have to kill someone," Calvin answered sternly but Jake could hear the sadness in his voice.

"Case closed" Jeff replied.

Finally the girl in the street turned around to see that her sure thing had walked off. She walked over to Calvin and Jeff, clearly not happy.

Jeff turned to Calvin and quietly said something. Jake couldn't quite hear it though.

Oh this should be good.

"Where'd he go?" she asked forcefully.

"He wasn't feeling too well so he went home" Jeff answered casually.

"What'd you say to him?"

"Nothing that wasn't true."

"What the fuck does that mean?"

"What was the plan exactly?" Jeff began. "You see Jared hitting on another girl at the bar and you decide to hit on one of his brothers? Real classy."

"That's funny because I didn't think you guys taught 'class' here?" she shot back, angrily motioning to the AZXi house.

"Not as far as you're concerned."

Jake had never seen Jeff maintain a level head. He always seemed pissed about something beneath the surface.

"You're a fucking asshole Jeff" she lashed out.

"At least I have morals," he said with a smirk.

"Fuck you!"

Clearly she's unfamiliar with not getting what she wants. And now some frat guy is telling her off? Forget about it.

"OK Buttons, let's head inside" Calvin interrupted. "Good night" he said respectfully to the girl before waiting for Jeff to move indoors. As they walked into the house Calvin patted Jeff on the back and said something which Jake struggled to hear. "You should have no trouble letting me take point on the meeting with the Dean next week" Calvin said as they walked into the house.

The girl turned away and stormed off toward the Orchards.

Jake sat there, still confused. *It's still early. She shouldn't have any trouble getting laid if that's all she's after. One hour of bar time is a year for chicks. She probably wouldn't be able to pick up another AZXi though...*

Finally Jake realized he was sitting alone outside in the bushes under the cover of darkness. It looked extremely sketchy. Jake made a move to get out from his hiding spot when he heard yet another familiar voice.

"What're you doing creeping around here bro?" Jared's voice hit him like a bullet. He felt insanely scared before he realized it was one of the few brothers he liked.

"Just looking for my phone man," Jake replied with a half-assed smile.

"Need any help?"

It took him a second to realize Jared had come from the same direction that Aaron had headed. *Good thing they didn't run into each other.*

"Nah I'm good. I found it a second ago."

"Alright nice."

"I thought you were heading uptown? Didn't you say that earlier?"

"No luck. They weren't biting" Jared responded, smiling like always.

"That's not like you at all."

"Can't score every night bro."

"Don't say depressing shit like that to me" Jake replied sarcastically.

"Shouldn't you be heading to Canada?"

"Oh shit yeah." With all the excitement he'd forgotten he was supposed to be somewhere. "As a matter of fact you didn't see me here."

"Well hopefully we're having after-hours tonight so I should black this out," Jared answered giddily.

"Beautiful. I'll see you Sunday" Jake said before jogging away.

His mind was spinning as he ran. Seeing how Calvin and Jeff acted when there weren't any pledges around was...weird. *Gretman always seemed like a legit dude but Jeff...no way.* Not only had the guy helped Jake's Big with something that he'd likely never take credit for, he'd acted kind of cool. He'd only ever seen the guy condescend and yell and swear. *I don't know who that guy was.* Jeff had been an ass to Aaron but it was actually for a good reason, not just because he could.

All through pledging Jake had always thought what Jeff and Jerry said was just a bunch of shit to make the pledges believe before Crossing. What was even more troubling was that he actually fully agreed with Jeff. Jake couldn't even imagine how he'd react if he saw one of the actives with Kelly. Just the thought made him weak.

But we aren't the same. That was another thought now eating away at him. Jake kept running, faster and faster. *There's no way Jeff is anything but an ass...*

Less than an hour later, Jake was still fervently against the idea that he and Jeff could be anything alike. Jake tried wrapping his mind around being a pledge-master and upholding traditions and yelling at underclassmen. He was ashamed to admit it did have a sick appeal to it.

It was entirely possible that he'd misjudged Calvin and Aaron at least. *Aaron did the right thing and Calvin handled the whole thing with respect.* Jake hoped that had pissed the girl off even more seeing a supposedly stupid, class-less frat guy act like that. *Even without AZXi, what Aaron was doing was a complete violation of guy code. And Jeff followed that code.*

For a few moments Jake started second-guessing everything ingrained in his mind since the day after Bids. *These could be the kinds of guys I'd want watching my back...right? If Jeff stops acting like a fucker then so could any of them.*

The thought was disconcerting. It threatened Jake's entire worldview.

For now at least, the situation could be left alone somewhere in the back of his mind. He and his pledge brothers were on their way to Canada to complete another wild goose chase from the frat guys back in Gladen Hills.

Who the fuck knows what kind of shit they want us to do when we get there? For the first time though that Jake could remember since Bids, he was excited for the future.

Chapter 12

It was eerie. The entrance hall into the EIPi house was usually filled with sound and yet here they were. The area would've been completely silent if not for the faint voices coming from the main party room about ten feet from where she and Tory stood. Of course, during the hours of midnight until the bars closed at two there was usually a severe lack of people wandering around the house. That was in no small part thanks to the fact that most of EIPi bordered on alcoholism, Riley included.

She looked over at Tory who was checking for text messages...again.

This feels so weird. "I called them ten minutes ago and told them to get here in five. What's wrong with this picture?"

"Somehow the pledges couldn't complete the impossible task of getting the six of themselves here that quickly when most of them live farther away?"

Somehow Tory managed to respond with equal parts sincerity and sarcasm. *Only T could pull that off.*

"*Exactly* what I was thinking. Zero respect."

Before long, Danielle's voice came rippling down the stairs from a floor up. Riley had put her up there to keep watch from the hallway window to see the pledges coming up the hill from Northwest, where most of them lived. Since the EIPi first floor entrance door didn't have a window that was the only option.

"They're coming up the hill!"

"OK I'll be in the main hall. Get them inside quick, we've got a lot to do tonight" she instructed.

"No problem Riles."

Riley walked down the small pathway and into the main hall that doubled as their party room. It used to be a lobby back when the whole building was a hotel.

Now this whole town lives and dies by the college.

The only hotel left in the middle of town was the Gladen Grove Hotel on University Grove. Even that was a bit of a stretch since it was technically more of a fine dining restaurant that just happened to have hotel rooms on the top floors. The only other option for visiting parents or travelers was a hotel down the interstate about five miles. Sometimes the 'drunk bus' would go that far on alumni weekends but it was rare. Both EIPi and Rho Beta had been converted to sorority housing decades ago. *The town's better for it.* Rather than destroy landmarks like these, they were updated and used for the Greek Circle.

Riley looked around the room and did a quick head count. *Only twelve actives. At least they all have EIPi letters on.* Most were wearing their pink and white jerseys but a few had sweaters and hats as well. It was about pride and showing the pledges what they were striving toward. It was a relatively small number of their sisters considering they had over forty actives. But with tonight being a last minute thing, most of the girls were still out at the bars or with their boyfriends or hook-ups.

Riley quickly got them all in a line and parked herself right in the middle.

"Get in the main hall now!" Tory's voice yelled from the hallway.

The six pledges came into view one by one with their arms interlocked at the elbows just like they'd been taught the day after Bids. Tonight the name of the game was expediency. She just wanted to keep the pledges on task and make sure they hadn't forgotten just what they were doing. They greeted only her and Tory quickly without a single mistake. After they finished greeting the two of them, they returned to the line and re-linked their arms. Every now and again she'd change it up and have them greet the sisters too but not tonight.

Once they'd formed their line Riley walked away from her own and started pacing in front of them like a shark circling a helpless meal.

"Just because the school says you need to be crossed by the end of six weeks doesn't make it true. It also doesn't give any of you a free pass to start slacking off and not caring about this sorority." *Don't scream. Not yet.*

"That's why we're going to try something new tonight" Tory chimed in.

In the past it wouldn't have been tolerated to have an assistant pledge mom add on to the pledge mom's speeches or thoughts but she gave Tory a fair bit of leeway since they were friends and she never abused it.

Tory moved to the bar area which had a single sheet of paper on it. The pledges eyes wandered along with her.

"Even though we don't really give a fuck about what the school thinks we still find it beneficial to cover our own asses. Honored sister Tory Brye is handing you a sheet of paper which you will all sign without question."

Tory handed the paper over to the pledge farthest left.

Angela always led the pledge line since she was the tallest. She was Danielle's Little and they were about the same height. Riley's Little was Brynn Wells. She was located two from the right. She wasn't short. Only when she stood next to her pledge sisters did it appear that way.

They all signed the paper using the pen attached. They used their pledge sister's backs for a flat surface to write on.

"If this pledge process goes past week six, so be it. Honored sister Tory and I have nothing better to do" she paused. "Actually we do but you can bet your asses we won't cross you until you earn it" she lashed out with enough contempt to fill the room. "The paper you just signed is an agreement between yourselves and this sorority. It states that you don't give a fuck when pledging ends. And should it go past that sixth week, you will continue on with it."

The pledges had a practiced look on their faces for callouts when they were getting yelled at. That came from learning the hard way that showing weakness in front of a group of sisters would get you nothing except more torment. It was like showing you were the weakest piece of meat in a room full of hungry predators. *Everyone always learns the hard way around here.*

Not one of the pledges changed their expressions when Riley finished speaking. She expected nothing less, especially from Brynn. There was no doubt in her mind that they were all feeling depressed but it was great that they weren't showing it. That discomfort would likely be expressed later with their pledge sisters. Normally the big sister's would fill that role but since they were on the end of week five all the Big's had severed contact with their Littles. *Just one more way to fuck with these girls.*

Brynn was always in a tough spot considering she was the pledge mom's Little. Complaining about pledging would be complaining about Riley to Riley. But Brynn was strong and she always kept her disgust to herself.

Riley knew the risks when she took a Little during the year she was pledge mom but she hadn't wanted to wait until her senior year. Selfishly, she wanted to spend as much time with her Little as possible. Her Big, Felicia, hadn't taken Riley until she'd been a senior and their time had been shorter because of it. Having a link to the past in the form of a Big was always a huge selling point for Riley and she wanted the same for her Little when she finally got one.

This was always gonna be a huge risk.

In the amount of time that EIPi had existed she'd only heard of a handful of instances when the pledge mom had taken a Little. *There's probably a reason for that but you had to do your own thing anyway.* Part of the reason she'd wanted Brynn to pledge in the first place was because she seemed like a very strong girl. *If anybody could get through pledging without having a full time Big, it's this girl. But what if you're wrong? What if she can't handle it? That's on you.*

Pledging wasn't easy here, or in most other places in Gladen Hills. *Unless its Rho Beta or DXA.* They weren't anywhere near as ridiculous as some of the bigger schools but it wasn't a relaxing time either. *There was a reason that Bigs were created in the first place right?* Every time she was drunk at a callout and had to look at Brynn and see the discomfort not in her face but in her body language she always came back to an argument in her head. Over and over she had to rationalize the decision she'd made.

It's already done now. You can't change it. Quit freaking out.

She'd often contemplated taking it easier on Brynn but that would put her in the awkward spot too. That wouldn't go over well with her pledge sisters *or* the actives. Riley wouldn't do that to her Little. *Fuck that. No one in this line will get it easy. Nobody will say Brynn didn't earn letters.*

Riley put her doubts aside and got back on point. "Some of you look confused," she said as she eyed each one. "Not shocking…some of them always look that way" Tory added with her own batch of contempt. Rachel alone chuckled at the line although Riley wanted to do the same. Generally, the sisters weren't supposed to show any emotion during a callout, happy or otherwise. *Whatever, Rachel's graduating this semester. She can have this one.* The girl was also the president currently so Riley wasn't going to step on any toes for something so trivial.

"That's definitely true sister Tory. Let's start with something easy. Pledges, you will begin by reciting pledge number three's family tree in order from her Big going up." The pledges didn't have names during callouts. They were only referred to by whatever number they were in the pledge line. In this case, it was numbers one through six, ordered from tallest to shortest.

They began speaking in unison. "…Sister Amy Brage, sister Tara Lync…"

No sooner had they gotten through the first two names did pledges two and five start fucking up. *What a surprise. The weakest links in the class…again.* The other four constantly paid for their mistakes.

Tory looked equally unimpressed. "Stop! Clearly *some* of you have no fucking idea what you're doing…as usual."

Riley looked over to Amy who was two down from her in the line of sisters. She looked disappointed too. *Can't blame you for that one Amy.* Her little sister Mary hadn't fucked up of course but it didn't matter. *Pledge class of one. Only one.*

One of the first things a pledge learned when they started was their own family tree. After they crossed it was extremely likely that these girls would meet a good chunk of their family lines at alumni weekends and other events. It'd be good to know their names ahead of time and it would also make the alumni feel special. *Win-win girls.*

Brynn had already nailed her tree about fifteen names down the line. Anything past that point was overkill since anybody past there was in their late thirties and forties and not likely to ever return to Gladen Hills. That didn't make them unimportant, just not as important as the girls still somewhat involved in EIPi.

"Let's try pledge four's family line" Tory suggested, essentially reading Riley's mind. The question was aimed to allow the pledges to succeed at *something*. It'd be nothing short of a travesty if they didn't know their own pledge mom's family tree that Brynn just happened to be a part of.

As expected, they rattled it off without flaws. "Pledge mom Riley Nichol, sister Felicia Crystal…"

They carried on for about twelve names before the actives started looking bored.

"I suppose I should be flattered that you haven't completely fucked up my family line but I'm not impressed at all." Riley left the line of sisters to pace in front of the pledges again. "No one is stopping you but you. I don't know what else I can say. Tory and I have done all we can. We've basically given you the fucking blueprint for finishing. I think I can confidently say that this is the worst pledge class we've ever seen." *Don't laugh. Don't smile.* Keeping a straight face was an extremely difficult task during these moments, especially when she was drunk.

"Your pledge mom won't say it so I will: keep up this level of disrespect and we'll have to spend more time on you worthless bitches. This will eat into our drinking time. That will affect our social lives, which more often than not eats into our sex-capades. Take away those three things and you will see a whole other side to us. And let me fucking tell you bitches: you will not like what you see."

Whereas Riley had to focus much harder on her speeches whenever she drank, Tory seemed to thrive.

"The translation ladies, is this: if you thought we were being too hard on you so far, you haven't seen a damn thing yet. Show them sisters," she said with enough venom in her tone to unsettle everyone. She didn't have to look down the line of actives to know they were all looking sadistic. *They know what's coming but the six of them don't have a clue. If Brynn can get through tonight she can get through anything.*

Riley hoped tonight wouldn't be the night she lost her Little.

****

It wasn't like he'd never seen such a side of his girlfriend before, but it was always jarring. Calvin knew Jennifer wasn't proud of it so he usually kept his thoughts to himself. He loved her but she tended to take things too personally.

He stood at the bathroom door, which was right next to his bedroom as Jen continued throwing-up the night's drinks. *She shouldn't be ashamed. My head's been stuck in that toilet more times than I can remember and it could've been again tonight.*

Calvin had been going uptown with Jared with the strict intent of getting hammered but Jennifer always took precedence so when she texted him for help he had to leave. He knew that made him seem like a pussy to the other brothers but he didn't care. *It is what it is.*

Jennifer took a break for a few seconds to look up at him. It wasn't a pretty sight but he still gave her a comforting look. She gave him a half-smile. He'd played this game enough with Jen to know what that meant. *I know Jen. You don't want me seeing you like this.* He knelt down and kissed her on the head, being sure to avoid her lips. *Neither of us wants that kind of action right now.*

Afterward, he shut the door and went into his room. He immediately noticed his guitar in the far corner looking sadly unused in its stand. Still having a solid buzz he picked it up. He sat down on his nearby bed and strummed a few chords. *Damn that feels good.*

Just as he was about to play his favorite song, one he wrote for Jen, one of his brothers walked in.

"You know someone's dying in that bathroom right?"

Calvin smirked at Jeff. "Yeah Jen's having a rough night."

"Dude she sounds terrible."

They both looked to the doorway and the bathroom beyond. As if on cue, out came another well-pronounced heaving sound. *At least she knows where she is and what's she doing. Can't ask for more.* Sometimes Jennifer overdid it but she never needed to be taken care of. The only real exception was alumni weekend last year.

"OK I'll give you that" he relented to Buttons.

"I'm still trying to drink but how can I work with that going on?"

"I don't know man. After seeing what's coming out of my girlfriend right now…I think I'm done for the night."

Calvin quickly looked around and noticed a full cup of beer sitting on the corner of his desk. He remembered bringing it up from the basement after they'd sent Jared's ex home. *I love when things work out.* With the look of disgust still fresh on Buttons' face he picked up the beer and chugged it.

"After-hours?" Jeff asked with a grin after watching Calvin finish the drink.

"I don't know Buttons…Biz isn't gonna be a fan of that idea."

"Then it's one against six. And I'll bet he's hammered. He won't mind at all."

All good points. It was refreshing to be on the same side of an argument, albeit one that they had with Eric every weekend. He was definitely the most cautious of the AZXis, which made him the ideal treasurer. That also made him a valuable ally most of the time when it came to all kinds of arguments with the other brothers, usually Jeff. *Thank God Biz joined our E-Board last semester after all that shit.*

"Guapo texted me to get up to the Midway because Biz was buying the bar again" Jeff added.

Well that settles it. He's hammered.

In general Eric Saren was a generous guy. He'd buy shots and drinks for people at all times if asked nicely. But when he went out of his way to spend money on others it was clear he was wasted. *Guapo would definitely exaggerate something like this but I'll bet it's legit.*

"Yeah he must be hammered then," Calvin finally agreed. "How much of the keg do we have left from the party?"

"Enough."

Game on. "Tell Guapo to get at it then. We'll throw it down." *Looks like I'll still get hammered tonight.* He had to stick around in case Jen needed anything so the only solution would be having a party here.

"Beer pong while we're waiting?" Jeff asked.

I wonder why he's so happy tonight. Maybe because the pledges are in another country? He personally felt that Buttons was a far better brother when he didn't have anything AZXi related on his plate. *He always seemed happier before this year.*

Calvin checked his phone and saw it was a little after two. *That leaves us about twenty minutes.* "Yeah there's still plenty of time to kick your ass."

"You good with leaving Jen like that?" Jeff asked just as another heaving sound filtered into the room.

Calvin grinned. "Yeah, she does this sometimes. She'll clear her system and then walk home."

Buttons looked confused. "Why doesn't she just stay home and defile her own bathroom if she's just going to end up there?"

"It's shocking I know but most of the other Betas don't drink as hard as she does and she doesn't want all the judgment. That sorority is changing for the worse pal."

"And here I thought she couldn't fall any further in their eyes once she started fucking you."

"I could say the same thing about Dana *if* she was in a sorority" Calvin replied.

"Ah yes...the age old question. To date a sorority chick or steer clear?"

"It's no question pal. Date within *if* you find a girl that isn't fucked eight ways from Sunday" Calvin answered with conviction.

"Sounds like a major loophole to me."

"Oh it definitely is. And Jen isn't even like the rest of the Betas, let alone like other sorority girls so yeah...I'm living the dream."

"While you're still here maybe...what about next year?"

That turned the conversation to a very dark place. It wasn't like Calvin hadn't given it a fair amount of thought. *I won't let Jen go so we'll date long distance if we have to. Jeff won't understand, he's not leaving 'til next year. No one will get it.*

"I'll worry about that some other time that *isn't* tonight." *Leave it alone please.*

Thankfully his phone went off with an incoming text that he promptly read out loud. "Guapo says he's doing work on spreading the word and Biz is completely cool."

They both said the same thing at the same time: "he's definitely hammered."

****

A little after two in the morning and she was wide-awake. *Nothing new.*

It was a Friday and she did have big plans for the night that would start around three. Danielle was sitting next to her since Tory had finally gotten a text from Brian. *He really had to work for that one didn't he?* Riley had to remind her assistant to be back within the hour since she was a key part of the latter half of their night.

"So you're gonna call them out again tonight even after all the shit we just gave them?" Danielle asked sincerely.

Sometimes I wonder if you can really handle being the pledge mom next year Dani. Riley had to admit they had yelled at the pledges pretty harshly earlier. *They deserved it. Week five is over.* "It's tradition" was all she could say.

"I think we should just cancel it and go to after-hours at one of the frat houses." Dani was never much for hanging at the frats, which meant she was either drunker than Riley realized or she just really wanted to give her Little a break.

She shook her head. "Next year when you're pledge mom you can literally do almost anything you want to the pledges but right now it's on me and I won't break tradition. The alumni would be pissed if we skipped the cleaning." Riley hoped she'd put enough finality in her tone to show it wasn't up for debate.

The 'cleaning' was always important to EIPi tradition but Riley had taken it a step further and added a non-traditional callout an hour before which they'd finished not five minutes ago. It wasn't unlike adding a stabbing to a gunshot.

"OK fine but this just might break one of them," Danielle said dismissively.

It hadn't gone unnoticed to Riley that the pledges were struggling. *That's exactly how they should be feeling. This is the end of week five, not week one.* Riley remembered how on edge she'd been.

"You cried during this callout when you were pledging didn't you?"

"Maybe I did" she began. "But those girls were so much meaner than we are."

Riley nodded. *So true.* The seniors from last year were out of control. It almost pushed Riley to the point of quitting and she'd never quit anything in her life. Dani hadn't pledged with Riley and Tory but both their classes had had the same batch of sisters to deal with.

"I wouldn't exactly say we're a barrel of laughs either."

"That depends which side of the process you're on. I happen to think we're hysterical."

She's gotta be drunk. She never talks this way. But good for her.

"I just hope they get it together with their projects so we can cross them on time. Going past week six is risky." Riley had no intention of taking the current Beta Theta class past six weeks but it could happen.

"You wouldn't really do it right?" Dani asked, concerned. "We can't put ourselves on the line for something with no real payoff."

There were even fewer instances in EIPi history than pledge mom's taking Littles than there were of classes going past six weeks. It wasn't done unless something crazy was happening. Even the concept of the pledges signing that document about pledging exceeding the time limit was a joke. It was in place for the sisters' amusement and to fuck with the pledges. They would never turn that in to the school administration. *That same administration that'll use any excuse to screw us. Might as well write them an invitation to take our charter away.*

"Yeah and sororities love turning each other in for breaking the rules" Dani said solemnly. *God girls suck.*

When it came to the opposite sex, they had an unwritten code not to turn on each other for stupid shit like that. *Or so Eric says.* There were times she'd heard of even recently where certain frats had gone over the six-week mark and were never turned in because frats didn't care what the others were doing. *But if we break a rule the nearest sorority would love to say something. The DXA's or the NDM's would turn us in so quick.* For whatever reason they'd developed a rivalry with those girls in recent years. *Something about one of their sisters getting into a fight with one of ours at the Midway God knows when over God knows what.* The whole thing made Riley sick. It was times like these she envied Eric and even Jake for the world they lived in.

****

Jake had to snap himself awake when they finally pulled into the Double motel parking lot. He'd fallen asleep in the car about twenty minutes from the border after some serious thought about what he'd seen at the frat house. The whole thing had mentally worn him out and it was showing on his face as he looked in the passenger side mirror while getting out of the car. *I look fuckin' awful. Thank God Kelly's not here.*

"Bill-Butt, is this the place Petey told you about?" J-Hood asked. He didn't sound like he'd be convinced regardless of whatever the reply was.

"Yeah the Double motel…this is the one."

"I doubt there are many places with that sweet-ass name" Jake yawned.

"Exactly" Will agreed. "Besides we won't be spending much time in the room and he said it was the cheapest around."

"It damn well better be for how terrible it looks." Jake was trying to be funny. *You aren't the little bitch you've been acting like. These guys should know that.*

Jake's phone started vibrating in his pocket while they stood there for a few seconds marveling at the state of utter disrepair the motel was in.

It was a text message from Riley. 'Eric told me you guys would be in Canada tonight. Please just have fun and try not to catch any diseases. In fact don't do anything Will says'.

"Jesus you'd think we were going to the fuckin' Middle East or something" Jake muttered. *Why would you say that out loud?* Summers shot him an inquisitive look. "My cousin doesn't want me to catch any diseases."

"That bitch" J-Hood said calmly.

Jake frowned. "You know what I mean. The girl is a year older but she makes me feel like I'm a ten year old. And when I'm doing anything fun it's like I got caught eating before dinner." *Yeah…that'll make you sound less like a little bitch.*

The lobby section was the on the far side of the building to the left. Will put his hand on Jake's shoulder as they walked. "She knows you lost your virginity right?"

"Bite me. Let's check in and go to bed. I don't want to clean on Sunday."

"Even if we do finish this scav list there's no chance we aren't cleaning on Sunday Raley" Will replied.

"You'd think they'd cut us a break after all that shit with the Trip E's this week," Jake lamented while looking right at Summers.

"I think that just pissed them off even more" he replied with no emotion.

We wouldn't even be in this fucked up situation if it wasn't for you dumbass. Jake felt his frustration rising. "Maybe you just shouldn't have gotten caught...."

"Might as well rest up boys" J-Hood cut him off. "It's a vacation so let's saddle up" he finished as they all walked into the lobby.

Fine. Jake followed his pledge class in quietly while deciding to keep his thoughts to himself for the rest of the night.

****

He tried hiding it as best he could but it was no use. Anyone looking at him would clearly see just how hammered he was. *Fuck it. Can't do anything now.*

When he'd finally reached the Midway after getting off the 'drunk bus' he was in a mindset to rip shots. He'd won over two thousand dollars from the previous weekend's online poker tournament and while he'd put a good amount into his savings account as usual, there was still a chunk ready to support the local bars. *I'm just a philanthropist really. I love supporting local business.*

The final row of shots was placed in front of him. Only three were present since he could only find that many AZXis. The floor lights were coming up. That meant the bar was closing although he had no real concept of time other than what others were telling him. It was just as well. Every week from Monday through Friday he was always worried about the time. Wondering if he'd have enough to finish assignments and get to his next class or lab so he could to look over his notes, setting aside stretches to eat and sleep while also maximizing his stay in the library. When the weekend finally came Eric always took full advantage. While the rest of his brothers like Guapo and Lance were out getting drunk on Tuesdays and Wednesdays he was looking over a textbook or working out problem sets, calculating for this variable or that one. *It must be freakin' nice being a communications major and doing absolutely nothing during the week. Nice catch Guapo.* Eric shook his head, almost violently. *What can I do? Biochem is my jammmm.*

He'd always known that later in life he'd be rewarded for working so hard now. It still didn't make watching Guapo and the others get laid constantly while fucking up in school any easier. *How the hell do they never get kicked out?* Eric was still reeling from the last hook-up he'd had with Tory months ago that he'd fucked up.

Suddenly there was a pat on his shoulder as the latest song swelled on the speakers surrounding the dance floor behind him. *Of course it's Guapo. Probably just finished chatting up the latest chick he'll be banging tonight ten feet from where I'll be passed out...alone. Fuuuuuck!*

"Shots up?" Guapo asked as Dylan drew closer, sensing the same. To his knowledge they were the only three brothers in the Midway, at least nearby. *Nice catch letting me buy the rounds. You...uglyyyyy...dudesssss.*

Eric nodded and slid one of the overflowing shot glasses toward Guapo and the other toward Dylan. Some of it spilled out but there wasn't much to be done about that considering how small the little plastic cups were.

"I am so down for after-hours tonight mannnnn," he slurred out with excitement.

"I know Biz. You mentioned that a few times already" Guapo smirked back.

Did I? Oh well. He was excited at the prospect of having a bunch of random girls in the basement dancing their asses off getting drunk. *Sooooo many good things could happen...*

"Let him get pumped. He looks ready to pass out," Dylan said.

Don't you worry about a damn thing Dills. I'm in...for the long haul...yup.

Dylan was a Biology major, which meant that by and large he spent a ton of time in the library as well. The difference between them was that somehow he never had trouble with girls even in the most fucked-up of states. *Well done Dills...*

Eric realized after a few long seconds that the other two guys were waiting for him to make the first move on the shots. He raised his glass as high as he felt comfortable with which wasn't all that much but the others followed. They all drained them in sequence. The Southern Comfort liquor went down very smoothly. Outside of Ice 101 it was Eric's favorite drink, even if it wasn't mixed with something else.

Not a second after Dylan put his shot glass back down did he turn to the group of three girls to his right. "AZXi's having after-hours tonight if any of you want to swing by. He flashed them his trademark 'drunk but harmless' smile. It worked. They smiled and giggled among themselves…like girls at the Midway always did.

"Middle of Arkridge Ave, free beer and we're partying all night!" Guapo added.

Eric felt compelled to add something, *anything* to the case. "After-hours!" he yelled loudly over the music. In his mind it sounded better. *At least now they know that I'm around right?*

Guapo shook his head. "I'll bet that totally sealed the deal Biz."

Eric grinned absently. *Guess we'll see…guess we'll seeeee.*

They moved to the nearest exit together while Dylan continued his crusade to talk to every attractive girl in the bar.

Always making moves…

"How do you just hit it off with the baby chickens man?" he asked Guapo with the utmost sincerity. 'Baby chickens' were for lack of a better definition, the hot chicks. It was a term he and Jerry used frequently.

I bet he doesn't even know how the hell he does it. It's so sick. I sound like a kid asking about Santa. I'm so uglyyyyy.

"It's just a talent Biz" Guapo replied with a grin.

Yeah right. There's zero chance he believes that…right? Guapo's not even that attractive. So how the fuck does he bang so much? Last time he'd heard, Guapo had banged like seventy girls. Add to that the fact that he hadn't lost his virginity until freshman year and something didn't make sense.

"I just can't get a bite," Eric said sullenly, trying to clear the child-like sounds from his tone and failing miserably as he stumbled out the door and down the steps of the Midway. *Damn…walking blows…*

Thankfully Guapo was propping him up whenever he needed it. "Don't put so much pressure on it. The night is still young," he said cheerfully as he moved him along past the science hall.

"Man the bar's just let out, this night is middle-aged at best."

"After-hours is where the real shit goes down, you know this."

"Yeah but Biz never makes it to after-hours" Dylan chimed in, having just caught up with them. He started walking on Eric's right so he had a brother on either side of him. That gave him the confidence to pick up the pace. *They won't let me fall over.*

"Last time I checked, you barely make it to those yourself" Guapo retorted.

Eric grinned but couldn't form the words. *Yeah! Good call Guapo!*

"Well we all can't stay sober and hit on the drunkest girls" Dylan shot back.

It suddenly clicked into place. Guapo being only buzzed by this point in any night allowed him to formulate good flirtation with chicks absent slurring and general creepiness. Whereas Dylan seemed to thrive under these circumstances, Eric would crumble into a stuttering heap of ruins.

"So that's how it's done," Eric finally replied, as though he'd just witnessed a massive scientific breakthrough.

"Yeah but he cleans up the bitches so I can't judge it."

"You do alright too pal" Guapo said.

He's obviously not talking to me.

"It's not all from skill though. When you drink as much as we do and head to the Midway it's a hunter's game" Dylan admitted.

What the hell does that even mean?

Suddenly Eric lost his footing and stumbled forward but Guapo caught him.

"When I'm stumbling around hammered, girls see that and pounce. I'm like a wounded fawn that gets poached when I'm in midtown" he answered Eric's confusion. "Don't kid yourself guys. Horny girls are just as ruthless as guys when it comes to the Midway. That's one reason why the buddy system is so key when you're blackout."

Eric listened in awe while Guapo just chuckled.

"Oh I'm preaching now" Dylan grinned.

Both Guapo and Dylan's methods clearly had merit based on either's track record and yet Eric never got 'poached'. *And I'm definitely never going out sober in Gladen Hills. Yeah, NOOOOO!*

****

It was the sound of sweet, sweet victory when the final ping pong ball hit the second cup in a row for Jeff. Hitting two back-to-back shots to win the game was awesome enough but given that it was against Calvin? That made it all the sweeter.

Chew on that one Gretman. He tried hiding his wide grin as he looked at his brother but he knew it was a wasted effort.

They were evenly matched all game and he had no doubt that Calvin could've pulled off overtime if given the chance. But such was the way of a final back-to-back hit. *No rebuttal shots, just me winning and you losing.*

"Guapo said he was on his way" Jeff announced to anyone listening. The basement was sparsely filled. A couple brothers had made it this far into the night and with them a couple girls too. "Said he was coming down with a bunch of girls and a hammered Biz and Dills."

"A bunch of girls? Good thing Guapo never exaggerates anything right?" Calvin asked sarcastically.

Jeff grinned. His pledge brother was known for stretching the truth whenever possible as long as it made him look cooler than he really was. *No stone left unturned right Guapo?*

"He's probably only got like two hideous chicks with him" Calvin laughed.

"Dude…that was really messed up to say about Biz and Dills." *They could stand to grow some hair on their balls that's for fuckin' sure.* Jeff chuckled at his joke while pouring the last beer from his rack into his side cup to drink. Even though Calvin hadn't hit his final cup he wouldn't let the beer go to waste. *Not on my watch.* He poured the remainder down his throat. Keg beer was never his preference but the effects were the same as most other beers. *That's all that matters on nights like these.* He moved over to the DJ booth to change up the song on the play-list computer but the basement door to the outside swung open and in walked his pledge brother Guapo. *He always has that same shit-eating grin.*

True to form, behind him walked a group of about fifteen girls and a few guys that had likely tagged along wanting to know what was good. When it seemed like everybody was inside, the final two stragglers came into view. Dylan was propping up Biz as they walked. To the casual and or drunken eye, Dills didn't look wasted but the guy was every bit as drunk as Biz. He was just better at concealing it. Dylan's eyes would always start rolling into the back of his head ever so slightly and his voice would get deeper. It was clear Dills had been the recipient of several drinks. *Probably from Biz's tab.*

"You see what I've been dealing with?" Guapo asked sarcastically as he motioned to their hammered brothers bringing up the rear. Before anybody could answer him he asked another question. "Who the fuck is DJ-ing this party?" He sounded angry as if some great crime against humanity had been committed.

"I don't know I just set the computer to shuffle the songs" Calvin replied casually.

"Oh weak. I got this guys." With that Guapo walked past them toward the computer in the DJ booth.

"Thanks because I was *real* worried about it" Jeff called after him.

He couldn't tell what it was but the song playing was extremely slow and only fast upbeat music should be played at after-hours. These types of parties were only for the hardcore. The people that always stayed up late looking for a good time.

"Don't worry Buttons. I'll get the girls real wet with this play-list" Guapo said subtly with a straight face.

"Jesus do you even listen to yourself?" Calvin asked.

Guapo either didn't hear him or flat out ignored him because he continued on his way without a care in the world.

"Who's trying to slam a beer with me?" Dylan shouted as he filled his cup at the keg by the door.

Eric had since planted himself on the couch near the beer pong table. He didn't even look alive but the son of a bitch heard Dylan. "I so will downnnnn," he slurred out while raising his right hand as if that'd signify his participation.

Yeah Biz...you clearly need another drink.

Dylan ignored Eric and turned toward the rest of the people in the basement. "Anyone *functional* trying to slam a beer with me?"

Oh hell no. A brother wouldn't be condemned to slam a beer alone while he sat here otherwise thirsty. "Fuck it, I'm down."

"Yeah why not? Fill 'em up" Calvin said from right beside him.

Maybe it was because he'd definitely be seeing Dana later or he was still riding the high from winning that beer pong game but as of now, he didn't mind Gretman's company. That was the first time he remembered feeling like that since sophomore year.

He gave himself even odds at beating Dylan who was clearly the favorite to finish his beer first. They all put their brimming cups into the center of the circle and began chugging. As expected Dills finished first with Jeff right behind him, followed by Gretman and then Lance. Afterward he turned his gaze again to a near comatose Eric on the couch. "Someone should really get Biz upstairs."

"Not it" both he and Gretman quickly replied.

Lance hadn't noticed Eric and wasn't really paying attention. *Like you would've helped out anyway.* Dylan was talking to some girl that just came in and also wasn't focusing on the issue. Jeff was about to suggest a chug-off to determine which of their sorry-asses would drag their hammered brother upstairs when Jerry stumbled over. *Clearly he's hammered too.*

"Great news Jer-Bear" Jeff began. "You get to be the one that gets Biz the fuck upstairs," he all but ordered.

Calvin stood there and nodded in agreement.

Ordinarily Jerry might've argued but he was easier to coerce when hammered. Of course he might've just told them to fuck off but Jeff was willing to risk it.

"Oh weaaaaakkkkk" he replied before agreeing to their ridiculous ploy. Thankfully Jerry was in decent shape so he had no problem lifting his pledge brother off the couch and over his shoulder to walk up the stairs.

After they were out of earshot he turned to a dumbfounded Calvin. "That was way easier than it should've been."

"No shit" Jeff agreed.

Not a second had passed before he hit him with a typical Gretman buzz-kill. "So I've been meaning to talk to you about some stuff."

Jeff just nodded. *You don't fuckin' say. Of course you have some shit to say.*

Calvin immediately backtracked when he saw the look on Jeff's face "I figured it'd be better talking to you when you're not pissed."

"I'd try tomorrow instead. I'm heading out now" he lied. He wasn't planning on leaving for Dana's so soon but it didn't matter.

"Tomorrow then?"

"Fine."

"At least we'll be drinking tomorrow too," Jeff said as he turned to leave. He reached into his pocket to grab his pack of cigarettes so he could smoke on the walk over.

"What's tomorrow?"

"Does it matter?"

He moved away from Calvin, weaving his way through the now full basement. He was pretty sure they had a breakfast with some sorority tomorrow. *If I'm gonna be forced to talk to Gretman about anything then I damn well better be fucking hammered when it happens.*

Chapter 13

Even though the motel was in a state of decay the likes of which Jake had never seen, he'd still gotten a decent night's sleep. At least it felt like he had. *I actually have no clue what time it is...*

The sound of the faucet running in the bathroom right next to the bed he and J-Hood had shared was loud enough to wake him up. The faucet wasn't the main problem; mostly it was the sound of pipes shaking in the walls to supply the faucet.

He looked over to the other large bed on his right and saw that neither Summers nor Will had even moved yet. *I bet those two could sleep through anything.*

J-Hood hadn't liked the idea of anyone sharing a bed with him but he conceded since he didn't want to get two separate rooms. Jake was sure to keep to the far end of his side so his pledge brother didn't freak out.

Jake continued to lie there, staring up at the ceiling with numerous holes. The wallpaper in their room had long since peeled off, leaving only a faint shade of paint underneath. With the way the pipes were acting because of a lone faucet running he sure as hell wouldn't be taking a shower around here. *It'd probably flood the whole room if I tried.* Fortunately after another few seconds it stopped.

J-Hood walked out from the bathroom looking refreshed. He abruptly began slamming his hand on the wall to wake everyone. Unfortunately this had the doubling effect of making the pipes go crazy again. *He probably just doesn't give a fuck.* Jake wouldn't have been surprised if the whole damn place collapsed right in front of his eyes. *That's what you get for paying fifty dollars a room.*

Bill-Butt and Summers finally moved in their bed after about a minute of J-Hood's fist on the wall. "Wake up boys. We're gonna get *real* productive today" J-Hood announced. *Is he happy?* "The list is straight forward, should be pretty easy."

"Anything on that list involve getting drunk?" Summers asked thoughtfully.

J-Hood positively beamed with energy. "As a matter of fact it does. We need to bring back three empty cases of Triple-X plus we need to take a picture outside Beers of the World. Two birds...four pledges...yuuuuupppppp."

Summers nodded as he walked past to use the condemned bathroom.

"Beer?! It's only like nine in the morning," Jake said while checking his phone.

"Is your vagina bothering you Raley?" Will asked as he got out of bed.

Summers came back out of the bathroom unharmed. "What's going on?"

"What's going on is Raley is getting his period and we're going to be clocking into the office early today" J-Hood answered matter-of-factly.

They all want to drink. I can't be the only one not involved.

Jake grinned and went along for the ride. "Did somebody say overtime?"

The morning went by in a blur. Most of the scavenger hunt was pretty entertaining even Jake had to admit. After starting at Beers of the World they headed to one of the local gas stations, also on the list. Jake bought some Gatorade while there. Since he wasn't a bona-fide drinker like Will or J-Hood he knew he'd need a chaser which he got while the others were taking a picture by the gas station's sign. Jake was confused about why they needed a picture there until he went back outside. The place was called the Beaver station and clear as day in the middle of the lot was a huge sign that simply said: 'Beaver does it better'. *That's awesome.*

Summers snapped the picture of Will and J-Hood standing in front of it with their thumbs up, grinning like idiots.

After that he'd had three bottles of Triple-X, which left only six to go throughout the day. The list had specified that the cases be twelve packs so that gave nine beers to each pledge. Will hadn't missed a beat in terms of making fun of Jake for needing to chase a beer but if he was going to drink early he was going to do it on his terms.

Since pledging started none of them had gotten a chance to just chill and enjoy the other's company. After getting a solid buzz they started working through the list. Thankfully everything they'd needed was within walking distance since the majority of tourism was basically confined to the three-block section where they were staying.

Getting Summers up into the mouth of the giant T-Rex statue at the local mini-golf course was easier than expected since there was a light rain coming down all morning and no one was there. Getting him down was a little more challenging considering no one wanted to catch him. Thankfully he landed all on his own. Jake was fairly certain it wasn't the first time he'd been jumping from spaces that high. *He probably uses windows for exits more than doors.*

Writing 'America Rules' on Will's ass was fun if not a little disgusting. One word was on each cheek and the idea was to take a picture of him with his bare ass hanging out in front of Niagara Falls. Getting it done without having anyone notice proved impossible so they just waited until there were no cops around. Some Asian tourists had noticed them and started laughing. When he and J-Hood explained why they were doing it they laughed even harder. That allowed them to take a picture with their family and check another thing off the list.

Apparently Jeff thought it would be funny to have the shortest pledge take a picture next to the tallest man statue outside 'Ripley's Believe it or Not'. That task fell to Summers and he did it with pride. The difference between the two was ridiculous. While they were there Jake had to get a picture of himself humping the giant marble sphere at the entrance. Thankfully nobody noticed as it was still earlier in the day so he went all out on the damn thing.

Asking a homeless guy for money was a little fucked up in Jake's mind so naturally Will volunteered for the job. He chatted up the first one they came across and smoked a cigarette with the guy and then mimicked asking him for money without actually doing it. After reviewing the picture they were all confident it would stand up to any scrutiny from Jeff or the others.

While on their way to the porn store they came across the Mounty statue. They had to mimic one of them giving the damn thing a blowjob. Will volunteered for that one too. Multiple people noticed and while a few looked disgusted, most found it funny. After he was done 'blowing' the thing he lit up a cigarette and put his arm around it to signify they were both relaxing after a job well done. That part wasn't on the list but they snapped a picture anyway since they were sure it would make the brothers laugh.

They picked up a few DVD's from the bargain bin at the store since they were supposed to get something for the brothers. Jake had to convince the others to get the cheaper ones. After their pledge class paddle and the regular scavenger hunt list his bank account was taking a hit. *Of course the bastards never said anything about the cost of pledging during Rush.* They agreed but only after they saw some of the choices in the bin. None of them were strangers to porn. Their laptops basically came preloaded with multiple scenes and movies.

The weirdest picture of the day was the one involving Jake needing to hold Will's hand as they skipped down the sidewalk in front of a strip club. *Only the minds of the AZXis could dream this shit up.* The others seemed to have no problem sucking it up and doing their own tasks but there were a few things on the list that involved Jake specifically. He knew he was going to have an issue with some of them.

Before they got to anything too divisive they decided to eat.

They'd been at it for about five hours and had almost everything done or in the planning stages so a break was earned. The pizza restaurant they went to was part of the list so it was a happy coincidence. As fate would have it they came across another piece of the puzzle right outside the restaurant: a group of four sorority girls from some national organization were in town too. Having such a miracle cross their path was amazing so they didn't take any chances. They sent in a specialist for the job.

J-Hood sauntered over to them like he was the Prime Minister and said just two words to open the conversation. "What up?" he said to the girl in the lead who also happened to be the hottest. She responded immediately and started smiling. In order to make things seem less sketchy than they really were, the three of them stayed a fair distance back and kept from looking directly at what was going on. Unfortunately that meant none of them could hear whatever magical words J-Hood was saying. Within less than two minutes he was typing the girl's number into his phone.

Jake and the others walked up to J-Hood as quickly as possible without looking like a pack of teenage chicks jumping a pop star. That was easier said than done. "They just ate but they said we should hit them up later for sure." J-Hood acted like that was the only outcome imaginable. *Maybe it was.*

Will had tried saying something to the second girl in line as they'd left but she just smiled and kept walking with the rest of her sisters. That put a smile on Jake's face.

They all walked inside the restaurant together and got a table within minutes. Their food was delivered quickly as well and the pizza was phenomenal. Among the best pepperoni slices he'd ever eaten.

After the meal was done he couldn't help but let his mind wander. He couldn't keep his confusion to himself for very long. "I don't get how you do it. You literally just met those girls and you got the hottest one's number right away." Jake tried keeping his tone casual but there was no denying how baffled he was.

"It's a talent Raley" Will said as if the thought was directed at him. "The best you can hope for is to catch the leftovers from J-Hood's handiwork."

"You mean like you tried to?" Summers immediately grinned in between bites of his white cheese slices. "As badass as J-Hood getting that number was, the highlight was probably watching that other girl not want to have anything to do with you."

"You bastards are supposed to be supportive!" Will joked.

"I am. I'm supportive of the fact that you're going to have to *handle* things yourself to make up for not getting laid tonight" Jake concluded.

"Trust me Raley. It's not over. Guarantee I hook up with one of them tonight" he said with a full confidence that Jake couldn't imagine the guy having after what he'd seen. *Yeah we'll see about that Bill-Butt.* "And what about you? One of the things on the list is Raley three-way kissing two girls. You gonna get on that?"

Jake shifted uncomfortably in his seat. *Just make things as plain as possible. Don't be an ass.* "I *won't* do that to Kelly" he all but lashed out.

Will just rolled his eyes. J-Hood and Summers said nothing.

"Just because I like having a girlfriend doesn't mean I still don't want to help you guys get shit done." It felt like he was abandoning them as soon as he said the words. *It's done. Between them and Kelly it's gonna be her every time. They know that.*

"Actually that's exactly what it means since this is your thing and you aren't gonna do it" Will said plainly.

"Don't pin this on me. I didn't choose this. I know Jeff chose me for this because he knows I have a girlfriend. And that's really fucked up by the way" Jake stated coolly.

J-Hood looked up from his plate and gave him a look that screamed for some kind of unity. "Can you just do it? We're in a really good spot here. The girls can help us with a lot of the pictures we still need and the water from the falls is something to get on the way back. We can finish this if you do your thing." He was still speaking in his regular tone but he was almost pleading.

"You know Hood...you kind of look like me" he started. "I bet we could get away with having you do it and making it look like me if we go from the right angle. And since I'm not doing it that's our best shot."

His pledge class took a few seconds to think it over.

Ironically it was Will that came to the defense of Jake's plan. "It would be easier getting J-Hood into that situation than Raley. And since he's being such a little bitch about it we might as well roll with this. Fuck it." Jake didn't care that he laced his comment with an insult. Unfortunately his face betrayed that he was unhappy about being called a little bitch by Will for the millionth time since Rush. "I still love you Raley but come on...I kinda doubt this is the girl for you" he said matter-of-factly.

What the fuck does that mean you asshole?

"She hasn't given me a single reason to think that."

"You're a sophomore Raley. It's a little early to think about that kinda shit" J-Hood added.

"Maybe...but I love her and I *won't* do this" he said with enough finality that even Will shut the fuck up.

"Fine. I'll do the three-way kiss guys. But I'm not happy about it" J-Hood said with enough of a smirk that it ended the argument completely.

"Raley just put this in your jacket and walk out. We'll meet you outside" Summers said, finally rejoining the conversation now that his food was gone.

He was of course referring to the giant beer mug J-Hood had ordered his drink in. It had the restaurant's name on the side just as the list specified. They were supposed to bring back one of these mugs for

Jeff. *Great. Now I have to steal something for that fucker.* Jake sat there for a few seconds letting his thoughts settle. *Don't say anything. If stealing the mug will put end this shit then keep your mouth shut and get it done.*

The sad thing was that outside of the conversation about the three-way kiss, he was having fun with his pledge class. He was still a little drunk from the beers they'd been ordering at various places but it was more than that. It might've had something to do with the fact that there wasn't a brother for a hundred miles.

Jake stared at the giant mug and finished his own drink before nonchalantly putting it inside his jacket so that he could feel the cold glass through his shirt. He did a quick survey of the area. Nobody was paying attention to them.

He got up from his spot on the outside of the booth and headed toward the front door. Sweat started forming on his neck as he walked what felt like a mile towards the exit. The hostess by the counter at the front looked at him quickly before going back to the computer in front of her. *Is she hitting some kind of silent alarm? Oh Jesus, the police are gonna be waiting out front. No way…it's just a mug for Christ's sake. They wouldn't call in SWAT for that.* Jake would've preferred buying one now given how uncomfortable he was feeling. *Fuck the money. This feels terrible.* Unfortunately had they asked to buy one and then been told they weren't for sale the waitress might've kept a closer eye on them. It was something they couldn't chance…or so Will had told them.

Jake reached the door and pushed against it for a few seconds. It might as well have been an hour before he read where it said 'pull'. He quickly checked around to make sure no one was watching him. Then he pulled it open and walked outside. Once there he immediately b-lined it for the nearest alley and some form of cover. After leaving the street he looked into his jacket at the mug. *All that for a mug because I didn't want to cheat on Kelly by kissing random sorority girls? Fuck my life.*

He probably had a few minutes before the guys reached him. Jake took out his phone and pulled up Kelly's number. *I need to hear her voice.*

****

Brynn Wells had never felt more abused in her life. At least not abused by actual people like she was here. She knew all too well that life could be cruel though. *ElPi changed that. That extra callout last night was so fucked. Who even thinks that shit up?*

The worst part was that while Brynn sat there in the car with her Big not saying a word, the rest of her pledge class was probably talking amongst themselves, venting about last night. That was a luxury she hadn't been afforded today. *Figures.* She never considered herself to be a scared little girl like Jocelyn or Mary could be on occasion, but these girls were pushing her to the limit, and fast. Riley was sitting right there in the driver's seat only inches away. *Why can't you just say something?*

Even when it was just the two of them, she still didn't feel comfortable bitching about pledging. *Riley knows how much of a pain in the ass this is.* It stood to reason that she would know how Brynn was feeling without her saying a word. Riley was the highlight of EIPi for Brynn and outside of callouts where she never paid much attention to her anyways; she was great to be around. With the good memories of her Big higher in her mind she'd started getting pissed at the other sisters in some twisted form of balance. Better she hate them than her own big sister. Chief among the bitches she hated was Tory Brye. *How could Riley be friends with that bitch?*

Brynn was confident that when pledging finally ended, she'd be able to put all this shit behind her. At least she'd felt that way until last night. She couldn't say why but for some reason Tory had seemed more evil than usual. And Brynn couldn't move past it once they left the house. *That's probably because last night was hell.*

"Tell me again why I'm the only pledge helping?" Clearing the disdain from her tone as she talked was a lot harder than she thought.

"Because you're my favorite" Riley replied happily.

"Some prize."

Over the past few weeks it seemed like Riley had come to enjoy Brynn's sarcastic nature. *Probably because she's got the same thing in her.* Riley had claimed that side of her came out more when she was with her cousins but Brynn had never met any of them.

"I know it's against the rules but I'm gonna be busy the rest of the day and you looked like you could use some family time" she added sympathetically. *Well at least you noticed the conditions we were rotting in last night.*

"What're you talking about?" she played dumb.

"The callout last night" she explained. "You weren't exactly keeping things hidden...especially with Tory. I knew you were pissed. I was too when I had to go through that" Riley cut into her thoughts. Her big sister pulled over into one of the empty spots outside the Center and looked at her. "I remember that night."

"So even me helping you get a keg is against the rules now?" she asked coldly.

Riley shook her head. "Pledges aren't supposed to do anything like this, especially with their PM. But if there's anything I can do to stop you from de-pledging, it's done." Her Big sounded almost motherly. *Five full weeks in and I'm gonna de-pledge? Fat chance.* Brynn had always felt she could get through pledging without a shoulder to cry on. *It's worked so far.*

"Your pledge sisters should be so lucky to spend time with me" Riley smiled again. *If I'd had a different big sister then I could actually have real conversations about pledging. Instead I have to sit here and take it all. At least the rest of my pledge class has Bigs to talk to.* Brynn shook her head as they sat in the parked car. *Don't think that. It's done now and it's almost over.*

"We've gotta wait for the owner so we can get the keg for the breakfast today."

There were times it was clear Riley didn't want to take things too seriously. Angela had a cousin in EIPi years ago and she'd told Brynn that Bigs never did things with their Littles during the final two weeks of pledging. But this was the third time that Riley had demanded they see each other. *It's just too bad she was never around during the first four weeks.* Curiosity drew her out of her own thoughts. "So why don't we get our kegs from the National? Isn't that like your favorite bar?"

"You know it is...and one day you'll feel the same."

Yeah probably the same day I start chilling with Tory.

"Trust me, it grows on you."

"That's what you said about Tory and that's fucking insane" she lost control of her thoughts as she spoke. *Good job keeping your mouth shut.*

"Anyways..." Riley began, trying to steer clear of that subject. "We get kegs at the Center because it's closer to our house and...that's all I got actually."

"Why didn't you just get one of your cousins to help with this? Guys carry kegs better than girls last time I checked."

"Jake's in Canada for the weekend and Alicia said she saw Eric stumbling around with his brothers last night. He was hitting trees and screaming about after-hours," she said, not sounding entirely sure of it. "So he won't be able to help anyone today."

"What about one of the Tau Chis then? They are the ones the breakfast is with today right?" *If they're gonna help finish the kegs they might as well help carry them to the house.*

"They never help when we ask and they get their kegs from The Cradle."

"Would your cousins even help? I thought AZXis didn't like Tau Chis?"

"All frats have something against other frats. It's the way of the world. Eric really doesn't care though."

Brynn shook her head. "Guys are so damn weird."

Riley just smiled. "So you'd throw a party with the Phi Thetas then?"

Good point. Brynn didn't know anything about them other than that they were stuck up, bitchy and from what she'd heard, complete coke sluts. "Fuck that, those girls suck" she said instinctively.

Riley grinned. "You're right though, it's stupid. But it's just what we were told when we pledged. Everyone around here is so sure they're on top. Every frat thinks they're the coolest. Every sorority thinks they're hottest. Every sports team thinks they're the best. The people not affiliated think teams and groups are a waste of time…welcome to college."

"Yeah, but why do the people not affiliated hate us?"

"What did you think of sororities before you came here?"

"They were all full of sluts and bitches." That time it was full on instinct with no real thought whatsoever. Brynn hadn't even hesitated. That wasn't what she thought now but she remembered thinking it beyond a doubt.

"Exactly…and *that's* the stereotype. The people that don't join anything still have that view and the longer you believe it, the harder it is to believe anything else."

Did Riley go through all this same shit when she was pledging? Did she question it? Did Felicia have to have these kinds of talks to calm her down too?

"That's why we don't see juniors or seniors pledging," Brynn said thoughtfully.

"And *that's* why you're my little" Riley agreed proudly.

Where the hell is this Riley when we're at callouts?!

"There he is" Riley pointed to a bulky guy walking in the front doors of the Center. "That's the owner. He handles our keg account."

Brynn was hesitant to get out of the car. *As soon as we're done getting the kegs Riley goes back to being my pledge mom. Fuck my life.*

****

The incessant knocking on his door could only be described as death. It had finally come to take him away. Eric couldn't remember feeling more awful in his life but that didn't make it true. For a fleeting second the concept of not drinking again flew through his mind and exited just as quickly. *Last night was still fun.* Whether it was worth it or not would depend on how long he felt terrible today.

"Come on cuz! We got a breakfast to rage at!" said the voice through the door. Even without seeing who it was, he still knew. Only one person could be that damn happy even after being at after-hours last night. *Did I even make it to after-hours last night?* The whole thing started getting hazy after he'd left the Midway. Either way Jared was entirely too happy right now. It was making Eric's headache that much worse.

On the third try he finally managed to get out of bed. Now that he was standing his headache went from awful to downright unbearable. *Damn you Jared.* He stumbled over his clothes that were strewn about on the floor to reach his door. It took him a second to make sure he was dressed at all. Thankfully he'd fallen asleep in mesh shorts and a t-shirt. He didn't recall changing last night so he must've woken up during his initial sleep to do so. That wasn't the first time that had happened.

He slowly opened the door to reveal Jared standing there with his trademark goofy smile like he'd just won the damn lottery. Eric looked at him with equal amounts of loathing for both waking him up and being so energetic. "What the fuck?" was all he could say.

"Rough night buddy?" he asked even though what he was seeing clearly answered that. It didn't help that his voice had gone slightly high-pitched during the question like it sometimes did. It caused another fierce ripple in his headache.

"No. I always wake up looking like this," he said dryly.

"The cure for a hangover is drinking" Jared said with amusing authority.

Eric had heard that line more times in the AZXi house than he cared to count. For him the only thing that *really* cured a hangover was time away from alcohol, usually spent in bed with zero noise. All drinking did was postpone the crash. *And by God the crash always comes.* "I'll bet that."

Before Jared could answer Eric's ill-advised bet the door next to his opened and a girl came shuffling out of Jerry's room. She smartly didn't look into his or Jared's eyes. Eric sure as hell wouldn't have said anything but Jared would definitely try to strike up a casual conversation while the girl completed her walk of shame.

She walked past them and down the stairs. Eric couldn't help but check out her ass as she left. Jared was doing the same. *Not bad at all.*

Eric then noticed Jerry was laying face down on his bed. That wasn't an uncommon sight. After a few seconds of them silently staring at the guy he raised his left arm to let them know he knew they were there. "Something to add Jer?"

Jerry didn't lift his head from the pillow but he was still talking loud enough for them to hear. "Drinking with a hangover just puts off a ridiculous crash," he said with unmistakable clarity. *That's why we're friends.*

"Whatever it does, it definitely helps me," Jared said gleefully.

At that point Jerry just started convulsing like he'd been attacked. "Jared is so ugly!" his now pillow free face said in their direction.

"Why the hell are you waking me up so early?" Eric turned to Jared, finally trying to figure out why he was conscious.

"It's two in the afternoon bro!" Jared joked as he nudged Eric. *Owwwww.*

Two in the afternoon?! No way I slept that long. If his memory could be trusted he was pretty sure his pledge brother had helped him upstairs. *So how did he find a girl to bang last night? He must've gone back down? Maybe?* The thoughts started to aggravate his headache.

"Alright just chill man" Eric waved Jared off before heading back to bed.

After he collapsed again Jared insisted on talking. "We got a breakfast with the ABI's in an hour" he announced, as if that was supposed to make a difference. *ABI kinda sucks these days and they never roll deep to a breakfast...never.* He shifted in his bed to get more comfortable. *I'm not going anywhere.*

"Kevin and Petey aren't around so apparently you're getting the keg," Jared said matter-of-factly.

Son of a bitch. He felt it coming and yet it still stung when he heard it. It was days like these where he really hated being treasurer. *Petey's the damn brew-master. This is his job. Kevin's the vice president so he should be all over this if Petey's missing. Why me?* His head throbbed again. All he could do was stare blankly up at the ceiling while Jared stood there patiently at the door, waiting.

"Giddy up!" the guy chanted.

Eric would never willfully ignore the frat as long as he could do something to help, within reason. Today was just one of those times where he'd need to pick up the slack from one of his brothers. It was happening more and more these days.

"Fine. Let me get dressed and we'll go to the Center," he said sullenly towards the doorway, not bothering to make eye contact. Eric stood up again and yelled past Jared towards Jerry's room asking if he wanted to come along. Jerry's response came in the form of a long laugh and his door closing. *Well-played Jer.*

"You think he's coming?" Jared asked. Now it was Eric's turn to laugh.

Once in the car, Eric tried keeping his eyes off the landscape outside considering how much his head was still hurting. *Just look at the floor, that's all.* Jared was an insanely weird driver on top of that. He was constantly changing radio stations even when midway through songs and his right hand was always playing with the spare change he had in the cup holder. *If his hands aren't always doing something he dies.* The coins falling out of his hand onto the rest of the pile coupled with the radio were making Eric wish he would.

Finally they pulled into the Center's parking lot and saw a larger guy Eric had seen work the door as a bouncer loading a keg into the backseat of a car he thought looked familiar. It took longer than it should have for him to realize that the car belonged to his cousin. Within a second of them parking Riley and some other chick were walking out of the bar. Given the disheveled look of the second girl he was going to assume she was pledging. Most of the time Eric could just tell by the dead look in someone's eyes if they were pledging or not given how he'd seen that reflection in himself only a year and a half ago. *Must be her little sister...definitely hot.*

Eric knew Riley was gonna give him a hard time about being so hung-over but unfortunately he wasn't driving and Jared parked right next to them. It took her all of two seconds to realize who was in the car and she immediately motioned for Jared to roll down the driver's side window. It was just as well because Eric definitely wasn't going to do it.

"Looking good Eric," she said happily. *Everyone in the world has it out for me when I feel this terrible.* "Did somebody have a rough night?"

He was willing to bet that one of her damn sisters had seen him stumbling around last night so she probably already knew the answer.

"I asked the exact same question," Jared yelled back.

"Can a kid just have a hang-over one time?" he asked, hoping that everyone would just chill for a damn minute while he rested.

"Of course" Riley said thoughtfully while getting into her car.

Without warning she honked her horn and yelled for them to have a good day. Eric couldn't even look at her because he was squeezing his eyes shut in pain but he was certain she was smiling her ass off. *Well-played Riley.*

He heard Riley's car move off and they were left in silence for approximately one second before Jared had to ruin it...again. "You coming in bro?"

"I'm not moving. Just find out what the account is up to and I'll write the check."

"Dude you gotta get moving. We got a long day today. Buttons can probably get you some coke."

"I'm not doing fucking coke" he bit out, leaving no room for debate.

"Well Dills could probably get you some Adderall too."

Eric stayed silent. *My God just let it go man...* "Come on dude. Just get this done so we can get back please."

Jared took the hint that time and moved out of the car. *Don't slam the door, don't slam the door.* As usual, his prayers went unanswered. Just like getting a winning card on the river at Hold 'Em he couldn't catch a break because the kid outright shoved the door back into place when he left. It sent a shockwave through the car and made a loud sound that sent pain shooting through Eric's whole body.

Fortunately as Jared's footsteps faded into the background he was left in peace. That lasted a whole minute before his phone went off. *Why couldn't I have just kept the phone on vibrate one time?*

It was a text message from Jake. 'Biz I'm taking your advice and we're drinking here and having a solid time'. He finished reading it and closed his phone. *I'll respond later.* Soon after, another goddamn message sent his phone into a ringing frenzy. It was from Jake again. Before even checking the likely less than important message he set his phone to silent. *If anyone needs me they can chill.*

****

Jake Raley had never been to a strip club. That was mostly because he felt he should never pay for something that was generally easy to get. He didn't think he was necessarily bragging or being arrogant with that mind-set but it was just that he had Kelly and Alison before her.

Lap dances were like hand jobs: teases that rarely went anywhere. Even with that in mind, Jake was ashamed to admit he was completely mesmerized by the blonde woman currently riding the pole on the center stage in front of him. *Those boobs are clearly fake but damn...still nice. Sometimes God needs help with the craftsmanship.*

"I feel like we came in here for a reason" Jake called out to any of the guys that would listen.

"You're looking at it" Will replied while keeping his eyes locked on the girl as she bounced around.

"I meant besides that."

Will had been getting on his nerves all day and even though the woman on the stage was doing her best to smooth things over, it wasn't working.

"There was something on the list we needed" J-Hood interrupted. He too was still looking at the chick up until that point. He pulled out the list and glanced over it while Jake did the same. They looked for one of the few lines that didn't have a check mark next to it. He found it a third of the way down. "We need to get a letter from one of the strippers about why AZXi is the best" J-Hood announced for everyone to hear.

"I nominate J-Hood for that" Jake immediately said while refocusing on the girl who was now sliding on the pole upside down. *I wonder if Kelly could pull that off.* Thinking about her again caused him to miss her even more. He'd talked to her an hour ago and she sounded sad. *She misses me too.*

"Seconded" Summers and Will both said simultaneously in response to Jake's idea. *At least we're all on the same page.* Out of the corner of his eye he saw J-Hood nod before finishing his mixed drink. Jake realized he was nursing his own and followed suit. *Maybe after it settles I'll feel less creepy about staring this girl down.* Will didn't care one way or the other because he was trying to yell things for her to do. Fortunately the song came to a close right when he'd put his last single on the stage at the request of Summers and Will. He'd been entertained so paying a price for it was fair.

They all turned their attention to J-Hood who barked loudly like a dog before getting up and heading over to two strippers standing off to the far side of the bar.

"What's the over-under here?" Will asked the two of them.

"Let's go with a full minute before either one agrees to write the letter," Jake said quickly. *That's about how long it took to get that sorority chick's number so why the hell not?* He smiled. *Why can't pledging be like this all the time?*

"Two minutes" Summers offered.

"No faith in Hood?" Will asked. He sounded a little disconcerted at even the notion of such a thing. *Bill-Butt is clearly in love with J-Hood.*

"Oh I have faith in him that's why it's two, not ten."

Not more than thirty seconds went by before one of the girls, the hotter of the two no less, was writing on a piece of paper J-Hood had given her. As she was writing the other girl continued to have a conversation with him as he turned and looked back at the three of them. All he did was give them a silent nod with no smile in sight.

"All business, all the time" Jake grinned. *We should've timed this.*

"The kid's got moves" Bill-Butt commented with a smile to match Jake's.

"Guess we were way off" Summers said.

"Speak for yourself pal. I gave respect where it was due" Jake replied.

After another minute the one who'd written the letter hugged J-Hood as if he'd been the one that did her a favor and not the other way around. He strolled back over to the table looking as serious as ever. He sat down in his former spot to the left of Jake. He tucked the letter into his pocket and started talking as if nothing had happened.

"What's next?"

They all sat there dumbfounded.

"Just like ten more things I think," Will answered in a somewhat confused way.

"We ready to roll then?" J-Hood asked.

Before anyone could speak a new song kicked up on the center stage as another stripper came out. She was a brunette with absolutely nothing fake about her body. They were all instantly focused on her as she walked out.

"I think we can afford to stay a little longer" Will said absently.

Jake didn't look away and neither did anyone else but he heard their responses.

"Definitely" they all said together.

Chapter 14

Hangovers never bothered Jeff much. That was probably a result of him staying up late past the point of drinking. He'd learned a long time ago that stopping around three or four in the morning and then not passing out until like five or six was beneficial. The result was that his hangover was never at the level it was likely to be for Eric, Jerry or Dylan today. Staying up late was the real trick. He usually gave himself a little bit of an edge by doing a line or two of coke with Dills around eleven or midnight. *Always does the trick.* Today he didn't feel bad at all. He hadn't done coke last night but he was up until five anyways. *Thank God Dana kept me up. Better than listening to Gretman bitch about whatever crisis he dreamt up.* It could've been any number of things. Each would've mattered less to Jeff than the one before it.

He and Dana had slept in until around two when her roommates finally decided they should wake up by giggling and pounding on her door. Dana found it cute. Jeff did not. He'd left shortly thereafter, stopping to get inside Dana one more time before leaving. She was happy with the sex, not so much with the leaving afterward. As of now they were kind of in a 'fight' but Jeff was sure he could fix it if she started responding to his texts at some point.

Jeff had hoped to catch another nap when he got back to the house but there was already a bunch of brothers chilling outside. That meant only one thing: a breakfast was in play. Jared was screaming about something with ABI today as he left with Eric to get the kegs. That poor bastard looked absolutely terrible as they drove off. Biz probably could've slept right through the breakfast had Petey and Kev both not been gone for the day. Petey was with his latest girlfriend and Kevin was visiting home…again.

He'd just started mentally preparing himself to party today when the inevitable knock hit his door. Just like Dana's roommates, the incoming presence was entirely unwelcome. Jeff knew who it was before hearing a voice. Calvin Gretman would never pass up a chance to condescend, especially to him. *You just had to tell him you'd talk today…you did this to yourself.*

"Yeah?" was as warm a greeting as he could provide given the prospect of *another* serious talk with the guy. Calvin walked in and thankfully didn't open with business. Jeff couldn't tell if that pissed him off or not. He'd rather get it over with but at the same time he didn't want to deal with it at all.

"You ready for the breakfast?" Calvin asked happily. It made Jeff sick.

"It's with ABI right?"

"I think so. That'd explain why I heard Jared yelling about it."

"It is the first nice day in a long time."

Jeff noticed it was a lot warmer today than in recent weeks. The snow was almost all gone from just the morning alone. *Leave it to upstate Ohio to be fuckin' freezing one day and have shorts weather the next.*

"It's like sixty-five" Calvin stated as he looked out the window at the brothers on the patio below. Jeff couldn't make out the conversations but he was willing to bet they were better than the one they were having. "So about that talk."

"Jesus this is starting early" Jeff interrupted.

"I know man. I just want to get it out of the way."

"Fine. What's the issue this time?"

"Kevin and Eric…and even Jerry think you're being a little hard on the pledges. We don't want any to de-pledge during week six." *So the rest of the E-Board and even my own goddamn assistant want to come at me together. Gretman probably loves it. Fuckin' guy loves the moral high ground…it's like his second home.*

"They won't de-pledge," he said in the most stoic fashion imaginable.

"I'm not that sure. Biz said Raley was really struggling."

"That kid doesn't have it in him to quit" Jeff said, maintaining his stance. *I don't tell this guy how to run the frat at E-Board meetings so what the fuck?*

"Ripping up their pledge books was one thing but now we've gotta deal with this shit with Raley and Summers and the Trip-E's."

"It's fine. It's not gonna lead back to us. I talked with my friend at the Sheriff's department yesterday."

Calvin looked shocked at the notion that something could've happened without his knowledge but that quickly faded. He must've forgotten that Jeff knew a lot of the local cops since they all drank at the National on Fridays. Last night there was only one topic on his mind and they'd given it to him straight like always.

"I figured as much" Calvin lied to save face. "But they aren't the real issue. That meeting with the Dean on Monday isn't going away."

Jeff had tried and failed several times since Raley and Summers fucked up to calm Gretman's over-working mind. "Nothing is gonna happen dude."

"They could suspend us from taking pledges next semester. Maybe even have the CGA take away our charter altogether."

"For what?! There's no way to prove they were acting for the frat. And they told the cops it was completely voluntary" he shot back with authority. He'd gone over the same line of thought the day after everything happened. It was a mess but there wouldn't be any lasting consequences.

"Still, as the president, I'm the one that's gotta deal with all this shit." Jeff fought not to smirk. *Calvin Gretman sounds bitter about his title for the first time.*

"I'm going with you. It'll be fine."

"Nobody's saying you aren't mad organized with all this. You're hitting all the traditional stuff but something...."

Jeff cut him off. He'd heard quite enough from Gretman over *his* program.

"You know why I'm doing things this way?" he lashed out. He didn't give Calvin time to respond. "It's so when these guys cross, there won't be any question that they didn't earn it." *He has no fucking idea...*

Calvin looked shocked.

"I've seen a lot of pledge programs and I wanted to make sure mine was considered the best, the most organized. For fucks sake, I saw how ridiculous it was when you pledged and that was the first one I saw from the brothers' side. It was so weak compared to mine."

"Dude I think our pledge program was fine..."

"How would you know? You were just a pledge" Jeff interrupted. *I let you talk until the end of time at meetings so you can shut the fuck up now.*

Entering the metallic barn still gave him an eerie feeling. *You're a brother now.* Guapo on the other hand, walked in like he was the ruler of the world. But that was pretty much how he always walked. It's what made him so much fun to hate. Almost everyone in the frat shared the thought and they showed it during pledging last semester.

Jeff and Guapo had pledged with Kevin and they'd crossed in the middle of week six, a few days before the standard pledging time frame ended. That was a point of pride considering most other pledge classes went through the *entire* six weeks. He'd been told by his Big that they'd done so well that they didn't need to go any longer and that was a notion he hoped his own Little would carry when he got one. Although he, Guapo and Kevin weren't allowed to haze the current pledges until week five so getting a Little was still a long way off. *It'll happen one day...*

Based on everything he'd seen Brandon do Jeff was sure these pledges were getting off easy in comparison to his class. The Phi class went through Hell left, right, and center from day one through Crossing. Brandon Sarce was the pledge-master now and he'd been a great assistant pledge-master the semester before. Great was a relative term considering that to be great as assistant was to be the worst hazer in the frat. *Congrats pal, you earned that title.*

He'd learned very quickly that simply being a good assistant pledge-master didn't necessarily make for a good pledge-master. The pledge-master had to run everything smoothly. Once a pledge lost faith in the process or thought it was anything other than perfectly constructed, the picture the brothers wanted to present fell apart. And once it was gone, it couldn't be put back together.

Jeff hadn't really gotten to know either of the two current pledges that well. Because of that he didn't know if their view of the whole thing had shattered or not. *I don't see how it couldn't have. This whole thing is pathetic.* Seeing things from a brother's perspective destroyed the illusion for him and that wasn't just because he was no longer blindfolded at callouts either. Brandon was just incompetent. He was a fun guy and great to party with but he didn't have any organizational skills.

Jeff and the rest of his class were still considered new fucks and had no real authority in the frat. On top of that any criticism they could level at things they didn't like wouldn't be backed up by any experience because they had none. It was frustrating but he didn't know what to do. His big brother agreed that the program was weak but he didn't really care since he was a senior and graduating a semester early. So Jeff had sat by these four weeks and just kept track of the inconsistency in his head since no one else seemed to give a fuck. *If they do they definitely aren't saying a damn thing at meetings.*

Jeff shook the thoughts from his head and focused on the walk inside.

The barn interior had been severely fucked up with all the parties they were throwing. The planks on the floor weren't even level anymore. *This place is on the edge of being flat-out condemned.* That was shocking since AZXi had been located at this address since its founding nine years ago. The barn raising was even a footnote in their history. Moving away from here would've been a huge switch. It didn't matter as much to Jeff personally but the older guys were going nuts over the possibility. The landlord didn't want to sink any more money into it so unless they wanted to fix the shit with money they didn't have they weren't going to have a place to party next year.

Jeff walked inside with Guapo. They were careful of their steps as they did. As expected, the whole place was filled with brothers wearing letters but Brandon was nowhere to be seen. The email of the callout schedule stated they should be good to go as of right now but nothing was happening. *That's typical.* He'd never considered becoming a pledge-master but with every callout he warmed up to the idea even though the job looked and sounded more aggravating than anything else.

"Yo Buttons! Guapo! What's good?" Boo-Yah called from the far corner where he was perched on the wooden bar one of the previous pledge classes had built from scratch. He was always the loudest at every party and usually the most entertaining too. His real name was Ronald Benjamin but everyone called him by his nickname of 'Boo-Yah' since that was what he constantly yelled at people when hammered. His goofy look and beer in hand instantly put a smile on Jeff's face and he forgot any bad feelings he had toward Brandon and the current Chi pledge class.

They walked over to greet him with the standard brotherhood handshake that everyone was taught at Crossing.

The three chatted for a bit before Boo-Yah pounded his beer and went to find a replacement. That left Guapo and him alone in the corner. The rest of the brothers were all talking amongst themselves.

"Looks like he's still not here" Jeff said out loud.

"What time was the callout supposed to start?"

It was already past midnight, which was when the email said to be ready by. Jeff could feel himself getting annoyed but he held it at bay. *Not my problem...*

"Should've started already" Jeff replied with no emotion.

"Weak man. I was tryin' to bang the girl I took to date party this weekend" Guapo announced as if Jeff had given the slightest hint that he cared.

"On a Tuesday night you're gonna bang? Get the fuck out of here."

Getting drunk with questionable girls and hooking up was one thing but practically nothing went on in Gladen Hills on Tuesday nights. That meant the girl wasn't drinking which meant she was fucking his pledge brother of her own non-alcoholic freewill.

"Gotta get with it Buttons. I've got mad game. Yo, but how'd things go with that Sig Lamb the other night?" Guapo had no problem talking about sex every minute of the day. It was a constant driving force in every aspect of his life. *Might as well humor him.*

"I fucked her," Jeff said casually. The whole thing had been awesome but he told himself he wouldn't say anything unless asked. He didn't like going around bragging about that kind of thing. Being unnecessarily vague to someone like Guapo was just the icing on the cake.

"I couldn't get a head's up?" he asked, sounding mildly offended as only he could be in that situation.

"Am I supposed to call you when I get laid?"

"How was it?" His pledge brother was practically drooling.

"It was a good time."

"Man…you always tell the best stories Buttons."

"Well we all can't spell out how and when we fuck."

"I don't like leaving anything to the imagination."

"No shit."

Fortunately Brandon finally entered the barn with an AZXi jersey slung over his shoulder. He was yawning like he'd just woken up. Jeff shook his head.

"OK guys, sorry I'm late. Thanks for waiting. I'm gonna call them in a sec so get ready. I know we were supposed to do the drop-off tonight but I'm gonna cancel that because I don't want to put them through it…and I forgot to ask people to drive" he smirked as he spoke.

Wow. Jeff felt extremely confused because no one was putting up a fight about canceling such a seminal part of pledging. One of his favorite times had been the drop-off. It was sort of miserable at the time sure but it was still good to have the memory. Guapo saw Jeff's discomfort at the news and shot him a look to ease up.

"Tonight's gonna be history intensive instead. Make sure they know the pledge classes. If they don't then stick to giving out push-ups, but not too many. It's only week four, we've still got plenty of time to fuck these guys up" he paused as if unsure about where he was. "…Hey Kraylin! Is the music ready to go?" he shouted toward Jeff's location. He hadn't even noticed that Kraylin was at the platform with the computer that housed their callout play-list. Kraylin gave the thumbs up.

Jeff checked his watch. The callout would be starting twenty minutes after the email had stated. *At least the pledges will never know the difference. I could've sworn a sound system check was the pledge-master's thing. After last weekend I definitely would've looked it over.*

Last night's callout had been cancelled so it really hadn't been run since Saturday. *It did sound a little off then too...I should just check it now.*

Jeff walked over Kraylin and greeted him before checking the wiring to make sure everything was good to go. *Why am I the one dealing with this right now?* If his own pledge-master Randy wasn't studying abroad maybe he could fix all of Brandon's fuck-ups. It stood to reason that he might be able to make a difference since Brandon was his assistant. *By the time Randy gets back it won't matter.*

With only push-ups being given out and "not many" at that? The Chi class might as well have been pledging the Gammas.

After a few more minutes of standing around Brandon finally gave them the head's up that the pledges were outside with his assistant. Jeff wasn't finished checking the wires to make sure they were all connected properly and just as the door opened and the pledges came in he noticed a short in one of them. *Perfect.* He motioned for Kraylin to stop the pledges. Everyone knew the callout play-list was the most important piece of the puzzle because pledging was mostly psychological at its core. Without the music blasting the intimidation wasn't nearly as high and then suddenly the brother greetings could be done easier, in a much lighter atmosphere.

Kraylin was too late. They were already inside. The silence was deafening.

There was no sound other than the pledges footsteps on the crooked planks as the assistant led them in. Brandon had a look of sheer indifference on his face. Jeff frantically tried to get the wires connected. Within a minute he tapped Kraylin to play it from the top. 'Bomb-track' from Rage Against The Machines began blasting at full power out of the various speakers throughout the barn. Now everything felt right.

The pledges began greeting the brothers after the initial scream from the opening chorus and the callout ran as normal. Jeff only hoped that that initial silent entrance hadn't shattered the illusion. If the pledges knew how dysfunctional everything was behind the scenes they might want out to go somewhere nationally recognized.

As he went through his own motions at the callout his thoughts kept coming back to one thing. He tried fighting it because he didn't want the responsibility but he knew he could do a better job than Brandon. Not only a better job, but a damn good one period.

Calvin and Petey still looked the same as they always did at callouts: disheveled, tired and miserable. It was a thing of beauty. They did know their shit and had most of the history memorized even by now in week four. They seemed like cool enough guys, which was basically what he thought at the formal blackball ceremony when they'd decided on what bids to give out. *I'll definitely be able to chill with these two after Crossing.*

****

Calvin listened intently. He knew the story wasn't made up because he remembered that night vividly. It was the first night the music hadn't blasted at the exact time of their entrance. He remembered feeling disoriented. The planks had been real unsteady on the floor and the silence made everything feel surreal.

When Jeff finished talking Calvin was grinning like an idiot at the memory. "I remember that night. We didn't know what the fuck to do. It was just pure silence. The actives weren't even talking."

"That's funny because Brandon didn't know what the fuck to do either. It was his job to check everything. But he overslept past the start time and didn't fucking check on anything. That wasn't even the first time he started late, that was just the first time anything bit him in the ass" Jeff said plainly.

Two and half years later and he's still pissed? He's gonna get an ulcer.

Calvin recalled the election where Jeff had gotten elected pledge-master as kind of a pity vote after everything he'd gone through with the school for AZXi.

A piece of his story finally clicked while he was thinking. "That's why we didn't do the drop-off? My Big told me there was just never a good time." *Why did I ever believe that?*

"Think about that Gretman. The hardest thing about pledging is finding times to schedule callouts when the pledges don't have tests or family shit going on. If we can find time to schedule everything traditional for six or seven person pledge classes then why the fuck couldn't we figure it out for the *two* of you?"

That's a good point. Actually that's a great fuckin' point.

He and Petey didn't even know the drop-off existed until the following semester when they saw the Psi class go through it. He remembered asking his Big about it then. He'd shrugged it off and given that flimsy excuse. *That was probably how he remembered it but Jeff remembers everyone's mistakes.*

"The drop-off is important for bonding because it's just the pledges by themselves. It obviously sucks but it's great to look back on. At least that's how I feel." He sounded sincere in that moment. Some things they put the pledges through were just designed to amuse the brothers but he did agree with Buttons about the drop-off.

"Well it's not like me and Petey are gonna re-pledge just for the drop-off because...fuck that."

"True but you never see stupid shit like that in my program do you?" Jeff asked point blank. Calvin took issue with certain things Jeff was doing but from an organizational standpoint the guy was flawless.

Calvin shook his head. Somehow admitting it out loud was too much.

"I wanted to make sure my pledge class earned their letters. And *no one* will be able to say they didn't. Not when I'm done."

"Yeah but nobody ever gave us shit after we crossed?"

"That's because most of our problems were with Brandon and how fucking terrible he was. It wasn't like you *really* knew what was going on behind the scenes."

Is he asking me or telling me?

"Even with that in mind, when we were drinking some things were definitely said about you two, sometimes even *to* you if you remember."

If anyone would remember that it'd be Jeff.

"The point is what happened when you were pledging wasn't your fault. But you still had to deal with it, maybe not as much but still. A strong pledge-master equals a strong pledge process equals a strong pledge class. Period."

Well he's clearly thought about this a lot.

For the first time in any of their conversations Calvin felt out of his depth. "You earned your spot in the frat. Not necessarily during pledging, but after when you became an active brother. That's why you're president." There was no mistaking the bitterness in his voice at that moment but he went on. "I didn't want these guys to have to earn anything after Crossing. That's why I'm so hard on them. This isn't a power trip. This is a template, maybe *the* template for everything that happens after. And that means a hell of a lot more to me than a couple of you guys thinking it may or may not be the 'right' way to go."

He wants our approval but doesn't care if he gets it.

Arguing about it anymore would just widen the rift between them. And that was the last thing Calvin wanted.

****

Jeff could tell Calvin was deep in thought. He wasn't expecting to lay his soul on the line like he had but it just came out the longer they sat there. The crazy thing had been the fact that Gretman hadn't remembered being hated on for pledging but Jeff remembered it perfectly. There were plenty of times that same semester after they crossed when they'd been out at a bar or in the barn where one of the older guys had given one or both of them shit. The more he thought about it the more it made some kind of sense. Calvin Gretman was one of those people that liked seeing and remembering what he wanted to.

"Alright Buttons...it's your call" he finally agreed.

"Thanks" Jeff said sincerely as he outstretched his hand. Calvin reciprocated and they gave each other the AZXi brother handshake. It had been a while for them.

"Come on, lets get drunk?!" Jeff said quickly trying to channel Jared as best he could. He was in no way ready to sit in an uncomfortable silence with the guy.

"Definitely. Biz and Jared should be back with the keg by now."

They better be back. I definitely need a drink.

Jeff got out of his desk chair and looked out the window just in time to see fifteen ABI's rolling up the driveway with their red and blue jersey's on. It was a small amount when since they had over fifty actives but it was more than Jeff was expecting.

Calvin was standing beside him looking out the window seeing the same thing. "Yeah...today's gonna be a good day."

****

Jake and Summers watched with full attention as J-Hood and Will continued their game of pool ten feet away. It hadn't taken long to find a close bar with a pool table so they could complete another item on the list. Somehow in a matter of eight hours they'd finished practically everything save for a few the sorority girls still had to help with. *Once J-Hood asks them.* Jake wasn't entirely convinced they'd get the list done but as the day wore on it was looking better and better. That allowed him to relax...a little.

Jake had been trying to get past that nightmare with the Trip-E's since it happened but he still had a hard time enjoying himself with something like that hanging over his head. The alcohol they'd been drinking all day certainly helped though.

"You think they'll be pissed?" Jake asked Summers.

"Nah they seem OK," he answered while taking another sip of beer.

J-Hood and Will had volunteered for the task considering he and Summers barely ever played pool.

"I don't know. They might be the kind of guys that'll try to kill us if this all goes the way we want it to."

Summers merely smiled back while drinking some more. "Good thing we aren't the ones playing then."

Jake was confused. "So you wouldn't help them if it came to that?"

"What should I do? Jump in front of the knife they might whip out?"

He's got a point there. I sure as hell wouldn't. Helping in a regular fistfight in a place like Gladen Hills was one thing but they were far from there.

"Point taken" he nodded. "Game's ending...moment of truth." Jake instinctively took a large gulp of his own beer to calm his nerves. He was remarkably on edge for not being directly involved.

J-Hood hit the eight ball into the corner pocket, ending the game. He and Will just stood there unsteadily as they looked at the two larger guys they'd played against. After a few seconds Will waved Summers and Jake over to the table. They went, albeit at a deliberately slow pace.

"What's going on?" Jake asked when they'd reached the table.

"I explained what's going on and they're down to help" Will remarked casually. *Of course they are. And I thought we were gonna fight them...*

"You guys won though right?" Jake asked tentatively.

"Come on Raley, it was me and Hood, of course we won."

Jake quickly got his digital camera out and set the guys up to make it look like they were still playing. Will stood stoically off to the side while J-Hood set up another shot with the eight ball, which they'd apparently stopped from going fully into the pocket. The two guys were good sports about the whole thing because they stood off to the opposite side putting on their best 'pissed off' faces. It was a stretch to get them all in the frame with their facial expressions so he had to cut Will out to make sure the other guy's were prominently shone. He smiled as he moved to cut his pledge brother out of the picture. *One less picture with Bill-Butt could never be a bad thing.*

After he took the picture they shook hands with the guys and bought them beers because J-Hood insisted.

Jake took out the list and crossed off the latest task: 'hustle Canadians in pool'.

"So that just leaves the eight things we'll need the girls for," Jake said triumphantly. It was only around four in the afternoon and they'd gotten practically everything done.

"That leaves us plenty of time to get fucked up" Will said happily.

They'd literally been drinking since waking up and Jake was feeling pretty good about where he stood in that regard but apparently he was the only one.

"I figured you'd had enough" Jake made the mistake of saying out loud.

"I haven't drank for real in five weeks Raley," Will said, almost depressed. "So no, no I haven't had enough."

"Back to the strip club then?" Summers asked happily.

"Let's find another bar to chill at 'til dinner," J-Hood suggested.

"Sounds good, I just gotta finish my drink first," Jake stated to the disgust of Will.

"Jesus you're still nursing that one. What is it your first?"

"Actually it's my third bitch" he lied. It was actually his second but he doubted even Summers would've known that and he was sitting next to him the whole time.

"So are you gonna sack up anytime soon and finish that?"

Jake drank the rest. He hadn't yet mastered the art of drinking from a bottle quickly because of the air bubbles but he finished it anyways. "Happy now?"

Will put his arm around Jake and smiled. "You bet your ass I am."

****

Not even five in the afternoon and Riley looked completely messed up. Tory always found it funny when her friend got so drunk, especially during the day. *This'll be fun to watch.* Tory knew Riley got weirdly competitive while drunk and flip cup was her favorite game.

When it started Riley was still staring off into space thinking about God knows what. She was fourth in line on her team out of five and when it came time for her to compete she slammed the beer in her cup in one gulp and flipped the cup on her first try in perfect rhythm. *Nice Riles.*

Tory grinned from ear to ear. *The poor Tau Chis just got schooled by a team solely of EIPis. Flip cup is a girl's game boys.*

As usual Brian was paying almost no attention to Tory today even after their session last night. That might've been because he was so hammered by the time she got there that he wasn't much good to anyone...especially her. *At least he's always generous when he's that drunk.*

After giving him truly meaningless head for a few minutes she got him to return the favor. There was no way he was getting hard so she didn't really try for him. Having walked all the way down from EIPi to Tau Chi in the middle of the night in between callouts hadn't been for nothing though. He may have been a little sloppy but he was still extremely thorough.

For one of the first times in their 'relationship' she'd been the sole one satisfied. It felt good and because of that she didn't mind being ignored today. If he wanted to get off with her again he'd have to work at it. As of now, she was ahead of him and if they never spoke again the last thing they would've shared was *her* orgasm. *I could live with that.* She took a large sip of her beer and walked over to congratulate her friend on a job well done on the game. "Even during a breakfast you're still playing such a great pledge mom" she quipped.

"What does that even mean?" Riley blinked at her.

"Making the pledges stand around linked in the corner while we get hammered in the middle of the day."

"It's tradition" Riley shrugged it off as she filled her empty cup with more beer from the pitcher that an unfamiliar Tau Chi brought over.

"Yeah maybe during parties, not usually at breakfasts."

Her cup was a little under halfway. "Right. And tell me again what the difference between a breakfast and a party is?" she asked while staring at the amount she'd poured in.

Tory was a little confused about why she'd put so much in. Traditionally, they weren't supposed to be that full for flip cup because it was all about speed. The less full a cup, the less to drink. That meant the quicker to get to the next person in line. She wasn't ashamed to admit she rarely filled her cup up more than a fourth, sometimes even below that. Her Big taught her how to play after she'd joined EIPi. She hadn't done a lot of drinking in high school so there were a lot of gaps in her party knowledge when she got to Gladen Hills.

"Breakfasts are day-drinking affairs, whereas parties are at night," she said confidently after realizing Riley was waiting. She might as well have been rattling off a definition from the Greek Circle handbook...if there had been such a thing.

"Good, so there's no difference. Plus week six is starting...they can deal."

Tory glanced over to the six pledges standing in the corner in their white t-shirts looking miserable. She thought she noticed Brynn glaring at her but she looked away as soon as Tory made eye contact. "Your Little must think you're bipolar."

She knew Riley had taken the girl to get the kegs earlier even though it was technically against the rules. She wasn't going to say anything though. Some of the older girls still held that tradition should never ever be fucked with. *Usually Riles agrees with them.* There were also some of the younger girls like Dani who could go in either direction in terms of tradition, with whether it suited them or not.

"I'm sure Brynn gets it" Riley finally said after realizing the next game wasn't going to start any time soon. She sounded almost too sure. *She must've had a hell of a chat with her Little.*

The 'cleaning' was always one of the worst callouts in terms of how much it affected the pledges. Given how late in the process it took place on top of the big sisters not speaking to their Littles, the ingredients for a disaster were firmly in place. She'd seen a few girls break and de-pledge around now and she'd only been in EIPi for three pledge classes plus her own. Thankfully no one from their pledge class quit. *One of the few that can say that.* Unfortunately her track record with Riley as the pledge moms hadn't been as fortunate. They had de-pledges last semester and this one. *And it's not over yet...*

"Besides" Riley cut in, "I'd gladly take bipolar to the raving maniac they think you are."

Tory grinned. *The worse they hate me, the better I'm doing.* "Thanks!"

"You're doing better than I thought you would."

"No faith in me Riles?"

"Oh trust me, I knew you could be crazy" she smirked, "I just didn't think you'd take it so seriously."

Tory nodded. There were few things in life she took seriously these days and school wasn't among those counted. "I knew it was important to you."

Fortunately the others around them were all involved in their own conversations. Nobody seemed to be paying much attention to them, which was great considering Tory didn't like when people knew she was being serious. *Nobody likes or wants me to be.*

"My God are we having a moment?" Riley asked sarcastically. *Maybe but it's gone now.* Tory grinned back at her.

"Line them up!" she yelled at the table to start the next game. *Classic Riles.*

Eric looks terrible. Calvin was about to say something to that effect when he realized the poor bastard probably just wanted to be left alone.

"So Jer-Bear, who'd you fuck last night?"

Calvin tried to live vicariously through his brothers and their random hook-ups so he could still feel connected. Jared had told them all within minutes of them sitting out front that Jerry had fucked some chick. That was weird in itself since most walks of shame took place between six and ten in the morning. That meant that either they were screwing all morning into the afternoon or there was something semi-serious going on with his brother and whoever the chick was. *Is Jerry in danger of getting wife'd up?* Calvin shook his head. *No shot.*

All he responded with was a smirk and his usual reply. "Don't you worry one bit about that." Jerry Culson was notorious for always being vague about who he was fucking. Calvin couldn't understand why. They didn't need play-by-play details like Guapo too often showered them with but a heads up one way or the other would be fine.

"So clearly the girl was hideous" Jeff instigated from his right.

Normally that would've been the first thought that sprinted to Calvin's mind but Jerry had a solid track record when it came to the girls he hooked up with. Most of them were hot and Jeff would know too which meant he was trying to get more information out of the guy in sheer defense.

Unfortunately Jared either didn't see the merit of that plan or else didn't care because he came to Jerry's defense. "Nah man, she was actually pretty hot."

"I think your definition on what's hot is completely different from everyone else's" Jeff said with a grin as he lit up a cigarette.

"Well I think Jennifer's hot" Jared defended himself and looked toward Calvin.

He just grinned. "Must be a coincidence."

"You think Dana is hot?" Jeff asked point blank.

"She's alright" Jared chuckled to himself as he took a large gulp of his beer to finish it off.

"I would be offended if you didn't think half the St. Gammas were hot."

Well played Buttons. The Sigma Tau Gammas were an interesting bunch in that there were only about ten actives and more than a few were questionable at best. Most frat guys titled them the 'Saint Gammas' as a nickname.

"What?!" Jared laughed. "They could get it for sure." He tried finding a friendly face among them but Calvin's instinctual look at the mention of their name wasn't going to help. Jeff and Jerry looked insanely disgusted at the idea and Eric looked disgusted at life. Jared just laughed even more.

"Was she affiliated?" Calvin asked Jerry, trying to get back on topic.

"Son, don't worry about that," he repeated.

"I really hate when you do that" Eric finally entered the conversation.

Jerry shot an inquisitive look toward his pledge brother. "You know you want to tell us so just get on with it."

"You're absolutely sure about that Biz?"

"One hundred percent" Eric shot back with all the strength he had which wasn't much. He held his ground for a few seconds before retracting it. "Maybe ninety-five."

"So clearly you have no idea" Jerry grinned.

"So what's the deal?" Jeff asked impatiently.

"She wasn't affiliated."

"Oh good that just leaves the other two thousand girls at this school" Calvin said sarcastically. Truthfully if the girl wasn't affiliated with a Greek Circle organization then the chances of any of them knowing her were slim. Suddenly the conversation became less interesting because of that.

Out of the corner of his eye he saw Eric come to life like he'd just discovered the cure for cancer. "I know who it was!"

"I...will...bet" Jerry responded, clearly not worried.

"I'm all in" Eric replied, holding his ground.

"Let's dance then Biz" Jerry kept grinning as he drank some more beer.

Jared still had that same absent look of joy on his face. Jeff just looked bored.

"Let's go with the captain of the field hockey team...for the win," Eric said smugly before leaning back in his chair.

"Well played. How'd you know?"

"I just remembered I wing-manned her for you" Eric replied. *That must've been what he just remembered.*

"You said she wasn't affiliated Jer."

"That question is reserved only for frats and sororities," Jerry replied with unearned confidence. *In this town as long as you're in a frat or on a team, it's the same.*

Jeff seemed to agree. "Bullshit" he called out.

"In this town, sports teams are just as crazy" Calvin added.

"Biz?" Jerry asked, looking for support. He didn't find any.

"I gotta side with these two" Eric said without a shred of remorse.

Jerry sat back in his chair and pounded his beer. "Oh weak" was all he said as he wiped the excess liquid from his mouth. He motioned for Jared to fill him up again.

The pitcher was getting dangerously low. *Why'd we have to send the pledges to Canada. Who's gonna fill up our beers?*

"So how as it bro?" Jared asked as he filled Jerry's cup. Right at the same time as Jerry said not to worry about it for the third time, Eric was mouthing the words off to the left side, doing a spot-on impersonation.

"Jerry can't fuck girls the right way," Jeff added with his trademark disdain.

If only to appease Jeff's apparent lack of interest in the current topic Calvin changed it up. "We got Phi Theta tonight right?" he asked anyone that could answer.

"Talk to Guapo. He's the social. I have no goddamn idea" Jerry replied.

Jeff just nodded because he too didn't have a clue.

"I'm pretty sure you're right," Jared agreed with Calvin.

"Gotta be a home game then" Calvin said. *Damn. A home party at our place means we're gonna have to clean the basement ourselves.* It was always a home game when they partied with the Phi Thetas since they only let the football team or the AK's party at their house. The problem was those guys usually destroyed it to the point where the idea of continuing to party there left a bad taste in the girl's mouths. Calvin had no idea why the cycle continued but he'd heard it was some kind of tradition going back a couple decades where the football team was basically considered another brother fraternity to those girls even though AK technically was their real one. *What a joke.*

"Those girls are all pretty hot though," Jared announced playfully.

"So who do you think is hotter? ABI or Phi Theta?" Calvin asked.

That was a hotly debated topic in AZXi and he loved bringing it up.

****

"ABI is definitely solid but it's gotta be Phi Theta" Eric chimed in with resolve. He was starting to feel a little better. He knew Jake agreed with that too. They tended to agree when it came to women. Except with Kelly who Eric agreed was hot but there wasn't much more he could see in her that his cousin apparently could.

"No way, ABI is much hotter" Jerry shot out with equal resolve. *Yeah well you already banged a few of them so you're biased. Lucky dude.*

"They're both straight" Jared said, walking the middle ground.

"ABI for me" Jeff said abruptly.

Jeff isn't pissed like usual today. Maybe Gretman and him sorted everything out?

Eric turned to Jerry and gave him a playful jab. "You're just saying ABI because none of the Phi Thetas would bang you."

Jerry shot him a grin. *That's what I thought.*

Then Jerry raised his cup for a 'cheers'.

Eric took a sip from his cup on instinct. When the beer hit his tongue he winced in pain. Jerry laughed along with the others.

Well played Jer.

Chapter 15

It had been a downright grueling bunch of hours since dinner and Jake was reeling from the effects of too much to drink. They'd met up with the sorority girls J-Hood had so expertly talked to earlier in the day. The girls had also spent the day drinking. On top of that they were apparently looking for a good time.

J-Hood called the one he'd talked to after dinner at Denny's and the girls suggested they all go to the club nearby both their motels. Of course the girls were staying in the motel across the street from theirs. The rest of his pledge class had called it luck. Jake wasn't as sure. He'd been texting Kelly all night but she'd seemed distant, only responding a few times. He told her he'd call her when the club let out.

Just like the Midway in Gladen Hills, the club was crowded, loud and generally not fun...at least for Jake. There certainly was no room for conversation. *There's no point in going to a place like this unless you're trying to get laid.* Jake had no interest in hooking up with any of these girls. Unfortunately as the night wore on, the line he wasn't supposed to cross was getting hazy.

Jake was never much of a dancer. Even in high school when he'd been in musicals he had to have extra instruction because the concept of rhythm was lost on him. That didn't stop Janelle from trying to dance with him all night.

As soon as they'd gotten to the club he'd found an open spot near the end of the bar and started ordering drinks. J-Hood couldn't be pried away from the girl he'd talked to earlier with a crowbar so he didn't join Jake. Will was too busy trying to catch the scraps from J-Hood's game so that just left him and Summers drinking a beer for the first half hour. *There are worse ways to pass the time.*

After that beer and a couple shots Summers demanded they take, he too left Jake. He didn't even go to chill with the others on the dance floor. He just went his own way and started dancing with some other girl. *Summers has no idea who the fuck she is. Typical Woodworks. Won't see him for the rest of the night.*

Jake wanted to enjoy as peaceful a night as he could in a situation where the music was blasting louder than a callout. For the first hour or so he was sipping his beer and texting Kelly non-stop. After a while though, he noticed Janelle constantly looking over at him.

What's her deal?

He tried not to stare.

She's actually pretty hot.

She finally approached him after the latest song ended and pulled him onto the dance floor. He may have been oblivious to the looks from single girls but Janelle was trying to grind on him like Kelly usually did. He didn't hate it but knew he should.

After one dance he felt sufficiently ashamed so he returned to the bar. Janelle wasn't happy and Will wasn't helping. He kept saying Jake was being a little bitch. All throughout the night it was his default phrase to say whenever he went to the bar to get a drink. It was driving Jake crazy.

It had carried on until the club closed. After a while Summers finally rejoined the rest of the gang on the dance floor and had hit it off with one of Janelle's sisters. In fact, each of the other three girls had paired off with one of his pledge brothers. The irony of the situation wasn't lost on Jake. It would've been the perfect time to call Biz and get his advice but since he hadn't responded earlier he decided against it. *There's probably some stupid-ass AZXi rule about texting pledges when they're in Canada. Or maybe Biz just never got them. I could maybe try calling…it's only two in the morning.*

Jake considered it as the lights came up. When the music started to die down he pulled out his phone and found Eric's name in the contact list. It rang about five times before going to voicemail. *Of course he didn't pick up. I'm about to have a problem and my cousin can't even pick up the damn phone.*

Jake took a deep breath to settle down. *He's probably just hammered or passed out.* Next he tried Riley but also got her voicemail. It was extremely depressing that the two people he needed weren't answering. He put his phone away and hoped one or both would call back soon. *There's no way they'll call back.*

Jake got a wave from J-Hood signaling their exit. He turned back toward the bar and finished the beer he'd bought only ten minutes before. He burped as he got out of the stool to catch up.

Everyone was leaving at that exact moment so he got caught behind a couple other groups. The rest of his group got out well before Jake did. Another two minutes of waiting and finally he was outside in the cool night air. It was a refreshing change from the stagnant heat of the club.

Janelle was waiting for him outside with a smile as he saw the other three pairs were all walking practically in tandem a little ways ahead. *This just keeps getting better and better.* He faked a smile. For the life of him he couldn't tell if he was fine with how everything was going or not, and that terrified him.

She walked slightly ahead of him at a quick pace to catch up with their group. *She's got a great ass...no...no she doesn't.* The idea that she was walking ahead just so he'd notice her definitely crossed his mind. She seemed like that kind of girl. *This whole thing is just some sick joke.*

Jake Raley was in a foreign country with seven other people. Not one of which was in a relationship besides him. Somewhere, somebody was laughing at him.

The latest beer he drank started hitting home and he found himself more and more lost in the ideas floating through his mind.

Then it happened. Exactly what he expected to happen happened.

"So do you guys want to come back to our room and keep drinking?" Adrienne asked from her place next to J-Hood, the spot she hadn't left all night.

Once they got back to their motel room, things were sure to get crazier. *People are gonna start pairing off and disappearing into bathrooms, alleys or cars...*

Reality came back to slap him in the face. "I think I'm out. I'm gonna head back to our room and pass out" Jake said, loud enough so everyone could hear. He did his best not to sound like a buzz-kill but that was surprisingly difficult. *I'm never coming back to this country...ever again.*

"Oh come on, don't leave early" Adrienne said.

He just shrugged back at her as they all continued walking. The motels were in sight now and the sooner he got back the sooner he could call Kelly and end the night.

"Raley if you try to bitch out one more time I might have to kill you" Will said.

Jake internalized his hatred for his pledge brother yet again...for what it was worth. It had been building for over three hours now and he was dangerously close to letting it all out. "Will...just leave me the fuck alone" was all he could say with an even tone. If he kept talking he probably would've started yelling right there on the side of the road. The guy must've read the obvious because he shut right up.

"I'm going back," Jake repeated firmly as they neared the motels. He smiled at everyone but his eyes held on Janelle's for a few seconds. *She looks so hot.* Her brunette hair moved with the soft breeze around them. All Jake could picture was how it would move if they were alone together.

He ignored the thoughts and got a hold of himself, turning to start the walk back to their motel as the sign for it was flickered across the road. That broke his frustration up slightly. *Oh right, we're staying in a cesspool.*

As soon as Jake hit the parking lot he heard the sounds of footsteps behind him. *If this is Will coming to tackle me then he's going to die...right here, right now.*

"I think you should come back with us" Janelle spoke up. Jake turned to see her all but one foot from him. He noticed she'd unzipped her jacket so her cleavage was showing. It immediately took his full attention. He tried not to stare while taking deeper breaths than normal. *Stop staring dumbass.* Fortunately there wasn't much light in the parking lot so she didn't notice his eyes. Jake doubted she'd mind even if she had.

"I just met him and I can definitely tell he's an ass," she added. *She must be talking about Will. Who else could it be?* Any girl that could see through his pledge brother's bullshit was fine by him since her one sister definitely couldn't. The poor girl that Will was with was probably mentally unstable. *She'd have to be to fuck that guy.*

Jake tried to hide the big grin hitting his face in response to her calling Will out. He failed. Before long he looked like a kid on Christmas morning. *Yeah, smile at her...that'll fix everything.* "I can definitely appreciate that" he paused. "I just want to call my girlfriend and get to bed." *Wow I actually do sound like a little bitch. Fuck Will.*

Janelle knew he had a girlfriend but repeating it made him feel better. That was when she hit him with it. "It's not cheating if she doesn't find out."

A guy would have to be blind and deaf to not see what was going on. Since he was neither, his fears...or maybe his hopes were confirmed with those words.

She wants me. My motel room is right there. We can just go there right now...

Time froze.

Jake looked at Janelle and saw how gorgeous she looked with her hair pulled back in a ponytail...her hands on her waist. She was standing there waiting for any kind of sign that she could follow him back to the room.

We could just go and be done before anyone else gets back. Kelly would never find out if only the two of us knew about it.

Janelle moved closer to him as if his silence was consent. Jake couldn't deny that the option was sounding better and better. She was within an inch of him when she reached her hand out to his waist.

In that moment he started picturing Kelly...in constant flashes. He heard Riley say what she would've if she'd been there. *Don't do anything Will says.* Jake remembered her text message from last night.

It hit him. *I don't need to talk to her or Biz...I know what they'd say. I can't do this. What the hell am I thinking?*

"Have a good night Janelle," he said when he finally found his voice.

She looked insulted that he didn't want her but the truth was he did want her...badly. But he couldn't and wouldn't do that to Kelly. *It's not right.* He turned and walked away as quickly as he could before another part of his body did the thinking instead of his head or heart.

After a few feet of walking he turned and saw Janelle storming back across the street. Jake breathed a sigh of relief. He wasn't sure what he'd do if she'd followed him anyways. Once they got within a few feet of the door anything could've gone wrong.

Finally, he reached their room and unlocked the door.

Looking back he saw that Janelle was catching up with the rest of the gang as they entered a room on the second floor. It was good that she was wearing such a bright pink colored jacket. It made it easier to spot her through the darkness. Again his mind shot to the idea of going over there...

Stop fucking thinking about it.

Taking a deep breath he realized he needed to call Kelly immediately if only to hear her voice again. Unlike his cousins she picked up on the second ring, not sounding tired at all. Just hearing her answer the phone made Jake feel better.

They talked for a few minutes before she started yawning and Jake told her she should get to bed.

"I love you."

She said the same and for a second he forgot everything that had happened tonight. *I can't wait to get back to school tomorrow...*

After they hung up his mind went back to across the street just like clockwork. Except now, at least at first, the list was on his mind. *They better get the pictures we need before they start banging.*

He moved toward the door and decided to sit on the bench outside their room to cool off. The night was still nice enough where he could sit without a jacket.

Inevitably his mind wandered over to what was going on across the street. He saw Janelle was sitting outside the girls' room. It looked like she was having a cigarette. Jake couldn't tell if she'd noticed him sitting outside too, looking back at her from across the street.

After a few minutes he noticed two figures leave the motel room and head toward the parking lot. It looked like Summers and the sister he'd paired up with at the club. Jake had heard all their names earlier but had forgotten them now. The two disappeared into a car that Jake assumed belonged to the girls. *I hope it does.*

Janelle finished her cigarette and stood up. It definitely felt like she was looking directly at him. He felt warm despite the cool in the air. After a second, Jake stood up too before moving inside to get to bed.

I need to sleep...this night needs to be over already.

The rest of the night had passed by painfully slow.

Jake had tossed and turned for an hour before finally nodding off. That left him with about three hours total. Under normal circumstances, that amount would've completely fucked him for the rest of the day but for some reason, he felt fine. Maybe it was the adrenaline of wanting to get to the presentation at the house. They all felt really good about their chances for success.

J-Hood was driving Will's car back because he and Summers were passed out in the backseat. *No morning people here.*

Summers had slept in a car with that one chick so that was expected. Will was fucking that other chick all night so he didn't get much sleep either...or so he claimed. How much of that was true was anybody's guess. J-Hood had fucked the hottest one in the bathroom and then gone back to their motel room to get a couple hours sleep. That was all after he'd done work on getting the last bunch of things on the list. They'd gotten pictures of three-way kissing and pictures of sorority girls in bed with each other. The best one was the picture of J-Hood in bed with his girl and Will's at the same time. *It looked legit...I'd buy it.*

Jake couldn't have been happier.

"So we got everything right?" he asked for the tenth time.

J-Hood humored him again by answering. "Relax Raley; the water from the falls we got this morning was the last thing. We're done."

Holy shit...we won't have to clean today. That's epic.

They'd done everything on the list and Jake was just finishing up organizing it on J-Hood's laptop. They'd wanted Jake to bring his own but he'd fought against it. He wasn't convinced it would survive the trip so J-Hood brought his instead. It was virtually the same as Jake's so he had no trouble navigating through all the pictures they uploaded to make a power point.

He put the final photo into place: 'Raley three-way kissing with two girls'. Even he had to admit he couldn't tell the difference from the angle. *Jeff will never know.* He closed the laptop cover and took a deep breath.

"Chill Raley, it's straight" Will suddenly chimed in to try calming his nerves.

Jake was the same kind of nervous before class presentations so it was nothing new. He figured there was no better to way to relax than to screw with Will like he'd done to Jake all night without remorse. "I'll be straight but will you be alright?"

"What does that mean?"

"No condoms or anything Bill-Butt? You're playing with fire."

Will had gotten in the car today and actually bragged about how he'd banged the chick without a condom because she said she was clean. That put a smile on Jake's face first thing in the morning.

"She said she was clean" Will repeated with a smirk. As if that was going to make everything OK. *That's basically like the girl saying she won't get pregnant. How the fuck would you know one way or the other?*

"Oh yeah? The girl you *just* met and banged said she was clean? Yeah...I don't see a single flaw in that" Jake finished with a smile of his own. He didn't want the guy to get AIDS or a child out of the deal but a good case of Syphilis or Chlamydia...that'd be fine by him.

J-Hood chuckled. *At least Hood was smart enough to wrap that shit up before fucking some chick we met in Canada. How is Bill-*

Butt not freaking out right now? He's probably on a first name basis with everyone at student health services by now.

"I can't believe you didn't fuck that girl when she followed you across the street last night Raley" Will said in disgust.

I wouldn't expect you to understand dumbass.

For once, Jake didn't feel combative toward Will. Last night would've felt great in the moment but sitting here in the car today knowing he hadn't betrayed Kelly was worth it. "Some things are more important…" Jake said firmly.

Amazingly, Will didn't say anything more.

"Yo Summers! Wake up!" J-Hood yelled to the only one of them still asleep.

Leave it to Summers to pass out in strange places and then sleep through the next day. He flinched at hearing his name, finally opening his eyes. He grabbed the bag that was sitting right next to him in the back seat. It was full of stuff for the presentation. "I'm ready, let's do this," he said while yawning.

J-Hood turned off at the exit toward Gladen Hills within another minute. That left about ten minutes for everyone to get their game faces on.

How did I get roped into being the speaker for this damn thing? Apparently Jake made an impression as being a clear and loud speaker at the previous presentation so the rest of his class made that decision unanimously. *Lucky me.*

Jake took a deep breath as he looked out the passenger window at the passing farmland. *We're gonna kick ass today…finally.*

****

He'd forgotten the cardinal rule of partying: always stay up past the point of getting hammered and the hangover won't be as bad. *I just went through this yesterday for Christ's sake.* Yet here he was, waking up next to Dana with a throbbing headache. *If this is how Eric felt yesterday how is he still alive?*

Of course there was a reason he'd gotten hammered before going to bed shortly thereafter. And it was almost as traumatic as his hangover at the moment. Jeff shook his head at what he'd seen last night before downing shot after shot. *I've gotta do something about that…but what the fuck is there to do?*

Knowing the problem would keep for another day he pushed the visuals from the Midway aside so he could refocus on what the day had in store. Jeff checked his cell to see there was about twenty minutes until he was due back at the house before the pledge's presentation. *Great. Just fucking great. Not even enough time for morning sex...damn pledges.* After all his talk to Gretman about being organized yesterday there was no way he could be late to his own meeting. *That'd be Brandon Sarce status.*

He got out of bed slowly, which caused his girlfriend to stir. As he pushed off the covers they came away from Dana as well. As expected she wasn't wearing anything. It was all a tease since he couldn't do anything about it. He slipped his pants on and moved around before he could find his shirt. It was in the far corner of the room. *How the fuck did it get way over there?* He assumed they'd had one of their wilder nights since Jeff really didn't remember all that much. *That breakfast really fucked me but at least Dana actually got over whatever she was pissed at me for yesterday.*

After the first hour he started playing beer pong and went on a winning streak with Aaron. He didn't sleep it off before the Phi Thetas came over either. He just went to the National in between and ordered more drinks. He was basically dead by the time the actual party started and Dylan was nowhere to be found. Jared said he went to a girl's lacrosse date party with some chick from his Bio class. With him out of the mix, he didn't do any lines.

Fortunately he did run into Dylan at the Midway later on, which is when all the shots had been taking, causing him to hit blackout status. From what he could remember Dana had finally responded to him around one in the morning and he'd gone back with her shortly after that.

Wow I'm a fucking idiot. Everything he'd done was basically another step in the perfect recipe for a disgusting hangover. Jeff thought he'd been done with these kinds of awful mornings after freshman year. Today would beg to differ with that concept.

"You leaving babe?" Dana asked as she sat up. Her tits were just hanging out and they weren't small. *I'm being tested. Look at that fuckin' body.* Dana always wanted morning sex. There were only a handful of times in their relationship where she didn't.

"Yeah I'm sorry babe. I've gotta take some Advil before this pledge meeting" he said, trying not to sound depressed.

"I thought your pledge meetings weren't 'til six on Sundays?"

Jeff nodded. "Yeah but they need to present the Canada scav list to me and Jerry at the house soon. Their regular meeting is still at six tonight." *Basically my day is shot because of these pledges. Great.* He wanted to go back in time and tell the sophomore version of himself that he was right: being responsible for a group of new fucks *was* actually very annoying just like he'd originally thought.

Dana did not look happy about the updated pledge schedule. *She's probably wet right now too…no…I have to get going…now. Fuck.* If he wanted to keep Gretman off his back and make sure the pledges' illusion stayed intact he'd need to get back.

"I'm sorry" was all he could say. He kissed her quickly so she couldn't try anything to get him to stay. Admittedly that probably wouldn't have taken much, which was all the more reason he hurried through it. He smiled at her on his way to the door. She did the same but he could tell it was half-assed.

As he walked out of her apartment building he started thinking about the items they'd put on the pledges' scav list. *They better have killed it on this one and not gotten arrested or something fucking crazy again.* Jeff had gotten his fill of their stupidity after the Trip-E shit. Thinking about the meeting with the Dean only got him more pissed.

When he reached the house he was nearly fuming mad. He tried keeping it under control but couldn't. Ironically the one thing that would've calmed him was staying with Dana. *That's not gonna happen.*

Now it was just him and the pledges.

****

J-Hood's laptop didn't have that big of a screen but it worked. The common room on the right side of the house wasn't huge so everyone should've been able to see. There weren't any other brothers around for the presentation. It was eight in the morning on a Sunday so it wasn't unexpected.

Jerry sat on the couch looking miserable. Jake internalized a smile at the thought that he was uncomfortable and probably in pain from drinking last night. *I hope you're in so much pain buddy.*

Jeff trudged in from the outer door two minutes before eight AM. *I should tell him he's early. He should give me some fucking push-ups for screwing up so badly.* Jake stopped himself from smiling again. He couldn't imagine saying that would go over well with Jerry or Jeff…or his pledge brothers.

There was no denying that with everything in order and only these two fucks to present to, Jake felt amazing. He'd love to see them try fucking them over on any of the items on the list. Everything was flawless and in perfect order.

He couldn't wait to be sent home *without* having to clean the house.

Of course it didn't go the way it had in Jake's head. It never did.

I did it again...I forgot the first fucking rule of pledging. Fuck my life.

Jeff and Jerry had torn apart a third of their presentation saying the pictures weren't good enough. *What a joke.* As soon as they'd gotten to the fifth picture it was clear that Jeff was pissed and they were fucked. Jake's presentation skills started suffering as a result. With every item they didn't count, he got more and more depressed. By the end he was just plain angry. The whole thing had been a train wreck from start to finish. Whatever Jeff was pissed about, Jake hoped it was serious. *I hope you're pissed about it all fuckin' day you jackass.*

When it was through they were in a very familiar position. In push-up stance on the floor in the kitchen where there was enough room. "After you count out these hundred as one you'll make this house look so damn spotless that I could eat off the floor if I wanted" Jeff screamed. Jake only hoped that his yelling was waking up other brothers. *I hope somebody beats his ass.*

All four Alpha Epsilons yelled back with a loud "Yes sir!"

If Jeff's yelling hadn't woken anybody up then their response definitely should have. *Unless you're in a coma you aren't gonna sleep through that.* Jake smiled at the floor as they counted through the assigned push-ups. *At least this is it. The final week.*

****

He'd never admit it to the pledges but the rest of the brothers would definitely be told what a phenomenal job they'd done on the Canada list. *Much better than the first list.* One thing he'd never admit to anyone was that they'd actually made him forget how pissed he'd been. There was a picture of Bill-Butt giving the Mounty a blowjob and then another of him smoking a cigarette next to the thing. It was all he could to not laugh with them right then and there. Jerry was having just as tough a time. The other ones of Raley chasing his Triple-X beer with Gatorade were priceless. *That's going in the history immediately.* Jeff was even considering wallpapering the house with them.

Jeff smiled while the pledges counted out their push-ups. *This is what it's all about. The pledges bond, the actives are entertained.* He only wished more of the brothers had seen what they'd done. *They will eventually.* Fortunately, Raley had put it all into a power point presentation that Jeff had told him to email out immediately.

He did think something would get lost in the mix though since the kid wouldn't be presenting it personally. It was the other actives' loss. He'd definitely enjoyed it. From the quick look Jerry had given him, he thought the same. Of course the pledges all thought they'd fucked up. *Just like it should be.* Truthfully they probably could've been given a pass on everything but there was no way they were getting off that easy. The house hadn't been cleaned since Friday. That couldn't and wouldn't be allowed to continue. *Not while they're still pledging.*

There'd be plenty of time for the actives to clean after Crossing. Jeff shrugged away that thought immediately. He hated clean teams and fixing a night's worth of partying. *We'll have to do it eventually. Fuck.*

He watched the Alpha Epsilons count out the push-ups in perfect unison. He had no doubt these kids would finish his program strong, and soon. *I'll make sure they do.*

Chapter 16

The Gladen Hills union building had a wide-open entrance showing the balconies of the second and third floors with wide, winding staircases going down to the lower two levels. Flags from several different countries were displayed proudly throughout the lobby level. They were hung from the ceiling but since the first floor entrance allowed for viewing all the way up they were always visible. The entire front of the building was made of slightly tinted plate glass so any student could see inside on the way to class.

Unfortunately, Calvin wasn't visiting the union for flag viewing or even to get a small respite from the cool breeze blowing outside. Today was the day of their meeting with the Dean of Students. *You just had to run for AZXi president didn't you?*

It was the Monday after two of the pledges fucked up the regular scavenger hunt. Since that fateful moment, he'd been dreading this meeting. If he'd been a lucky AZXi president, he would've never had to meet with the Dean at all. But Calvin was unlucky, so the bastard was practically on a first name basis with him although he still had to call him 'Dean'. *This is why I don't play poker.*

Today was the second time he'd had to meet with the guy during this school year. And today promised to be the worse of the two visits. Jeff had said time and again that it wouldn't be a big deal but Calvin had a very bad feeling about the whole thing. If he'd had his way, he'd have met with the Dean on his own but the bastard was smart. He demanded to meet with both the president *and* pledge-master. That meant Buttons was coming along for the ride no matter what. *At least he wasn't smart enough to meet with us separately…who knows what the fuck Jeff would do alone in a room with that guy.* Calvin didn't think it was out of the question for him to throw a punch after everything that happened during their sophomore year. It was clear that that specific timeframe was on Jeff's mind as he sat there next to him practically seething in the leather chairs in the Dean's outer office.

His secretary was typing on the computer nonstop. *Probably writing up a form letter expelling or suspending someone. The Dean will sign and never give it a second thought.* It was no secret that in the recent years, the Gladen Hills administration legitimately believed it was better than pretty much every other school in Ohio. That meant their admissions standards had gone up. *I doubt I'd even be able to get into this school these days.* With the increasing standards came the desire to remove certain 'older' elements. Frats and sororities were relics of a time when the school was renowned for being fun as well as a great school. That time was reaching its end. Expelling or suspending students for what Calvin considered minor mistakes was how the school was 'cleaning' itself up to allow for what they considered 'more appropriate' kids.

One thing that was constantly on his mind recently was if AZXi or *any* organization like theirs could survive without going through some drastic changes. He was fortunate to have had a great experience here with no real problems…save today. *Are the younger actives gonna get the same experience?*

"I'm surprised you didn't want Eric or Kevin here for this" Jeff said quietly enough not to bother the secretary. She hadn't paid much attention to them since they'd arrived twenty minutes ago. Calvin assumed she knew why they were here and because of that, they weren't treated with much respect. *Even dressing up in khaki's with shirts and ties…we're still frat guys to the people around here.* Most adults at the school could just tell if a student was affiliated or not. With or without letters, they generally carried themselves differently. That was what he'd been told by one of his professors who'd been in a frat here himself years ago. Calvin wasn't ashamed to be in AZXi, even at times like these. *It'd be great if we weren't labeled right away though.*

He realized he hadn't responded to Jeff's remark yet. "They both have tests tomorrow so I figured I'd let them have one less thing to worry about."

"So they're where they usually are: in the library" he replied with a smirk. Calvin winced. *He thinks this is all gonna be fine otherwise he wouldn't say a word. Fuck.*

"More than likely."

"So what's the plan here?"

At least he remembers that this is my show. That's something.

"I know you hate the guy so your job is to only talk if he talks to you. And even then, keep it short" he said succinctly.

"No faith in me, Gretman?"

"When it comes to you and the Dean? Not a chance in Hell." He tried keeping his voice low enough not to attract notice. Fortunately whatever was coming out of the printer was making a fair amount of noise to cover up their talk. The outer office was about three times the size of the AZXi common area on his side of the house so they were also a good distance removed.

"So why am I here then?" Jeff asked impatiently.

Believe me it wasn't by my choice pal.

"He wanted to see the president *and* the pledge-master which means me and you are stuck here together. Believe me I wish it wasn't the case." *Just keep pushing him you dumbass.* Fortunately Jeff didn't take it all that seriously…probably because he agreed.

"I'd rather be studying for a physics test with Eric in the library right now."

"You aren't the only one" Calvin agreed.

They neared the half hour mark of just sitting in the outer office and Calvin's nerves started to fray. "If this guy wasn't such an ass then waiting forever out here wouldn't be such an issue" Jeff whispered.

Calvin wouldn't have put it past the Dean to keep them waiting so long out of sheer spite. But there could've also been another part to the plan. The longer they sat, the more nervous they'd become.

"You think it also might have something to do with the fact that you aren't graduating on time with the rest of us?"

"It might" Jeff replied gruffly before looking away to stare at the wall.

"I know man. I'd be pissed too." Calvin wasn't even sure he would've come back to Gladen after being suspended for a year like Jeff. It was something he'd thought about a lot after it happened.

"You have no fucking idea. The bastard *enjoyed* telling me I wasn't allowed back here for a year."

Calvin didn't appreciate the venue for Jeff's honesty but it was always interesting hearing his uncensored thoughts. Jeff never talked about what went down. Not when it happened and not when he came back. And every brother knew not to ask.

"Well we already knew the guy isn't a big fan of frats," Calvin said tentatively. He wasn't sure how far the conversation would or even should go right now.

"No shit" he paused. "And I had to deal with it...for the frat." There wasn't anger in Jeff's voice now, only regret.

"Anyone who was there respects the hell out of you for what you did."

The problem was that most brothers who were around then weren't around anymore. And since Jeff never talked about it, most people didn't have a clue about what *really* happened.

"That didn't make explaining it to my parents any easier" he choked out.

I don't know how I'd even have that conversation...

They sat in silence for a few minutes after that. Calvin was thankful. They needed time to regroup. As they were reaching the forty-minute mark the secretary finally spoke up as if she'd just remembered they'd been sitting there.

"Boys, the Dean can see you now."

****

There wasn't a sound to be heard on the third floor of Cordan library; just the way Eric liked it. There was a reason he was always in the library during the week instead of at the house. AZXi always had some kind of event going on throughout the day and into the night whereas the third and fourth floors of Cordan were reserved for 'quiet study'. Most of the time, no one even talked up here. When Eric was staring down the barrel of two chapters in his advanced chemistry textbook, zero talk was a necessity.

Jerry had similar views because there he sat, across the table from Eric. They weren't speaking or even working on the same thing but he'd rather have Jerry sit at the same table with him than anyone else. There weren't enough tables for everyone to sit alone so sharing with his pledge brother was preferable.

It was later in the day and his lab had gone longer than normal so he hadn't gotten to library until after five. Jerry had already been there for what looked like a couple hours. After a few more minutes he nodded at Eric and made his way over to the bathroom twenty feet away on the other side of the stacks.

Eric leaned back in his chair and outstretched his arms to unwind a little before pressing on. As he lowered his arms he heard a weird noise. He looked to his left and then his right before spotting his cousin cowering behind a bookshelf in the opposite direction of where Jerry had gone. *How long was he just standing there waiting for Jer to leave? Probably too long.* He nodded at Jake and motioned for him to follow downstairs to the first floor where talking wouldn't annoy anyone.

Jake did as silently instructed and followed right along.

Once they made it to the first floor foyer Eric moved over to an alcove in the back where they wouldn't be noticed by anyone walking into Cordan. Seeing any other AZXis here on a Monday would be a real stretch but he didn't want to take any chances. He knew Jake wasn't supposed to be here right now. After six in the afternoon the pledges were all supposed to be in the basement for their library hours. Even having Jerry see one of them out of the basement between six and nine would likely make their next callout far worse.

"Why are you up here and not downstairs?"

"I would be if I hadn't just finished hanging out with Kelly" Jake grinned.

"If any brothers see you walking around here, you're gonna be fucked."

"Good thing I stopped giving a fuck then" Jake said proudly.

At least he's not freaking out. "Dude you're almost there, don't go off the deep end now."

"Going off the deep end sailed when I took the bid Biz. Now I'm just on cruise control, trying to get through it all."

Eric sighed. He'd been worried his cousin might quit after the pledge books were torn up. Jake had never said anything to him personally but he could see a look in his eyes that night at the last Raley's Ring party. *Something wasn't right.* Riley had told him Jake needed help but wouldn't go into detail. It wasn't surprising but if Jake had quit when Eric could've stopped him then he would've been real upset...at both his cousins.

"I knew you weren't gonna quit" Eric lied. He always thought his cousin could get through pledging but it was on him to see that in himself.

The formal blackball for the Alpha Epsilon class had been interesting to say the least. Most of Jake's bid had hinged on Eric. He'd taken a chance that Jake was strong enough to see he could do it. He doubted he'd ever tell Jake that. He hadn't even told Riley as much and none of the actives were dumb enough to say anything either.

"You're sure about that?"

"Well I hoped you wouldn't" Eric corrected himself.

Jake smiled. "I appreciate the faith."

"So what's up?" he asked, trying to find the root of Jake's visit.

"Hadn't talked to you in a while, wanted to see what was good."

Probably because I didn't respond to those calls or texts from Canada. Eric hadn't ignored them on purpose. Saturday was just a long, rough day.

"You hear about the second presentation? I haven't talked to Jared yet."

"The Canada list? Yeah I heard" Eric replied, being deliberately vague.

"And?" Jake asked, sounding a little pathetic.

Might as well throw him a bone. It couldn't hurt.

"You guys did a great job from what I heard" Eric said with a straight face. The news lit up Jake's though.

"You don't seem to be getting the point of all this," Eric continued promptly after letting him have a second of victory. "Doing anything right in pledging is completely out of the question. Everyone goes through this semester after semester. We weren't gonna let you guys have a free ride to Crossing. Jerry and I went through this same shit."

"We did the paddle right," Jake answered casually, still smiling.

Jeff had thrown out the term 'acceptable' when he'd been presented with their pledge class paddle. Eric more than agreed with that description but thought Jeff was being overly kind.

"Besides that, when's the last time before or after the paddle that you got even a hint you were doing well?" Eric didn't even give Jake time to respond. "Exactly" was all he said into the second's worth of silence.

"At least give me time to think!"

Eric smiled at him. "I could give you all night. It wouldn't change the outcome. It is what it is J."

"Fuck that…it just makes me hate Jeff and Jerry even more."

"You knew what you signed up for."

"That's not even close to being true. I literally had no idea what I was signing up for. You knew…and you know me…" Jake tensed up.

"You're right and that's why you're still here. It's just one more week."

Pledge classes never go past six weeks. At least not in over five years.

His cousin wasn't convinced but there wasn't much more Eric could say. He certainly wasn't going to let him see the callout schedule for the week.

Eric assumed he'd just gotten through banging his girlfriend so the fact that he was still stressed boggled the mind. But that was how his younger cousin always was.

"Alright I'll head back down. Thanks Biz."

Eric nodded before slapping up his hand, being careful not to give him the AZXi shake…not yet at least.

****

"Alright gentlemen, tell me what happened" the Dean calmly ordered from behind his massive desk. Calvin had walked into the office first because he didn't want Jeff's face to be the first thing the bastard saw.

He'd greeted them with a pleasant enough smile as they sat down in the two available chairs opposite his. Past the desk and the Dean was a gigantic window that looked down on the parking loop. Fortunately it wasn't too late so there was still some sunlight filtering inside. That was fine by Calvin since the meeting was ominous enough without adding darkness to the mix.

"Well sir, as I'm sure you know, some of our pledges were caught playing a prank on one of the sororities." The Dean showed no emotion so he continued. "I'm also sure you're aware they were not acting for AZXi," Calvin finished confidently.

"And I'm sure you're aware that I don't really believe that" Dean Standor interrupted his train of thought right then and there.

Calvin felt a chill go up his spine. "Sir?"

Out of the corner of his eye Calvin saw Jeff shifting in his chair to the left. It was very subtle. *Yeah Buttons, I heard him too.*

"You know my feelings about hazing Mr. Gretman and if you don't, let me refresh your memory. I find it immoral. I have zero tolerance for it. There is no place for something so juvenile at Gladen Hills."

Well we certainly can't have anything 'juvenile' at a school now can we?

There was no question now; the Dean was throwing out veiled threats. That was a problem for Calvin so he could only imagine what was going on in Jeff's mind.

"Yes sir" was all he could think to say.

"Unfortunately" Dean Standor went on. "Since neither of your pledges will confirm that it was in fact part of your hazing 'pledge' process, there isn't a whole lot I can do."

Don't sound too disappointed fucker. Calvin remained stoic while looking the Dean right in the eye.

"Hazing will not be tolerated at this school...or any other school. This is the twenty-first century boys; we aren't living in the nineties anymore. But I can't prove anything without someone willing to come forward. And since Mr. Raley and Mr. Summers don't seem apt to help me I'm at a loss. However, being Dean still affords me certain powers."

The pause between the Dean's statements made Calvin's blood run cold.

"I want your pledges initiated and listed on your chapter roster by the end of the day. Give it to my secretary tomorrow morning. Alpha Zeta Xi pledging stops right now." He didn't even try to hide a threatening tone that time.

They aren't ready. Not yet. Calvin's mind whirled. *There's no way around this? He's ordering us to cross the pledges early.*

Dean Standor was making it abundantly clear that from now on he'd be watching them closely. For the first time in his life, Calvin was silently thankful he was graduating soon and wouldn't have to deal with any possible repercussions. He shut the thought out in shame as quickly as it had come in.

"You can't do that," Jeff argued in hushed tones.

"The Gladen Hills administration disagrees with you Mr. Chester."

"Sir I think that..." Calvin started in to take the focus off Jeff.

"This school sanctions Alpha Zeta Xi's ability to exist Mr. Gretman. As such, we can tell you, if we deem it necessary, to initiate your pledges whenever we want. That's why pledging will never go past six weeks. And even though six weeks haven't yet passed, given recent events, I think you can *both* agree that these actions are warranted."

Calvin noticed the Dean's eyes shift from him over to Jeff when he used the word "both" as though tempting him to speak out again.

Is he really trying to fuck with Buttons right now?

There was nothing left to do but signal defeat. Dean Standor was standing on the high ground with no weak spot in sight. *Jeff's gonna be pissed but what am I supposed to do? Arguing with this bastard will just put us in deeper shit. There still needs to be a frat left when we graduate Buttons.*

"I think that's reasonable sir" Calvin said solemnly. He tried hiding his defeatist tone but it wasn't working. He could almost feel Jeff fuming in the chair next to him.

Dean Standor nodded. "Good. Anything to add Mr. Chester?"

There seemed to be an insanely long pause in the time between the Dean's question and glare to Jeff's response. At least it seemed that way for Calvin.

He imagined all the different ways Jeff could start fucking AZXi with his rage. *He could just stand up and punch this guy...that'd be sick...for a second. Then it would really suck for the rest of his life. He might just start swearing and tell the guy off... which would basically have the same result. Except it'd be a little less awesome.*

I'd pay to see either of those things right about now...

"I didn't feel it was my place to add anything," Jeff said calmly, maintaining eye contact with the Dean as he spoke. Of all the scenarios currently whirling around Calvin's head, that one didn't even make the top five.

"Mr. Chester...given your past circumstances, maybe you even more than Mr. Gretman should have something to add here."

Calvin realized just how fuckin' annoying it was that he kept referring to him as 'Mr. Gretman'. *I'm only twenty-one and I still go to school here. I'm not 'Mr. Gretman' yet.* It was almost offensive. He didn't want to be an adult, not yet at least. Suddenly the thought of wanting to graduate just so he wouldn't have to deal with the Dean's shit next year was sickening.

"I'd like to leave the past out of this if you don't mind" Jeff replied with a lack of emotion. Calvin wasn't sure how much more he could take before his brother's clear head ran screaming from the room.

"Given what transpired between you and the school, I think the punishment was more than fair. I hope you agree," Dean Standor finished, purposefully leaving the statement open-ended. *Don't take the bait Buttons. Don't do it.*

"I'm just happy it's over" Jeff choked out after a few seconds.

"I believe we understand what we need to do sir" Calvin stepped in, if only to stop the river of shit the Dean was currently sending at Jeff.

Dean Standor looked shaken that the second student sitting in his office had spoken while he was addressing the first. *Like I was going to just sit here while you fuck with my brother from your high horse with your thoughts on morals.*

"Good" Dean Standor finally said, resuming his earlier posture. "I'll expect your chapter roster on my desk tomorrow morning then. Have a good evening." He smiled thinly at them as he finished speaking.

"Thank you sir" Calvin said as politely as he could before turning and leading the way out of that god-forsaken office. Jeff followed right behind.

Calvin noticed, as he was sure the Dean had, that Jeff didn't say thank you or even goodbye as they left. It wasn't unexpected but he would've liked to see his brother kill the fucker with kindness as much as possible. *That would've driven the guy crazy. He thinks he's so above us all with everything we do.*

The world probably looked so clear to Dean Standor, sitting in that third floor office with a great view of University Grove and the Northwest dorms.

Gladen Hills at your feet...all those students to expel and so little time.

****

He kept his mind firmly focused as they exited the outer office.

Once they were in the union's halls, Jeff b-lined it for the nearest bathroom. Calvin followed, probably out of sheer curiosity, or just to make sure he didn't outright kill an innocent bystander. It was about thirty feet away from the Dean's office. Neither of them spoke on their way to it. Jeff forcefully pushed open the door, praying no one else was inside.

The bathroom was tiled, likely reinforced with cement. Jeff decided against punching a hole in the wall because of his anger, but only because his hand would get fucked up. He headed to the sink and splashed cold water on his face three times to see if that would calm him down. He was settling slightly when Calvin made it inside. His face was solemn and he didn't say a word.

"I can't believe you thanked that bastard for pissing on us...again" he bit out with enough contempt to keep even Gretman's condescension at bay.

"Dude it wasn't like I could tell him to go fuck himself even though I wanted to" Calvin replied.

Jeff cracked an unintentional smile. "You bet your ass you could have." *God damn the look on that fucker's face would've been so priceless if Gretman had the balls to say that. Oh well. Standor probably got balled from every frat at college. That's why he hates us all now. Fuck him.* That was too perfect a reason so Jeff doubted it was true. Some people just liked flexing their power even if no one was being hurt in the processes they were dead-set on disbanding. Dean Standor seemed to be one of those people.

"Well I'd like to keep the frat *out* of trouble, so I figured bending over was the best strategy."

It made sense but Jeff still wasn't thrilled with the idea of the guy fucking them again on what Standor considered to be the moral high ground. "I know I know," he said instinctually. He didn't mean to agree out loud but his emotions were still running high. He slammed his hands down on the sink counter. "I just wanted to jack that fucker in the face..." he lost his voice mid-way through as he shook with fury.

"You weren't the only one Buttons."

It hadn't gone unnoticed to Jeff that Calvin had stepped in for him during their meeting. Jeff wasn't sure what he would've done if that conversation had continued. *I might've gotten expelled completely this time. No warnings, no suspensions, just gone.* He would've lost everything: Dana, AZXi, his degree...all of it. For that he was thankful that Gretman had stepped in, whatever his motives were.

The two forms of punishment being decided on in the wake of his 'infraction' sophomore year were expulsion and suspension. Thankfully the Dean was just one vote of seven on the administrative board back then. It wouldn't have surprised Jeff one bit if the guy had voted for expelling him. Unfortunately, the administrative board didn't vote on student punishments anymore. Now the buck stopped at Standor.

Jeff looked at himself in the mirror. He wasn't proud of the reflection. There was an inconsolable rage in his eyes that wouldn't go away.

Even recently, Jeff couldn't figure out why he was always so mad every single day. But today's anger eclipsed all other times. It all led back to sophomore year when his life had been put on hold. *I'd be graduating this semester...I wouldn't have missed the senior year of all the older actives that rushed me to pledge AZXi.* Those were memories Jeff was never going to experience and it was killing him even more now with his original graduation date coming.

He grabbed some paper towels and dried off his face before walking out of the bathroom with Gretman close behind.

"So what're you gonna do about the pledges?"

"Guess we'll have to talk to the guys about that because I have an idea. Let's get a drink."

****

It was a little cold out but it wasn't nearly as bad as it had been. Jake was walking back to Cordan after his time in the quad nearby. He should've still been in AZXi library hours but he didn't like the idea of returning to that same table he'd been sitting at for five weeks straight so soon. He needed some fresh air first.

The six double doors making up the main entrance were all made of plate glass and they were always unlocked until two in the morning. Jake couldn't imagine anybody needing to study at one or two in the morning. *Not even Biz is that dedicated.*

Jake was happy he'd gotten a chance to talk to him, if even for a few minutes. It was also great to hear that they'd done well on the Canada list. He'd suspected as much but getting confirmation still felt good. *Just one more week.*

His pledge brothers were sitting in the same room they'd taken control of on the first week of pledging. It was off to the far right side of the basement. They could do whatever they wanted without really bothering anyone. It had its own standalone computer and a projector hooked up to a large white screen on the right wall. It was the perfect spot for them to question their recent life choices in peace.

Will was on the computer while J-Hood and Summers were working on their laptops. J-Hood was typing up what looked to be a paper while Summers was watching a show. *Some things never change.*

"What's up boys?" Jake asked happily as he entered the room. Having just gotten inside Kelly about twenty minutes before, he was as content as he could be.

"Where you been?" Will asked immediately.

The mantle of responsibility didn't look good on Bill-Butt. In fact Jake found it laughable. *Who died and made you Jeff Chester?*

"Just living life man," Jake answered as he sat at the same narrow table as the other two. He lifted up his backpack and took out a notebook. The silence coming from his pledge brothers was deafening. "I was with Kelly and Eric."

They all looked confused bordering on disgusted.

"What!? Not at the same time. I swung by the third floor after I hung out with Kelly. I saw Eric and said hey" he lied. He'd practically scoured the top floors of Cordan before finding his cousin.

"We're lucky none of the brothers came by to check on us," J-Hood said coolly.

The last time one of the actives had swung by was last week so they were due for a check-in at some point soon.

"What more could they do to us?" *Even if they had shown up it would've only meant a few more push-ups at the next callout. After the first hundred who really cares?*

"Since when are you so damn laid back?" Summers asked.

"Since I realized the end is here and we can't do anything right so why bother?"

"Word" J-Hood said before returning to his work. Summers hadn't even waited for Jake to respond before he'd put his headphones back on.

"If it makes Raley easier to deal with for this week then I'm all for it" Will announced as he shut off the main computer and joined them all at the table.

"Glad you're on board" Jake said sarcastically. He wanted to make it clear that he couldn't give a fuck if Will supported his thoughts or not since he was still not happy about Saturday night in Canada.

"Does this mean you've given up studying your pledge book too?"

"Is there some particular reason why I shouldn't?" Jake asked with an edge.

Will looked to J-Hood and then back to Jake.

"I was talking to Petey yesterday, when Jeff was blasted Saturday he was saying some things." That got Jake's attention. "He said as long as at least two of us knew the AZXi credo, we could cross earlier."

If that was even remotely true then it sounded great.

Jeff could've been lying at the time or just too fucked up to know the difference. Petey could be fucking with Will hoping we'd waste our time memorizing more shit in our pledge books. Will could just be trying to fuck with me too.

"And you believed that?" Jake asked tentatively.

"Petey was black-out when I talked to him so I don't think he meant to tell me. Besides he doesn't fuck with me, he's my Big."

That still doesn't make it true. "Petey was the pledge-master last semester, Jeff was his assistant; this is definitely up his alley. And when the heck was he so blasted that you got this out of him?"

"Some brothers were having a Sunday-Funday yesterday after we got back."

"Of course they were" Jake rolled his eyes.

"Could it really hurt for you and Hood to memorize the damn thing?"

Jake had already resolved not to study any more of his pledge book. *We're gonna cross by the end of the week so what the fuck does it matter? But what if it's true? Even having one less day of Jeff being a general ass...memorizing the credo could be worth it.*

"Why don't you do it if you're so sure it's for real?"

Will shrugged before answering. "You know I hate giving you credit for anything Raley" he began. *That's for damn sure.* "But you remember shit the fastest so can you take care of this?"

It nearly sounded like begging. It felt refreshing.

"It'd be such a pain in the ass," Jake groaned with a smile.

"And?"

"You're right" Jake nodded. "I deal with you on a regular basis. How hard could this be?" It wasn't as much of a joke in his head.

He pulled the pledge book out of his backpack and unwrapped it from the black t-shirt it was in. Turning to the credo in the back, he looked it over. He'd read it before briefly but it never registered.

Looking over the page long AZXi credo, Jake decided to put his faith in Will's story. *We'll be done pledging by the end of the week. If I can speed it up I will...*

Chapter 17

It was amazing how fast things could change around here. That was true anywhere but in Gladen Hills things were always in a state of flux. When Jeff and Calvin sat Jerry and him down (absent Kevin who wasn't answering his phone), he'd been happy. Buttons said they were ordered by the Dean to cross the pledges immediately and list them on the chapter roster by tomorrow morning.

Aside from the fact that they wouldn't be able to throw a legitimate Crossing party on such short notice, it was actually a good thing. It meant his cousin Jake and his friend Will would become brothers of AZXi. Yet Eric was watching all that slip away.

"So you want to underground the pledges?" Eric asked unsurely. He was certain that was what Buttons said but he wanted to make sure that he was absolutely serious about such a ridiculous plan.

Calvin was remarkably silent. Eric would've expected him to make the arguments he was being forced to make right now. *Was the meeting with the Dean that bad? Good God.*

"Basically, yeah" Jeff replied casually.

How does he not see that this is a big deal?

"I don't know man…this isn't smart."

"How is anyone gonna know the fuckin' difference?" Jeff shot back. *And there's the Jeff Chester I've seen all semester.*

"Look I'm just saying…would it really be so bad to cross them early?" *It's less of a gamble than what you're proposing.*

"Would *you* want to cross on a Monday night? I doubt it. What is there to do on a Monday night around here? Nothing. We were just at the National and it was dead. Plus there's no way we'll get every brother down here for an unscheduled event. It's just not going to happen." *OK true.* It was hard enough getting all the brothers to show up for a scheduled event let alone one put together at the last second.

"We could just do the same thing we do almost every night. Get wasted" Calvin interrupted diplomatically.

"You and I both know there are less people to do that with on a Monday of all goddamn days" Jeff responded in his usual gruff tone. Calvin just nodded in concession before Jeff turned his attention to Eric and Jerry. "Look, I've been told by certain people, namely Gretman, that my unilateral decisions are pissing people off. I don't give a fuck about that so much but I think this more than anything else affects the frat. So I'm open to *real* suggestions if anyone has any."

Eric doubted that he was actually serious. It was more likely he was trying to save face. He'd run the whole program without so much as a word from any brother and now he wanted suggestions? Eric wasn't buying it but he kept quiet. Even the appearance of Jeff trying to get along was good enough…for now.

"OK but you obviously don't want them to cross early" Jerry interjected. "So options are kinda limited."

"Even when we're doing regular pledging shit, we're breaking school rules. I don't see a big difference doing this, " Jeff countered.

"It's different because now Standor is specifically watching us" Calvin finally contributed something meaningful. *Welcome to the conversation Gretman.*

"Fuck that son of a bitch. Unless he actually stakes out our house, he can't do shit because *none* of us will talk. I'm asking you guys to trust me. It's only for a little longer. We've already done five weeks with these kids."

There was a hint of pleading at the end of his tirade that Eric wasn't expecting.

"You know *if* we get caught, at best we can't take pledges for a semester. At worst our charter is suspended, maybe indefinitely" Eric responded calmly.

"Yeah but there's always a risk of that."

"And now the stakes are higher" Calvin added solemnly.

"Will you guys support this or not?" Jeff asked sharply.

If he's looking for a vote, he won't be happy with the result.

"Despite a few things I would've appreciated a heads up on, Buttons has done a good job with this program. I think we're stuck in this situation because of a pledge's dumbass decision alone. I think we can afford to underground them for a few days. That's how I see it" Calvin said directly to Eric and Jerry.

"Even if you guys don't like it I've been running this program with the sole concept of making these kids *earn* their letters. Crossing them early and before they're ready pissed all over everything we've all been a part of. Now I'm asking you for a few more days. And I'd appreciate the support because I shouldn't make this call alone."

At least he's got that much straight. The pledge-master alone didn't have the right to underground the pledges when the consequences could potentially affect the entire frat. Eric appreciated that. He took a deep breath. "I don't like the idea but if Buttons thinks he can pull it off...and if Jerry is down...I could live with it."

Jerry smirked. "Yeah I'm down to help."

"Thank you" was all Jeff said.

"Good, then we're set. If we get caught we'll blame the whole thing on Buttons" Calvin joked. The moment of levity was a nice change although Eric wasn't sure how Jeff would take that considering his past history with AZXi but he stayed cool. *That's a miracle right there.*

They all gave Jeff the brotherhood handshake in solidarity.

We can all go down on this ship together boys.

"So when do you want to tell the pledges?" Jerry asked.

"You and I are going over there right now. You're driving."

"That's good because Standor wants that roster by tomorrow morning. We might as well put on a good show for the fucker," Calvin said with a grin.

Eric had to admit there was a certain appeal to breaking the rules. He didn't hate it. For so much of his life he walked in between the lines and stayed out of trouble. The only real times he'd gotten in deep shit were when he was with Jake or Will. And now he was breaking the rules and by extension fucking them over.

They weren't supposed to cross this early anyways. Jake better not freak out about this...please don't let him freak out. Eric knew he'd have to keep his phone on vibrate for the rest of the night just in case he had to talk his cousin down one more time.

****

As they got into Jerry's white Camaro, Jeff was still shocked. *I can't believe they all agreed. Eric and Gretman both.* He had to have multiple drinks with Gretman at the National before he was on board and even then, he was unsure of where he'd fall in the conversation with the others. *He could've easily just fucked me when we talked to the other two guys...but he kept his mouth shut for most of it...unbelievable.*

Jeff knew he couldn't get away with undergrounding the pledges without the support of the E-Board so he needed their say so to finish the program the way he wanted to. It made him sick that after five plus weeks of doing everything his way he was now forced to get permission. *Fuck Dean Standor.*

All the same it was nice to know that his brothers had his back now.

Eric supporting him definitely must've felt weird considering Raley was his cousin and Will was one of his good friends. It meant a lot to know AZXi was still the place he originally wanted to join freshman year. The players might've changed but the general attitude and lifestyle was still the same. He'd always attributed his frat's internal mechanics to everyone having gone through a similar process in pledging. They could all reminisce about past callouts and it didn't matter if you were long graduated or a new fuck, everyone was connected.

He'd be damned if he let Standor cut off the Alpha Epsilon's experience.

****

The beginning of the end was finally here. *Thank God.*

Week six of pledging had started and they were almost through another day. The pledges were all still awake and working on their pledge books and other projects Riley and Tory had given them. Since the beginning of the week, the pledges were sleeping in the chapter room at the EIPi house.

Riley had personally hated that part of pledging. Getting yelled at during callouts was one thing. Being forced to spend every waking minute at the EIPi house when class wasn't in session? That was quite another matter. Getting back to her own warm bed in the dorm was part of what got her through some of the more terrible callouts. Even that one small comfort was ripped away during week six.

Looking in on the pledges, Riley felt pity. *Almost done girls.* Her Little was standing next to her. She'd asked about some piece of history Riley had to bullshit through. Fortunately she'd done a good enough job to fool even Brynn.

"Is there anything else you wanted?" she asked Brynn sternly. She had to keep her pledge mom persona on at all times now that they were so close to the end.

"No that was it" Brynn replied solemnly.

"OK then get back to it" Riley motioned back to the chapter room where the rest of her class was.

"These projects all better be perfect" Riley yelled into the chapter room. She was sure to keep a straight face. After the pledges made eye contact with her they all went back to work.

Tory appeared from the stairwell and pulled Riley aside into it to be out of earshot. The pledges weren't aware of even the slightest detail so every sister took steps to make sure it stayed that way.

"What'd she want?"

"I don't know. Something about a pledge class from like a decade ago. I took care of it," Riley answered confidently. *I think I did at least.*

"They're all so worthless with those things." *With all the shit those books need to hold it's no wonder nobody ever has them perfect.* The basic concept of their pledge books, at least in Riley's eyes, was to give them a connection to EIPi's massive history.

"No kidding but at least they're pretty much done" Riley replied happily. She enjoyed her job as pledge-mom but after two semesters she was happy to let it all go. She'd done her time with two separate pledge classes and now it was time for someone else to take care of it. *Probably Dani if things go well at elections.*

"At least we're almost done with *them*" Tory nodded in the pledges' direction. "I don't know how much longer I can pretend to be interested in educating them."

"I knew the responsibility had to be getting to you" Riley smirked.

"It's no secret Riles…it's not a good look for me."

"Then why take the position at all?"

"Just because I don't like something doesn't mean I'm not good at it. I don't like giving hand jobs but I'm great at it."

"Of course you are" Riley smirked.

"Ask anyone."

"I'd rather not."

"So you think they'll be ready for Crossing in two days?" Tory quietly asked.

Riley made a motion for them to walk further up the stairs and into the hallway on the next floor. Whether or not the stairway door was shut didn't keep her from being uncomfortable when talking about Crossing so close to the chapter room.

Once they were up in the hallway and Riley noticed that most of the doors nearby were closed and no one was around, she responded. "When is someone *ready* to cross?"

"I don't know…I just don't think they know enough history, but their pledge projects are OK" she replied unsurely.

Riley chuckled. *Knowing EIPi history is the most subjective thing about Crossing. How much should a pledge class know before they're considered proficient?* As the sorority got older the question became more confusing.

"EIPi has been around over twenty-five years. It'd be insane to memorize it all…even half is a stretch." *Thirty years worth of pledge classes, family trees, Bids and more? There's no way anyone could memorize all that in six weeks on top of school and a lack of sleep.* There had to be a point where a pledge-mom said it was good enough.

Tory nodded. "I think they've done enough with what we've given them. And I'm personally tired of dealing with all their shit so yeah…Crossing is Wednesday" she made sure to tone down her voice. Even being a floor up didn't feel *that* secure.

"Well as long as you're good with this."

"We go through the same cycle every semester. Take a pledge class and it starts off strong with all the actives involved. But week after week goes by and we all just want it to be over." It was as clear as Riley could make it. It was also one hundred percent realistic. She accepted that fact when she took the job.

"It'll be nice having our nights back," Tory said thoughtfully. "Alright you're the boss. Let's do this."

"For another three nights yes I am. Then I'm back to being a nobody and not caring about pledge education…ever again," Riley promised.

Tory laughed. "Yeah until you get on the E-Board again at elections."

Riley immediately felt uncomfortable. Felicia had tried telling her what to do at elections but she wasn't sure she wanted to be one of the responsible ones around here anymore. She loved EIPi but a year of 'pledge education' had taken its toll. For those six weeks each semester she'd had to keep a certain kind of presence about her all the time. Even at parties she had to remain somewhat stoic because the pledges were always there, watching and waiting…standing in the corner with linked arms. An E-Board position wouldn't be the same but more responsibility didn't sound like something she'd want to experience during her senior year.

"Who says I want an E-Board position?"

"Please" Tory played it up. "You couldn't go a few weeks without a position, let alone a full year. You love having control."

"Maybe you're right. I just hate that you know me that well" she lied.

"You think I like knowing you that well?"

"Um why wouldn't you? I'm awesome."

They both stood there just laughing at the face the other was making.

"I need a drink. There's gotta be somebody in this town that wants to get crazy with me on a Monday" Tory announced abruptly.

"Sorry T. For once I'm not one of them." She'd had a rough enough weekend between AZXi on Friday and then the Tau Chis and K-Nus on Saturday. She hadn't felt nearly as bad as Eric looked on Saturday but it still hadn't been pleasant.

"Maybe I'll just text that K-Nu from the other night."

"For drinking or sex?" Riley asked and was immediately sorry.

"What night is complete without both?" Tory smiled in her usual devious way.

"God you're sick" Riley said sarcastically.

"You sound surprised."

Riley checked her cell to see how much time they had before the next callout. "OK you have two hours to make whatever bad life choices you want."

Tory nodded before walking away while texting on her phone.

"Two hours T! Then get your ass back here!" she all but ordered. Riley didn't think her assistant would be late but it never hurt to drive the point home. Subtleties were sometimes lost on her sister.

"Don't worry Riles, guys never last that long" she winked and kept walking.

Yeah...Tory would yell something like that without a second thought.

"Amen girl!" she heard one of her other sisters yell from her room.

****

Will had gotten a text from Jeff telling them to leave library hours early. That was pretty weird considering the rigid schedule they were expected to follow. It made Jake feel far from good. *You just had to test it didn't you? You had to ask what more they could do to all of us, didn't you?*

He looked over at Summers who was sending a text and then to Will who looked liked he was memorizing some pledge trivia from his book. Both Jake and J-Hood had their pledge books open to the credo, which took up a full page with all its bullshit.

Jake needed a break from the monotony. "So I was going to post on your Facebook wall last night except you don't have a wall to post on. What's the fuck?"

J-Hood didn't look up from his book. "I just got tired of girls writing about how great it was meeting me or how much fun they had. It was fuckin' annoying."

He's not serious. He can't be. What guy wouldn't want that attention? Ninety-nine guys out of a hundred would've killed for that. Justin Henksin was the hundredth guy. It seemed like the more Jake got to know him, the more he realized that the weirdest shit got under his skin.

"Let me get this straight, you got tired of girls jumping on your dick, so you just took it away?" He asked as sincerely as possible and it still sounded ridiculous.

"Yup."

"Unbelievable."

"I don't know Raley. Really think about it, that's definitely something J-Hood would do" Will said with confidence.

"Yeah I'm not even that shocked by him anymore" Summers agreed.

Just as they were all getting settled, in walked Jeff and Jerry. *Oh good. I was just thinking we were all too happy today. Thank God they're here.* Jeff led the way, Jerry followed. They looked angrier than usual and that was definitely saying something. Jerry made sure to shut the door to the study area so it just left the six of them in a space the size of the common room at AZXi.

Just relax…nothings happened yet.

"Brother Calvin and I met with the Dean tonight about Raley and Summers' fuckup at the Trip-E house last week" Jeff began gruffly.

"What'd they say?" Jake blurted out.

"We were talking solely about AZXi, not about you two. You guys will have to work that shit out on your own" he replied, sounding annoyed.

Jake could share the sentiment. *You could at least feign interest that we might get completely fucked by this whole thing.* Jake didn't even want to think about it anymore. He'd re-run that night in his head so many times it was starting to hurt. Eric kept telling him it would make for a great story one day but Jake couldn't see that day.

"The Dean said we need to cross you guys immediately and list you on the chapter roster" Jeff continued. He didn't sound nearly as sad as Jake thought he would be when he finally lost his control over them. They all started showing looks of happiness except for J-Hood who only looked *a little* happy.

"Don't get excited" Jerry bit out.

Fuck you. I'll get excited if I want to. They were finally done with all the bullshit. What could they do now that the Dean of Students had told Jeff to cross them? The endgame had arrived. *I should send the Dean a fuckin' fruit basket or something.*

"I've spoken with the E-Board and we've decided that in the eyes of the school, we will cross you. But nothing will change. You are still pledging. And as usual if anyone asks about what you're doing or why, this is all one hundred percent voluntary. Is that clear?" Jeff finished.

Any excitement or happiness to come about in the last minute was being replaced with anger and depression and the sudden urge to swing at one or both of the fuckers in front of them. *How can they? The school ordered them. How could Eric have gone along with this?* Jake noticed he wasn't alone in these feelings as even J-Hood looked put off by the news.

"Yes sir" they all responded bitterly. There wasn't much they could do given that they were technically still pledges. If not in the school's eyes then in the brothers'. At the end of the day the latter was the more important of the two.

"So everyone is clear?" Jeff asked again. He got the same sullen and bitter response before he stood up at the head of their table. "Anything to add Jerry?"

"No I'm good. Just make sure those damn books are memorized," he threatened before turning to leave with Jeff.

"Just to be clear here" Jeff began. "Whether your friend, your girlfriend, or your mother asks if you've crossed, you say yes. End of story."

If my mother even knew I was pledging that might be a problem.

They all nodded, having apparently lost the will to speak.

Jeff and Jerry exited the room, being sure to slam the door behind them.

"Well that fucking sucks" Jake let out when he was sure the two were far enough away from the door. He couldn't believe what just happened and he'd sat through it.

"It really doesn't change that much" J-Hood said calmly.

"Doesn't change much?! We essentially thought it was Christmas and then were told it was only fucking Labor Day!" he yelled. The sound was a lot for them all to take in the small room but Jake didn't give a fuck.

"It really does suck when you put it that way" Summers agreed.

At least one of them sees how messed up this whole thing is.

"Well it's pretty much guaranteed we'll be called out tonight so I'd get some more studying in before eleven boys" Will said solemnly. Even the always sarcastic and asinine Bill-Butt had been shut-up by Jeff and Jerry. Jake had often prayed for that but definitely not like this.

What about Crossing at the end of the week? The only reason it always ends six weeks after Bids is because of the school and that's clearly not a concern. Could this just go on 'til whenever Jeff wants?

****

After three different callouts during the week, the pledges were broken.

That was exactly where he wanted them and also exactly where they should be. Between the sprinkles separation and the pennies search, they were running on no sleep.

Raley's face had been priceless when Jeff told him he'd have to miss class tonight for an AZXi event. The pledges hadn't stopped trying to sneak around house hours though. It was a point of admiration for Jeff to see that they were still functioning well enough to be that creative but he still had to keep up appearances.

"So why is it none of you have been to house hours this week?" he asked as he looked at the three sitting there. Where exactly Summers was right now was anybody's guess. *Probably jerking off to '24' somewhere.*

"I've been going to office hours pretty regularly this week sir. And I believe they have been too" Raley answered for everyone.

In his multiple semesters in AZXi, Jeff had never seen office hours work out quite so perfectly for a pledge class so that house hours could be skipped altogether. *It's a great plan.* School and family were the only two things that could come before pledging and since a family crisis every day would stretch credibility, school was the best option. *How did none of us ever think of doing this before?*

"Let me see your syllabuses" he growled. He was attempting to call their bluff but if he knew Raley at all then he'd have planned for that.

"Yes sir" he said while turning to his backpack.

Jeff surveyed the three syllabuses he'd been handed, and he noticed each had office hours perfectly stacked on top of each other. It was a work of art. "You really need to be going to all these Raley?" he probed a little further. Ordering the kid to miss a class was one thing and since it was a special occasion tonight he didn't think too much of it. But he knew he couldn't force the kid out of getting extra help whether it existed at these times or not. He was just curious to see what the response would be.

"I figured it couldn't hurt sir."

Jeff knew Raley was trying his hardest not to show how happy he was. The kid knew he had him fucked for probably the first time since they'd met and he was savoring every second of it. *Well done Raley.* Had Jeff really wanted to, he could probably prove they were all lying about being in office hours by going to the respective spots and checking up on them. *Even if office hours are given at these times, there's no way these sleep-deprived fucks are making it to all of them.*

Jeff had to do his best to hide a smile. "Fine. I better not hear any bitching about your grades. We are over halfway through week six. If you aren't good at budgeting your time by now, you never will be."

The ingenuity at play was more entertaining than it was frustrating. These pledges would've literally had to re-type each syllabus up to include specific times. *For that much work you can have this one Raley.* Giving them a victory every now and again was important. It was the same reason he'd called their pledge class paddle "acceptable". It was a brilliant paddle but "acceptable" was as high a compliment as a pledge-master could give.

"Yes sir" Raley responded stoically. *Good poker face kid.*

He all but threw the papers back at Raley to illustrate how unhappy he was...even if he was impressed. He glared at each of the three and then stormed out of the room, allowing himself to smile when he'd turned from them.

Jeff Chester knew in that moment that he was doing the right thing.

They're getting there...

****

Jake allowed himself to smile as Jeff left the room. He never had a problem calling the bastard "sir" when he knew it was pissing the guy off. Whether or not Jeff actually believed they all had office hours so perfectly stacked was of little consequence since he was banking on the fact that it would require too much effort to actually prove they were lying. *And I was right.* If the look on Jeff's face was any indication, it looked like he believed it. Not only that, Jeff had actually stuck to the fraternity's stance during Rush that school and family came before pledging because he hadn't ordered them to stop attending 'office hours'. *Except he told me I'd have to miss my business ethics class tonight for some unknown activity. What the fuck does he have planned now?*

"Where is Summers anyway?" Will asked.

"You know the rule: if you don't know where he is, he's in the woodworks" Jake answered with a smile.

He felt phenomenal right now. *So this is what victory feels like.*

They heard the outside basement door slam signaling that Jeff had left the house. *No brothers left...perfect.*

"Well played Raley. Sleeping during *office hours* is so prime" Will complimented him. It took a second for the shell shock to wear off but Jake grinned at him in thanks.

"How about that callout last night?" J-Hood asked out of nowhere. None of them had really talked about it at length after they'd been yelled at to leave the house but Jake definitely thought it had been a weird one.

"If you could even call it that" Will began. "All they did was just keep asking us if we trust them before putting us through that trust falls shit."

No push-ups, no loud music, no yelling...definitely not a typical callout. There was a lot of whispering and a lot of talk about trust before they were put through the exercise. The whole thing couldn't have lasted more than forty-five minutes. It had been a welcome break after two nights spent sleeping at the house on crappy couches.

"I don't know...all I wanted to say when a brother would ask me if I trusted him with my life was: motherfucker I wouldn't trust you to watch my cat, let alone with my life." *If only I could've actually said that.*

"I'll admit it was fuckin' nerve-wracking being blindfolded and then pushed off a high rise; not knowing what the hell was going on" Will added.

"So it's Thursday, how many more callouts can they have this week?" Jake asked. He was hoping they were all thinking the same thing. *We should have a night off tonight...we've already gone three for three this week.*

"Well let's see...if it's Thursday and there are three more nights in the week I'm gonna go with...three." J-Hood was trying to be sarcastic but his voice never changed.

"Alright you ass, I meant how many do you think they're gonna have?" he rephrased the question, hoping to get a different answer.

"My bad, when you put it that way...three. It's 'Hell Week', not 'let's put it on cruise control and coast to Crossing' week."

That time he sounded bitter but he still didn't change his tone.

"I have class tonight and Jeff told me I needed to miss it even though attendance guarantees extra credit. What the fuck is that about?"

"Raley, who the fuck knows what they have planned next?" Will replied.

"It's just weird. During Rush they all said school and family came first but that was all bullshit." Despite having just gotten one over on Jeff with the fake syllabuses, he couldn't wrap his head around why he needed to skip class tonight. *There better be a damn good reason.*

"They have to say that shit. How else are people going to pledge? If someone is trying to sell you something they don't mention the negatives, they focus on the positives" J-Hood said calmly, as if it were the most natural thing in the world.

The happy feeling about lying to Jeff about office hours was completely gone by now. The worst part was that Kelly was in tonight's class with him. It was sad to say but their time in business ethics was basically a date night since Jake wasn't finding much spare time recently.

"Yeah except complaining to the Better Business Bureau is kinda out of the question don't you think?" Jake shot back.

"Either way we've gotta be almost done" Will said hopefully.

"We better be."

****

Eric's earlier lab had been a pain in the ass but fortunately he'd gotten out at the same time that Jerry was leaving Cordan. He said he wanted to get a nap in before their event tonight. *God knows I could definitely use one too but I have that damn group meeting at four today…*

As they hit the AZXi driveway Jerry renewed his assistant pledge-master persona. Eric didn't care if he walked in and found the pledges all having a miserable time or not, he wasn't going to pretend to be pissed when he walked in like Jerry did all the time.

They found three out of four pledges sitting on the various couches not doing much of anything. Their notebooks were out but if Eric remembered anything from his week six it was that he didn't do any history memorizing at so late a stage. He doubted *anyone* could still be motivated by now.

When they noticed who had walked in, all three got up from their seats to give the standard brotherhood greetings. According to tradition, the pledges had to greet any brother throughout the day whenever they saw them. They had to rattle off the same greetings reserved for callouts albeit in much more low-key fashion. Most of the time if they were in public the pledges would just whisper the information to the respective brother so they didn't draw attention. Eric found it more annoying than anything else. Making them do it at callouts was one thing but not during the day and definitely not on campus. With that in mind, he waved each of them off. Jerry on the other hand reveled in it and made each of the three greet him in turn while he kept his face rigid.

Eric remembered one time where Jerry literally walked in and out of the room the pledges were in three separate times within minutes and made them greet him each time. Jerry had been pretty blasted at the time too.

They both left the common room and made their way into the kitchen where Jerry poured himself a glass of water. After he turned the sink off they both heard faint whispering in the other room. Jerry grinned. "I hope to Christ that you fucks are whispering about pledging related activities!"

Eric didn't know how his pledge brother could keep a straight face when he yelled those threats, but fortunately the pledges weren't looking at him.

After Eric checked the fridge for a reminder of what he needed to get at the grocery store, his cousin trudged in.

"I'm heading to office hours sir," Jake said plainly. He wasn't asking permission.

Eric knew his cousin well enough to know there was very little chance he would be going to office hours anywhere but he kept his mouth shut. After all, it was Jake's game to play.

****

The nap Jake had taken while at 'office hours' had been one of the best of his entire life. He was able to relax by himself in his dorm room. That was a rarity in terms of both Kelly and Wayne being gone. Wayne was never around but Kelly usually was whenever Jake had free time. Today he'd just wanted to be alone though. It had paid off because he felt great when Jeff and Jerry had come to pick them up from library hours later in the day.

He still wasn't happy about missing an easy chance for extra credit in his ethics class but it was done now. It had already started without him. *I'm in the custody of Warden's Chester and Culson now...fuck my life.*

They'd gotten to Cordan at exactly half past six like they said they would. As soon as they got there, they ordered the pledges to follow them out.

They were led across campus back to the house. The whole thing was insanely weird...not unlike the trust falls night. *What are they doing?* Jake dared to hope that tonight was Crossing. It seemed like a long shot at first but then he started thinking more about it on their walk. Given that they were almost through week six and they'd never had four callouts in a row, it stood to reason. Plus, the longer they weren't crossed, the more likely the school would find out and fuck AZXi.

They walked in a straight line with Jeff leading. Jerry brought up the rear. No one spoke or gave eye contact to any of the other students walking by on their way toward the house. The whole thing felt surreal just like it did on Bids when each pledge was picked up in the same fashion. But Bids marked the beginning of their suffering and tonight was hopefully marking the end of it. It felt better the closer they got.

Once they reached Arkridge Avenue Jake had convinced himself that it was the end. *By the end of the night I'll be wearing letters.*

They reached the driveway and walked to the back of the house just like always. There wasn't a soul anywhere on Arkridge Avenue and the same could be said of the AZXi backyard. It was remarkably quiet for a Thursday.

Once Jeff and Jerry had them lined up facing the house with those two between them he said the words Jake would never forget.

"Put your blindfolds on."

Those fateful words had started every callout since the second one and each night that had followed was a study in destroying confidence. *And you thought tonight would be different.* Broken and dejected, they all did as they were told.

As the blindfold covered his eyes, Jake promised himself he would never forget the cardinal rule of pledging again. But that was only if he made it through tonight.

Chapter 18

It felt good to be back in Gladen Hills after the long winter break. It had always shocked him to know that most people thoroughly enjoyed their breaks away from school. Scribner on the other hand just wanted to get back. *Scratch the classes and this place would be insane. Even more insane.*

Winter break consisted of a month and a half away from school. That was all fine and good for the first two weeks. Once the holidays ended though, he just wanted to get the fuck out of his parent's house and back to his own space, even if he had to share half of it with Dukes. Scribner was close with his parents but sometimes a guy just needed to be on his own.

Fortunately there were plenty of people who felt the same way. Raley had wanted to get back as soon as he'd stepped out of his cousin's car. His mom tended to get under his skin in very amusing ways so the less time he spent in her house the better.

She'd always let them do their own thing with Raley's Ring so she was all right in Scribner's book. On the flip side he sure as hell wouldn't want to live with her for extended periods of time so he gave his friend credit.

Raley had gotten back to school for the spring semester a few days before Scribner. Basically the second the dorms were unlocked Raley was there. He'd gotten a ride back from his cousin Eric since that guy always wanted to be around for his frat parties.

Can't blame him for that.

He'd known Eric a long time, since the Raley's Ring days but he'd never pictured the guy joining a frat. Of course it was even less likely that Raley would join one and yet last semester he'd tried convincing Scribner to join the sketchiest one of all.

SIMS was the dictionary definition of shady and there was no way Scribner would ever pledge there.

Interestingly enough, after that one conversation at the dining hall last semester, Raley had never mentioned pledging again, at least not to Scribner. Raley wasn't usually the type to let things go so he figured the thoughts were still swirling around the kid's head in some way.

The first thing his friend wanted to do when Scribner walked back into their suite was play Mario-Kart. It was within seconds that he'd somehow talked him into playing instead of unpacking. Scribner still wasn't fully sure how he'd gone from wanting to take a nap to having a controller in his hand.

Dukes and Wayne still weren't back and their RA suitemate Derek was MIA as usual so Scribner was the first form of company Raley had, especially with Eric being knee-deep in beer at the frat house.

Raley crushed him in every race they played through. Not too surprising when taking into account the fact that this game was pretty much the only thing he'd done to pass the time during his first semester at Gladen Hills last year.

Thank God I didn't transfer into this school like Raley.

Most, if not all of his current friends were ones that he'd met during those precious first few weeks of the fall semester when everyone was looking for company.

His friend hadn't had that. Raley transferred in during the spring semester and missed the fall completely. With it he missed that short window of time where everyone was adapting. He tried getting the kid to come out with him more but he seemed content to hang with that girlfriend he had. It seemed like a very lonely existence every time Scribner thought it through. He knew deep down that most of the reason he agreed to live with Raley was because the kid didn't have many other options. He knew he'd never say that out loud though, just thinking it made him feel depressed. It was still a nice catch to be a freshman living in a suite since Raley was a sophomore and had that luxury built into his class year.

After the final race Jake put his controller down and grinned at Scribner. The last race had been more of a slaughter than the previous three combined so he wasn't all that happy about it. That was fine though because Raley was clearly happy enough for the both of them.

Scribner grimaced. *Damn him. I should've just unpacked.*

"Find me anyone who can beat me in Double Dash and I'll find a porn star for you to fuck."

"I didn't know you knew any...except through your computer."

It was no secret Raley had tons of porn on his computer but which guy didn't have a stash in one form or another? And with his girlfriend not around Gladen Hills these past few days there was little doubt what he was doing to pass the time with no one in the suite.

Oh yeah. Definitely giving that hard drive a real workout.

"Don't pick apart my joke Scribbs" Jake replied as he set up the next match.

"I wouldn't have to if you didn't make bad jokes."

"Yeah well at least I'm getting laid."

"You have a girlfriend pal. You aren't out there in the field working every night," Scribner said with more bitterness than he'd planned. He hadn't gotten any in a month.

"That's just the beauty of being me."

"Call it whatever you want."

"You should really try losing with grace sometime."

Scribner frowned. "Race me in the real world with my Camaro and we'll see what's good" he challenged the self-titled Mario-Kart expert.

"I don't know how you're dealing with separation anxiety from your car this year."

Scribner shook his head in dismay. *Damn campus housing for keeping freshmen from having cars.* The thought was sour. Getting dropped off somewhere by his parents was a feeling of embarrassment he thought he'd left behind when he'd gotten his damn car to begin with. "Fuckers" was all he could say.

"What do you wanna do tonight?" Jake asked suddenly.

Maybe the long car ride had screwed with Scribner's head since what was happening never happened. *Raley never asks what to do on a Friday night.*

Classes didn't start until Monday so there would probably be a ton of people out getting hammered. He never would've guessed that Jake Raley would want to join in on all that fun.

"I heard a couple of frats are having Opens on Arkridge tonight" Scribner said thoughtfully as if it hadn't been the sole thing on his mind the entire way back to school. He would've gone with or without Raley but he preferred company. He just didn't think it'd be easy to convince the kid to leave his cave in the suite.

"Which ones?"

"Tau Chi and that other one further up the street."

"Eric's frat? That's AZXi" Jake said wearily. "I'll text Eric and find out. I'm really just trying to get hammered. It might as well be with you and Biz."

"I could definitely go for a few drinks," Scribner replied sarcastically. A few would turn into a lot which would turn into a ridiculous hangover not unlike the one he'd had during Raley's speech about pledging SIMS last semester.

"Dukes isn't back yet right?"

"He's over at Daryl's place. He texted me to let him know where we're going when we knew" Jake said while checking his phone. "Biz says they're having happy hour until like nine. You trying to go?"

Scribner smirked. He doubted the kid had been prepared to go out so early but he wasn't going to sit by when there was fairly priced alcohol not two miles from where they were. "Happy hour? All day yes" he answered with a huge grin.

It'd be a pain in the ass to walk all the way from Northeast to the far end where Arkridge Avenue was but it didn't matter. Even with the snow on the ground and the cold air filtering its way into every building, beer was still beer, and being drunk was still the best way to pass the time in Gladen Hills.

"Alright I'll tell him we're rolling then," Raley finally said. "It should be a good time." It sounded like he was trying to convince himself but Scribner was sure once they got there he'd see the light. Maybe it would even lead to the kid wanting to go out more but he didn't want to push his luck.

Scribner put his bags down in his room where they'd likely sit until the following morning, untouched. For now, there were more pressing things to do then unpack.

Scribner found himself playing Mario-Kart a lot more these days since Raley was never around. He could barely remember the last time they'd sat and raced a few tracks. A feeling of nostalgia washed over him as he recollected the last memory of it.

He shook his head absently to the vacant room. *It's been way too long*.

Not only was Scribner playing it more, he found himself getting better and simultaneously wishing he could play against his friend again to see how he stacked up now. *Maybe he'll be down to run a few races when he gets back from wherever the fuck he is tonight.*

As he rounded the final corner in the last race Scribner realized he'd just been reliving the last time he'd played with the kid. *The first night back this semester...I had to convince him to go out.*

He chuckled as he realized that that might've been the night Jake had actually truly decided to pledge a frat.

Scribner never meant for it to happen in that way...but it had. Now Raley was the one out every night and he was the one sitting alone playing Mario-Kart.

How the fuck did this happen?

****

Jake instinctively put his blindfold on in short order given what he'd just heard from Jeff. It was crazy to think that only a minute before hand he'd convinced himself that tonight was Crossing. *This doesn't have to end this week...it doesn't have to end next week either. Maybe it never will...*

Being underground from the school's eyes meant pledging was completely at the will of Jeff Chester. *This must be what Hell feels like.*

It took all of five seconds once they'd been led into the basement in a straight line like they had so many times before for everything to truly hit home.

"Welcome to the end of week six fuckers!" he heard the familiar voice of Calvin Gretman scream as they walked down. The heavy metal music kicked up right on cue once they'd all gotten inside.

"Week seven is when the real fun begins boys!" Guapo screamed at J-Hood who was in line ahead of him.

"Let's go bitches!" Brent yelled from farther back, still just as audible as the rest.

Week seven was all Jake was focused on for the moment. *Week seven. Six weeks wasn't enough for these fuckers? Now they want more?*

It took a moment for him to even realize there was a brother in front of him asking for a greeting. It was Aaron Ajersul.

Jake hadn't really thought much about him since that night he saw Jeff read him the riot act getting him the fuck away from Jared's ex. That was because even though they'd all had to greet him at callouts, Brent and Aaron had never gone out of their way to haze them. With the exception of Brent's issue with Will a few weeks back the two Alpha Deltas were saints compared to the other actives. The first time they'd ever gotten push-ups from either one was last week.

"Greet me Raley" Aaron repeated.

From the sounds hitting his ears, the basement sounded full. There were people brushing past him at regular intervals and the whole room was warmer than it usually was while still being cold. That didn't bode well.

Why couldn't you have just told Jeff to go fuck himself and gone to class? Jesus, I'd rather be in class than a frat house. How the fuck did I get here?

There couldn't be a more sobering or defining thought than that.

"Greetings brother Aaron Ajersul. Nineteen, Alpha Delta class, political science, Reesewood, sophomore." Jake rattled off his greeting as he had a hundred times before, although that might've been the quickest he'd ever been. *Chew on that Aaron.*

Jake felt a pat on his back. "Good job Raley. Now why didn't you make it to house hours that much this week?" Aaron asked kindly.

"Office hours sir" he replied, trying to hide a smile for his expertly crafted alibi.

The kind tone of Aaron evaporated and condescension rained down in its place. "Give me a break Raley. This isn't a fucking game. Nobody goes to office hours *that* much. Get the fuck on the floor and give me fifty!"

After the shell shock passed he did as commanded. Jake lowered himself to the cold basement floor into push-up position. Slowly the thought of being in class with Kelly came back to him and he felt his restraint slipping away.

He went to a different place in his head, trying to steel himself a little longer.

He'd swung by Eric's frat a few times before but had never stayed long. Tonight would be the first time he was actually going with a full-on invite from his cousin. *Only took a year for that to happen.*

I've got Scribbs at least. Jake knew his friend would come back to Gladen Hills after the break with an itinerary full of drinking so he'd been warming himself up to the idea of getting hammered for the past couple of days.

Having been one of the only people in the dorms when they were unlocked on Wednesday was incredibly lonely. In the past three days he hadn't done much with his time save for videogames, TV, and using his laptop.

Wayne wouldn't be back 'til Sunday at the earliest so Jake had the room to himself…like usual. He was only sorry Kelly wasn't coming back until Saturday. She'd had family stuff to do with her parents so he was on his own.

After the long walk through the frozen wasteland that was Gladen Hills in winter, they finally made it to Arkridge Avenue. Unfortunately Jake didn't really have a great memory of which house was AZXi. Thankfully as they walked down the street it became apparent. The Greek letters of Alpha Zeta Xi were stretched across the front of the house in a loose wooden framework. The letters themselves were outlined in gold and colored in with black. It looked extremely old but still in decent shape.

The memories started coming back as they walked down the snow-covered gravel of the left side driveway. They reached the back door that led into the basement and upon walking inside they found his cousin.

"Hey! There he is! What's up man?" Eric asked happily as Scribner shut the door behind them.

The basement wasn't nearly as cold as it had been outside but it wasn't overly warm either. There were a ton of people flooding the area and Jake wondered just how cold the basement would be if there was no one around.

Nobody had been in the dorms all week but apparently the off campus houses were full of people just like AZXi was now. It was quite the shock considering how quiet the entire campus had felt on their way over.

At least forty people were standing around, mostly guys but still a few girls, with cups of beer in hand.

"I'm doing alright Biz. I just kicked Scribb's ass in Mario-Kart" Jake announced as he shook his cousin's hand. Eric reached over to shake Scribner's hand as well while Jake put his coat on the pile on the couch by the door.

"When I ask what's up, I'm hoping for actual news," Eric said with a grin as he looked over to Scribner.

"Yeah yeah…fuck you" his friend shot back sarcastically.

"Grab a beer boys. I'm trying to win this game right quick," Eric announced casually as he pointed toward the keg before turning back to his beer pong match.

It was a good bet that during any party Eric would be posted up at the beer pong table. Failing that, he'd be playing 'pound' or 'flip cup'. Jake and his cousin both loved drinking games to an almost unhealthy level but they were also better than most people at them so they didn't care.

"Yo who's next Biz?" Jake asked immediately, getting down to business.

"Not sure...you are I guess," his cousin replied absently while looking around.

Exactly what I was hoping for...

"Nice. You and me Scribbs. Let's get some beers."

They walked past a few people on their way to the keg in the corner.

There was another guy filling up his cup. He looked shady. The guy pumped the keg a few more times to make the beer come out faster while eyeing the two of them as they approached. He didn't smile or nod, only electing to stare them down.

As Jake got two cups from the stack off the wide handmade wooden bar nearby he finally spoke to them. "Hey, who are you here with?" the guy asked in a neutral yet still threatening tone. He finished filling his beer and stood up straight. He was about the same height as Jake but a little under Scribner. He had an unlit cigarette in his ear and an AZXi jersey on. The guy looked more intimidating than friendly.

"Hey man, I'm Eric's cousin Jake, this is my friend Scribner."

"Dan works fine too," Scribner added with a stretch of his hand for a handshake.

The guy responded with what looked to be a very firm handshake before beating Jake to it and moving to shake his hand too. *Why didn't I shake his hand first?!*

"You never told me your name was Dan" Jake said sarcastically to Scribner, trying to lighten the tone. It didn't seem to have much effect on the guy at the keg. *Maybe he just didn't get the joke?*

The guy kept looking at them while sipping half the cup he'd just filled without so much as a head-tilt or sign of fatigue. "I'm Jeff."

"Twenty-five, twenty-six..." Jake rattled off as anger started flowing freely through him.

Jeff was an ass from day one.

"Thirty, thirty-one…" Jake yelled as he continued his push-up punishment for Aaron to hear. No sooner had his thoughts strayed to his hatred for Jeff did the bastard's voice hit Jake's ears like a hammer.

"What the fuck did this kid screw up now?"

****

Jeff had been standing close by for the entire interaction. He'd heard Raley greet Aaron perfectly and yet he was on the ground doing push-ups. That was probably due to the fact that Jeff had posted on the AZXi forums that the kid was trying to fuck with house hours by making fake syllabuses. He'd let him have the earlier victory because it helped him convince the kid to miss his class tonight without any arguments. *This is all for your own good Raley. You'll be thanking me for this one day.*

Now it didn't really matter considering his class had already started and all four of the Alpha Epsilons were under his control for the rest of the night. *Perfectly planned out.* There was something to be said for the power a pledge-master held.

Jeff watched Raley continue his fifty push-ups for Aaron who was still watching intently. His own thoughts turned to how the kid had been when pledging had started. *He could barely do twenty without keeling over. Now he's pounding out fifties without breaking a sweat. You're fucking welcome Raley.*

He tried remembering his impressions of the kid the first time they'd met. *Did I even guess this kid would pledge?*

Intimidating the non-AZXis at their happy hours was something of a hobby for Jeff. And so it was that he found himself in a similar situation with two new dudes while he pounded his fifth beer of the hour.

"I thought I saw you here a couple times" Jeff continued from his introduction.

"Yeah. I've been to a couple of other parties," the kid admitted. "I transferred in last year and I don't really know too many people."

Given how little of this Jake kid he'd seen during the parties that he'd come to, that revelation wasn't exactly surprising. *Maybe if you stopped following your cousin around like a lap dog you'd meet more people.* The kid didn't seem all that social. *If he's this freaked out now he probably can't meet any new people by himself.* Unfortunately, Jeff couldn't give himself all the credit for scaring the underclassman. *This kid was terrified before I said a damn word.*

He decided to throw the kid a bone since he was clearly making an effort with the joke he'd just tried telling about his friend's first name. "Dude relax, you don't have to explain yourself. Family is always welcome here. Grab a beer boys" he invited them over to his spot at the keg.

The Scribner guy grinned while moving to the tap. "I wouldn't say no to a beer."

"Good. You'll fit right in."

Clearly this Scribner kid is the social one. It wouldn't have surprised Jeff to hear that the scared one followed him around just like he did with Eric. In either case, the Raley kid seemed nice enough.

Jeff thought back to his first time on AZXi property and felt sorry for the two kids almost immediately. *Everyone's nervous their first time here.*

He watched as they filled their cups. He finished his cup in the mean time and proceeded to fill it again after they were done. Once all three had full cups Jeff raised his in a cheers motion that he was hoping the other two would be down with.

As expected, the two kids didn't come close to beating him in the race. He finished first, followed by Dan a few seconds after. Not surprisingly, Eric's cousin brought up the rear.

"Wow that was embarrassing" the kid admitted. "Good thing there aren't many girls around here."

"Yeah what's up with that?" Dan asked. He sounded disappointed as though he'd finally noticed the lack of females.

"When we have happy hours it's usually just for guys looking to go to Rush. So they can chill with us and not feel pressure or any other bullshit," Jeff explained. "Still, some girls just can't stay away. Most of the ones here are from Rho Beta down the street."

"It's definitely a cool place," Jake said. Jeff couldn't tell if the kid was just trying to suck up to him or if he was being sincere. He bet it was a little of both.

"I always thought so," Jeff agreed with a little sarcasm. "I gotta piss. I broke the seal and now I'm paying for it."

"Alright man it was good meeting you" Jake said quickly.

"Likewise. I'll be right back anyways," Jeff said as he turned for the back door.

I could see either one coming to our Rush but who the fuck knows?

Jeff had been told by his Big after Crossing that he'd seemed shy and reserved during Rush. AZXi had opened him up in ways he'd never expected so why couldn't it do the same for someone else like him? Although he wasn't sure just how like him the Jake kid was. *He sure as hell can't pound a beer nearly as well as he should. But that's something we can teach.*

Either one could be AZXi material…

As he opened the back door into the frigid outdoor air, Jeff gave himself fifty-fifty odds on ever seeing either one again.

"Forty-five…" Jake continued on.

Jeff remembered thinking Raley was terrified and for the most part, weak. Most of their first meeting hadn't revealed much more. *That Dan kid was pretty straight though.* If he recalled correctly, he'd bet that his friend would be the one to go to Rush and not Raley. To that he chuckled inaudibly under the blaring music of the callout.

****

"Fifty" he said through stunted breathing.

Jake moved to get up out of the all too familiar push-up position. Aaron's yelling accompanied his new stance. "Brent and me never missed house hours! You have no respect! You will never get letters! You will never get laid! Your parents don't love you! Your name is beat! And you make me sick! Get it the fuck together Raley!"

Jake could've sworn he heard Aaron's tone change mid-way through his rant. It almost sounded like he was smiling through it although it was impossible to tell.

Before he could put too much thought into it, Aaron's pledge brother entered into the mix. "You disrespect him again and it'll be a lot worse than fifty push-ups Raley" Brent said in his usual deep and raspy tone.

I can't believe they let you stay in this frat after what you did to Will you fucker.

Before Jake's resolve could crack any further, Brent walked away.

"Greet me pledge Raley" Jeff's voice ordered. It hit Jake like a semi-truck. The guy that forced him away from class and his girlfriend was standing right in front of him acting like it was business as usual. Sadly it kind of was.

"Greetings brother Jeff Chester. Twenty-one, Phi class, computer science, Lenchter, junior" Jake concluded stoically. Then something happened that hadn't happened since the day they'd met.

"Good job" were the words that came from his pledge-master's mouth. They were as foreign to Jake as Latin. He started prepping himself for the worst. Even though they both knew that Jake had been flawless in his greeting, it didn't matter because it never did. He always got push-ups from Jeff and Jerry after their greetings were done, perfectly or not.

A few seconds passed. They felt like years.

Instead of being ordered to do a wall-sit or some keg-lifts, Jeff just stood next to him. Finally, he grabbed Jake's hand and moved it over the jersey Jeff was wearing making sure he felt the letters of Alpha Zeta Xi that were stitched into the front.

"Do you know what those are?"

There wasn't the usual hatred in his tone that Jake had heard so many times in the past. It didn't feel right. "They're letters sir" he answered unsurely.

"And they feel good don't they?"

If it means this shit is over then you bet your ass they feel good. "Yes sir" Jake shouted, although even he wasn't sure why.

"Don't give up on me Raley. Not when you're this close..." he paused for a second as the callout music swelled. "All this...it all comes down to how badly you want it. *You* are the only thing standing in the way."

Jake just stood there, completely dumbfounded.

Usually Jeff's speeches were designed to simply torment and insult the pledges under his command. Sometimes they could even be entertaining. Not in the moment but after a while when Jake could look back on them.

This was completely different. He was essentially giving encouragement out just like he usually did push-ups. All Jake could think to do was nod back at Jeff who he assumed was still standing there.

He got a pat on the back before he felt the guy move away. *What the fuck was that about?*

****

Calvin stood there in complete shock. Usually after a pledge greeted Buttons they had a look of utter defeat plastered on their blindfolded faces that was just as easy to read in their body language.

Jake Raley looked like he'd just gotten blown right there on the basement floor because his stance had the look of absolute confidence. Calvin couldn't help but smile widely at the sight.

The happy hour had been pretty solid so far considering it was the first weekend before classes started. Calvin hadn't been convinced that any potential rushes would show up but more than a few had come to chill and drink. They were about halfway through the night and there were at least six or seven potentials in the basement. *Not bad at all.*

It had been Jeff's idea to have a happy hour since they were designed to drum up interest in pledging. That only worked if the underclassmen were around and ready to drink. Unfortunately most of them weren't back at school yet so Calvin hadn't been convinced they'd get a good showing. He'd only agreed because it was an excuse to drink with his brothers and with graduation looming in four months he would run with any chance for that.

He'd also silently hoped that with Kraylin around maybe tonight would be the night he'd do something worthy of a 'good and welfare' story at the weekly meetings. Too often he'd agree to be skipped because he hadn't done anything worth talking about unlike the other brothers who were banging in random classrooms or getting head in bathrooms.

Calvin couldn't say anything like that even if it did happen since they'd all know he'd be talking about Jen. She was adventurous but he wasn't sure he wanted his brothers knowing about that half of his life with her. Telling Biz or his Little, Dylan, about it was one thing. 'Good and welfare' stories were a completely different beast. They were designed for everyone's entertainment whereas his sex life with Jen was somewhat private.

Even though it was pretty cold outside he and Kraylin were sitting out at the back picnic table with jackets on, sipping on their beers.

David Kraylin had graduated last year in the spring so whenever he came back to Gladen Hills Calvin always made it a point to chill with him. Kraylin had been one of the key brothers that convinced him to pledge when he was a sophomore.

They were finishing up their chat about the upcoming elections and who they thought would be running when out walked a kid neither of them recognized. He definitely wasn't a brother so that made him a potential rush. And who better to talk to the kid than two of the best rushers in AZXi history?

The kid moved off to the far side of the backyard area and started pissing in the opposite direction of the house. There was nothing past the house in that direction, save for old factories and farmland.

"Hey kid" Calvin yelled in a non-threatening tone once he was done pissing. The kid looked confused and more than a little unsure of himself. He made a motion to make sure Calvin was talking to him. *Of course I'm talking to you...there's only three of us out here.* "Come here for a sec."

"What's up?" he asked hesitantly. "Should I not have pissed back here?"

Kraylin started laughing as Calvin cracked a smile to disarm the clearly frightened underclassman. "Please" he waved it off. "Sometimes even chicks piss back here."

"Damn this place has just gone downhill since I left" Kraylin said quickly.

"I'd rather have everyone piss outside than in my house any day of the week."

Kraylin nodded. Having lived at the house himself when he was still active, Calvin knew the guy could get behind that thought.

"What's your name?" he asked the frightened kid.

"Jake...I'm Eric Saren's cousin."

"Are you asking or telling us?" Kraylin joked.

Calvin grinned. *He might not even know.*

That finally brought his guard down slightly. "No I'm definitely Eric's cousin," he said with more confidence. *Glad we got that cleared up.*

Calvin decided to go right for the jugular since he was feeling a little drunk from the beers he'd been slamming with Kraylin all night. "So you interested in rushing then?"

Any confidence Jake had gotten a minute ago vanished immediately.

"It seems like a cool place...but I mean...I don't want to step on Eric's toes or anything like that. It just seems like this is *his* place. I don't think he'd want me to pledge here..." his voice trailed off.

"Whoa whoa kid. We're talking about rushing, not pledging. Don't assume you'd get a bid here just because of Biz" Kraylin said in a more authoritative voice.

"I'm sorry…I didn't mean anything by it" Jake apologized quickly.

Calvin tried salvaging the situation. "So if Biz wasn't here what would you do?"

"I'm not sure. I never really pictured myself in a frat."

"Yeah but you're in college now. As far as Eric's concerned, you could find your own way at this place just like he did."

"Yeah but I don't want him to feel like I'm following him." The amount of shame in the kid's voice was palatable.

"Look, if one of your friends got a great job making a ton of money, wouldn't you try to get into the same thing if it was what you wanted?" Calvin asked.

Thankfully it looked like the kid forgot about whatever was making him uncomfortable a second ago.

"That's not following, that's called playing it smart" Kraylin interrupted.

"If you and Eric are alike and I can definitely see some things that would make me think you are, then this is the place to be," Calvin said diplomatically. He'd almost forgotten what Biz had been like the first time he'd walked into AZXi.

"I'd have to talk to Eric about this before I do anything."

"It's your life. You don't have to ask for permission."

"Yeah but I'd feel better about it if I did" Jake said with conviction.

This kid will never make it to Rush without a full-on blessing from Biz.

Calvin doubted Biz would stand in the way but he didn't know what kind of family dynamic was at play.

"Just think it over. Rush will show you what we're all about. Plus you don't have to just rush us…go everywhere. It's a great way to drink free beer and meet people."

The basement door opened abruptly and a high-pitched voice rang out. "Hey Raley, I aint shakin' your dick for you so get your ass back inside, Biz wants to play!"

"Just chill" Jake yelled back at whoever was shouting.

"I thought you said your name was Jake" Calvin asked confusedly.

He smirked. "Raley might as well be my name. Everyone around here calls me that even though my first name is Jake."

"Welcome to the club kid," Calvin said as he motioned to himself and Kraylin. "We have first names too but you'd never know that around here. I'm Calvin Gretman by the way," he added once he realized they'd never introduced themselves.

"I'm Dave Kraylin," his brother quickly added, noticing the same error.

"You're both seniors right?"

"I am" Calvin replied somewhat somberly. It was getting harder and harder to admit it to anyone who asked.

"I graduated last year," Kraylin said. "I'm just visiting for the weekend."

"How often do alumni come back here?"

"A lot actually. It's still their frat too" Calvin quickly answered.

"Yeah except now we have all the fun and none of the responsibility."

Must be nice Kraylin. Calvin was knee deep in all the presidential shit while also warming up to the fact that he'd have to go head to head with Jeff over his pledge program this semester.

He'd been dreading it since they'd elected him assistant pledge-master during Kraylin's last semester. They'd had friction ever since sophomore year and it hadn't gotten better. *I helped it along. Now I've gotta deal with it. This new kid doesn't need to hear about our internal shit. I might as well point him over to the Tau Chis if I do.* Any rush or pledge had to be absolutely convinced that everything going on behind the scenes was on the up and up.

"Soon enough I'll be washed up like you," he said to Kraylin in a joking manner but it was hard to deny that the words still tasted bitter.

"And I can't wait for that day" Kraylin replied happily.

"Well it was nice meeting you guys. I've gotta get back to the table" Jake said quickly before nodding at them again and walking back inside.

"You think he'll rush?" he asked Calvin as soon as the basement door shut.

"I think he should but I doubt he will."

"This is week fucking six Raley and you still can't tell it's me by my goddamn handshake?" Calvin yelled at him. "What the fuck is wrong with you?"

"I have no excuse sir."

"You bet your ass you don't have an excuse because there isn't one!"

Calvin didn't have it in him to give the kid push-ups tonight. Not when he was feeling so nostalgic. Yelling at him he could stomach but that was about it.

He motioned for Kraylin to follow him outside since he wanted to chat with him. He hadn't seen much of his old friend in the past few weeks since he hadn't been visiting much this semester. Somehow they'd all convinced him to come back for the night even though it was the middle of the week.

"That kid looks familiar to me," Kraylin said once they got outside.

Calvin smirked. "He should. Me and you talked to him the last time you were here…like two months ago right?"

"I gotta work man, believe me I'd rather be here" Kraylin replied with a little sorrow. "Life isn't nearly as fun after graduation."

Hearing about the real world after graduation was a dangerous road. Calvin was so close to experiencing it all in two months that it was becoming a lot harder to ignore.

"Nothing can ever come close to what we all did here," Kraylin said after a few seconds of thought. "What're you planning to do after all this?"

Calvin knew what it was he was really asking but he ignored it and answered in much simpler terms. "I plan on getting drunk and then getting laid."

"I meant after that," Kraylin corrected himself.

"Probably fighting a wicked hangover."

"You and me both."

They both grinned and fist-bumped instinctively.

"You know what I mean though. After college?" Kraylin clarified fully.

"I guess the plan is for me to go work with Adam at my dad's company" he said. "I just don't know if I'm ready for all that shit. This is place is…it's just insane."

Unfortunately he'd spent a lot of time thinking about what would happen after his time at Gladen Hills ended. Working for his dad at his company was as good a choice as any and at least this way he'd get to spend more time with Adam. Despite the age difference, they were always close.

"Adam was graduating right when I joined the frat so I didn't really get a chance to know him that well. He seemed like a good guy though. Plus he was the treasurer and I hear it's not that easy" he finished with a grin.

The irony wasn't lost on Calvin. Kraylin had been the treasurer during his senior year and he always talked about what a pain in the ass it was. Outside of maybe his own job as president, treasurer had to be the most work in the frat.

"So Eric keeps telling me" Calvin agreed without stroking Kraylin's ego, which was a delicate balancing act.

"Come on, I'm trying to fuck with the pledges a little, can't let them get too comfortable" Kraylin announced abruptly.

"Fair enough."

He didn't really want to head back in again so soon but he'd follow Kraylin's lead. *He's the one visiting. Might as well let him have some fun.*

Jared walked out as they were turning to head back in. His face lit up when he saw them. "There you are bro!" he said happily to Kraylin. "Callout's gonna be going a while, you wanna rip some shots?"

"At the National?"

"Nah, I got a bottle in the fridge I brought from my dorm."

"Are you sure no one's taken it?" Calvin asked immediately. *I always have to pad-lock the fridge when we have parties.*

"It's still there, I just looked" Jared replied.

"Fine let's have a few shots" Kraylin responded with a sarcastic sigh. *As if there was ever a chance you were going to pass up shots.* "I'm really trying to haze some of the pledges though."

"I hear ya. Just make sure you leave that Jake kid alone."

Kraylin looked back at Jared with a questioning stare.

"Come on bro" Jared began to explain. "That kid's your Little-Little."

Chapter 19

It was a crazy feeling of déjà vu that suddenly hit Eric while he sipped on his drink. He'd just picked it up from the beer pong table when it hit him. The table obviously wasn't being used for its actual purpose right now since the callout was in full swing but almost everything else about the moment felt lived in. Kraylin and Calvin were walking in from the basement together like they had so many times before.

The more he thought about it, the exact last time he'd seen those two walk in from out back was the night of *that* happy hour.

Eric finished his beer quickly. As usual, that gave way to his mind wandering.

It was definitely good to see Kraylin back so early in the semester. In most cases, alums that just graduated made repeated trips back to Gladen Hills. The closer their actual homes were to the college, the more likely they were to get sucked back into the AZXi lifestyle, even after they were supposed to be done with it by society's standards.

That was one of the things Eric liked the most about the frat. Alumni, recently graduated or not could always come back to immerse themselves in college one more time. He'd seen guys with kids come back to pound a few beers with undergrads just to feel young again. He definitely saw part of that future in his own when he graduated. *Another year and a half...*

When the cold air hit him from the open door, he'd automatically looked up to see who was coming in. Eric only nodded at Gretman and Kraylin as they came inside because he had to get his mind back into the game.

Fortunately this game was going a lot better than their first one. That was in no small part thanks to Scribner being drunker than he was earlier. It had been readily apparent to Eric after he'd met the kid years ago that when he got hammered, he lost focus on everything. That was a general rule for most people but not Eric or his cousin.

In another three turns, their fate was sealed. Scribner had only hit one cup and Jake three. Thankfully Jerry had done his part this time by hitting two cups so Eric hit the remaining four with little trouble.

I told Jerry two cups was the minimum I'd accept and he delivered.

He and Jerry walked over to the other side of the table to shake hands with the game's less fortunate players. It was a begrudging handshake from Jake but he maintained eye contact.

"It's alright son. You got us once, and we got you. Not a bad showing."

"I would've still preferred an undefeated night," Jake lamented.

"Yeah well that's never gonna happen down here" Eric replied quickly.

He'd been in AZXi long enough to know that most of the brothers were at least average at the game. Some were above average and a few were sickly good.

Just like a typical sibling rivalry, when a team was having a good night on the table, the best ones among the remaining brothers would step in to put an end to their reign. No one could be allowed a perfect night at the AZXi house. It was practically a rule.

"We've had undefeated nights back home."

Eric shook his head. "We aren't back home."

Jake looked puzzled as if it wasn't completely true. More likely though, he still thought the parties back in Reesewood were the apex of drinking.

Eric had fun at Raley's Ring but AZXi socials were a different breed entirely. He didn't want to get into it with his cousin now since he was already on edge from the loss. Scribner on the other hand couldn't seem to care less. He'd headed right back to the keg and was now chatting it up with Calvin while filling his cup.

"I gotta piss. I'll be right back," Eric announced.

"I'll head out with you...I have to go too," Jake replied.

Once they got outside they went behind Jeff's van and started pissing. They were no more than eight feet from each other so Jake picked up the conversation. "Are you saying you didn't have fun back home?" he asked sullenly.

Eric had to be tactful. Saying the wrong thing might piss Jake off. *I refuse to deal with that shit for the rest of the night.*

"Come on dude. That's not what I said. I'm just saying that...partying here, drinking with new people...that's the way it should be. We can't get that back home."

"Alright" Jake said quietly.

Eric couldn't figure out what was bothering him. He'd been keeping a close eye on the guy all night since he'd gotten there an hour ago. Outside of taking trips to piss out back, Jake had been posted up on the beer pong table.

Then it hit him. *Maybe he talked to some other guys outside? Calvin and Kraylin were out here...maybe they talked to him?*

Eric shook his head. *Gretman's awesome. No way he'd intentionally screw with my cousin.* That didn't necessarily preclude the fact that something they said hadn't screwed with Jake anyway. He tended to get a little too caught up with people's words, even if they didn't mean what he perceived them to mean.

"Isn't the concept of just going to Opens at random frats getting old?"

"We drink in the dorms too Biz."

"And that carries the added bonus of possibly getting written up for your trouble."

"Nothing has happened yet and it doesn't matter anyways. I'm not living on campus next year so who gives a fuck if they write me up during my last semester under their watch?" Jake replied harshly.

"All I'm saying is that it got old for me J" Eric said calmly.

Jake stood there, staring off into the darkness. Only the sparse few lights on the edges of campus were visible past the trees on Arkridge. The factories and farmland beyond the outer rim were shrouded in the lack of light.

"Is that why you pledged?" Jake finally asked, breaking his silence.

Up 'til now, Jake seemed content to never ask Eric about anything AZXi and he was fine with that. These days though, it was getting harder to keep the two things separate.

"Part of it was yeah…it just felt like the best move for me. It was all I could do."

Eric remembered how it all felt that first day when he'd gone to Rush at this house last year. It hadn't been easy at all and that was with Jerry by his side. He never saw Scribner pledging so it stood to reason that *if* Jake was considering this lifestyle, he was going to be doing it alone.

"Why don't you pledge here?" Eric blurted out absent thought.

Silence reigned freely for a few seconds while the cousins looked at each other.

"I never thought you'd be cool with that" Jake finally responded quietly.

"If I could find a place here then why shouldn't my family?"

"I've thought about it…it's just that…I already feel like you and Riley looked down on me for coming here…to the same school as you guys."

Eric smirked in the darkness. He'd often thought it was more than a coincidence that Jake had chosen Gladen Hills after he and Riley had been there for a year. He knew he was never going to say anything about that to his younger cousin because it would obviously strain their relationship with no real benefit for either of them. He didn't mind having him around anyways. They were too much alike not to have fun together.

"J, there's over six thousand kids at this school and I'm sure we aren't the first family that wanted to stay together. This is a good school and I couldn't look down on you for wanting to come here when I wanted the same thing."

Jake turned to face him. "I can't say you two weren't part of the reason I came here. I thought if I could just hold on to something…anything…that was the same before I graduated high school, then everything would work."

Eric nodded. "It's tough for everyone J. All I know is that what comes after we leave this place…*that* is really going to change everything. I have no clue where we'll all end up. But right here, right now…why wouldn't I want to go through all this with my best friends. That's why me and Jerry pledged together. It's why Will wants to pledge too. Nothing bonds people like a common experience…" Eric felt his voice trailing off. "I don't want you to miss all this."

"Thanks Biz. I don't know though…you really think I could get through pledging?"

Eric turned to look off toward the edges of campus as he thought it over. *That's the million-dollar question. Getting a bid and accepting it…those are the easy steps compared to the six weeks that come after.*

"You can be a pain in the ass when you want to be" Eric smiled through the darkness between them while putting a hand on his younger cousin's shoulder. "And your temper is…a lot, but it's only six weeks. Six weeks of Hell for sure…but if you knew that you'd be signing up for all this after, wouldn't that be worth it?"

"It would be if I knew that for sure."

"You trust me right?" He didn't wait for a response. "I'm telling you it's worth it. This place can change your life. And I don't just mean the partying. You're gonna meet a ton of people and make new friends every weekend. This stuff is gonna stick with you."

"And that's what you're getting out of all this?"

"Well selfishly I'd get somebody to talk about all this shit with after it's over. Not just somebody I could tell the stories to."

"Reminiscing is better than reciting" Jake replied skillfully while nodding his head.

The flood light over the back door was now on so he could see his cousin was looking pensive. They began the walk inside not long after.

"Look, I say you just talk to the other brothers and see what they have to say about all this" Eric offered.

"I'd be pledging with a girlfriend though. Isn't that gonna make things hard?"

"You aren't the first one to go through that. It might be hard yeah, but it could also give you the support you'd need to get through something like pledging. Jeff and Calvin both have girlfriends. I'd talk to them and see what they have to say." Eric regretted mentioning Jeff's name as soon as he said it.

"I met them both already actually. Jeff seems a little...intense" Jake said hesitantly, as if trying to choose the right words. *Intense is probably the nicest way of putting it.*

"Come on man, enough of this serious shit. We've gotta help finish the keg."

"Always happy to help Biz."

Eric had never undersold his ability to talk Jake into doing anything with a little pushing and prodding. Jake may very well have been considering pledging *somewhere* before their talk that night, maybe even AZXi. But there was no way on God's green earth that he would've gone through with even rushing here without talking to Eric first. *He needed my permission.*

There were other people out there who'd resent being so close to their family for so much of their lives. Jake didn't have siblings so he and Riley and their other cousins were all he had to latch onto. He'd never thought less of Jake for following his lead so he told his cousin exactly what he needed to hear that night.

Eric knew it was the best call for someone like Jake to be involved in something like AZXi. And if giving his blessing to go through with it was all he needed then there was no way he wouldn't give that.

Even so, there was no question that what he'd done in pushing Jake to pledge wasn't a severe gamble. There had been two de-pledges in the Alpha Epsilon class already. *What if Jake had been one of the ones to quit instead of Ron or that Stan guy? Could we have gotten through that?*

Quitting would've resulted in Jake never really being welcome at AZXi again, whether Eric had enough pull or not. De-pledging was the epitome of sacrilege in Gladen Hills and nobody ever got past it. Was Jake really ready for pledging when Eric had pushed him into it? He'd often thought about what he'd done in terms of getting Jake to the point of accepting the bid that morning in February. He'd always shrugged it off thinking that Jake could make his own decisions. *What if that's not true? He'd follow me anywhere. Did I lead him the right way? Did I help him make a choice that he shouldn't have made?*

Eric remembered the night they'd talked about all of it and from the way he was framing it, Jake was essentially waiting for his approval. *And I gave it to him without thinking. Was it just for me? Reminiscing is better than reciting.* Jake's words were almost haunting him now.

He wasn't sure what changed in terms of being positive that Jake wouldn't quit to now being deathly afraid of it. Ron and Stan just walked away after a week of pledging. Why couldn't someone like Summers or Jake quit after six weeks of being treated like shit? It had happened before in AZXi and more recently at other frats in town. Had he been fooling himself the entire time Jake had been pledging?

Eric finished filling his beer and then proceeded to slam all of it before repeating the process. Being drunk was clearly freaking him out but the moments when he was drinking made him feel better. The cycle was vicious.

Looking around, he found Jake immediately. He was being reprimanded by Jeff in the corner with Will right nearby.

Eric walked over with his freshly filled beer to get a better idea of what was going on. He nearly tripped over J-Hood doing push-ups on the ground.

"Either of you know the credo?" Jeff asked gruffly.

"I do sir!" Jake yelled back while Will stayed noticeably silent.

Will Anthony would never quit, of that much Eric was certain. Jeff could yell at him all day and it wouldn't make a difference. If that just happened to simultaneously be taking the heat off his cousin, he was fine with that.

"Why didn't you answer pledge?" Jeff immediately turned his attention to Will.

"I don't know it fully sir" Will replied sullenly. Eric doubted if Will cared all that much about learning the frat's history but for the sake of this callout, he was pretending that not knowing his shit was bothering him.

"Then you better hope your pledge brother can man the fuck up for both of you," Jeff shouted before immediately flipping to the credo in Jake's pledge book.

"Any fucking day now Raley!"

****

"The credo of Alpha Zeta Xi provides the following statement of principles…" Jake began rattling off the words he'd looked at so many times before. He could feel Jeff's disproving eyes hitting him through his blind-fold. Even though they'd shared an almost human moment earlier the guy was still the pledge-master through and through.

As he continued saying the words absently he felt a hand touch his shoulder warmly. "You got this J" Eric's familiar voice said from right beside him.

His thoughts abruptly flashed to Kelly while he continued saying what was expected of him. He needed to go some place comforting in his head while he danced to Jeff Chester's tune.

Jake had spent as much time with Kelly during the first week of school as he could. And he loved every second of it.

The bedroom was deserted except for Kelly so he took advantage by slowly and quietly creeping up behind her. She jolted straight up from her desk chair as he quickly put his hands on her shoulders.

"You know I hate when you do that," she said with a smirk.

"Yeah or maybe you secretly love it."

She flashed him a disproving look that was more for show than anything else.

He leaned in to kiss her but she turned away still playing up the fact that she was 'upset'. Finally after a few seconds he landed his lips on hers and everything stopped. She pulled away quicker than he would've liked. "Drank a little over at Eric's frat house again baby?" she said with some judgment in her tone.

"I swear it wasn't my idea Kel. You know how weak I am when it comes to peer pressure" he joked. Eric had invited him to his second happy hour in two weeks. He'd had fun at the first one and tonight had been even better.

"I'm sure they really had to twist your arm" she replied sarcastically.

"Whoa, are you calling me fat?!"

Kelly smiled back as she turned to save whatever she was working on.

"What're you working on?" he asked, powerless to stop his curiosity.

"Not much. I'm just looking over everything for this computer science project we got assigned on the first day of class" she replied, sounding aggravated.

She had a point. Her professor could've at least waited past what all students had termed 'syllabus day' to assign a huge group project like the one she was currently looking over. *The first day should only be about handing out the syllabus and getting a quick rundown of the class. Nobody gives a fuck on day one...except apparently Kel's computer science professor.*

"That's a group project right?" Jake asked unsurely.

She nodded. "See? I do listen," he said triumphantly.

She closed her laptop screen down and smiled. She kissed him quickly as she stood up to wrap her arms around his neck. "Yes you do," she said supportively.

"So why bother starting anything on it now?"

"I just have a feeling my group is gonna be worthless and I want to get an idea of how much work I'm gonna have to do."

"I'm guessing you aren't going out tonight then?"

"I don't really feel like it tonight babe" she said while looking into his eyes. "You can go out if you want."

"Yeah like that's gonna happen" he replied while kissing her forehead.

"How 'bout we order a pizza from Masterson's and watch a movie?"

Kelly smiled back as they kissed again, longer this time.

"Your roommate coming back tonight?" he asked hesitantly. The answer could either make or break the night. *Come on...come on.*

Kelly smiled seductively. "She's out with her boyfriend."

"And he's got his own place doesn't he?"

"I thought you were a great listener?" Kelly asked sarcastically as she playfully pulled away from his arms.

"Umm when it relates to you yeah, you bet your ass I am" he smiled as he followed her movement backward to the bed.

"What's my mom's name?" she tested him.

"Linda"

"What pets do I have?" she tested again.

"Two cats, two dogs and a couple ducks that hang around your house in the summer" he answered victoriously.

"What's my brother's birthday?"

"Does it turn you on when I get a question wrong?"

"What if it does?" Her eyes said it all. They had a deep, sizzling glow.

He inched closer to her, making sure to keep his eyes locked on hers. "Then I think I might be getting amnesia."

"Then how are you gonna remember what I want?" she asked as she sat down on the bed opening her legs.

"You're just gonna have to trust me."

He couldn't hold out any more. He lunged inward at his girlfriend and kissed her as passionately as he could while she laid back onto her pillow.

As soon as her head hit it Jake's hand was moving in between her legs. It felt as warm as it always did and he felt himself following along. She moaned between their kissing as he ran his fingers against the fabric of her pants that separated them from what he was after. He leaned in while looking down at her waist to see her legs spreading in preparation for his next move.

It was then that Jake went for her favorite spot. He kissed her neck just hard enough to get his point across without leaving any marks. Kelly always loved when he kissed her neck and no matter where they were, that got her going immediately.

She reached down and grabbed at him. It wasn't hard to find considering what they'd been doing these past few minutes. By this point in their relationship, they could undress each other with their eyes closed. In practiced rhythm they were naked within seconds and Jake was inside her.

Thankfully there was no one else in the suite tonight. He wasn't even sure they'd closed the bedroom door but it was too late for that. He knew neither of them would want to stop until they'd finished.

Jake started speeding up as he looked into Kelly's eyes. She knew what he was thinking so it didn't need to be said. *I can't ever lose you...I can't ever lose this...*

Jake nearly lost where he was in the credo since what was going on in his mind was exponentially better than his current reality.

"Finish it Raley" Jeff s ordered angrily.

"...In pride and for the wisdom of its traditions" he said while exhaling.

For a few seconds he'd forgotten the final words. If that tripped him up it wouldn't have ended well.

"I didn't think I'd live to see the day when you impressed me Raley" Jeff began. Jake straightened up his stance a little to mirror the pride he was feeling at being complimented by Jeff, however back-handed it was. "But it could've been quicker. So now you and Will are both gonna do keg-lifts until you finish it a second time faster."

He felt another person grab his arms and stretch them out in front of him. He wondered if it was still Eric right next to him. Within seconds a near empty keg was put into his hands. Jake's fingers laced the handles on the upper metal rim and he started lowering and lifting it in sequence while beginning the AZXi credo all over again.

The keg couldn't have been more than twenty or twenty-five pounds but he was sweating during the lifts. He could hear Will right next to him huffing like he usually did during the physical shit but there was no sound of him dropping the other keg.

Even though he was sweating Jake felt cold all over, not because the basement was cold, he just felt sick. He tried to bury himself in his thoughts again. It had worked out before minus the fact that he'd nearly fucked up the credo's ending. *Just don't think about sex this time...*

Thankfully Kelly's roommate hadn't come back last night. That was good because when he'd gotten up to go to the bathroom after their first time Jake noticed the door wasn't locked or even shut all the way. One of Kelly's other suitemates had gotten back in the middle of it and heard their admittedly loud sounds. They'd laughed about it afterward but it still felt a little weird.

Jake hadn't thought much about it for the rest of the night while they watched the movie she'd chosen. Thankfully it wasn't 'The Notebook' again. *I can't sit through that travesty one more time...not even for Kel.*

Jake was usually the first to wake up in the morning, especially when he stayed over at Kelly's. It wasn't that he was uncomfortable next to her but he always liked sleeping in his own bed. There was just something inherently better about it.

He shuffled slightly next to her to get into a better position. He leaned over and kissed her softly on the cheek as she began moving in response to him.

She opened her beautiful dark blue eyes.

"Morning gorgeous."

She replied with one of her typical morning lines that Jake never understood. "Stop...I probably look terrible." She shrugged away and turned over so her back was up against him.

"That's not even close to being true."

It was a fun little game they played pretty much every morning. He would call her beautiful, she'd say it wasn't true and around and around they'd go. He loved it almost as much as he loved her.

"What time is it baby?"

"Like noon" he answered, not really all that sure.

"We slept in that late?"

"Hey, don't blame me. I've been awake for a while now," he lied.

"Well I didn't feel you wake up."

"Yeah…I may have been watching you sleep in the least creepy way possible."

To that she turned to face him again. "There's a non-creepy way to watch someone sleep?"

"You know I wish you'd just let me have this one."

She leaned in to kiss him while returning his smile with one of her own. After her lips left his she moved to rest her head on his chest.

"I meant to tell you something last night Kel" he began, realizing they hadn't done a whole lot of talking after he'd gotten there.

"I actually think you told me a lot last night" she said in a seductive voice.

"You're damn right I did. I just didn't use words."

"What's going on Jake?" she asked innocently enough as she raised her head to look him in the eye.

"When I was with Eric last night I got a chance to talk to some of the older guys."

"OK" she said hesitantly.

"What would you think if I pledged?" he blurted out.

Kelly fully sat up and continued keeping her eyes on his. "Are you really serious about it?"

"I wanted to talk to you first. I mean it's definitely something I've been thinking about" he treaded as lightly as he could.

"For how long? Just last night?"

"It's been a while but last weekend…Eric talked to me about it…I never thought he'd actually go along with this but…I think he wants me to do this."

"That's great baby." She sounded confident but he could see through that to how unsure she was.

"So what do you think?"

"I think you should take a little more time to think about everything before you make any decisions" she said blankly. Her eyes were on him but it was clear her mind was whirling.

"So you don't like the idea?"

"You know that's not what I said."

"Not directly no."

She put her hands in his. "I just don't know how you'll handle pledging."

"Oh that's easy...I'm gonna hate every minute of it."

"So why do it at all if you know you'll hate it?"

"Because of what comes after," he said confidently. "Eric said it'd be worth it and I've always trusted him."

"Jake...just because it worked for your cousin..." she began before he cut her off mid-sentence.

"Cousins" he corrected her, referencing Riley.

"Right" she followed the correction. "Just because it worked for them doesn't mean it's right for you."

"Yeah I know but I think it might be...and I need you to be OK with it."

I won't do this without your help Kel...

"OK baby. If you *know* you need this then that's good enough for me," she said before leaning in to kiss his cheek lightly.

"Thanks Kel" he paused. "I love you so much you know that?"

"I know baby, I love you too" she smiled. "What're you gonna do now?"

"I'm gonna talk to Eric and Riley later today and see what they both think. I'll figure it out from there."

Once again he finished the AZXi credo.

This time he didn't stumble at the end because of the imagery in his mind. Remembering the warm times in Kelly's bed with her head on his chest was good enough...for now.

He lowered and raised the keg one more time for good measure after he'd said the last words. Then he dropped it casually for effect. *Because I don't give a fuck about you or your keg deposits...*

He knew he'd been flawless again and this time he'd also been quicker.

Right on cue he heard about his apparent lack of 'respect'.

"I didn't tell you to stop Raley" Jeff's angry voice came through clearly. "Pick up the damn keg and give me the most recent pledge classes and go *all the way* back."

Jake could deal with that demand too since it would take forever and Jeff would likely get bored with it long before any mistakes popped up with the earliest classes.

Let's dance Jeff.

He started listing off the names starting with Brent and Aaron's class. Then he moved onto Jared's class. When he got to Eric's class he wasn't even sure Jeff was still standing there.

Chapter 20

Classes had gone by pretty quickly. Riley was definitely thankful for that. She was hoping to get the boys together for dinner tonight because it had been a while since it was just the three of them together. *He'll have to skip pledging dinner but Jake won't care about missing that.*

She reached out to Eric first. Unfortunately he told her it wouldn't be a good night for that because Jake would be busy. Riley was not at all happy with that answer. *He might as well have just said there was a callout tonight.*

At first she didn't understand why a callout after eleven would affect having dinner at six. Then it dawned on her that the callouts must be at all hours of the day now just like they'd been for Eric and Jerry last fall.

I never had time to worry about Eric because I was pledging at the same time. Not that I would've had to anyway. He'd never let pledging get to him...but Jake...

Considering that now her own EIPi pledges were crossed and her job as pledge mom was done forever, she was focused on just one thing today: family.

The second semester of her junior year had only just started but she was in the same familiar spot she'd been in during the first weekend of freshman year.

Riley was in the fetal position wincing from the pain of last night's misadventures, except now she was doing so in the confines of her own personal room at the EIPi house.

These types of mornings had perfectly coincided with meeting Tory Brye. They'd met in the dorms and that same night gone on their first college bender. This morning was simply an extension of that relationship.

Why? Why did I let Tory talk me into after-hours...again? Full cup flip cup should never be played past two in the morning.

Thankfully today was Saturday so she didn't have a thing to do besides preparing for another ridiculous night. Unfortunately she'd also agreed to a lunch date with her cousins. Jake had caught her at the perfect time last night. She'd been perfectly buzzed and agreed to it on the spot not taking into account how she'd be feeling after a night like the one she was settling into. Now she was reaping the rewards of her lack of foresight.

It took a massive amount of strength to even open her eyes to look at the clock on the nightstand. It was a little past noon, which meant at any moment she could get a text from either Jake or Eric asking her to meet them at the Lancaster dining hall.

Riley stared absently at the ceiling, trying to make sense of everything.

Maybe they'll forget? No...not Jake.

Funnily enough she didn't feel all that bad once she was upright. After trudging over into her bathroom it became clear that she'd taken off her make-up before passing out last night. She smiled into the reflection. *At least I got that much right.*

Her thoughts flashed to a memory of the Midway before they'd gotten back to the house. She remembered seeing Jerry there. *He looked so good...ugh.*

Sooner or later he was going to wind up in her bed again. She only hoped that she'd remember the circumstances leading up to that point.

After freshman year they'd taken a step back and hadn't done anything since but it wasn't for a lack of wanting to...on either side. It just never came together. *It's gonna happen again...it can't not happen. Damn he looked good last night.*

Her text message alert jolted her out of thoughts about Jerry and away from the warmth she was starting to experience.

She moved to check it. It was from Jake. *What a shock.*

He sent it to both her and Eric saying to meet at 'the Lance' at one. That should give her enough time to shower and throw on a hoodie. *Maybe then I'll be presentable.*

Ironically, Riley and Eric got to Lancaster before Jake did. The dining hall in the middle of campus had that name but everyone called it 'the Lance' for short. It was easily the best of the three main dining halls so obviously it was only open for half the day everyday except Sunday when it wasn't open at all.

They'd both already gotten their food and were now sitting at a table awaiting their cousin. Riley's parents had insisted on giving her a partial meal plan for the on-campus locations so she'd used her card to pay for Eric's meal too since he didn't have one. She didn't mind though since he usually bought her shots at the Midway whenever they ran into each other.

She was content to wait for Jake before she ate but Eric didn't see things that way. If the general look of her cousin hadn't given away that he was hung-over then his over-compensating appetite would've done the trick.

"Didn't Jake say one?" she asked Eric. She already knew the answer since she'd double-checked the text twice since they sat down. Eric just nodded because his mouth was full.

She decided waiting for Jake any more would just cause her more pain than she was already in so she took a large bite from the taco she'd gotten upstairs. As she was chewing her phone went off. *Right on time*. It was a text message from Jake saying he'd be right there.

"So how'd your night go?" Riley asked the punctual cousin.

"The usual" Eric said between bites. "Had a good crowd for happy hour and every brother showed up for the girl's lacrosse social."

"Did Jake go to your happy hour thing last night too?"

Eric nodded and continued shoveling food into his mouth.

"Figured as much. I got the usual drunk text around nine when he left your place."

"All those shots at the National did me no good last night" Eric announced.

"They never do," she agreed. *That won't stop either of us from doing the same thing again...probably tonight*.

"We had a party with the Lambdas." She offered the information freely since she wasn't sure her cousin would ever ask, at least not with a plate of food in front of him.

"Ewwwww" was the sarcastic response she got back.

"Oh stop it, they're nice guys."

She was about halfway through her meal when their younger cousin finally walked in from the north entrance.

"Trouble getting up this morning" Eric asked playfully after he sat down.

"Nah, been up for a while. I was over at Kelly's."

Riley rolled her eyes. *Of course you were.*

"I figured that's where you bounced to last night."

"Dude I told you where I was going" Jake replied while patting Eric on the back.

"Eric when your blackouts start going retroactive it's time to seek help," Riley commented with as much fake-concern as she could.

"And that's never happened to you?" Jake asked while Eric grinned.

"Let's focus on one problem at a time please."

Her two cousins just leaned back in their chairs with contented smiles.

"Remember much from last night Biz?"

"Yeah, yeah," Eric replied, shrugging it off. "You won at beer pong, I get it."

"I mean besides that? I talked to Calvin and Jeff again...I mentioned my plan to you real quick."

"You mean about pledging?"

Riley felt concern welling up. *That can't be it. Jake would never pledge.*

"Yeah" Jake said confidently while turning to make eye contact with Riley.

"I don't know Jake, it's a lot to handle." It was abrupt but she didn't know how else to get her point across. *No point in being subtle.*

"I've actually been thinking about it a lot," Jake said calmly.

"You never said anything to me," Riley answered, still sifting through the shock.

Eric returned to his food. *He knew and didn't say anything to me.*

Jake picked up on her glare at Eric. "I didn't really mention it to Biz until last week. I told him I'd think about it."

"What brought this on?"

"Transfer students are fucked from the start" he responded, being equally blunt.

"I don't know if I'd go that far."

"It definitely isn't easy being a transfer," Eric interrupted.

"I'm getting the sense you don't like this idea Rye."

"I just don't get why you're considering this," she said plainly.

"You think I'm just following Eric again right?"

"Are you?" she shot back, regretting it immediately.

Jake stood up while keeping his eyes locked on her. He looked more upset than angry. "Biz said he was fine with it *and* he actively encouraged me. But it's pretty obvious you don't trust me to know what I'm doing."

That's not fair. You're dating Kelly Frazer so what am I supposed to think?

"I'm gonna get some food. I'll be back."

"OK so what's the problem?" her cousin immediately asked once Jake was gone.

"Do you really think he can get through pledging, Eric?"

"I wouldn't have said anything if I didn't."

Riley sighed. *Great…now they're both being impulsive idiots.* "You know I love you both…but is there a chance that you want him to do this so you can be close again?"

Eric stopped focusing on his food for the first time since they sat down. "That's not it, and stop making it sound weird." Riley could see she touched a nerve.

"We are still close…we all are," he added quickly. "And I think it'd be the best thing for him since he doesn't really have friends here except for Scribner and us. This will open everything up. You know that."

"No you're right. It will," she conceded. "But that's only if he makes it through pledging. I just think he might be better off joining an easier frat."

"Anything that's easy to get through isn't really worth it. And if I'm around to help him through a harder one like mine then it'll work out."

"You really do believe that don't you?" She could see it in his eyes but still wanted to hear him say it. "Yeah I do. Pledging sucked for sure…but damn if it didn't feel amazing when it was over…wearing that jersey for the first time."

"And what if he quits?" she said quietly while looking off toward their younger cousin waiting in line for the grill. "You have to admit it could happen."

Eric looked Riley directly in the eye. "I won't let him quit."

Eric knows what he's doing…you trusted him before.

Jake had to be getting close to the end. Most other frats and sororities had already crossed their classes. Then again AZXi was always one of the final pieces of the Greek Circle in Gladen Hills.

This last week had been nerve-wracking for her and she wasn't even the one pledging. Hopefully she'd get a chance to see Jake tomorrow to see how he was doing.

She sat down on her bed. The stillness of her room made it easy to hear the squeaking of the mattress beneath her. Everything felt empty and devoid of warmth.

Riley took a deep breath and tried to think of something she could do. Instead of just worrying about Jake so much, she wanted to try and take a page from Eric's book.

****

With Kraylin off yelling at J-Hood for not knowing his family tree and by extension, Raley's family tree, Calvin was left to his own devices. He immediately found his way to the keg and filled up. Jeff made his way over not long after and the two slammed their beers in accordance with the tradition of getting hammered at daytime callouts. *Tradition is important.*

Jeff motioned for Calvin to follow him over to where he'd left Raley and Will. There were a couple brothers standing around the two, listening to them drone on about pledge classes and the names therein. They were over halfway through the entire list but still going strong.

As usual, Jeff cut in to the proceedings. "Alright stop. I've heard enough. Brother Calvin, what did you think of that?"

He took a second to acclimate himself. "If this were week four I might be fucking impressed but since it's week six that's not how it's gonna be. I say it's about damn time," he said gruffly, doing his best 'Buttons' impression.

"Let's change gears a bit and deal with the Executive Boards. Start with the current one and go backwards. Let's see how far you get," Jeff ordered.

Calvin noticed a distinct lack of movement from either pledge. That wasn't unexpected. Executive Boards were tricky in that they were barely ever asked about during callouts but there were always exceptions.

"What a goddamn surprise. Let me know when these two decide to show some fucking respect" Calvin yelled with annoyance.

"It might be a while."

"That's fine. We've got all night."

"Come on Buttons, we don't have all night. We're up now," he said to his frat brother. He was shouting across the basement to be heard over some bullshit pop song. *This has to be Guapo's doing.*

"Hey Guapo! Can you play some decent songs please," Jeff yelled back, taking the words out of his mouth. Jeff then walked over to join Calvin at the beer pong table where he'd already started setting up the cups.

"I only play the hottest shit!" he heard Guapo shout from the DJ booth.

Well that's a fuckin' joke. He plays whatever will give him the best shot at getting laid based on the girls around. Too bad there's no girls at Rush events Guapo. Calvin didn't even want to think about what was going on in the guy's mind without women around. *Probably some real sick shit.*

"Then why am I listening to this garbage?" Jeff yelled in that direction while he helped fill up the last of the six cups in the rack.

Guapo was still shouting something but they couldn't hear it over the continuing onslaught of his play-list. It was probably a good thing considering most of what their brother said was complete bullshit.

They finished setting up their cups and began the pre-game stare-down at their opponents. One was Eric but the other was an AZXi rush. Apparently he was a good friend of both Eric and Jerry as well as an acquaintance of Brent and Aaron. That made him almost a shoe-in for a bid considering that kind of backing. Short of the guy trying to murder one of the other actives he was likely to get in, and even then, it depended on the active in question. *I bet we'd give him a pass if he went after Guapo.*

"Should we let the rush win?" Calvin asked honestly.

"Fuck that" Jeff answered without hesitating.

"I was hoping you'd say that. This kid's so full of himself already."

"The best there is...the best there was...the best there ever will be!" the kid yelled to the full basement as he slammed the contents of his side beer down his throat and threw the cup to the floor before stomping on it. Calvin would've sworn his eyes were making it up if he hadn't just witnessed it. Jeff looked equally baffled by someone who could be that ridiculous in a room full of people he didn't know.

"Oh boy am I gonna love hazing that bastard" Jeff grinned.

Good call Buttons. Will is the kid's name I think? I'll have to remember that.

There were times throughout his tenure at AZXi where he genuinely liked hazing the pledges because they'd had preconceptions before walking through the door. Preconceptions based on the idea that they were better than others. People like that had a way of getting what was coming to them. When he saw somebody acting high and mighty, he tended to overcompensate to balance things out.

"That's the kind of kid I'd bid just to fuck with for six beautiful weeks," Jeff said quietly enough so that only Calvin heard it.

Jeff Chester was coming up on being the pledge-master in a few days and Calvin wanted to extend an olive branch to keep things going smoothly. That was mainly why he offered to have the guy be on his team for beer pong tonight.

"Let's start by beating this kid."

"Done."

Their opponents' hit both cups on the first volley and got the balls back just as the rules specified.

As they were returning the balls, the backdoor opened and Eric's cousin walked in.

"Gotta be here tonight to show I'm serious about getting a bid" he heard the kid say to Eric as they shook hands near the middle of the table.

"You ready to do this thing Raley?" Will asked louder than he probably should have. It was pretty clear he'd be getting a bid but a little effort to hide the fact would've been appreciated.

"That depends if I get a bid or not" Jake responded coyly.

Calvin smirked. *Exactly like that kid is doing. Don't take anything for granted.*

"Yo J, make sure you say hey to the other brothers down here too" Eric suggested, ever the diplomat.

"Thanks Dad" Jake said sarcastically before turning his attention to Jeff and Calvin.

"Hey Calvin, how are ya doing?" Jake asked, warmly enough.

"Not bad Jake, good to see you" he shook the kid's hand firmly before stepping aside for Jeff to do the same.

"Thanks, I appreciate that" he stopped and turned to Jeff. "Hey Jeff, what's up?"

"Not much, good to see you came" Jeff responded without any emotion, as though he was reading from a script.

"You want a beer?" Calvin asked, if only to get Jake away from Jeff whom the kid was clearly terrified of. *No point in overdoing it on the kid tonight Buttons.*

"Not tonight man" Jake apologized. "I've gotta hang with my girlfriend but I wanted to make sure I stopped by."

Too many kids these days only wanted to use the sororities and frats to drink and party. Forming relationships with the people in your organization was becoming an afterthought for a sad majority of people. That was why formal blackball was such a big deal to Calvin every single semester. It was important to him and to the future of the frat that they let in kids that were going to help the frat continue on and grow.

"Do me a favor and don't let Eric win this one. His head shouldn't get too big" Jake joked to Calvin.

"I hear ya" Calvin agreed as he turned in time to see Will miss his shot. *At least now we'll have a chance to shoot.*

By the time he turned back around Jake was off saying hey to Jared and Dylan in the corner by the keg. Jared had immediately handed him a beer as soon as he got within arm's length. The goofiest smile he'd seen on Jared was fully present.

Calvin turned his attention back to the game. They waited for Eric to shoot and hopefully miss. "What do you think of that kid?" Calvin asked Jeff.

"You know I like to save my thoughts for blackball," he said, stone-walling any chance for a conversation. "We'll find out tomorrow what I think. But if these rushes knew what they were in for there's no way they'd accept their bids" Jeff smirked as he prepared to take his shot.

It was so clear even in the beginning. Thank God it's almost over.

He watched Raley and Will struggle on the Executive Boards from ten years ago and he smiled at the absurdity of it all. *At least we fucked with Bill-Butt. Buttons kept his promise on that one.*

****

"What the fuck do you mean you don't know the fifth Executive Board from eight years ago?" Jerry screamed at both him and Will after appearing nearby. At least it should've been directed at both of them. For some reason it felt like it was solely at Jake.

Anywhere else on planet Earth that question would've been met with laughter and looks questioning the sanity of the person asking. *Just not down here, not tonight.* Tonight that question was just another in the long list of things keeping Jake from being left alone.

"You both had one goddamn job. You just had to memorize the history and that's it. But you couldn't even get that done" Jerry continued screaming. Jake couldn't tell if the fucker was smiling or not. *This bastard never smiles at anything.*

"Yes sir" was all Jake could think to yell back. *I wonder if Bill-Butt is keeping a straight face.* It was a fair question considering he and Jerry were friends before their lives all went to Hell after Bids.

"I'm sick to death of dealing with your shit Raley. I just can't take any more god-forsaken disappointment from any of you! Do either of you even know why we bothered giving bids to you morons in the first place?"

"No sir!" they both yelled.

"That makes three of us! I just hope you can get it together during week seven because this shit aint gonna cut it anymore. If it goes on, we'll just keep you pledging until the very end of this fuckin' semester!"

He heard Jerry slam his pledge book closed even with the music still blasting from the various speakers throughout the basement. He then felt somebody putting the book into his backpack.

"How long did the Alpha class pledge for?" Jerry screamed.

"Eleven weeks sir" he and Will responded, somehow still in sync.

"Does that give you guys an idea of how far we're willing to go when we have to? Because it damn well fucking better. Nobody wears letters around here unless they earn them. This isn't the goddamn Gamma house!"

Jake felt his arm being raised and subsequently rested on a shoulder of the guy in front of him before he was lead over to a different section of the basement.

Within the next minute or so the music suddenly stopped. Jake's ears were ringing as if the speakers were still blasting. It was far from pleasant but Jeff's voice came filtering through all the same. *If only I went deaf down here…*

"Since learning the history isn't a priority for you fucks, we thought we'd try something different. You are going to *attempt* to entertain us. And I say attempt because I'm not convinced any of you are up to the task."

If only I skipped Dirty Rush six weeks ago, I could be in the dorms with Kelly right now. But no...I had to go to that party and suck up to all these bastards.

He hadn't wanted to drink at all tonight, but Jared had handed him a beer as soon as he'd laid eyes on the guy. They'd proceeded to pound one and then another and by the time the third one was done, Jared had to go piss out back. That left Jake alone at the keg before Will sauntered over.

"How'd the game go?"

"They hit two cups back to back to win the game" Will replied in as solemn a manner as Jake had ever heard from him.

So that's what upsets Will: losing at beer pong. Jake made a solemn vow right then to try his best to beat the guy whenever they played from now on.

During Informal Rush last week Jake had seen Will try to drink two individual cups of beer at the same time. He remembered laughing hysterically at the guy before Eric introduced him as a friend from high school.

"Ah, Biz's favorite way to lose a game" Jake remarked.

"Having no rebuttal is like being neutered," Will commented as he finished the cup of beer he'd just filled.

"You know a lot about being neutered Bill-Butt?"

Will paused to fill his cup again before staring right back at Jake. "Raley, let's just say I could teach your girlfriend a thing or two about the million things you're probably doing wrong."

That didn't sit well with Jake and his face must've said as much because Will backtracked immediately. "Come on, you know I'm just messing with you."

"Just keep that shit to yourself man" Jake said as calmly as he could.

Thankfully Justin walked over immediately as if on a mission. A mission that apparently involved filling his own cup. "I'm guessing you two are friends?"

"Damn is it that obvious?" Jake replied sarcastically. *Acquaintances at best pal.* With the way Will could regularly push his buttons he wasn't overly sure they would *ever* be friends. *Pledge brothers maybe...not friends.*

"Will and I went to the same high school as Eric and Jerry...and Brent and Aaron" came a fourth voice from off to the side. Another rush named Matt had spoken from Jake's left. *How long was this guy standing there?* It seemed like he was always lingering in the background of every Rush event. Jake had never really spoken to Justin or Matt before now. Eric had told him Rush was primarily for meeting the brothers so he hadn't spent much time with the other rushes.

"Word" Justin said as he looked around the party. He probably just wanted to make sure there were still no girls around. The first time he'd seen this Justin kid was also at Informal Rush last week. He'd been chatting with a chick that looked like his girlfriend.

"Hey was that chick you were with last week your girlfriend?"

"I don't have a girlfriend" Justin replied without a single change in tone.

Why didn't he ask me which girl I was talking about? The only reason he could come up with was he'd been talking to so many different girls last week that going over them would've been a waste of time. *There's no chance he didn't fuck that girl last week.*

"Did you go to the same school as all of them too?" Justin asked casually.

"No. Eric is my cousin though. I grew up across town from all these guys," Jake said proudly.

The difference between 'Reesewood' and 'East Reesewood' was something inherent that everyone living there knew. Explaining it to someone who hadn't lived there wasn't worth the energy.

"Sounds like you guys are guaranteed bids."

"Maybe…who knows what'll happen" Jake replied carefully.

"Relax Raley, it's only overconfidence if you don't win" Will said proudly. "Raley can't get overconfident though because he went to school on the wrong side of town from the rest of us. East side is so beat."

There he goes again. Jake took a large gulp of his beer to calm his nerves. He wasn't convinced he could spend six weeks with William Anthony and not want to kill him at every turn. *Is it too late to walk away?*

"Might as well slam a beer boys. If we get bids then we're spending six weeks together," Will said, reading Jake's reservations like a book. "Well actually, I'm still not convinced Raley will go through with it."

That turned the attention of both Justin and Matt over to him.

"I'm here aren't I?"

Will nodded. "Coming to a party is a whole lot different than accepting a bid. We'll see what happens Saturday morning when they hand them out."

"Yo J! Are you trying to slam a beer right now?" Eric's voice came from behind them. Both he and Justin turned on cue as if he was talking to both of them. They gave each other a weird look.

Eric made his way over to them. "Two J's around here is definitely not gonna fly. We'll have to get nicknames for you guys right quick," he said with a smile before reaching for the tap.

Jake had never even spoken to J-Hood before that night at the final Rush event and now they were finishing up their sixth week of pledging together.

With how much Will had constantly been pissing Jake off during the past few weeks, it was hard for him to remember or even think about the night that started it all.

Jake knew early on that Bill-Butt was going to be a pain in the ass. *Just wish I would've known how fucking psychotic Jeff was gonna be.* Now that had been nothing short of a fatal flaw.

****

The 'mock' portion of the night could either be stupidly entertaining or incredibly dull. It all depended on the pledges.

Jeff had high hopes for both Bill-Butt and Raley in that regard whereas with J-Hood and Summers it could go either way. Tonight could very well be the perfect storm of creativity from both the actives and the pledges. Only time would tell.

Jeff looked from the blindfolded pledges up against the back wall to the brothers all sitting behind him. He and Jerry were the only two standing in between the actives and the pledges since they'd be moderating the whole thing.

"Let's see some impressions," Calvin yelled out from his spot in the back by the couch. That got a bunch of cheers and agreements from the various other actives. Jeff wouldn't argue with what the crowd wanted.

"Bill-Butt, give us your best impression of brother Jerry" Jeff ordered.

The pledge stepped forward off the wall he was leaning against and made his voice deeper like Jerry's. "This isn't a fucking game boys. You are all fucking worthless and I'm sick of wasting my time on the likes of you" he yelled while waving his hands around frantically.

Jerry never waved his hands when he spoke to the pledges but there was no way for them to know that since their eyes were always covered. Other than that it was damn near perfect. The brothers agreed because he saw smiles and heard laughs from a bunch of them. *Not a bad start.*

"Yo Raley, impersonate brother Jeff!" Brent yelled out from his spot next to Calvin on the couch.

Raley took a step off the wall without much prompting and moved around to stretch out. That already got some of the actives anticipating what he'd do next. Since there was no need to stretch out before impersonating someone it was clear Raley was aiming for crowd approval. *If he's anywhere near as creative as he was the night we gave them 'the mamba' then this kid is gonna do just fine.* Jeff still smiled every time he thought about what Raley had said that night to a room full of brothers at the callout.

"Pledge Will…why the fuck don't you know the credo!?" Jake yelled out in a raspy, gruff voice. "Don't you have any respect? This is week fucking six and you are a pledge class of one! This isn't the fucking Gamma house now get it the fuck together!"

Does my voice really sound that dry?

Based on the reactions from the brothers it was clear that Jake was spot on since they were all laughing. Jeff too, allowed himself a smile. *Finally they're getting it.*

"Pledge Summers, tell us which brother is the most likely to get laid on any given night" Jeff ordered sternly after the laughter calmed down.

"Those with girlfriends sir" he said more quietly than Jeff would've liked.

"Besides the pussy-whipped ones" Jeff corrected.

"You do know you have a girlfriend right?" he heard Calvin say from behind him as Jeff continued keeping his focus on the four pledges.

He was doing his best to ignore Gretman. The point of questions like this was to see if the pledges had learned anything about the ones they'd be calling brothers one day. He wasn't sure what Calvin's angle was since he should know their purpose too.

"Pledge Summers, answer the damn question!"

"Brother Aiden Multayza" he said, more confidently.

Damn. Jeff knew that was probably the best answer to the question but he'd never admit it out loud. The brothers in the room all started ripping on Guapo while he danced before taking a bow.

"That's *incorrect* but we'll move on."

"Haters!" Guapo yelled before sitting back down.

"Pledge Raley, whose game could use the most work?" Jeff asked loudly to calm everyone down. Keeping control during 'mock' nights was a tricky line to walk. He had to make sure he was entertaining everyone at all times or there'd be chaos.

"Brother Eric Saren" Jake answered so quick Jeff almost felt whiplash.

That got all the brothers laughing and pointing. Eric smiled and took it all in, accepting his fate. He must've agreed with it on some level too.

"OK" Jeff moved his arms to quiet his brothers down. "Group question, you can conference about it. "Which brother is most likely to black-out on any given night?" After he finished with the question the four of them huddled together to discuss the possible choices. It wasn't unlike watching an episode of 'Family Feud'.

When about a minute had passed, Jeff ordered them to hurry up. Too much time spent debating and the brothers would grow anxious. Besides, this should've been a relatively easy question, at least in his mind.

The pledges all turned to face forward again. The other three let Will speak. "Brother Aaron Ajersul" he said confidently. *Well at least they got that one right.*

Jeff turned around to see all the brothers nodding in agreement before they looked and saw Aaron back by the keg filling up his cup for the thousandth time that night.

"Good to know you fucks were actually learning something since you clearly weren't studying the history."

Jerry stepped in to take over while Jeff finished his beer and reached for the nearest pitcher from Jared. "Which brother do you hate the most? Each of you can respond individually," Jerry ordered. "Summers you're first."

Jeff filled up his cup while he watched. Every time this question was asked the pledges needed no time to think it over. Every semester for every pledge, this was the easiest question. No doubt the person they hated most was seared into their memories.

"Brother Jerry Culson" Summers stated clearly.

"Brother Jared McAlpin" J-Hood said coolly.

"Brother Brent Segcand," Will announced strongly.

"Brother Jeff Chester" Raley hissed with enough contempt that Jeff smiled. At least he'd gotten one vote from his pledges. *I must be losing my touch.* He knew he couldn't get Will's vote because of what went down with Segs during week three but he thought Summers might pick him. Raley was always going to be a shoe-in.

Jeff took a large sip of the cold beer and rejoined Jerry in the middle of the basement. He wanted to see if any of them had learned anything about themselves in the past weeks so he switched things up.

"This question can be answered by any of you. Tell us something about one of your pledge brothers that none of us would know." He realized after he said it that they were already at a disadvantage. There wasn't a thing any of the other three pledges could tell them all about Raley that at least Biz wouldn't already know.

Surprisingly Raley stepped forward and paused for a few seconds as if regretting the decision to move at all. "Are you gonna say anything Raley? Or did you just take a step forward to waste our time?" Jerry asked immediately.

"Sir my pledge brother...William Anthony...he dated a girl in high school and got his heart ripped out. He loved her and it didn't end...well...he hasn't dated anyone since." The basement went quiet except for the sound of Raley stepping back.

His words were solemn but they had a ring of truth in them. If Jeff hadn't already thought it was true, then Will's body language would've convinced him. He obviously couldn't see the kid's eyes through the blind-fold but his head turned toward the source of Raley's voice as he slouched.

"Pledge Will is that true?" Jeff asked calmly.

"Yeah."

He was clearly trying his best to hide any reaction. That all but proved it was true. Even still, Jeff turned to Jerry who gave him a subtle nod approving its validity. It didn't matter that Jerry knew in this case since it was an emotional fact. Most pledges opted for the fun facts like someone having syphilis once upon a time. It was all Jeff could've hoped for. During the countless hours these four pledges had spent together they were talking about themselves and learning. He wanted to march back to the couch right now and tell Calvin to chew on that while fucking himself. His pledge program was doing all it needed to and if nothing else, what Raley just said proved it.

"Alright then, on that note, let's try something different."

"Yeah because that was fuckin' depressing" he heard Guapo yell.

Yeah...but it was worth it.

"Son I got this."

Jeff turned and saw Eric moving toward him and Jerry. "Raley really likes Star Trek" Eric began before Jerry picked up on it. That was appreciated because Jeff had no fucking clue where he was going with it.

"Let's have Raley impersonate one of the characters and Will can attack him as another one" Jerry offered with a huge grin. *That could either be really weird or epic.*

Jeff decided to roll the dice.

"Done" Jeff agreed. "Raley, pick a character from Star Trek and if anybody here recognizes the name you'll all do wall-sits."

"Thomas Eugene Paris" Raley shouted without pausing.

At first he thought Eric might've brought up the kid's love of Star Trek as a kind of revenge but that clearly wasn't the case.

This type of situation seemed to allow Raley to thrive.

"Anybody recognize that?" Eric asked the brothers.

Everyone looked like they'd just heard Raley speak Latin.

"No because we actually know what a clitoris is" Calvin yelled.

Again the basement lit up with laughter and cheers.

"OK Raley, Bill-Butt…you can begin" Jeff ordered with a smile on his face.

"OK Bill-Butt you can play a Klingon and I'll be in Starfleet" Jake explained as if Will would know what the fuck he was talking about.

Jeff followed the words but only a little. He liked Star Trek too but he wasn't nearly as big a fan as Raley apparently was.

"Raley I have no idea what that means" Will replied casually.

"Just follow my lead" Jake said as he kneeled down and acted like he was typing on an invisible console. He was really getting into it.

"Shields at sixty percent captain, we're taking heavy fire!" Jake yelled out.

Will just stood there, entirely unsure about what to do. Then he just threw himself into the game. He started roaring and screeching at Raley and clawing his hands into the air. All his noise just made his pledge brother kick it up a notch.

"Shields are failing captain; I'm diverting emergency power to compensate. Evasive maneuvers!" he continued yelling.

Jeff was again following some of the words but it was sounding increasingly like gibberish. But it was very entertaining gibberish. And he was powerless not to smile.

Chapter 21

It was a question that had been particularly prevalent recently. *When is it too early to start drinking? It's after seven...and it's a Thursday. That's good enough for me. But I've been wrong before... Riles will know what to do.*

Tory headed in her best friend's direction. *I need an answer to this right now.* She knocked before she went in since last time she hadn't and been told she never would. She liked to throw a curveball every now and again.

"Come in!" she heard through the door before she entered.

"Hey girl, what's going on?" Tory asked as she walked inside.

Riley was standing at the large rectangular window along the back wall of her room. She looked deep in thought. That was never a good thing so close to the weekend.

"Let me ask you something T. What's it like having no siblings?"

Well that's fucking random.

"I know it's random but I want to know."

Tory frowned. *This is not a good time to ask about drinking times.*

"It's kinda lonely I guess..." her voice trailed off.

"But you don't have to worry about anyone but yourself."

"What's going on Riles?"

"Eric...and Jake."

"They're your cousins, not your kids" Tory said immediately while stifling her negative emotions. *Seriously? This is what you're worrying about right now...on a Thursday night?*

Eric could definitely take care of himself and even though she hadn't met Jake, she'd been told they were a lot alike...mostly from Riley.

"You're right."

"Why exactly is it your job to deal with any trouble they get into?"

Tory moved toward Riley's bed to sit down. It made a slight creak the way her own did. She knew that Riley's wasn't getting the same constant workout hers was though. "Riles?" she choked out hesitantly into the unnerving silence.

"Because our family makes it my job" her friend lashed out suddenly. "They always say I'm the responsible one…that I need to watch out for those two. I knew Eric was right about Jake pledging but if he quits now then I'm gonna be stuck dealing with him for the next year and I fucking can't. What's he gonna do after we graduate?!"

"You could always just do what I do with family advice. Don't pay attention to any of it" Tory said with a grin while hiding any negativity percolating beneath the surface, of which there was plenty.

"I can't drown out something I hear so much" she said sullenly as she turned away from the window again. It was getting too dark outside to see much of anything, even with the campus lights coming on one by one in the distance.

"Last time I checked, Eric's been going here as long as we have. Unless he just killed someone…then I don't see why you're freaking out now."

"It's not about Eric" Riley admitted. "One of the Tau Chis just texted me saying he heard screaming and shit coming from the AZXi house when he walked past. He wanted to know if my cousins were being raped again."

"How is that different from any other night at that house? They're always going nuts at their callouts."

"Eric told me Jake couldn't go to dinner tonight because he had class except he didn't mention that until after, saying that he'd be busy with other things."

She's worried about her younger cousin de-pledging. "So the kid's getting hazed a little earlier in the day, it's not that big of a deal."

"Jake might finally lose it on this one. It just feels wrong. Being told to miss class so he could get fucked with all night? We don't even do shit like that! Class is class! It's a sanctuary. It's practically the only time I've been in college where I've wanted to go to class because the sisters couldn't do shit."

Riley was practically hyperventilating now.

They're not your responsibility Riles. It's just family…

"I'm just afraid he might quit tonight," Riley added, interrupting Tory's thoughts.

"I doubt it."

"You don't know Jake like I do."

"Yeah but that's only because you don't want me to" Tory smirked at her innuendo. That finally got Riley to smile, if only briefly, while she headed over and flipped on the light for her room. It was a welcome change.

"I'm serious though T. You know what it's like for de-pledges around here," Riley said sadly, as though she wasn't part of the same system she was bitching about.

Every member of the Greek Circle in Gladen Hills had at least a vague idea of what it meant to de-pledge. It didn't help a person's social standing…for frat Opens or at the bars. It was pretty weird that everyone took the same stance given how different they all were but it was like that long before any of them started college.

"Yeah but Eric knows too. There's no way he'd let him quit."

Eric and Tory weren't exactly on speaking terms these days but he always seemed like a nice enough guy. Nicer than a lot of the guys she'd been with, especially recently. *He always at least tried getting me to finish.*

"Did you talk to him at all about this?"

"I tried texting him like twenty minutes ago but he hasn't said anything yet."

"Good. Just calm down Riles. I'm sure everything is fine. Just treat it like a pregnancy test, there's nothing to worry about until there is." She winced instinctually at her own joke but Riley thankfully didn't notice.

"While we're waiting though, you wanna help me with my wine?"

Riley smiled and nodded. *Guess it's not too early to start after all.*

****

Eric was laughing so hard at what was happening that he forgot to check if they'd sent somebody outside to monitor the noise level. It was a minor thing to forget really since they were rarely so loud during this point in the night to warrant suspicion. If anyone had been walking by and heard anything it might've sounded extremely weird. Some of the brothers laughed in weird ways. They almost sounded like they were screaming. And there was no shortage of laughs in the AZXi basement tonight.

They were about done with the rap battle portion and all four pledges had done a sick job. Jake was a few points away from taking the whole thing home. He'd mentally laid odds based on the competition that either Will or Jake would win, but he'd been leaning more toward his cousin. As it went on it became clear his faith wasn't misplaced.

"Summers, you're up! You need another point to stay in this" Jeff yelled from his spot to the left. Eric was over sitting to the right next to Jared. Jared tended to screech when he started laughing. He wouldn't have been surprised if people were hearing that out in the middle of Arkridge Avenue.

"Raley's so ugly and he watches Star Trek, he's also real beat and his dick is low-tech" Summers rapped while Guapo mixed a beat from the DJ booth. *That guy would have a special program for doing stuff like this.*

The crowd of brothers went nuts at Summers latest throwdown but Jake didn't let that sit long. "Oh good one there Summers" Jake said in his best, high-pitched nerd voice. It was a thing of beauty.

"OHHHHHHH" a group of the brothers all shouted, commending Jake.

"Summers says I'm ugly because I watch Star Trek, but his mom didn't mind when I slit her throat and took a shit in her neck" Jake said in perfect sync with the low beat coming from the speakers.

Eric couldn't hide his wide smile. *Well that settles it.*

That was the final point Jake needed to get to five and win the rap battle of the Alpha Epsilon class. Eric mentally patted himself on the back for calling the winner right from the start. The basement was still lit up with cheers and laughs.

Out of the corner of his eye Eric noticed Jeff pull Jerry aside from everyone else and whisper something in his ear. With all the noise around him, especially from Jared, Eric couldn't hear what they were saying.

Jeff moved to the center of the room between the actives and the pledges shortly after so Eric couldn't ask Jerry what was going on. He had an idea though.

"OK pledges, you did a decent job tonight" Jeff began.

Eric chuckled. *This was the best one I've ever seen and you know it Buttons.*

"But I expect better things when we do this again next week. For now, I want you to think about everything that happened tonight. The rest of us are heading to the Beta house for a party since I feel like we deserve it after dealing with you fucks. All four of you are going to stay standing down here without moving."

Eric saw the immense grin on Jeff's face as he finished up his speech. He then threw a nod in Jerry's direction before following Calvin and the others out the door. There were only a handful of actives left after Jeff walked out, Jerry and Eric included.

"I drew the fucking short straw tonight so now I have to watch you failures and miss the party. So just stand still and don't piss me off any more than I already am. The Betas are absolutely crazy about me. You'll probably have to write a letter to them apologizing for keeping me away tonight" Jerry said loudly as he paced in front of the four of them. He somehow always kept a straight face.

"That's outrageous!" Eric heard Guapo shout as he walked up the far side stairs out of the basement. *Classic Guapo. Always has to have the last word.* He had basically proclaimed himself king of the Betas since he'd fucked five of them during the current semester already.

Eric turned to see Jared was still down in the basement too. Eric nodded in his direction because none of them were supposed to make any sounds anymore.

Eric headed out the backdoor, leaving his cousin and the others in Jerry's hands.

It wasn't late but it felt like it was. The formal blackball for the Alpha Epsilon class had just ended. It had been a little more awkward for Eric than he would've preferred but at least it was over. Now the bids would fall where they may.

He loosened up his tie and unbuttoned the top button of his shirt. The blackball had been fast-paced enough in that classroom that he hadn't thought to undo it until they were leaving. Eric had shared some casual words with Jerry after the session but other than that he hadn't said much to anybody.

Formal blackball was either going to be very straightforward because everyone was on the same page or monstrously long because people needed to be swayed one way or the other on which rushes to give bids to. Tonight was definitely quicker than the Alpha Gamma one had been but that was because they'd only gave bids to six people this time and not the ten from that particular semester. *That night was such a mess.*

"Yo Jared! You riding with us?" Eric heard Dylan shout past him to where Jared was standing with AJ. He was so zoned out that he thought he'd been the last one out of the room but he was wrong.

"Nah, I'll catch back up with you at the house bros!" Jared shouted back.

Most of the brothers had already made it to their cars in the lot next to the interstate. Fortunately he'd driven himself so he didn't have to wait for anybody.

AJ walked past him on his way to the parking lot. "You ready to get hammered tonight Biz?"

"I'll get there" Eric replied with a fake smile.

AJ didn't seem to notice. He nodded and followed the rest of the brothers out.

Eric felt like he wasn't alone as he stood outside of Maxen Hall. A couple of the brother's cars were already full and leaving. They beeped at him while they turned out and cruised by.

"Pretty easy night" he heard Jared's voice say from behind him.

"You forget something in your dorm again?" Eric asked.

"My jersey. I didn't want to walk there and then all the way back to the house if you wouldn't mind driving me there bro."

"I hear that. Which dorm are you in again?"

"The first one on Northeast" Jared answered quickly.

Northeast was far from practically every other piece of the campus. Fortunately Maxen was also the closest academic building to that part of Gladen Hills so they weren't too far away. "Northeast might as well be its own sovereign nation" Eric said to nobody. It was a miracle Eric had lived on Northwest for both his underclassmen years.

"Where'd you park at bro?"

"I left my car near the library. Parked on Hadren" Eric replied.

"Bro I feel like you're always in the library" Jared said sympathetically. As sympathetically as he *could* sound at least. He was always happy so sounding sad wasn't within his reach most of the time.

"You would not be wrong in thinking that" Eric confirmed.

"That's real beat Biz."

"Yeah but what can I do?"

Jared nodded and shrugged.

"You're right though, that blackball was pretty straightforward. Nothing to be ashamed about with six bids" Eric circled back to Jared's original statement.

They walked past Cordan quickly enough. Its lights stood out brightly against the black backdrop of the sky. Truthfully Eric could probably stand to spend another hour in there at least but he didn't want to be late to the blackball tonight so he'd cut his time short. That meant he'd just have to make up for it on Sunday. *Sunday is gonna blow...*

"Here's hoping all six accept."

"You know most of the rushes don't you?" Jared asked.

"I know Jake, Will and Matt yeah."

"You think they'll be down?"

That was the million-dollar question of the night. He'd pushed Jake toward that outcome but now that everything was out of his hands he didn't feel all that comfortable with the road ahead.

"Jake is the only one I'm not sure about. He says he's down but I think it'll really hit him when the bid gets delivered tomorrow morning" Eric answered honestly.

"You tried talking him into it right?"

"I said all I wanted to say. It's his call now."

Jared nodded. They'd all been through this before: getting a bid and having to accept or not within hours of receiving it. It was nerve-wracking. *Signing your life away for six weeks isn't for everybody. That's probably why only twenty percent of the kids here ever join something like this.*

"If he takes the bid though…I'm not sure who would wind up being his Big" Eric said quietly. They were walking past some kids and he always liked keeping internal AZXi matters close to the chest. It wouldn't do anyone any good to have rumors fly on campus about any particular organization or person involved.

"What do you mean?" Jared asked quickly once the group of kids had passed.

They had just hit the corner of Hadren and College Curve so they weren't likely to run into that many more students. Eric was no stranger to seeing the road so deserted since he usually left the library after midnight during the weekdays. Of course since it was Friday, most kids didn't bother staying at Cordan that late.

"There's a bunch of older guys in the mix to get Littles but I don't know if any will want to take him," Eric answered with sad confidence. He was hoping to avoid taking Jake as his Little personally since it would just make him lean on Eric even more. It would be more helpful, at least in his mind, if someone else took him so then he could branch out.

"I'd definitely take him. He seems like a cool kid," Jared said gleefully. "I'm sixth in line to get a Little so if all six accept I'll be down. I actually was hoping we'd only get five so I'd get first pick next semester but if Raley is the last one that'd be straight."

Leave it to Jared McAlpin to put a positive spin on his cousin being passed over by the older guys in the frat. His worries were well founded given that a group of the older guys were less than enthusiastic about the rushes this semester, his cousin included.

Finally they reached his car. Even in the minor moonlight coming down through the trees on Hadren Drive, it was clear how faded the paint was. It wasn't terrible though, considering the car was from the nineties. Eric sat down in the driver's seat and reached across the passenger's side to manually unlock the door. *Power locks would be nice.*

"They have 'til noon to accept their bids so make sure you're at the National by one to choose Littles" Eric reminded him as Jared sat down in the passenger's seat.

"I'll be there at eleven ready to get hammered."

"Jerry and I are getting there at ten when it opens. Tryin' to get some quick-draw in before we tap the keg."

He started the car. The engine turned over immediately which was a nice change of pace. Usually it took two or three tries. He turned onto Croftlin Rise and went down the hill away from the campus toward University Grove.

"Hey man…if you do end up being Jake's Big, just don't tell him everyone passed him up OK?" Eric said as he put the car in park within the dorm's loading dock.

"I got you bro," Jared said, still smiling. "I'll be right back out."

"Alright. And try to keep him out of trouble too. He's not that big of a drinker," Eric added hesitantly. *Good God I sound like his parent.*

"Maybe now he isn't" Jared continued smiling before getting out. He moved quickly up the loading dock pavement to the door and went inside.

Eric felt better about everything now that Jared had all but guaranteed he'd be Jake's Big. *How much trouble could they really get into anyways?*

Eric walked along the side of the house across the gravel. It crackled under his shoes as he made his way to the front. *Maybe I should've just been his Big…he might've not gotten banned from the Beta house on Bids weekend…*

As he crossed their small front lawn to the front door he realized he probably would've made the same decision all over again. Good, bad or otherwise, Jake had created an AZXi memory on Bids that didn't involve Eric. And he'd be damned if he ever did anything to take that away from his cousin.

****

Calvin was opening the front door at almost the exact same moment that Eric was reaching for the handle. They nearly ran into each other since there wasn't much light outside. Eric nodded at him as he passed by on the way inside.

Eric made his way inside to look for a seat that hadn't already been taken. *Good luck with that one Biz.* Having a large amount of actives, there was bound to be a couple people left standing when everyone was accounted for. Calvin didn't have to worry about that though. His spot was already called and couldn't be taken so he left to stretch his legs by himself.

He'd been through plenty of callouts like these and he'd learned during junior year that he should take some personal time before anything else happened. It usually helped him refocus. It was always asking a lot of any AZXi to stay quiet after drinking for a couple hours.

At the end of the grass, he hit the pavement of Arkridge Avenue. There wasn't anyone on the street. *That'll work.* What they were doing would look pretty weird to outsiders. Then again most of what they did would look weird to everyone. But this was his life and he was enjoying it immensely. What other students thought was irrelevant.

It was definitely time-consuming at certain points but that was part of the draw even when he'd first joined two and a half years ago. There was always something going on that interfered with sleep patterns and class schedules.

Late February in Gladen Hills was always a cruel, cruel time. Early in the mornings like now just exacerbated the issues. Even classes never forced him outside into the windy chill of the campus this early.

Seven in the morning was hardly a time he spent outside. But the bids had to be delivered early every Saturday after formal blackball so the rushes could have as much time as possible to think over their decision. Would they go through with it and make the jump from rush to pledge or let the opportunity pass them by? Time would tell which of these six would make the right call. While Calvin couldn't necessarily agree with someone turning down a bid to AZXi, he could respect that some people just weren't ready and or built for the Greek Circle. It wasn't for everybody.

Back in his sophomore year, he'd accepted as soon as he'd been handed his bid.

There were times during pledging when he'd second-guessed himself but not once since Crossing had those thoughts gone through his mind. He imagined it was the same for most if not all his brothers. Jeff was probably the only one that may have contemplated de-activating during all the shit that went down that same year.

Ironically, he was one of the three of them delivering bids today. Jeff, James and Calvin were traditionally supposed to deliver bids. That is, the pledge-master, rush chair and president were involved in bids drop-off.

Jeff and Calvin had stayed up most of the night drinking at the brotherhood lock-in after formal blackball. James had turned in early like he usually did. Jeff had to swing by his place on Hadren to pick him up.

James Brock or J-Bro as they all called him never really partied like the rest of them and in fact barely made it to parties at all. There were definitely times when Calvin wondered why it was the guy even bothered to pledge a frat at all. The more he'd gotten to know him, the more he realized J-Bro never looked like he was having fun, regardless of what he was doing.

After J-Bro had gotten into Button's soccer mom van they made their way around the campus making sure to hit Northeast first. Three rushes lived on that side of town.

This was the second semester that Calvin had gone along to drop off bids. It was awesome the first semester because it was still September at that point and not disgustingly cold like it was now. They'd even walked across campus to deliver the bids since it had been so nice out, even that early in the morning. Not today though. One look outside this morning and Calvin knew they were driving.

They pulled up outside the first dorm on the list and made their way toward the loading dock entrance. Fortunately there wasn't a lot of traffic on Saturday mornings in Gladen Hills so they could leave the van parked without any trouble.

Jeff reached the door first and swiped the ID card to let them inside. They'd had to borrow one of the underclassmen's ID cards the night before, in this case Jared's, otherwise they wouldn't be allowed inside. None of the three of them lived on campus anymore so their college ID's wouldn't allow them access.

The scanner beeped and the lock released. All three quickly made their way inside away from the blistering cold.

Calvin shivered when the door closed behind him as he adjusted to the warmth inside.

Buttons' van was so old the heating system hadn't done much on their drive over. Fortunately the dorms on Northeast were newer than those on Northwest so the heating systems here worked fine.

After Jeff made sure they were all inside, he led the way down the corridor. He checked his phone while they walked. No doubt he'd stored the addresses for all six rushes. Fortunately they always made sure everyone that came to Informal Rush write down where they lived for the day when they might be given a bid.

The particular rush they were starting with lived on the basement floor, which was right near the entrance they'd used.

Jeff reached the wooden door in the far left corner of the basement quad first and started knocking. Knocking on a dorm door this early was always the sketchiest part of bids drop-off because nobody knew they were coming. No one could prep for it. Usually if the rush lived in a suite it wouldn't be the rush that'd answer the door first. Such was the case now as a kid with bright red hair answered the door in shorts and a t-shirt. Clearly he'd just been woken up. And he looked anything but happy. Calvin immediately recognized him from their happy hours but knew now wasn't the time to make small talk.

The kid was still alert enough to notice that all three of them were wearing AZXi jerseys. He looked over the gold lettering and black background of their jerseys under their unzipped jackets.

"He's in the first door on the left," the kid said groggily.

"Thanks" Calvin said with a smile as Jeff nodded and walked behind him. After the kid had spoken, he'd turned and headed down the hall back into the suite. *I'd go back to bed too if I were you.*

As soon as they all walked into the common area connecting the rooms in the suite, the red-haired kid pointed to the door on the left from the corridor. It was a good thing too since Jeff looked like he needed the adjustment.

Calvin reached the door first since Jeff was heading toward the other one. His knock didn't get a response. He checked the doorknob and surprisingly found it unlocked. He twisted the handle after getting a nod to go ahead from Jeff and J-Bro.

The door creaked open the rush lying in bed under the covers with a girl next to him. The guy's eyes opened when he heard them. The girl was still lying next to him asleep. Calvin smiled at him for lack of a better idea.

The three walked inside. He heard Jeff reaching into his pocket.

Calvin saw the envelope out of the corner of his eye since Jeff was handing it to him from behind. He grabbed it in seconds and gave it to the kid in bed.

"Hey man" Calvin said warmly as he sat up. The girl was sitting up now too. She was wearing a pink tank top while looking confused. He immediately thought of how awkward it would've been had she been naked under the covers that had slipped away when she'd sat up. *Awkward...but still funny.*

"What the...?" he began to say while opening and closing his eyes rapidly to get his bearings. He looked a little less confused than the girl but still not quite alert.

"The brothers of Alpha Zeta Xi would like to formally extend a bid to you to join our fraternity" Calvin announced in his practiced formal tone. It was his first intro of the day but he thought he nailed it all the same.

Jake Raley immediately opened his eyes widely and looked at the envelope being put in front of him. He reached out and grabbed it after a little hesitation.

"Wow...thanks guys," he said as he looked at each of them.

Jake opened the envelope and read the contents before looking back up to Calvin. It became clear to him immediately that Jake wasn't going to be one of the guys that instantly accepted.

"You have 'til noon today to let us know if you'd like to accept or not" he explained cordially.

Jake nodded back at Calvin and the others. "OK...I'll let you know by then," he said while glancing at his alarm clock on the windowsill.

"Sounds good man. Hope to see you later" Calvin finished before nodding again.

As he turned to leave Calvin saw that Jeff was just blankly staring at the kid.

It was nothing short of poetic that Raley had been the first one to receive his bid and now he'd be the first one to walk through these doors tonight. It was also interesting that even though he was the first one to receive his bid that morning, he was the last to accept. *We're a long way from that frigid morning in February.*

Calvin took another look up and down Arkridge. There was still no one in sight. He took a deep breath before turning back toward the house. His eyes were locked on the AZXi lettering hanging out front.

Those letters had come to mean a lot more to him than he ever expected. He could only hope that the incoming Alpha Epsilons would look at them the same way one day soon.

****

There was some extremely sketchy music playing throughout the basement at the moment. If Jake didn't know any better, he'd think they all were about to be sacrificed before some kind of satanic cult. Come to think of it, he wasn't all *that* sure.

Jeff had told them all to stay still right before everyone but Jerry had walked out. It was just another in the long line of slaps to the face they'd endured since Bids.

It was actually a little unsettling to Jake that he'd had such a fun time during the latter half of the night doing impersonations and answering questions. Having fun in the AZXi basement wasn't normally something that happened. Of course that happy feeling vanished as soon as Jeff said they were going to stay here the rest of the night.

Nothing's changed. Nothing's ever going to change.

He started shifting more and more in his stance as the night wore on and the music started seeping into him. Anger was the only thing he was feeling after a while. Anger at the fact that once again, all the bastards he'd had to memorize greetings for were out having a great fucking time while he was stuck down here with his pledge brothers. Nothing about any of it was even remotely fair.

Once the next track of suicidal music kicked up to full blast Jake felt a hand touch his arm. His own hand was brought up to rest on the shoulder of whoever was in front of him. He felt himself being led away from the rest of his pledge brothers. After a few seconds he felt the cold air of the night wash over him as the basement door opened.

He was led up the stairs slowly. Once his feet hit the gravel of the driveway he became thoroughly confused. He'd never been blindfolded and led outside after a callout besides when they'd done the trust falls exercise. But by now it didn't matter because it was all just more of the same: white noise that tried his patience.

"You OK bro? You looked like you were getting pissed down there" his Big's voice came into focus as they walked.

"Yeah well I guess I'm supposed to be happy about pissing away points toward my class average so I could come down here and chill at a fucking callout." Jake was talking louder than he was sure Jared wanted but he was in no mood to play by AZXi rules right now.

"You're way too close to quit now."

"That's the same bullshit Jeff was feeding me tonight. And that might fucking mean something if I had some idea about when this was all gonna end."

"If you quit now, you'd just be throwing away the past six weeks" Jared said as seriously as Jake had ever heard him. It was spoken like somebody who had an idea about what to expect next, someone who had a callout roadmap that a pledge like Jake would kill for.

"Those six weeks are already gone pal. And to top it all off it's still not over!"

He felt a hand on his shoulder as they stopped walking. With how little they'd actually traveled, they could only have been around the corner of the house, close to the front. "This town is a bubble. We can get away with some ridiculous shit. But that only happens if you're affiliated with something. It's just how it is. Now just relax. You're going inside first," Jared said calmly.

"What the hell are you talking about?!" Jake asked, exasperated. "And why the fuck am I still wearing this goddamn blindfold?!"

"It's tradition. You're gonna knock on the door and Jeff will ask what the vigilant words of the fraternity are. And you're gonna say: "Equality and Brotherhood. Got it?" Jared asked as if it was the most natural conversation on the planet.

All it did was frustrate Jake even more.

"Whatever" was all he could say without biting the guy's head off any further. *Great...just another stupid drill like that trust falls bullshit.*

Jared just chuckled. "Once you do that they'll walk you inside and we'll wait for the rest of your pledge class. I'll be in there with you. Just follow my lead bro."

"Let's just get this over with."

Once Jared led him to the door Jake's fist connected with the wood, being sure to avoid the upper glass windows.

"What are the vigilant words of this fraternity?" he heard Jeff's scathing voice come through the wood and glass.

"Equality and brotherhood" Jake all but shouted. He hoped there were people watching him from Arkridge Avenue a few feet away. *Yeah that's right...I'm in a fucking cult and I can't get out.*

"You may enter" he heard Jeff say more quietly as the door opened. He felt Jared walk in front of him again as he was led inside. He couldn't have taken more than five or six steps before he was made to stop.

There wasn't much sound coming from the common room but that didn't matter. It was clear to Jake from his other senses that the room was packed with people, probably the rest of the brothers. *Eric's gotta be in here somewhere. I should rip this blindfold off and kill him. He didn't warn me about any of this shit when I accepted the bid. He couldn't even help me when it happened...*

"Congratulations baby" Kelly said as she stretched out in bed.

Jake had been so blown away by the entire situation of AZXis being in his dorm room at seven in the morning that he'd almost forgotten she was there.

"Thanks Kel" he finally managed to say through his swirling thoughts.

"Why didn't you just accept it now?" she asked.

He hoped she wouldn't ask it because he was asking himself the same question.

"What're you gonna do?"

That was another question he was hoping not to hear, both from her and in his own head, yet both sides were coming in loud and clear.

"I don't know," he admitted after a few more seconds of silence. He wasn't trying to keep anything from Kelly; he legitimately had no idea what to do. *That son of a bitch Will was right. Damn him.*

"Well it's only seven in the morning, there's still plenty of time." Her words echoed throughout the room as if they were taunting him. He looked back to his alarm clock as the minutes changed. Now there was even less time to make the right call, whatever that was.

"Yeah...I'm gonna get some air babe. I'll be right back" he lied.

He hunched over and slipped his sneakers on over his chilled feet. His shorts and t-shirt would be adequate for a walk through the suite and maybe the basement quad if he deemed it necessary.

Jake reached for his cell on the windowsill and frantically began typing a text message to Eric. He needed his cousin right now. After it was sent, he just continued sitting there for a few seconds, frozen in place.

"You're sure you're OK?" Kelly asked again. She sounded concerned. Jake couldn't blame her for that. *He* was concerned.

"Yeah…I just need a sec," he repeated.

He leaned over the bed to kiss her gently. She kept her gaze on him without blinking. There was love and concern in her eyes and for a moment it took the edge off Jake's anxiety. Then he turned away and it all came flooding back.

He walked out of the dorm room, not turning around again. Quietly, he closed the door behind him and leaned up against the wall right next to the door. His eyes were still shut, his thoughts going in a thousand different directions.

"Raley?" a voice shot through his mind, except it was coming from a few feet to his left. Jake jolted upright when he heard the sound.

Scribner sat there on the far couch up against the common room window just grinning back at him. "So I'm guessing those guys didn't swing by here this early in their letters to say you *didn't* get in."

It didn't sound like one but it was definitely a question.

"This would be pretty easy if that'd been the case" Jake replied.

"So what's the problem?"

"The problem is now it's put-up or shut-up time and I don't know if I'm ready for either" Jake admitted. He wasn't entirely sure why he couldn't talk to Kelly who was literally just a few feet away but something felt more comfortable about talking with a friend over his girlfriend.

"I thought you were dead-set on this?"

"I am…I was…" he said quickly. "…I really have no fucking idea Scribbs."

Jake stopped leaning against the wall and took a seat on the chair closest to him. He wanted to be sure to keep his voice low so that Kelly couldn't hear or get worried.

"Well that covers all the bases" Scribner said sarcastically but also with his trademark honesty.

"Do you have any advice or do you just want to let my thoughts continue to bounce off you" Jake said, angrier than he would've liked. Scribner didn't deserve to be yelled at for the mess he was in. But he was the only one around.

Jake checked his phone again. No response from Eric yet.

"Can't decide this one for you" he replied, much the way Jake expected him to. "But I know you...and I think you want this."

Somehow his friend's words were more paralyzing than the bid he'd just received.

"Why are you even awake right now?"

"Because somebody had to let those bastards in. It's seven in the morning and there's no way Dukes' ass was getting out of bed," Scribner answered.

"Right because it's not three in the afternoon yet" Jake agreed. *Dukes wouldn't get up for a fire drill this early on a Saturday let alone for a knock on the suite's door.*

"Don't change the subject though kid. What do *you* want to do?"

"I know you're probably right."

"I always think so" Scribner cut in with a smirk.

"I just need a second to think. I'm gonna take a walk."

"It's freezing outside Raley."

"I'm not going outside, just around the building. I don't want Kelly to hear me pacing out here."

"That's completely healthy."

"Get back to bed Scribbs...you look terrible."

With that Jake turned to walk down the short hallway past their bathroom to the outer door.

"You aint no fuckin' beauty queen yourself kid!" he heard Scribner's voice come after him just as the main suite door closed between them.

Jake grinned to himself as he walked to the nearest stairwell fifteen feet away.

Briskly, he went up all three floors to hit the top level. He found the nearest corridor and found himself looking outside as snow fell gently across the campus.

The corridor overlooked a courtyard that one other dorm shared with this one. It looked very peaceful outside. There wasn't anyone within sight.

Jake stared longingly out the window trying to make sense of what it would mean accepting the bid or walking away. Almost frantically, he checked his phone again. Even though not seeing a message from Eric was bad, Jake also was unlucky enough to notice the time. And it was moving much faster than he wanted it to.

Chapter 22

After Jared placed Jake in the farthest open spot nearest to the kitchen doorway the room fell silent again. It was an unfortunate truth of the current AZXi house that there was really no good place to hold this particular ceremony. In the old days it would be done in the barn where he, Kevin and Guapo had pledged. *That damn thing could hold every member with room to play pong and pound.*

Those days had passed. They were here now.

The common room on Gretman's side of the house was better than the one on Jeff's in any case so they'd held these meetings here for the past two years.

There were three different couches throughout the small room built for three people each. Tonight each one held four brothers, not to mention the ones sitting on the arms of each couch. Then there were the brothers standing in the corners, in the doorway, and sitting on top of the large TV stand. The room was packed past capacity.

Being the pledge-master carried the added bonus of having his seat chosen for him before anything even started. It was always in the same place. Front and center on the middle couch with the lone coffee table in front of him where the AZXi binder was placed. In front of the binder were twelve short candles, all lit. The flames were dancing even without any movement in the room.

Jeff was standing by the front door when the next knock came. "What are the vigilant words of this fraternity?" Jeff boomed to the closed door.

"Equality and brotherhood" Summers' voice came through clearly.

"You may enter" he replied the same as he'd done with Raley. Summers was then led into the room by Eric and placed right next to Raley. Eric then took his place behind his Little, next to Jared. They were standing up against the tucked-in legs of the brothers on the couch behind them.

Much quicker this time, the next knock came. "What are the vigilant words of this fraternity?" Jeff asked for the third time.

"Equality and brotherhood" J-Hood's toneless voice replied.

"You may enter" Jeff repeated.

The same as before, J-Hood was led into the room by his big brother Kevin and placed next to his two pledge brothers. Now only one spot remained.

The final knock came. Jeff's excitement kicked up a notch unexpectedly. He hadn't expected to feel much of anything at the completion of tonight. But now a sense of accomplishment was taking over. It felt good in a way he hadn't felt in a long time.

"What are the vigilant words of this fraternity?" he asked one last time.

"Alpha Zeta Xi" Will's voice came through confidently.

Jeff was about to tell him he could enter before he realized he'd heard the wrong answer. Fortunately in that time he heard what he thought was a slap on the back.

"Shit…I mean equality and brotherhood" Will corrected himself.

In the shallow light of the room, Jeff smiled at the mistake and its quick correction, courtesy of Petey no doubt giving Bill-Butt a love tap to speed things along.

When he allowed them to enter Petey was shaking his head. Once Will was placed next to J-Hood the table was set. *Time to go.*

Jeff looked briefly at each pledge he'd molded over the past six weeks. The only one he stopped on was Jake. He knew why the kid was weighing on his mind but he couldn't bring himself to think about that now. *I'll deal with that later.*

Jeff made sure each of the Bigs had a tall white candle in their hands as tradition dictated. Last semester that had been fucked up and he didn't want a repeat.

"Pledges, you may remove your blindfolds" Jeff instructed coolly.

In unison, the four before him took off the t-shirts they'd been using as blindfolds for the past month and a half. It didn't take long for their eyes to adjust to the low light of the room they were in. The only source was coming from the twelve short candles on the coffee table in front of Jeff, Jerry, Calvin and J-Bro.

"Brothers, it is my honor to introduce to you the pledge class of spring 2007. The candidates for initiation are: Jake Raley, Matthew Summers, Justin Henksin and William Anthony." As Jeff said the names he made eye contact with each pledge along the way, making sure to give them the respect.

"Alpha Epsilon class, you have dedicated yourselves to Alpha Zeta Xi for six long weeks. You have shown us all that you are indeed worthy to be called our brothers."

Usually the pledge-master had to keep his eyes locked on the binder in front of him so he could read the words directly from the pages. But Jeff had been studying the paragraphs for a week now. He wanted to be able to look his pledges in the eye as much as possible when he finally said the words to them. *They memorized page after page of the AZXi history from their pledge books for me so I can memorize a few lines from the Historian's Binder for them.*

"The twelve candles you see before you represent our twelve founding fathers that started Alpha Zeta Xi twelve years ago. May they light your way into the future the same as they have done for all of us here before you."

Jeff was constantly looking back and forth between all four pledges.

"When God asked Cain: where is your brother Abel? Cain replied: Am I my brother's keeper?" Jeff stopped for a moment. "Truly we are our brother's keeper. May the four of you find comfort in knowing that each member of this organization will always be there for you in the days ahead. We will now recite our credo. Brothers, return to these words often and find solace in them.

Jeff turned the page to the credo of Alpha Zeta Xi that he'd once been forced to memorize all those semesters ago. It felt unsettling to look at it again, even under these happier circumstances. There were still times when he remembered pledging and the Hell it had brought on him and the others.

He took a deep breath before plunging back into the words on the page.

****

She read the text message. Then she read it again just to be sure she wasn't hallucinating. Sadly that wouldn't be the first time her mind had caused her to see something that wasn't there.

"Thank God" she let out a sigh of relief before finishing the cup of wine Tory had poured for her a few minutes earlier.

"What?" Tory finally asked as she polished off her own cup. Her third if Riley was recalling correctly.

"Eric just messaged me that they're crossing them right now" Riley answered quickly. It made her feel even better to say it out loud. It made the whole thing seem real, almost as if it hadn't before that moment.

"On a Thursday?! That's weird."

Riley had been so happy about Eric's message that she hadn't stopped to think about it in that way. *Wow, that is weird.* Most organizations crossed their pledges on the weekends, not during the middle of the week. Even though Thursday was technically the weekend in Gladen Hills as much as Friday was, it was still un common for a Crossing to happen then. From everything she knew about Jeff Chester it just seemed off somehow that he would play things this way.

Riley shook her head fiercely. *Who cares? Jake's crossing! It's over.* He hadn't quit. He hadn't de-pledged. Most importantly, she wouldn't have to baby-sit him anymore. *He's got a fraternity full of brothers now.* She was proud of him but in some ways she was very happy for herself.

"You're right but who gives a fuck? It's over!"

"You're right" Tory agreed. "It's great. Does this mean you're gonna stop worrying now?"

"Definitely not nearly as much although putting the two of them together like this in the same frat could be trouble" Riley replied as she finally let that new fact sink in.

Her face must've shown apprehension at the thought. *Jake's already been banned from the Rho Beta house for God knows why.*

"Just let it be someone else's problem" Tory urged her slyly.

Riley nodded at Tory and faked a smile. The thoughts were still on her mind as were all the times her aunts and mother had said to 'keep an eye on the boys'.

"Does this at least mean you're going to start being 'fun Riley' again?"

"Well it at least means I'm going out tonight to congratulate him. Who's our party with tonight anyways?" Riley asked.

There was little doubt in her head that her best friend had come to her room earlier to start drinking. Unfortunately she'd been neck-deep in paranoia at the time so it wasn't until after being talked down that she'd agreed to let Tory bring down the wine.

What kind of friend would I be if I let her drink alone?

"The Kappa Nus" Tory responded almost instantly.

The last time they'd had a social with those guys only like ten brothers showed up. They must've figured that since EIPi wasn't ABI or Phi Theta they couldn't be bothered to attend. *Typical Kappa Nu.* They might've been the most attractive guys on the campus overall but they sucked to party with most of the time. *Everyone loves a drunken frat guy until he tries to fuck your best friend.* Riley grinned. No statement could was better suited to Kappa Nu.

Tory poured her another cup full of the red wine they were currently downing. "I've got another bottle in my room. You game?" she asked as if the answer wasn't painfully obvious. Riley was committed to going out and celebrating with her other family. Pregaming was already part of the plan.

"Nothing wrong with starting our party early" Riley stated with confidence and a smile to match it.

"I hope not. We'd have a serious problem otherwise" Tory grinned as the bottle emptied itself into her own cup.

"Don't worry T. We've definitely got problems. That just isn't one of them."

"I feel like I should be insulted. So I guess I'm gonna drink the wine by myself."

"What the hell am I supposed to do then?"

"Moral support?" Tory responded dryly.

"Very funny."

"Oh relax. I'll go get it for you princess. Who wants to drink alone anyways?"

Riley sat on her couch smiling as she looked toward the darkened window frame.

EIPi's pledges were crossed along with AZXis. Life could finally start getting back to normal. Or at least as normal as things could be in Gladen Hills.

****

"Before we initiate you into our order, we must present to you one final test" Jeff began. Jake didn't even wait to hear what the rest of it was. *Of course you have to test us again. You put us underground from the school. It was never going to end that easy.* Whatever these final tests were Jake was sure they'd be impossible.

"If for any reason you can't answer these questions fully and honestly then please see your big brother who will see you safely escorted from this chamber" Jeff went on as Jake continued stewing in his place.

Jerry started speaking about something or other but Jake was getting too frustrated to listen to any more of their telegraphed bullshit. After reading a few lines out of the binder on the coffee table, Jerry stopped and looked up at each of them before the other continued onward.

"Please list in alphabetical order the founding father's full names," Jeff stated casually as though he wasn't setting them up to fail. Jake doubted a single person in the room had any clue what the answer was. The twelve names in their pledge books had the founding father's first and last names but not their middle names. Jake could only assume that Jeff was asking for those as well.

The four of them started their pointless response and as soon as they finished with the first name Jeff told them to stop while shaking his head. "I asked for their *full* names, not another half-assed answer," he responded icily.

"I would now ask you to please recite, as a pledge class, the credo of Alpha Zeta Xi." Jake flinched again. As it stood, J-Hood and himself were the only ones that knew it. Of course Jeff made sure to ask for them to recite it 'as a pledge class'.

They all started with the first line in sync and then when they reached the second sentence it all fell apart. Will was saying gibberish trying to find the right words and Summers just stopped speaking completely as if no one would notice. *Two down and one to go 'til they can continue fucking us.*

Jeff again stopped them with disgust in his eyes before proceeding to the final question. The options started whirling through Jake's mind. What would the final question be? Something along the lines of the birthday's of the founding fathers parents? Maybe what each of their favorite beers is? What about what the weather was like on the day the CGA had accepted AZXi's charter? Nothing would've surprised Jake.

He was so lost in his own daze of hatred and contempt that he almost didn't hear what Jeff asked for the last question. "What are the colors of this fraternity?" he asked with a straight face that was clearly hiding a smile.

"Black and gold sir!" they all yelled in unison…one last time.

"Very well" Jeff said, still keeping a straight face. "I would now ask everyone to raise their right hands and repeat after me: I swear before God and these witnesses!" he boomed. "To be entirely committed to the welfare of my brothers. Their concerns will be mine. Their mistakes will be mine to challenge. Their victories will be mine to share." Jeff looked around and waited for everyone in the room to repeat every word.

Once they'd caught up to him, he continued. "I swear that I will renew this day…the affirmative responses to my initiation examination!" Jeff's voice continued booming throughout the crowded room.

"I swear that I so shall live my life…as to bring honor and credit…upon my brothers…myself…and the Alpha Zeta Xi Fraternity!" By the end they were all shouting the lines back to him. It felt good to be a part of that even Jake had to admit.

"You may now lower your hands" Jeff ordered, not unkindly. "In life's dark hours a brother will always help you find your way. If any of you are ever called upon to assist a brother, then do so with steadfastness...for this day you have sworn to do so. Alpha Epsilons, you have earned the right to call yourselves Alpha Zeta Xis. If you would turn around, your big brothers will now show you our fraternal handshake which bonds us all together" Jeff finished.

They all turned around as instructed to see their respective big brothers standing there. Jared was grinning as widely as Jake had ever seen and it was contagious. He felt himself smiling as he extended his hand to learn the handshake. It felt just like a normal one except for Jared's index finger being outstretched to hit the underside of Jake's wrist.

"Our final test is one of three questions, so too is our grip one of three fingers" Jeff continued.

Jake extended his index finger to Jared's wrist to mimic the maneuver. That got his big brother smiling even wider, which he didn't think was physically possible. He finished up the handshake and turned back around. The candles their Bigs had been holding were now being lit and handed to the four of them to hold in their place.

"Now your big brothers have lit your path. There's one final task to complete before the night is over" Jeff exclaimed. "You must complete this fine bottle of liquor that we've procured just for you before leaving this house." As he spoke he picked up the bottle that had been resting unseen on the floor and placed it on the table in front of the binder but between the twelve candles.

Jake wasn't that big of a drinker, especially in the past six weeks but even he caught the irony of calling that big ass bottle 'fine'. *That's the kind of shit we'd serve down at a Raley's Ring party.*

The lights in the room came up as Calvin hit the switch and the cheering began right after. It split the silence like nothing Jake had ever heard. Everyone that had been quiet throughout the entire proceeding was now cheering like they'd just won the lottery. It was unreal. Jake didn't know how to react. He'd hated practically everyone in this room for so long and now it was over?

"Get it started boys!" he heard Calvin's voice through the constant barrage of screams and cheers.

"Let's get hammered!" Jared yelled from behind him as he patted Jake's back.

Jake looked over to see Eric hugging and congratulating Summers right next to him. After that he immediately turned to see his cousin. Jake never felt a hug so overpowering with emotion as Eric's now did for him. "Congratulations J. I'm proud of you" was all he heard Biz say through the overwhelming noise.

"Thanks Biz, it means a lot," Jake confessed. Even he was surprised at how good he felt hearing those words from his cousin.

Eric pulled Jake aside through the crowd of brothers now congregating around the pledges. The other actives took the hint not to bother them as they made their way through to the corner.

"You know I never told you about this and you never asked…" he started saying hesitantly. "That morning the bids were dropped off…I was fucking hammered still but I got up to piss. My head was pounding and I felt like I'd been hit by a truck after the lock-in." Jake assumed he wasn't supposed to know what the hell a 'lock-in' was so he just stood there and listened. "But I got that text message you sent me asking for help. I knew what day it was and because of the time I knew the guys must've dropped off your bid. You wanted advice on what you should do right?"

Jake looked at his cousin with confusion. He'd always just assumed Eric had slept past noon that day and by the time he'd read the text he wouldn't have been able to help anyways so he'd never brought it up since. But now he was telling him that he'd gotten it and flat out ignored it.

"Yeah, that's exactly what I wanted. Why didn't you say anything?" Jake asked harshly. How could his cousin, his family, not say anything or help during the time when he needed him? It was like hearing it about somebody else. Eric would never do that to him intentionally, not with all their history.

"I didn't say anything because this decision was yours. No matter how much I wanted to tell you to accept. That it'd be the best decision of your life…I couldn't. Because that would've been *my* decision and I wouldn't take that from you. I never will. This is your experience J."

His harsh feelings toward his cousin washed away while he listened. Even with the white noise coming from all the actives chanting and yelling he heard every word Eric said. Jake knew he was right but somehow he couldn't bring himself to say it. He just nodded and put out his hand. For the first time they shook hands as brothers of Alpha Zeta Xi. In that moment he knew he couldn't be mad at his cousin…his brother.

"I think I should call Kelly and let her know" Jake choked out. He still hadn't found his full voice after what Eric had said.

"I guess so. It's a big day for her too."

"It just feels so weird to be done with all this shit."

"Weird?" Eric looked shocked as he repeated the word.

"Don't worry I'll get used to it Biz" Jake assured him with a smile.

****

Eric watched his cousin smile before turning to walk out the front door to call his girlfriend. He didn't agree with that idea but what could he do? Tell his cousin to leave it alone and enjoy tonight with his new brothers? Somehow he didn't see that particular conversation ending well.

"Hey Eric, do you have anything to mix this with?" Summers asked from behind him. He turned to see his Little holding the huge bottle of vodka, waiting for guidance. To be fair Eric wasn't even sure *he'd* drink that garbage straight but there was also no way he would lighten the task.

Every semester they'd been giving the crossing pledges a bottle of bottom shelf vodka and calling it a 'fine batch of alcohol'. He and Jerry suffered through it just like Brent and Aaron had and the Alpha Gammas along with every other class before them.

Jerry beat him to the punch. "A mixer?! For that fine batch of alcohol?!" He spoke the words as if reading them from a script. The words were the final mind-fuck the actives gave to the new fucks at Crossing. It wasn't meant to be malicious in any way. They just couldn't afford to buy Grey Goose for the incoming class every semester. Not when they had below thirty actives, some who didn't even pay dues on time. That on top of parties three nights every week stretched the budget. Something had to give and Eric had to cut corners wherever possible. And this was a corner.

He always imagined when the frat was starting out the founders had given some kind of top shelf liquor to the incoming classes but as time went by, things changed.

Jerry turned toward Eric, feigning shock. "Did these ugly dudes just ask for a mixer? I'm absolutely ashamed."

"Somehow I think you'll manage Jerry" Jake's voice reentered the conversation just in time. His cousin was grinning from the sarcasm he'd just shot in his assistant pledge-master's direction. *There ya go J, welcome back.*

"You talk to Kelly?" Eric asked, if only to get the question out of the way.

"Nah, she's still in class. I got her voicemail." He wasn't as sullen as Eric expected, which was good. They had a long night ahead and there was nothing that should stand in the way of the new fucks having a great time now that it was all over.

"I don't know Raley. It'll be tough I think. I might just have to blackout and forget this ever happened," Jerry said with a grin.

"Doesn't sound like anything out of the ordinary" Eric jumped in.

Finally, as if everyone noticed at once that Jake had reentered the room, the throng of actives came toward him, all wanting to congratulate him. It was a thing of beauty. Eric Saren was in no short supply of pride at the moment.

****

By the time he was done shaking hands with all the actives that had surrounded him, Jake felt hammered. And that was before he'd taken even a sip from the gift bottle.

The final piece of the puzzle was the pledge-master himself who seemed to be gingerly making his way toward him. It looked weird. It felt weird too. Usually the bastard just stormed up to him and asked the impossible, whatever that may be for any particular time. That would generally be followed by some kind of physical activity.

He tried remembering the week's events. There'd been four callouts, one on each of the weeknights. Jake was finding himself hard pressed to recall Jeff ever being his usual full asinine self as he'd always been during the first five weeks of pledging. He'd still given out push-ups, wall-sits and keg-lifts but something just felt different about those memories. Almost like Jeff was holding back. *Why would this guy ever hold back anything? He hates me and I hate him.*

"Congratulations Raley" Jeff said as he reached out for the brotherhood handshake. Jake didn't know how to react. He'd wanted nothing more than to punch the guy in the face so many times. Shaking his hand now without having to give him a flawless six-second greeting was somehow wrong. Jeff actually looked sincere in the moment. Jake begrudgingly shook hands in the AZXi way. His former pledge-master didn't notice or just didn't care about his underlying emotions.

"Did you just leave for a second?"

"Yeah I went outside to call my girlfriend" Jake replied as they stood there. Some of the brothers had already started filing out toward the basement to refill their beers. He and Jeff were standing off to the side now that Eric and the others were moving away toward the kitchen.

Jeff didn't move at all when Jake replied but his apparent lack of a response put him on edge. He seemed to be actively trying not to show a reaction. Ironically, that's what caught Jake's eye. *Who cares what his problems are?*

"You know I was real pissed at you about all this tonight" Jake began in earnest as he motioned around the room. He wanted it to signify the entire fraternity but wasn't sure if Jeff was getting the point. "I was pissed for missing class…and yes I know how that sounds. I was ready to walk the fuck away from this," he said confidently while staring right into Jeff's eyes. Neither of them blinked once.

Funnily enough, Jeff's hardened gaze cracked first and he smiled back like he'd heard something amusing. He immediately felt sheepish like he had so many times before in the guy's presence. *What the fuck?*

"I figured it was something like that. It just means Jerry and I did our job" he replied casually. "The general rule around here is that if you aren't ready to quit, you aren't ready to cross."

Jake let that sink in. It made sense in a really twisted and warped way. *Just like everything else in this frat.*

"This is where the fun begins Raley so just keep that shit in the past or deal with it later on if you want…like when I'm not around" Jeff smirked.

Jake let out an inadvertent smile.

"Come on kid, you've gotta sign the Historian's Binder" Jeff motioned to the table by the couch he'd been reading off of earlier. The page was opened to a near blank one. There were only five names listed on it: Brent and Aaron's and then Jake's three pledge brothers who'd already signed.

Jeff handed him a pen and Jake started writing right below Will's name.

A sudden urge hit him so he flipped back a page. He read through the nine names in the Alpha Gamma class and then found Eric's name right above Jerry's. One more page back he found Calvin and Jeff plus his Big-Big Kraylin.

They've all been here before…right where I am. Signing their name to something they probably didn't understand. It was making his mind numb to think about the history of the organization. He'd memorized names, pledge classes, Bids parties and Executive Boards but it never really sunk in about just what it all meant.

Pride and for the wisdom of its traditions. That sole line from the AZXi credo started repeating in his thoughts. He was now a part of something bigger than himself. It felt good and yet somehow terrifying. He realized after a minute that he hadn't signed his last name. Jeff hadn't said a word but had kept watch the whole time.

Jake signed it completely and put the pen down.

"Do me a favor Jeff. Tell me to do twenty push-ups" Jake ordered after he looked up from the binder.

Jeff looked extremely confused at the request but he humored his former pledge nonetheless. "Get down and give me twenty Raley." Jake Raley just smiled. "Go fuck yourself."

****

It had taken a little longer than even Jeff had expected to get everyone into the basement. The pledges were doing their best to get through the bottle but he'd slowed them down in preparation for what was planned. It was best if they weren't completely hammered for now. *It'll be safer too.*

Jeff raised his hands and called for everyone to quiet down. Of course there were some that just weren't getting the message. Not surprisingly, it was the drunkest ones that weren't shutting up. "Aaron and Dills! Shut the fuck up!" Jeff called them out by name. Finally he got enough of a lull in the bantering to speak clearly to the pledges if no one else. The four of them were standing in front of the bar. J-Hood had the bottle in his hand and was sipping on it. He handed it to Raley who looked ready to throw-up at the thought of drinking more.

"Now I don't know about you guys, but when I was pledging I always wondered about the pledge class paddles lining the hallways of the house. Specifically, I used to wonder why the hell some of them were so fucked up, missing letters and shit. The answer to that is something you're about to learn."

Jeff lifted up the Alpha Epsilon pledge paddle they'd created three weeks ago. Jerry had been nearby to hand it to him. He looked it over once again, if only to take one last mental note of how sweet it looked before its inevitable destruction.

"See guys...your paddle is in great shape. That's something we can't allow. We need it to have battle wounds. You guys have another task to complete in addition to finishing that bottle Raley is nursing like a bitch." The basement lit up with laughs not unlike the kind that had accompanied the kid's rap battle victory an hour before.

"You guys understandably have some pent up rage against the brothers around here. And what better way to get that rage out than to use this paddle of yours to get back at them" Jerry added on.

"Each of you is going to get the opportunity to paddle the ass of two brothers of your choosing" Jeff stated as clearly as he could. "Raley" he smiled at him as he approached. "You're up first."

He handed the kid the paddle and began to walk away before he heard exactly what he was expecting to hear. "Where do you think you're heading pal?" Raley's voice echoed through the basement even with the background chatter from other brothers.

"Ohhhhh!" half of them exclaimed in unison when the kid called him out. *Good. Better to get it out of the way first.*

Jeff smiled knowingly before going to the nearest wall to the right of the pledges. He slid his pants down a little to expose his bare ass. He cupped his balls in his hands since there was no worse feeling on planet earth than having a hard paddling hit those things as well. Every active knew to cover those suckers up during a paddling.

Jeff looked back to see Raley being instructed by Jerry on how to paddle appropriately. The last thing they needed was one of the pledges flipping the paddle and hitting one of the actives square in the back with the side of it to really hurt somebody. Not that getting a paddle on the ass was pleasant. It was just that it was the best place to get a paddle without any real lasting damage.

After Jerry's tutorial ended Raley wound back and took a step forward. Jeff turned away at the last possible second to absorb the incoming impact. The pain that shot through Jeff's body was well earned. He'd been paddled the past two semesters by the incoming new fucks but Raley's was on a different level of pain entirely.

A millisecond after he caught the brunt of the pain, he heard the giant thwack sound the paddle made when it connected. He could've sworn it echoed off the walls. *Son of a bitch...*

Jeff was now fighting a losing battle with his legs to stay standing from the pain. He was too busy trying to stay standing that he didn't notice Jerry's hand on his shoulder letting him know that he could move out of the way for the next victim of the Alpha Epsilon class. He'd created a force to be reckoned with. Once he was able to sit down again he'd be proud of that.

"J-Hood! You're up next!" Jerry called out since Jeff was still in no position to speak clearly.

"Jared!" he called out calmly. "Get over here" he pointed to the space Jeff had just slowly vacated.

Jeff hadn't noticed until now that the Alpha Epsilon paddle had already lost some of the lettering from the hit Raley just gave him. *No surprises there.*

Jerry walked J-Hood through the proper paddle swing and then backed away in a hasty fashion.

Thwack! The sound hit Jeff's ears. His own body reflexively winced at the familiar sound. Jared let out a high-pitched yelp. Jeff hoped he hadn't made a similar sound but couldn't remember one way or the other. Opening his eyes, he saw his pants being pulled up as the guy stutter-stepped out of the way toward Jeff. He hadn't even noticed that the bringer of pain was standing right next to him.

Jared started talking to Raley as soon as he got into earshot of him.

"Son of a bitch that was ridiculous" Jared exclaimed as if it wasn't entirely obvious to everyone down there. The people walking out on Arkridge probably heard it.

"Well I did hear you were kind of an ass to the rest of my pledge class."

"Well...don't any of them have a sense of humor?"

"I'm sure J-Hood could ask the same thing about paddling you" Jake quipped.

"I just wish my ass wasn't on fire."

"And I'm sure they wanted to be able to lift their arms after a callout too" Raley smirked back at him.

"I guess we'll call it even."

"Don't look at me pal, you'll have to take it up with them" he motioned to the other three Alpha Epsilons.

Jeff would've told Jared not to count on anything like that but he didn't want to resurface on anyone's radar and possibly get paddled again. At least not so soon.

He needed a beer and quick. Fortunately he wasn't that far from the keg. Slowly, he made his way over to it and filled a new cup. He'd lost track of his previous one. As he chugged the cool beer he noticed Raley was now slamming the vodka bottle down. He must've taken a good three shots worth in the gulp alone.

Jeff felt bad for whoever was going to get paddled next by the kid.

He only had one more thought circling his mind as he drank the beer and looked around the basement. The pledges all had smiles on their faces for the first time since Bids. It was great to see.

Pride was filling him where just moments ago pain reigned. *This is the real Gladen Hills.*

****

Jake hadn't felt this kind of a throbbing headache since the last Raley's Ring party he'd thrown two weeks ago over spring break. *This one feels so much worse. What the fuck happened last night?* He quickly tried getting his bearings. After adjusting his eyes to actually function he figured out that he was in Kelly's room.

She was already up and typing at her computer. "How did I get here Kel?" was the first thing he asked. It even hurt to speak those words.

"I picked you up around ten last night after I left class. It sounds like missing the extra credit was worth it," she replied warmly.

"Ten? That means I couldn't have been at the house more than two hours after we crossed" he said thoughtfully. He was desperately trying to get *any* recollection from last night.

"You know babe, watching you unable to function after promising to do so much to me on the way home is such a turn-on" Kelly said sarcastically.

Yikes…

"Well I'm sorry about that Kel. Why don't we take a shower and talk about it" he gestured. He wasn't sure how much better off he was today from last night but figured it was worth a shot.

"You know I'm so proud of you baby," she said as she leaned down to kiss him lightly. "Now I get to see you more right?"

"I think I might reverse the situation from pledging actually" he sighed. She looked at him inquisitively. "I'm not going to have time for the frat because I'll be with you every second" he promised as he sat up to kiss her. Her lips made his headache a little easier to bear.

"That sounds like a great idea."

There was no way that Eric, Jared and the other guys would be OK with that plan but Jake didn't care. *I'm free from all their bullshit now…*

He was sure Biz would be pissed about him leaving so early last night. If he remembered correctly though, they were all planning to go to the Rho Beta house. Last time he checked, he still wasn't allowed there for whatever happened on Bids.

"Come on, let's get to the shower before one of your suitemates does," he begged her. The thought of getting inside her again was turning him on despite the massive hangover. *At least that part of me still works…thank God.*

"Go ahead and get it started. I just want to finish up this email."

Jake did as instructed and stumbled toward the doorway and down the hall. Thankfully there was no one in the bathroom. *What a miracle that is.* He got the water running to a nice warm temperature before heading back to her room. Jake's plan was to kiss her neck until she agreed to come with him immediately.

When he reached the room she was texting. She seemed a little pensive even from behind. Facing the window on the opposite side of the room, she still hadn't noticed he was in the doorway. Kelly finally put the phone down before staring out the window at the campus below.

"You ready babe?" he asked after a few seconds standing in the silence with only the faint sound of the shower running in the background.

"Yeah I'll be right there."

Jake didn't even realize it but he was swaying back and forth in the doorway from his recent inebriation. *Good God what the hell did I drink last night?*

Kelly must've assumed he'd just gotten there because she played it off as such. She grabbed a towel from the back of her desk chair and left her cell phone where it was. "All done," she said as she approached him.

His mind was appropriately fixed on the way her body swayed as she walked toward him. He couldn't wait to get those clothes off and take her under the warm water of the shower. *It's gonna feel so good.*

Even now the euphoria from Crossing didn't seem real.
I can't believe it's over.
Now everything can be normal again...just me and Kel.

Chapter 23

Perfect serenity. And then it all came crashing down.

Screams and cheers erupted from Jerry's room next door.
Why Jerry? Just why?

Eric tried and failed to get back to sleep. Whatever was going on in that room next door was winning the battle.

Finding his bearings, he managed to slink his way out from under the warm enveloping covers on his bed. His head was throbbing in ways no one should ever be subjected to.

Twisting the doorknob before him, Eric stumbled into Jerry's room where he found the guy playing Super Smash Bros. with Brent like usual. Most of the time he'd be invited to play along with Lenny but not today. *It's probably not their fault.* For all Eric knew, they could've knocked fervently on his door to see if he wanted to play but were met with no response. *That's probably exactly what happened actually...*

Eric had learned a long time ago that locking his door after a night of partying saved him all kinds of headaches the next day. If someone like Buttons, Dills or Kev wanted to get in, they could probably card their way through. Thankfully, not everyone in AZXi could card doors. That kept his room from being a rest area from the after-hours parties at the frat house.

Taking a quick glance at the flat screen TV Jerry had mounted on the wall Eric noticed his pledge brother was winning. Not surprising since he would've bet against Segs all day in this match-up.

"Uhhhhh" was all he could manage to say before collapsing on the bed that the other two weren't using. Jerry's room often doubled as the main venue for Smash Bros. games so he had folding chairs ready to go.

Jerry and Brent were deeply focused. They didn't even seem to notice Eric's presence. He couldn't blame them for that. The day's bragging rights were on the line.

Eric finally heard the sweet sound of victory that could only belong to his pledge brother. Only then was he given the courtesy of his existence being noticed. "Rough night Biz?" Jerry asked as he kept his eyes clearly focused on the TV to view the stats of his victory over Segs. Brent on the other hand seemed to take no pleasure at seeing that screen. *I wouldn't look either Segs.*

"You know some people just can't handle our Thursday parties" Brent commented to Jerry while doing a quick once over of a decaying Eric.

He lifted his head up from where it had fallen on the bed and spoke, if only to help his cause. "I usually don't hit up Thursdays."

Jerry knew that better than most people since he was usually side by side with Eric in the library. "You didn't have class today?"

"Professor had some family thing to do today so he told us last week we'd be off today. It was a miracle catch."

"You've only got one class on Fridays? That's a miracle right there Biz" Brent commented with a hint of jealousy.

Just how late in the day had Eric slept? He didn't even bother checking his alarm clock on the way out of his room. He immediately noticed the clock on the corner of Jerry's desk. *Noon.* He'd gotten a solid eight hours of sleep. *Not bad at all.*

"Yeah but that one class is a three hour physics lab," Eric said sullenly.

"Yikes. Sounds like the *perfect* way to start the weekend."

"You know...I'd rather be in the lab than feeling this way" Eric said to no one. "Actually that's not true at all." In truth that lab was downright terrible and he found physics pretty interesting most of the time. It was just such a long damn time to be stuck in a single room.

"Well wahhhhh" Jerry mockingly cried out. "I haven't been out since Crossing."

"Since that was three weeks ago I *highly* doubt that son" Eric shot back. He knew for a fact that Jerry had gone out and partied at least twice in the past three weeks since the Alpha Epsilons became brothers.

"Oh I've gone out," Jerry corrected. "I just haven't drank like I usually do."

"OK, now *that* I could get behind" Eric agreed.

"Yeah you're right. I really haven't seen you out at all since Crossing" Brent joined in, as though he just realized Jerry's point.

"Gee thanks for noticing my absence Segs."

"Where you been at?"

"No less than three projects son. But I turned in the last one this morning so I'm celebrating by kicking your ass" Jerry grinned.

It was at that point that Eric noticed that both Jer-Bear and Segs were sipping on long neck bottles of beer. Maybe he just didn't want to notice since he was still feeling like hammered shit.

"You want one Biz?" Jerry asked with a grin.

That looks disgusting...but it might help.

"We have a party with the Phi Thetas tonight" Brent added.

Son of a bitch. I'll probably end up going to that.

Eric did have a girl in that sorority he'd been trying to get with since his own Crossing. Every time they partied with those girls it seemed like he was making progress only to go home empty handed...every single night. *Tonight might be the night though.*

Jerry didn't even wait for an answer. He took a bottle from the case he had on the floor next to his chair and handed it to Eric. "Was the party hot last night?"

Eric was still contemplating cracking the bottle open. *Is it worth it?*

"Not bad at all" Segs answered in Eric's place.

"Who was it with again?"

"St. Gammas."

"Oh weakkkkk."

His pledge brother always extended the adjective whenever he was mildly disgusted like he was now. *Some things never change.*

On paper the St. Gammas were nothing special, and they were not to be confused with the regular Gammas, which was a fraternity. The sorority didn't have many actives and none of them were drop dead gorgeous like most of the ABI's or Phi Thetas. Even most of the NDM's and Betas were better looking. But what they lacked in attraction they made up for in their ability to have a good time. *The*

ABI's could definitely use a lesson on that much. Eric still wanted to bang more of the ABI's than St. Gammas but the latter was infinitely more fun to party with.

"Hey man, it was still a really solid time" Eric defended them.

"What happened?" Jerry asked with only a vague hint of curiosity as he powered up the next game.

****

It was a Friday afternoon and his classes were done. By all logic in the universe Jake should've been dancing in the street. *If* he enjoyed dancing. But here he was feeling…off. And he couldn't figure out why.

Fortunately his day was about to get significantly better. Hopefully that would snap him the fuck out of his current daze. He'd just finished off typing a wall post onto Dukes' Facebook page when his girlfriend walked in. *Is she done with class?* He checked the time on his laptop to confirm she was done for the day too.

Kelly placed her purse and books on his bed before moving over to kiss him gently the way she always did when they greeted each other.

"Hey babe."

"Hey" she smiled. "Did you go to class today?"

"Of course I did. I'm a phenomenal student."

Ever since Crossing he'd been making it to class regularly. She knew he was going but always wanted to make sure.

"I wasn't sure you would. You mentioned you were gonna go to a party at your frat house last night."

It was one of the first nights in the past few weeks that the two of them hadn't spent the night together. Eric had been all but begging him to come out and experience life as an active brother but Jake had basically been ignoring him. Finally since he and Kelly were taking a break from staying over at the others' dorm he decided to humor Biz.

"Yeah I did go," he confirmed.

"Did you have fun?"

Jake was decidedly unsure on that topic.

"I guess so. I left kinda early."

Kelly flashed a look of concern.

"I just didn't feel like being hung-over for class today" he lied. He wasn't sure why he'd left the party early but that was definitely *not* the reason.

"I didn't realize that was ever a concern for you" Kelly smirked. Jake should've known better than to try that excuse with the girl he loved. She knew that had never stopped him in the past when they'd partied at a frat Open on Thursdays last semester. They'd woken up next to each other countless times only to have sex before stumbling to class together.

"Fair enough" Jake conceded with a smile.

"Is something wrong babe?"

"No, not really."

Even he was shocked at how flimsy his responses were. He was practically begging for her to dig deeper and Kelly never needed much prodding for that.

"Talk to me Jake," she urged.

He turned to stare blankly at the white wall in front of him on Wayne's side.

Eric was indifferent to him about never coming around AZXi. Scribner wouldn't really understand the situation and Riley was constantly busy were her new little sister to care much about what he was going through so that only left Kelly in his inner-circle.

"I guess I just don't fit in," he finally admitted painfully.

****

Eric wasn't entirely sure that anything he said about the previous night's party would sell Jerry on the fact that it was a great time but he pressed on anyways.

"We all started drinking at the National before the party even started. The girls actually showed up ready to go at like half past nine too so that was sweet."

So many times since he'd crossed Eric noticed that the girls they partied with weren't even remotely interested in showing up before ten. The St. Gammas were like a lone oasis in a dry world. It was yet another reason why he liked partying with them.

If there was ever a time when Eric Saren felt completely content, this would probably be a hallmark moment. Standing around the old, decrepit pound table with his brothers just enjoying beer and the game at hand. There was no greater feeling that he could remember. There wasn't any worry about class since the lab had been cancelled tomorrow. The nearest test was two weeks away and the next project was a month from being turned in. Tonight, at this moment, life was good.

Gretman, Bill-Butt and Buttons were the only other guys at the table; decently attractive girls took the other four open spaces.

More to the point, the girls weren't so hot that they would pass on looking at Eric. That was more than he could say for the ABI's.

He'd gone without any for too long and the feeling of desperation was setting in. Guapo had told him so many times that thinking along those lines wasn't going to help him get laid and in fact ran counter to his chances. He never put much stock in what Guapo said but the guy was more of an expert at banging sorority chicks than anyone.

One of the girls rolled an eleven and now had the opportunity to fill up the communal cup and hand it off to whomever she chose. She filled it almost to the top and then slid it over to the space in front of Eric. He was no stranger to pounding full cups of beer and in fact was one of the better AZXis at such things. Hopefully she was one of the girls in Gladen Hills that actually appreciated a guy that could chug. *One time please.*

More often than not everything about pound was luck based since it revolved around the roll of the dice. A person would have to drink the contents of the cup in front of them before the person giving the beer rolled a seven, eleven or double number.

If Eric could finish the full cup before any of those were rolled then he'd be free and the next person in line would roll. If he failed then he'd have to drink another cup full of whatever amount the same girl chose. It was a game that got him hammered quicker than flip cup or beer pong ever did.

Unfortunately now that the pledges had crossed there was nobody but the actives to fill up a low or empty pitcher for these games. Nobody ever wanted that job. Usually Eric would be stuck filling them since he hated waiting for others to step up.

After a few more seconds of just staring down the girl who handed him the beer in the least creepy way possible he grabbed the cup and started chugging. As soon as his hand hit the cup the girl started rolling. He finished before the second roll even set on the table. That was fortunate since the second roll came up with double twos. A tie always went to the drinker so there was no room for debate.

"I love when girls do that," he announced triumphantly to Calvin after the girl passed the dice onward to her right.

"Because you get to show off?" he asked bluntly.

You know it Gretman. Bragging about it to his brothers was one thing but he'd have to be a lot drunker to flaunt his chugging ability out loud.

"Too bad you can't translate that into getting laid" Will joked from his left. It was his friend's turn and he rolled double sixes. He went the gentlemanly route and filled up the cup a little below halfway and handed it to the most attractive girl at the table.

She picked up the cup immediately and Will rolled within the same second, getting another double six on the first try. "My rolling is so hot tonight!" he shouted for the whole basement to hear.

It's all luck you ugly dude. Of course there was no way he'd be able to convince Bill-Butt of that.

Jeff joined in on the conversation from across the table in between two of the St. Gammas in his usual gruff, condescending tone. "Who the fuck gave that kid a bid?" he asked with a grin.

"I was just thinking the same thing," Calvin agreed.

Eric smiled. The silver lining of pledging being over, aside from the fact that he didn't have to worry about Jake anymore, was that the tension between Buttons and Gretman seemed to be subsiding. *It's about damn time.*

"You haven't regretted it for a single damn second" Will grinned as he filled up the communal cup with little more than a shot of beer before giving it back to the same girl.

"You'll always be new fucks to me," Jeff mockingly warned him.

Eric could've sworn he was simply reminding the new guy of his 'place' in the frat. Wearing letters was great but being a new fuck still held inherent issues. Buttons would always be the first to remind new brothers of that.

"Yo check it out" Calvin nudged Eric's arm and motioned behind him past the center of the party. "Looks like J-Hood and Guapo are after the same girl."

Sure enough, the hottest girl in the St. Gammas was in between Guapo and J-Hood. She looked to be talking to both of them intently although the latter looked to be mentally checked out while Guapo was devoting his full attention.

"That's so sick...I love it" Eric admitted.

It was always entertaining watching any brother score. Living vicariously through them was pretty much the only way he was getting any chicks these days so he ran with it.

"Best...bid...ever," Calvin said confidently with a huge grin.

In the background he noticed Jeff looked noticeably indifferent to the entire situation whereas Bill-Butt was also soaking up every second.

While they were paying attention to the scene unfolding, the girl at the table had taken advantage and finished her beer without anyone noticing. It was an amateur move on their part but it was still good to see a savvy sorority girl take advantage of their limited attention spans. *Well played, well played.*

Looking around, Eric found Summers near the center of the basement dancing with a couple girls. Eric hadn't even noticed him there when he'd been watching J-Hood a second ago but he saw him now that he was really looking.

Where the hell is Jake?

"Yo Biz, where's Raley at?" Calvin asked with genuine concern.

"I thought I saw him a second ago" he lied.

Fortunately up 'til now only Eric seemed to really notice how little Jake was actually around since Crossing. That wouldn't last forever, and then it'd be a problem.

"I swear I've only seen that kid once since Crossing" he reiterated Eric's own unsettling thoughts. "I mean seriously Biz…what the fuck?"

"Who knows man?"

Once again he noticed Jeff's look from across the table. This time it wasn't one of indifference like it had been with J-Hood, it almost looked like there might be concern. As soon as Jeff noticed Eric looking his way he put on the look of 'not giving a fuck'.

Thankfully Calvin took the hint that Eric didn't have a good answer and let it go.

Fortunately his cousin chose *that* moment to make his entrance.

He looked a lot like he did the first time he'd walked through those doors as a rush: scared, intimidated and not sure he wanted to be where he was. Eric hoped no one else could see what was painfully obvious to him.

"It's about damn time," Calvin said. "Yo Raley! Get over here!" he urged his cousin over to a space he was making at the table by sliding away from Eric.

Jake hesitantly made his way through the guys and girls littering the basement and arrived at the old pound table.

"You're playing pound," Gretman announced. It sounded more like an order than an invitation.

"Am I?"

"I've barely seen you around and that's not gonna fly so you're pounding beers with us" Calvin repeated.

"Yeah I'll play a few rounds," Jake said, sounding mildly defeated.

"Alright now Raley can finally get some beer in him. Maybe now he can stop being a little bitch all the time" Will said almost immediately.

Jake had barely taken up the spot between Eric and Calvin before he heard Will's comment. He looked uneasy and pissed. Both guys were acting like their textbook selves and they didn't mix well together.

Eric tried to shoot Bill-Butt an under the radar nod to leave Jake alone but he didn't notice. And there was no way he was going to say it out loud and actually be caught coming to his younger cousin's defense. That wouldn't look right.

It took longer than it probably should have but Eric finally realized the dice were his. He rolled and came up empty. After a faked expression of disappointment he passed the dice along to Jake who also came up with nothing. The dice then passed to Gretman.

"So what's up son?" Eric asked his cousin during the lull in their game.

"Just chilling man. Same as always" Jake responded casually. "Been pretty busy actually" he corrected hesitantly as if that was what he was expected to say.

"Busy is what you were before Crossing" Eric corrected him again. "Now you should have more free time than you know what to do with."

"I don't know Biz. I can handle quite a bit" Jake smirked. "Besides, I'm getting really sick at Mario-Kart these days. Like world record status" he announced happily as if that was going to get him some kind of praise. He was met with the only reaction he was bound to get.

"Do me a favor and never talk about videogames at a party again" Calvin all but ordered with a smile.

The dice reached Buttons and he rolled a seven. It was the first legitimate roll on the table since Will. Jeff filled the communal cup to the brim and slid it over to Jake just like Eric was expecting. He would've gone all in on that possibility from the second Jake joined the game.

"Time to live a little Raley" Jeff said haughtily.

His cousin kept a stoic face while nodding at his former pledge-master.

"Bring it on " was all the response he gave. Jake took the beer to his face and started drinking at an alarmingly slow rate, even by a new fuck's standards. Jeff took his dear sweet time rolling and before Jake even reached halfway, he'd rolled a set of threes.

"We need to teach this kid how to drink" Jeff said directly to Eric.

No kidding. "It's not like I haven't been trying Buttons."

Once again Calvin nudged Eric's arm behind Jake's back and motioned toward the corner of the room. "Jesus look as this" he said while subtly pointing. Pretty much everyone at the table picked up on what Calvin was looking at, including the girls.

J-Hood was now full on making out with the girl he'd been not really paying attention to not five minutes earlier. It wasn't a playful make-out either. This girl was enjoying it immensely from her body language. Hood was grabbing her ass in full view of the party. The girl's arms were wrapped around his neck so tightly that breathing could become an issue at any second.

"I fucking love that guy" Will said, echoing the thoughts every man in the room.

"Good thing he's an AZXi now" Calvin said happily.

Eric agreed but it was the lack of a response from both Jeff and Jake that caught his attention the most. When he turned back to see what his cousin was doing his heart sank. Jake was sliding the leftover beer in the communal cup toward him.

"Yo take the rest of this for me Biz, Kelly's calling me" he said quickly while he checked his phone and moved toward the stairs away from the party. Eric rolled his eyes instinctively at the mere mention of his girlfriend's name.

Looking at the half finished beer in front of him with a touch of regret he again caught something out of the corner of his eye. Jeff looked different. *Is he disappointed?*

"So J-Hood has some sweet game...nothing new there" Jerry grinned as he turned back to the TV.

"It was still great watching him beat Guapo while he wasn't really trying. I don't know…I thought it was great," Eric admitted. Nothing was sweeter than watching the self-proclaimed 'king of pussy' get his ass handed to him by a new fuck.

"Yeah true" Jerry agreed. "I *hate* Guapo," he said with gusto like he had so many times before. Of course his pledge brother didn't really hate anyone.

"Nothing new there either Jer-Bear" Eric said with a smirk as he cracked open the bottle he'd been handed ten minutes before. *Just one and we'll see how it goes.*

****

"I got to the party later than Eric wanted and as soon I got in the door, one of the older guys ordered me around. It felt just like a callout except the music wasn't that weird heavy metal shit" Jake started in. "I hate playing pound because I suck at it. But Gretman didn't give me a choice. Of course fucking Jeff gave me a full beer even though he already knows I can't chug. And that whole damn game is based on chugging. He just wanted to fuck with me again."

Kelly's eyes had nothing but concern and comfort in them. "Jeff was your pledge-master right?"

"Yeah. I hated him then and I hate him now. He's trying to act like nothing happened. Actually they all are but he's the one that pisses me off the most. He led the whole fucking thing…" his voice trailed off.

"I'm sorry baby," Kelly said sympathetically while resting her head on his shoulder. He felt her hand rubbing his back to soothe him further. He was actually starting to breathe heavily while venting.

"And then to top it all off…I gotta watch J-Hood making out with *another* girl and hear everyone talk about how great the son of a bitch is." Jake did his best to stave off any feelings of jealousy when he said those words but he wasn't sure if he did.

"I always thought that's just what guys did."

"Well…yeah" Jake agreed. "It's just that people put that guy on a pedestal for everything he does. There were four people in his pledge class but you'd think he did everything himself." Now he could hear the jealousy in his voice.

"I don't know Jake…maybe you should just take a step back from that place for a while" his girlfriend said supportively.

Yeah…wouldn't that be fuckin' nice. "Biz would never be OK with that, absolutely no chance."

"You didn't quit pledging. You're in his frat now. Why would he be mad at you for doing your own thing now?"

It made complete sense when she said it like that and yet Jake didn't see his cousin responding kindly. He wasn't sure he would respond that way if the roles were reversed. How could he expect Eric to do what he couldn't?

"You know...I knew when I was pledging that even after it ended I wouldn't want to be friends with or even hang out with half the fuckers in the frat. I just didn't think I'd still actively hate most of them still...not this long after it ended."

"I'm sorry Jake."

Jake sighed. "Maybe I should just steer clear from that damn house 'til next semester at least. Then I can avoid going off on any of them," he said with confidence. The last thing that would help was yelling at one of the actives for reasons even he couldn't understand. It'd be even worse if that active was his cousin.

"Whatever you think you should do baby."

"Thanks" he smiled down at her. His lips touched hers lightly and again he felt better than he had a second before.

"I'll be right back...bathroom," she said before getting up off the bed they'd been sitting on.

"I'm guessing you don't need help finding it."

She gave him a quick amused look before leaving the room.

Once he was alone the feelings from the previous night flooded back as if on cue.

"Good thing he's an AZXi now" Calvin's voice said from behind him as they all remained focused on Jake's pledge brother.

Jesus it's not that big of a deal...so he gets laid a lot...who the fuck cares?

There was a time when Jake was of the same mindset but since Crossing he'd gotten tired of hearing the *real* thoughts from all the actives. None of them had been able to compliment any of the pledges during actual pledging. Now that it was over the dick-sucking J-Hood was receiving annoyed him to no end. Even Bill-Butt was lining up to kiss the guy's ass.

Jake continued watching his pledge brother grab the ass of the girl who only moments before was talking to Guapo intently. *How does he get away with all this shit?* The thoughts swirling in his mind were uncomfortable at best. *Why can't girls do that with me? Why am I not good enough to get that kind of attention?*

Jake looked away. *Why does it matter? I've got Kelly...she's all I need. She's better than some random girl from some sorority.*

He didn't want to feel this way...to feel...jealous. But he couldn't stop it.

Abruptly, Jake turned back toward his pledge brother. The more he saw how turned on the girl was, the more it hit home. *I want her.*

Jake turned away again, back to the table and his half-full beer that Jeff gave him. Instinctively he took out his phone to check if he'd gotten any texts.

No new messages or missed calls.

The only thing he knew for sure was that he couldn't stay. He couldn't continue to watch half his 'brothers' fuck any girl that wanted action while he sat there powerless.

It's not right...it doesn't make sense. I've got Kelly...I'll never cheat on her.

Jake nudged Eric who was right next to him. "Yo, take the rest of this beer for me. Kelly's calling" he lied.

His cousin rolled his eyes but did as he was asked. Jake tried to hide that he was almost running out of the basement but by the time he was halfway to the door he didn't care. He just wanted out.

Chapter 24

Walking to the ElPi house brought up bad memories. It had been over three weeks since it had all ended with that final ridiculous night and Brynn Wells hadn't expected to still be so entranced by pledging.

Fortunately now that it was over, she was allowed to drink just like normal. She'd rolled out of bed around eleven today and immediately sent out a mass text to her five pledge sisters. Ironically, the one she was the least close with responded immediately. Madison and Olivia were busy at some group meeting for a class they were in together. Jocelyn and Mary just hadn't responded even now so that just left Angela.

Normally it would've been at least her and Madison making this trip but her best friend had started believing class was more important these days. Brynn didn't share that thought. She meant to cancel the plan to go to the house at some point in the two hours before hand but just didn't have the heart to go through with it. It wasn't that she didn't like Angela; Brynn just didn't know her or Mary all that well.

Part of her believed she couldn't cancel just so she could hang out with Angela, only the two of them. *It couldn't hurt, that's for sure.*

The crazy part about the Beta Theta pledge class dynamics was that between Brynn, Angela and Mary, their Bigs were all really into hazing. Riley was the pledge mom so it was no big shock that she was devoted to making pledges suffer. Amy Brage was Mary's Big and she basically just went along with whatever Danielle said since they were best friends and pledge sisters. The rumor was that Danielle wanted to be pledge mom next year after Riley was done. Between the three of them, they suffered quite a bit. At least the other three had big sisters that didn't give them Hell *every* callout.

Walking past the library on a Saturday wasn't ideal but if they wanted to get to EIPi, Cordan was part of the journey from Northeast. It was directly in the center of the outer ridge of campus so it wasn't easily avoided when coming from their dorms. The weird feelings always stemmed from the idea that she could've spent a little more time there during the week but never did.

Brynn wasn't a bad student. She usually averaged B's in all her classes but rarely paid attention in them. Her mom always gave her shit for 'not applying herself' among other things. *Like getting B's is that big of a deal. Seriously who cares?*

"So what's the plan again?" Angela asked as they walked up the hill.

"Get to the house and convince people to drink" Brynn repeated. She could admit it was a loosely defined plan at best but that's how she felt most comfortable.

"I think I'm still hung-over from Crossing" Angela lamented, albeit proudly.

"That's just plain sad."

"Well I'm not a big drinker."

That makes absolutely no sense...for you or Mary.

They'd all just joined a sorority, one that wasn't a stranger on the party scene and yet neither really drank much. That was easy to see on Crossing when Angela and Mary had gotten hammered very quickly in relation to the other four.

"We'll fix that" Brynn assured her.

"I don't know if I care all that much" Angela replied quickly.

Brynn stopped walking and motioned for Angela to do the same. "Please don't ever say that to me again." Brynn tried maintaining a serious stance but Angela wasn't fooled. They shared a short chuckle before continuing on.

"I really should be in the library today. There's so much shit I missed."

Brynn's conscience and her pledge sister had something in common it seemed. They both wanted to make her feel bad about not being in Cordan. *Fuck that.* "Who goes to the library on a Saturday?! That's a Sunday event at best...even then it's weird."

"Well we all can't be naturally good at school," Angela said sarcastically.

Brynn could tell there was a hint of jealousy in her tone. People loved trying to make her feel bad about not having to study while still getting by. It never worked. She didn't give a fuck about what others thought and she sure as hell wasn't going to feel bad.

"It's called information retention, get it right Ang."

"Sorry, guess I didn't *retain* that during our last chat" Angela fired back.

They both laughed before reaching the side door of the EIPi sorority house. From the sounds they heard, it sounded like they wouldn't have to do much convincing on the drinking front. *Perfect.*

Brynn entered the four-digit door code and they walked inside. There was a party already going on just like the noise level led her to believe. Their brother fraternity was littering the party room along with a handful of EIPis which included both their Bigs and the one sister Brynn was indifferent on at best: Tory Brye.

"Good you're here" Riley said as she neared Brynn. "I need a partner in beer pong and I'm up next." It wasn't all that shocking considering her Big usually didn't like playing with Tory in that particular game since she wasn't all that good at it. Riley liked winning, but only when she was drunk. Sober she was indifferent.

"And you didn't think to text me?!" Brynn said with faked disgust.

Riley just grinned back at her while also handing over her cell phone. On the screen was a half-typed message to Brynn. 'Get to the house NOW!' was all it said.

"Just like pledging all over again," Brynn quipped.

"Yeah except this time you'll actually have fun here," Riley promised.

"Oh I always had fun at the EIPi house."

"Sweetie…you're terribly confused. Let's get you drunk and it'll all make sense." Riley motioned her to the keg as she put her arm around her.

Brynn hoped Riley wasn't lying although it wouldn't have been the first time her big sister said something that wasn't entirely true.

****

"Why weren't you at the party Thursday?" Tory asked abruptly.

"Better yet, why weren't you at the party Friday?" Danielle followed up.

Tory and Danielle may not have seen eye to eye on some things but their ability to team up and intimidate the younger girls was almost unmatched. Tory thoroughly enjoyed it. Now that pledging was done she wasn't assistant pledge mom anymore, so she took her enjoyment where she could. That meant fucking with the newbies.

Angela looked like a deer in the headlights when faced with both Danielle and Tory's questions. The poor girl looked completely out of her element, not unlike the first few times Dani had come through the doors of the EIPi house.

There were definitely times when Bigs chose Littles that were completely wrong in terms of chemistry. Then there were times like Riley and Brynn and even Danielle and Angela where they couldn't have been picked better by someone seeing the future.

"Is there any good response to this?" Angela finally asked hesitantly.

"Not even slightly" Tory confirmed.

"You know the point of Crossing was to get you to have fun again," Dani agreed.

"I am having fun" Angela replied. She wasn't even remotely convincing.

Tory swore there were times when Angela regretted pledging since she seemed to be way out of her depth during parties. That was where Tory felt most at home, with alcohol inside her and a frat guy nearby. *Nothing is better…nothing to worry about.*

"Do you want me to do a keg-stand or something?" Angela foolishly asked.

"Um…yes…definitely…now" Tory said, unable to control her happiness.

"I was kidding."

"Oh good...I wasn't" Tory said with more authority. *We'll get you to loosen up.*

Tory looked over at Brian and a couple of his brothers that were standing by the keg. "Bri! She wants to do a keg-stand" Tory shouted at the four guys. It was the first thing she'd really said to Brian since their last meeting. It was as good a segue-way as any to get back on his radar. She didn't care if they fucked again, seeing that look in his eyes was good enough for now. *Yeah...you still want me.*

"Fuck yes!" one of his brothers shouted back.

Brian grinned and moved the others out of the way. "First keg-stand of the day at...one thirty" he confirmed while checking the time on his cell.

"That late?! We're slacking!"

The girls followed Tory along, even if it was more tentatively than preferred.

"Do you want to do this?" Dani subtly asked her Little. She was trying to keep her voice low but Tory heard it all the same. *She just needs a little push.*

"I guess so," Angela mumbled. "I've never actually done one before."

"They are a little rough," Danielle agreed.

Well don't say that before she even tries one, come on.

"I'm only gonna do it if Dani and Tory do one after me" Angela shouted.

Tory grinned at the turnaround. *Well done Angela.*

Now they were all resigned to being flipped upside down to drink straight from the tap. Tory didn't mind but she doubted that was something Danielle had planned on. It was a rare thing for her to go so hard so early but this was Tory's bread and butter.

The boys at the keg all shouted and cheered as there were now three girls in line to do keg-stands instead of one. Tory did a mental check to remember what kind of underwear she was wearing. If she was going to be flipped upside down on the keg it just might be noticeable even though her tank top went down over her pants. *It's my purple thong. Brian's definitely seen that one before...good.*

"My Sunday self isn't going to like this at all," Danielle said as they watched Angela get helped into position.

"Probably not" Tory confirmed. "But that's tomorrow's problem."

Might as well be my goddamn motto.

****

Today seemed familiar in a lot of ways while still being different. Thinking about how things had changed in Gladen Hills since he'd signed the Historian's Binder two and a half years ago was always a jarring road to travel down.

Calvin took another sip from the plastic cup he had in his hand. The beer was chilled just like usual. Even after a night of partying, the keg would sit in the basement and remain decently cold. *Three or four more cups and it won't matter anyway*.

Right now his focus was fixed on the fraternity composites hanging on the walls of the common room. The newer ones hung on his side of the house while the older ones from the frat's earliest days were on Jeff's side.

There were times when Calvin liked to just look over all the names of the brothers who came before him. They'd built what he'd come to love about Gladen Hills. Tonight he was looking specifically at the previous era before his own. It had seen the graduation of the guys that had hazed and initiated him into AZXi. There was no one else nearby although he could hear cheering in the basement thirty feet away.

After taking another few sips of beer, he heard approaching footsteps coming upstairs. His back remained turned to the doorway leading to the kitchen.

"What the fuck are you doing?" a voice asked indignantly.

It was just as well that the owner of the voice was an older guy too since the younger guys wouldn't appreciate his reminiscing.

"Chilling Buttons...chilling" Calvin responded pensively.

"I think most of the guys are at the National right now. You're not trying to go?"

"Let me ask you a question Buttons: do you ever think about how things used to be when you joined AZXi?"

Jeff paused and even though Calvin wasn't looking at him he could tell from the silence that he was unsure. "Considering most of the finer details from that time I can't really remember I don't think about it *that* much...but sometimes...yeah."

"I just remember things being a lot crazier than they are now" Calvin replied sadly. It was strange considering most of the time he wanted nothing more than to have everything quiet and calm as the frat's president. Any major outburst from them like what the Alpha Epsilon's had done at the Triple-E house would come back to haunt him specifically. And yet...he couldn't shake the feeling that their lifestyle, and by extension his own, was missing something.

"Yeah those were the days" Jeff grinned as he moved to the left of Calvin.

"So what the fuck happened?" Calvin blurted out.

"Speak for yourself. I'm still having a great fucking time."

Of course. He wasn't sure why he expected to have a legitimate conversation with Jeff Chester of all people. He'd be better off talking to Petey or even Guapo. *Well maybe not Guapo.* Somehow that conversation would get turned around to how awesome the guy thought he was. *It always does.*

"I am having a good time but it seems like it's Jared, Dylan or Jerry doing all the crazy shit these days." It started feeling clearer as he talked. There was definitely jealousy in his inability to cut loose the way those three could. He'd even seen Buttons do wild shit with a katana sword prop he'd bought online at after-hours a few times when they were all younger. It wasn't an intelligent way to pass the time but at the very least it was memorable. Even though they'd never seen eye to eye on most things, especially after sophomore year, Calvin still remembered *those* times.

The younger guys won't have any memories like that of me...

"I've only got five weeks left at this place," he thought out loud. "Then I'll walk the stage and that'll be it. College is over."

Jeff clearly didn't know what to say to that since he kept his mouth shut. *What can anyone say?* There wasn't any witty comment or drinking game that was going to change the fact that he'd be leaving Gladen Hills soon.

"Five weeks is plenty of time to do something crazy. All you need is one night."

Calvin pried his eyes away from his Big to the third on the composite in front of him and looked at Jeff. He seemed almost brotherly in that moment.

He's right. It's not over yet...

"I just can't do anything that would piss off Jen."

"Maybe that's our problem. We both have girlfriends," Jeff said evenly. "Dana keeps me in line in the best and worst way possible."

That might've been true but Dana sure as hell hadn't kept Jeff from doing more coke this semester than he'd ever seen him do previously. It was only during parties that he did that shit but it still seemed excessive.

"You remember the time Boo-Yah threw himself through Guapo's door because he thought he lived at the house?" Jeff asked with a grin.

Calvin laughed. *Who the hell could forget that?*

"Yeah and Guapo came back with that DXA and tried waking him up but it wasn't happening. Then he tried convincing you and me to let him bang out in one of our beds" Calvin added.

"No amount of money would make me let Guapo fuck in my bed."

"I doubt there's enough bleach on the planet to clean the sheets after he finished in there either."

Guapo had tried convincing the chick to fuck him on the couch when all else failed but the girl turned him down. *Lucky her. She dodged a bullet on that one.*

He finished the beer in his cup and found Boo-Yah's picture on the composite to his right. He was a stout, well built but definitely goofy looking bastard through and through. "Fuckin' Boo-Yah. Every alumni weekend he reinvents drunken stupidity."

****

"I'm definitely trying to fuck something tonight" Will blurted out. It would've taken him by relative surprise had it been said by anyone other than Bill-Butt. *Maybe Guapo.* "You really need to get back in the game Biz" Will continued.

Eric grimaced. *It's not for a lack of trying son.*

The main thing preventing him from achieving success unlike Bill-Butt was that he had some form of shame. "You know the stats Biz. Hit on seven girls at the Midway, the eighth one is gonna take you home" Will said with authority.

"Who the heck has the time or patience to deal with seven failures before finding the eighth?" Eric asked sarcastically. If he had the backbone to do what Will was saying he wouldn't mind wasting the time sifting through the crowds of girls at the Midway.

"You're looking at him" Will grinned.

While it was impressive that Will got laid as much as he did given how much of an ass he made of himself when they drank, the stats were still misleading. There was no way that one out of every eight girls would bang *any* guy that was willing to go through the trouble of looking that much. If he were sure that wasn't true he'd probably be able to drink enough to try it.

They both looked over at J-Hood who was playing flip cup by the window of the Sigma Lambda house. *There's no way that kid has to go through eight chicks to find one that will bang him. He probably doesn't even need to look that hard for a threesome.*

"What I wouldn't give to be that kid for a night" Will stole the thoughts right from Eric's head.

"Seriously" Eric finally contributed another line to the one-sided conversation.

Eric switched his focus from all the sex talk to his current surroundings. It always blew him away the way sorority girls lived versus the AZXis.

The Sigma Lambda place was huge just like every other sorority house in Gladen Hills. Multiple rooms, most of which were doubles or triples, littered the two floors. The room that would've been the dinning room in a normal house was where they were partying. The far room that would've been the living room housed the beer pong table. *They have so much freakin' space.* The first floor alone probably had equal the square footage of the entire AZXi house.

Turning away from the décor, Eric saw Jeff standing with Calvin while they filled their beers at the nearby keg.

It was nothing short of a shame that they hadn't brought over the keg they still had leftover from last night's party. Nobody wanted to drive it over so Eric was forced to pay the Sig Lamb treasurer for the new second keg. He would've preferred not to but it didn't really matter at the end of the day. That extra half keg at the house would just get used up for the inevitable Sunday-Funday tomorrow.

"It's a shame we all can't be banging supermodels regularly." Eric said loudly enough about J-Hood to catch the others' attention.

"I'll tell Jennifer you gave her the compliment," Calvin replied with a grin.

"While you're at it remind her she has to hook me up with one of her sisters still too" he grinned back. It was far from nonchalant but he was reaching the point where he didn't care how obvious it was.

"Shouldn't have to" he replied knowingly. "Every time we're in midtown you get really hammered and that's the one conversation you always have with her."

"Maybe we should just get you a hooker or something Biz" Jeff said in a serious tone, although Eric hoped he was kidding. He could never really tell if Buttons was trying to be funny or not.

"If you're buying Buttons, then by all means make it happen."

It was scary how quickly Will's face lit up at the possibility. "Really Biz!?"

"Get the fuck out of here. Of course not" Eric said in disgust. He might be toeing the line of desperation right now but he was still not prepared to pay for sex. Tipping strippers was one thing but this line he wasn't prepared to cross.

"It would be a bit extreme" Calvin joked.

"Gee ya think?" Jeff said immediately.

"I think it serves him right for ending things with that hot EIPI" Will added.

"That was mad long ago though," Calvin said directly to Will.

Eric couldn't tell if it was a question or if he was defending his honor...what little there was.

"Yeah but she was hot and she was content fucking Biz. Tell me that's not one in a million right there" Will said.

He was clearly joking but Eric could definitely see how someone like Jake could get fed up with the guy talking all that shit *all* the time.

"They do know I'm right here right?" Eric questioned Jeff while Will and Calvin carried on. Jeff just shrugged, obviously enjoying the show.

"So you've never ended things with a sure thing?" Calvin asked quickly.

"Gretman...you can't end things with a sure thing" Will paused. "Because they're a sure thing."

"Then how did Biz pull it off?"

Will looked as though he was about to say something but realized it wouldn't answer the question. "I guess Biz is just better at that part of banging chicks."

I need more beer. A lot more beer.

****

A blunt that Bill-Butt had gotten somehow was being passed around the room when Calvin finally snapped back into reality. Jeff had it now and was taking a few drags before passing it on. *Did I just take a hit?*

Eric was sitting between them in the circle they'd fashioned on the couches at the AZXi house but they all knew he didn't smoke weed. *I don't feel high.*

They'd only gotten back from midtown fifteen minutes ago from what he remembered. Since then the only thing on Calvin's mind was that another night had passed and nothing wild had happened to offset his feelings of regret. Only one thing had happened that was out of the ordinary, and it wasn't good.

"I can't fucking believe I lost my phone" Calvin complained loudly to the room.

"Dude...shit happens at the Midway" Eric slurred out while barely conscious in the seat next to him. Will just nodded as he took the blunt from Jeff.

"You should buy Biz a bottle for calling Jennifer for you" Jeff joked.

Even being fairly drunk Calvin could still sense Jeff wasn't entirely kidding.

"How do you not know your girlfriend's phone number?" Will asked.

"Because who the fuck memorizes numbers with a contact list?" Calvin answered.

"Nobody" Jeff agreed. "Except the dumbasses losing their phones at bars."

"Fuck off."

"A bottle would be sweet though," Eric finally agreed to Jeff's earlier comment.

"You know I love you Biz but that's not gonna happen" Calvin said as diplomatically as he could.

"So walk me through this again Gretman" Will started in. "You're at the Midway, you leave early because you want to smoke...and you don't take Jennifer with you?" he asked pointedly. There was severe judgment in his face, as though he couldn't comprehend where it all went wrong.

How do I explain this without sounding like a fucking idiot?

"She wanted to stay and dance. I didn't. I told her I'd call" he started to say before Jeff interrupted him.

"But you didn't have your phone?"

"I forgot I lost it!" he said for the millionth time.

"Three times I've heard that and it's still funny," Jeff said with a grin.

The other two in the room laughed along with him. Calvin cracked a smile when he saw how everyone was reacting.

They were all still chuckling when Jen walked in the front door. "Hey boys."

"Jen" Buttons said while nodding in her direction.

"Hey girl" Will said with a shit-eating grin.

"Hey Jen" Eric waved at her.

Between the four of them, they were an ugly bunch. It made Calvin smile to know he'd done something sort of stupid tonight, even if it wasn't what he'd had in mind.

"Can we just head to your place" Calvin all but pleaded with his girlfriend as she sat down next to him on the couch. It forced Eric to slide over from where he'd sprawled out but he didn't seem to mind moving.

"Sure" she said hesitantly.

"I'm mad tired and I don't want to be here for after-hours."

That perked up Biz right away. Calvin doubted adderall would've even had that much effect on the guy. "Who said anything about after-hours?"

"We're definitely having them Biz" Jeff announced.

"I don't know about all that son" Eric responded unsurely. He was clearly getting a second wind, now looking fully awake.

Jeff looked to Will for support. The two of them together could definitely sway Biz into making it happen *with* his blessing. "Guapo won't leave me alone; he wants to know if it's on. He's still at the Midway."

Will flashed a weak puppy-dog face at his friend hoping to crack his resolve.

"I don't know man" was all Eric said.

"See? It's a done deal," Calvin said softly. "He'll fold like a napkin." Between himself, Jeff and the rest of the brothers, they'd basically perfected this dance around Eric as he bent to their plans.

Suddenly a group of Rho Betas appeared in the doorway.

"Thought that was you Jen," the lead girl said. "We saw you walk in here from the Lambda's backyard."

"What were you doing over there?" Jen asked.

"We were uptown smoking blunts with the Phi Psis and wanted to hit up after-hours but apparently the Lambdas aren't doing anything tonight" she said, disappointed. Calvin had seen the girl around at their parties before but never caught her name. Or maybe he had and just didn't remember.

"We're still trying to party" the girl reiterated to the room of AZXis. She was clearly hoping someone would take up the cause.

"Sorry, we actually just agreed that we aren't having after-hours tonight..." Will started to explain slowly in a very formal way.

Eric interrupted him so quickly the room felt whiplash. "Please don't talk about things you don't know!" he said as fast as Calvin had ever heard. "There's still a keg left downstairs" he directed them toward the basement.

The girls didn't need to be told twice. They smiled and followed Eric and Will out of the common room. It hadn't happened exactly as Calvin expected but the result was the same. "Told ya," he grinned at Jen.

She smiled back and kissed him once Jeff left the room too. "My place?"

"Your place" Calvin agreed as he kissed her again.

****

"Thanks for staying in with me tonight babe" Jake said as he squeezed Kelly against him for more comfort.

"I was planning on relaxing tonight anyways because my group meeting is tomorrow," she explained again. Whatever the reason for her being by his side tonight, he wouldn't argue.

They were watching some chick flick but Jake was so bored by it that he really hadn't been paying much attention to anything except Kelly. That seemed to be perfectly fine for both of them.

"I can't believe they scheduled one on a Sunday. Don't they know there's drinking to do on the weekends?!"

It made him feel slightly off because he hadn't had a real desire to drink since Crossing. When the six weeks of pledging was thrown into the mix he could count on one hand the number of times he'd gone out at all this semester.

Kelly nestled up next to his front with her back and nodded in agreement.

"You could just skip it" Jake pointed out.

"I wish I could but each person has to grade the others on the work they do," she said unhappily. *That's a great call by the professor.* Of course if the group was comprised only of friends then there was an easy loophole but most times in the lower level classes, *that* many friends in one class was a stretch.

"Baby, why didn't you want to go out tonight?" Kelly asked point blank.

Jake wasn't looking forward to discussing his lack of enthusiasm with his girlfriend who generally always wanted to leave the dorms for one reason or another. They had two very different mindsets these days.

"What? Out with the guys?" he played dumb. "I just wasn't feeling it tonight." It wasn't a flat out lie but it still felt like one.

"Didn't Eric text you?"

"Course he did. Jared too. I'll just tell them I passed out early."

Kelly turned away from the TV to face him. She looked concerned while also wanting more of an explanation.

"Kel, they're just gonna bitch about why I'm not out...at least Rye doesn't do that shit to me."

"I haven't seen her in a while. How's she doing?" Kelly abruptly changed topics.

"Now that pledging is over for everyone she's her usual self" Jake said, more upbeat. "I'm actually having lunch with her this week if you want to come."

"She'd be cool with that?"

Jake shrugged. *Why wouldn't she be?*

Kelly and Riley weren't close friends but they'd never been uncomfortable around each other either. At least not that he'd seen in the past. Now was as good a time as any for them to get closer considering how close he was with both of them.

"Trust me it'll be fine."

****

Now that they were halfway down Arkridge Avenue his thoughts shifted back to what was going down at the house. He wasn't really feeling up to being at a party right now but he couldn't help but want to be there all the same. His thoughts went back to Boo-Yah and the older alums like it had all throughout the night at the Sigma Lambda party and then again at the Midway. His whole day felt like a patchwork of him going through the motions and nothing else.

"I'm not gonna make it" Calvin lamented as they walked. Or rather as Jennifer walked and he stumbled next to her.

"You always say that when you get this drunk" Jennifer assured him. "But somehow you always make it."

"Well that fuckin' sucks. Now I'm unoriginal too…" he paused while his clouded thoughts organized themselves. "You know the alumni we used to chill with…they were all so damn crazy and awesome" he exaggerated.

"And since when has being like that been so important?" she asked abruptly. Either she didn't quite get where Calvin's head was at, which was plausible, or she just didn't like where it was currently. *Just terrific.*

Given how much he'd drank tonight he wasn't exactly filtering his thoughts well so he let it all out. "Since I'm graduating in five weeks and I have no stories of my own to remember. And it's not because I drink too much or not enough. It's because I haven't done anything worth repeating to anyone. Let's face it Jen: I'm fucking boring."

Jennifer quickly pulled away from under Calvin's arm where he was lending some of his weight, the look on her face was anything but happy.

"Come on Jen…you know I didn't mean anything about you."

"Really? Because that's exactly what it sounded like" she shot back with a high-pitched voice. *And now she's pissed at me.*

"I meant guy stories Jen. Nothing to do with us…"

"What the hell does that even mean? Guy stories Cal? You want to get drunk and fuck a random girl every weekend like your

Little or Guapo? Is that what you want?" She looked to be on the verge of tears. *She's almost as hammered as I am.*

"How could you even think that?" he asked, losing what little composure he had.

"I didn't before now!" she turned away to walk toward the Beta house.

For a millisecond he actually thought it might be best for both of them to just go their own ways tonight since he wasn't helping either of them at all.

No...I can't leave her like this now...

Calvin moved quickly after her and lightly reached for her arm so she could turn to face him. "Jen...I've never done anything worth mentioning to the *guys*" he tried emphasizing the last word as much as possible. "They don't want to hear that I met the perfect girl in college at a frat party."

She didn't look convinced or even less upset.

"That's not how guys work. Guys don't really give a fuck about other guy's relationships. Especially here." He waved his arms around ungracefully to show he meant the entire town.

"God...guys are so messed up," Jen vented to the otherwise empty street.

"I didn't say it made sense but this is the world we live in."

After a few seconds of having her uncomfortably far away she moved into his arms. He hugged her tightly and kissed her head.

"I love you Jen...it's just...there are times when I wish we hadn't met so soon."

The look of disgust on her face at his words made him cringe.

"But I'm glad we did, nothing about being here would feel right without you...but neither of us really had any single time. We met in freshman psych and then hooked up at a frat party. That was it. Doesn't that ever bother you?"

"Sometimes, when I see Abby hooking up with a guy she's been flirting with for a few days I miss the rush...but she wants what we have, everyone does."

"I don't know Jen...I just feel like I did something wrong but I wouldn't change anything from how it all happened."

There was silence between them even as a group of girls and guys headed up the road to find a party. Calvin was so focused on the look in his girlfriend's eyes that the group might've been full of his brothers but he didn't care.

"So you think you had me from the beginning?" Jen finally asked playfully.

Calvin smiled inadvertently. "You saying I didn't?"

She smiled her mesmerizing smile and nodded. She'd fallen for him just like he had for her, less than a semester into college. Neither of them had looked back.

"I'm sorry. I just wanted to do something crazy before I left this town for good."

"There's still five weeks left. Who knows? We might break up."

Calvin wasn't laughing. "Don't even joke about that Jen. I don't know how to be here and not be with you."

She hugged him tightly as they stood in the middle of the street. "Why can't you be like this all the time?"

"You mean like an emotional little kid?"

"No Cal. Just honest. I mean, you always are…but you don't show me this part of you…at least not in a while."

What does that even mean?

Calvin always thought he told and showed her how much she meant to him. "You know how much I care about you right?"

"Of course Cal. And I hope you know that's always been good enough for me. You might not get arrested every semester like some of your brothers…"

"That's right!" he cut her off. "Even the damn pledges have a wild story already. And they just fucking crossed!"

"Don't interrupt me when I'm giving you a compliment" Jennifer ordered. "Maybe you don't have run-ins with the cops. Maybe you don't catch syphilis regularly but these guys will remember you for always being there, ready to have a good time. Not everyone can be wild and crazy; otherwise the frats and sororities here wouldn't exist. The responsible people keep them standing while the crazy ones try to tear it all down. Like you said: it's the world we live in."

"It sounds kind of gay when you say it like that" Calvin admitted.

"Hate to break it to you babe but sometimes you guys do act kind of gay." She stopped for a second when they reached the parking lot of the Rho Beta house. "You're amazing Cal…and your brothers know that. At least the ones that care about you the most know who you are."

"I guess I can't argue with such a beautiful girl."

"Good boy" she said as she cut off their kiss abruptly. He would've preferred to continue that right out here even though it was getting cold.

"Let's get inside. And you better not black this part out" she said as she flashed her seductive eyes at him. "I'll give you a crazy story."

The music was blasting so loud that he had to check the floor for pledges doing pushups to ensure it wasn't a callout. He didn't see Raley anywhere so it couldn't have been a callout.

An after-hours party was a free-for-all in terms of what happened. The keg was nearing its end but that didn't necessarily mean that the party would clear out. Girls liked dancing regardless of the booze situation and guys liked to watch them and or join in. Most people who came to after-hours were already hammered so more drinks were rarely needed even if they were wanted. It was just as well since the beer was still cold but decidedly flat.

Jeff slammed the remnants of his cup. He couldn't enjoy these types of parties unless he was blasted. With the beer on hand he doubted it was possible to get him there. Fortunately he'd had quite a lot between the Sig Lamb party and the midtown trip so he didn't need much to keep him in a good spot.

He moved back to the keg to fill up again even though the tap required more than a few pumps to get the beer out.

Eric was in the corner dancing with probably the least attractive girl around. She'd been one of the original Betas to come through their doors earlier. If nothing else, hopefully she'd snap the guy out of his dry streak. *He could use the fun.*

Jared was leading the flip cup game about five feet from Eric and screaming loud enough to be heard over the music. *Nothing new.*

Jeff's phone started ringing and he immediately picked it up. He had a quick conversation before making his way to the back door.

There were a few people out back chilling by the picnic table.

"Where've you been?" Jeff asked with a smile as he saw his visitor. His girlfriend Dana was standing there in a slim jacket with tight jeans on.

"Didn't make it to the bars" she explained. "The party at Criss-Cross was really crazy so we all ended up staying there."

"Missing the bars for an apartment party? That sounds wild" Jeff replied sarcastically. He'd never really understood his girlfriend's fascination with going to parties at Criss-Cross. He hadn't gone to one of those since sophomore year and he didn't miss it. Not when AZXi supplied everything he wanted in a party every night.

"Definitely not as wild as all of this" she replied evenly. It was hard to tell if she was being sincere or sarcastic since she toed the line so well. It was one of the things he loved about her.

"Just another night at AZXi. You want a beer?" he asked knowing full well the keg was close to being tapped. *We might even get one if we hurry.*

"No I'm fine. Me and Kaylie killed a box of wine."

Then it's a miracle you're still able to form sentences.

"She had more than I did but I held up my end."

Jeff smiled back at her and leaned in for a kiss.

"Get a fuckin' room Buttons!" he heard Brent's drunken voice call out.

"I've already got one so what the fuck is your excuse for still being here?" Jeff challenged his brother after breaking the kiss. "Jealousy isn't a good look for you Segs."

"True true. Nice catch tonight" Brent complimented him while he did a once over on Dana. *Subtlety is not lost on these idiots.* Some guys tended to dislike when *other* guys checked out their girlfriends but Jeff didn't give a fuck. *As long as she's with me alone by the end of the night who the hell cares?*

"What makes you think he's got me?" Dana asked with a confused face.

"Yikes." Brent quickly turned away to continue drinking his own beer.

"You saying I'm not?" Jeff asked her immediately.

"Depends if you're coming back with me now" Dana said plainly.

Jeff had just started coming around to the idea that they could stay and hang out before heading back to her place but clearly they weren't on the same page. Right now he wanted it both ways. He'd been spending a lot of time with Dana the past few weeks and even though she looked amazing now he was leaning toward staying at after-hours.

"I'm really tired Jeff. I just want to get home and go to bed."

"Yo Buttons! I need a partner for beer pong!" Jerry shouted from the steps leading down to the basement.

"A little late to be asking don't you think?"

"Chill son" Jerry started in. "Aaron was my partner but he's passed out upstairs."

Jeff quickly checked his phone to look at the time. "At least he made it to three in the morning this time" Jeff admitted. *That might as well be a record for Aaron.* He looked back at his girlfriend who was still waiting for an answer. *I can definitely hang out with Dana tomorrow if I stay tonight...*

"Go home and get some sleep babe. Can I call you when the party ends?"

"I'll be asleep by then. Just text me tomorrow."

"You sure?" he asked, making sure to cover his bases.

"Yes. Go have fun."

Dana leaned in to kiss him again before she left.

Even in the reigning darkness beyond the floodlight coming off the back of the house he could see her perfect ass as she walked away. Of course the buyers remorse shot through him instantly. He tried justifying it in his head. The options whirled as Dana got further and further away. Jeff watched her walk down the driveway until she hit Arkridge. Only then did he turn around and head toward Jerry.

"How'd you fuck that one up Buttons?" Brent asked while cackling.

"Maybe you should worry about your own lack of pussy" Jeff shot out before he realized it was insulting both ways.

Brent laughed at it all the same. Jeff cracked a smile too. He wasn't sure if he was laughing at Brent laughing or his own ill-conceived joke. Maybe it was self-deprecating considering he might've just made a mistake in letting Dana walk away when she clearly wanted him. It was done now though and he sure as hell wasn't gonna run after her down Arkridge Avenue.

That's something Gretman would do. And I'm not Calvin Gretman.

Chapter 25

Seriously, how much time do I waste on Facebook every day?

She'd just finished putting the final touches on a funny post to her big sister Felicia when she heard a knock.

"Brynn! You can just walk in!" she shouted at her door. There was no way she was getting out from underneath the covers she'd perfected in the desk chair.

"And you knew it was me how?" Brynn asked as she walked inside.

Because I'm awesome. "Not many people knock on my door. That means it was somebody who didn't live here and you're on that short list my dear."

"Hmm, it's weird. I just can't get used to having free reign over this house."

"Jesus we really did a number on you during pledging."

"Don't flatter yourself Riles. Tory was way worse than you" Brynn clarified.

Well that makes a little sense. She'd always tried to go easier on her Little more than the other five, intentionally or otherwise.

"She has that ability on both sexes actually" Riley joked. "So are you two gonna be BFF's now pretty please?"

"Let's not get crazy here" she smirked. "Where is she anyways?"

"She's at the National, it's Trivia Night. A couple of the girls went along too."

Riley had been asked to go but hadn't really felt like leaving the building after she'd gotten back from class. She still wasn't feeling one hundred percent after the past weekend. Breakfasts plus a standard party rarely helped her future self.

There was a brief bit of silence between them before Riley decided to bring up something that had been on her mind since Crossing. "So elections are coming up soon..." she broached the subject slowly. "Did you have interest in doing...*anything*?"

Judging from the look she got back it was clear that the subject was off-putting.

"I figured since I *just* crossed that I wouldn't even bother until next semester" she replied casually.

That sounded rehearsed.

It wasn't entirely uncommon for the new girls to not want to jump right back into having responsibility after Crossing but Felicia hadn't given Riley that option years ago.

"Oh no, no way any Little of mine is going to be a sister that just skates by."

"What does that even mean?"

"You're smart enough to know as long as I'm around here you'll be doing stuff and helping out."

"OK mom, just relax" was the sarcastic response she got.

Ironically enough, that wasn't unlike the phrases she threw at her own mother and aunts back home when they told her to watch out for Eric and Jake. *My God I'm turning into an old lady...or worse, my mother.*

"Do you really not want to do anything?" she eased up her tone.

"I honestly hadn't thought about it."

"That's fine. I never did either."

"So how exactly did you get roped into it all then?" Brynn asked genuinely.

Where's Felicia when I need her?

"The thing about most Greek Circle organizations, including ours, is they attract all kinds of people. And within most groups, there are people who do work and those who don't. I'm sorry to say you and I are in the first group. That means like it or not, you're going to have to help carry the team." *At least I hope you're like that.*

"And why would I want to do that?"

"OK I'm about to get serious with you here so maybe you should get a beer or something" Riley offered with a smirk.

Brynn didn't need to be told twice. She grabbed a can from the mini fridge in the corner and returned to her seat on the bed.

"Look, you're only a freshman." Riley said more sullenly than expected. *Why can't I be a freshman again?* "You've got three plus years ahead at this school, and at EIPi" she stopped to think for a second. "And I want you to keep this whole thing going after I leave."

Brynn looked like somebody who'd just been told they were now in charge of an entire country of people. *Great...she's not ready at all...*

Riley tried switching gears. "You know, the biggest oversight for most of us is the Big-Little relationship. It's essentially like having that cool older cousin. It can be awesome depending on who gets matched up...or it can be nothing. That happens more often than it should but I never had that problem with Felicia. And I told myself that I wouldn't have that problem either. You're going to have two years at this school without me. So with that in mind we only have one year to drink, get crazy and generally make bad life choices. And that's exactly what we're going to do."

That put a smile on Brynn's face at least. Even if she couldn't get her excited about running for something they still had that much. *We can build on that.*

Elections are still a ways off...there's time to make this work if she wants it.

"One of the more depressing days around here was when Felicia graduated. But I bust my ass every year to make sure the alumni want to come back on their weekends or for Bids. We keep EIPi as awesome as we can however we have to."

"Alumni weekend is coming up soon right?" Brynn asked.

"Two weeks, four days and six hours but whose counting?"

Brynn looked like she was both impressed and disturbed by Riley's knowledge of the timeline. *I'm gonna take that as a compliment.*

"Trust me, when you see the shit-show that goes down around here that weekend...you'll understand why we get so excited. Oh and you'll meet your Big-Big too." She threw it out like it was nothing even if it was the single most important part.

"Sounds great to me" Brynn replied casually.

"Sorry, I get a little into this stuff. I'm hoping you will too," Riley said hopefully. She headed to the mini-fridge to get her own beer.

"We'll see how I feel at elections," Brynn said pensively as she looked away.

Riley smirked. "I guess I'll take that."

****

Eric Saren liked to think of himself as a patient person.

Then there were times when his cousin pushed the limits of that patience past its breaking point. It hadn't happened in a very long time. Not since they were in high school had Jake done something so completely ridiculous that he just lost it. Unfortunately the next occurrence seemed to be getting closer every day.

Why can't he just act like a normal freakin' person?

He'd been sitting and talking with Scribner so long in the common room he'd almost forgotten why he was in the dorms in the first place. It was a talent that Jake's friend had. He could bullshit for hours, days if Eric had to bet. He wasn't even sure what they were talking about now so he switched topics.

"This Friday son" Eric reminded Scribner again. "Just come by at like nine."

"Sounds good man. And thanks for the invite" he replied from his spot on the couch in front of the TV. *Freakin' underclassmen…must be nice.*

Jake was sitting at his desk in his room alone. He was also staring at a TV. The difference was he was playing a videogame whereas Scribner was just watching some farming show on the Discovery Channel. Eric had to admit the bits he'd caught sounded pretty interesting but he didn't have time to sit and watch.

"What's up man" he greeted his cousin warmly even though Jake's eyes remained leveled at the screen. Eric wasn't even sure he noticed him come in. His cousin tended to get lost in a deep focus when he was playing most games.

Eric picked out the game immediately because he'd played it with Jake over and over again when they were in high school. Once upon a time they'd both been sickeningly good at it. *Good old Perfect Dark.* The game brought up plenty of memories of going through every challenge, side-by-side. *What the hell changed?* These days getting an invite from his cousin to hang out was as foreign a thought as any.

"Hey Biz" Jake said blankly without turning.

"Haven't seen you in a while."

Jake looked shaken although he still didn't meet Eric's eyes. "It's only been a few days…right?"

"More than a week actually" Eric corrected him.

"I don't see much difference from how its been."

Eric winced. "Yeah but that's when you were pledging J. Freedom kind of comes with the territory now."

Still Jake kept his focus on the TV.

Is he trying to imitate his pledge brother or something? J-Hood could pull off this sort of thing without being an ass but J definitely can't.

"You're right. That's why I'm sitting here playing a game instead of studying AZXi history" Jake replied coolly.

Eric kept his cool but was losing ground. "Speaking of freedom, where's Kelly?"

"Had a group meeting at Cordan. She'll be back in an hour."

Between his casual response and the various female clothing around the room it was clear they'd been spending a lot of time together.

Even Gretman and Buttons can make time for the frat…

Eric hadn't had a girlfriend in a long time but he remembered what it was like. A guy could get lost in that sort of thing and cut people out that were better left involved. He saw that happening but didn't know how to stop it. Especially since the people being cut out were himself and the other brothers, maybe even Riley too.

"Are you coming to any parties this weekend?"

"I don't know yet."

That was pretty much identical to the response he'd given Eric last week when he asked. Jake hadn't come to any of their parties then either. *He might as well just tell me to fuck off.*

"J you should really try getting more involved." He was almost pleading.

It was really weird to be in the position of having to talk his younger cousin into anything related to him. Something had definitely changed. That much was clear.

Jake paused his game and turned to face Eric eye to eye for the first time since he'd walked in.

"Why?" was all he said. He kept his eyes locked on Eric as if daring him to give a good reason. Or at least a reason he'd think was good enough.

What the hell do I even say to that?

Eric kept his eyes locked on his cousin's while he gathered his thoughts. "Because you crossed Jake. You're in AZXi. You have a right to be there."

"I'll keep that in mind" Jake replied coldly before returning to the game.

Eric stood up from his spot on the bed to move toward the door. When he started opening it he turned back to his cousin. "Did you even want to pledge?"

Jake didn't pause the game but Eric did notice the screen stopped moving as he stopped controlling his character.

"I don't know," he said quietly.

"Then why do it at all?"

"I thought I wanted to" Jake said as he stood up and moved to the window. It looked like he was just staring out at nothing. The sun was almost completely gone and the campus lights were coming up. Even with the blinds half opened Eric saw his cousin's reflection in the window.

"What changed J?"

"I just don't like what I saw. It was a hell of a lot different from the shit we were spoon fed at Rush."

"Those guys were just doing their jobs man…"

"And again, why exactly is it their job to haze us? It doesn't make any fucking sense. Like none at all."

"I went through it too…I know it sucked. But it's done, you finished it" Eric said as he inched closer to the window. The closer he got to him the more uncomfortable everything became.

"Just because it ended doesn't mean it never happened."

Eric shook his head. He hadn't felt that way after Crossing. The only feeling at the time was relief.

"You've gotta let it go J. None of it was personal. If you think any of the brothers actually hate you that's insane."

"Even if they don't I'm not sure how I feel. I can't even stand being next to some of them right now."

"If you don't like Jeff then don't talk to him…who cares? You crossed. You earned this. *You* deserve to enjoy yourself. Do you really want to spend college with *only* your girlfriend?" As he said it he realized it sounded more like he was challenging him but he didn't regret it.

"You should fuckin' talk pal. You can't even get past how you feel about me and Kelly" Jake shot back. He'd gone from sad to angry in seconds.

Yeah and there's a reason for that. Knowing how the two of them got together in the first place Eric had never been sold on their relationship. Neither had Riley. But they'd both decided to keep their mouths shut. His cousin was losing himself to some girl at the expense of the rest of college.

"I don't hate her J...I just don't like how you are when you're with her."

"I'm still your cousin," he snapped.

Eric just nodded as he turned to leave. *I've gotta get out of here before we start yelling about something this stupid.* "I'm sorry J."

Jake kept his back to him as he continued looking out the window. Now that he was further away from the reflection Eric couldn't tell what was in his eyes.

"I'll talk to ya later Biz."

Eric turned and left the room. *I hope so.*

****

How the fuck is it only Tuesday right now?

That was the lone thought on Scribner's mind as he walked with Justin through the campus back to Northeast. The only good thing about the current moment was that class was done for the day. *Thank God for that.*

"When do you want to work on this paper?" Justin asked.

Raley and the rest of his fraternity were all calling his friend 'J-Hood' but Scribner wasn't sold on the idea yet.

"This weekend?" Scribner offered before realizing how completely fucked an idea it was. Especially with the guy he was offering it to.

"Nah can't do it" Justin answered diplomatically. Most other guys would've told him to get the fuck out immediately. *They wouldn't be wrong.* "Got a date party Saturday and Friday is a four-way at our place."

"Shit that's right. Eric invited me to that one yesterday. Whose it with?"

"No idea. You gonna go?"

"After you made it sound so awesome? How could I stay away?"

"Word."

Scribner was sure Justin had gone to a date party last weekend too. He was also sure that neither of those were AZXi events which meant sorority girls were inviting him to theirs.

"You wanna grab a beer? I've got some in the fridge in my room" Scribner offered. He wasn't trying to do much more than just chill and drink but he never liked doing it alone, although he still would on occasion.

"Yup" Justin replied without hesitating.

Scribner smiled while walking ahead to lead the way to their basement suite.

"You've been in here before haven't you?"

"During pledging."

"Yeah...Raley didn't handle that well at all" Scribner said softly even though he knew full well there was only one other person in the suite and it definitely wasn't Raley.

"No" Justin agreed before pausing. "No he didn't."

Scribner took solace in the fact that pledging was over and he was starting to see his friend a lot more often. Of course the only time he was seeing the guy was when he was with his girlfriend. They were a package deal now. Scribner wondered if the guy actually had any other human contact these past few weeks.

Scribner handed a beer over to Justin from the mini-fridge in the common room. He cracked it open immediately and took a large sip. Within a minute of them getting into the suite his roommate came out of the cave that was their shared room.

"Well look what's awake!" Scribner said brightly. The *thing* standing before them could be classified as a 'who' but that was pushing it.

"What time is it?" Dukes asked, still groggy.

"Only about three in the afternoon" Scribner grinned. He knew that wasn't what the guy wanted to hear, which made it all the more fun to say.

Justin just sat there on the couch. He didn't seem to know what the hell to make of Dukes. *Can't blame him there.*

"Damn you Scribner. I could've easily slept 'til four."

"I know. I've watched you do it."

"You watch me sleep? That's fuckin' weird" Dukes jabbed as he surveyed the common room. Only at that point did he notice there was another person there.

"Man...what did I say about having guests in here?" Dukes asked.

"Not sure actually because I don't give a fuck what you think" Scribner shot back with a grin.

Dukes shook his head as he made his way to the unoccupied second couch in the room. "You did that pledging shit with Raley right?" Dukes asked as he trudged.

"Yup" Justin said between sips of beer.

"And how'd that work out for you?"

Justin remained cool. "Well it's over...and that's really all there is to say."

"I respect that, short and to the point. You could learn something from this guy Scribbs" Dukes said plainly.

Scribner flicked him off on reflex. It was a common motion in their suite, particularly when it was directed at Dukes.

"You want a beer?" Justin asked as if it were his to offer.

"Sure why not" Dukes replied after pretending to debate it in his head.

"Yeah why not" Scribner chimed in. "You've definitely earned it."

"You listen here Scribner. You think it's easy sleeping all day and staying up all night?" Dukes asked with fake anger.

"No...I personally don't know how you do it."

"It damn well isn't easy that's for sure" Dukes pointed an accusing finger.

"You trying to drink this weekend?" Scribner asked as Justin handed Dukes a fresh beer from the mini-fridge.

"I'm trying to drink right now."

"Raley's cousin invited me to their four-way party on Friday."

"I'm happy for you" Dukes said sarcastically.

Scribner smirked. *Like you've ever been happy for anyone else in your entire life.*

"I'm sure it'd be straight if you came too." He didn't want to go behind frat lines alone since he wasn't sure if Raley would go or not. *Depends on what his girlfriend has to say about it...*

"Didn't get an invite, can't do it" Dukes answered plainly.

Justin finished the can of beer he'd been handed not five minutes earlier, all but slamming it down on the arm of the couch. He looked directly at Dukes. "I'm inviting you." The guy's tone was the same as it had ever been but it demanded attention.

Scribner finally started to see why all the AZXis called him J-Hood.

****

It was Tuesday afternoon and Kelly was stuck in one of her damn computer science classes until later in the day.

Fortunately Jake's big brother had texted him earlier asking to chill. He never minded hanging with Jared because he was the only brother who was the same person to him at the beginning *and* end of pledging.

Jared had been at the AZXi house for most the day after his classes. There was no way in Hell Jake was going there to meet him so he suggested they meet near Lancaster. Jared hadn't complained about the suggestion. He never complained about anything.

"I'm telling ya bro, you missed a great party last weekend" Jared exclaimed as they walked past the Union.

Jake rolled his eyes. *It's always the same story from every damn active I ever talk to.* "I feel like if you've been to one of our parties, you've been to them all."

"You bite you tongue! That's outrageous!" his Big said in a high-pitched voice.

Jake knew better though, the guy wasn't really upset.

"Was it too clichéd?"

"Forget that. How many parties have you even been to since Crossing?"

"I don't know man" Jake lied. He knew full well what the number was. Given that it would fit on one hand he knew it would be awful for Jared to hear.

"See that right there is a travesty."

"I didn't realize you knew so many big words."

Jared laughed. "When the situation calls for it I do. And this is unreal!"

"So I didn't go to a few parties…that's a problem?" Jake asked sarcastically. He knew full well that to the brothers, it damn well was a problem.

"No the problem is you not knowing it's a problem! But either way, Biz told me he invited your roommate to our four-way on Friday."

At the mention of his cousin's name Jake tensed up but Jared didn't notice.

"If your roommate who isn't even in the frat comes to our party but you don't…I'm going wild" Jared promised.

Right because usually you're completely calm.

They reached the Union and walked inside. Jake was grateful to get in away from the brisk winds.

"You want to play some pool while we're here?"

"Pool!" Jared screeched. "Who the hell plays pool? Ewwwww!"

Jake looked around to make sure no one was paying attention. Fortunately no one was. "OK so what do you want to do?"

"I'm 'bout to play some DDR, cut up a rug real quick!"

Now it was Jake's turn for an outburst. "Ewwwww!"

"You don't get down with DDR bro?"

"I don't dance...period," Jake answered with finality.

"Haven't I seen your chick at the Midway mad times though?"

A couple doesn't need to dance together to function. "She can dance all she wants pal. It doesn't mean I have to.

Jared looked like someone was stabbing him. "Dancing is the perfect pre-game for sex!"

"Thanks footloose" Jake replied dryly.

"It's true. The Midway is where it's at."

They finally got to the main game room on the first floor. It was lined with pool and ping-pong tables as well as huge arcade games. In the far corner was a set of Dance-Dance-Revolution machines that his Big was so dead-set on playing. There was barely anybody there. *Not too many, not too few...perfect.*

"The Midway is always way too packed," Jake said confidently. That was the worst complaint he could level at that bar. There was barely any room to move and no space to chill and talk. The actual bar was always surrounded so getting a drink was practically impossible after midnight when most parties let out.

"Yeah...it's packed with tons of horny girls. How terrible!" Jared exclaimed.

"I have a girlfriend."

"I'm just stating a fact bro. Speaking of which...how long you two been dating?"

"I don't know" Jake lied. He wasn't comfortable sharing the details.

"You blackout the specifics?" Jared laughed at his own joke.

Jake smiled. "Nah, we just didn't start dating at a specific point. It was weird" he failed in his explanation. "It's been a year at least."

"OK now you've gotta tell me what happened."

Freshman year was not shaping up to be particularly memorable for any other reason beyond being miserable. Jake was hours from his home and friends and his cousins were usually busy all the time. He'd never felt so alone.

Generally his days consisted of going to class and coming back to the dorm to do homework and or watch a movie. Rinse and repeat. Nothing changed for the first month or so until meeting Kelly. That had been both a good and bad thing.

She'd definitely helped him feel less lonely...when she was around. The problem was that her attentions were divided and his weren't. That was why he was sitting here today after class watching another mindless movie from his collection just to pass the time.

Jake could feel himself nodding off to sleep when an abrupt knock came at his door. It couldn't have been Kelly; it was still too early for that.

"Come in!"

His cousin Riley walked through the door with a purse slung over her shoulder and a notebook in her hand. She couldn't have just come from class; it was too late in the day. He checked the time and saw it was well past six. Most classes didn't go that late although there were exceptions. Of course none of that explained what she was doing in his dorm.

"You know we missed you at dinner tonight" she said curtly while putting her purse down on his desk chair.

It was then that Jake realized today was Thursday because he'd had economics. It all came flooding back after that. He'd been invited to dinner with Eric and Riley tonight at the Blue Hold. In that moment Jake felt bad about having his cousins make the trek over to the far side of campus only for him to be a no-show.

Jake leaned over to check his phone and sure enough there were a few missed calls and texts from his cousins. His cell was on silent so he hadn't noticed a thing.

"Sorry Rye, I forgot that was tonight" Jake apologized half-heartedly.

Riley didn't look remotely convinced. She had a point. Jake didn't care one way or the other. Dinner would've just consisted of more talk about how great Eric's frat was and how much fun her sorority was. All of it would've probably depressed him more now than he was already. And that was saying something.

"What's going on Jake? Is it problems with that Kelly girl again?"

"I can't get her out of my head...it's driving me fucking crazy."

Riley shook her head furiously. "She has a boyfriend Jake. Girls don't leave their boyfriends for other guys" she said with authority.

Girls don't leave their boyfriends for other guys. And I am the other guy.

A part of him knew she was right. "They sure as hell don't have trouble cheating on their boyfriends with other guys though" he said sourly.

"Listen to what you're saying. You don't think that should be setting off alarms?"

Jake drowned out her words. All he could think about was how he felt. He'd never met a girl like Kelly before and everything about her excited him whereas every other part of his life was failing at that same task.

"She's screwing with you. You aren't dating her but you're still the emotional support. Trust me, you don't want this."

"Kelly isn't happy with that guy. It's gotta end soon." He was speaking with more confidence than he actually had and hoping his cousin wouldn't notice.

"Why the hell would you want to wait around for that?"

Jake looked Riley right in the eye. "Because I care about her." *I'm falling for her.*

Riley looked away to stare at the floor. "Sometimes I wish you would just go out and get some from somebody else to get over this girl."

"It's not about sex," he said firmly.

Riley just smirked back at him with a look that screamed disbelief.

Jake felt himself getting frustrated. "It can't be because we aren't having any!"

"You're putting yourself through all this shit for a girl with a boyfriend and you aren't even getting laid for your trouble?"

"What's wrong with that?" he asked without thinking.

"Um...what's right with that?"

"Look Rye, I don't need your permission."

It seemed like all Eric and Riley ever did was look down on him for what he was doing although they rarely said it. *Who the fuck asked her to look after me? I can handle this without her or Eric.*

"No...you'll just need my help when you need the pieces picked up" she said ominously. "And I'll do it because we're family."

She was breathing heavily while on the verge of shouting.

"I'm sorry" was all he could think to say.

The idea of Riley losing her patience somehow settled him down.

Riley took a deep breath before picking up her purse again. "OK, I just wanted to swing by to make sure you were alive."

"Well I am" Jake replied with a small smile.

Riley smiled back at him before leaving although she didn't look convinced she'd found what she came for.

An hour went by after his cousin walked out. An hour spent going into a near catatonic state in front of the television. *Girls don't leave their boyfriends for other guys.* The words were as fresh now as they'd been when Riley had said them. *Why would she even say that to me? She doesn't know how Kelly feels.*

Jake looked out the window, watching the sun descend.

The one good thing about his dorm was that he was on the top floor. As such, he had a great view of the surrounding campus. It was a phenomenal sight even though he lived on Northeast, away from everything else.

He turned away from the landscape that captivated him since the first day he'd arrived in Gladen Hills. Back when his dad and cousin had helped move all his things in. That day he remembered looking out the same window and thinking about how everything had changed. Unfortunately, not much had changed from *that* moment to now.

Footsteps on the stairwell next to his dorm shook him from his memories.

"Well hey there" he said, grinning like an idiot. He never could help smiling whenever he saw Kelly. She always looked so beautiful, better than any window view.

"Hey cutie" she greeted him in return.

His smile somehow got bigger. "How was practice today?"

"Ugh" she groaned as she sat on his bed. "Too many sprints to count. I probably look terrible."

Jake sat down next to her to kiss her cheek lightly.

"Yeah I don't miss those days" he recalled his own practices in high school playing soccer. He'd given it up before college since everything was more competitive and frankly he didn't care that much about the sport. *There's no way I'm ever going through six weeks of pre-season Hell for anything.*

"That's because you stay thin regardless of what you do or eat" she commented with a hint of jealousy.

He just kissed her cheek again. He couldn't help himself.

"So what do you want to do Kel?"

Truthfully he'd do anything she wanted. All she had to do was ask.

"I can't move" she exaggerated. "Let's just watch a movie."

"Hey you're the tired one. Are you sure you can handle that?"

"Your DVD's are in the top drawer of your dresser right? Because you somehow had extra space there."

Jake nodded absently. In his mind he had more than enough clothes but he learned when he got to school that what a guy thought was enough and what a girl thought were two completely different concepts.

"I can't believe you don't have any extra space" he joked.

"Hey do you want me looking hot?"

"Well I happen to think you're hot regardless, and without clothes...I think that speaks for itself."

"Yeah because I'm out of shape" Kelly lamented.

She can't really believe that. "That's ridiculous. You're gorgeous," he said on cue.

Kelly reciprocated by kissing him on the cheek and hugging him tightly.

They just sat there for a minute, holding each other. Jake felt more content than he had all day. It held strong before his mind circled back around to what Riley had said earlier. The urge to say something took over.

"Are you ever gonna tell your boyfriend about this?"

He knew it was a huge risk considering how these talks had gone in the past but he did it anyway.

As expected, Kelly broke off the hug and pulled back. "We've been dating since high school...this would kill him. I can't say anything," she said succinctly.

Every word was a knife stabbing him and his face said it all.

"Why do we have to talk about this Jake?"

"Because I don't want it to be this way," he admitted freely while sitting up.

"I'm sorry...I can't break up with him. He means a lot to me...but so do you."

With that Kelly moved back to the door and picked up her duffle bag.

"You're leaving?"

She nodded solemnly. "I just don't want to talk about this right now."

"And when would be a good time to talk about this? The next time he visits?"

"Stop it Jake" she said sternly. There was no affection in her voice.

"I'm serious Kel. I can't keep going through this."

"Then why are you?"

Jake couldn't find any words to speak. He wasn't sure why he was stuck in this loop with Kelly but he couldn't get out of it either.

"Because I want things to change."

"I care about you Jake," she repeated. "But I can't end things with Dean."

There was finality in the statement that crushed him as soon as he heard it. He lost control almost on the spot. "Then what was this all about?"

"I didn't mean it to go this way...you just make me feel so amazing."

If her intention was flattery it was a long way off the mark.

"Well it's good to know I was just here for emotional support." He was the one speaking them but they were Riley's words. It didn't feel wrong.

Kelly didn't even give a response, only shaking her head while walking out.

Just like that, Jake was alone again.

Jake wasn't even sure why he was thinking about that day in particular. Sparing details left and right, Jake gave Jared the cliff notes version of their story.

Once he was through, the judgment came swiftly. It always did.

"Bro all that tells me is why you *shouldn't* be dating this chick."

Jake steeled himself and tried to keep from getting too defensive.

"It's weird. Yeah it sounds ridiculous but she ended up breaking up with the guy and we got closer...I think it worked out fine."

"Hey if you're straight with it then so am I" Jared offered cordially.

I'm definitely fine with everything now.

Time was still passing but Jake didn't feel like he was a part of it. The days going by felt like minutes the more time he spent with Kelly alone. Nothing else even came close to mattering the longer they were together.

The only reason he knew it was Friday now was because it had been over four days since he'd hung out with anyone else and today he was supposed to see Riley.

Was Jared really the last person I saw this week besides Kelly?

Jake shook his head. *Who the fuck cares? I'm happy, that's all that matters.*

The burgers in Lancaster tasted much better today than they normally did. That was probably due to Jake's mood though. He felt great about everything, especially after such a phenomenal week spent with his girlfriend.

Jake was actually planning on going out tonight and felt somewhat decent about the idea, if only because his roommates were coming along with him. Somehow the concept of going to AZXi with non-actives made it seem not quite as daunting. On top of that, he was planning on going over to Kelly's after the party and ravaging her all night and probably most of Saturday too. He doubted he could have planned a better weekend if he wanted to.

Jake was also looking forward to seeing Riley today. He hadn't had much time to see her since Crossing and even before that during pledging so it was a welcome change. Even if he was indifferent to Eric right now he still wanted to see Riley. They were both his family but at the moment, she was the one he wanted to be around. That was probably because she tended not to judge him for skipping AZXi parties whereas Eric couldn't leave it alone.

Looking around the lower level of the dining hall again it was apparent that she hadn't gotten there yet. She'd rescheduled twice already: from Tuesday then to Thursday and now today.

"She's usually not late" he lied to Kelly, who was sitting across the table looking as stunning as ever. "It's a good thing I texted her for what she wanted because that grill line sucks" he commented while watching the next crowd of people increase it.

"You're just so special like that, baby," Kelly said sarcastically.

"Yeah I'm just a team player."

Kelly leaned in to kiss him. There was more passion in the kiss than he'd expected for being in the middle of the dining hall but he reciprocated all the same. Maybe they'd have time to get back to her place after lunch? Their quick unplanned sessions were usually the hottest.

"So I was hanging out with Jared the other day. He asked how we met."

Kelly's peaked interest disintegrated on the spot. She didn't look happy.

"I just don't like when people ask that about us" she admitted.

"You're not ashamed of anything are you?"

"No baby...but people still judge us for it."

"I don't think there's any reason for that" he tried comforting her.

"You're right but people judge me for what happened with Dean."

He leaned over to look directly at his girlfriend. "Hey" he said as he met her eyes. "I love you and I don't care what anybody thinks."

Kelly smiled and leaned in to kiss him again, this time with even more passion. It got to the point where they were fully making out at the table. He didn't hate it either. It was best to just go with it when his girlfriend got worked up. Jake could almost feel the stares coming from the people at other tables but when he checked, no one was paying any attention to them.

He turned back toward her as she was surveying the room in the same way. "Besides...it's not like there's any problems now. We're doing great...right?" He didn't know why he felt compelled to ask that every so often but he did.

"Obviously we're good, why wouldn't we be?" she asked. It almost sounded like a challenge.

They started kissing again. It was getting harder and harder to keep his hands off her body and he felt himself getting excited at the thought of being alone.

Then his punctual cousin interrupted it all.

"Hey guys" Riley chimed in loud enough to get her point across.

Jake greeted her as happily as he could. Kelly did the same although she sounded hesitant. Riley didn't look all that happy about what she'd just seen them doing.

He motioned to the tray full of food on his left, directly across from where Kelly was sitting. By design, Jake was between the two girls.

"You're welcome for getting your food for you Rye," Jake said while motioning to the now enormous line at the grill.

"What would I do without you?" she asked sarcastically.

"He's so modest isn't he?" Kelly chimed in while rubbing his shoulder.

"Glad you noticed that too" Riley replied.

"It's kind of hard to miss."

They were going back and forth at his expense, which he didn't really mind considering any common ground was fine by him. He sat there grinning like an idiot while they bantered about him.

"So what's your plan this weekend?" he asked his cousin as she sat down.

"Drinking" she answered quickly before eating a few fries.

"Wow that was insanely detailed Rye."

"Did she need to say anything else?" Kelly asked.

His girlfriend defending Riley was another welcome sight. "You're right."

"Good boy" she said with a flash of seduction in her eyes that made him want her right there on the table. It bothered him a little that a simple look and some making out could turn him so much but what could he do?

"How are classes going?" she interrupted their staring contest.

"Ugh, I have a bunch of worthless people in my groups for three of my classes so it's not too fun" Kelly complained.

Jake had heard that particular song before so he changed the channel in his head.

Riley smirked knowingly. "Believe it or not, it doesn't get any easier."

"Any advice?"

"Use the weekends for everything they're worth…but I probably don't need to tell you that" Riley said curtly.

Did Eric tell Rye I haven't been going to the parties? That's just fucking perfect. Riley was supposed to be the neutral one and now she was listening to Eric? *Just perfect.*

"We usually have fun all the time" Kelly added.

"During the weekdays too? That's impressive."

"A boyfriend usually has that effect," Kelly said icily as she turned from his cousin to him, as if trying to make a point. Whatever point it was, Riley seemed to catch it because her face fell neutral and she resumed eating. "I'll look into it."

Kelly too removed the ice from her stare and smiled warmly back at Jake. "You definitely should." She reached out to hold his hand.

Riley swallowed her food. "Well we all can't swap guys out like tampons right?"

Jake nearly choked on his own food. "Come one Rye, that was a little much," he intervened, trying to calm the situation. He wasn't sure how Kelly would react.

His cousin pried her eyes from where they were on Kelly to look back at him. As soon as she turned from his girlfriend to Jake they went from cold to warm in an instant. "I'm just kidding. I'm gonna get another drink." With that, she left the table.

Jake waited patiently to see Kelly's reaction although he definitely saw where she was coming from about people judging them. Even his family wasn't off limits for that.

"I told you she hates me," Kelly said with the appropriate 'I told you so' attitude.

"She doesn't hate you" he replied unsurely. "She's just protective."

"I'm probably just tired and bitchy. Do you just want to stay in tonight babe?" she asked innocently.

The temptation to simply agree was overwhelming in that moment.

"I would but Scribbs and Dukes are coming to the party tonight. I told them I'd go. I guess it kind of is my frat now too" he echoed Eric's own words.

"So now you want to go hang out with those guys?"

"Mostly just those two actually but it'd still be good to relax with a couple drinks too. You wanna come?"

"No. Like I said I'm tired," she reminded him calmly.

"Should I call you after the party? I'm probably not gonna go to the bars." He posed the question like that wasn't what he was planning all along. *Come on Kel…say yes, please say yes.*

"Sure but I might be asleep."

"OK…are you mad at me now?" He touched her hand again. "How can I fix it?"

Going out with the guys would seem hollow if he was in some weird fight with Kelly at the same time.

"I'm not mad, it's fine."

Yeah right, like I believe that. Most of the time when a girl said she was fine, she meant the complete opposite, but that was just his personal experience.

"I'll go get you some ice cream from upstairs" he offered. It wasn't much but it would at least prove he wasn't ignoring her.

Kelly gave a half-hearted smile while he kissed her. He was only allowed her cheek, which he kissed lightly before heading upstairs.

What the hell is even happening right now?

****

They didn't even notice I already had a drink before I left the table…wow.

It wasn't lost on her so just for show she went and got a cup of water to compliment the orange soda Jake had seen fit to get her. Other days it would've made her laugh if she wasn't sharing a meal with *that* girl.

There'd always been something about her that made Riley feel uncomfortable. She wasn't alone in that either since Eric felt similarly and according to him, even Jake's roommates saw something wrong. Of course none of that really mattered in the end because Jake didn't see any of it and he was the one holding all the power in that decision. *If he ever starts thinking with the right part of his body he'll figure it out.*

Riley couldn't recall how many times she'd warned Jake it was going to end badly, both before and after they'd started 'dating'. *If it can even be called dating.* So far she'd been completely wrong and they'd gone on for a full year. Although there were bumps along the way, they were still together. Riley wasn't sure how.

Walking back from the drink dispenser she caught a glimpse of something she was hoping to avoid. Kelly was alone at the table. Jake was off somewhere else.

Great. He's probably off somewhere doing something for her that she doesn't even really want. Typical. Every time she gets upset he runs off to fix it...

Riley sat down across from Kelly while setting her water down. The girl was sending a text message on her cell.

"Texting one of your boyfriends? Or just Jake?" Riley said coolly.

"Since he's right upstairs I wouldn't text him. We aren't madly in love like you think we are" Kelly said.

She kept calm but Riley could see resentment bubbling under the surface. *At least she does have real emotions.*

"Oh trust me Kelly; I'm definitely aware of that."

Kelly looked back at her with a deep, piercing glare.

Riley took a sip of the cold ice water and lightly smacked her lips together for effect. "You know I don't like this: you and him together. I never have."

To her complete surprise Kelly just smiled back at her. But there wasn't any warmth behind it. It was filled with something else.

"Finally you come out and say it. I was wondering if you ever would."

In an equally surprising turn, Riley could feel herself getting angry whereas a moment before she was sure she was pushing Kelly toward that fate.

"Jake doesn't get it but I'm the one that had to deal with him when you were busy screwing with him and actually screwing your last boyfriend."

Kelly kept her cool composure but the smile vanished. "If he's gotten over that then why the hell can't you?"

Riley looked her directly in the eye with steel in her gaze. "Because when this is all over *I'm* the one that's gonna be there for him. Not you. Me."

"Who said this is gonna end?"

Riley had to stop herself from laughing. *Right girl, keep telling yourself that.* "We aren't playing games. Jake's not here and I've seen you in midtown. Not exactly keeping your hands to yourself are you?"

"I haven't cheated on him" Kelly defended herself.

Finally her smug face vanished just like the fake smile before it.

"I didn't say you did…because *if* you did he'd know in seconds." Riley tried discerning any guilt from the girl but her poker face appeared flawless.

"It's good that you're looking out for him" Kelly mocked her.

"It was clear when this thing started one of us had to."

"I think I'm done listening to this" Kelly said while finally turning away.

Riley smirked. "I'm actually surprised you let me go on this long."

"You think I won't say anything to Jake about this?" Kelly threatened.

She'd waited since sitting back down for *that* threat. *And there it is.* Now it was her turn to smile where her opponent thought she'd crumble. "Not for a second. And I figured you would."

"He's gonna be really pissed at what you said."

Riley shrugged it off. Most of it was for show. She never liked fighting with Jake but most of the time it couldn't be helped. "It's not the first time he's been mad at me and it won't be the last."

If she hadn't known better she could've sworn Kelly looked somewhat impressed.

"So that's it then?"

"Yeah it is" Riley said plainly.

The two continued staring at each other with malice as only two girls could. Guys would just throw punches after such a talk but Riley would never hit the girl unless she came at her first.

"I got your ice cream" Jake's upbeat voice entered their private cold war.

Thank God. Riley didn't want to stare at Kelly all day. She had things to do.

"Thanks baby" she said to Jake without taking her icy stare off Riley.

Jake leaned in and kissed her on the cheek and she finally turned away to face him. "No problem. I can't have you being upset" he smiled.

Kelly smiled in return while throwing a quick look at Riley as if threatening her all over again.

It was the first point since she sat down that Riley felt powerless.

Kelly must've sensed it because she smiled at Jake again although this time it was clearly aimed at her. The girl then kissed her cousin. *At least she's got the good fucking grace to not make-out with him right in front of me. She saved that for earlier.* Riley could feel the frustration rising like a poison but she kept still. *Don't give her that.*

Jake finally pried his eyes from Kelly. "How's the food Rye?"

"A little off today I think."

Her poor cousin had no idea what girls were capable of but she knew he'd eventually find out the hard way. And knowing his girlfriend's thirst for all things new, it was probably going to be soon.

Chapter 26

It wasn't a regular frat house Open or even a typical happy hour. Tonight marked the first time since he'd gotten to Gladen Hills that Scribner had been invited to a frat party that would've been otherwise closed to non-brothers.

Eric Saren was one of the smartest people he knew and he usually had a reason for everything he did. The guy knew that now was as good a time as any to start rushing for next semester's pledge class. Justin was probably thinking the same thing, which was why he insisted on walking with them to the party.

"Who's the party with tonight anyways?" Jake asked.

Scribner gave him a look that probably went unnoticed on the dark, near-unlit Arkridge Avenue. "Aren't you in this frat?" he asked, shaking his head. "I figured you'd know which sorority you guys were drinking with on any given night."

Now it was Raley's turn to shake his head. "It's not like it really matters all that much. The night is going to turn out the same whether we're with the ABI's or the Phi Thetas. It's all the same."

That's not even close to being true. Even I know that and I'm not even in a frat. No way all the sororities are the same.

"You're really selling me on this pledging thing Raley" Dukes said dryly. He might as well have taken the words right out of Scribner's mouth.

Maybe he just doesn't give a fuck about any of it these days. If Raley's talk with Eric earlier this week was any clue, then that was probably true. He hadn't meant to overhear but the walls were thin in the dorms and Raley never spoke quietly. Scribner had lowered the TV volume all the same just to hear things a little clearer.

"It's the Sig Lambs and the D-Chi-As Guapo said" Justin answered for him.

"That's basically French to me," Dukes said casually.

Arkridge was being pummeled with shouts and screams from the various frat parties. They all sounded like they were having a great time. *No Opens, of course they're having fun.* Scribner thought about all his friends back in the dorms who were likely doing nothing or just drinking in their rooms. *That'd be me tonight if Eric hadn't said anything...*

They reached the left-most driveway and Scribner noticed Jake had slinked his way into the middle of their grouping. Justin was only too happy to take the lead so he blazed down the gravel path to the back.

There were a couple brothers wearing letters out back having cigarettes. Justin went full 'J-Hood' status and slapped up each of them. He didn't say a word, just nodded at each one. Jake only spoke in half-assed greetings. The brothers didn't really pay much attention to Dukes or Scribner. Apparently being escorted by two other actives gave them clear passes. *I could live with that.*

They were then led down into the basement that Scribner had seen only a few times before. *Hopefully Raley will cheer the fuck up once we get in here.* The view inside was nothing short of spectacular. With spring around the corner the girls had started dressing in less and less clothing. Short shorts and tank tops were the order of the day. *God Bless America.*

"I could get used to this," he said although no seemed to hear him with the music playing so loud.

"It can be fun…I'll give them that," Raley agreed despite the heavy noise.

"Says the guy that never comes here" Dukes added. Raley just shot him an angry look. "Sorry, didn't realize there was more sand in your vagina than usual."

"Alllllright, what's up boys?" Eric greeted them with a slight slur as only he could pull off. *I wonder what time this kid started knocking 'em back.* He still had the hand-eye coordination to shake each of their hands in any case. He got to Jake last. "Glad you're here man" he said warmly.

"Thanks" was all he got in response from his cousin, who took it in unfazed.

He's probably just happy to see the kid somewhere without his girlfriend…even for a night. Scribner could share that sentiment.

"You're a bitter son of a bitch you know that?" Scribner said to Raley with a smile. His friend actually ceased his hardened stare and smirked.

"Tryin' to get some beer boys?" Eric asked happily.

Justin was already way ahead of them. Somehow he'd managed to get from where they were over to the keg where he was currently filling a pitcher. He was right next to another active. Scribner thought it was another one of Raley's pledge brothers he'd seen hanging around the suite.

"I'm offended you have to ask" Dukes replied casually.

"Biz, I'm pissed I don't have one yet. This would never fly at Raley's Ring."

As if on cue another guy came strolling through the crowd with five beers in his hands. The fact that he was able to keep them all steady while walking through all the people was enough to warrant immediate respect.

"You were saying?" Eric replied as if the whole thing was planned.

Scribner took a beer from the guy before it hit him. They'd met this guy at that one happy hour earlier in the semester. *Jeff I think? Was that his name? So this is the bastard that was fucking Raley for six weeks? He doesn't look so badass…but I've been wrong before.*

Jeff handed out the other beers while keeping one for himself. He patted Jake on the back. "Good to see ya man. Missed ya last weekend."

It was as warm a greeting as the one the guy had gotten from his own cousin but Raley stuck to his indifference like glue. "Thanks" he said again, equally as cold.

"Let's pound these and get it going!" Eric cheered.

****

They'd only had half full cups but the pound race hadn't gone in Brynn's favor. She may have liked drinking but doing it quickly time after time was a skill she hadn't learned yet. Tonight was the first night where she'd had to chug so much so fast.

"You're getting there" Riley lied to her. She wasn't even close to being able to drink as fast as her Big or even Tory though she was getting closer to beating Danielle.

"Gee thanks" was all she could manage to say. Even that came out bitterly.

"Hey let's try to be positive here," her Big said happily.

Brynn smirked reflexively. "I'm just not used to seeing that from you…or you" she motioned to Tory who'd been nodding in agreement to Riley the whole time.

"Well I wouldn't get used to it," Tory said quickly, still smiling.

"That's what I love about you T; you're always so warm and fuzzy" Danielle added as she put her cup down on the customized EIPi bar.

"Anyone wanna play quarters?" Tory asked, ignoring the quips.

Rachel, and Amy had left the corner table open for use.

"I'm in" Riley exclaimed.

Riley and Tory b-lined it for the empty table, which left Brynn alone with Danielle. Fortunately Angela came up right then.

Dani smiled at her Little. "I never like partying with the Tau Chis."

Gee…I wonder why?

Tau Chi was EIPi's brother fraternity but they seemed to be partying with them half the time while the other eight frats fought for the other half. *Whatever…I'm not the social chair.* That honor fell on Amy Brage. She was dating a Tau Chi so it didn't take a detective to figure out why their social schedule was stacked the way it was.

"I don't know" Angela said hopefully while surveying the room. "Some of them are pretty hot."

Danielle didn't look convinced. "Ya think?"

"Dani it's clearly been too long for you" Angela said honestly.

"It has been a while."

"I don't get it" Angela shook her head. "Aren't you like best friends with Tory?"

Danielle frowned quickly. "Riley is but even she's not *that* into frat guys."

Brynn couldn't help but laugh. "She is one of a kind."

Keeping the bitterness out of her voice when it came to Tory was getting harder and harder as the semester wore on.

****

Raley's other pledge brother Will had graciously gone on Scribner's side of the flip cup table when Dukes and Eric wound up opposite him. It had been for the best since Biz had completely fucked up his turn to cost his team the win. Fortunately he was last in line so the rest of his team had at least been allowed the courtesy of finishing their own beers.

"Biz is so whack" Will said plainly.

"Chill chill" Eric replied in a goofy, high-pitched voice.

"It's a good thing I don't really care about this game" Dukes interrupted.

Eric looked astonished. "See that's the kind of attitude that won't win us games."

"Damn...you're absolutely right" Dukes replied sarcastically.

"Yo, you want to fill the pitcher for the next game?" Will asked innocently enough. Scribner hadn't even noticed they were out of beer.

Fortunately Biz had different thoughts. "Son, these two are trying to chill, you fill it," he all but ordered Will.

To his surprise, Will didn't argue. "Only if you come with me." Biz agreed and followed along.

Scribner looked around again like he had a dozen times since they'd gotten here. "It's a pretty legit place," he announced to his roommate.

"Yeah sure, if you're into that sort of thing. Legit parties I mean."

"Yeah you're right, what dumbass would want all this?"

Scribner found himself looking around the basement again, but now *really* looking at what was going on.

Raley was in the corner talking to one of the older guys. *The son of a bitch still looks uncomfortable and we've been here an hour. What the fuck is his deal?*

Shaking his head, Scribner looked away to find Will over by the keg with Eric. Not surprisingly, the latter was the one actually filling the pitcher while his accomplice just poured beer from his cup into his mouth a few inches from his face. He didn't spill any. *He's definitely done that kind of thing before.*

Finding Justin or "J-Hood" wasn't particularly hard. Scribner found the highest concentration of girls around and sure enough, the guy was neck deep in between all of them. One girl was dancing in front of him, grinding away and the other was letting him grab her ass as she did the same from behind. *They crushed it with that nickname.*

Past J-Hood was the other recent pledge he hadn't caught the name of yet. He was talking to some other chick in the corner. *Yeah...she could definitely get it.*

"I just don't get it," he said openly.

"How you get laid with that red hair? I know me either" Dukes replied instantly.

"Please, I'm adorable."

Thoughts of the last Open they'd gone to were fresh on his mind. Tonight was technically a four-way with two sororities and another fraternity that he couldn't make out the letters for and yet it still wasn't as crowded as that Open had been. A person could actually move freely and get to the keg if needed. It was a welcome change.

"This is so much better than Opens" Scribner said thoughtfully.

"How do you figure? There are less people here."

"Exactly. We don't have to wait ten years for a fuckin' beer."

"I don't know about that. Raley's cousin has been gone a long time."

It's only been like two minutes. I'll gladly take that over the Opens. And Eric's getting a pitcher, not just one cup.

"What do you think of it?" Scribner asked honestly.

"I think I'm trying to drink more and this wait time is ridiculous."

Scribner frowned. "I just can't ever have a real talk with you can I?"

Dukes gave his trademark stare. "No, but it doesn't stop you from trying."

****

Unfortunately, besides her and Tory, nobody wanted to play quarters so their game lasted all of five minutes. It was just as well since they were on to bigger and better things. Flip cup was her game of choice and they'd already destroyed the opposing team three times in a row. She didn't want to be sexist but even an idiot could tell it was because her side was all EIPi sisters and the other team had three Tau

Chis on it. *Girls are always better at this game.* The losing team had to fill the pitcher so for the second time since Tory and her had gotten to the table, the boys were off at the keg.

Riley surveyed the party room to see if anything interesting was happening. Nothing caught her eye except for one of the Tau Chis playing beer pong in the room's center. He had a nearly shaved head and was about six feet tall. *He clearly goes to the gym...a lot.* She'd seen him around at a few parties but never really paid that much attention to him. Tonight there was something different. It might've been her.

Without warning she found herself staring at him and smiling.

Of course he chose that moment to turn and see her looking like a stalker. It blew her mind when he actually smiled back. For a second the only thing in the room was them. That came to an abrupt end when she felt a nudge on her shoulder. It was Tory letting her know the next game was starting. When she looked back he was paying attention to his own game. The moment was gone. *Thanks T.*

"You know, you have the worst timing," Riley said to her best friend.

"You wouldn't believe how many times I've heard that."

She could only imagine the circumstances that would lead others to tell Tory that.

The novelty of flip cup was starting to wear off with no real competition since Riley's side dominated again. The most recent game hadn't even seen the final two on the opposite side drink before their team finished. The fact that she was still drinking every game was the biggest bright spot. *This just feels like beating up a defenseless kid.*

"So what's the deal?" Tory asked abruptly. "I saw you checking that guy out."

"And you interrupted anyways?" Normally something like that would've been better than Christmas for her best friend.

"We had a game to play" Tory replied innocently.

"Whatever, he's not my type" Riley lied. "Just fun to look at."

Riley couldn't stop herself from looking back over at him, still on the beer pong table. Her eyes must've given away more than she was hoping for. Tory could read expressions like that from miles away, mostly because she made them herself. Out of the corner of her eye she saw her friend nearly choke on the beer she was drinking.

"I'm sorry, it almost seemed like you wanted to fuck him."

Riley felt shameful. *Please say that louder next time.*

"It's just...you know, you usually give me shit for doing things like that."

"I just want Luke!" Riley announced without thinking. *Oh I'll pay for that one.*

"Ugh!" Tory exclaimed. "This is the problem with fucking a guy that studies abroad for a semester." No truer statement had ever been said by Tory Brye.

Riley had messed around with Jerry on and off for most of freshman year before meeting Luke during pledging. They hadn't been 'dating' exactly but they might as well have been. As far as she knew they were only hooking up with each other. Toward the end of last year they'd even started hanging out and *not* hooking up every time. *He just had to go to England this semester. No way he's not with other girls over there.* The thoughts soured her mind.

Riley didn't want a boyfriend although she'd be open to it if the right guy came along. She just wanted someone to have fun with whenever she felt the need…kind of like how she'd been feeling the past couple of weeks. Since pledging had ended all her focus had gone back into herself. With no pledges and nothing else to keep her mind occupied, guys and sex were center-stage again.

If a previous hook-up was around and willing, she'd be all over it in an instant.

"I haven't done anything since last semester" Riley said quietly.

That time, Tory didn't choke on the beer she was drinking; she flat out spit it up just like a movie would portray it.

"Wow, that actually happens in real life," Riley said calmly.

"It happens when you say something like that to someone like me" Tory exclaimed, the shock still clear on her face.

Her best friend never fully believed she and Jerry hadn't hooked up earlier in the semester when he stayed over in her room. Riley was starting to think she had a point. *He was right there and he clearly wanted me so why didn't I just fuck him?*

"Not all of us can get guys as easily as you" she lied.

Tory picked up on her indecision immediately. "Look in the mirror Riles, you're hot. You could get some any time you want but you *choose* not to."

She shook her head on reflex. Compliments on her looks never sat right so she generally denied them whenever possible. Now was no exception, even if it had come from her best friend.

"It's definitely true girl. So do yourself a favor and choose *to.*"

"It's that simple?" she half-asked, half-stated.

Tory nodded. "We're in college and while there will never be a shortage of horny guys in the world; never will they be so concentrated around your bedroom."

Riley grinned without thinking. *I do live in the house.* Her bed was literally a stone's throw from where they were standing.

Suddenly she felt an urge to grab the guy playing beer pong and take him upstairs. It felt strangely hot to picture. *Does Tory feel this way all the time?*

She came crashing back down to earth when she thought about how it would feel *after* they finished. Awkward small talk followed by a return to the party where everyone would talk about and judge her. His frat brothers would know in seconds and they'd all be laughing about it. *It's not worth it. Not like this. What if he's terrible in bed?*

"God you have a sick mind" Riley joked. *Sick maybe, but realistic for sure.*

"That's why you love me" Tory smiled. "Don't worry Riles. Tonight at the bars we'll find you a nice hot mistake to make."

Danielle walked over from the far benches. "What's going on?"

"Just getting some good bad advice from T" Riley answered plainly.

"Oh good" Danielle said happily. "And I thought tonight was just gonna be more of the same."

****

"So what's the deal Raley?" Calvin asked point blank.

"Not much Gretman, just chilling."

Calvin grimaced. By and large the new fuck in front of him seemed content to avoid AZXi most of the time and give half-assed answers when he actually did show up.

"Well you might be chilling, but never around here" he cut to the root of his thoughts. Raley looked completely confused but also uncomfortable. "This is just one of the few times I've actually seen you around here" he clarified.

"Jesus man, I didn't think you were gonna start in with this shit now too."

Calvin figured at least Biz had tried convincing the kid to show up a little more but from the sound of it, he wasn't the only one. "So other people have said something and you still want nothing to do with us?"

Raley looked around the basement like he was trying to find something. After a few seconds he motioned toward the flip cup table.

It looked like he was specifically pointing out the two guys that he and J-Hood had shown up with.

"See them? *That* was me before pledging."

Calvin smiled inadvertently. "Still so young and clueless."

"This is me now" Raley concluded in a darker tone.

"Yeah...I'm not really a fan of this version."

"You know what the difference is?"

He looked at the full beer in the kid's hand and then at the almost drained one in his own. "Now you've given up drinking," Calvin stated without posing it as a question.

"Now I've pledged. Now half the people here piss me off," Raley answered with very angry authority.

They'd all seen cases of bitterness with recently crossed new fucks but Raley was elevating it to an art form. He wasn't just bitter, he was downright furious.

"Dude you've gotta get over that. It was all just part of our system."

"Yeah...and it's a system that guys like him have way too much fun with" Raley said while looking directly at Jeff.

No kidding. For a second he considered telling the new fuck he agreed with him but fought the urge. *I let Buttons do what he wanted so it's on me too.*

"Would you rather we have no fun with it? I think if we took it too seriously we'd have a much bigger problem."

Calvin didn't want to say too much but the first thing that sprinted to his mind was his suitemate coming back bruised from Kappa Nu pledging during sophomore year. For whatever reason, that frat thought it was cool to beat their pledges. For Calvin, that's what a 'serious' pledge process looked like.

"Having fun with it is our way or getting through it all too" Calvin continued explaining, letting the previous thoughts go.

"Right...I'm sure it's so hard for you guys to deal with giving orders and shit."

Fortunately Jerry was walking by at that moment. "Observe" Calvin said while waving Jerry over. The guy was clearly one of the drunkest there.

"Jer-Bear, what do you think of callouts?"

"Oh weakkkkk. They're a pain in the fucking ass" he said without hesitating although he was slurring a lot. "You think it's bad that you get called out every week? The brothers have to be right there too and usually for longer than you fucks."

"The only way to make it worth it is to have fun" Calvin added.

As if sensing his part in the conversation was over with, Jerry walked away.

"Look Raley, one day this is all gonna be over" he motioned to the party taking place around them. "One day you'll be old and washed up like me and *then* you'll graduate" he said in enough of a self-deprecating way to get his point across. "The real question is: do you want to get to that point and have no memories of the guys you *earned* the right to call your brothers?"

"I don't consider any of these guys my brothers," Raley replied sullenly while looking around. "No offense."

"That's because you're still bitter as hell. But that'll pass" he responded assuredly although he was anything but. He wasn't entirely convinced that AZXi was the root of Raley's issues so he couldn't say it definitively. *How could an underclassman like you be so pissed? I'd kill to be back in your place.*

"Just think of it like when you work and earn money. You don't throw the cash away." The kid looked positively distraught over throwing money away. *He just might make a solid AZXi treasurer one day...if he ever comes around enough to be noticed.*

"Obviously not otherwise what's the point?" Jake replied quickly.

"Exactly. You pledged, you worked, you crossed. You *earned* this. Now you can enjoy it, otherwise what was the point?"

Finally the kid looked contemplative at the very least. Calvin could accept that much for now. *Biz looks that way all the time. Must be a family thing.*

"When I come back for Rush next year, your ass better be hammered, having a fucking great time" Calvin ordered.

Raley smiled. "Well that's something to look forward to."

****

"Dude that was a solid party" Scribner proclaimed happily.

"It was pretty cool. But why the fuck did they let Raley in?" Dukes retorted.

"I've been wondering that myself" Jake answered by focusing on the question and ignoring the insult.

"Oh damn it's the depressing Raley again, do something Scribbs" Dukes urged.

"I don't know what's wrong with me."

"It's not like we haven't tried to make you cooler but it's a lost cause."

"Chill Dukes" Scribner said quickly with a forceful tone.

"You know I probably could've gone to the bars tonight with the other guys. Biz knows the bouncers at the National. But I'm going back early to mope around the dorms because Kelly is mad about something I can't figure out." There was more depression in Raley's tone than anything else.

As far as his girlfriend was concerned, any number of things could've been pissing her off today, each less rational than the last.

"Probably cause you didn't fuck her right last time. Got him!" Dukes exclaimed.

Raley shook his head and ignored the jab, walking further ahead of them.

"Come on man, shut the fuck up" Scribner said plainly.

They both caught up to Jake as they neared Northeast.

"What the fuck is wrong with me?" he asked openly through his cracking voice.

Scribner held his breath for the inevitable insult from Dukes.

"Too easy" his roommate whispered.

"I love you Raley but you hold grudges too long" Scribner explained. "So they hazed you...they hazed everyone. They got hazed too at some point I'll bet. Shit happens, it's over."

"That's just it Scribbs, I know you're right...but here I am."

Dukes walked into the dorm ahead of them after realizing he couldn't contribute much more to the conversation.

Raley sat on the step right outside the lower entrance. Scribner was pretty tired so he wasn't sold on staying up and chatting but he would if that's what his friend needed.

"Just sleep it off Raley, we can talk tomorrow if you want" he urged. "We can hit up breakfast if you want, like old times."

That at least got his friend smiling again.

The last time they'd had breakfast was when Raley had tried convincing him to pledge. It was feeling more like regret these days. Not just for himself but for Raley too. *If I'd pledged with him maybe I could help more now but who the fuck knows?*

"Yeah sure" Jake answered. "Just give me a sec, I'll be in soon."

Scribner stood there unsurely as his friend looked blankly up at the sky.

Fuck...should I really leave him alone?

"You got your ID card right?" he asked before going inside. He wanted to make sure he at least had a way of getting back into the dorm.

Raley nodded that he did.

Scribner quietly retreated. *He just needs some time alone...*

****

The night was quiet and still, which felt weird on a Friday. They'd passed a ton of people on their way back from AZXi but there wasn't anyone in the main courtyard outside the dorm. Northeast was far enough from the beaten path that he'd likely be outside alone for a while. Thankfully it wasn't that cold and even with just a Gladen Hills track jacket on over his button down shirt and jeans, Jake felt comfortable.

His friends had retreated inside to leave him alone, just like he wanted. He wasn't sure why he was feeling the way he was these days but he couldn't shake the loop he'd gotten stuck in.

It was peaceful out tonight though. The silence was calming. That was more than he could say for most things in his life recently.

Jake loved spending time with Kelly but for some reason after their lunch with Riley today, she'd gotten cold. *What the fuck did I do wrong?*

Reaching into his jeans pocket, he pulled out his cell phone and flipped through the contact list until he came to Kelly's name. He hit the call button and heard the first outgoing ring in seconds.

Jake couldn't remember being so happy since before he left home. Kelly brought out a side of him he wasn't sure he'd ever see without her. Spending time with her was his way of coping with being so far from Reesewood.

Transferring into Gladen Hills in the spring had done him no favors. He hadn't been able to make many friends. He'd practically pleaded with his parents to just let him start classes in the fall. That way he could potentially just meet the incoming freshmen which he'd essentially be even though he'd be taking sophomore level classes. It had made the whole idea seem less intimidating but that was probably because he'd be putting off leaving home for a little longer. His parents had actually sided together on that argument for the first time in years.

"You sure I can't just walk you back to your dorm?" he asked even though it was the last thing he wanted. Kelly just smiled like she did most of the time.

Thank God I found her tonight.

Jake had gone to another crowded Open tonight with some kids from his dorm. He'd essentially just been tagging along but he hoped to run into Kelly after their sort of fight earlier in the day. *Why'd Rye have to fill my head with all that bullshit?*

"Absolutely not" she said happily. "I'm staying and watching a movie with you."

"That can definitely be arranged" he grinned like an idiot as they went inside.

Thankfully once again, his roommate was nowhere to be found. *Probably off with his girlfriend again I bet.* Tonight, Jake was actually appreciative for his absence whereas most of the time having Wayne around actually helped make him feel less lonely.

For once, things had just worked out perfectly. He'd 'bumped' into Kelly at the frat house they'd gone to. It was nothing short of amazing that neither of them seemed all that interested in talking about what happened earlier in the day. She seemed more content than he was to leave their issues behind.

"I'm thinking a classic is in order," he said while opening the dresser drawer where he kept all the movies he'd brought with him to Gladen Hills. "Remember the Titans," he announced as if it was the only logical choice.

"Oh my God" Kelly exclaimed. "I love that movie!"

"It's fucking amazing right?" Jake asked. Again there was only one logical answer. She agreed just as expected. *God she's perfect.*

For a few seconds everything stopped. They were just frozen in place, smiling at each other. Abruptly, Kelly kissed him forcefully. It turned him on that she wanted to kiss him like that. It all felt exciting in a way he'd never experienced before now.

Jake moved one of his hands away from where it rested on her waist and felt behind him for his bed, which he found quickly. Leaning backward, Kelly followed along, not wanting their kiss to end.

They fell back onto the mattress in one fluid motion while exchanging their tongues. He motioned backward farther so his head could rest on the pillow at the end of the bed. Kelly followed. She straddled him and started rubbing against his waist to feel the swelling from her actions. Their kissing grew more passionate which didn't seem possible until the moment it did.

Suddenly Jake felt vibrations from Kelly's leg, which was currently beside his own. She cut off her kiss to take her cell phone from her pocket.

Jake wasn't really paying much attention to what she was doing. He was just looking up at the beautiful body on top of him. *I want her…right now…I need her.*

From his peripheral vision, he saw her silencing the phone before putting it on the dresser next to his bed.

"Who was it?"

"Just Dean again" she answered with no emotion.

Jake just smiled even though he felt bad. "That's like the eighth time he's called. I mean, doesn't he get you aren't able to pick up?"

"You'd think so," she agreed with a matching tone before leaning back down to kiss him again. Just like that, the phone ringing and her boyfriend were distant memories as they picked up right where they left off.

She took off his shirt and hers followed shortly after. He was hesitant to take off her bra at the moment since her chest looked so perfect as it was.

Jake felt her hands reaching down his pants as he struggled with indecision. When she found what she was looking for he felt himself grow even warmer.

Kelly broke off their kiss and started maneuvering around so that her pants could be taken off. She took off his jeans in one quick motion once his belt was undone. She did both so fluidly that Jake felt impressed even with all the other thoughts and emotions swirling inside him. They started rubbing against each other with only two pieces of fabric at their respective waists separating him from feeling all of her.

Just then, something inside him started screaming to stop. He was so aroused that ignoring it was the easier option but it was insistent. Finally he gave in.

"What's wrong?" she asked with some concern and a little annoyance.

"You're still with Dean" Jake put his thoughts and emotions into words quicker than he thought he'd be able to. *Why would you say that out loud you dumbass?*

Kelly sighed. "I know Jake...I just want you so bad" she confessed.

There's gotta be a better way than this. "It doesn't feel right" Jake made his own confession. No doubt it would've felt amazing to finally get inside her but taking her like that just felt wrong.

"I care about you so much Kel...I don't want our first time to be drunk, while you're dating someone else. It'll stop this from ever going forward" he admitted. *My God I sound like a little bitch...stop talking and fuck her.*

"What do you want Jake?" she asked pointedly. There was something else in her eyes now. It looked like affection but things were blurry from the alcohol. He might've been imagining it because that's what he wanted to see.

"I want you...just you" he said softly. "I just don't want you to regret our first time. Does that make sense or am I an idiot?"

"Baby you're amazing" Kelly immediately replied before kissing him again.

There was a completely different feeling in the last kiss from the previous ones tonight. She must've have felt it too.

If I had anyone to tell this story to I'll sound like a fucking idiot.

Kelly un-straddled him to assumed a cuddling position on the left side of the bed. Her head rested on his chest as his breathing slowed from what it had been moments before. It felt so comfortable having her next to him. That was the moment he knew Riley had been wrong. *It was never about sex...it's about how we feel...why can't she see that?*

Jake got up to put in the DVD. As he lied back down he saw her phone was going off silently again but she wasn't paying any attention to it. Her eyes were fixed on him so he offered her the same respect.

No one else matters tonight.

Jake knew now that he made the right call that fateful night during his first semester in Gladen Hills. Now they were a year into being together.

Jake couldn't wait to tell her how much he missed her and was thinking about her non-stop all night. He hoped she was still awake so he could maybe even go over there. *Come on Kel, please pick up.* After another ring the call went to voicemail.

The lights from the campus were comforting at least. He heard some laughs and cheers from people heading into one of the nearby dorms across from his. He couldn't have been sitting silently for more than a minute before his phone started vibrating. He nearly dropped the thing as he took it out of his pocket; he was so excited to talk to Kelly.

His heart sank. It was only a text message from Eric.

When he first got to Gladen Hills, a text from either of his cousins would've made him feel special. That was a long time ago though. Now a text from either of them, especially Eric, left Jake feeling hollow. It was a nice enough message all the same. It said he hoped Jake had a good time and that he should bring Scribbs and Dukes back to the house more often. *Yeah that'll be the fuckin' day.*

He deleted the message after reading it. The background of his phone came into view just like it always did. It was a picture of him and Kelly that he'd taken over winter break when he'd visited her house. *She's so beautiful.*

Jake resigned to calling her again, purely on instinct. *Maybe she'll pick up this time.* He quickly hit the recent calls list and found Kelly's name at the top.

He dialed again; still unsure of why he was trying so fervently. It rang...and rang...and rang...

Chapter 27

There was a time when a locked door meant no entry to Eric but those days were a distant memory with Calvin's sealed bedroom door stood before him now. He was definitely still drunk from last night's four-way party and the subsequent shots at the National afterward but he couldn't sleep. He had to talk to Gretman immediately.

A text was sent to Jake last night that Eric was sure he got and yet there was no response. Not last night and none yet today. As of now he was pretty sure he wouldn't get one at all. That was just the latest in the line of sketchy things his cousin was doing. Before they got to school and even right when he got to Gladen Hills, a text would be answered within an hour maximum. *God forbid I ever get a response now though.*

Eric gave Gretman the benefit of the doubt and knocked loudly first. He heard muffled talking behind the door. It was tough but Eric was pretty sure he made out the words "can't move".

After no more than three attempts he carded his way into the room and thankfully found Calvin underneath the covers without Jen. It would've been nothing short of awkward if one or both of them were naked. He hadn't really given that much thought before he charged. *Next time I'll think that through.*

"Please tell me you didn't come in here today just to show off your carding skills" Calvin rasped with his face half covered in pillows.

Eric smirked. "As much fun as it would be to describe how learning to card was part of a response to being in this environment and it all leading back to adaptation, no that's not why I came in" he slurred quickly.

Yet again Eric found himself consumed by the sight of the hammock Calvin had hanging up in the corner. *I could never figure out how to hang one of those things inside a house.* "It's so sweet that you have that thing in here" Eric gushed.

"Dude...banging in that thing is fuckin' sweet."

"You and Jen get down in this thing?" he asked, unable to wrap his head around the logistics.

"Swinging her back and forth while I get it...it's awesome. I'm surprised the housing struts can even handle it."

"Good to know you checked the structural integrity before putting it up."

"Yeah...let's assume I did" Calvin said shiftily.

He rolled over from the position he was in and looked up at the ceiling. Taking a deep breath seemed to help but he still looked awful.

"Raley still can't hold his alcohol well," Calvin blurted out suddenly.

"What do you expect man? He barely drank during pledging and he barely comes around now. He's always with his girlfriend."

"Some people just can't manage both lifestyles...dating and all this."

Eric hadn't been active as long as Gretman so he obviously hadn't seen as much. That didn't stop him from hearing things about certain past brothers never coming around even though they were considered 'active'. That was what worried him.

"I know. That's why I was hoping you could talk to him."

"What for?"

"You have a girlfriend and you're active. It couldn't hurt."

"I actually did talk to him last night...at least I think I did."

That was the first time Eric fully noticed just how destroyed Gretman's room really looked. There were clothes all over and empty plastic cups strewn about the floor. *Does it always look like this?* Eric struggled to find a memory to support that thought. He didn't have much luck so he gave up just as fast.

"Yeah and if the complete disaster that is your room didn't sell him on the fun of this place then we might as well send him to Tau Chi" Eric joked.

"It looks like I had after-hours in here by myself last night."

"You don't remember any of it?"

"Hey don't judge me because your room is spotless."

Eric laughed immediately. His room was rarely ever in perfect order although not for a lack of trying. With the constant flow of brothers in and out, upkeep was a lost cause. "Please, I think there's still some coke left in there from the last time Buttons and Dills rented it out" he said dryly. *It's probably true.*

Eric wanted to talk more about Jake but Jennifer walked in and his mind abruptly shifted back to how she must've looked on the hammock swinging back and forth. She was almost as much of a sister to him as Riley since she was essentially married to Gretman so he cleared the thoughts immediately, ashamed they'd been there at all.

The bigger issue today was the same as it had been for weeks. His cousin needed something to snap him out of the loop he was stuck in and for one of the few times in his life, Eric Saren was unsure of what to do next.

****

"Hey Eric" Jen greeted him warmly as she strolled into the bedroom. She looked dressed like she was ready to go out in public. *Did we have something planned for today? Fuck...what happened last night?*

"Hey Jen" Eric replied pensively. The guy was greeting Jen but it was clear his mind was elsewhere. *Probably on Raley...but come on Biz, it's not like we can force the kid to come here.*

"Missed you in midtown last night sweetie" Jennifer smiled directly at him. *Well at least that explains why my room looks like shit...I never made it to midtown.* Economically it was a smart move but it had stopped him from getting laid, both last night and this morning so it was a wash in his mind.

"We didn't have anything going on today did we?"

"Nothing official outside of you being my boyfriend and me being dumb enough to want to see you" she answered. *Ah, that's exactly what I thought.* "Since you clearly don't remember one way or the other, you're gonna take me to breakfast" she all but ordered. *So much for saving money at the bars last night. Easy come, easy go.*

"I could live with that" Calvin said as he sat up in bed. "Breakfast Biz?"

Eric stopped his subtle retreat when he heard the question. "The drinking party in the daytime or the actual meal?"

Fair question. "The second one first but then let's get the first one going" Calvin said cheerfully. *A double-header breakfast sounds perfect.*

"Not this weekend. We can't keep paying for breakfasts every day. Next weekend for sure though," Eric answered diplomatically.

"OK fine, you wanna get actual food then?"

The question was more of a courtesy than anything else. They both knew he shouldn't be going since it was clear Jen wanted some alone time.

"Just so Jen doesn't kill me or forget she owes me that favor with her sisters…I'll sit this one out" he smiled at her innocently.

"Good choice Eric" Jen smirked.

"I'll call you when I get back" Calvin assured Eric as he left the room.

"You invited your brother to *our* breakfast?"

"I knew he wouldn't go" he lied. "And that you wouldn't care." *I was hoping…*

"You just think you're so smart don't you?"

"Well I have been on the Dean's list every semester."

"Book smarts and street smarts are too very different things Cal."

"I'm definitely aware" he assured her. "I know I'm lucky to have both."

"You're kinda hot too," Jen added.

He motioned for her to come over to the bed. "I was hoping you'd notice."

****

Four weeks after she'd earned the right to wear EIPi letters, it still felt weird walking through the house unattended. The same halls she'd been forced to sprint through only a month ago. The place she'd had to answer all kinds of ridiculous questions and memorize useless facts that meant absolutely nothing now. Surreal was the only word that came close to describing how it all felt.

It was weird to think that none of her pledge sisters seemed to be having trouble adjusting to sorority life. Even her best friend Madison seemed completely fine with everything. *I can't be the only one feeling like this.*

Her swirling thoughts were cut short when she noticed someone actually sleeping on one of the hallway couches. Brynn hadn't quite yet memorized where each sister's room was but she had a good idea of whose room that couch was outside of. *At least these bitches had the common sense to move the couches when we were sprinting up and down the halls. If I'd hit one I would've been fuckin' pissed.*

She got closer to the contorted body laid out on the couch and just as she'd guessed, it was Tory Brye. She nearly laughed right then since the girl had passed out on an uncomfortable couch only ten feet from her actual bed. The door to the right of the couch was decorated with Tory's name and pledge class just like the rest of the doors in the EIPi house. Fortunately their landlords allowed them to paint the stairwells and doors of the house with all things EIPi. Pledge classes, family trees, and EIPi history covered the place much like wallpaper and pictures would a regular home.

"Umm...Tory?" she said quietly.

"Yes?" Tory said groggily without moving any other muscle in her body.

God she looks terrible. "Whatcha doing?"

"Taking in the sights obviously...what's it look like?"

Brynn smiled, more so for Tory's assured suffering than her actual comment. So many times during those six weeks had the roles been reversed. Brynn was the one in pain and suffering, getting yelled at for nothing and Tory was the one towering over her enjoying all of it. The reversal was euphoric.

"It looks like the ass-end of a walk of shame," Brynn replied haughtily.

"Close actually but this is where I passed out when I lost my keys." There was no shame in her voice, even with the ridiculously stupid act she'd just admitted to. *She really just doesn't give a fuck about anything.* "I think I left them in Riley's room but she passed out before me. She locked her door because she sucks. I swear that girl could sleep through anything...and she has."

It took Brynn a week and a half before she developed that same skill...by necessity. Going through each day of class and then pledging on one or two hours of sleep wasn't something she'd wish on anyone, except maybe Tory.

"I'm heading to her room so I'll see if I can get her up and find your keys."

Tory rolled over on the couch in a futile attempt to get more comfortable. "Thanks...when she does get up do you want to get some breakfast?"

She really thinks she's ready to go out in public? Fuck me.

"I can't actually. I told my roommates I'd hang with them today. I just wanted to grab my cell from Riley's room. I guess that's the place to leave shit if you're drunk."

Tory smirked while still keeping her eyes shut. She moved her jacket over her face to keep the light from reaching her eyes.

"Alright, see ya tonight then" she heard the girl's muffled voice through the fabric.

Brynn didn't even respond as she walked away down the hall.

Her Big had a room at the end of the hall that was no bigger than the other rooms on the second floor. That wasn't to say it was small by any means. Every room in the building was disgustingly big in comparison to the dorms Brynn was living in.

To her surprise, Riley opened the door just as Brynn reached it. She looked pretty refreshed considering how early she'd passed out last night. *Wish I could get wasted and pass out early and feel great the next day. Must be nice Riles.* Riley had Tory's keys in her hand already so Brynn motioned for them.

"Got your keys Tory!" she called down the hall.

"Just leave them on the floor or walk them down to me. I can't move" Tory replied in hushed tones through the jacket over her face.

Without any hesitation Brynn simply dropped them on the floor. They didn't make much of a sound when the EIPi lanyard hit the ground. Riley didn't look all that amused but she didn't move to pick them up either.

"What? You heard her, she didn't really care where they were."

"Still, kind of cold."

"I don't see you moving to bring them to her" Brynn replied with a smirk.

"That's because she does this weekly and it's getting old."

Brynn looked back down the hall to Tory's deformed position. *She wants to go out to breakfast when she can't even get off the couch for her own keys...wow.*

"You ready to get breakfast?"

Brynn grinned as she kept her eyes on Tory, alone on the couch. "Absolutely."

****

Fortunately a few days had passed since the weekend and Jake had been able to connect with Kelly. She'd fallen asleep early on Friday just like she'd said and they'd spent the following night in bed together straight 'til morning. It was exponentially more fun than Friday had been.

"Try not to work too hard in class today Kel, it makes me feel kind of bad when I don't do as much."

"OK babe but try not to give your cousin such a hard time, he's just trying to help" Kelly replied supportively.

"Yeah well, all he's succeeding at is annoying the shit out of me."

The only reason he'd agreed to have lunch today was because Jared was going to be involved. At least he could act as a buffer between the two. After their last one on one chat, Jake believed that was a requirement. That was especially true with the topic of conversation he had picked out today.

"Be nice Jake" Kelly chastised him. She leaned in for a kiss to further get her point across. It worked like a charm.

"Fine fine, you win. But it's only because of that outfit you have on." *If we can even call it an outfit.* A pink tank top and very short jean shorts were all that was covering his girlfriend today and he loved every second spent staring at her.

"It's spring babe, this is the style."

"Believe me Kel, this isn't me complaining."

He kissed her again before retreating inside Lancaster to eat with his 'brothers'.

Jake found Eric immediately. Jared and he were sitting on the upper level. Most of the time when Jake ate here it was on the ground floor but the upper level essentially doubled as a balcony, which had a much better view.

"I got your food son" Eric declared triumphantly as he sat down.

"How'd you know what I'd want?"

"Come on J, your diet consists of the same food...all the time."

OK, fair enough. It had been a major point of contention for his family when they were all growing up. His grandparents in particular couldn't understand why he was so averse to trying new things. His cousins had learned to accept it but the older generation kept trying to force-feed him salad and other healthy foods.

"Fine" Jake admitted, "but did you get enough ketchup?"

"Please bro, this isn't amateur hour" Jared said from his chair to the right, directly across from Eric's seat.

Jake forced out a small smile as he looked over the plain hamburger and fries his cousin had gotten for him. The ketchup was in several small paper circlets on the edge of his tray. It looked like there was enough but he could never tell until he was done.

"How long have you guys been here?" Jake asked innocently.

"A little while actually. Jared wanted to talk with me about something."

And so it begins huh Biz? "OK?"

"Your attendance" Eric said softly.

"What about it?" *Another day with the same fucking story. Another lecture from my older, brilliant cousin, the one I should try to be like.*

"Well it's kind of non-existent bro" Jared interrupted subtly. For once there was no smile on his face, which was jarring.

"I'm glad you went with the delicate version," Jake said sarcastically, switching his attention from his cousin to his Big.

Only then did Jared start laughing like he always did. "It's kinda true isn't it?"

"I suppose this is a bad time to mention that I'm thinking about going inactive next semester then." There was no regret or second-guessing in his voice.

Eric caught onto that immediately and looked anything but happy. "I'm sorry; I don't think I heard that right. It sounded like you wanted to throw away six weeks of your life," he said coolly, bordering on condescension.

"I think that ship already sailed Eric" Jake bit out. *You don't want to bring up pledging to me right now pal.*

"No trust me Jake...that ship will sail when you leave the frat...for a girl" Eric shot back, just as venomously.

Jake tried eating his burger while ignoring the glares from his cousin.

Jared wasn't smiling anymore and his eyes remained neutral.

Going inactive in an organization was like taking a step back from it. After that, a person could either return at any point or just leave it behind altogether. *There's no way I'm the first person to go inactive in this fuckin' frat. Not that anything like that is in the history. Why would it be? Everyone gets along with everyone in AZXi; there are never any problems between actives. The same shit we get spoon-fed at Rush. It's all bullshit.*

"It's not about Kelly."

"Oh...here we go" his cousin said sarcastically with a hint of anger. "You've been dating over a year; let's hit the facts real quick J. This is the same girl you had a ton of shit with because of her last boyfriend. How'd that go down again? Oh that's right; she cheated on him with you. Then she waited a while before breaking *that* dudes heart. Then she moved right on to you...and you don't see anything wrong with this picture?"

Jake and Jared kept their composure while Eric looked to be on the edge of rage.

"Look, whatever's going on; it's possible to split time between the frat and your girlfriend bro. I did it when I was with Jess" Jared explained, keeping his tone flat.

That must've been the chick I saw Aaron with that night before Canada.

"And what if I don't want to split time?"

Eric shook his head. "I just don't get why you wouldn't want to. You earned the damn letters. This is it."

He'll never understand what it feels like to be with someone like her so fuck it. He hasn't had a girlfriend in years.

Eric saw the look of contempt in Jake's eyes and read it like a book.

"Get the fuck over it Jake. Quit being a little girl."

Jake felt his anger rising. Their last fight four years ago had started with Eric saying something just like that. "I'd watch how you talk to me Biz" he said the nickname with hatred. "We aren't kids anymore...I don't follow you around like I used to."

Eric laughed condescendingly. "Says the kid that came to the same school as me and Riley. You pledged the same frat. Is that the same kid that doesn't follow? If you weren't being so insane maybe you'd see what we're trying to do."

There was enough that had already been said. And Jake hadn't liked any of it. He did the only thing he could to avoid doing something terrible. He picked up his tray and stormed away from the table.

Jake felt one of the two he'd left behind following him but he didn't turn around.

"Cut him some slack man" Jared said calmly while walking beside him.

"I suppose I should thank him for calling my girlfriend a slut and telling me to get drunk with your guys to make up for it? I wanna fucking kill that guy."

"No you don't...and there are worse ways to pass the time bro. You wouldn't have gotten a bid if we all didn't wanna have you around. That's what it's all about."

I heard that same shit during Rush. I bought it then but not now...not today.

"I don't see the problem with wanting to chill with Kelly. She barely got to see me during pledging...and now I'm supposed to drink with AZXis and sorority girls all the time? What's the fucking point? Why would she keep me around after that?"

"Some people never get what we have. You're losing it before it even starts."

Jake took a deep breath as he found an open table on the ground floor. He felt better once he sat down with his tray. Jared followed suit and sat across from him.

"I hear what you're saying," he admitted. "I just feel like I owe her for not being around during pledging. I missed Valentine's Day because Jeff needed the house cleaned right then for whatever reason. And after all that shit we went through at the Trip-E house, I'm not exactly feeling the brotherhood. It's all fucked."

The one exception to all that was sitting in front of him. Jared was the only person he bonded with since Rush. He hoped that was apparent to his Big because he didn't want to offend him. Fortunately, as usual, he didn't take any offense, at least any that was noticeable.

"It does take a little while to get used to. But you're skipping what's supposed to help with that. Hanging with everyone after Crossing gets you involved with how things work. Alumni weekend is coming up too. That's the perfect time to go balls deep."

What the fuck is so special about alumni weekend? So a bunch of old guys come back and drink beer in Gladen Hills…what's so crazy about that?

With the food getting cold Jake was content to let the conversation drop. He knew Jared wouldn't push it like Eric so he kept quiet and continued eating; hoping his Big would change the subject on his own.

Jake never looked back to the upper balcony but he couldn't help but wonder if Eric was still up there, watching him.

****

Eric wasn't sure how long he sat frozen in place after his cousin walked away.

His shock spread out from each of the things that had happened. Shock at Jared being serious, even briefly. Shock at Jake saying he wanted to go inactive, which was just a polite way of telling AZXi to fuck off altogether. Most of all, he was blown away by losing his own temper. *That could've gone better.*

Finally, he forced himself to look down from the balcony to see that Jake and Jared had sat at a table on the ground level. *At least he'll still talk to Jared.*

"Stalking isn't a good pastime Biz" Jeff's voice filled the air. Quickly, he turned away from where he was looking to see Jeff standing there with a tray of food. Eric didn't see anyone else. *Is he about to eat alone?*

The guy sauntered over, looking down to the ground floor to what Eric had been staring at. "It's even weirder that you're stalking your cousin though. But I guess you've probably seen about the same amount of him that I've seen since Crossing, which now that you mention it, is zero."

"That's funny Buttons. He just stormed off when I asked him if that was ever gonna change" Eric said bitterly. "He's my family..." his voice gave out.

Jeff sat down at the table as though Eric had invited him. "What's his deal?"

"All day everyday, girlfriend time."

Jeff winced but Eric had no idea why.

"I tried telling him that separation of friends and girlfriend is like having separation of church and state...it's essential. But he won't see it. What's worse is I don't think they work together." *They shouldn't be dating at all...end of story.* "She cheated on her last boyfriend with Jake. In my opinion that means she's just biding her time 'til she does the same thing to him."

It was plain as day now, Jeff looked beyond uncomfortable. He shifted in his chair while leaving his food untouched. "What if I told you that already happened?"

"You better explain that to me Jeff" Eric ordered, feeling his pulse race.

"I've seen her cheat on Raley."

Eric stopped blinking. *What the fuck does he mean by that?*

"It was the Saturday they were in Canada. I saw her getting pretty close to another guy at the Midway."

Eric stared him down, demanding a further explanation with his eyes.

"They were making out and grinding. I think the guy was a Kappa Nu" he finished solemnly. If he'd been talking any lower Eric would've been hard pressed to hear him and he was hanging on every word.

He felt his temper flare again. "And you decided to keep this to yourself?"

"You bet your ass I kept it to myself, for two reasons" he started explaining.

Eric didn't want to hear any of it but Jeff kept going.

"I didn't know him well enough to have that kind of chat with the kid..."

"Then you fucking tell me! And *I'll* decide what to do. He doesn't deserve to be kept in the dark on this," Eric lashed out.

People around them were looking on with morbid interest.

"That brings me to reason two. *If* you or me said anything to him he would've de-pledged so quick it would've made your fucking head spin...and for what? For a girl he wouldn't give a shit about in a few years. Now the program is done and he's got us when it all goes to Hell."

Eric was angrier than he'd been in years. For all he knew, the guy may have just wanted to avoid another de-pledge in the Alpha Epsilons. That would've marked half the class telling him to fuck off if Jake had left. That wouldn't sit well with a guy like him...or the rest of the frat.

"You might be my brother in some fraternity," Eric said coldly "but he's my family. That means *I* get to make that decision if you can't."

Jeff remained remarkably calm even with Eric yelling at him. The curious onlookers from other tables hadn't quit either.

"Why tell me now at all?"

"I kept trying to talk to Raley alone but I've literally only seen him three times. Even then, he ignores me. I haven't been able to get this done."

For the first time since Jeff sat down, Eric looked back out over the balcony and saw Jared and Jake still talking below.

His anger at his cousin was a distant memory.

****

"He needs to know" Eric said sternly from across the table. His eyes weren't on Jeff though. He'd resumed his one-sided stare down with his cousin.

"You're right he does" Jeff agreed. *It's been too long already.* "We'll tell him together. This is my problem Eric. I saw it; it's on me to say something. And if he asks why he didn't find out sooner I'll tell him that too."

Eric turned back toward him with less anger in his eyes. Now they were filled with a mix of that and sadness.

Jeff didn't have any siblings or close family so he couldn't really imagine what was going on in his brother's head.

"He's gonna lose it" Eric said quietly. "I need to be there."

"That's why I called it a team effort," Jeff reiterated while he too looked down at the younger AZXis.

The Midway really does blow.

Jeff darted his eyes around the largest bar in Gladen Hills. It was filled with undergrads dancing their asses off to blaring music in the warmest atmosphere around. It was no wonder he rarely came here whenever he made it to midtown from Arkridge Avenue. The amount of times he'd come here without being near blackout drunk were even less and yet here he sat.

Fortunately his brother was not having the second problem at all. Dylan was already fucked up before Jeff ordered a round but that didn't matter because he sure as hell wasn't going to rip shots alone. That required a level of depression he wasn't at.

"I might be tryin' to make moves Buttons" Dylan declared as if it was newsworthy.

You don't say Dills. The music was blasting louder than a callout. Most of the time he couldn't stomach the 'pop' shit they played here but the chicks fucking loved all of it.

"Dude I never see you at the Midway. Why the fuck are you even here?"

"I didn't think I had to run shit by you first" he shouted back just to be heard.

Dylan just smiled while his eyes rolled around in their sockets. It was a miracle he was actually able to remain upright in his bar stool. "I would've liked a head's up so I could've brought money for shots." Dylan said it like he was in some desperate need to drink more when he'd clearly be good for the rest of the night and most of tomorrow.

Jeff smirked and paid the bartender.

"You're the man" Dills flattered him. *Anyone who buys you shots right now might as well be named godfather to your children.*

"But for real, why you here?" Dylan asked again.

"Some kind of fight with Dana. Figured I might see her here to talk since she isn't answering my texts," he answered honestly. Even though he was shouting he doubted if anyone other than Dylan heard him.

"Everything straight?"

"It will be. She's probably just drunk. If I can talk to her it'll be fine."

He and Dana had little fights every couple weeks over stupid shit. This time he believed it was because she thought he wasn't making enough time for her. Of course he'd warned her ahead of time that that would be the case when he was the pledge-master so she either hadn't believed him or just ignored it altogether. *Now the pledges are in Canada 'til tomorrow and she can't even answer my texts for Christ's sake.*

It looked like Dills had had enough of their chat since he was off to go dance in the crowds milling around the bar. Jeff sure as hell wasn't going with him so he stayed put. As he was turning back toward the bar something caught his eye. There was a girl and guy full on making out back to front not five feet from his bar stool. That by itself wasn't a rare occurrence at the Midway since half the people there came just for the chance to hook up. Still, the couple in front of him struck a nerve. At first he couldn't figure out why. Then it hit him like a line of coke. *Holy shit...that's Raley's chick. And that's definitely not fuckin' Raley she's shoving her tongue into.*

He continued staring, not realizing how creepy it probably looked. Fortunately, they were too involved with themselves to notice anything around them. The more he looked, the more he became sure it was Raley's girlfriend. *They couldn't have broken up? No shot. Raley would've been more of a bitch than usual. And Biz definitely would've said something. That's definitely her though. Fuck my life.*

Jeff had only seen her once, the night she dropped Raley off at the AZXi house before Formal Rush. His first thought had been that she was too hot for Raley so obviously he'd done a phenomenal job for himself.

"Son of a bitch" he said out loud to no one.

His eyes remained locked on the two dancing heatedly in front of him. He thought he recognized the guy she was with too. Jeff was pretty sure he was a Kappa Nu and as such, more in line with the girl's looks and type.

Kappa Nu was known for being full of pretty boys and preppy types. *I knew this bitch was all about the looks.* He'd been able to guess that the second he saw her outside AZXi six weeks ago. It made the fact that she was with Raley all the more impressive.

Finally Jeff turned away from them. *At that rate they'll leave the bar soon or just starting fucking right here in front of everyone.*

He ordered another two shots for himself. This time he'd drink them alone.

Jeff reached into his pocket for his phone. Cycling through the contact list he found the name he was looking for. The highlighted line was resting on Raley. He'd needed all the pledges names and contact information when pledging started. He was moving to hit the call button before going outside where it was quieter.

For some reason he couldn't bring himself to hit send.

Raley had been pledging for five weeks but Jeff still didn't know the kid all that well. *What am I gonna say to him? He probably won't even believe me.*

Moving down the contact list he found the next name he was looking for.

Eric's his cousin. He'll definitely know how to handle this. What's he gonna do though? Call Raley immediately and tell him? The pledges are probably close to the motel if not there already. What good will it do to say anything right now?

The shots were poured in front of him. He paid right away. He slammed one without hesitation and let it sit for a second before doing the next one. His thoughts started shifting around in his head. *We tell him before Crossing and he'll quit without thinking.*

Jeff closed his phone and ripped the second shot. It went down smoother than the previous ones. He took one look back at the girl with her Kappa Nu boy-toy. They were moving toward the exit. She was the one leading the way out of the bar. When they hit the exit Jeff caught sight of Dana coming in with a group of her friends. Even though she was clearly a little drunk she locked eyes with him right away.

He sighed heavily before resigning himself to this fate. *One problem at a time.*

His stomach rumbled as he continued looking down at Jared and Raley. His food sat on the table, still untouched. *At least I told Eric. Now we can deal with this and get it over with. That bitch doesn't deserve our brother.*

Chapter 28

Jake had only had sex with a few girls before getting to Gladen Hills. Even with that in mind, he couldn't imagine any one ever topping how amazing it felt every time he got to have Kelly.

Every time he went inside her felt like a new high, one that was reset with each passing session.

And Wayne had to pick tonight to actually sleep in his own bed. Fuck.

Kelly's dorm room was always occupied by her own roommate but that tended not to matter in most cases since Jake's room was almost always clear. *Except tonight.* Wayne was usually either out at lacrosse practice or with his girlfriend at her place over on Northwest. Jake could count on his hands the number of times he'd seen the guy in the past month.

Jake and Wayne had bunk beds in their room so when one of them rocked, the other moved in sequence. They knew that well enough because they'd tried going at it earlier in the semester during another occasion when Wayne was actually in the room and he hadn't been happy about it.

Kelly broke off their kiss and started saying the same things he was already thinking. "I can't believe the one time we need your bed is the one time your roommate is here" she exaggerated. Jake smirked. They needed his bed almost every time they were alone. They couldn't keep their hands off each other. They'd been lying on the couch so long with the lights off that their eyes had adjusted and she read his expression perfectly.

"That's why I can't get mad Kel. It's his room too," he said through near gritted teeth. He knew he shouldn't get frustrated because it was so rare an occurrence but that didn't change how much he wanted Kelly right that second. "And it's the first time this has happened all month."

"Where are the other guys?"

"Dukes and Scribbs are at the house I think, not sure." J-Hood and Eric had invited them again that weekend for another smaller party. *Never too early to start rushing the next pledge class...or so they tell me.* "The other one is on duty tonight." Derek happened to be an RA and they all saw less of him than they did Wayne. He was manning the front desk in the building's lobby tonight so he wouldn't be back until after two in the morning. Jake didn't feel all that comfortable getting inside Kelly in either of those rooms but their options were limited.

The more they made out and she rubbed at his waist the more he warmed to the idea. "What about their room then?" Kelly half-asked, half-urged as she motioned to Scribner and Dukes' room. She reached down Jake's pants to find him hard and ready. Kelly ran her hands up and down and within seconds he moved away to check to make sure their door was unlocked, which it wasn't. *Locked...of course...Scribner's not an idiot.* His friend often referred to them as rabbits and because of that, there was no way he was leaving his room unlocked for them to defile.

He shook his head solemnly back at Kelly who was still on the couch with her legs spread. She was still wearing clothes but the view mesmerized him. Jake lunged back at her and aligned their waists. Even with both of them still wearing pants he could feel how warm it was between her thighs. *I need her now.* She offered to relax him, immediately reaching down his jeans after expertly unzipping his fly. Within seconds her mouth was moving away from his, heading down.

Her mouth felt wet and warm, almost as much as his favorite spot between her legs. She went up and down. Everything else drained away. After a few minutes he couldn't take it anymore. He didn't want to finish without giving her something too. Jake pulled her up from what she was doing and motioned for her to follow him to Derek's room. "I'm done waiting," he said between heavy breaths as they walked the short distance to the third door. *Unlocked...yes.* As they walked inside a ton of screams, shouts and laughter from outside the dorm ripped through the otherwise silent suite. It sounded like whoever was outside was having a phenomenal time.

"What if he comes back?"

"He's an RA. He'll be gone until at least two" Jake assured his girlfriend. She smiled and started kissing his neck while she slid his pants off. *Hopefully he doesn't come back to his room before then.* Jake ignored the thought as his clothing fell away. *No point in boring Kel with details like that.* Abruptly he felt her mouth on him again. He nearly got lost in the feeling but fought against it, if only to keep things even. Jake stood her up from where she'd been on her knees and nearly ripped her clothes off, throwing her onto the bed to let his mouth do the work for her now. She tasted so good, better than usual. Her continued moans turned him on to the point that he couldn't put it off anymore. He slid inside her with ease.

The blinds in the room were cracked slightly so the campus lights outside were streaming through. It made Kelly's face easier to see. Jake liked watching her when they had sex. His enjoyment came directly from her pleasure. Jake kept pumping away, with Kelly getting louder each time. She kept begging him to go harder and faster. He couldn't keep the rhythm up long without finishing. He warned her. She didn't care.

Fortunately he'd done a good job getting her close too. He kept thrusting as long as he could before pulling out and finishing all over her the way she liked. She was rubbing herself to climax when he looked down at the same moment. It was an unfortunate side effect of pulling out. Sometimes she had to finish herself off since she wasn't on the pill and they hated using condoms. Kelly didn't seem to mind. And it turned him on seeing her rub herself the way she did.

For a few minutes after they just lied on his suitemate's bed. Nothing but the continued sounds of the drunken masses beyond were audible outside of their mutual heavy breathing. Jake smiled up at the ceiling. *That was the best sex we've ever had.*

****

Calvin could only stand in awe of what he was hearing.

"So I'm shoulder deep in cow snatch, I grab hold of the calf's legs and pull that sucker right out of his mother. The damn thing comes out, hits the ground, shakes it off, and heads for the nearest tit."

If he'd had any beer in his mouth he might've felt compelled to spit it out, either from being sickened at the story or just the ridiculousness of it all. Either way Calvin hadn't taken more than a small sip during the whole story he'd just heard from this Dan Scribner kid. He was apparently a friend of both J-Hood and Biz and maybe Raley too. *If that kid even still counts.*

"Jesus that's ridiculous" Calvin finally commented while shaking his head. He knew nothing about cows other than that parts of them tasted good.

"Just another day on the farm" Scribner said while taking another drag from his cigarette. Calvin had been outside pissing when the kid had come out to have a smoke. He hadn't recognized him so he went to introduce himself. Not five minutes into their conversation he'd heard the cow story. Apparently he routinely helped birth calves.

"I didn't picture you as a farmer and now I can't un-picture it" Calvin confessed, still in mild shock.

"Dukes says it's the red hair and beard that give me away" he said with a grin. Dukes was apparently another friend of Scribner's and by extension, Raley. Calvin was having a little trouble managing all the connections.

He gave the kid another once over and focused on his hair and beard. Even in the fading light of the backyard it started becoming clear. *OK...yeah. Now it makes sense.* "You're right. That definitely does the trick."

After a few seconds, Calvin noticed the kid's eyes had shifted to the frat house, like he was seeing something nobody else could. "This place is pretty straight though."

"I always thought so. Let me guess, you never thought you'd find yourself in a place like this." Scribner started looking uncomfortable so he eased off a bit. "Let me ask you ask this then: what do you usually do on the weekends?"

"Usually just head out wherever there's an Open and drink 'til the kegs run out," Scribner replied. His tone would've suggested that he was making it sound better than it really was, or at least trying to.

Calvin wasn't fooled. "So what changed?"

Scribner blinked before diving headlong into an answer. "I go out with the same people to the same parties. I pay the same five bucks for the same three beers that I push through the crowd to get. I never meet anyone."

Taking another sip from his beer to almost finish it he looked directly at the kid and tried sounding sincere. Rushing undergrads was fine line to walk. It was guys' hitting on guys without letting it seem like that's what was happening. "That's never a problem here."

Scribner grinned back. "I noticed that during the four-way party. Even with the people packed into this house it was still better than an Open."

"That's one of the perks of having closed parties. They're more intimate. You can actually chill with people and talk. You can even hit on chicks" he finished with a sly smile.

"Yeah…that's if J-Hood left any behind" Scribner grinned.

****

It was clear which way the conversation was heading in the last few minutes but that next question from Calvin still threw Scribner off. "You ever thought about rushing any frats?" Scribner didn't want to hear that question because he was both unsure of and a little ashamed of the answer. It'd be hard enough having such a talk with Biz or Raley but he barely knew the guy in front of him. *He seems legit though.*

"I've definitely thought about it," he answered in a half-truth. It was the best he could do with how conflicted he felt. The next Rush wasn't until the Fall and at least then the summer would be separating him from the nerve-wracking decision. In truth it was so far off in his mind that he didn't want to think about it. Yet here he was constantly putting himself in the position where conversations like these would happen.

"It can't hurt to go to Rush" Calvin said a little sullenly, sadness creeping in.

He felt it was only fair to level with the guy. "I just always thought of frat guys as collar-popping douchbags," he blurted out. *That's great, insult the guy while you're at it…dumbass.* To his surprise, the look of sadness on Calvin's face vanished as a giant grin took its place. *What the fuck?*

"You think it'd be fucked up if you decided to join one after all this time hating them?" He might as well have been reading thoughts straight from Scribner's head.

"You saying it wouldn't?"

Calvin finished his beer. "People look at frats and sororities and they see what they want to see. You want to see a bunch of jackasses making bad decisions or a group that excludes everyone, then *that's* what you'll see."

He said it with such authority that Scribner was tempted to believe it. "What's your point?"

"My point is if you look closer, there's practically a place for everyone in this town but most people can't get past what they've been told or the judgments they've made." Scribner thought it over. Truthfully he hadn't formed a whole lot of opinions on frats other than what was based on shit he'd heard from friends or people he'd just met. "You could die trying to please everyone."

Scribner smirked inadvertently. "So I should say fuck it and rush?"

"You tell me. Is this frat what you always thought it would be when you heard about places like it in high school?"

He looked from Calvin back to the house in front of them and started sifting through the experiences he'd already had here in the handful of times he'd been invited. They were few but they'd left more of an impression on him than the three dozen or more Opens he'd been to in Gladen Hills.

"You can only find out so much out about a frat from going to its parties. Rush is designed to show you what happens *between* those parties. There's more to this place than just the drinking." Calvin patted him on the back as the look of sadness from earlier returned.

Was that what Scribner could look forward to if he joined a frat: the downright awful depression that came along with graduating? He assumed that was what was going through the guy's head. *If I graduated tomorrow the only thing I'd miss is living on my own...not much else. There's gotta be something better... He's upset because he's losing something that was worth caring about in the first place.*

****

Her Little was later than she would've liked but it didn't matter. Sunday afternoons were notorious for being filled with absolutely nothing important. Even the people like her that procrastinated on their homework all weekend had the good sense to wait until past seven or eight at night to finally give in and go to Cordan. That left the hours between noon and then up in the air.

Brynn had shown up at two. That had allowed Riley to watch more of her Grey's Anatomy DVD's than originally planned. That was a Sunday ritual along with procrastination. Actually it was more of an 'anytime she was hung-over' ritual. Her cousin had told her a while ago that the best thing to do when being hung-over like they all were so often in Gladen Hills was to go into a vegetative state and watch season after season of TV on DVD. Riley was now a full-fledged supporter of that idea. Jake had aided her further by getting her the latest season for Christmas last year. He might as well have been a crack dealer for how addicted it had gotten her.

Riley had wanted to go to University Grove for lunch before things got too busy. *The lunch rush should be over by now.* Considering how sloppy Brynn had gotten last night it was amazing she was able to show up at all.

"OK here's how it's gonna go" Riley began. All she got in return was a hesitant murmur. *That'll work.* Riley had learned a long time ago that Brynn was much more attentive when she was standing upright. As soon as they sat down to eat, her Little would mentally check out. Given how disheveled she looked, Riley couldn't blame her but that was all the more reason to power through the facts while they walked to University Grove.

"The E-board positions get voted on in two weeks. Any assistant positions get appointed by the person who has the main position" she stated as she locked her door behind her.

"Got it."

"If you want to run for a major position you need to have a speech ready." That stopped Brynn in her tracks and they'd only walked ten feet. Riley motioned for her to follow along. "Relax. You don't have to worry about that this year" she assured her. *Next year's a different story.*

"What are the E-Board positions?" Brynn asked almost sincerely. It was probably coming from a place of curiosity as much as it was her wanting to change the subject. Riley obliged in any case.

"President, VP, treasurer, recording secretary, house president, Rush chair, social, pledge mom and chapter relations." Riley rattled off the list with no trouble. Brynn looked like she'd been dunked in frigid water. They rounded the far corner of the hallway and hit the first stairwell leading down from the second floor. "Then there's the associate board. That has all the assistant positions for house chair, social and pledge mistress...plus the CGA rep," she added with practiced contempt. *Who knows why the CGA rep is on that board but whatever.*

"CGA rep?" Brynn asked as they reached the first floor landing.

"It's for the Council on Greek Affairs. The school administration says jump and we jump. It's their way of keeping track of all the organizations that they've sanctioned on campus." She tried keeping the cynicism out of her voice but it was tough. *No point in worrying about that now. That'll keep for next year too.*

"Then there are the positions I think you should be trying for."

Brynn's pace slowed. It looked like she was stalling for something. "Which position are you going for?"

"Anything on the E-Board would be good. Ideally President or VP I guess." Her big sister Felicia had graduated almost a year ago but there were still times when Riley felt like she was right next to her. Brynn picked up the pace again as they left the stairwell and moved into the ground floor hallway. "You don't have to vote for me if you don't think I'll do a good job."

"Wait...seriously?" Brynn asked, smirking.

"You damn well better vote for me" Riley quickly replied, only half-kidding. Brynn's support would ensure that her pledge class went along too and given the slight situation they were in with the Beta Zetas, it couldn't hurt. "It's gonna be tricky. The Beta Zetas are kind of a roadblock" she said plainly. She wanted to see how Brynn would react. Confusion was the first response. "The Beta Zetas have ten in their pledge class. And for whatever ungodly reason, they vote as a unit...every single time." The Beta Zetas didn't specifically have an issue with Riley being on the E-Board; it was Tory she was lobbying for in a roundabout way. Amy and Danielle were part of the Beta Zetas and they'd basically handed Rachel the presidency last year. If any of them wanted to be on the E-Board over Tory then there wasn't much to be done about it.

"Sounds like that whole 'pledge class of one' thing kinda came back to bite you guys in the ass" Brynn answered sarcastically.

Riley frowned. "It's fine when you're actually pledging, if not absolutely necessary. After Crossing you aren't supposed to create an island away from the rest of the sorority." Brynn didn't look content with the answer and Riley couldn't blame her. *She* wasn't content with it. Dani, Rachel and Amy basically ran Jessie, Brianna and the rest of the girls in that class. Fortunately since Dani was her niece she'd been able to get closer to her than most of the other actives. Her Big had been tight with her too but she'd graduated the same semester Danielle had pledged which left Riley as the sole girl to look up to.

Even so, Riley doubted she could change her mind if Amy or another girl in that class wanted positions that Tory or anybody else was interested in. "Sorry Brynn. This is how it looks on the other side."

Inter-sorority politics were just as messy if not messier than anything going on in a fraternity. She was willing to bet they were messier, especially with the Beta Zetas. There were forty-three actives in EIPi but a solid twelve votes swinging one way could change an election, and it had. It hadn't been pretty during last year's elections with Felicia and some of the older girls being shocked by how firmly Rachel had gotten the support of the other eleven. Rachel Hager had been a solid president so far but she was only a sophomore when she'd been elected. She was a junior now but generally it was the seniors doing the higher-level jobs. The Beta Zetas made a statement with that election. It was one Riley hoped wouldn't need a repeat lesson. "It doesn't always happen though" she said modestly. "It definitely didn't happen for the six of you."

To be frank, it had *never* happened before the Beta Zetas. At least not in her time with EIPi or any she'd heard about. With forty-three actives and over one fourth going toward one person for any given position, things could get messy, or in their case, remarkably smooth. Those girls were the first ones to figure that out. Not only had they seen what everyone else seemed content on ignoring, they ran with it.

"No, definitely not" Brynn replied thoughtfully. Riley felt relieved but she was still hoping her Little could do a little persuading for Tory if not herself. *If the Beta Zetas and Beta Thetas both go the same way on anything it's game over.* It was going to be interesting too considering Angela and Mary were the Littles of Danielle and Amy. That was another reason that Riley had wanted to take a Little this semester despite being the pledge mom. *No one else needs to know that reason...*

The two of them reached the outer door and immediately started making their way up to University Grove past the bottom of the hill. It was where all the local businesses were and where some of the best meals could be had. Even Jake liked some of the food on the Grove.

"Anyways...there are a few positions I think you should go for. There's the song mistress, corresponding secretary, judicial rep, gossip and awards, public relations, athletics and quarter-mistress" Riley finished with a heavy breath as they reached Cadren Drive. Once again Brynn looked completely out of her depth. "Don't worry I'll explain what those are" she tried calming the girl's obvious whirling mind.

"Good because I have no idea what the fuck you're saying to me right now."

"Don't worry" Riley smiled. "By the way though, Tory wants to be the house president so plan your votes accordingly."

Riley made sure she said it quickly enough for it to be heard but not enough that they'd dwell on it. She wasn't blind to how weird her Little was when it came to her best friend but she was hoping Brynn would get past whatever it was.

****

...Tory wants to be the house president...

She couldn't stop thinking about it. It was added so sparingly to all the other gibberish being thrown at her that she almost missed it.

They'd walked down most of University Grove before deciding on a place to eat. By that time, Riley had explained or at least tried to explain which positions she thought Brynn should run for. After another ten minutes, they got into Uncle Rudy's sub shop and sat down with their food. By then, Brynn's thoughts were swirling around so furiously that the hangover she was already fighting had actually gotten worse. It was clear Riley wanted the request about voting for Tory to seem like a joke and that's what was tripping Brynn up.

Now Riley was saying something about how Tory had tried hooking her up with some guy earlier last week but she couldn't focus. There were too many memories violently finding their way to the surface.

Danielle was leading them into the party room at ElPi. The six of them had their arms linked at the elbows like they'd been made to do too many times before. *And this is only week five?! Pledging won't end until at least next week but now who knows? They made us sign that form to the school earlier tonight about extending pledging.* Brynn tried shaking the negativity from her mind but it wasn't working.

Once they'd all gotten into the room she started using her peripheral vision. Strictly speaking, none of them were allowed to look anywhere other than straight. That didn't stop Brynn from looking all around her, just in a less noticeable way. As expected, the room was filled with ElPi sisters all clad in jerseys or sweatshirts covered in pink and white, the sorority colors. She couldn't tell for sure but they all looked more evil than usual. That was saying a lot.

"I've always thought God loved me because I'm so amazing. Then I got stuck with all of you and I realized it couldn't be true. But I don't have to be OK with that. I will make you all into better pledges if it fucking kills me. So tonight we're going to get a little exercise. And by we, I mean you."

Brynn tensed up. *There's no way Riley isn't bipolar.*

"Sisters…let's get to it" Riley ordered after finishing her customary pacing in front of the six of them. *Even she looks meaner.* Of course no one held a candle to just how sadistic their assistant pledge mom was. *Tory's in a class all her own.*

With that order from her Big, the rest of the girls in the room all grabbed a cup from the table in the room's center. There had to have been at least twenty, each of which looked to be half full of something Brynn couldn't see. Once all the cups were picked up, the sisters spread out around the room and with simple nods from Riley and Tory they all started dumping the cups' contents on the floor. They weren't filled with any kind of liquid. Instead the cups were filled with small spherical beads about half the size of a penny. They rolled in a thousand different directions. They weren't the same color either. From red to pink, blue to purple, green to orange, white to black, every color was present. Brynn didn't have to see her pledge sisters to view the looks of horror. She knew they were there. They couldn't have been much different than the look forming on her face.

Tory moved in front of her and Brynn saw a smirk come across the girl's face. Generally, neither she nor Riley gave out any kind of emotion at callouts other than anger, immense anger. This time it was clear as day that Tory Brye was enjoying herself. *Yeah…you would enjoy this wouldn't you bitch?*

"We have another party tomorrow night" Riley stated gruffly. "And if there's even a single one of these left on the floor, someone could slip and break their neck. None of you should want that to happen right?" she asked rhetorically. *Depends on which sister is breaking their neck. There's some acceptable options…*

"No, pledge mother Riley Nichol" the six of them shouted back in unison.

There were a few sisters moving around behind the flip cup section in the corner that doubled as a bar but Brynn couldn't see what was happening. "Good, so you won't have any trouble cleaning all of these up?" Riley asked in a kinder voice.

"No, pledge mother Riley Nichol" they all repeated.

"After they're all cleaned up, the floor needs to be cleaned too. Since we're so nice, we'll help you. Sisters…if you please" Riley motioned for the second time. The first order had let the beads loose and Brynn shuddered at what was going to come next.

Brynn looked away toward the flip cup table and saw what the girls had been doing a few seconds ago. They were lifting up buckets they'd stored on the floor in the corner. She definitely hadn't noticed them when they'd been led in but that was probably the point.

The actives started dumping the ten buckets of water all over the floor. There was a ton of soap in the water so the foam and bubbles spread across the entire room in seconds. The beads became harder to see underneath it all. "That should do it…" Riley paused as she stepped lightly across the mangled floor of the party room. "Actually we should probably at least give them some music to work to."

Brynn noticed Tory once again smiling darkly as she hit the play button on the boom box in the opposite corner of the room. It must've been set at the maximum volume because the high-pitched voice of a female singer split the air and Brynn's eardrums.

The six of them lingered there for what felt like an hour before her big sister ordered them to make the room spotless. They all knelt down and de-linked their arms. It was the first time during a callout that they were allowed to do so. It felt liberating and weird in equal amounts.

Brynn reached out and swept away a grouping of foam and bubbles to reveal a mass of beads. She reached down to grab as many as she could. Her pledge sisters were doing the same. Even over the music, Brynn heard Riley's voice screaming from above.

"What the fuck are you doing? Why aren't you grabbing the pink ones first?"

Tory moved over from where she'd previously been in the corner by the boom box to get closer to the six of them. "Pink is the most important color in your life! Pink is what you'd bleed right now if I stabbed any one of you!" she screeched while towering over them. "I don't want to see any fucking crying in here!" she yelled as if daring one of them to shed a tear. *You won't get that satisfaction from me bitch.* "We all had to go through this and it made us better sisters. You should all be so fucking lucky!"

They all shuffled around in the bubbles and water to find the pink ones first. Their pants were all soaking now from the knees down. Riley and a few of the others were kind enough to actually place the empty cups on the ground so they could store the beads they picked up. The six of them continued on for a few minutes, making a decent amount of progress. *This is gonna take forever...*

As the music continued blaring from the corner the song started to reach its climax. *At least play a good song next...this chick sounds like someone stabbing me in the ear.* Brynn continued picking up more pink beads as the lull between songs on the CD came up. For those few fleeting seconds the only sounds came from the sloshing of water being moved from one point to the next. Then it happened. The same song they'd just listened to came up again in all of its Hellish glory. *The exact same song? On repeat?* Brynn couldn't believe what was happening but that didn't stop it.

Around the song's fifth play-through Riley started yelling again. "This is taking way too long." Tory agreed with her Big like she always did. The girl's smirk was still plainly obvious even though Riley still had a hard, stone-faced look.

"Give them some coffee to wake them up!" Riley yelled.

Just like that, where before there was only soap, water and beads, now there were coffee grinds being added to the mix on the floor. The brown-black powdery substance came from three buckets that must've been brought in after they'd started the insane task. It turned the floor where it hit into a disgusting slush-like mix. Now the beads had to be picked clean through the coffee grinds and bubbles. Seeing them plainly on the floor without moving anything around was impossible.

Without saying a word, the six of them just continued on with retrieving the pink beads first. Any progress Brynn thought they'd been making was a distant memory now. *We're never gonna get out of here.*

"It's still taking too long!" Tory yelled during the break between the repeats of the song. This time Riley agreed and she subsequently ordered the sisters to give them some breakfast to speed things along.

Beads, soap, bubbles, water, coffee grinds and now all kinds of cereal were being dumped out like it was completely normal. Now every bead they found was a victory in itself, pink or not. So many times Brynn found what she thought was a bead but it was really just a piece of colored cereal.

When she looked up around the room, all the girls had sinister looks in their eyes except for Danielle and Amy in the corner. They looked almost as pissed as Brynn felt. *Almost. You can't be as pissed because you aren't down here on the floor.*

The same grating song continued repeating as they suffered through it all together. The cups around them were slowly filling with beads. Pink ones first of course but then they started on the other colors as well. White was the next one in line. During one point in their 'cleaning' Tory had accidentally slipped and knocked over one of their cups of beads. Brynn didn't believe for a second that Tory had slipped. Even if the ground was slick in certain areas, it had to be completely intentional.

She's fucking evil.

"You are a pledge class of one. You will finish this task and make this room spotless again. You will stay next to your pledge sisters the entire time you are doing this. You are ElPi pledges, nothing more!" Riley yelled between lulls of the song. Brynn felt her self-control slipping away. The next time the song repeated she felt it sprinting away.

Every few minutes she found a pink bead and quietly made a movement to put it in the right cup. Hopefully none of the sisters would notice or care that pink wasn't being *specifically* looked for underneath the river of shit they'd tried drowning them in.

"Scratch the rest of the night" she heard Riley's voice say through the twisted music that continued playing. By what felt like the thirtieth play-through Brynn's hearing had gotten accustomed to the scratching sound so she could catch bits of the girls' conversations when they got close enough.

"Really?" Tory asked in a surprised tone.

"Yeah definitely, no point in overdoing this, let the girls know we're done for now." Riley almost sounded regretful.

"You big softy" Tory mocked her.

Brynn grimaced at the floor and at last made herself look at how fucked up her jeans had gotten by kneeling in all of the muck. Thankfully the actives at least had been nice enough to tell them to wear old clothes that they didn't care about.

She looked up from the floor again and saw Tory talking to some of the other sisters. *She better be passing along Riley's orders or I'm going to kill her...slowly.* After a few more seconds, she resigned herself to continuing. Her pledge sisters probably felt awful too but they weren't stopping, so she couldn't either.

The 'cleaning' session, if it could even be called such a thing had indeed taken the entire night. They'd gone straight through 'til five in the morning. That was when they'd finally been sent back to the chapter room for rest.

Tory just kept on ticking. At least Riley had the decency to stop whatever *else* was planned that night. Brynn never had the stomach to ask what she'd stopped from going forward. She wasn't sure she wanted to know.

Her sub sandwich was still sitting in front of her, awaiting the first bite. Riley was finishing up her story. Brynn had no idea what she'd been saying but she doubted she'd missed much. Any story that had to deal with her assistant pledge mom couldn't have been that interesting.

Brynn hadn't meant for it to happen but somehow just the mention of Tory wanting an E-Board position flooded her thoughts with all the negative emotions from pledging. A flood she couldn't stop now even if she wanted to. It wasn't unlike how she felt that night the beads hit the floor.

Chapter 29

"We should be able to get this done today right Hood?" Will asked from his spot towering over their kneeling pledge brother. J-Hood didn't bother to turn around from his work on the raised platform in the basement. He was using a tape measurer as well as Jake had ever seen. *No shock there.*

"Yup" was the only thing he said back as his eyes continued focusing elsewhere.

Today marked one of the few times since Crossing that the four Alpha Epsilons were all in one place. Ironically they were all back in the AZXi basement where their nightmare of a journey had started.

"What do you want us to do?" Jake asked nervously from his spot behind Will. Much to the chagrin of his father, he'd never mastered the ability of handling any tools so as usual he felt useless.

"Grab the stencils from the bar for the names" J-Hood replied as he allowed the tape measurer to re-roll. Summers nodded and wandered over a few feet away toward the makeshift flip cup table where the stencils were. Jake took a step forward so he was right next to Will. The son of a bitch had the same weird smile he always had when he was indulging his man-crush on J-Hood.

"Doesn't J-Hood look like the freshest dude when he's working with power tools?" Will gushed like an idiot.

Jake rolled his eyes instinctively. "Jesus here we go again."

"Oh J-Hood is so fresh" Summers parroted back.

"Thanks Summers…get with it Raley" Will chastised him.

Jake bit his tongue. *One thing at a time.* Their pledge class project still wasn't done and Crossing had happened over five weeks ago. Very rarely since then had at least one of them not been constantly reminded about the fact that pledge classes *always* finished their projects before Crossing. *Jeff crosses us early on a random-ass Thursday and now we get bitched at for not finishing this fuckin' project. It never ends.*

"Is that gonna be done by today?" Jeff's gravel-coated voice echoed through the basement. *Might as well be nails on a chalkboard.* His pledge brothers didn't seem to mind the ass-clown being cordial now after six weeks of shit.

"Should be" J-Hood replied.

"What's the difference?" Jake bit out.

If Jeff was rattled by his cold question in the slightest, it didn't show. "Not much really…except a pledge class usually finishes this *before* Crossing. Other than that though, you take your time."

"Well I know I feel more complete knowing that" Jake shot back.

Jeff patted him on the back as he strolled by to check the progress for himself. "I'm happy for you."

"You could always just help us finish it faster Buttons" Will chimed in happily.

"Fuck that" he spat out. "I'm not part of your pledge class." *Thank fucking God for that.*

"It's crazy how much I can sense the brotherhood down here," Jake said bitterly in Jeff's direction.

Jeff once again stayed calm. "Come on guys, could you just this once follow the guidelines."

Jake smiled as warmly as he could. "The last time I followed AZXi guidelines I wound up at the sheriff's office." He may have been smiling but his eyes were filled with contempt, and they were pointed at Jeff.

"You got a good story though right?"

"Oh yeah sure, just as long as we don't get fucked at court" Summers chimed in. Jake had almost forgotten he was down here.

"At least the school didn't give a fuck," Jeff replied defensively.

Jake had never gone into full detail with his pledge-master about that night. He'd only given him the summarized version of what went down at the Triple E house. As he was shaking his head and moving to where J-Hood was working he saw Jeff open his phone to check an incoming text from Eric of all people. *Didn't know those two ever talked outside of this house.* The look on Jeff's face after he closed his phone was one of complete confusion and deep thought. It looked like he was planning something. "Alright Raley, come help me with the kegs and cups" Jeff ordered in his rediscovered pledge-master persona.

One of the only benefits of wearing letters now was the ability to question Jeff to his face. "What for?" Jake asked with an edge. The look on his face was priceless. *It must suck not having me jump when you say so.*

"For the breakfast today" Jeff replied coolly.

Wait...there's a breakfast today? What day is it? A breakfast on a Sunday? Breakfast parties on Sundays were rare but since the weather was cooperating recently and the semester was winding down, people started getting more brazen with their drinking patterns. "No wonder you wanted our project done today."

"Nah Raley. We wouldn't be able to use it today. The paint and lacquer will take a while to dry" J-Hood said confidently.

Will just stood beside him. "Yeah come on Raley" he practically mimicked the guy. *Like you fuckin' knew that before he said anything.*

"OK let's roll" Jeff repeated as he motioned upstairs. *Why does he want me to go with him? Maybe he wants to kill me for asking questions.*

"It's cool Buttons, I can help you. Let them work on the project together" Calvin said as he came down the stairs from the other side of the house. *Sounds great to me, thank you Calvin.* Jeff admitted defeat and agreed.

Jake nearly had to do a double take. *Why does he look disappointed now?*

****

It was nothing short of sacrilege that her best friend had forgotten about the breakfast with Alpha Zeta Xi today. Tory wasn't really a fan of that fraternity but she definitely felt like drinking today. Add that to the fact that she'd failed in trying to get Riley some action last weekend and she was excited for the day's possibilities. The only guy Riley had even touched this semester was in AZXi. *She could fuck Jerry again if she wanted. I can't be the only one of us who likes getting laid.*

She met up with Riley and Brynn when they got back from lunch up on the Grove. Her Little had been acting weird all day but that wasn't unusual. Brynn always acted weird whenever Tory was around but she never understood why. *Maybe the breakfast today will change it up.*

Fortunately today was beautiful so the boys had the good sense to move all their tables outside so they could take advantage of the weather. They must've moved some of their cars to different lots or onto Arkridge because their backyard driveway was conspicuously empty. 'Backyard' was a loose term to use considering there wasn't any grass around and the ground was covered with gravel. It made it a real pain in the ass to wash off the beer pong balls with water every time they went off the table. *Small price to pay for drinking outside though.*

"You guys called next already?" a familiar voice asked from beside her.

Tory had been so focused on the game they were watching that she'd completely forgotten who else was around. Riley's cousin Eric was standing next to her looking pretty hot in his AZXi jersey. *He must've just gotten a hair cut. He did always look cuter with shorter hair.*

"Yeah. We've been waiting like twenty minutes because this game is taking forever!" Riley exaggerated only because Rachel and Amy were among the four playing the game in front of them. Tory didn't recognize the two guys opposite them.

Eric smiled at his cousin's dramatic response. "The breeze back here can really mess up a good shot," he stated diplomatically. Tory had forgotten how much of a beer pong fiend he was. *Typical frat boy.*

"Sounds like a real convenient excuse to me Biz" Jerry said from his right.

Tory smiled slyly toward Riley because of the close proximity they were all now sharing. It wasn't lost on her best friend. Fortunately the boys weren't paying attention to it at all.

"Oh yeah Jerry? Tell me you disagree then" Eric challenged his friend.

"Absolutely not because I don't" was the reply. They both just chuckled.

"God you two are so gay sometimes" Riley interrupted their weird moment.

"Sometimes?" Tory joked. As expected, neither of them were remotely offended.

Riley had mentioned once that Eric was actually the one who took the brunt of most jokes from her cousin and older brother. Tory could never picture that, even though she knew first hand how nice Eric was.

"Oh come on Tory!" Eric replied with a smile.

"Wow and here I thought you wouldn't talk to me at all" she lied. Part of her had been hoping he would say *something* to her.

"Why would you think such a thing?"

Out of the corner of her eye she saw Riley move to Jerry so they could talk and leave Eric and her somewhat alone. *Good girl. Two birds, one stone.*

"You haven't talked to me at all since the beginning of the semester." *I haven't talked to you either but that's beside the point.*

"That just doesn't sound right to me" he confessed. She could see the wheels turning in his head. It wasn't unlike how she probably looked while trying to recollect a drunken night's activities.

"So you don't remember not talking to me?"

"I guess that's true..." he stopped for a second. "But you haven't talked to me either." *Riles did say you were smart. Too bad that never extended to girls.* Tory had practically done all the work to get him back to her room the first time they hooked up. She didn't mind though. Situations where she was in control more turned her on.

"Well...it doesn't matter now but you were the one making out with a DXA when we were still hanging out" she said accusingly. *Relax girl, don't scare him.* All Tory knew was that it felt good to throw it in his face.

Eric looked positively shocked by the accusation. "When the heck did that happen?" he asked quickly.

"It was at the Midway," she answered vaguely. It was anything but forgotten. The image of Eric and that ugly girl he was with was a permanent fixture.

"I never go into the Midway unless I'm blackout so I don't remember."

"That doesn't mean it didn't happen," she said coolly. *If only forgetting what we do erased it then we'd all be happier.*

He smiled back at her with his warm yet somehow confused look. "Oh I'm not saying it didn't happen. I just wish I knew."

Tory rolled her eyes. *They're all the same at the end of the day.* "Like I said, it doesn't matter now" she lied blatantly, more to herself. *We weren't dating. It doesn't matter.* She'd seen hook-ups move on or actually done the same herself so it wasn't anything new, yet the feeling gnawed at her. This instance felt different somehow.

Unfortunately Eric agreed with her reasoning, even if she didn't. "Yeah true" he said while continuing to smile.

"Don't expect me to take it easy when we play you" she referred to their upcoming beer pong match. It was a completely ridiculous threat and they both knew it. Still, Tory couldn't find a problem with spending a little more time around Eric.

****

Riley looked back to where her cousin and best friend were talking across the beer pong table. *She's just going for it like it's nothing.* Jerry was standing right next to her and for once, he wasn't completely obliterated and or surrounded by his brothers. It was ideal. *What would T do right now?*

"You think they'll ever get over that awkward stage?" she asked Jerry in what had to have been the most self-aware question she ever posed.

Jerry either didn't pick up on it or didn't want to dive into that topic right now. "Who the hell knows? I can't ever tell with Biz."

Riley grinned. "I usually can actually" she said haughtily. "It's Tory that's hard to predict."

"Don't know her well enough to judge."

Suddenly she felt an urge to put Jerry on the defensive. There was an elephant in their room that she wanted out. "So why didn't you respond to my texts last weekend?" she asked abruptly. It had the desired effect; Jerry looked completely out of his depth.

"I did too" he covered with a blatant lie. Riley smirked immediately.

In an attempt to prove his point the guy whipped out his phone and started scrolling through his texts. After a few seconds the light in his eyes vanished. "Well I meant to. I just never sent it. Figured you were hammered."

Riley looked at him incredulously. "Since when has that been a problem?"

Maybe he's just being polite...maybe he didn't want to see me. The next day when she'd woken up alone and saw the texts and the lack of a response, Riley had blamed Tory instantly. Her best friend had somehow talked her into trying to hook up with him again. Rather than hook up with some random frat guy Riley had gotten worked up enough to at least try to repeat with Jerry. The lack of a response stung more than she thought it would.

Jerry smiled coyly. Riley felt a rush or warmth go through her. "Well at least you weren't actively avoiding me." Giving him the benefit of the doubt was a stretch considering it was possible Jerry hadn't responded because he was with another girl. Riley wasn't so starved that she would take another girl's sloppy seconds on the guy she'd practically broken in during freshman year. The thought of him with her after being with someone else made her sick. Instinctively she drank the rest of the beer in her cup to get rid of the ill feelings.

"How could someone avoid you?" he flattered. "You usually get what you want."

Riley smiled innocently. *He must have me confused with Danielle...or Tory.* "You say that like it's a bad thing."

"Should everyone get their way *all* the time?"

Abruptly Riley had a flash of one of their many times in the dorms where she'd all but demanded to be on top. *He might have a point.*

"I think I should," she answered, only half-kidding.

"So why'd you text?"

Even Jerry couldn't be *that* dense about what her intentions were. *You got a text from a girl after midnight and you don't know what it was about? Come on.* "I wanted to see if you were heading to midtown." *It's not entirely a lie.*

"That's usually a safe bet."

"Clearly you should've answered me then."

"Let me guess...you were trying to get some drinks bought for you?"

Riley smirked. "I definitely wouldn't have said no to that."

"I bought you so many drinks freshman year," Jerry said, trying to play the high and mighty card.

"I like to think I made up for that" she grinned knowingly. *If he can't read between the lines there then kill me now.* Fortunately he returned her look and agreed instantly. *At least he still remembers how great it was.*

For a few seconds they just locked eyes and Riley could feel her body getting warmer. She wondered if her face was turning red as a result. Of course the moment didn't last as the beer pong table victors started shouting. One of Jake's pledge brothers was the loudest. *Leave it to another frat guy to ruin the moment, like always.*

"Victory!" Will screeched as if he'd just won a life-saving battle. Everyone on Arkridge Avenue easily heard the guy. *At least it's not just my day he's messing with.*

****

"Yo you banged her right?" Jared asked with all the tact of a four year old.

It was enough to snap Eric out of his daze of staring at Tory across the table. She was playing with one of her sisters that he'd seen around but never caught the name of. "That was really subtle" Eric commented dryly. Fortunately for once the guy hadn't said it loud enough to be heard by everyone. Eric was thankful for that.

"You did though right?"

"Just chill on that," Eric pleaded in hushed tones.

"Nice bro!" Jared patted him on the back. "She's mad hot!"

No kidding man. Was she hitting on me earlier? I should ask Riley and see if she's said anything about me. Surveying the immediate area, Eric came up empty on his search. Riley wasn't anywhere nearby. He could've sworn she'd just been outside a second ago. *Wasn't she talking to Jerry? Where's he?* Eric continued looking from face to face but found neither of them. Then it hit him. *No way. Again?*

"Yo if Jerry isn't back when we're up then you're my partner" Eric announced.

Of course his answer came with a huge smile. "Definitely! I haven't lost a step bro" he replied happily while practicing his beer pong throw.

Within minutes Tory and her other sister beat the other two girls on the table. It was a miracle that he'd be playing against Tory at all considering Will had just been on the table. After his latest victory the guy had 'retired' for the day citing that there were no challengers good enough to hold his attention. It was all bullshit though. Eric knew he'd barely beaten the previous two EIPis he'd been playing against with Lenny. That meant he was slipping and didn't want to lose any subsequent games, especially to girls.

"You next Eric?" Tory asked warmly from her spot on the winning side.

"You know it!" Jared exclaimed from right next to him.

"We good to go?" he asked unsurely as the opposite end of the table was vacated by the losing team. They looked like a couple older EIPis that Eric had seen in passing a few times before. Generally speaking, the older the EIPi, the better they were at drinking games. So if Tory and her other friend could beat them then maybe they were playing well today. *Good thing I like a challenge.*

Tory smiled and motioned for Eric and Jared to head to the other side of the table to set up for their game. "I hope you've said your prayers ladies!" Jared announced as if the game's outcome was already decided. Eric knew better. The game wasn't over until it was over. Too many times overconfidence could be the decisive factor in a loss for the better team.

Setting up the loose cups in the standard triangle formation didn't take long. Getting the pitcher filled up enough for both sides took a little longer. When Jared got back to their side he started filling up the empty cups. It was never lost on Eric how unsanitary it was using the same six cups game after game. That problem could sometimes be solved with side beer cups but more often than not, he forgot to use them.

A tap on his shoulder snapped Eric out of his daze again, except this time it wasn't from Jared. He turned to see Jeff standing beside him although he was swaying slightly and the look in his eyes made it abundantly clear that he'd drank a good amount. Eric stared at him inquisitively. "Raley's here. Over by the keg with J-Hood" Jeff motioned subtly behind him. His cousin was right where Buttons pointed. "Well?" Jeff said impatiently. Eric looked again and saw that Jake was actually talking and laughing with J-Hood. Of course the latter wasn't laughing so much as giving off the appearance of being amused.

"It's a start," Eric replied sarcastically.

Jeff looked confused by his comment but then quickly agreed. "Definitely...you wanna do this now or what?"

Finally...there it is. He'd been sitting on the knowledge of Kelly for a few days but somehow hadn't gotten around to talking to Jake about it. *That's on me.* Between the past week with his labs and the presentation on Friday morning, Cordan had been his home. He'd only gone to the house to shower and sleep. "Absolutely not. Not today" Eric answered brazenly. "We aren't doing this when we're drinking."

"But he needs to know."

"Yeah he does, but you're the guy who's known for weeks," Eric shot back with condescension. He quickly looked around them to make sure no one was paying any attention to what they were saying. Thankfully everyone was too preoccupied to notice. He noticed Jared talking to Tory out of the corner of his eye. The two were laughing and joking with Tory's teammate. *Good God what is he saying to them?*

The options ranged from embarrassing to the downright disgusting. Of course that pretty much summed up *any* interaction with Jared.

Turning back to Jeff finally, he saw he'd hit a nerve with his last comment. Eric took a deep breath and looked back over at his cousin. *He actually looks happy. I won't take that away...not now.* "You want to come along with me when he finds out? We do it sober, that's it."

Jeff sighed and took another sip of the beer he clearly didn't need. For whatever reason, his buzz today was causing submission. *First time for everything.* There'd been a time where he would've been sure that Jeff would've blazed ahead and just told Jake whatever he wanted and damn everybody else. "Fine. It's your call."

"It is...we'll deal with it tomorrow" Eric declared firmly.

"Tomorrow?"

"You think you can handle it?" Eric asked with an accusing stare. Jeff nodded coolly. Eric eased off from his forceful posture. At the end of the day, Jeff had only done what he thought was right with the information he had. Whether he agreed with it or not was irrelevant now.

Eric couldn't help but feel apprehensive about what tomorrow would bring. The recent happy state his cousin was in likely wouldn't make it through the day and it sure as hell wouldn't last tomorrow.

****

Whatever Eric had been talking to his other brother about before their beer pong showdown, it caused him to lose focus. He'd still played well in the beginning but as the game wore on it was Jared that hit the remaining two cups. Her pledge sister Brittany hadn't contributed *anything* to the game at all, just like the one before it. It was a miracle they'd stayed on the table for a second game but Rachel and Cameron had played truly terribly in their first game. Tory would've preferred Riley on her team but she'd disappeared with Jerry before they'd gotten up. She'd almost laughed out loud when she witnessed how sly the two of them *thought* they were in sneaking away separately during the middle of the party. Tory had practically invented that move.

The game hadn't been a total loss though. She was back on Eric's radar and she'd been flirting with his partner before the game even started. Tory was sure that Eric had noticed it but whether it had bothered him or not was up in the air. Now that the game was over she was heading to the bathroom. She was going to the one on the right side that was usually reserved for parties but Eric insisted she use the other side. As Tory went up the stairs she came into view of the other bathroom at the end of the hall. Brynn was standing there with the door open looking in the mirror. She could've sworn she saw the girl roll her eyes as Tory approached.

"Hey Brynn" she greeted her as if they hadn't seen each other in weeks.

"Hey Tory" Brynn replied in a much less upbeat fashion. "Taking a break from beer pong?"

"Yeah. Let's call it that" Tory replied with a grin.

The fact that she'd lost wasn't very well hidden and Bryn wasn't an idiot. "You got your ass kicked didn't you?" she asked with obvious happiness.

Tory shrugged off the negative emotions like usual. "Well Brit didn't play well" she defended herself with an even smile.

"The AZXis beat you then?" Brynn asked for clarification.

"Yeah Eric and one of his brothers."

Brynn's smile twisted. "Isn't that one of the guys you hooked up with?" she asked innocently. At least it seemed innocent.

"A while ago yeah" Tory answered calmly. Of all the frat guys she'd slept with, Eric wasn't among the ones she would ever be ashamed about, not that she was ashamed of any; they'd all served a function at the time.

"It's a shame beer pong skills aren't sexually transmitted" Brynn said coolly as she turned her attention back to the bathroom mirror.

It was getting more and more difficult to shrug off the constant veiled insults coming at her from Riley's Little. "Yeah it is." Brynn didn't seem to hear her because she continued fixing her hair while Tory stood in the doorway.

After another minute she asked the question that had been on her mind since Crossing. "Do you have a problem with me?" She asked it as calmly as possible. Even Tory was surprised by how genuine it sounded.

"No more than usual" Brynn replied plainly as she finally turned away from the mirror and made her way past Tory.

"What does that even mean?" Tory asked in an almost pleading way.

"It doesn't mean anything."

Tory watched Brynn walk away down the hall. *Well that was fucking weird.*

****

It was enough that Tory was probably insanely confused by their latest exchange that Brynn was completely satisfied. She strolled mightily down the hallway away from a girl who just five weeks ago had been the bitch they called the assistant pledge mom.

How many minutes and hours had Brynn spent looking up at the ceiling of the chapter room these past few weeks? If there was any way to actually track the time she'd wasted in here the answer would've made her throw up. Tonight was no different.

Five days after the 'cleaning' callout as it had been not so affectionately named by her pledge class and things hadn't improved. The constant lack of sleep had become a problem during week five and now that they were halfway through week six Brynn didn't have much self-control left. One wrong move could set her off. She was afraid of what she might do when that happened.

The only light in the chapter room was coming from a dim lamp in the corner. The light bulb must've been on the verge of burnout since it was flickering more tonight than it usually did. *Maybe it'll start a fire and burn this whole fucking house down.* She shifted in the sleeping bag the sorority had gifted each of them with. None of them had actually brought a sleeping bag to school and why would they? But in order to give them some semblance of sleep over the past week and a half the sisters had given out the ones in storage. Allegedly these were the ones they used for the pledges every semester. Brynn always hoped that Riley or somebody else had them washed between semesters but she doubted that had happened.

None of her pledge sisters were fidgeting in their own spaces on the floor. They'd probably all fallen asleep the second their heads hit the pillows. Not Brynn though. She couldn't sleep. There was a nagging feeling gnawing away at her. *I can't get too comfortable. They'll come back...*

Once again, she tried counting the dots on the ceiling hoping that would get her to nod off. As she got past two hundred the door to the chapter room swung open just like it had dozens of times before. The voices that accompanied it were anything but comforting.

"Get the fuck up!" Tory screamed into the silent room. On command, the other five pledges jolted awake at the sudden sound. Brynn was standing before any of them.

"Could tonight actually be the night that you start thinking pink?" Riley followed Tory's screams with her own.

"I fucking doubt it" Tory answered before any of the pledges could. All of it was par for the course. None of it was new or novel. The screaming, the insults, the constant sleep disruption, it was all part of Brynn's life. It made her sick.

The six Beta Thetas linked arms with practiced rhythm. Once they'd done that Riley and Tory demanded greetings. By the time it was Brynn's turn, she'd become numb to the constant yelling.

"Greetings Riley Nichol, pledge mother, education major, an honored sister from Harrisville. I, ElPi pledge Brynn Wells am honored to greet you and I hope you have a great day. Keep thinking pink" she replied to her Big. Brynn tried keeping her tone even and upbeat but it was a lost cause. Riley hinted at a smile but never let one appear.

Tory followed right behind her. The look in her eyes made Brynn want to jump out the nearest window, preferably taking the bitch with her. "Greetings assistant pledge mom Tory Brye, mathematics major, an honored sister from Pendleton. I, ElPi pledge Brynn Wells am honored to greet you, and I hope you have a great day. Keep thinking pink," she said in much the same way she'd greeted Riley.

Once the six of them had greeted the two pledge moms Riley paced back and forth in front of them, walking over their various sleeping bags. "Tonight the games are going to stop. We are going to make you respect us!" she shouted.

The next hour passed by in a blur. Brynn couldn't recall the finer details of what had happened even if her life depended on it. They'd all been made to sprint down the second floor hallway, down and back. On their second run they were supposed to stop at each of the open doorways and answer a question about whatever the sister therein was holding in their hands.

When it was Brynn's turn, she finished the run quicker than the girls before her. The first sister she ran into was Danielle. Fortunately she asked an easy question. "What does your candle mean to you?"

That one had been beaten over each of their heads so the answer came immediately. "It signifies the light of knowledge to help me find my way!" she exclaimed while panting slightly. Trying to hide her disdain at all the bullshit was the hardest part.

Unfortunately not all the doors had been that easy. When she'd gotten to the door Amy was at she was asked a more ridiculous question she wasn't prepared for. "What does your egg mean to you?" Amy asked while holding out a pink egg in her hand. Brynn wasn't sure how the girl kept a straight face while asking such a dumb question.

Once the six of them had finished their runs they were led into the far side's stairwell where Riley and Tory were waiting with lit candles in their hands. It was fortunate that they were lit since the hallway lights were off. "You aren't done yet" was all Riley said. She spoke so threateningly that Brynn had all but forgotten that it was the same girl who could be so warm to her during anything not ElPi related.

In the corner of the second floor stairwell landing there was a small end table with two candleholders on top. Riley placed her candle in one of the slots and Tory followed suit. Her Big then vacated the landing with an obvious look of disgust on her face. Unfortunately, Tory didn't follow her that time. Danielle and Rachel entered through the same doorway Riley just exited through. They looked almost as sadistic as Tory did.

After the door shut behind their entrance it went silent for a few brief seconds. That was when the loudest music Brynn had ever heard started filling the void. She wasn't even sure what was playing or where it was coming from since there was no sound system nearby that she could see.

Then the shouting started. She could only hear bits and pieces of it because of the screeching music. *At least it's not that same fucking song we heard at the cleaning.*

"You are all worthless! I can't believe we gave any of you bids! You disgust me right to my fucking core!" she heard Tory scream. The three sisters were circling the six of them while they stayed linked and huddled together. The landing was wide enough but they were still being pressed together like live bait for roaming sharks.

"You are making sister Riley and sister Tory look awful because none of you can do a fucking thing right! Rachel shouted. She kept talking but the music drowned her out. Brynn didn't mind.

"I'm at the end of my rope right now because no matter what the fuck we do, none of you deserve to be in this sorority. We might as well send you over to the sluts at DXA. God knows they'll take anyone, even you!" Tory yelled some more.

Rachel then shouted something along the lines of asking why none of them were speaking. *Like you could hear us if we said a word.*

"They have nothing to say. They're incredibly stupid, every one of them. I'm ashamed we bid them at all!" Danielle raged.

"What more do we have to do to show you this isn't a fucking game! This is real life! This is serious! This is mother-fucking EIPi! Epsilon Iota Pi! You got that pledge four!?" Tory directed her onslaught directly at Brynn.

Even through the lack of light in the stairwell she locked eyes with the bitch and replied the only way she could. "Yes assistant pledge mother Tory Brye!" she said with contempt. Fortunately the tone of her voice was lost in the barrage of music and constant screams from the sisters. Rachel and Danielle continued their ranting to compliment Tory but they weren't nearly as loud. The music kept blasting. The screams continued.

Brynn felt her legs shaking from the lack of energy. It felt like she could collapse...

The fresh air from being outside did wonders for Brynn's state of mind.

Five weeks after Crossing and certain memories were haunting her like they'd happened yesterday. Being around Tory and some of the other girls certainly wasn't helping but there wasn't any way around that unless she wanted to steer clear of EIPi altogether. She shook her head at the thought. *Who the fuck would be dumb enough to pledge and then just disappear?* After all the shit she'd gone through with pledging she'd be damned if she didn't get some kind of enjoyment out of life at Gladen Hills.

Brynn found her way to the keg very quickly once outside. Danielle was standing nearby. Her current mood was probably written on her face because she asked what was wrong instantly. Shrugging it off as nothing was no easy feat but Dani backed off within a minute of her insistence that it was nothing.

"So you're alright?" she asked one last time.

Brynn sipped her refreshing beer. "I'm getting there."

****

Riley hadn't felt so satisfied in a long time.

Jerry had improved since the last time they'd hooked up. He'd always been decent enough that she could make herself finish while on top but today he'd done most of the work getting her to climax. She was nearly shivering when it happened. He'd finished roughly around the same time so it made her own orgasm that much hotter.

After they'd finished Riley had made her way around Jerry's room collecting her clothes that had been almost ripped off when they'd gotten upstairs behind his closed bedroom door. She was almost positive that they'd left the breakfast in such a way that nobody had really noticed them. That was fortunate considering it'd be embarrassing getting the third degree from Jerry's brothers about their mid-day session.

Once dressed, she leaned in for another kiss just so she felt less dirty about the whole thing. Somehow the act of kissing or cuddling after screwing a guy made her feel somewhat fine with it. Such was the case today. She'd yet to meet a guy who wouldn't indulge her in one of those ways afterward. Jerry reciprocated the kiss once he'd finished putting on his pants. He was decidedly drunker than she was but that didn't bother her. Today was about her and she'd made that clear from the start.

Fortunately the far side of the house where Jerry's room was had been completely empty except for the sounds of someone else having sex at the end of the hall on the ground floor. *I'm glad I wasn't the only girl around here who wanted some today.*

All the good feelings she had about today vanished the second she walked outside and locked eyes with her cousin. Eric had just finished pissing off to the side of driveway between some bushes bordering the Lambda house. *Must be nice being a guy and not having to go inside to use the bathroom.*

Her cousin walked toward her without being asked. "Alright I don't want to know a damn thing as per the agreement ..." he paused slightly. "But I'm glad you're here. It saves me a call."

She looked back at him with cool reserve. He wasn't going to ruin the moment for her. *I wanted to hook up and I did...end of story.* "I would say grow up but I think you're already at your limit" she chastised him. "What's up?"

"It's about Jake" he began.

Riley rolled her eyes. "When isn't it?"

That caused her cousin's serious face to crack slightly. "Good point" he chuckled. "Kelly's been cheating on him...like for sure."

She only found herself mildly shocked. Riley had always assumed it was going on but at the same time didn't know for sure. *I'm gonna kill her.* "How do you know?"

"Buttons saw it at the Midway a while back, nothing major" he backtracked.

Riley winced. *A while back? How long has this been going on?*

"They were just making-out and shit but I kind of doubt it ended there...and Buttons thinks the same."

Riley tightened her stance. *Maybe I need another drink after all.* She'd previously resolved to head back to EIPi so she could sober up for a trip to Cordan tonight but that was looking less and less likely. "Knowing that girl, I wouldn't be surprised if she fucked whoever it was on the dance floor."

"How'd he take it?" she asked, trying to keep the anger out of her voice.

"I haven't told him yet. I just found out Wednesday" Eric admitted sullenly. *Wednesday? It's Sunday. What the hell is the hold-up?*

"He needs to know Eric" she said firmly. *How could you keep something like this from me? What the fuck is going on with you two?*

"I know," he confessed. "I just didn't want to do it when we were drinking and I had a ton of shit to do this week with my classes..." he went on, trying to convince her of his reasons. Riley was unimpressed.

"Jake was at the party today?" she asked blankly. *How the hell did I miss that?* She could practically hear the shouts from her mother and aunts now.

"Only for a little bit. I think he was working on his pledge class project in the basement. He looked like he was having fun though" Eric replied thoughtfully.

Riley nodded. *Well that's a start.*

"Buttons wants to tell him since he's the one who saw it."

I don't give a fuck what that guy wants. This is something family should handle, end of story. "How long has he known?" Riley wanted clarification immediately. Even a blind man would've been able to see how much Eric was shying away from answering that question. His whole body almost contracted. "How long Eric?" she repeated, losing patience. The high Jerry had just allowed her to feel was gone.

"A couple weeks at least."

Riley seethed. "And he didn't tell anyone!?" she blurted out loud enough for anyone passing by on Arkridge to hear clearly.

Eric found his backbone again. "I've already talked to him about that so it's done. We need to focus on *this* problem now. The plan is to tell him tomorrow."

Riley looked at her cousin fiercely. "I want in."

****

Happy wasn't in the same realm of emotions Jeff was feeling since Eric had all but ordered him to keep quiet about Jake's girlfriend 'til tomorrow. It wasn't the first time in the past five days that Jeff had the distinct thought that Eric probably shouldn't have been told in the way he had. *I should've talked to Raley myself, man to man. But no, I had to be a little bitch about the whole thing and spread it around like a chick.*

Thankfully the breakfast had ended recently and save for a pretty funny encounter with Calvin between bedroom doors; the whole thing was uneventful. Although rumor had it Jerry had fucked one of the EIPis during it.

Jeff made his way up the steps on his side of the house and unlocked his door before stumbling inside. After collapsing onto his bed he reached out for his desk. He resolved to sit up after a few seconds of fruitless movement. After he got upright he found what he was looking for. The frat's latest composite picture had been sitting on his desk for a week. He hadn't had time to put it up on the wall yet with the others. It was a smaller one than the standard pictures adorning the main walls of the house. These ones were laminate copies of the original that were given out to each of the actives toward the end of each school year. *Another year…another composite to put up.*

Jeff's eyes stopped on Jake's picture in the lower right corner with the rest of the pledges from the year save for Will. His absence was likely to be unnoticed by most of the brothers considering half of them didn't pay much attention to the finer details of the frat. *None of them really care.* Shaking his head, Jeff laid the composite back on his desk and leaned back again. His head was spinning, only partially from the drinking.

"You OK baby?" Dana's velvet voice crept through the silence in Jeff's room.

"Fine" he lied. "Just taking a breather before the National."

"I thought we were hanging out today?"

The last thing he wanted to deal with right now was an argument with Dana. "I don't have to go," he corrected himself.

His girlfriend moved through the bedroom, navigating it perfectly despite the fact that it was barely lit. The only light came from the windows and since the sun was setting, there wasn't much.

"That's the quickest I've ever seen you give up on going to the National" Dana said as she sat down on the bed next to him. Jeff should've known better. *Of course she'd notice me not wanting to go there. What was I thinking? Now she'll never let it go unless I tell her.* "What's going on Jeff?" she dove right to the point.

"Just some fuckin' drama that came up..." he stopped to think. "Let me ask you something babe. You've known people who've cheated right?"

Dana looked confused. "Like in a relationship?"

"Yeah."

She shrugged absently. "It's tough to be in college and not at least know somebody who has."

It's fucked up but completely true. "At least we've never done that to each other."

She rubbed his back to comfort him. It had minimal effect. "I'd kill you if you ever did...and I'd expect you to do the same" she added cheerfully.

Jeff almost smiled but stopped himself when the thought really sank in. "Yeah and *that's* the only reason I'd never do that, because of the reaction" he said sarcastically.

"Hey I'll take what I can get" Dana replied, still trying to get him to relax.

"I just think it's so fucked up," he said abruptly while looking away.

He kept trying to put himself into Jake's position of just what it would feel like to find out the girl you loved was fucking somebody else. *I don't know what I'd do...*

The thought of Dana doing that made him sick. Sicker than he'd ever felt. It wasn't a physical sickness either. The pain hurt his mind and body in a deeply emotional way. Jeff wasn't used to processing things like that and the idea of legitimately telling someone else something and *causing* that kind of pain was too much. *Is that why I told?*

There was silence filtering back into his room. "OK Jeff you're scaring me" she admitted uneasily.

He turned back to her to match her gaze. "Relax Dana, this isn't me we're talking about" he explained. "One of our new guys has a fuckin' slut for a girlfriend...and I saw something..."

Dana was obviously happy that the situation bothering him had nothing to do with them because her tone shifted. "How'd he take the news?"

Jeff looked away to stare blankly at the wall. "I'll let you know tomorrow."

Chapter 30

Walking through the halls of the EIPi house just made Jake feel uncomfortable, even with Riley escorting him. According to his cousin there were twenty-six girls who lived in the house whereas the AZXi house only held seven total. He'd never actually been inside EIPi before but he'd obviously seen it on his way to class. The only reason he was here today was because Eric said he had to talk to him about something. He'd been in Cordan for most of the day, which was close to the EIPi house.

Jake hadn't been thrilled by the idea but he decided to give Eric the benefit of the doubt. They hadn't talked at all since that day in Lancaster last week. The more he thought about it, the more worried he became. It could all be a double team effort by Eric and Riley to convince him *not* to deactivate next semester. At first the thought pissed him off. Would Biz really go down that road again and drag Riley into it?

With things going so well with Kelly recently he felt he could stomach a little more prodding from his family, but only a little. His decision was made. Starting next semester he would be completely done with AZXi for a while. It would always be there *if* he ever felt the need to go back.

After going up a flight of stairs they finally found their way to Riley's room on the second floor. It was a little shocking when Jake realized he'd never gone out of his way to visit his cousin. *I'll have to work on that.* Once they made their way inside, the obligatory small talk ceased and Riley got down to business. "You know Eric is pretty upset about that lunch."

Jake nearly cracked up. "It's only been five days, how messed up can he be?"

Riley didn't look amused. "Quit acting like avoiding each other is a good time. I know you hate it. You haven't gone five days without talking in the past five years."

"He was being an ass." Jake felt like he was defending himself to his mother in a very 'he started it' fashion.

His cousin must've caught on to that too because she cracked a smile at how immature the whole thing sounded. "You know I love you both but maturity isn't something either of you have gotten the hang of, especially you."

"Come on Rye, tell me how you really feel."

"Maybe you two should end this because life's too damn short. Who knows, maybe that's what he's coming here to say."

Jake shook his head. *Like you don't already know what he's coming here to say.* "He said it was important but it better not take long. I'm supposed to head over to Kelly's soon."

Riley swiveled around in her desk chair to turn from Jake. She started doing something on her computer, which he couldn't see because she was sitting between him on the couch and the laptop screen.

Overall the room was sickeningly huge. Even if Wayne didn't exist Jake's dorm room was half the size of hers. *What the hell could she need all this space for?*

Realizing there was now an uncomfortable silence coming between them he decided to change the topic. Rumor had it they'd crossed the recent class a day before Jake's but he hadn't heard much about them. "How are the new girls doing?"

The topic seemed to catch her interest because she turned back around in her chair. "Well my drinking has gotten even more ridiculous so there's that."

"And you started at insane…then went to ridiculous. It might be time to take a step back."

"The semester is over in three weeks. I'll take a step back then," she promised. "It's not my fault my Little is wild and drinks a lot."

"Sounds like she'd get along great with the AZXis" Jake replied dryly.

"So would you."

The silence re-entered the room. Jake smirked. "And now I've got two cousins anxious to give me advice on the same shit."

"If only you listened…at all" Riley shot back with a continuing smile.

Jake missed the conversations he used to have with his cousins over weekly family dinners at their grandparents. He hadn't had a chance to experience things like that since he left for college. It felt warm and comfortable.

Then it all came crashing back down when Eric walked in. He wasn't alone either. Jeff Chester strode in right behind him looking hard and cold as ever.

Oh great, is he gonna haze me in this house now too? Jake felt tense immediately so he sat up straight on the couch. Greeting each of the guys in turn with the signature AZXi handshake felt weird enough, especially under the roof of a sorority but he went through the motions regardless. *Why the hell are we all here?*

****

"What're you doing here?" Jake finally asked. It was a surprise he waited as long as he had. When his eyes hit Jeff the tension could've been cut with that prop sword he used to slice beer cans open with at after-hours. *If anyone were to line up the four people in this room I'd be the one that doesn't belong.*

In classic chick fashion, Riley went from her desk chair over to the couch to sit next to Jake. *Good, that won't make him feel more anxious at all.*

"What's this about Biz?" he turned away from Jeff to face Eric who took up a spot on the bed facing both of his other cousins. He joined him there quickly if only to avoid being the sole one left standing.

After five days of holding it all inside Eric came right out with it. "There's no point in sugar-coating it Jake…Kelly cheated on you."

It was the equivalent of watching a multi-car pile-up on the highway. Eric's words were the car that stopped suddenly and blocked all other traffic and the rest of them just came hurtling toward him. *Fuck. That's one way of doing it.*

Shockingly, Jake actually smiled at first. Then he found his voice. "I don't think I heard that right." His tone demanded a further explanation. Like clockwork Riley started rubbing his back to soothe him. *That won't make a difference.*

Eric sat there as grim as ever. "You heard me J. I'm not repeating it." He matched Jake's demanding stare with an impassable look of his own.

"How do you know that?" the kid stammered.

"Jeff saw it happen."

All the focus in the room from the three family members shifted to him. Riley and Eric both looked to him for clarity but it was Jake's eyes that hit him like a sledgehammer. They were filled with judgment and accusation…and loathing. For the first time in as long as he could remember, he couldn't say a word. He wanted to, he even tried to but nothing happened. *Stop being a little bitch and say something.*

"When?" Jake finally asked, his voice cracking.

"It was a while ago" Jeff choked out. His mouth was drier than sand.

"When?!" the kid screamed.

Jeff looked to Eric for guidance but all he got in return was a look of complete indifference. *You knew it was going to come to this and I walked right into it because I stayed quiet for so long.* "It was during the fifth week of pledging...right after you went to Canada. She was dancing with some Kappa Nu at the Midway and they were making out pretty hard." He tried keeping the description tactful but it became clear that wouldn't help anything.

"That doesn't mean it went any further" Raley tried rationalizing out loud.

Riley and Eric's faces looked identical. *They both know how this girl is, maybe even better than me.* "...there was a good amount of grabbing going on too...and to be perfectly honest, she wasn't fighting it. She was enjoying it...a lot."

All Jeff could see in Jake right now was his own face and the look of pure depression that would come along with knowing Dana was with some other guy and enjoying his touch over Jeff's. *This isn't about me. Raley needs the focus.*

Jake only stayed seated for another few seconds after Jeff finished speaking. Then he stood up and started for the door, getting all of two feet before Eric was on him, forcing him to stop. He hastily wrapped his arms around his cousin, immobilizing him. "I'm sorry about what I said before but you need to hear this." Raley didn't look convinced. "We're family J. Now sit your ass down." Jake didn't move any further toward the door. Whether that was in direct response to being held in place or Eric's order was anyone's guess.

"Why the fuck didn't I hear about this sooner?" Jake yelled. It was clear he was looking for *anybody* to respond.

"That was my call" Jeff interrupted. "I wanted you to finish pledging and I knew this would stop you."

"You mean you didn't want to lose your favorite kid to fuck with right?" Jake turned around violently to look past Eric who was between the two of them. The kid's eyes were burning holes through Jeff.

"If that were true then you wouldn't have crossed on a Thursday!" he yelled, losing his temper. The confused faces around him were easy to spot. "Didn't anyone find it weird that I had them cross on a weekday?" he looked directly at Eric. He was caught off guard but by the look in his eye it appeared as though he'd at least thought about that before now. "You crossed two days before you were supposed to on Saturday because *I* couldn't deal with it. You were supposed to get told that weekend by me but you were never around and whenever you were you wanted nothing to do with me...or any of us. What was I supposed to do? I didn't fucking know what to do!" When Jeff finished talking he was out of breath. He never wanted to admit that.

For a while the four of them didn't move. Even Riley was baffled and she wasn't even in AZXi. Jeff broke the silence after losing the ability to sit still. "You're my brother now Raley. At the time I saw all this you weren't. I wanted you to finish pledging. I made the call. Nobody deserves what she did, but to have it happen during an already rough time is just fucked up…"

Jake wrestled free of Eric's hold and stormed toward Jeff. They were right in each other's faces although Jeff hadn't moved. "That time was rough because of you for Christ's sake! How much could you really fucking care about that?!" He screamed at him with such hate that Jeff was sure a punch would come any second. *What am I gonna do? I can't fight him.*

The tension in the room kept rising until Riley's voice cut through. "He's right Jake. I know you. You would've confronted Kelly. Hopefully she would've told you the truth for once. After that you would've quit pledging right then. That doesn't have to happen now that you're a brother. They can help with this."

Jake didn't look at her while she talked. His legs started shaking when she began. Thankfully he stopped staring at Jeff in that moment. He looked away toward the ground while leaning against the bed. Riley motioned for Eric to move over to help.

"The Greek Circle was practically founded for helping with the opposite sex" Eric began hesitantly.

"Yeah" Jeff agreed. "Whether it's getting with them or getting over them…"

Riley rolled her eyes but kept quiet. The room went silent again. Jake took a deep breath and turned back toward all of them. His face had a few tears running down. *Don't worry kid. We're still here.*

"I need a minute," he said calmly while turning back to the door.

Jeff saw Riley motion for Eric to stop him again but he shook his head. Jake didn't notice. All three of them sat there helpless while the youngest walked out. As soon as the door shut behind Jake the accusations flew.

"Why didn't you stop him?" Riley demanded.

As usual, Eric didn't flinch. "He heard what we had to say. Every word. Until he actually believes it there's nothing we can do. He's still fighting what we told him, anybody can see that."

Jeff agreed with him but didn't want to take sides. *You couldn't pay me to jump into this argument.*

"What're you gonna do?" Riley asked.

"I haven't visited his dorm in a while and I could use a good smash session. I'll head there and chill with Scribner 'til J gets back."

Riley looked sullen. "Just text me when he gets back."

Jeff stood up. "Me too."

****

I fucking hate Jeff. I hate him. Those were the only words circling his head at the beginning of the long walk from EIPi to Kelly's room on Northeast. The walk seemed longer than normal. *He could've been lying; he could've seen another girl who only looked like Kelly. Kelly wouldn't do that to me.* The closer he got to the dorms the more his doubts crept through. The thing he continuously couldn't get past was that Eric and Riley were completely and utterly sure that Jeff was telling the truth. *My own family believed what that fuck was saying. How could they know Jeff was telling the truth?*

After finally getting to Kelly's dorm and going up three flights of stairs he found his way to her suite. Sweat was practically pouring off his hands when he reached up to knock on the door. *What am I gonna do? What the fuck am I gonna do?*

Kelly answered and smiled immediately when she saw Jake. She leaned in to kiss him just like she always did. He leaned back to avoid it while fighting the tears forming in his eyes. Once she realized he wouldn't kiss her back she asked what was wrong.

"Have you ever cheated on me?" he asked plainly while continuing to look away from her. Looking into her eyes hurt too much. He'd only locked eyes with her when she'd opened the door and seeing her nearly made him collapse. *She's so beautiful.* Since then he kept his gaze focused in any other direction. The thought of seeing her and almost knowing that she'd been with somebody else was enough to make him pale and weak. He felt like he was ninety, lacking any energy or will.

The question froze the world and there was silence between them as he stood in the hallway. Fortunately there wasn't another soul on the floor for now. Finally he looked back at his girlfriend if only to speed along her answer. The uncertainty was throwing knives around his stomach. Once his eyes met hers it was clear what the answer was going to be. Jake's legs started to buckle.

"Yes" she said softly. The word cut through him like nothing he'd ever felt before. "But it was a while ago and I haven't done it since" she tried explaining. That was when the first tear came trickling down his face. He tried stopping it but couldn't.

"What the hell happened?" his voice cracked. A second tear rolled down.

Kelly sighed before continuing. "I was at the Midway…really drunk. One of the guys in my computer science class was there…he bought me a drink. I don't know…we just started dancing and things…happened."

"I had to hear this from one of the brothers Kel!? How could you do this to me? What did I do?" he asked pleadingly as two more tears fell.

Kelly reached out to console him but he'd be damned if he was going to allow her to touch him again. "I'm so sorry Jake…I just feel like maybe we started dating too soon after I broke up with Dean" she choked out. "I think I might want…I think I need to be single for a while. But I love you so much I couldn't choose between the two."

"You already did" Jake choked out with as much confidence as he could before turning to leave her standing there in the doorway. He didn't want her to follow him but at the same time that's all he wanted.

"Please don't leave like this Jake," she pleaded.

Once again he turned to look back at her, maybe for the last time. She was crying now too. *Good, she's upset. It must hurt being in her place.*

"I'm such an idiot." He was only inches from her. He could reach out and hold her, feel her lips again. The urge was so much that it shocked him to think he still wanted to hold her after what he'd just heard. "I never thought you would do to me what you did to Dean." *What you did to him with me. How could I have been so stupid?* "But I guess most people can't change right? I can't even look at you Kel…please…just leave me alone." He wished it sounded more confident but he couldn't find the strength for that. He was using all he had just to remain standing.

Finally Jake turned away from his former girlfriend who had more tears running down her face than he did. *At least you have feelings.* His heart was hardening on his way to the stairs. She didn't follow him. Someone else was coming up at the same time he was going down. He kept his eyes leveled at the floor as they passed. Jake didn't want whoever it was to see him crying. Even with the sounds of footsteps echoing around them in the stairwell Jake heard the sound of Kelly's door closing down the hall a floor up. The sound sent waves of every kind of emotion through his body. *I'll never be in that room with her again…*

****

Calvin couldn't tell if it was just the fact that he'd drank four days and nights in a row or if he was just getting past his prime, or both. *If this were sophomore year that much wouldn't have even touched me.* Unfortunately he couldn't shake the immensely hung-over feeling right now.

Fortunately the day's activities hadn't been that strenuous. Classes were getting to be more and more of a joke the closer they all got to finals, which were now a few weeks away. Calvin noticed that some professors would simply stop around now and focus on reviewing the previously covered material. He rarely skipped classes so he went even though he didn't need the review.

Now that classes were through for the day he was lounging in the common room on his side of the house. Normally he could do so by himself since Jerry and Eric were *always* at Cordan during the week regardless of what time of the semester it was but today was different. Eric and Jerry were still nowhere to be found but Dylan and Jared were both there, by design.

"I'm actually depressed about being hung-over today," he announced to anybody who would listen.

"That's fuckin' sad man," Dylan said while keeping his eyes locked on the TV.

Calvin had called Dylan to chill since he was trying to get as much time with the actives as possible before the semester ended, Dylan maybe more than the rest since he was Calvin's Little.

"Want a beer?" he motioned to the remnants of a thirty rack he'd come over with. Jared didn't need any prompting, he reached over and cracked one open. The smell of the beer was enough to get Calvin nauseous. *What's wrong with me?*

Wherever his little brother went these days there was likely to be some kind of alcohol or drug in tow. *That's probably why he does so much fucked up shit most of the time. It's a miracle he's still in school.* After a few moments of indecision, he reached out for a beer that Dills was handing off to him. *No point fighting it.*

They all sat in relative silence and watched whatever reality show garbage Jared had chosen for them. In any event, most of the shit he watched was good for mindless viewing, which was perfectly acceptable today.

Jeff walked in a few minutes later and sacked out on the couch next to Jared opposite the one he was sharing with Dills. Calvin took a long sip of the beer he'd been handed and felt the weight of it decrease in his hand. It tasted awful but it usually did when he was hung-over. *Hitting up the National last night was definitely not a smart move.* He took another sip and scrunched up his face. *This probably isn't either.*

"Let me guess Buttons…you're pissed because you don't have any pledges to haze anymore?" he asked playfully.

"Not tonight Gretman" was all Jeff said. His tone was gruff but it sounded like he was pleading too.

Calvin decided to take a stab in the dark. "Trouble with the girlfriend?"

"Not mine."

"You bangin' somebody else's!?" Jared asked giddily.

Calvin shook his head. *Thank you Jared.*

"I just had to tell Raley that his chick was fucking around on him" Jeff said with a hint of sadness.

"Damn" Jared replied immediately. His smile was completely absent from his face but there was no real surprise anywhere. The complete opposite could be said of Calvin and Dylan who were blown away by the revelation. *That's so fucked up.*

"Did you know something?" Jeff asked Jared immediately after also noticing his lack of surprise. "Nah but after what he told me about her I figured it'd happen" he answered quietly while continuing to drain his beer.

Calvin had never met Raley's girl but it was never a far off topic when he'd talked to the kid in the past. "Who is this chick? She affiliated?"

"Just field hockey I think" Jared answered unsurely.

"Sports teams are loaded with condescending bitches" Jeff replied.

Commiseration always needs a jumping off point.

"Well sororities aren't exactly filled with nuns either" Dylan said after finishing his second beer. Calvin smiled at his Little's comment. *He would know.*

"There are bitches in every organization…outside of them too" Calvin said with finality. There was some truth to be had there so he hoped everyone would agree. Organizations, Greek Circle or otherwise had both good and bad types just like anything else. It wasn't particularly fair to stereotype them that way. *We sure as hell don't like when it happens to us.*

"Chicks…" Jared said quietly while finishing his beer. "He alright?"

They all focused on Jeff, waiting for his response. "He didn't take it well.

Calvin nodded. *Who would?* "I'm surprised Biz let you tell him." It didn't seem plausible to Calvin that Eric would leave something like that to someone else, even another brother.

"Oh don't worry, he was there supervising the whole thing with their other cousin." Calvin nodded again. Jeff was talking about the girl cousin that Calvin had only met once or twice at their parties. They all seemed pretty close.

"I should call him," Jared announced while reaching for his phone.

Jeff motioned for him to stop. "I'd wait. Biz wasn't even sure he believed us."

Calvin turned to Jared. "Let me know when you talk to him...the last thing that kid needs is more drama."

"He barely comes around as it is" Dylan said from off to the side. Calvin noted that his Little was being remarkably quiet, and he always had an opinion on everything.

"Maybe this'll help with that," Jeff said evenly.

The only way Jeff could've been involved was if he'd seen something related to Raley's girlfriend...he must've been the one that saw shit go down...

"Man...fuck chicks" Dylan said authoritatively.

Calvin smirked and took another sip. *Chicks probably say the same shit about us.*

****

There was only one thing to do at times like these: stalk on Facebook. Riley had resolved to check the website the second Eric and Jeff had followed Jake out of her room. She sat there scrolling through picture after picture taken of Kelly at the Midway. She was surrounded by guys while dancing in most of them. *The signs were all clearly there.* Jake wasn't in many of her recent pictures and it was no small wonder why. *Can't have him seeing what you're up to at night.* Riley found her way back to the main profile page and saw that her relationship status hadn't been changed. 'In a relationship with Jake Raley' it still read, clear as day. "I can't believe it got this far," she whispered while shaking her head.

"I thought we talked about how creepy it is when you talk to yourself Riles" Tory said as she entered the room. Tory had no idea what had just gone down in here not an hour before. For her, everything was still bright and cheery.

"We did but it helps me stay sane."

"That's weird. I figured it'd be the other way around."

Her sister moved to the bed and sat down at the foot of it so she was right next to Riley. "To what do I owe this visit T?" Riley asked, not yet sure if she was in the mood for company.

"Just missed you" Tory said sarcastically. Ironically it probably wasn't far from the truth. Just like Jake and Eric, her and Tory really never spent all that much time away from each other. The girl's eyes shifted toward the end table in front of the couch and made a move to grab one of the magazines off it. Of course she came back with the latest issue of 'Cosmo' that Riley hadn't read yet.

"Haven't you already read that one?"

"Obviously. Usually on the day they come out too."

"So why read them again?"

"They're so entertaining" Tory explained.

Riley just smiled while turning away. "Those are always one and done for me."

Tory lifted her eyes from the magazine and started grinning at her. "Usually you make fun of me for that kind of behavior."

"That's only because you can't have a healthy relationship with anything but a magazine" Riley shot back quickly. She wanted to take it back as soon as she said it. Projecting her anger onto her best friend wouldn't help either of them. Thankfully Tory didn't care.

"You're awfully angry today Riles" she said sweetly. "I would've thought Jerry took care of that for you."

Riley rolled her eyes. "I knew I shouldn't have told you."

"And yet you did...although it was pretty clear what happened when you too went all shady serial killer on the way out of the breakfast. Seriously...it's called class girl. So what's the problem?"

I shouldn't say anything but whatever. The news is probably doing the rounds at AZXi by now anyway so what's the difference.

"There's nothing wrong but we might need to slash some whore's tires tonight" Riley said. It was only partially a joke.

Tory flashed an evil grin. "Ooooooh, I do like causing mayhem."

Riley smirked. *Yeah, no kidding.*

"Did some girl try to interrupt you and Jerry yesterday? You never told me that!" she went on, already assuming she was right.

"Come on T, you've gotta let the whole Jerry thing go already."

"Oh. Well then it must be a cousin problem" Tory deduced brilliantly. "But don't look too impressed. It's usually a guy thing with you Riles, family or otherwise."

Riley nodded once she thought about it. "It's Jake's soon to be ex."

The look on Tory's face lit up like she was a kid at Christmas. "Jake's single!?" she gasped in delight.

Riley winced. *Maybe it wasn't such a good idea to mention anything to the one with the constantly raging hormones. But maybe...actually...he might need someone to get him through all this. Not Tory...just someone like her.* "Of course that's what you would take away from what I said."

"How can I not? It's not my fault you have beautiful cousins."

"Focus T, this bitch cheated on him" Riley clarified.

"What a bitch" Tory immediately parroted back without a second's thought. *It's just what she expected I'd want to hear. She wasn't wrong.*

"You've never done anything like that right?" Riley asked hesitantly. She was almost positive of the answer already but wanted one hundred percent certainty.

"Have to be in a relationship for that to apply" Tory answered in a roundabout way. Riley was ashamed to admit she didn't know if her best friend had ever slept with a guy who had a girlfriend. She was afraid of what the answer might be.

"True" Riley agreed unsurely. "Plus I doubt the magazines care either way."

"Your support is really touching."

Mentally she shook her head and let her doubts fade away. *Tory may be Tory but she cares about me and we'd never do that to each other.*

"She's not a DXA is she?"

"No, only field hockey." That seemed to calm her down although Riley wasn't sure why she was still pissed at that sorority given how her and Eric had hit it off again yesterday. The DXA's were immaterial now unless she chose to fixate on them...and she just might.

"She could be a lesbian then" Tory announced with a serious face although the comment was meant to be anything but.

Riley shook her head furiously. "No definitely not. Not this one. She's definitely straight...she'd almost give you a run for your money."

"So you think I'm like this girl?" Tory asked quickly.

The joking nature of their conversation turned abruptly cool.

"No chance T." Her friend didn't look convinced. "The difference is to my knowledge you've never done what she did to Jake." Riley could feel her own restraint slipping as she continued thinking about what Kelly had done to her cousin. *He wanted to deactivate from a frat he pledged just so he could spend more time with that girl...this has gotta be a sick joke.*

Tory sighed. "I haven't really dated anyone since high school. I just never saw the point. Here especially...relationships are pointless." It was as honest a thought as Riley had ever heard from her best friend. She never talked much about what high school was like. Riley on the other hand told her everything throughout the course of their freshman year. Some of it was in an attempt to get Tory to open up about her own experiences but she never seemed interested in reciprocating. She always seemed much more interested in creating new memories in Gladen Hills.

"What would you think of me if we weren't friends?" Tory asked point blank after a few moments of silence. The question hit Riley like a freight train. She never wanted to allow herself to think about that because she was terrified of what that world would look like. More over, she was afraid of what Tory might think of her answer.

"Lucky for us we *are* friends so it doesn't matter. We're Facebook official and everything" Riley played it off as a joke. At first it looked like Tory wasn't going to accept her answer but finally she cracked a knowing smile and continued reading Cosmo.

****

"I don't know if he wants me telling you guys but I figure you'll know eventually. Jake isn't the kind to keep secrets. Until he says something though just act like everything's normal," Eric ordered Dukes and himself.

Scribner wasn't shocked by what Eric had just said about Kelly. *Right on schedule.* That was the first thing that came to his mind. Scribner knew he never liked Jake's girlfriend and with this latest news it was clear he was spot on with his original thoughts. *I'm just ahead of the curve.* "Alright that's fine."

"You're the boss" Dukes replied, only half serious. Half serious was better than the norm for his roommate so Scribner was impressed. It was probably lost on Eric though since he wasn't familiar with Dukes' personality. *Lucky him.*

Eric had come over under the pretense of playing smash brothers, which Scribner hadn't bought for a single second. No matter what the problems were between the two cousins, there was zero chance that Eric would come over to play a videogame without including Jake. Scribner had asked him point blank after the first match had ended with little to no talking. On top of the ridiculous lie Eric wasn't saying much so he clearly was thinking a lot about *something* and he wanted to know what, especially considering that it was likely about Raley. That had been when Eric folded and told them everything.

After they played through another few matches they heard the suite door open. Within seconds of the door shutting, Jake walked into the common room. The first person he noticed was his cousin sitting on the couch, controller in hand. Eric had the good sense to pause the game as soon as they heard the door open so the three of them just sat there looking at Jake.

"Hey man, sorry about what happened" Dukes said cordially.

Wow Dukes. If he hadn't just completely disregarded what Eric had told them Scribner would've been impressed by how sincere the guy sounded.

The look of annoyance on Eric's face was almost comical but Dukes didn't care.

"Wow...good job" Eric said miserably.

Jake waved his hand to stop his cousin from getting more annoyed at Dukes' comment. "It's straight Biz. I figured you'd be here."

"How are ya doing?" Scribner asked honestly.

"OK " he answered although he didn't seem it. Nobody in the room bought that either. The four of them lingered in their stances for a few seconds before Jake found the energy to move into his dorm room.

Once he reached his doorway he discovered for himself that Wayne wasn't around, as usual. Scribner could see the wave of relief come across his face. He turned back to the room and asked if he could talk to Eric. *Like you'd be able to keep him away even if you wanted to Raley. Jesus, even Dukes knows he's only here for you.*

Eric dropped his controller to follow Jake into his room. As he did Jake looked over to Scribner briefly. They shared a quick nod before he turned away. *Yeah...I'm here when you need me kid.*

****

Once Eric followed his cousin into the room he was sure to shut the door behind him. He was fairly certain Jake would be having a similar conversation with Scribner at some point within the next day or two but now was their time.

Jake sat in his desk chair and quickly moved his laptop mouse to stop the screensaver slideshow that was playing. Eric thought he saw a picture of Jake and Kelly smiling as he cleared the screen. *He'll have to fix that quick.*

"I know why you did what you did Biz."

"What do you mean?"

"You didn't tell me what was happening with Kelly because of pledging right?"

Eric sat down on the bottom bunk bed and looked sincerely at his cousin. "J, I didn't find out about it until last Wednesday...I should've told you then but it was right after that day in Lance so I didn't. But you don't deserve to be led on by her."

Jake nodded at him with a look of understanding. *At least he cooled down since our last talk but what the hell has he been doing for the past hour?*

"Well you wouldn't have been wrong in telling me right away but I don't know that you would've been right either" he confessed. "I wonder if how well you know me and how I've been acting would've changed things. Jeff holding it back the way he did might've been the smartest thing. Because we all know I probably would've walked away from it all, just like Riley said. I am easy to read I guess..."

"Whether that's true or not doesn't matter...I couldn't keep that from you. Waiting those five days with that secret was already too much. There's no way I'd make it five weeks J."

If Jeff hadn't done what he had then Jake wouldn't even be in AZXi now. He'd have nothing left, no brothers, not even his chick he said he loved. Could I have stood by him if he quit just because of this girl? "You've still got me J" Eric assured him as much as himself.

Jake's response came swift and heavy. "Yeah but for how much longer?" It was clear that tears were welling up in his eyes, and not for the first time that day either. "You're graduating next year Biz."

Eric was immediately swept up in that statement. *One year...that's all I've got left.* The thought chilled him immensely.

"Riley is too...and God knows what the hell you two are gonna do after this...head off somewhere new...I don't know..." his voice trailed off as he looked away.

Eric couldn't find the words to help. There was nothing he could say that would change the fact that by Jake's senior year, his cousins wouldn't be going to school with him anymore. He didn't want that day to come so how could he expect his younger cousin to deal with it? *He's the one having trouble today, not me. He needs to hear me say something.* "No matter what happens next year or after, we're still family...that won't change." The words came to him as he spoke. They weren't filtered between his brain and mouth like so many of his thoughts were. He couldn't explain it.

Shaking his head, tears started rolling down Jake's face. "I've been a complete ass ...with her...and you've been dealing with it...with me."

Eric fought the urge to tell him he told him so. It didn't take much effort.

"So it's over then?" he asked hesitantly. *Please let it be over.*

"I couldn't stay with somebody like that Biz" Jake answered sullenly. He almost sounded disappointed.

Eric felt the tension in his body draining away at the answer. "I'm proud of you."

"You didn't think I would go through with it?"

"I gave it fifty-fifty" Eric lied. He'd laid odds much worse than that. *He doesn't need to know, he just needs to know I'm still here.*

****

His cousin's warm smile was comforting. It almost made him forget what the purpose behind it was. Then it all came rushing back like it had on the walk to his dorm. *Kelly fucked another guy...and she enjoyed it.*

"Let me ask you something Biz." The thoughts circling his mind made him want to throw up worse than tequila. "If you cheated on someone would you keep it to yourself and just hope it didn't happen again..." he paused. "I mean do you buy all that shit about telling the other person is a selfish way to get rid of your own guilt? Kelly said it only happened once but she still never told me...I don't know..."

Eric pondered the question. "I think both sides have a point but I guess it really depends on the situation...I'm guessing you don't right?"

At least he's still perceptive about that kind of shit. "For me it's black and white. If you fuck up you need to say something. Fuck all that shit about just doing it to clear your own conscience. You tell the other person because it's the *right* thing to do. If you care about them then they deserve to know the truth. You know what's really selfish? Keeping it to yourself to keep your own perfect little world in one piece. *That's* worse than telling the truth." He finished ranting and took a deep breath.

On top of the thought of Kelly fucking somebody else from another frat no less, those were the things circling his mind on the walk back to his dorm. *The place I'll be sleeping by myself from now on.* The thought of being lonely started creeping into his mind. It stung as much as any of the thoughts before it.

What could cause a person to cheat on somebody? Weakness? Lust? The thrill? I don't fucking understand...at all.

"I guess you're right" Eric agreed after thinking it over. "But neither of us has been in that position before and hopefully it'll never come to that."

Jake nodded. *It will never come to that.*

"Come on J, let's go kick your roommate's asses in some smash," Eric offered.

Jake couldn't argue. He could use a guy's videogame session after today. "Sounds good…just give me a second."

Eric looked unsure about leaving his cousin alone in the room but he walked out anyway when Jake nudged him to do so. Once Eric closed the door Jake took out his phone and for the first time ever he scrolled to find Jeff's name. It had 'jack-ass' listed in parentheses. Jake smiled before deleting the nickname altogether.

He typed up a quick text message to his former pledge-master thanking him. Jake wasn't fully on board with being kept in the dark but he was hopeful that in the days to come he might see things clearer. After the message was shown as sent Jake put his phone into the charger on the corner of his desk. He sat in silence for a few minutes, just letting his thoughts settle. Abruptly he felt the urge to check Facebook. Once he got to his profile page he saw that he was still listed as 'In a relationship with Kelly Frazer'. It was both calming and unsettling. He hovered his mouse point above her name for a second and then clicked away to edit his profile. With a few more clicks his relationship status said 'single' and once again, the idea unsettled *and* calmed him.

How can a few clicks on the computer erase everything we went through?

That didn't matter because their relationship was now in the past.

Chapter 31

Northeast was an island, far away from the rest of Gladen Hills. Even the university police tended to ignore it because it was so out of the way. That tended not to matter in most cases since nothing ever happened on campus that the police were needed for anyway.

The track and field section was located just south of the main dormitories. Besides those two things, there was nothing college related on that side of the interstate that cut through the town. It was pretty unnatural for anyone who didn't live there to venture over. The dorms on this end were a recent addition to the school. They were far younger than their counterparts on Northwest. The school administration had decided in its infinite wisdom to build dormitories about a mile away from the nearest academic building. Maxen Hall was the closest and it was still a decent distance removed.

Riley Nichol had been over here a few times over the course of the semester. Once to pick up Brynn and Madison on Bids, another couple to console with Jake whatever his problem of the day was. Tonight was just a simple visit with her Little. *A little exercise never hurt anyone and God knows I could use some.*

Now that spring had come, the season for looking good was upon everyone, specifically the girls. The days of hiding in class behind heavy sweatshirts and hoodie's were in the past. *Until next year...my last fall semester.*

Once they almost finished eating at the Blue Hold Riley went over more about the upcoming elections. After a few minutes it became clear that there was something else on her Little's mind. Tory had told her she'd acted bitchy at the AZXi breakfast but Brynn had been insanely hung-over and cranky that entire day. *She might've punched me if I gave her a reason.*

"Let me ask you something" Brynn started in hesitantly.

Riley tensed up slightly. She didn't want any more drama after the shit three days ago with Jake and Kelly. "I don't think anything good has ever followed that line."

Brynn's demeanor cracked and she smiled. "Maybe not, but it still stands. Did you have problems with anyone *after* you crossed?"

Riley was glad her Little had taken the time to emphasize the word 'after' because it would've been too easy an answer if she hadn't. *No one in their right mind didn't want to kill somebody or ten somebody's during pledging. If I hadn't had Felicia...*

"You knew something was wrong didn't you?" Brynn immediately asked.

"Obviously. I was wondering how long it'd take you to say anything. Well that and T said you might be dealing with some stuff." Riley was hoping for even a hint of embarrassment at the mention of her attitude toward Tory but if Brynn felt that way it wasn't registering. "And to answer your question...there were definitely moments...but I think everyone deals with that. Some just deal with it better than others."

Brynn was clearly clamoring for more detail.

"Tory didn't give a fuck about any of it. No grudges, nothing. She just dove into EIPi headfirst like she always does. It didn't matter who hazed her or left her alone she was down to chill with everybody. That's just how she is."

Brynn smiled uneasily.

"Since she works that way it's hard for her to picture anyone else acting differently. I think sometimes she took her assistant pledge mom job a little too seriously and went harder than she should have because in her eyes, none of it would matter after Crossing." Riley was trying her best to give Brynn the benefit of the doubt. She'd never actually noticed Tory treating her any differently from the other pledges but then again she'd made a conscious decision to largely avoid her Little during callouts.

"So you're saying I shouldn't take it personally," Brynn sighed.

Riley frowned. "I'm saying I don't think Tory has it in her to hate anybody and she sure as hell didn't mean to offend you specifically…that I can promise."

Brynn didn't look convinced but her icy demeanor was starting to show some cracks. "How'd you handle it then Riles?"

"I needed a little time. There's only so long I can deal with being bitched at by actual bitches before I lose it. There were a few callouts I had issues. The floor cleaning in particular I was ready to walk out on to just be done with it all."

****

Riley was ready to walk out and be done with it all? There's no way. EIPi and her big sister were synonymous in her mind. "What stopped you?" she blurted out, thoughts still swirling.

"Felicia" Riley replied, equally as candid.

Well it must've been a whole different world actually having a Big who wasn't your pledge mother. The whole idea soured Brynn's mind. Neither of them had asked to be put in that position. She knew she definitely hadn't. *Riles did the best she could; there's nothing else to think about.* That aside, Brynn still couldn't shake the thought of how different things might've been if she'd had a different big sister. "I can't picture anyone else being my Big" Brynn replied, fully tasting the lie.

"Well that's because I'm awesome" Riley smiled. "I just think everyone needs to go into this world at their own speed. You have two sides of the coin. So you just gotta ask yourself: Are you a Tory or are you a Jake?"

Who the hell is Jake? One of Riles' fifty cousins?

"So where does that leave you and me?" Brynn asked hesitantly. She knew for a fact that she wasn't in Tory's half of the equation but she was willing to bet she didn't want to be fully on Jake's side either, whoever he turned out to be.

Riley looked thoughtful for a few seconds before saying anything. Even before that, she took a large sip of ice water to wash down her food. "We're somewhere in the middle. But seriously, EIPi and the world...neither of them could handle another Tory."

Brynn smirked. *Amen sister.*

"I know Tory didn't mean to piss you off so just let it go. We've only got three weeks left this year and I doubt you'll still feel like this in September."

"I better not" Brynn replied immediately. She was already tired of the constant tug of war in her head over how to feel and what to say at parties. That was part of the reason she drank so much, so she didn't have to think about it. "But I don't know Riles...I can hold a grudge pretty well."

Riley didn't look surprised. "I don't doubt it," she agreed. "But it's just not worth it. Not for something like this. My cousin Jake was ready to deactivate because of how pissed he was. Now *that* kid can hold a grudge, and it's not helping him either."

Deactivate EIPi? That'll never happen. Why walk away from everything I suffered through for those six weeks. Revenge is better than surrender. Brynn looked across the table at her Big and smiled through the memories now beginning to take root firmly in her mind.

The room was full of EIPi sisters all laughing and joking...and drinking.

Where am I right now? This can't be a callout. No, there's way too much happiness in here for this to be a callout. They're all wearing EIPi letters so I'm not in the wrong house so what the fuck is going on?

Brynn never got the chance to ask anything because she was being snapped out of her deep dream by more screaming. It wasn't the usual voices doing the screaming though. She hadn't even gotten her eyes fully open and adjusted to the low light yet but she knew there was a difference.

When she finally got acclimated she found her assessment was right on. Danielle and Amy were standing in the doorway to the chapter room. They were in the spots customarily reserved for the ones who'd be doing the most yelling on any given night. *They did just mind-fuck us in the stairwell a few hours ago so maybe they want Riley and Tory's jobs. They can't be any worse.*

"How the fuck can any of you be sleeping at a time like this?" Danielle screeched at all of them. Brynn felt anger rising. *That better be a rhetorical question.*

They were all still struggling to get up and link arms. Their response time to a sleep disruption was usually better but it was around one in the morning. *They let us sleep for an hour after the hallway sprints...yay.*

"They're just getting more and more disrespectful as the day goes on I guess" Amy said, sounding proud of herself.

Brynn grimaced. *Trust me sister, you haven't seen disrespectful yet.*

"You'd think after that class in the stairwell that they might've learned something," Danielle said, more to Amy than to them. It was just as well. Most of them were still yawning so the sisters' screaming was coming in as white noise. "Pledges, this is a sad day for EIPi. Your pledge mom and assistant pledge mom have both walked out on this program. They've walked out on you!" she yelled, as if that was supposed to mean something profound to any of them.

"They walked out because all of you are completely worthless!" Amy continued. "This has never happened before! Never in the history of EIPi! But we've never had pledges as awful as you!"

The six of them just stood there with their linked arms, unsure of whether they should say anything or not. Brynn was betting they were better off keeping their mouths shut so she tensed up her elbows to let the girls linked on either side know to keep quiet.

Thankfully, Danielle picked up just when the silence was reaching critical levels. "Sister Amy and I are going to fill in for sisters Riley and Tory until you all step up and find them. You need to bring them back to this house. We believe they went down to Tau Chi to relax after you all failed so miserably tonight."

Brynn assumed that meant they were all supposed to leave immediately and head downtown through campus to Arkridge Avenue to look for the two girls. *I'd rather we just leave them down there...forever.* Unfortunately they weren't given that option. "Get the fuck down there and look for them. Tell them you're sorry. Tell them you love them. Tell them you want them back so they can continue at least trying to teach you what it means to be an EIPi" Danielle continued screaming.

Fortunately these days they all slept in their clothes so they didn't need to dress. They were at least allowed to put jackets on before they left. It was still March so it wasn't that warm yet, especially at night. That small mercy was appreciated. It was a long walk from ElPi to Tau Chi.

Brynn had never gone out of her way to talk about pledging in any detail once they'd crossed. She figured she didn't want to know anything until she was on the opposite side next semester. *There'll be a whole new group of unsuspecting girls to torment…just like us.* Riley must've been able to see the wheels turning in Brynn's head because she asked what she was thinking about.

"That final week of pledging. The night the two of you walked out for the first time in ElPi history," Brynn said sullenly. Part of her never believed that was the first time it had ever happened but she'd never asked. *It doesn't matter now.*

Her big sister's face said it all.

****

"Sweetie that was all a big joke" Riley announced through laughter. She didn't want it to come off quite as condescending as it had but it was insanely funny to her. "That same thing happens *every* semester at the same time regardless of how well the pledges are doing."

Brynn didn't seem amused.

She heard the screams from the chapter room clear as day even though they were a floor up and a couple rooms over. *Danielle is gonna make a great pledge mom next year.* Riley smiled again while they continued listening. Amy wasn't being a slouch either during the pledge mom replacement callout.

Abruptly the screaming stopped and Riley took that to mean the pledges had been exiled to Arkridge to 'look' for them both. Of course they wouldn't find them down there. All they would find was house after house full of frat guys ready to be amused by a search they all knew was completely pointless.

Part of her job as the pledge mom was to check with each of the frat houses on Arkridge Avenue to make sure they were cool with the pledges swinging by and 'looking' for her and Tory. Most of them agreed without a problem considering the sight of the pledges running through their house was entertainment enough. The girls had to chant "we love you, we miss you, we want you back" through the halls of each house while Dani and Amy yelled at them. *Who wouldn't want to see that?* Each frat house had agreed to allow the pledges to come through around now and continue their search.

It made Riley smile when she thought back to her and Tory's own experience. Tory had caught the eyes of a few brothers on their search even with how haggard they all looked during week six.

"This has never happened before in the history of ElPi! Never!" Tory did her best Danielle impression while they sat in her room.

Riley laughed and picked up the charge. "You pledges are completely worthless, get out there and find them!"

"I wonder if any of them actually bought all that."

"Didn't you believe it when we were pledging?"

Tory blushed. "Kind of yeah."

Riley had been on the fence at the time considering how much of pledging revolved around assorted mind-fucks like that. "So gullible T."

"Oh please, like you didn't believe it too."

"We aren't talking about me."

"We've got an hour before they get back, what do you want to do?" Tory asked although it was clear she was hoping Riley would answer in only one way.

She was only too happy to oblige her friend. "I recorded the latest episode of Grey's," she answered gleefully. Part of her was ashamed to admit that the newest episode was on tomorrow night and she hadn't yet watched last week's. Between school and managing the pledges and their schedule she hadn't had time to watch it.

"Wine and Grey's? I could live with that" Tory said, as if there was some better option out there. Riley poured her best friend another cup of the boxed wine she'd bought earlier in the week. The two girls smiled. *Just another night in the ElPi house.*

She couldn't tell after the story was done if Brynn was laughing along with her or simply at the idea that she'd once been intimidated during pledging. Either way she felt that her reminiscing about it had been helpful in at least *some* way. When Riley really thought about it, pledging was all just one big mind-fuck and the sooner somebody accepted that the sooner they could get over whatever grudges they were clinging to.

She took another sip of ice water but then almost spit it out when she continued laughing about her memory of that night. Brynn started laughing too. *I can bring her around just like Felicia did with me.* They kept laughing even after the people at the tables around them started staring. Neither of them cared. Sisters had their own world.

****

The first night after he lost Kelly he'd been fortunate enough to have Eric, Scribner and even Dukes around him until well past midnight. They'd played smash brothers for three hours before Eric said he had to head back to Cordan. Jake had wondered how behind he was since he'd spent most of the night taking care of him.

It had been Riley's turn to hang out with him the next night. She'd come over and watched TV with him at his dorm until a little before midnight. Originally his cousin had wanted to take him over to EIPi to drink in her room with a few of her friends. At first the idea had thrilled Jake but the closer he got to the time he'd have to leave the more fearful he got about the whole concept. He kept thinking he wasn't ready to be around girls like that, not yet.

During their mindless TV session Jake chewed Riley's ear off with all kinds of scenarios regarding Kelly. A few times throughout the night some tears came down his face. Somehow he just felt more comfortable letting Riley see that side of him than he'd been the previous night with Eric. He'd still cried with him in the room but he felt weird about it. That wasn't the case with Riley.

The third night both his cousins had been busy. Eric was in the library the entire day. Riley was with her friends that she'd ditched the previous night for Jake. They were likely drinking again. He got the obligatory invite again from her but turned it down in the same fashion as before. *I'm such a pussy I can't even leave the dorm to go to a sorority house.*

As the night had drawn on he found himself checking Kelly's Facebook profile every ten minutes or so just to see what she was doing. He was looking just to get any idea of if she was feeling as badly as he was. Around ten he saw that she'd just accepted a friend request from some guy named Alex. That sent Jake on a downward spiral even though there was no context. Was that the guy she'd fucked while they were dating? Were they fucking at that exact second? The thoughts were paralyzing.

He'd knocked on Scribner's door within seconds of reading it and they'd talked through all the implications of what that friend request meant. Jake had been extremely thankful for his friend's patience on the matter considering how stupid the topic really was. Stupid or not though, Jake needed to talk to somebody about it and with his cousins on a temporary break from watching him, Scribner was the best option. He sure as hell wasn't going to bear his soul to Dukes. *Not in this lifetime.* Dukes seemed content to steer clear of Jake during most of the week. Doubtless he wanted to make all kinds of jokes at his expense so it was good enough that he kept his mouth shut.

Getting a text from Bill-Butt had been the highlight of Jake's day today though. *Day four of being single.* He never thought he'd feel that way but a lot had changed over the course of four days. His pledge brother said they were gonna be putting the finishing touches on their pledge class project tonight so he should swing by the house to help. It was strange to think that just a week ago the prospect of going to the AZXi house for anything had filled Jake with feelings bordering on contempt. Today they made him feel strangely happy. It was enough that he'd be doing some kind of manual labor. That would keep his mind occupied and hopefully away from Kelly. He'd replied to the text almost immediately even though it had been during a class. Jake was almost certain his professor had seen him typing out the response but he didn't give a fuck. He was just excited at the idea of being with people again. Scribner, Eric and Riley could probably use the break after the three nights he'd worked them over with all kinds of Kelly topics.

Now here he was, almost in a state of perpetual bliss. He was just standing by J-Hood and Summers tracing out the brother's names on the huge plank they'd bought down the interstate at the local lumber supply company. The more they worked the more the project started to look more and more like what they'd originally promised the actives. A new, up-to-date pound table with a black top board and a bigger yellow board behind it glued together. Both boards were octagonal. On the upper board they were tracing out six names in yellow lettering. Jeff and Jerry's names were listed with their appropriate titles of pledge-master and assistant pledge-master, respectively. After that came their four names in alphabetical order under the Alpha Epsilon banner. In huge lettering across the top read their current semester of 'Spring '07'. It hadn't seemed possible a week ago but Jake actually felt something resembling pride in what they were doing. His name was right there, third in line on the board, between Justin Henksin and Matthew Summers.

"This'll definitely be done by this weekend right Hood?" Will asked their pledge brother. It had been the same question posed only four days ago.

"No doubt."

Of course on Sunday when he'd said something to that extent the situation was a little different. Originally they were working up until the breakfast kicked off. Once the EIPis started rolling in his pledge brothers had all but abandoned the project in favor of drinking and chilling with the girls. Even Jake had joined them outside for a beer, if only for a little while.

J-Hood had told him some story or another about one of the girls grabbing his ass while he pumped the keg. Jake remembered laughing about it, especially when he pointed out the girl who had done it. *She was so fuckin' hot.* Jake specifically remembered holding his jealousy at bay because he had Kelly.

"I'm just glad this is the last thing Jeff can bitch at us about" Jake commented as he lightly touched up the lettering. He was using a small paintbrush to stay between the lines they traced. They all agreed with him that that was definitely a good thing.

"Raley I was completely shocked when you answered my text today…within like seconds" Will commented off-hand. "I didn't think you'd want to show up."

Jake smirked. "That's part of why I'm here pal. There's nothing quite like proving you wrong."

As usual Will got a little too physical for Jake. He wrapped his arm around him in a playful enough manner that he let it go though. "Glad to hear it Raley."

J-Hood bid them all to take a step back and stop working. He surveyed the pound table for a few seconds before saying anything further. "Alright, one or two coats of lacquer and this thing should last forever."

"Alright, let me get in there to help" Jake announced, acting happy enough for both of them.

"And here I thought you were just around to supervise" Will joked.

"Don't kid yourself Bill-Butt, it's a critical role."

J-Hood handed him a brush to start coating the boards with lacquer. After a few seconds Jake felt the need to say something. He took a deep breath and stepped back. "Let's put all the cards on the table guys" he began in earnest. The other three looked confused. "I was a fucking idiot. I got fucked over…but I'm here now for real."

In a moment that took Jake completely by surprise J-Hood cracked a hint of a smile and put his hand out for him to shake. Index fingers outstretched to the wrist. For the first time it felt like it was being done with a purpose for Jake. "Trust me Raley, bitches aren't worth your time…you might as well cheat on them before they cheat on you." He appreciated the sentiment his friend was trying to make if not the overall idea.

"Oh word Hood?" Will asked jokingly.

"No question. Raley could probably tell you better than I could though."

Feeling slightly uncomfortable, Jake ignored the opening to agree. "You guys did a sick job with this whole thing." Considering he hadn't helped all that much, taking only a little or no credit was fine by him.

"Glad you approve kid" Will patted him on the back.

"The supervisor's gotta sign off" Jake replied sarcastically.

After another twenty minutes of lacquering the surface they appeared to be nearing the end. Oddly enough, it was Will that came through and once again asked if everything was cool. Jake sighed and played it up as best he could. "Yeah...the girl's a bitch and it's not even worth thinking about." *If only I could take my own advice instead of checking her Facebook every hour.* He knew he'd probably look again as soon as he got back to his dorm.

J-Hood took up the cause almost instantly. "Damn straight. Out of sight, out of mind. There's plenty of ass in this town...giddy up."

If it hadn't been for the severe monotone voice that came along with the comment Jake would've sworn the words had come from his own big brother. Jared had been texting him non-stop since Tuesday asking him to come out and drink but Jake had never felt like it, at least not yet. "You know it's not as easy for everyone to get laid as it for you Hood."

"You just gotta know what to say and when to say it" J-Hood said casually. It was as if it wasn't the same thing that confused guys the world over.

Will looked like he was about to piss himself in delight. "Hood just please teach me how to do it" he begged.

J-Hood shook his head. "It's not something that can be taught."

Now it was Jake's turn to pat Will on the back. "Looks like you're fucked."

Summers finally decided to speak. "I think I'm gonna like this new Raley."

Jake smiled in spite of himself. *You and me both pal.*

Chapter 32

Tory Brye shook her head. Watching her best friend pace around the room was always surreal. *She always gets like this...every single time.* Riley didn't notice her movement. She was too fixated on her own thoughts.

"You know it's a good thing you don't wear heels much" she remarked. It was more of a test to see if Riley was listening to anything outside of what was going on in her head. Surprisingly, she stopped to look at Tory. She noted the marks on the carpet that flowed in the direction she was currently walking. It didn't look as worn out as it should have. Riley smiled before picking up right where she left off. Tory shook her head again as she moved to the door. *She won't even notice I'm gone.*

Moving into the hallway she noted how quiet everything felt. *Just the calm before the storm.* It got her all the more excited about the things to come. Lost in her own thoughts she started paying less and less attention to her surroundings. She almost didn't hear the question being asked of her. Tory turned around to see a girl coming toward her. "Where the fuck is she?" the girl repeated, quickening her pace.

Tory felt a huge grin form in a millisecond. *Oh my God yes.* "Well it's great to see you too" she replied sarcastically, ignoring the question entirely.

The girl shrugged it off like she always did. She tended to ignore any sarcasm that didn't come directly from her. "I know it is T now where is she!?"

Tory felt a little bad keeping her in the dark so she folded. "It's that room right there" she pointed behind her. "You don't remember? I'm pretty sure that's where you slept last time you were here."

Once again the comment was waved off like it had no business being brought up. "Do you remember my last time here? Because I sure as hell don't."

For a second, it might've looked like the two had entered into a standoff. To the trained eye of an EIPi however, it was simply how this particular girl acted every time she was in Gladen Hills. The girl dropped her duffle bag to the floor and reached over for a hug almost at the same time that Tory was reaching in herself. *Yes, yes, yes!*

The hug was longer than any one Tory had ever given her own parents but then again she liked this girl more than those two. Once it broke off the girl started talking again. "I'm so pissed at Kayla for not coming back. I may never talk to her again."

Tory agreed with that statement. She'd gotten the news a few weeks ago that her Big wasn't coming back for alumni weekend. The reason had to do with some bullshit about her work schedule. Truthfully it was something she didn't really care much about except that it was keeping her away from EIPi when it mattered the most.

"But it's fine, it's fine. We'll just have to take mad pictures and send them to her to keep her jealous."

Tory smiled. "What else are sisters for?"

"You're ready to go right?" the girl asked.

"It's only six…" Tory started to say.

"Yeah, we leave in ten minutes." With that she blazed past Tory much like a car on the freeway. She made her way to Riley's room and right on cue the screaming started. Tory followed her shortly thereafter. Seeing Riley hug her Big only got her more upset that Kayla wasn't around. Riley was clearly happy enough for all three of them though. Her friend even picked up the visiting girl at one point during their hug.

"I'm so freaking glad you're here!" Riley continued screaming as if it wasn't already obvious. It was only the third or fourth time she'd said it in the span of the minute they'd been hugging. *And I thought we had a long hug…*

Felicia Crystal was the same height as Tory and Riley but she always towered over them. It was humbling but also extremely comfortable. She was a senior when they'd pledged as sophomores. Kayla and Felicia were part of the same huge pledge class from spring '03. They were the last ones to take Littles because they'd been the pledge moms during their junior year just like Tory and Riley. The four of them had only been active in EIPi for a few weeks and a semester after Crossing. Tory could only imagine the types of shit they could've gotten into had they been together longer like most of the other family trees in the sorority.

Tory was getting so lost in her thoughts that she almost didn't respond to Felicia's words again. "Don't you love when Riles goes nuts?" she asked while prying her body away from her Little.

"You love it and you know it" Riley said casually, finally settling down.

"Who are you kidding Fels? You get the same way when you're hammered" Tory burst her bubble quickly.

"Well at least I only get that affectionate with my friends and not random guys" Felicia shot back.

"I wouldn't exactly call it being affectionate…" Tory fruitlessly tried defending herself before she realized there was no need or point. Both girls in front of her didn't really judge what she did.

That didn't stop them from giving her shit about it whenever possible though.

"You know I love you" Felicia started in as if reading her mind. "If you're happy then I'm happy."

Tory turned her gaze from Felicia to her Little. "See Riles, why don't you take a page from her book?"

Riley didn't look fazed or impressed. "I only give you a hard time *because* I love you. Get it together."

"Alright! That's enough of that. Are you two ready to go?" Felicia cut in.

"I've been ready for the last half hour" Riley replied giddily. Tory nodded in agreement. She might as well board the train now because it was clearly leaving the station with or without her.

"Good, glad to see you two have finally gotten your shit together" Felicia teased.

"Funny how that didn't happen until *after* you graduated…" Tory shot back.

"Well I definitely wouldn't be maxing out my credit card in midtown if you two were slacking, that's for damn sure."

Felicia's eyes started darting around Riley's room. She haphazardly threw her duffle bag onto the couch to claim that spot for the weekend ahead. "Where the fuck is my Little-Little?" she asked after a few seconds of pointless searching. They all knew there was no one else in the room besides them.

Riley calmed her down as best as she could. "Don't worry, she'll be around."

Tory smirked knowingly. *Maybe she'll be more fun with Felicia visiting…*

****

The AZXi house was flooded with brothers, active and alumni both. Every one of the actives was here as well as over thirty alumni, down for the weekend. Eric's blood rushed at the thought of how much fun it was all going to be. *Only a little after six on a Friday and this place is rocking.* Part of him started feeling a little apprehensive about all the problems that might come along as a result of so many guys being there. He beat that feeling down by drinking more beer. *It's all gonna be fine, relax.*

Another upside to the weekend was that his cousin had actually retreated from his cave he'd created in the dorms and showed up. On top of that he was around relatively early too. Eric couldn't ask for more, but he would anyway. Jake's was still subdued given all the shit that went down with his ex earlier that week. Eric had caught the brunt of it on Monday and then a little more on Thursday. Thankfully Riley and Scribner had picked up some of the slack too. Now with alumni weekend in full swing, he knew their female cousin would be attached to her own big sister like Eric usually was to a beer pong table. *Can't fault her for wanting a break.* Jake may have been at the AZXi house but it was abundantly clear he wasn't there mentally. *One step at a time, he'll get there.*

Eric handed his cousin a beer while taking a large gulp of his own. He was hoping Jake would see him and follow suit but it wasn't that easy. Jake just held it in his hand for a second while his eyes moved around the room. "I didn't expect it to be this packed so early" Jake commented quietly so only he could hear him. Eric smiled. He remembered how awesome his first experience with alumni weekend had been last year. He could only hope that Jake's memories of the weekend would measure up to his own. Anything to help him would be a plus.

"We're talking about alumni weekend J," he stated with gusto, as if that would drive home his point better. "This is the one weekend a year that these guys can come back and revert. They go wild like they used to when they went here."

That wasn't entirely true of course. Any active would be the first to admit that any alum was welcome at any point throughout the year to visit. Alumni weekend was just the best time because all the organizations across campus were taking part together. If people had friends in other organizations it was as good a time as any to come back to Gladen Hills and see as many old faces as possible.

Jake nodded his head although he didn't seem to be grasping the situation. "Right, right" he replied absently. Only then did he take a sip of his beer.

Eric carried on as if Jake had asked for more detail. "When that's the case everyone wants to soak up every possible second" he motioned around the room at everyone laughing and pounding their beers. *Come on J. Enjoy yourself for once.* "That's why they come back so early to hang out."

"I'm sure it doesn't hurt the actives' perspective with the alumni dropping so much money at all the bars either" Jake quipped.

Good call. "It definitely doesn't hurt. But more than that I think they actually like buying us broke actives drinks." He embellished their economic situation whenever possible if only to generate sympathy for donations. "It's a way for them to feel like they're still connected."

"Is that how you're gonna be when you come back?"

Eric's expression went from happy to indifferent in a flash. *Only one more year before I'm like them.* He shook his head. "Let's not talk about that right now son" he all but ordered while finishing off his beer. *I'd just as soon not kill my buzz before I even get one.* "But yeah probably" he admitted once the beer was down.

When Eric looked at Jake's nearly full beer he shot him a look that begged for an explanation about why it was largely untouched. "I don't know man. I guess I just didn't mentally prepare for this." *Come on man. This is our time. This is your time.*

Fortunately Jerry was close by to speak his mind. It was convenient that his pledge brother's thoughts mirrored his own. "I'm absolutely offended by that Raley," he slurred his way into their conversation.

To his credit, Jake simply grinned before saying anything. "Well now I feel much better about it."

Jerry ignored his wise-ass remark. "Did you ugly dudes finish your pledge class project yet?" He stood their patiently slamming his own beer while waiting.

"I'm glad you're staying so involved. We finished it yesterday. It's good to go so try not to throw up all over it this weekend" Jake taunted. Eric cracked a smile. He was at least grateful that his cousin's sarcasm didn't seem deterred after the week he'd had.

"I make zero promises Raley" Jerry smiled before turning away. He was probably on his way to get himself another beer. *A glorious pursuit.*

"Yo I'm gonna get some more beer...and that better be finished by the time I get back from the keg" he referred to his cousin's lingering cup. Jake smiled knowingly before he turned to walk away. Eric gave it fifty-fifty on his cousin still being there when he came back. *Even fifty-fifty is being optimistic.*

****

A light rain had started falling throughout Gladen Hills as Jake made his way outside. Bobbing and weaving through the swarms of AZXis inside was no small task but he needed some air. By avoiding eye contact nobody had stopped him but he was sure Calvin, Jared and some others were wondering what the fuck he was doing and more importantly where he was going. With the weather beginning to turn, there was nobody left outside. Jake turned his gaze up past the lone tree in the front yard and looked toward the sky. The soft rain on his face felt refreshing and for a few brief seconds the rest of his problems melted away. There was no sound around him save for the raindrops kissing the pavement on Arkridge Avenue.

"It'll get easier you know" a coarse voice shook Jake from his thoughts. Quickly, he turned around and saw Jeff standing on the side of the house underneath a portion of the outwardly jutting roof. He was putting out a cigarette.

"You honestly believe that?" Jake asked once the rainwater cleared from his eyes. It was still coming down slowly enough that it would take hours to actually soak him. For a second he almost believed Jeff was going to be like any other nice person but that didn't last long.

"Once you sack up...yeah I bet it will" he grinned as he made his way out away from the house, closer to him.

Jake turned away. *Even Rye knew not to try this shit with me now.* He wasn't even sure what he was feeling anymore. Everything seemed harder than it should be. "What the hell does that mean?"

Jeff continued walking until reaching a spot right next to Jake, so they were both looking onto Arkridge. The road was barely wide enough for two lanes but thankfully there was never much traffic since it was a dead-end street. Jeff lit up another cigarette. "It means that a bitch fucked you over and you can let it run who you are for however long you want or you can say fuck it and move on. Don't fixate. Don't check her Facebook or any of that bullshit. It's not gonna help."

Yeah right. Easy for you to say. You don't know what this feels like. Kelly Frazer was still dragging Jake down in every conceivable way and he wasn't even speaking to her. *How am I supposed to get past this?*

"You know what helps get over a girl like that?" Jeff asked rhetorically. It was just as well considering he didn't pause long enough for Jake to get in a word, not that he had one to say. "I'd say other girls except with how you are I doubt you could get your dick up for a porn-star let alone a co-ed." If Jake had the drive to do anything other than just exist these days that might've offended him. As it stood he just went with it.

"God you have no soul."

"Thank you" Jeff grinned as if it was a compliment. Maybe it was to a person like him.

He took another step out onto the road to further get away from the mild cover that the lone tree was providing. The rain was soothing as it hit him. "Is there a point you're trying to make?" Jake asked in earnest as the droplets kept falling.

"The point is that you need to spend time with people. Not alone like you were trying to be just now. Being alone won't get you through this, being with us will."

Jake stopped looking up at the sky and the incoming rain to face Jeff. "So that means I'm walking in the wrong direction?"

Jeff didn't mince words. He never had. "Fuck yeah you are. There's a house full of guys and beer behind you that can keep your mind off that bitch. That's as good a plan as any right now."

"Yeah…maybe I even agree with you but…" his voice trailed off as his thoughts took over. Not a week ago he hated everything about Jeff Chester and here he was now having an honest conversation with the guy. "But that doesn't mean I'm gonna listen. I know it sounds fuckin' stupid but I can't explain it." It felt shameful to say out loud.

"Of course not. That'd be too easy" was the reply he got. Jake was expecting to be ripped apart not unlike he had been at callouts for saying something so unbelievably stupid but nothing came. *Maybe he does have a soul or at least some part of one.*

"Way too easy" Jake agreed.

Almost on instinct Jake reached out his hand to shake Jeff's. *Index finger to the wrist.* Jeff reciprocated while finishing his cigarette. He stepped on the butt and returned his gaze to Jake. "Just be sure to come back when you're more fun."

****

The Center was the most up-scale bar in Gladen Hills. Of course up-scale in Gladen Hills didn't account for much. It may have been a step above the National and the Cradle and ten steps above Thirst Point but that just made it less fun in Tory's eyes. Plus it was more expensive. That didn't matter much today considering Felicia was only too happy to buy her and Riley drinks whenever they were running low. The Center was actually significantly smaller than the National and even a little below the Cradle but for pure aesthetics it couldn't be beaten. The walls were made of a polished oak that glowed dark when the light from the overhanging lamps hit them. There were leather booths lining the wall up against Cadren Drive outside. The bar itself was the first thing anybody had to walk past once they came through the sole entrance at the far end. The Center was basically a long rectangle with the bar and booths on one end and the pool tables and dartboards on the other end with the bathrooms. The place wasn't for playing flip cup or beer pong but she guessed that was the kind of point the owner was going for. A person would rarely come to the

Center if they were looking to get plastered. People came here if they wanted to sip on good beer and have actual conversations. Tory couldn't argue that there was definitely a time and place for such things but she rarely wanted that. Just sitting and talking weren't her speed at all.

For the life of her she couldn't figure out why Felicia and most of the older girls liked coming here so much but it was their call tonight. A ridiculous amount of EIPis if not the entire sorority had come along with them when they'd left the house. Between the actives and alumni, they basically had the bar to themselves. It was just as well, Tory tended to enjoy herself more when they were all together. So often during the past couple weeks there were fractured groups that didn't go to their parties or breakfasts. That wasn't the case with alumni weekend…ever. Everybody came out during the course of the weekend, and with damn good reason. It was always a good time and usually insane as hell.

Riley and Felicia had left her at the bar to go play darts with a few of the Kappa Nus that had also made their way up from Arkridge to drink. That was fine by her. She didn't feel like playing darts on top of the fact that it was only being played in two person teams right now. She hadn't been alone long though. Danielle found her way to the bar in short order once her departing friends had vacated the stools. She ordered herself some drinks without a problem. "I love that carding just stops on alumni weekend" she commented with a smile. "Gotta love it."

Alumni weekend amounted to big business for the locals. Bars and restaurants were always packed for these few days. Even though all the alums were over twenty-one they came back to hang out with the actives, most of which weren't that old yet. In order to keep the system afloat certain corners had to be cut, or just ignored altogether. Riley and Tory had had a long discussion about it last year. "No point questioning a good thing" was all Tory managed to say.

Fortunately Danielle's drinks were delivered quickly and Tory's own shot was still sitting untouched in front of her on the bar. Felicia had bought them each two but the first had burned her throat so she took a second to regroup and by that point the other two had pressed ahead. Now was a perfect time to catch back up. She raised the shot glass and Danielle followed along. The tequila burned her again but not nearly as bad as the first one. *We're getting there.*

"When you're right you're right," Dani agreed as her own shot settled.

Tory smiled through the slight pain. "Just remember that at elections." It was terribly unsubtle even for Tory, especially on alumni weekend.

Danielle smiled knowingly at her as if she didn't mind the topic being introduced. "You don't have anything to worry about." The words didn't have their intended effect. Tory was still worried even though Dani had told her otherwise.

It was no secret to anyone in EIPi that Danielle's pledge class voted as a singular unit during elections. That was why Rachel Hager was president during her junior year. It didn't matter that she was graduating a year early. It was unheard of before that point for a junior to be running the sorority she'd only recently crossed into. Unlike Felicia and Kayla and a few of the older girls, the idea was lost on Riley and herself: they didn't think it was that big of deal. Now that she was staring down the barrel of her own possible election to the E-Board the whole thing terrified her more than anything had in a long time. If any of the other Beta Zetas wanted to be the house president in Tory's place then she could kiss the position goodbye. Add to that the fact that she wasn't entirely sure where Brynn and her class sat and she could toss those eighteen votes right the fuck away. With only forty actives voting that was quite the piece of the puzzle to have against her. It wasn't the first time Tory had felt a little jealous of Danielle and her seat within her pledge class. *Well at least we beat home the pledge class of one thing with that group.*

"Sometimes I wonder what it's like being you," she thought out loud.

Danielle seemed amused at the comment. "You're gonna be fine. None of my pledge sisters have said anything about wanting to be house president over you." She motioned over to the booth that housed seven of the other eleven Beta Zetas. As usual they were keeping to themselves just like they did most of the time. Tory swore that if Danielle, Amy and Rachel didn't branch out the way they did then the entire class might as well just become their own sorority. *They'd probably be happier that way too.*

Brianna, Jessie and the rest of them just did their own thing and Tory couldn't understand why. That didn't make the rest of the sorority from bonding together to outvote them at elections though. For better or worse, EIPi was filled with all kinds of different personalities so getting everyone on the same page with anything was nearly impossible.

They weren't even supposed to know how people were voting at elections since they all kept their eyes closed but with how outspoken Danielle and Rachel were it was clear how they were all proceeding. With the rest of the sorority split voting between any number of girls having that solid twelve going one way almost guaranteed a victory depending on which way everyone else was going. Considering that Amy or Brianna could easily change their minds the day of elections and decide they wanted house president over her it was tough to fully relax. *All they have to do is wake up that morning and decide to run and I'm fucked.*

It was sad to think about. While Tory was definitely loved by most of the sisters for being herself, most girls didn't think she could handle any *real* responsibility. Sometimes they had a point. Her grades were nothing to write home about and she seldom referenced them when she *was* home but she could take things seriously when she wanted. Getting appointed assistant pledge mom by Riley was hopefully the push she needed to be taken seriously by the other girls. *It couldn't hurt to have the Beta Zetas support though.*

"If you think it's gonna be an issue I can talk to them again. Amy doesn't even want a position" Danielle reaffirmed. "But working on that particular angle couldn't hurt" she motioned toward the entrance.

Brynn Wells had just walked into the Center. Riley hadn't noticed her yet but once she did all Hell would break loose. Tory looked forward to seeing that.

"You ever figure out why she hates you?" Danielle asked as she sipped the mixed drink she'd ordered. It looked like a sex on the beach but Tory didn't know for sure. *I could use one of those right now. The drink and the act.*

"I haven't even found out *if* she hates me yet, so definitely not why."

"Some girls hold grudges after pledging I hear" Danielle said thoughtfully.

Tory had heard that same rumor although she didn't understand why. Pledging was all just a big joke. It was serious at the time and as assistant pledge mom she took it as such but once Crossing was over the fun really started. It didn't make sense to her when people couldn't just let it all go. If high school had taught her anything, it was that the past was better left behind.

"She's only in a pledge class of six. And there's no way they're as close as mine is" Danielle said haughtily. *There's no point hiding it when you're on top I guess.*

"That girl and I are gonna bond this weekend if it kills me" Tory promised herself out loud. Danielle cracked up. Tory did the same once she really thought about it. "Why can't that girl just like me the way everyone else does?" Tory said with less modesty than planned. Danielle only seemed a little amused.

"You want to be on the E-Board because me and Riles are gonna be on it right?"

Tory shrugged uncomfortably. "I still want to do something next year...I don't know." She'd run through the positions in her head so many times over the course of the past few months that it hurt to do it now. *President, vice president, treasurer, recording secretary, house president, rush chair, social chair, pledge mom, chapter-relations.*

Riley will go for president or vice president. She's gotta be one of the two.

Taking only those two out of the mix left a lot open. Social chair had to schedule all their parties three times a week and fill in gaps as they came up. Tory felt she could do that but didn't think it was likely she'd get that responsibility considering how integral it was to every sister. Pledge mom was never going to happen. It was considered the highest position in EIPi. Riley nearly lost in that election last year so Tory wouldn't have a chance. Chapter-relations was another one she thought she could handle but didn't really want to handle. Recording secretary was integral in working with the rest of the E-Board but it didn't amount to much. It was only as essential as whoever held the position chose to make it. That left treasurer and house president. They were similar in some ways but Tory wanted house president more if only because she had enough trouble managing her own bank account. She didn't want to be responsible for managing the entire organization's funds.

House president was integral and held responsibilities that she felt comfortable enough with. Like treasurer it involved collecting dues, but only for the house, not for being active. Whoever held the position had to make sure that their landlord got the rent checks on time as well as making sure the kitchens were all stocked with cleaning supplies and also that all sensitive rooms were locked during parties to make sure frat guys weren't raiding freely. Not that they wouldn't but there was no point in making things too easy.

Danielle must've seen the gears shifting in Tory's head so she waved a hand in front of her eyes. That snapped her out of her thoughts. "Just try not to piss off Brynn any more" Danielle said diplomatically.

Tory just smiled as she felt the day's alcohol setting in. "Please! Who could stay mad at me?!"

Chapter 33

The only thing missing was Kayla.

As Tory looked around the insanely dense party at EIPi she couldn't help but notice her big sister's absence yet again. There were more alumni down here than there were active sisters. All of Felicia and Kayla's Alpha Omega pledge class were visiting and getting hammered with all the rest.

Somehow she and Riley had managed to get up on the beer pong table despite the ridiculously long list. Tory was sure they'd cut a ton of people to get there but that was a thing of the past since the game was already winding down. Out of everyone nearby, she might've been the least drunk, which both shocked and appalled her.

"Seriously, you need to play drinking games more!" Riley slurred at her Little.

Brynn looked amused. "And seriously, like why?"

"Because you're really like…so good at them!"

Tory smiled. A drunken mind had its own way of rationalizing the talking it did.

"OK Riles just calm down and shoot the ball" Tory ordered, turning her friend's attention back toward the opposing side that still had two cups left. There were four left on their end.

"I got this," she said with more confidence than anyone should've had after missing six shots in a row like her. It was nothing short of a miracle that they were still winning the game. The biggest surprise was that Tory had actually hit three of the cups so far. Buzzed, she always played her best. *If Eric could see me now.*

Even though Riley was sucking right now they were up against some alums that pledged in the nineties. *They've probably barely played beer pong since graduation.* It didn't seem to matter much to them that they were losing. They were just enjoying being a part of the tradition and party once again. Tory couldn't blame them for that.

Out of nowhere Riley finally shot the ball and to everyone's shock it went in the left most cup. It didn't even hit the rim, just straight into the beer below.

"How 'bout that" Tory thought out loud. Even with the music blasting and the constant chattering around them her friend still heard her disbelief.

"I'm offended you're shocked."

"Hey she was shocked too!" Tory replied while motioning to Brynn who also looked stunned about the precision from her Big.

Riley darted her rolling eyes past Tory to see Brynn…and the truth. "Say it aint so Little" she demanded.

"What? In your condition you think that's common?"

Tory looked around to find Felicia. She was sitting down on a corner bench looking entirely more hammered than even Riley was. *Looks like all those shots they just had to do as a family line aren't sitting too well.* Even with their obvious condition Tory still felt jealousy and sadness at not being involved.

Brynn had gotten to the Center later so she hadn't endured the previous rounds of drinks Felicia had insisted on. *We might as well have been pledging again with the orders we were getting.* That was the only reason Brynn wasn't stumbling around like her two big sisters.

"Erroneous! Erroneous on both counts!" Riley all but yelled to both of them in a joking manner.

"Don't you just love it when she quotes movies like that?" Tory asked Brynn who definitely heard her but pretended otherwise. She immediately looked away to say something to Madison. *Good thing that's not awkward…*

"Just hit the last cup and finish the game!"

Tory nodded at Riley and actually tried to concentrate before stepping up. After a few seconds of having no luck at drowning out the massive amount of sound coming from every corner of the room she shot the ping pong ball. It circled the rim of the cup twice before falling into the beer below. *Concentration actually does pay off in this game…who would've guessed that?*

All she could do was turn to her best friend and sport the haughtiest smile she could manage. Riley smiled back before starting to sway like she needed to sit down. Tory was about to make her friend take a seat but Riley wanted to drink a victory beer. Hesitantly she moved to the side of her friend as opposed to directly in front of her where she was. *If she throws up it sure as hell won't be on me.*

They lifted their cups to drink and as soon as it hit Riley's mouth she nearly dropped the cup back onto the table and pushed her way through the crowds of people to make her way outside.

"Too much too fast" Tory explained diplomatically to Brynn, who'd just walked over to get the story as though it wasn't painfully obvious. The girl just shook her head.

Casually, the two of them looked over to where Felicia was still sitting on the bench. She was at least carrying on a conversation with one of the older girls that Tory didn't fully recognize. *At least she's still conscious.* "Looks like you're my new partner," she said, leaving no room for argument.

Brynn didn't look happy at that prospect.

While they reorganized the cups for the next game the two girls they'd just beaten came over to congratulate them on winning. Their names were Ana and Desi, from the Alpha Kappa class. Even after being out of college for a decade they still read between the lines on Riley's sudden disappearance.

After the two alums walked away, Brynn and Tory were the only ones in the immediate area. The others around them were talking amongst themselves and not paying much attention to them. Tory was feeling pretty good and buzzed so she went for broke. "Hey sis, what's the deal? Why do you hate me?"

****

Brynn nearly froze when she heard the question.

She tried making her movements seem more fluid than they really were but she didn't know how successful it looked. For all she knew it could've looked like she was having a seizure right at the table. "Wow that was subtle" was the only reply that came to her mind.

"Oh it definitely wasn't but neither am I and I don't wanna fuck around" Tory replied, equally as abrupt. She didn't look mad. As a matter of fact the only thing Brynn could read off her face was legitimate curiosity and maybe a little sadness. *What the fuck is going on right now?*

She turned away again to make sure their rack of cups was in perfect order. It was a stupid hope but she thought that maybe Tory would leave it alone once she saw that Brynn was in no way interested in talking about it.

"So what's the problem?" she asked again, still sounding only curious.

Brynn winced. *Of course she wasn't just gonna let it go, come on.* "I don't hate you," she replied as convincingly as she could. *I don't even know what to think of you.* The whole thing hurt her head when she thought about it. Letting go of all the pledging memories was proving to be a nightmare.

"What would you call it then?"

"I'd say I have absolutely no idea what you're talking about." Brynn only felt a little bad about blatantly lying to the girl. It wasn't a bad enough feeling to stop.

"Because if it's about pledging..." Tory began. "Then you should know I didn't mean anything by it...it was just my job."

It might've been the alcohol or just Tory's general attitude but Brynn could feel her self-control slipping away. "Sure Tory, a job you did insanely well" she said coolly. Funnily enough the girl actually smiled at that like it was a compliment. Brynn was only too happy to correct her.

"Maybe it wasn't a compliment but I'm gonna take it as one" Tory said happily. "Either way Brynn...we're both sisters now. Pledging is over. Dwelling on it isn't gonna help...either of us."

Brynn found herself smirking. "You're probably right but I'm way too stubborn to just let it go." Tory didn't seem to mind her honesty.

At that moment Brynn started to get an uncomfortable feeling flowing through her. Was she about to throw up just like Riley had minutes before?

"Hey Dani!" she called over to her other sister who was by one of the kegs with Jessie. She wheeled around almost immediately at the mention of her name and walked over shortly thereafter.

"Can you play for me? I wanna talk to Felicia before she completely blacks out" she lied. It felt like such a lie that she was sure it was written all over her face. There was little doubt that at least Tory would see through her bullshit but Brynn didn't care.

Danielle looked past both of them to where Felicia was sitting in the corner. "I think that time has passed...you know...like two hours ago. But I'll play."

Brynn thanked her before smiling at Tory half-heartedly and making her way to the corner. Once she was sure the two girls' eyes were off her she broke off from her path and looped back around to the exit hallway. Maybe she could find Riley, wherever the hell she was. The feelings she was getting at the table with Tory were making her feel almost comfortable. That was something she didn't want to feel around that girl. *She doesn't deserve that. Not after everything.*

It was cold.
It was late.
Those were two instances that Brynn was getting to be all too familiar with. As if being woken up from a sound sleep wasn't enough torture for the actives anymore, now they were being forced to do increasingly insane things with their time. Leaving their warm sleeping bags to be forced down to Arkridge Avenue at one in the morning on a weekday was bad enough. And that wasn't the end of their torment. Not by a long shot. *Why stop there when there's so many other fucked up things we could be doing?*

Their 'new' pledge moms had ordered them down to Arkridge to search all the frat houses for their 'old' pledge moms. The irony wasn't lost on any of the six of them as they walked through the brisk night. Going into each frat house was bad enough even though Brynn stopped giving a damn about her appearance around week four. Before they even got there she had a sinking feeling that there would just be more misery waiting for them.

The first house they got to was the Tau Chi's. Brynn had hollowly hoped that given the late time they were arriving that there wouldn't be many brothers up. If she hadn't known better though it would've seemed like their entire fucking fraternity was there. And they all yelled at the six of them the same as Danielle and Amy already were. The two girls had driven down to supervise the whole thing. *It's so nice of them not to leave us alone with a bunch of frat fucks.*

After the Tau Chi house it was the Kappa Nus, then the AZXis. After them it was the Lambdas and finally the Gammas. After the first house the rest passed by in a blur of yelling, swearing and generally demoralizing behavior from everyone who wasn't an arm-linked pledge. The six of them were forced to run through each house shouting the same thing every time: "We miss you! We love you! We want you back!" they chanted fruitlessly and furiously.

Every time they did so they were met with mocking from either Danielle and Amy or the multitudes of brothers at whichever house they were stuck in. There was one guy at the AZXi house in particular that was insanely mean for no reason. He just looked like a complete ass the first time Brynn saw him and he'd lived up to that in full. Thankfully none of the frat houses came even close to the size of ElPi so their runs didn't take long.

Danielle and Amy at least had the good sense not to make them go through the SIMS house or even the Phi Psis. Both of those places were sketchy as hell and Brynn had no desire to even go there for a party *if* they ever made it to Crossing.

Their new pledge moms let the frat guys in each house fuck with them as if they were ElPi sisters. It made Brynn sick. Being hazed by the sisters of the organization she wanted to join was one thing. And even *that* was wearing thin. The only thing that kept Brynn insider herself was the idea that freaking out would only make things worse. For her and her pledge sisters. *Pledge class of one. Pledge class of one...*

Fortunately the search through the five houses had only taken an hour. Riley and Tory were nowhere to be found of course. If they'd ever been down there to begin with which Brynn doubted, there was no shot that they were going to find them running through houses screaming like idiots.

After Danielle and Amy told them what a bunch of failures they were for not finding them they began the long walk back from Arkridge Avenue to the ElPi house on College Curve. The new pledge moms drove up in their heated car of course.

They made their way up hill, walking through the lit campus before coming down the other side. Only then were they finally coming up on the house. Once ElPi came into view it was clear that the night was just beginning.

Danielle and Amy were standing out front in their ElPi jackets looking annoyed. *We're the ones suffering. What the fuck do you two have to be pissed about?*

Behind them, in each of the windows lining the front of the ElPi house was a sister standing there in a darkened silhouette with only a single candle in each of their hands for light. It was mesmerizing and intimidating in equal amounts.

It was well past two in the morning on a weekday so there was no one, campus security, student or otherwise nearby. It made Brynn feel completely helpless as they entered the parking lot to stand before Danielle and Amy.

After a few seconds of uncomfortable silence in front of the fifteen or so sisters in the windows and the two out front they finally got the idea that they should do their greetings. Once Angela and Olivia got through the greetings for the new pledge moms a familiar voice rang through the cool air.

"Please tell me just what the fuck you all think you're doing?" Riley demanded from off to the side in the shadows. *How long was she standing there? Fuck.*

"There's no point. There is no explanation for this. You all make me sick" Tory was only too happy to chime in from right beside Riley. They both looked a lot more sinister than usual. Even her big sister looked like she was planning world domination with the look on her face.

"I've never been more offended in my life" Riley started in. It even sounded like she meant what she was saying. "We leave and you had only one job to do. You just had to find us! You didn't even think to look in the house that we fucking live in!" Riley was talking loudly while still being reserved.

"It shouldn't be hard to figure out! When we're depressed as shit because of how terrible the six of you are we'd want to spend time with our sisters! Seriously, get a fucking clue!" Tory followed up with a decidedly less reserved stance. None of the sisters even batted an eyelash behind them. Danielle and Amy took a few steps back and Tory lined up next to them.

Riley paced away before turning around slowly. "Welcome to Hell bitches" she said with ice in her voice. As soon as Riley spoke every sister in the windows blew out their candles at the same time. The entire front of the house went dark against the starless night sky. She lost track of everyone, save for the four sisters out front. "Get in the house right now."

After the shock had worn off from the sisters' synchronized actions they finally followed Riley's orders. At least the house had some semblance of a heating system in place. Anything was better than staying outside.

Danielle opened the door for them on their way in the side entrance. Someone must've had the door code pre-entered because they walked through the threshold quickly and quietly without stopping. Once they were inside they were lined up in the party room, their arms still linked at the elbows. The ceiling lights weren't on so the only light came from four flickering candles in the room's corners. It lent an eerie feeling to an already foreboding picture.

They all knew the room was filled with active sisters even though they could only really make out the ones in the front row. The shadows did a phenomenal job concealing the true number of actives who were no doubt looking on all of them with hatred and contempt. That's how Brynn always assumed they were looking even when she couldn't see them.

After some time standing in silence Riley ordered them to follow Tory out of the room one by one. Angela went first, Olivia next, then Mary. Brynn was the fourth. Each of the previous three pledges had been gone a while although she couldn't say how long. They'd been led back into the room but none of the returnees even gave eye contact to the rest of them who were still standing linked in line.

Finally Riley ordered Brynn to follow Tory out of the room. *Just my luck. After all this I'm finally gonna get murdered by Tory Brye.*

Reluctantly Brynn de-linked her left arm from Madison as Mary took her spot. She followed the assistant pledge mom out of the room. She could feel all eyes on her as she walked. Her footfalls on the ground were the only sound coursing through the air.

As she left the room she heard Riley start yelling again. "If I never see any of you cross I wouldn't feel deprived at all! Your actions are too fucking worthless to ever deserve our letters!" The words became less audible the farther they got from the party room.

She followed Tory hesitantly up the poorly lit stairwell until they reached the second floor landing. She waited for Brynn to catch up before pressing on, moving up to the third floor landing. Tory pushed the door open into the hallway and held it for Brynn to follow. It was the first time she'd done something remotely friendly for any of them since Rush. *There aren't enough doors in the world to make up for the past six weeks bitch.* They made their way down the third floor hallway hastily. Tory wasted no time leading her to the slaughter or wherever they were going. Once they hit the far end of the hall she abruptly turned and went inside the corner bedroom. Brynn followed.

Short of a quick trip to Riley's room she was entirely unfamiliar with who lived in which room at the house. Fortunately each of the hallway doors were decorated and painted over with the name of whoever was currently living there.

Brynn read the name on the door when she made her way through. Just like every other room in the house there were no lights on, just the flickering candles on the end table in front of a couch along the back wall with the window. The blinds were shut so no one outside could see what they were doing. *Probably because it looks so fucking crazy...even to me and I'm neck deep in this shit.*

Only one girl was in the room: Rachel Hager. She was sitting as stoically as any pledge mom. Tory sat down right next to her on the couch so that only the coffee table with candles was between them. Brynn remained standing.

As her eyes adjusted to the even lower lighting level in the bedroom they began to wander around even though she knew it was a bad idea. Brynn was sure that neither Tory nor Rachel was looking anywhere other than directly at her. She couldn't help it though. She always tried looking around if it was her first time in a place.

Rachel's room seemed bigger than Riley's and it was different in subtle ways. There was a huge flat screen television in the corner by the bed. There were strings of beads hanging by the entrance to her personal bathroom even though the door was closed. Posters of hot models and actors lined the walls as well as movie posters for comedies and chick flicks. *So these girls actually do have lives.* Brynn always just assumed that most of the rooms doubled as torture chambers for unsuspecting pledges.

Finally her eyes found the way back around to the two girls sitting in front of her. They seemed to be waiting for her to meet their gaze. That was when Brynn realized the small table between them wasn't only holding candles. There was also a row of six shot glasses as well; each one filled with a clear liquid. It could've been anything from poison to vodka.

"Pledge four, the shots in front of you represent you and your pledge sisters. To show that you are committed to Epsilon Iota Pi you're going to take all of them right now" Rachel said calmly but with an edge of menace.

Brynn nodded at the sorority president slowly before picking up the glass furthest to the left. *Left to right...one at a time...you got this.* She took the first shot immediately after picking it up. *One quick motion.* The liquid burned her throat on the way down. *Vodka...lovely...why couldn't they have gotten tequila? At least I'm not a Beta Zeta...I could never do twelve shots in a row.*

After she set the first shot glass down the five full ones left in front of her somehow seemed larger and fuller than they had a second ago. Hesitantly, she reached for the second and took that one down quickly as well. It burned even more than the previous one had. *Different brands of vodka? That's just sick...even for these girls.*

She set the second one down and reached for the third. Trying to keep the thought about how disgusting the next one would be out of her mind was a challenge in itself. If she didn't know better Brynn could've sworn she heard her brain screaming for it to end. All the while Tory and Rachel stared her down with accusing eyes.

Raising the third glass to her lips, she poured the liquid inside. She closed her eyes to mentally prepare for how awful it would taste on her tongue but nothing happened. There was no taste to the third shot. Brynn blinked. *Water? No way they'd just let me take shots of water. Not now.* Quickly she set the third down and did the fourth, then the fifth and the sixth. Each one left no taste in her mouth and had in fact helped to wash out the truly awful aftertaste from the first two.

Once she set the sixth glass back down on the table a smile started to form around Rachel's lips although she was trying to hide it. "Very good pledge four," she said coolly.

It looked like she had more to say but it was Tory that continued on. "Brynn Taylor Wells...I want to be you sister. Do you want to be mine?"

Everything stopped as thoughts began swirling around Brynn's mind. She'd often fantasized about what she would say back to Tory if and when the time ever came to answer a question just like this. The moment was finally here but she couldn't bring herself to say any of the admittedly terrible thoughts that were begging to be voiced.

"I guess so" was all she could choke out. It was as honest and mean as she could be without one side overpowering the other.

Rachel looked astonished at what Brynn had replied with but Tory remained collected. All she did was smile. "Not exactly a glowing recommendation but fine" Rachel forced herself to say after regaining her composure.

"When we take you back downstairs we're going to place you in line next to your pledge sisters again. You won't say a word until they've all come up here and gone back down" Tory explained.

With that Rachel nodded at Brynn while Tory got up from her place on the couch to lead the way out of the room. She followed. Upon reaching the hallway Tory spoke. "You know you're probably one of the only girls not to respond with a definite 'yes' to that last question."

"Just trying to be different," Brynn muttered defiantly.

Tory smiled again as they made their way down the two flights of stairs. "Riles is gonna be so proud."

"I hope so."

"I'm happy for you" Tory said, exposing full sincerity.

Thankfully they were making their way back to the party room and were too close for Brynn to say thank you in any meaningful way. Not that she would have at all.

The two made their way into the darkened room where the rest of Brynn's pledge class was waiting silently. Now that her eyes had fully adjusted to never having real light she could fully see the entire sorority standing there facing her five pledge sisters.

She could've sworn she saw Riley smile as she made her way back into line but the shadows from the candles were moving too quickly. Her Big was still yelling about their lack of respect but Brynn wasn't paying attention. *Almost there.*

Fortunately that night had marked Crossing for the Beta Thetas. It had come and gone. Now they were all sisters. Alumni and actives alike had all gone through the same shit and had come through wearing the pink and white letters of Epsilon Iota Pi. That was good enough for her pledge sisters it seemed but Brynn couldn't help still feeling cold to some of the experience...and some of the people.

****

Calvin's final alumni weekend had passed by in an intense blur. The feeling of whiplash was prevalent throughout his entire Saturday. Now that the final stretch was here, he found that for the moment he just wanted to reminisce alone. That was what brought him to the AZXi front yard.

About twenty to thirty alums had rolled through all within the same hour and the drinking started immediately. He and a bunch of the actives like Kev, Petey, Buttons and Guapo had started drinking around two but Calvin wasn't even sure what they were doing before most of the alums got there could still be considering drinking. Most of the older guys came through with six or twelve packs of high-class, high ABV beer. Not the usual shit they filled their kegs with. Others had brought bottles of Grey Goose and demanded they all rip shots immediately upon arrival. Today being the last alumni weekend Calvin would spend as an active he soaked up every experience like he'd never have it again. Part of him knew it could be true.

His brother Adam had come through just for Friday night and although Calvin was busy talking and drinking with a hundred others he still made time to slam a beer or two with him. He was the one that originally told him he should check out AZXi when he and Petey started going to Rush events sophomore year.

Brandon Sarce, David Kraylin, Ronald Benjamin or Boo-Yah as he was titled during his active years were all here. They'd all come through looking to relive the crazy days they'd spent here together in years past. Calvin was only too happy to indulge them.

Whether it was playing beer pong, flip cup or just having a chug off, the whole thing just felt right. There was no place he would've rather been during the past thirty-six hours. He'd barely seen any of the actives, and if he had they hadn't taken up much of his time.

The weekend was all about the alums. Since he was a senior, he knew more alums than actives. So many of the guys that came back were the same ones who'd hazed him when he accepted his bid two and a half years ago. It felt like the completion of everything he'd done at Gladen Hills to be able to relax and have some actual good beer before he walked the stage for his diploma in a few weeks. Every time he checked his cell phone for the time he wanted it to be earlier than it really was. And every time it was later than he wanted it to be.

He'd barely seen Jennifer in twenty-four hours but there was rarely a time like now where he could just stop and think about how much he missed her. Despite the whirlwind feeling of it all, the memories would stay in his mind for a long time. Forever if he had his say.

Surprisingly, there weren't actually any AZXis nearby right now. It was still early enough in the night where most of the alums and actives were down the street at the National where they'd all been pretty much all day.

Every guy who called himself an AZXi had great memories of the National. It wasn't much to look at but most of them called it a third home behind their actual ones and the frat house itself. Buttons, Boo-Yah, Guapo and a few others probably thought of it as a second home. *Crazy ass alcoholics.*

Calvin had been there with everybody for most of the day but he found himself needing a breather. The non-stop drinking taking its toll, exhaustion was creeping in.

Boo-Yah had broken his doorframe at seven in the morning when he stumbled in and demanded they all start drinking. Brandon was right behind him with a full bottle of Ice 101. Twelve hours later and Calvin was feeling tired although he'd never admit it. Fortunately his Little had been able to give him some adderall earlier. *I need to stay up all night. If I pass out now I'll never get back up and I'm not missing this.*

He looked down at the ovular orange pill in his hand. He tended to steer clear of drugs most of time. The only time he'd needed one was that semester's Bids when he felt himself waning very early after the walk. One pill from Dills and he was good to go the rest of the night. He'd stayed up so late that Jennifer couldn't walk right after they were done fucking all over her room at the Rho Beta house. It had been one of their hottest times ever. Jennifer always said it was the best she'd ever felt being that sore. Calvin concealed the pill in a fist when he heard a couple voices coming in his direction. Biz and Buttons rounded the line of hedges that separated AZXi from the Lambda house.

A few of the Lambda alums had almost gotten into a fight with Boo-Yah and Buttons over some truly stupid shit. Calvin's blood had risen along with everybody else's when it was happening. Had it truly come to it he would've thrown punches with the best of them. Fortunately Biz, Petey and a few others had cooler heads so they calmed everyone down.

"Yo Gretman! What're you doing?" Eric asked as they approached.

"Just relaxing. What're you two up to?"

"I know Buttons is about to do some lines and I wanna make sure he stays out of my room for once."

Jeff grinned knowingly. Whether or not he would've used Eric's room for more lines or stuck to his own side of the house was anybody's guess. Biz was probably smart to follow him. Calvin smiled and nodded. He'd barely spent any time with either of them in the past day and a half so he followed them inside.

Outside of Jeff's room in the hallway was where the frat had displayed all of the pledge class paddles including the most recent: the Alpha Epsilons. Jeff went into his room as Eric and Calvin stayed in the hallway at the top of the stairs. The noticeable gap in the wall full of paddles always caught his eye and not in a good way.

"We should really fix that" Eric commented, noticing the same thing.

Jeff was already cutting two lines on his desk but he knew what they were talking about. It was far from the first time they'd brought up the missing paddle. "Fuck that" Jeff said abruptly. "We should find out who took it and burn their house down."

"Sounds completely reasonable" Calvin agreed sarcastically.

Jeff just shot him a look from the adjacent bedroom. He and Eric were standing in the doorway so he caught the brunt of it like he was meant to. "Come on Buttons. The damn thing has been missing two years" he exaggerated. "Ever since we moved in here."

"I remember" Eric said confidently. "Me and Jerry had to screw all those damn things into the wall. I still have no idea how they got away with that one."

"That's pretty easy Biz. Obviously you and Jerry did a terrible fucking job securing them," Jeff said matter-of-factly. In his mind that was probably the only plausible reason. Calvin knew better. Sororities in Gladen Hills were just as cunning as any frat. There was little doubt in his mind that it was the work of a sorority. EIPi, the NDM's, maybe even the Rho Betas although Jennifer wouldn't have been involved nor would any sister have told her if they had.

"Yeah sure Buttons" Eric rolled his eyes.

After another minute Jeff was done snorting the lines. Calvin had taken the adderall pill he'd kept clenched in his hand when he realized that neither of the two that were with him would give a fuck. And they hadn't. Jeff didn't even bat an eye and Eric looked disinterested at best.

Jeff secured the lock on his door for all the good it would do. If a hammered alum wanted in, he'd get in. No amount of locks would stop someone like Boo-Yah, and the guy's entire pledge class was back with him. Buttons had to know that but Calvin guessed it was a habit. He couldn't blame the guy. He'd locked his door too even though it had already been proven worthless.

They all moved down the hall and outside into the dry airy night. Jeff and Calvin were walking a little faster than Eric so he was behind them.

"So this party tonight dropped us to around zero" Eric started in unprovoked. When he was drunk sometimes he liked to start crying poverty. Neither Calvin nor Jeff took it seriously, having heard it all before. "I don't know how we're gonna pull off senior hazing next weekend" he continued.

That got their attention. They both stopped and turned to face him, their eyes fully incriminating. It was then that Biz realized he might have overstepped slightly. "Don't worry guys we'll still be able to have your precious day."

That's more like it Biz. There better not be any problems with senior hazing.

"Just wait 'til it's your turn in the spotlight Biz" Jeff warned.

"We've got the sickest place to hide when it goes down" Calvin taunted their younger brother. Jeff had finally gotten around to explaining what his great idea had been that day of the EIPi breakfast last weekend when he tried barging in while he'd been fucking Jennifer. Even Calvin had to admit at that point that Buttons had been right in wanting to tell someone as soon as possible. It was an awesome plan.

"Please. All the actives versus the five of you? You guys are fucked."

Calvin and Jeff just grinned at each other when they heard Eric's hollow threat.

"There's plenty of time for that next weekend. Let's just get fucked up now," Calvin announced with a smile. He could feel the adderall kicking in. His energy came roaring back.

"Way ahead of you Gretman" Jeff grinned.

They made their way down Arkridge toward the loud music and yelling currently filtering outside from the National. *Just one more night...*

****

There were few times since arriving at Gladen Hills when she could remember having a hangover as terrible as the one she felt earlier when Felicia had shaken her awake. Riley was expecting it though considering she'd thrown up around ten at night then drank some more before passing out a little after midnight. All that added up to the soul-crushing headache she had today. Fortunately, Felicia essentially forced her to start drinking around ten in the morning although she must've been feeling just as terrible as Riley. Felicia knew probably better than she did that alumni weekend was not a time to sit on the sidelines and mope about the pain their horrible decisions had caused. Alumni weekend was a marathon and yet somehow they'd both forgotten that over the course of Friday and treated it like a sprint. Riley was taking it easier today than she had yesterday. Not that she was steering clear of alcohol but she was taking care not to overdo it, at least not until later.

The plan worked out well enough. It was later now and they were all at the customary EIPi-Tau Chi party. Saturdays of alumni weekends always had them partying with their brother fraternity. Every organization worked that way including the AZXis who were with the Rho Betas tonight for how much fun that would be.

Felicia had wanted to meet her younger cousin Jake since she'd found out he went here a year ago. Unfortunately since Jake was mixed up with Kelly from basically the second he got to school there wasn't a lot of time for them to interact. She'd met Eric a few times and loved joking with him so Riley guessed that she was just looking for more of the same in terms of Jake. Both her cousins were right across the street at their place. Unfortunately the Betas tended to look down on girls from other organizations that crashed their parties, even if it wasn't at the Rho Beta house. Riley couldn't really blame them for that since she would probably act the same if other girls came to EIPi when they were partying with a fraternity. It didn't stop her from being mildly annoyed that she couldn't go over and at least say hey to her cousins and finally introduce Brynn to both of them and Felicia to Jake. Hopefully she'd get to at least see Eric out at the bars later even though Jake would probably head back early. Eric had texted her yesterday saying Jake left their party pretty early. *He left the dorm though, that's a start.* Jake hadn't even had the drive to drink with her and her sisters earlier that week. It was nothing short of a miracle that he was out now.

She looked over at Felicia who was nudging her forcefully to let her know they were about to have a family race. Riley looked at Brynn who was wavering with each passing drink. Felicia wasn't messing around though. She lifted her cup and shot a look to the two of them demanding they follow along, which they did.

Riley finished the quickest with Felicia being a second behind her. Then Brynn came along. She took a little longer to get the beer down with how much she was swaying around. After it was done Felicia turned around again to fill up her cup at the keg beside them. Thankfully they were near a keg that was barely being touched considering there were an additional six separate ones at Tau Chi, inside and out.

The Tau Chi house looked similar to AZXi from the outside, save for the fact that they had a huge unscreened porch that jutted out from the front. Their colors were dark blue and green. That was apparent to anyone with eyes considering that's how the house was painted: mostly dark blue with green siding. The porch was entirely blue as well. The entire structure looked trashy more than anything else.

The house had gravel driveways on both sides and a gravel backyard that was bordered on its backside by a small ravine. On the other side of all the trees and shit was the road that led to the townie apartment section or TAS as they all called it. Fortunately they were far enough away from the residents that their noise level never caused the policed to be called. Not yet at least. They'd be pushing the boundaries of that tonight judging by what Riley was seeing.

"Great job picking this girl for our tree Riles" Felicia commented after she finished filling her cup again.

"I know. I'm freaking awesome," Riley agreed happily. It was always good to get a compliment from her Big, especially when she had originally been apprehensive about her taking a Little that semester at all.

"Hey I picked you didn't I?" Felicia asked rhetorically.

"Yeah I guess you're kinda cool too."

"We're all awesome!" Brynn shouted. That pretty much sealed the deal. *Yeah, she's hammered.* Riley felt a surge of pride at being able to stand there with her Big and Little having a few drinks, even if one of them was blasted.

It was insanely fulfilling having her Big back in Gladen Hills like she was when Riley crossed last year. *Things were a lot simpler.* She could constantly defer to Felicia whenever she needed help with anything. Sometimes it was easier getting advice and following it than coming up with her own plan of action. Just having the security of a big sister around, even for a short time, was liberating. Riley wasn't in charge right now and she was surprisingly OK with that. Felicia could take the lead with whatever she wanted to do and Riley would follow without a problem. *Why couldn't she have stayed an extra year?* It wasn't the first time the thought crossed her mind.

"I love this girl!" Felicia yelled as she hugged Brynn. It looked like it was in a partial attempt to help keep the girl propped upright.

"Hey she's my Little so hands off!"

"You should...like stick around...hanging out with you is sooooo fun," Brynn said slowly as if the words were having trouble forming in her head.

"I wish I could. Graduating was the biggest mistake I ever made."

Riley noticed that her tone suggested she was being sarcastic but her body language screamed that she was being somewhat truthful.

Felicia reached over to hug Riley and Brynn at the same time. In the process of the group hug her Big dropped her beer on to the gravel-strewn driveway. It looked like she didn't even notice it was missing from her hand. "Promise me that neither of you will ever graduate" Felicia ordered as solemnly as she could.

Both Brynn and Riley humored their older sister and made the promise. *If only that promise was worth anything.*

"Where the fuck did my beer go?" Felicia finally asked.

"Maybe you dropped it?" Riley replied while trying to keep a straight face.

"Damn that sucks" Felicia replied while looking around the ground.

Brynn stayed quiet next to them. It almost looked like she was having a hard time tracking what was being said. Riley instinctively reached over to help keep Brynn level as Tory walked over. Felicia was busy looking for a replacement cup.

"Jesus what did you two do to her?" Tory asked after seeing Brynn.

"I have no idea. She was just drinking with us like normal."

Tory shook her head. "Well normal for us isn't normal for her."

"*Yet*" Felicia interjected after apparently finding another cup to use.

Seeing the look on Brynn's flushed face made it clear that she was about to pass out and needed to be taken care of. *Well that pretty much settles it for me tonight.* A sad look came across her face as Riley realized she'd miss the last night with her big sister. The sting was worse considering the previous night was such a blur, and would likely remain so forever. *I just had to overdo it last night.*

"You guys can stay I'll take care of her" Tory interrupted Riley's self-pity.

Wait...seriously? Riley shook her head at her best friend. "No. She's my Little. I got this" Riley replied. She wasn't happy about the station but she couldn't let her best friend leave the party early because she and Felicia had gotten their Little too wasted too early. Fortunately Brynn didn't seem to be registering any of the conversation taking place in front of her.

"Come on Riles. Felicia's never here. It's not a big deal. I don't really like the Tau Chis anyways." Riley took that as a coded message that she wasn't a fan of the 'talent' around the party tonight. Brian was either ignoring her or she finally decided to toss that option aside. "I'll take her to the house and come back" Tory added.

"You sure?" Riley asked, trying to cover all her bases. It was clear which way Felicia wanted this to go since she was keeping quiet right next to them. The girl always had an opinion but knew well enough when her own thoughts would harm the outcome she was pushing for.

"Well you both will owe me a lot for this" Tory grinned.

"I'll adopt you and steal you from Kayla when you get back T" Felicia smiled.

"Now that's something to look forward to."

Riley smiled back at both girls before leaning in to talk directly to her own Little. "Tory's gonna take you back to the house now OK?" she asked although it wasn't even close to being a question. *If this girl is anything like me then she'll say she can stay and make it through. And we'd both be ridiculously wrong.*

"I just need a quick nap" Brynn nodded absently back. Her eyes were locked on Riley's but they weren't looking at her. *How about that? She still has common sense.*

Tory moved in to put her arm around Brynn. Riley was kind of shocked to say that it felt good seeing the two of them together, even if it was only because one was way too drunk. "That's what we're gonna do Brynn. Just take a quick nap and come back out," Tory said soothingly.

Riley and Felicia watched Tory walk Brynn down the driveway from the rest of the party. Nobody else seemed to notice what was going on. She felt bad that her Little was missing out on the rest of alumni weekend but there wasn't much she could do. She didn't have any adderall and Brynn didn't do coke so keeping her awake wouldn't work.

Riley still had Felicia though, for a few more hours. Then she'd lose her all over again. The Sunday after alumni weekend was always the single most depressing day in the history of college. She hated saying goodbye to all of the alums she'd met and drank with over the weekend. And tomorrow would be the hardest one yet.

Chapter 34

Even the light movement of fingers across a keyboard was sending waves of agony through Brynn's body. It might as well have been the sound of a monster truck revving its engine right next to her ears. Not just her head was in pain, her arms and legs felt completely fucked too.

She finally found the courage to open her eyes knowing that it would probably hurt immensely when she did. And she was absolutely right. Once her eyelids moved back to allow the rush of light coming through the nearby window, the feeling was nothing short of how she imagined Hell.

"Whoa" Brynn muttered when she realized she had no idea where she was.

"Oh hey there Brynny" a cheerful voice said. At least it would've been cheerful had it not sounded like nails on a chalkboard. It certainly didn't help once she realized who was speaking to her. Tory turned around in her desk chair to stare happily to where Brynn was lying on the couch. *Please don't tell me I ended up in Tory's room last night somehow?* Horrible thoughts started circling her mind even though it hurt to think that much. *Maybe I'm in Riley's room and Tory is just in here.*

"What the fuck happened...?" was all she could say without causing her body to ache even more.

Tory reclined a little further back in the chair and smiled. *She's probably loving that I'm in pain.* Even if it was true or not Brynn found herself wanting to believe it was. "If I had a nickel for every time I heard that...even in this room" Tory replied with an even bigger grin.

Brynn cut her off if only because she was in no mood for jokes, especially from her. "Yeah I know...you'd be rich but it still doesn't answer my question," she replied curtly. It was meant to convey as much impatience as possible. From the look on the other's face, that had come across very well.

"Nothing new…you got hammered, I drew the short straw" Tory answered. Something about the way her eyes wouldn't quite lock with Brynn's made her suspicious. That didn't change the fact that she couldn't say what happened last night any better than somebody absent.

"Why not Riley or Madison?" her mind reached for any possible reason about why Tory Brye of all people would take care of her. The only explanation that came to her mind was that everyone else was dead and the apocalypse had come.

"Just the lucky one I guess" Tory said kindly as she turned back around to continue working on her laptop.

Not surprisingly, Tory's room was pretty much laid out in the same way that Riley's was. Most rooms on the second floor had the same floor plan. That made the choices for how to organize a room pretty limited.

The thing that really caught Brynn's eye was how her four walls were painted different colors, or actually two sets of colors. The walls to her left and right were white and the walls in front and behind were pink. *EIPi colors.* Brynn found herself wondering if Tory had inherited the room as it was or if she'd actually painted it herself. *She probably just got some guy she was fucking to paint it for her.*

"What're you working on?" she asked forcefully, if only to snap her mind out of the severe hurricane within.

"I'm finishing up a paper for my psychology class. It was due last week but I got an extension from the professor because of home stuff."

Brynn squinted because she wasn't sure she heard that correctly. Tory would definitely have lied to an unwitting professor about that kind of shit just to cover her own ass and save a grade. But then she found herself wondering if there really was something that had gone on back home with her family that was a legitimate cause for an extension. Something didn't feel right about asking.

"How late did I make it last night?" Brynn asked, quietly changing the subject and all but ignoring Tory's previous comment.

"Oh not too bad at all" she said while turning around again. "Almost 'til nine."

I hope that's not supposed to make me feel any better. Inadvertently Brynn found herself lowering her head in shame. Not since the week of Crossing had she passed out so early. At that point she'd sworn never to miss a night again unless it was by her own choice. Clearly that hadn't been the case last night because she couldn't fathom the circumstances that would've led to her being in Tory's den of sin by her own will. *Not in this fuckin' lifetime.* She would love to have even a single memory of what happened right about now. The mystery surrounding how she got here was killing her almost as much as the headache was.

"Oh relax. Me and Riles didn't make it through our first alumni all the way either. Besides I don't know how far I would've gone if I'd split a bottle of SoCo with two of my pledge sisters before going out."

The memory of calling Angela over early in the day to help her finish a freshly opened bottle of Southern Comfort with her and Madison came flying back at just the mere mention of it. *And it seemed like such a good idea at the time.* Brynn had been making leaps and bounds in hanging out with her pledge class since Crossing. Angela had been the only real hold out since she was always with her Big Danielle but she'd caved yesterday too. She and Madison had convinced the girl to join them for some pre-gaming in the dorms before they went to EIPi.

From what she remembered it had been positive. *At the time it was.* The farther the memories went the more she could see the three of them talking and laughing although she couldn't remember any specifics.

"Did I tell you that?"

"Oh yeah we chatted on our way back from Arkridge last night" Tory smiled.

Just what the fuck is she so happy about? "You remember any of it?"

"Not a damn thing" Brynn replied unhappily, admitting defeat.

"Don't worry about it" Tory said, minimally hiding her disappointment. "It was nothing crazy. I think Angela might be worse off today than you."

"Then she must be dead too. At least I didn't suffer alone."

Brynn kept looking around to get her bearings. Turning her head for better viewing sent shooting pains through her body. There was a bulletin board near Tory's desk with pictures full of her and Riley. There was a poster-board in the corner with half naked men just as expected.

"You need help getting back to the dorms?" Tory asked genuinely. It sounded so sincere that Brynn nearly lost her newfound footing as she attempted to stand.

"No I'm good," she stammered. "I'm just gonna go back and sleep 'til Wednesday. Tell Felicia she's awesome and I'll miss her."

"When she gets back from lunch with Riles I'll let her know. They swung by here earlier to see if you were in any condition to go…and you weren't. But if you leave now then you'll miss Sunday-Funday."

Brynn shook her head slowly. The pain continued. "Never…ever…ever again" she answered unhappily.

Tory started laughing. "There's another thing I should collect money for hearing. God knows I've said it enough…about a few things…"

Brynn smiled but it wasn't for being amused. *Now that I can believe.* "Alright… I'm gonna go…so thanks." The words tasted like acid. It felt unnatural.

"Wow don't hurt yourself Brynny" Tory replied gleefully.

Turning to the door, she made her way out of the room and started shaking her head instinctively again upon reaching the hallway. The sound of the bedroom door closing sent another sharp spike of pain bouncing around her head.

Brynn would've sold her soul for a real memory of last night.

****

Tory knew the second she heard the door hit its frame that it would definitely cause a little more pain in the headache Brynn was already feeling. *Clearly the girl hasn't mastered quietly leaving a room.* Tory had pretty much perfected the technique of a silent exit during freshman year. *I might as well be a fuckin' ninja.*

Even though Brynn claimed to not have any memory of the previous night it was hard for Tory to believe that completely. Not when the memory was so fresh for her.

Riley's Little may not have been obese by any stretch but it still wasn't easy to keep her propped up on the long walk uphill back to ElPi. The sorority house was the only option. Tory couldn't leave her in the dorms like she was. An RA would have a field day if they saw Brynn. They were already on the lookout for drunken acts like sex in the bathrooms and throwing up in the halls so they wouldn't hesitate to write her up for barely being able to stand. As nice as it would be to just drop her off and leave her so Tory could enjoy her night it wouldn't be right, at least in the strictest sense of the word.

Brian hadn't been at the Tau Chi party and Tory didn't want to go for a hat trick in that frat so her options were limited. That added to the fact that Riley didn't deserve to have her night cut short because of Brynn's lacking tolerance and she didn't have much choice in taking care of the girl. Brynn had been in a near catatonic state the entire walk down Arkridge Avenue until they reached Castle Lane. The girl had been breathing that whole time so Tory wasn't concerned. As they hit the corner of Castle and Arkridge Brynn finally started talking.

"You knowwwww. I used to be so sooooo scared of you…" Brynn slurred. At first Tory couldn't make out what the hell she was saying. *I should've drank more before I left.* Drunken minds could better understand each other. "But you aren't even like… that… scary" she continued.

"I don't know if I'd go that far" Tory tried defending her assistant pledge mom persona. *I scared the shit out of all six of you and you know it.*

Brynn nearly tripped on the uneven sidewalk as they made their way up College Curve, which cut directly through the campus and led to EIPi. After she regained her footing by simply leaning on Tory she finally replied. "Oh yeahhhhh? If I redid pledging it'd be so fuckin' different."

Tory laughed. "Why the fuck would you want to do it again?"

Brynn clearly hadn't been expecting that question because the look on her face was priceless. "You're right," she stammered. "When you're right, you're right…and you're fuckin' right."

"Right" Tory joked.

They walked in silence the rest of the way up College Curve. There were still plenty of sounds coming from all around them. Hadren Drive was a block away from EIPi and the Phi Thetas, ABI's and NDM's all lived there. By and large Tory couldn't stand the first two but the NDM's were kind of fun. The last time they'd had a four-way party with those girls it had been a great time. They were probably the sorority most similar to EIPi in Gladen Hills. *And still only an imitation.* Their parties were all still going strong even as Tory prepared to get Brynn to bed.

As they reached the bottom of the hill that marked the end of College Curve Brynn decided to become a human girl again. "Did you really have to be such a bitch though?" Even though she was slurring and falling over the question was sincere.

"Probably not but it was kinda fun actually" she answered honestly.

"See!" Brynn said, as if she'd just discovered treasure. "And you wonder why I don't like you."

I wasn't nearly a raving psychotic like our pledge moms last year. She should be thanking me, not hating me for giving her and the rest a hard time. Tory had gotten past pledging the second she'd done those shots in the third floor corner room. Once she'd definitely said yes to becoming a sister that was the end of it for her. No grudges, no hard feelings, just good times.

"That's ridiculous" Tory answered with an edge.

"If you'd just been nicer then we'd be friends" Brynn explained in her own way.

Tory shook her head. "You're absolutely right" she patronized the drunken girl. It didn't feel bad. She clearly didn't notice because Brynn smiled and thanked Tory for admitting as much. Tory took a deep breath. "I'm sorry I was mean to you during pledging" Tory said, trying to sound genuine.

Brynn turned to her while unwrapping herself from the crutch that Tory had been serving as. "See! Now what was so hard about that?" she asked innocently as if the apology had actually meant anything. Tory wasn't really sorry. They all went through a ton of shit during pledging, most girls didn't give a damn when it was done.

"Nothing at all" she humored her. "So are we friends now?"

"Sisters and friends" Brynn announced as she fell back onto Tory as if she'd been a pile of leaves in the fall.

It was only once Tory got the girl inside to lie down on the couch in her room and moved a bucket next to her that Brynn finally realized she wasn't in her dorm room. When she asked why, Tory had to explain that she was trying to avoid her getting written up. She kept quiet about the fact that she was sure she shouldn't be left alone now though.

"Just make sure if you have to throw up that you use this bucket" she motioned to the yellow one that she'd used herself just last weekend. "We don't have pledges to clean up the house anymore."

That lit up Brynn's face like a kid at Christmas. "Yeah! We don't have any fuckin' pledges because we mother-fuckin' crossed!" she yelled. Her voice could've probably been heard throughout the entire house. Not that it mattered since nobody was there at the moment. *Lucky them.*

"Hey Tory...I'm not keeping you from the party tonight am I" Brynn asked innocently enough that it melted her heart.

"Don't worry…the Tau Chis aren't much fun this semester." It was only a partial lie. It wasn't that they weren't fun they were just partying with them so much that it got old. *That's what happens when the social chair is fucking one of them all the time. And people get weird when I do shit like that.* Tory smiled through her veiled lie and sat in her desk chair. *I could always do some of that paper that was due last week…or I could just check Facebook until Brynn passes out.* With that she opened her laptop and went straight to the website.

After a few minutes checking Brian and Eric's profile pages Brynn talked again. "Seriously Tory…you can go back to the party…I'm completely fine."

That made her laugh. Pretty much every ElPi at one point or another and probably every person that drank had probably said those words. And each time, they were a lie. "There's no way I'm leaving you alone in my room. God knows what kind of damage a drunken Brynn Wells could do in here."

Brynn just nodded absently. "That's so true." After that she settled down onto her side and stretched out on the couch. The newly cleaned bucket was right next to her on the floor so it was easy to access. Once Tory was sure the girl was sleeping she moved over and gave her a blanket. She knew it got pretty cool in the house at night, even during the spring. Tory also moved her slightly so that Brynn was on her stomach.

Her mother had always warned her never to fall asleep that way when she'd been drinking because a person could potentially choke if they threw up in their sleep. She never really believed it but didn't want to take any chances. It was the same principle for using condoms although she never did. *It feels so much better without them…and there's no point now anyway.*

Tory went back to her desk and stared blankly at the screen for a few minutes trying to figure out what to do. It was still a little before ten so she could easily make it back out and have a good time. *Decisions decisions…*

Tory sat at her desk silently. The sounds of Brynn's footsteps had long since disappeared. She just hoped the memories came back to the girl before elections.

****

All things considered Riley actually felt pretty great by yesterday's standards. No overwhelming headache or feelings of shame that usually plagued her the night after a drinkathon. Not that last night had been tame by any means but she'd actually treated the whole thing like the marathon it was and made it 'til four in the morning because of it. The same couldn't be said for her Big. The look of regret that permeated her face all morning was clear as day. It made Riley smile every time she looked at her.

"I can't believe I stopped my own Little from getting laid" Felicia announced for the hundredth time.

Riley dropped the sandwich she'd been intently focused on and laughed. "It's fine. I'm sure Jerry will get over it." *It might take an hour or two but he'll come back.*

She'd called the couch in Riley's room almost the second she'd gotten back to Gladen Hills and she always followed through with that sort of plan. Jerry had stumbled through the EIPi house looking for Riley and likely a repeat of last week's breakfast. Unfortunately there was no way she was going to sleep with him with her big sister passed out mere feet away on the couch, hammered or otherwise.

"He wasn't happy when I wouldn't leave the room."

"You could barely walk let alone find another place to sleep…especially at that point so it's fine" Riley tried comforting her even though it was fun making her think it was solely her fault.

"It's just downright shameful" Felicia complained of herself. "This would never happen if I was still active."

Riley shrugged. "Yeah but that's only because you'd still have your own room and wouldn't need to sleep in mine. Besides, the one good thing about frat guys is they *always* give you a second chance for sex." They both agreed on that.

Felicia took another sip of coffee. "I miss this place so much" she said while looking around. "Not *this* feeling but just being here…having no real problems."

I can only imagine what it feels like driving back home from this place today…back to whatever real life is. The thought chilled her. She knew it probably wasn't nice or fair to talk Felicia into staying for at least lunch today but Riley didn't want her to leave. She was actually praying that the longer she stayed the likelier she'd be to start drinking and get stuck here another day. *God invented sick days for a reason.*

"You know how many times you said something like that last night?"

"Knowing me it was probably every fifth sentence," Felicia guessed. It was remarkably accurate.

Felicia finished off her sandwich after that while Riley did the same. They sat in their booth at the diner on University Grove for a minute before her Big decided to get down to business. "So with elections next weekend what's the plan Riles?" she asked abruptly. Dancing around topics was never her Big's style.

"I loved being pledge mom but it took up so much time. I'm glad it's over."

"I heard you were amazing at it." The look of pride was practically bursting out. "I'm an alum, I'm not dead. Even though it feels that way," she laughed. "I like to keep tabs on my tree. I didn't think you'd go through with taking a Little this semester either."

Riley always knew her Big would have an opinion on that considering Felicia had waited until the first semester of her senior year for that. She'd been pledge mom during her junior year the same as Riley. The following year when she pledged Felicia had been the president. Whether Riley wanted it or not, *that* was what was always expected of her.

"I'm a trailblazer like that, what can I say?" she joked, trying not to go on the defensive. She didn't want to justify the choice of taking Brynn when she did even if the reasoning behind it had at least been *a little* self-centered. With the way she'd gone about it now she'd have an entire year to spend with her Little whereas Felicia only had a semester and a month to hang out with Riley.

"So you're going for president right?" Felicia cut through the bullshit and went to the core of her thoughts.

It set Riley on edge. "I really want VP actually" she answered confidently. *That* put her Big on edge. "I'm not dealing with all that bullshit during my senior year Fels."

Being pledge mom had been great but it was so central to everything in EIPi *and* it took up too much time. The idea of stepping into that fire again for her final year was not attractive. Riley still wanted to be involved but not nearly to such a huge extent.

"What about treasurer then?"

Riley shrunk back in her seat at the mention of doing something so crazy. "And try to collect money from our sisters? Umm...fuck that," she said as cordially as she could. They both laughed and agreed. Treasurer had to be the most brutal and thankless job in *any* organization. Even now, she wasn't sure why Eric had ever signed up for it.

Once their laughter ceased they went to the counter to pay. Felicia took both their checks and covered Riley's food. She tried to stop her Big but she wouldn't hear anything of it. "I'm the one with a job now. I remember the finances of an active in that house so it's done."

After how much food she'd bought for her cousins with her meal plan it felt good that the universe was paying her back. The fact that it was coming from her big sister and not the ones that were actually using her parent's money was a hiccup but she ignored it knowing how stubborn Felicia could be.

Once they walked outside and the sunshine hit their faces Riley felt a moment of clarity wash over her. "Sometimes it doesn't feel like the same EIPi I joined. Like what it was when you were still active," she admitted.

Oddly it didn't take Felicia by surprise. "That's the thing about organizations like ours. How they are is so dependent on who's in them at any time…that when the people change the place changes. When I graduated it wasn't the same as when I crossed. It's not like that for anyone. Everything changes…but it's all really the same. You're still here" Felicia smiled warmly back at her. "Although your Little could use a higher tolerance." They both laughed again. It only made Riley sadder when she realized Felicia was about to leave Gladen Hills and her all over again.

"Just as long as it stays this much fun when I come back, I can deal with the other changes. They aren't all bad Riles."

Riley nodded. "That's why I want to stay on the E-Board actually…to make sure it doesn't change *that* much."

They walked to Felicia's car and got inside. There was a fair amount of traffic on the Grove today considering so many alums were anxious to get the hell out of town and back home to sleep off a weekend's worth of bad decisions. *Just like Felicia.*

"You won't have any problem getting that at least" her Big assured her. "But I still say president is the better move. They won't let you be pledge mom again so it's the next best thing." The light pushing would never stop and Riley didn't really want it to. It was just another piece of the puzzle that made Felicia who she was. Riley shot her a look of annoyance all the same. "Hey I'm just saying, it'd be nice to have another president in the tree" Felicia commented before starting the car.

Riley smiled. *Elections are next weekend. So much can change here in a week.*

****

Once he'd woken up from the long nap Eric only felt slightly better. He wasn't even sure he'd call what he just went through an actual nap so much as an extension of the previous night's sleep. He'd gone to bed around three in the morning after Jerry had said something about going to the EIPi house, which Eric wanted nothing to do with.

With his pledge brother gone and the rest of the alums just hanging around drinking out back he'd decided to call it a night. Calvin and Buttons had both called him a pussy when he said he'd be heading inside but that hadn't stopped him, much to their disappointment. Eric had woken up early enough in the morning to go to the bathroom but then he managed to find his way downstairs to see what was going on. People were awake and moving around but not much was actually happening so he hung out for a little and then retreated back to bed.

Somehow he'd managed to sleep straight through 'til five in the afternoon, which was unheard of when living at the AZXi house. He'd missed a few text messages but nothing important. Jake had said he was going back to sleep around one and to text him about their planned dinner tonight with Riley. Riley had also texted to confirm that plan. Dinner was still on for six tonight at Hanoran on Northwest. Getting there from Arkridge would be a pain but less so because it was so nice outside.

More often than not one of his two cousins would give him a swipe at the dining halls when they ate considering he didn't have a meal plan and they both did. He could pay Riley back by buying shots at the Midway or wherever and he usually did just that. Jake was usually just happy to see him so he never expected reimbursement.

Amazingly, Eric was the first one at Hanoran but Riley arrived a few minutes behind him. After she swiped them both through Eric got his own food and Jake's too.

The dining halls were only used sparingly by students on the weekends so the place was pretty dead today. Jake had gotten there about ten minutes behind the two of them, which was perfect since they were just sitting down with their food.

"You pick out my food again Biz?" Jake asked more cheerfully than Eric would've imagined given his lack of enthusiasm all weekend long.

"If you ate anything different then I wouldn't be able to but as it stands, it's a guarantee. Plain hamburger cooked medium, only ketchup, nothing else, side of fries." Eric finished so confidently that it must've been radiating from his face. His cousin was a severe creature of habit, which was probably why he was having such a hard time being single now.

"How are you doing Jake?" Riley asked warmly.

Eric noticed she looked pretty tired, which was probably a result of the weekend. If he remembered correctly he saw Riley and her big sister only briefly at the Midway last night but they really hadn't talked. Eric did specifically remember wondering where Tory was at that point though.

"Alright I guess" Jake answered hesitantly. It didn't really convince anyone.

"Eric said you were at the party last night. How was that?" she probed further.

"You missed it man, it was crazy at the bars last night" Eric chimed in happily.

Jake just smiled half-heartedly. "I'm sure I'll have more chances later."

"At least you have the guys to hang out with now," Riley said comfortingly.

"Yeah you're right" Jake conceded. "That bastard Jeff had a point." He might've called him a name but there wasn't any malice that Eric could detect. *That's a good sign.*

"Just chill on telling him that J, he's already full of himself" Eric joked.

"Like I didn't know that" Jake smiled again.

"I say you just let me kill the bitch so we can all move on" Riley offered with an evil grin. She'd acted the same way when both of them had broken up with their respective high school girlfriends.

"I'd hate to see you go to jail over killing a girl like her" Jake replied morbidly.

"Yeah but it'd be worth it" she continued grinning.

"I couldn't live with that and besides I don't think Jerry could or would continuously do the conjugal visit thing."

"Really Eric?" she asked, staring directly at him. She only seemed mildly annoyed, which was what he'd been planning on. He'd only told Jake to change the subject of their Kelly conversation during the previous night's party. It had done the trick and shut him up about his ex, at least for that moment.

"What?" Eric asked innocently. "I thought it was relevant." The look he got back from her didn't show any belief or amusement but he still doubted she was all that upset. "OK maybe not relevant but at least entertaining."

Jake cut in after that, just as Riley was softening a little bit. "Under the terms of our pact I'll say nothing except...yikes."

"I'm pretty sure that 'no judgment' was a part of that very agreement."

"Maybe but it's kind of hard not to" Eric pointed out.

"Plus you two were judging me and Kelly all to Hell anyways" Jake added. The mention of her name usually sent his cousin into a frenzy of sorts but he skated right by it without issue.

"So now Eric and I look like prophets" Riley chuckled haughtily.

Amazingly enough, they all laughed. It was the first time in a long time that Eric could actually remember the three of them just being together and not having any real drama on their plates. It felt good. He hoped it wouldn't be a one-time thing as much as a sign of things to come.

Time would tell.

Chapter 35

There they sat, the five most senior members of Alpha Zeta Xi. Three of them would be walking the stage to get diplomas in two weeks. The other two would be staying behind. For the life of him Calvin couldn't figure out which of the two groups was in a better position.

It was daunting but also exciting striking out and away from the bubble he'd built for himself and his brothers over the past four years. But there was also something enticing about staying in Gladen Hills. But that was all pointless to think about now. Change was here now. There was one thing Calvin was absolutely certain about though, and that was that as of right now, there was no place he'd rather be.

The AZXi president sat there just looking around the metallic structure they were bunkered in. The other four were laughing but Calvin wasn't paying attention.

The building they were in, if it could even be called that, looked almost identical to the way it had the last time he'd seen it. That was both a good and bad thing. It meant that it was still damn near unstable like it had been when it was deemed 'unsafe' two years ago but also it meant the memories were easier to see. The barn at the previous AZXi house was where all five seniors had pledged. That was where Buttons had thought to hide for the day. The barn held memories for them all, good and bad alike. For the rest of the actives it was just a place they'd heard stories about. Today, that lack of connection would keep the five seniors out of reach from the rest of the frat. No one would think to look for them here. *Well played Buttons.*

Calvin refocused on the moment after seeing a younger version of himself doing push-ups on the ground mere feet away. Brandon was standing above him with Petey off to the side yelling something Calvin had since forgotten. *Just another callout.* Most of them had blended together as the years passed.

Fortunately the guy's soccer team who currently rented their old house had neither the drive nor thought to use the barn for any thing other than storage, which was why there were still chairs back here. That was helpful since it meant the five of them wouldn't have to resort to sitting on the cold, uneven wooden floor. *If I never sit or lie on this floor again I won't feel deprived.* "This is it boys" he said proudly while lifting his cup. It was a full week after alumni weekend but the hangover from it had only just disappeared two days ago. He'd likely have one to match it tomorrow.

"Yup" Kevin agreed quickly. *Few words…no wonder J-Hood's his Little.*

The other three reciprocated. They knocked their cups together before drinking. They still had plenty of work to do to finish off the handle of whiskey Kev bought. The goal was to finish it between the five of them, which would likely amount to six or seven shots each. Calvin was good with that.

"I never thought we'd get rid of you guys," Jeff added sternly, holding back the burn of the whiskey like the veteran he was. It only bit Calvin lightly but he still made an inadvertent face. Jeff didn't even flinch.

"Please, you two bastards will be completely fucked without us" he motioned to himself, Kevin and Petey.

Jeff smirked casually. "Right right. My only real regret is that you aren't taking Guapo with you when you go."

"Eh wahhhh Buttons" Guapo cried sarcastically.

"What was your GPA again this year? 0.6 I think?" Jeff asked quickly.

"It was lower than that" Petey chimed in.

"0.5 was the magic number for our boy here" Kevin proclaimed happily.

Ganging up on Guapo was a cherished pastime for pretty much anyone that called himself an AZXi. Calvin could just add that to the list of things he'd miss when he left Gladen Hills. *It's gonna be a long list.*

"I'm still here!" Guapo defended himself giddily. It never seemed to bother the guy when people made fun of him. Knowing how he was it wouldn't have surprised Calvin to know that Guapo had been dealing with that kind of thing all his life. He'd likely gotten used to it long before pledging AZXi.

"That's because God hates me," Jeff added casually while pouring them all another round. He'd insisted they get no chasers and that was just now coming to bite them in the ass on their fifth round.

"At least you get to stay here another year man," Petey said almost sullenly.

Calvin's pledge brother was no doubt suffering through the same emotions that he was dealing with regarding exiting Gladen Hills. "Fuckin-A."

"Yeah but we all know why that is" Jeff answered somberly.

"One more year isn't bad" Kevin said, trying to comfort his own pledge brother. Calvin doubted it would do much good. He doubted Dana could even make much of a difference as far as Jeff was concerned on that score.

"Nah it could've been a lot worse" Jeff agreed while keeping his eyes down.

"There are far worse ways to get fucked over by this school," Guapo added, as if he would know about such things. The guy had consistently failed each semester with little to no repercussions surrounding his actions. He was even able to avoid STD's.

"I don't know about that" Jeff grinned. "I am stuck here with you."

After some more jabs between them they started reminiscing. From their own wild Bids nights to Crossing and having to finish that terrible bottle of vodka, the barn had a very lived-in feel, even two years removed.

After their fifth shot the alcohol was starting to settle in for each of them. Calvin's thoughts started swirling to subjects that would probably be best left untouched. "How do you guys feel about the elections tomorrow?"

"I'm liking my chances for VP re-election" Kevin replied sarcastically.

"No way Kev, you're fucked."

"You thinking there's gonna be trouble Gretman?" Petey asked.

He shrugged. "That depends if people accept their nominations." He stared directly at Jeff when he answered. Buttons knew what he was talking about.

"Biz versus J-Bro for president? Now that'll be a show," Kevin announced.

"Does Biz even want it?" Guapo asked. It was the first time in a while that Calvin could remember his brother actually showing any kind of interest in the E-Board elections of AZXi. He'd never wanted those positions and generally kept quiet at the elections surrounding them. Pledge-masters and social chairs were the ones he raised the biggest fuss about.

"That's the million dollar question," Calvin replied unhappily.

"It's not a question about what he wants" Jeff interrupted. "It's about what's better for the frat."

Here we go again. "I don't know if Biz sees it that way" Calvin confessed. He hoped it would settle Jeff down but he doubted it would.

"I know James wants it real bad" Kevin added.

"You think he'd do a good job?" Petey asked. They were talking as if neither of them could see the gears shifting in Jeff's head.

"Maybe he would but I think Eric would be better" Calvin responded confidently.

After everything he'd seen of his younger brother throughout the past semester and a half of him being treasurer he knew he could handle being president. Knowing he would have no say in AZXi active problems after elections, it made him feel better thinking Eric could step up. Whether or not Eric Saren followed through on that was another question entirely.

****

"We'll see if he steps up" Kevin replied. Jeff immediately saw through the bullshit. He wasn't any more convinced that Eric would make the move than he was.

"Guess so" Calvin said. The defeat in his tone wasn't close to hidden.

Jeff hadn't gone out of his way to talk to J-Bro regarding what position he wanted in the upcoming elections but he'd heard from Kevin among others that he was angling for president. Sure he'd done a decent job being the Rush chair for the Alpha Epsilons but that didn't necessarily mean he was a good fit to run the fraternity. James Brock had always struck Jeff as a guy who had joined a frat thinking he was better than everyone in it. He'd actually rallied against him during the formal blackball for the Alpha Gammas but he'd been lost among a sea of older guys that were scrambling to get the frat's numbers back up.

During the time the Alpha Gammas were being rushed AZXi's numbers were down into the mid-teens with a large graduating class on the horizon. Coming off a semester where they'd only gotten two pledges in Eric and Jerry, they were all concerned. Unfortunately with that kind of fear comes an unselective Rush and that's what landed them with a group of admittedly apathetic actives. Dylan and Jared had been the only bright spots in a group of nine who had come with that class. It didn't help that AJ and J-Bro were both angling for E-Board spots either. If Jeff ever stayed up at night worrying then those would be the things keeping him awake.

If Eric didn't step up then J-Bro would have a clear line to the presidency. That didn't sit well with Jeff Chester. Something felt wrong about having that guy run the frat. Calvin shared his thoughts but not nearly the amount that Jeff was feeling. They'd both laid their case at Eric's feet a few weeks ago to get him to at least consider the idea of being president but he wasn't satisfied with how it had gone.

"Fifty bucks says he accepts it" Petey said cheerfully.

"No shot" Kevin and Guapo said simultaneously. Jeff was inclined to agree with his pledge brothers. *We're so fucked if Petey pays that money out...*

Elections were three weeks away and it would take an idiot to not see how things were shaping up. He and Gretman had actually been on the same page for what felt like the first time ever in terms of getting things to where they should be. Unfortunately that meant it was going to be an uphill battle. Jeff wasn't unaccustomed to that type of thing, especially in AZXi. With a limited time frame to work with Jeff had actually approached Calvin. With the pledges crossed, Jeff's full attention was on the upcoming elections. He hadn't even fully decided if he wanted to run again or not but he was leaning toward yes. He knew that getting president or VP was out of the question given how many people were still questioning his tenure as pledge-master so he'd always assumed that secretary would be the best bet in terms of remaining on the E-Board. That meant he was likely going to have to run against AJ. Jeff liked the guy well enough and he was definitely fun to party with. They did coke every now and then and the kid almost bled black and gold. Even so, he couldn't shake the thought that AJ just didn't take things as seriously as they should be for an E-Board slot. *He won't do what needs to be done if he's elected.*

Fortunately Calvin had actually agreed about Eric needing to succeed him so they made time to chat with the kid about it. Today was the best time considering that next weekend they had a breakfast with ElPi planned and the following was alumni weekend, so there'd be no meeting at all.

The E-Board always met before the actual meetings and with Kevin again visiting home for the weekend that left him and Calvin alone to talk with Eric. Kevin wouldn't have likely cared one way or the other about what Eric chose to do so it was almost better he wasn't around.

Jeff had gotten up early today before wandering to Calvin's room immediately after getting dressed. He'd put on his AZXi jersey with a renewed sense of purpose. They'd exchanged small talk before driving up to campus together for the first time all year.

The AZXis always had their Sunday meetings at Lenthan Hall up near the Cordan library. It was the biggest building on campus and it housed almost half the lecture halls in Gladen Hills. They always met in the same room on the second floor: room three hundred. It was the closest room to the entrance they all used.

Their early arrival gave them time to prep what they would say to their brother. Eric was generally punctual so they'd had about ten minutes to talk through things before he got there. Those ten minutes flew by and before Jeff could even look at the clock again Eric was walking down the aisle between the desks toward them. The first thing he thought of was the guy's cousin and how he still had yet to go over all that shit he'd seen with his girlfriend during their Canada trip. He'd meant to deal with it so many times before but no time ever seemed right. *I'll have to deal with that later on my own. I can handle Raley alone.*

"Morning guys" Eric greeted them warmly as he took up his seat at the front table.

The president always stood at the lone podium that the professors used during classes. The VP, treasurer and secretary all sat at the rectangular table to the right of the president. The design was to have the Executive Board facing the rest of the frat who would sit in the assorted desks spread throughout the smaller rectangular room.

Once Eric sat next to Jeff at the table Calvin spun around a desk and sat on top of it so they could both face their younger brother. "Kev's home for his mother's birthday so it's just the three of us" Calvin announced without prompting.

"So what's on the agenda then?" Eric asked as he flipped open his notebook.

Jeff always found it weird that his handwriting was so damn illegible considering how often he wrote notes. *Hopefully a bus never hits the guy since none of us will be able to read his notes on who owes what.*

"We got elections in three weeks…" Calvin began.

It was clear to Jeff that he was going to dance around the issue and they didn't have time for that. The rest of the actives would start trickling in within a half hour. "What's your plan?" he interrupted Gretman.

"My plan?" Eric's eyes went from Jeff to Calvin and back.

"Yeah" Jeff reaffirmed.

"I just figured on being treasurer again" Eric replied, shrinking back into his seat.

"Fuck that" Jeff blurted out, instantly getting a look of judgment from Calvin.

Eric looked confused and uncomfortable.

"Why stop there?" Calvin asked diplomatically. It upset Jeff that Gretman had translated that well for him.

"I'm good at it man" Eric answered confidently. It was a rare moment for the guy to admit one of his strengths. It took Jeff by surprise.

"No question" Calvin agreed while Jeff found himself nodding as well. "But what about going a step up? We think you'd be a sick president."

Jeff smirked. *How about that? He actually said it.*

"Where the hell did this even come from?" Eric asked.

"Me and Buttons were going over next year's roster and we wanted to see where you stood," Calvin explained. "You know this is it for me Biz. Four more weeks and I'm done. Just like every other year we need the best brothers to step up and take control."

"I still want to be on the E-Board…that's good enough."

"Not by a long shot" Jeff interjected. He'd kept silent too long already.

"You know the E-Board is a team. You know that better than most of the frat because you've gone through it with us" Calvin added, quelling Jeff.

"Why can't Buttons do it?"

"I'll be lucky to keep secretary after all the shit that happened with the pledges this semester" Jeff replied. The words tasted like week-old beer on their way out. He hated admitting defeat but he knew which way the wind was blowing. That coupled with the fact that he wasn't sure he could even handle another loss at the presidency to match the one last year made him angry beyond words.

"I think it still worked out" Eric responded.

Whether he believed that or if he was just trying to keep himself out of the fire was completely up in the air. Fortunately neither of them cared. "Yeah but shit still happened. Whether or not it worked out...there was still a problem that needed to be worked out," Calvin clarified.

Eric nodded although it looked like it killed him to do so. "I'm taking too many three hundred level classes next year...there's no way I could pile on being president to all that" he confessed.

"I took a lot of classes this year too Biz. I got through it."

"International relations isn't biochem or even physics, no offense."

Jeff nodded. There was no doubt on that and even Gretman agreed. Jeff's major was harder than Calvin's and even that couldn't touch what was on Biz's plate. That aside, he had no doubt that if anyone could balance the two lifestyles it was going to be Eric Saren. He'd known that since the moment they'd talked during Rush two years ago.

"Yeah, so you keep telling us" Calvin added levity to the increasing tension.

"I just don't think Brock is going to be that bad," Eric said plainly.

"James is going to be a train-wreck. He was when he was pledging. He was when he crossed. He doesn't give a fuck about this frat; it's all just a means to an end."

"J-Bro isn't that bad. He doesn't party with us much but that doesn't make him a bad brother. Plus he's willing to step up" Calvin stated calmly. Jeff wasn't sure if that comment was designed to spur something in Eric or just counter what he'd said but it didn't have much effect either way. "That being said," he continued. "*You* are the one I want in this position."

Eric looked speechless. He'd had the same dumbfounded look pretty much since he'd sat down. *There's no way he was ever expecting to have this conversation.* "I'll think about it guys" he responded timidly before getting up from the table and heading toward the door he'd come through earlier.

As soon as he was out the door Jeff could feel Calvin's eyes staring knives through him. "A little less being an ass might help" Calvin immediately accused him.

Jeff was undeterred. "Oh come on. He's the better choice and we both know it so why dance around the fucking obvious."

Calvin didn't look convinced.

They sat there in limbo until Eric got back and by then most of the frat had arrived. Any follow-up would have to wait for a different time.

Jeff grimaced as they did their next shot. The time for the three of them to talk again had never come. Knowing Eric like he did, that was probably by design. *Adding Raley's cheating whore girlfriend into the mix sure as hell didn't help either.* That had taken precedence over any follow-up that Jeff might've been able to have with Eric. It was partially his own fault, which only pissed him off more. Tomorrow would be the end of it…one way or another. The chips would fall and there'd be a new E-Board when they left Lenthan Hall.

****

The entirety of the frat stood before him not unlike a general facing his troops, even his cousin Jake had made the trip over from Northeast to join the fun. *Thank God J-Hood brought him. Today isn't about him though, it's about the seniors.* It was weird standing up front with all the actives looking at him, Jerry and James. It almost felt like a meeting except they weren't at Lenthan. At least during those times he'd had Calvin there to take the lead. He could just sit back and worry about his treasury notes while Calvin and Kevin took care of the big issues. The uncertain future gave him pause. *Worry about now.*

"Alright! I doubt they're in any building up on campus" Eric announced loudly.

"But we've gotta check them anyways" Jerry added.

Eric nodded. He believed in being thorough even if it amounted to a waste of time. "Jer is gonna take a group up to check Cordan, Lenthan and the auditorium. The rest of the buildings should be locked." *I hope so at least…*

"Everyone keep your cells on, they're our walkie-talkies today" Jerry reminded everyone while moving away to gather willing participants for the drive to midtown.

"Dills, Segs, Raley, you down for a ride?" Jerry asked the three nearby.

"Count me in Jer-Bear" Brent answered.

"Shotgun" Jake chimed in, more upbeat than Eric would've expected.

"Let me finish this one first" Dylan replied before slamming the beer in his hand in two seconds flat. Then he nodded and followed them all out the backdoor to where Jerry had his car parked.

"What're we gonna do bro?" Jared asked giddily once the four had left.

Eric turned from him and poured over the map of Gladen Hills that James had picked up that morning. Having an aerial view of the playing field would allow for a better plan even though they all knew the town in its entirety. It took only a few seconds of staring at the buildings and houses off campus for Eric to decide on a course of action. "Alright guys, I want everyone to get out their phones and call any sorority girl that owes you a favor. All you want to know is if there are any AZXis in or around their house. Only call the ones you can trust. Stick to the girls that we would know better than the seniors. We don't want them getting tipped off."

Jared just started smiling before nearly ripping his pants to pull out his phone. "Good call Biz."

"That's what it takes to be a science major these days pal" Aaron chimed in as he prepared to make a call. *It's too bad none of us can call Jennifer...but would she even know where they are?* They might be better off calling a girl that wasn't close with Jennifer. Considering the Betas weren't exactly a tight-knit group that left a lot of possibilities. For the first time in the history of his life Eric actually wished that Guapo was there considering he'd banged enough of them to warrant getting a number or two. Eric wasn't entirely sure if Guapo fucking one of them was more or less likely to get a girl to help though.

"I've got EIPi!" he announced in case anyone was thinking otherwise. There wasn't a person in the room who could boast a better inside connection to that sorority than he could. "Who's got the Betas?"

Funnily enough most of the brothers immediately looked to Jared as a joke considering he was the last one they'd help. Considering they banned him from their house for whatever happened with Jake on Bids Eric found it funny.

"I got it" J-Hood declared in his usual serious tone. Nobody questioned it and they moved on down the list of the other sororities on campus.

"What about the DXA's?"

"I've got a friend there Eric" James answered stoically from his spot beside him.

"Nice, thanks Brock."

From the ABI's to the Phi Thetas on down to the NDM's and the Sig Lamb's there was at least one active that had some kind of 'connection' they figured they could milk for information.

"Let's get to it so we can find the seniors and drag their asses back here to finish that keg!" he yelled cheerfully. It felt simultaneously liberating and frightening to be front and center in such a way but he tabled his reservations for the time being.

"Right because we all know how Biz hates wasting alcohol" Aaron joked.

If you only knew how true that was today pal. Eric just smiled before hitting send on his phone listing of Riley's name. As he listened for the ringing over the constant chatter radiating off the walls of the basement a thought popped into his head.

Suddenly he knew where the seniors were before his cousin picked up the phone.

****

"Come on Eric. Of course they aren't here. I'd hope by now they know I'm your cousin." Even as Riley said the words she wasn't sure how many of the ill-conceived guys down at AZXi really had the mind to let a fact like that sink in. Fortunately her cousin glossed right over that fact. From the sound of it he had something else on his mind. "Yeah I'll give you a head's up if I see Jeff or any of the others." After that they said their goodbyes and hung up.

Eric had listed off the names of those hiding today for their Senior Day but Riley hadn't really recognized any of them. They were just names to her. She couldn't really say she'd recognize them even if she ran into them. She knew who Jeff was so she figured he'd be with the other guys in question. She'd heard the name 'Guapo' mentioned a few times since a few of her sisters had slept with him but he was more of a phantom presence.

"Are the AZXis doing their Senior Day today too?" Danielle asked. Her tone seemed to suggest that EIPi should have a monopoly on such a thing. Riley ignored it. Most organizations waited until today to do some kind of send-off for the graduating class. It made sense since it was the last weekend before the final full week of school that included finals.

"It looks like it" she replied. "We'll probably have to see some kind of stupid frat shit today." She kept her tone condescending even if she didn't feel that way.

"How so?" Brynn asked innocently from her place on the couch.

It was no mystery that Tory wasn't present considering what Riley wanted discuss had to do with both of them supporting her best friend. By now Riley was more confident in Danielle's ability to support Tory than she was Brynn's. There wasn't much she could say one way or the other that hadn't already been said. "Nothing too bad" she replied to her Little. It dawned on her after a second that Brynn had never experienced a Senior Day in Gladen Hills. "We just might have to witness my cousins tackling seniors and dragging them off somewhere…the usual" she answered as casually as possible.

"Wow…that sort of shit actually happens?"

"Not too often actually but don't let that fool you. They all love this kind of stuff. Any chance to be immature is gold." She did her best not to look down on that kind of thing especially since her younger cousin could use some of that behavior these days.

"You jealous?" Brynn asked immediately.

"Yeah kind of" Riley replied, equally fast.

All three smiled. There was something to be said for just not giving a damn and running around chasing your friends like the kids they sometimes were.

"So what exactly is the plan today?" Brynn asked.

"Same as always" Danielle answered. "Just get the seniors hammered."

"Wow you really meant 'same as always'?"

Riley smiled again. It sounded similar on paper but any upper class EIPi would know how important today was. "Today is special," she explained. "This is the senior's last real EIPi event to drink with all of us at while they're active." The depressing nature of the statement really sunk in as Riley was saying it. That wasn't lost on either Danielle or Brynn.

"Fuck that's sad" Brynn said with all the tact of her years.

"You're not gonna get emotional when it's your turn are you?" Brynn challenged playfully. Riley didn't even want to think about that right now but since it had been asked it was hard to keep it from processing.

"I think I'll be fine" Danielle replied.

"You better prep yourself because I'll cry like a little girl." It was partly meant as a joke with the other part designed as a prediction. She knew herself well enough to know that when the day came for her to leave Gladen Hills behind like Felicia had she was guaranteed to cry.

"Oh good…something to look forward to" Brynn responded, dripping sarcasm.

"You better lock it up girl. There'll be plenty of waterfalls today from the seniors. It can get pretty messy." Riley's thoughts were focused squarely on how she'd felt when Felicia's turn had come. *That was a sad freakin' day...*

"There's zero chance I'm crying when I graduate" Brynn assured them.

Riley made a mental note to try to be present during that time even if she'd be two years graduated by then. *I don't buy that for a second Brynn, everybody cries here at some point.* "Those are big words coming from a lowly freshman" Riley retorted.

"It's hard to remember back that far" Danielle grinned even though she was only a sophomore.

"Jesus that makes me feel old" Riley confessed, hoping for someone to disagree.

"Relax Riles, you're only a year past me, it's not like you're my mother or something." Danielle answered her silent pleas.

"I appreciate that Dani" Riley smiled at her niece.

The door to her room swung open and in sauntered Tory Brye. *Only she could enter a room in a blur like that.* "Time to saddle up girls, the seniors want to start now. We apparently have some of a keg left over from last night," Tory yelled at them. Thankfully she left any questions she might've had about not being invited to their meeting unsaid.

"Who's on cleanup?" Riley immediately asked, fearing the answer.

"Let's cross that bridge when we get to it" Tory replied happily while failing to answer the question. *Classic Tory.*

"We'll be at that bridge tomorrow and I'm not dealing with it" Riley swore in front of the three witnesses. Even with that promise she still had a sinking feeling she'd end up being the one to spearhead anything of consequence tomorrow.

Seven shots later with an eighth in their cups and the five of them were feeling phenomenal. Calvin knew they'd eventually have to leave but he didn't want to be the one to suggest it even though the handle was now gone. Pretty much all the fun of senior hazing was based on the concept of the seniors running from the rest of the actives. That couldn't happen without abandoning their admittedly awesome hiding spot. He'd already complimented Buttons more on the idea than he probably had in the entire time he'd known the guy so he was fighting the urge to add to that number.

The final shots were still sitting in their cups even as they started to move around the barn. It was being used for furniture storage although from the look of everything most of the shit inside would be better served in a landfill rather than awaiting use. The floor was still uneven in most spots so they stayed close to the door where the floor was still somewhat supported. For bathroom breaks they just pissed in the corner where the floor gave way to the muddy ground beneath. Once they'd all gone through their favorite memory from the barn Jeff raised his cup. "To Alpha Zeta Xi boys" he said, trying to keep his balance.

"Hell of a run" Calvin added.

"Speak for yourself" Guapo said from right beside him, grinning like an ass.

"Well some of us actually wanted to graduate on time" Kevin joked.

Calvin winced at the comment if only because he wasn't sure how it would affect Jeff. It was always hard to tell how he would take things meant as jokes. Fortunately he let that one pass without incident even though Calvin couldn't help but stare while waiting for the inevitable explosion.

"Sounds beat as fuck to me" Guapo answered.

"I hate that I'm jealous of you for the first time in my life" Petey replied.

"It was bound to happen…especially when you aren't getting pussy!" Guapo chanted loudly. They were all raising their voices in an effort to outdo the others around them. Even Calvin fell victim to it. Fortunately the barn was far enough back from the main house that the soccer guys therein wouldn't care.

"Here we go again" Buttons rolled his eyes. "It's all about getting laid."

Calvin guessed that was meant to sound like an insult but Guapo would never take it as such. "Gotta stick to what's important," the guy continued grinning.

Calvin just shook his head laughing. "God you're so damaged."

"Alright let's do this" Jeff announced sternly. He was clearly getting impatient that they had shots left. And with that they all went along and drank the final remnants of alcohol in the barn.

"OK so what now?" Kevin asked as he reached behind him to find his chair. It almost looked like he was going to fall, which would no doubt have fucked up the floorboards even more. Fortunately he found the chair and avoided the tumble Calvin had feared, and at the same time had excitedly been awaiting.

"I've got another bottle," Jeff announced as he threw the cup toward the back of the barn. It was plastic so it couldn't break anything but Calvin still felt weird about littering in a place that wasn't theirs.

"It's back at the house though" Calvin interjected before Jeff could say the same.

"Your point Gretman?" Jeff challenged.

"There's no damn way you get into the house to get that bottle and then back here without any of the actives seeing you."

"I have no problem staying in here all day as long as there's alcohol but since we're out we need more. I figured the actives would be smart enough to search this place by now but here we are." Calvin detected a hint of happiness in the fact that they hadn't been found yet. It was shocking that they hadn't been attacked but at the same time it had given them all time to chill and simply enjoy the moment.

"I could use some fresh air anyways" Petey exclaimed happily. Clearly he was on board. One by one they all agreed, and the plan was set.

"Try not to get caught guys" Jeff joked as he reached for the door handle.

All four of them turned to Guapo immediately since he was the least athletic. "What?!" he asked, faking surprise. "I've got a plan."

Calvin wasn't even remotely convinced but at the same time he didn't much care. Right now he had no problem feeding Guapo to the actives to make sure they weren't losing focus on their goal today. *Sometimes you gotta shoot a hostage.*

Jeff opened the door and the sunlight hit all of them immediately. It took a few seconds for them to adjust, hurting all the while. There was no overhead lighting in the barn since it didn't have power currently so the only way they saw what they were doing was by way of the broken rotted roof letting daylight creep through in patches.

"OK let's move" Jeff whispered as he led the way.

"What're you whispering for?" Calvin asked in his usual voice. Gladen Hills wasn't a big town by any means but it was still big enough that he felt safe using his normal voice outside.

"Gotta be stealthy about this pal," Jeff commented almost happily as he ducked low and made his way over to far side of the barn. It looked like his plan was to cut through the smattering of woods separating the TAS (townie apartment section) and Arkridge Avenue.

Calvin grinned. *The actives will never look for us back here.*

Chapter 36

Most non-affiliated undergrads knew better than to hit up the midtown bars on the final weekend of school. That left everything pretty much open for the sororities and frats to use at their leisure. Groups like the Phi Thetas got all dressed up like it was a date party on steroids to have dinner at the Gladen Grove Hotel. As far as Riley was concerned they could have it. There was a bar there too but it was more expensive than any other in Gladen Hills and they had a certain standard overall which prohibited any sloppiness. Riley always just looked at it like they didn't want anyone to have any real fun, which is why she tended to steer clear of the place.

Most of their seniors had wanted to go to the Cradle to start. They'd all left the EIPi house together in one giant forty-girl parade. If anyone had been in the Cradle when they'd rolled through they'd since had the good sense to close their tabs and clear out.

Generally speaking, most bystanders didn't want to be around them when they were getting drunk and crazy, unless they joined in. With Tory off talking to Amy, and Brynn with her own pledge class Riley was sitting at the counter with Danielle and Rachel, the latter of whom was graduating a year early for some unholy reason. "This is one of the last times I'll ever wear our letters" Rachel said solemnly yet still loud enough to be heard over the shouting and laughing around the bar.

Riley rolled her eyes in the direction of the bar rack so that neither Danielle nor Rachel could see. "Come on Rach not this early" she pleaded.

"Hey it's my day and I'll get completely depressed if I want to."

Riley couldn't argue. *It's their day. It's their day.* "You're the boss."

Rachel smiled back while taking a sip from her rum and diet coke. "Glad you can finally admit that" she answered haughtily.

"I don't think Riles ever had a problem following your lead Rach" Danielle interjected in defense of her aunt.

Rachel shook her head. "I don't know, seemed like a problem sometimes."

Damn, I thought I did such a good job hiding that too.

Following the presidency of a girl who'd pledged the semester *after* Riley had been tricky. It was a little easier for her since she held the other top spot of pledge mom at the same time. For Felicia and the older girls, there were times it still felt weird, even if most of them had already graduated. "OK let me make it up to you then" she offered as she motioned for the bartender. "Three SoCo limes please."

"Are you trying to get me drunk or something?" Rachel asked incredulously.

"No no no. Drunk was five minutes ago. Now I'm shooting for hammered."

"It's her specialty" Dani explained cheerfully to her pledge sister. "It's a good thing she isn't a bartender otherwise we'd be dead."

"Oh come on!" If the looks Danielle and Rachel were giving back to her were any indication then they definitely didn't believe that for a second. "OK fine, but at least it's always fun with me."

"That I'll give you" Dani agreed kindly.

The bartender finished mixing up the shots and subsequently placed the three of them in front of the girls. Riley handed one to Dani and one to Rachel, keeping the final one herself. "OK let's do this…it's gonna be a long day."

"Riles I can't wait 'til you're graduating, it should be an eye opening experience" Rachel commented dryly. *That was a little bitter.* Riley let it go. *It's their day…*

"No more sentiments girls, at least not 'til later. We have another marathon on our hands today. This is only the first bar of the five. Shots up!" As usual the shot went down smooth and easy. As far as alcohol was concerned the one thing that she and her two cousins could agree on was that Southern Comfort was the best. It generally went down without issue.

Not two seconds after they put back down their empty plastic shot glasses a group of Beta Zetas grabbed Rachel from her bar stool and demanded that she help them with the ice runoff race that was about to start at one of the tables. Rachel went along with them even though she pretended they were forcing her. Brianna motioned for Danielle to go with them, which would've left Riley relatively alone but she didn't accept for whatever reason. Riley reached down and took another sip of her own diet sprite vodka. She was getting nostalgic because of Rachel's comment about her own impending graduation. Maybe that was the girl's intent all along, she couldn't say.

"One more year Dani" Riley announced calmly.

Danielle just shook her head in what looked like mild-confusion. "I didn't think I'd ever get to see you get depressed like this…at least until you were closer to where Rach is."

"Well I don't like to broadcast it but I do actually have feelings too."

"I'm sure you do Riles."

Riley lifted up her cup to make Danielle do the same. "Pledge mom Dani…I'm gonna be so proud of you if you get it." That comment elicited a look of confusion mixed with mild condescension so Riley corrected herself quickly. "OK *when* you get it." That got Danielle back to an even stance.

"Thanks sis" her niece answered evenly.

"It's a good thing you've got me to show you everything you'll need to know."

"Yeah about that…" Danielle began before Angela grabbed them to play flip cup on a row of tables they'd just lined up.

****

"Summers just called. He said the seniors were running up College Curve to University Grove" Jake announced. That perked up everyone in the car. Jerry immediately pulled into the nearest parking lot to make a U-turn in that direction. "He said they caught Petey in the woods behind the TAS and Arkridge. They're bringing him back to the house now. Buttons and Kevin should be coming up our way."

Dylan's phone rang; Larry was on the other end relaying the same information Jake had already gotten from Summers. "You're sure you saw Buttons and Kevin heading to midtown?"

"Is that them?" Jake practically yelled as he pointed to two figures sprinting up the sidewalk heading into the residential area.

Dylan nodded. "Got 'em," he relayed before hanging up.

Jerry gunned his Camaro into the nearest parking spot on University Grove. They sat in the car for a second as the two seniors came closer and closer to where they'd parked behind a row of cars, which somewhat obstructed the view. *Fish in a barrel.*

"If we run at them they're going to split up," Brent predicted.

"True. You and Dills take Kevin, he's not as fast as Buttons" Jerry ordered.

"That means me and you take Buttons?" Jake asked.

Jerry nodded. "That's not a problem is it?"

Jake smiled back in what he could only assume looked like the Cheshire cat. "None whatsoever. I've waited a long time for this." His other problems seemed like distant memories.

"I know you were half-assing it during that mile run on Hell Night so just bring your A-game and we'll get him" Jerry smirked. He surveyed the car's occupants and smiled as widely as Jared normally did. "Let's go to work boys."

Thankfully there was no parking meter payments needed on the weekend so they all jumped out of the car and made a mad dash toward the two seniors. Just as predicted the two immediately jolted in opposite directions. Jeff headed toward the bars further down the Grove and Kevin ran toward Northwest.

While he and Jerry were chasing Buttons Jake saw a car pull up next to Kevin as he was running down the sidewalk from Dylan and Brent. Out of the car jumped his Big Jared. He tackled Kevin to the pavement with almost perfect timing. They rolled around a little bit as Kevin tried to escape but the other two actives were on him too quick. They all surrounded the senior, picked him up and threw him into the backseat of the car, jumping in after him. The car then took off down College Curve. Jake laughed as he ran after his former pledge-master. *That would've looked like a kidnapping if anyone was paying attention.*

"Son of a bitch is fast," Jake panted as they ran.

"That's why we're chasing him" Jerry exhaled sharply.

Buttons made his way to the end of the Grove and made a hard right onto Croftlin Rise toward the residential area. If Jake was right then back here there were actual normal non-college people mixed in with some off-campus housing. Hopefully they'd be OK with the shit-show coming their way.

****

The flip cup game had been quick. It actually was a little unsatisfying in that way. Of course by the time it was done Riley's old barstool was occupied by Amy who was talking to Danielle. They'd just sat down. Fortunately there were two empty stools on the end by the front windows that she and Tory could use.

They couldn't have been sitting for more than a few minutes, having just barely ordered their next round. Out of nowhere a blur shot by the window. *That kind of looked like Jeff.* Riley instinctively moved to call Eric. She wanted to let him know she might've seen Jeff when two more blurs shot by in pursuit. That time there was no mistaking the two. *Jerry and Jake.*

Tory had seen them too. "Weren't those...?" she started to ask before Riley cut her off immediately while subtly putting her phone back into her pocket.

"No...no they were not" she assured her friend. She took a large sip from the SoCo and diet coke she ordered in an attempt to move past what had just happened. Tory knew what she'd seen but was quietly keeping that to herself since she wasn't the only one to see the flashes of dumb frat guys sprinting by. Riley would just as soon not confess that she was sleeping with one of them and related to another. Fortunately Tory had her own issues that she wanted to talk about. It was painfully obvious for Riley to see even though she hadn't said anything up 'til now.

"So it all comes down to tomorrow and I'm just telling you Riles, if Amy runs then I'm fucked" she blurted out. *Well that would definitely complicate things since the Beta Zetas would definitely vote with her and give twelve votes away. Depending on what Brynn and the Beta Thetas do that could be almost half EIPi against T.* There were only forty-three actives and three weren't allowed to vote so eighteen being all for one person would certainly be a challenge for her best friend.

"Didn't you and Brynn like bond over alumni weekend?"

"Yeah we did but I don't think that your Little remembers any of it…and I can't really blame her, she was pretty fucked up."

"Felicia would be so proud" Riley joked. Tory wasn't laughing. An E-Board slot was something she wanted more than anything Riley could remember. It was almost unnerving how driven she was. *If she were like this in class she'd easily have the highest GPA in EIPi.*

"Can't you just talk to her so she stops hating me?"

"Please. If I had that ability then you'd be paying me for it."

In truth Brynn was as stubborn as they came and Riley wouldn't have any better luck convincing her to do something than the girl's own parents would. Not that she ever talked about her parents or home in general. She was like Tory in that way. *One day I'll get them both to spill it all.*

"What does that even mean Riles?"

"It means with how many people around here that find you a little too much to deal with…a publicist probably wouldn't be a bad idea" she replied sarcastically. The alcohol must've been getting to her because her words sounded cruel.

"Do I have a problem or something?"

"Hell no. You're way too entertaining for it to be a problem" Riley joked.

Truthfully there were plenty of EIPi girls who were similar to Tory in that they hooked up with a lot of guys. The main difference between her and them was that Tory tended to flaunt that ability whereas the other girls, even if they thought that way, at least pretended to be ashamed when the truth came out. It kept the girls who weren't sleeping around in check. Tory Brye on the other hand, just didn't give a fuck. Riley could see how that could be intimidating to other girls, in EIPi or not, but she never found a way of explaining that to her best friend. It didn't bother her so she never brought it up but still knew it was a problem in EIPi. Tomorrow it would shine brightly, especially if she was up against Amy. *Another Beta Zeta going for an E-Board position.* Riley always found it to be more than a little weird that

Danielle seemed to be almost in control of that particular voting bloc even though she was among the youngest in the group. Amy, Brianna, Jessie and Rachel were all older and yet they all loved Dani.

"Listen T, we just have to go with it at this point. Whatever happens happens."

"The words I live by" Tory smiled but there was only so much happiness.

"I'm personally a fan of 'let's get drunk' myself" Riley grinned back.

That time Tory smiled with more conviction. "I like it…simple, easy to remember. Might as well be the school motto."

****

They knew he was out here, and they were getting closer with each step. *Petey must've sold me out, the drunk bastard.* Multiple thoughts were going through Calvin's mind as he hid under the brush in the woods that he; Guapo and Petey had run into. They'd made it all of thirty feet from the barn before the actives were on them. Kevin and Buttons had run toward midtown while the rest of them had made for the safety of the woods. *It should've been safe.* Petey hadn't been as fortunate. Calvin never would've predicted in a million years that Guapo would've outlasted his pledge brother during senior hazing. And yet Petey had been tackled and captured by a couple new fucks and seasoned actives, thrown into a car and taken away. Unless he planned on pulling off some kind of daring rescue plan then Petey would rot there. Of course if he'd given up the locations of Guapo and himself as they took him then that would be far too lean a punishment. *Why the fuck did we talk about where we'd hide back here?*

Eric and Aaron were being relatively quiet while keeping their focus all around. Clearly they were hoping for Guapo or himself to make some kind of break for it and give away their position. Guapo had done just that even though he'd done so about ten minutes ago. That was what had landed the younger guys deeper in the woods than Calvin had hoped. He figured Guapo was still somewhere close by but had no way of knowing for sure. Calvin knew his best chance, especially back here where he couldn't run full speed was to hide. Fortunately with all the snowfall Gladen Hills got year after year there was plenty of brush to hide in. If anyone other than Eric Saren had been out searching he would've given himself a better chance of not being discovered but that particular active was a meticulous one.

Suddenly he heard a bunch of sticks and leaves breaking and crackling under the footfalls of someone very nearby. Calvin prepared to run. He was almost about to take off but realized it was just Jared joining the search.

"Raley and Jerry are chasing Buttons through midtown. We've already got Kevin and Petey back at the house," he announced, panting slightly. He was reporting in to Eric like the latter was commander of their ragtag army. *And this is the guy who doesn't think he can be president?*

"Who's watching them?" Eric quickly asked, looking for more details.

"J-Bro, Segs, Dills…almost the rest of the frat. But J-Hood drove back up to the Grove to help with Buttons" Jared reported.

Eric nodded, clearly liking what he'd been told. "Good, they'll need a car to get his ass back down to Arkridge."

If Kev and Petey are back at the house and Buttons is up on the Grove then that means nobody knows where the fuck Guapo is. Did the son of a bitch actually have a plan? Calvin wasn't sure how he'd react if Guapo outlasted the rest of them today. It was always actives versus the seniors but something would feel hollow about the victory if Guapo were the one to get it for them. He shook the thoughts from his head. He and Buttons were still OK…for now.

"Guapo and Gretman ran back here after we got Petey," Aaron added afterward.

The three actives split up, heading in different directions. Of course the closest to him was Eric. *It fucking figures.* He was getting closer and closer to the fallen tree that Calvin had concealed himself under. With the help of some branches and leaves he was fairly confident that most of his body was covered well enough. The closer his brother got the less sure he became until finally he leapt up to grab Eric. Calvin twisted him around so that his left arm was around his back. If he pulled it too far it would hurt like hell. Eric was smart enough to know when he was outmatched so he didn't fight.

"Whoa!" he shouted, as if all the movement hadn't alerted the other two already. Aaron and Jared appeared in front him quicker than he would've expected.

Once he had their attention Calvin started speaking. "Alright boys this is how it's gonna go: you're gonna give me a twenty second head-start from here by backing the fuck off or I'll snap the kids arm" he threatened. Thankfully they were far enough back in the woods that no one else could see them because otherwise it would've looked extremely weird. His admittedly hollow threat wouldn't have helped make it look any less so either. Jared and Aaron looked unconvinced but still took slow steps backward. When they were far enough Calvin started moving away with Eric in tow.

It was at that point that he saw Guapo run off from a layer of brush thirty feet behind where Calvin had been hiding. *Was he there the whole time? Damn him.* Guapo cut a swath through the woods by the time Jared yelled the word 'twenty'. With that he nodded at Aaron and took off after Guapo. Even with a head start it was unlikely that Guapo could evade Jared for long, even back here.

"Why would he run back toward the house?" Aaron asked anybody that had an answer. Eric shrugged. Calvin couldn't think of a good reason either.

"That wasn't part of the deal."

The three brothers formed an uneasy truce for a few seconds as they just stood there sizing up their next moves. Eric was helpless but Aaron was always a wild card who tended to be crazier than most other actives combined. It wouldn't surprise Calvin even slightly if he did something unconventional. Even so, Calvin stared right back at Aaron, warning him again not to come any closer. Of course none of them believed he'd actually hurt Eric so Aaron didn't pay much attention to the warning. He edged along after Calvin as he moved backward with his hostage.

"Yeah you're right" he answered the silence and Aaron's unlikely thoughts. "I'd hate to have Eric's broken arm on my conscience too." Calvin continued moving back through the woods. Finding his footing was tricky. With how many shots he'd done on top of the uneven ground the whole concept was fucked.

Abruptly his heels hit another downed tree and for a split second he looked backward and saw how big it was so he could judge his steps. He noticed a huge pile of dead leaves on the other side of it. Unfortunately Aaron must've noticed it too because before Calvin could turn back around he felt the force of a body hit both him and Eric, driving them both to the ground into the leaves. He lost his hold on Eric. Both he and Aaron were on him in seconds, wrestling until Calvin was pinned.

"It was a good try Gretman" Eric complimented. It had a hollow feel. *Guapo used me for an escape just like I planned on using him. Well played.*

"I wouldn't say it's over Biz…how the fuck do you expect to get me out of here and back to the house?" he asked. The look on Eric's face clearly showed he knew he had a point. The kid looked over their current situation. He was pressing down Calvin's left arm and leg with his whole body and Aaron was holding down his other side. If either moved then it would give him the chance he needed to break away.

"It's OK Biz, I got this" Aaron assured him as he moved to Calvin's stomach to basically lie on top of his entire body. Once he was in position Eric got on his phone and started calling in their location. *If any other actives get back here I'm so fucked.* He started thrashing wildly to no avail.

"Yeah…in the woods behind the TAS…hurry up man!" Eric ordered as he closed down his phone to resume his place holding Calvin. He couldn't have much time before other actives arrived. He kept trying fruitlessly to break free but with the running and the drinking he'd already done he wasn't in any condition to get away.

The next thing he saw made his heart sink. "Hey there Gretman" Will said cheerfully as he strolled through the brush toward them. "Fancy meeting you back here." It wasn't so much who was coming as it was the tools he was bringing along. There was a heavy chain slung over the guy's shoulder.

"You aren't really going to use that are you?" Calvin asked, knowing full well once they did he'd be done.

"Well we don't want to" Eric grinned. "Actually that's a lie."

Once again he tried fighting his way free but now Will was helping the other two and it was even more impossible. They started wrapping the chain around and around his upper body to keep his arms at his sides. They were at least kind enough to leave his legs untouched so he could walk in shame back to the house.

"If it makes you feel any better Gretman, I just won ten bucks off Jerry for needing to use that chain on you" Eric laughed. "He thought you'd come quietly once we caught you."

"Well I'm fuckin' offended."

"Yeah I would be too," Aaron agreed. "You can always paddle him when we get back to the house though."

Calvin grinned. *Now that's food for thought…*

****

The scene unfolding behind AZXi as Will's car pulled up was a thing of beauty. With Kevin and Petey already subdued inside and Calvin in the car's trunk with a chain wrapped around him that only left two seniors outstanding. That made seeing Guapo nearby all the sweeter. He'd locked himself in Gretman's car with the keys in his hands. Still, he was basically as trapped as the guy they had in the trunk. *Four out of five…not bad for three in the afternoon.* "You can take Gretman in from here right?" Eric asked as Will parked on the opposite side of the backyard.

"No problem" Will assured him as Aaron nodded too.

Eric got out of the passenger seat and made his way over to car currently housing Guapo. He felt pretty good about everything considering how well the actives had done under his direction. He started thinking more about elections tomorrow than he had in weeks. Fortunately he snapped out of that daze as soon as he got up next to the car where Dylan, Jared and Brent were already circling like vultures. Guapo was already caught; his brain just hadn't caught onto that fact.

"It's a great plan and all Guap' but there's one huge hole in it" Dylan said in a very self-satisfied way. He held up a cell phone so that their brother inside the car could see it clearly. The look on his face went from arrogant to utter horror in seconds. Eric caught on immediately. Dylan had taken Guapo's phone from his room.

"Look at that Dills, there's no lock on his phone" Brent stated matter-of-factly.

"Damn...no lock on your phone?" he asked Guapo through the car door. "Practically anyone could get at the thing...I mean just imagine what they could send to people..." Dylan said innocently enough although his eyes clearly conveyed a threatening nature. Eric just sat back and watched it all play out with a big smile.

"I'm thinking a mass text," Brent suggested.

"Subject?"

"Keep it simple: I have Chlamydia." That got a roaring laugh from Jared who was also watching while catching his breath. That run through the woods must've been more trouble than Eric had thought. *It's a miracle Guapo got this far...*

"Right to the point. I like it" Dylan agreed as he went to work typing out the mass text. He clicked through and chose ten random female names from the contact list. He arched the phone in a way so that Guapo could look on in horror. It was brilliant.

"Yo that's so fucked up!" Guapo complained through the car door.

"I haven't hit send yet," Dylan said evenly as his thumb hovered over the button. Even a small slip could send it accidentally. Eric was tempted to let him hit it just to see what would happen, his jealousy over Guapo's success with women was momentarily overpowering his good sense.

"Alright fine! Put the phone down and I'll come out."

Dylan and Brent didn't look satisfied. They both shook their heads in almost perfect sequence. "Come out and we'll put the phone down" Brent ordered.

Guapo knew he was fucked. *And there it is; now he gets it.* He popped the lock and opened the door. As soon as he stepped out Jared and Brent were all over him. Dylan cancelled the text and closed down the phone. He didn't even fight once the younger guys got their hands on him. The look of defeat was a thing of thing of beauty to rival any he'd seen all day. "That makes four out of five Biz" Dylan said happily as Guapo was dragged from their sight into the basement. The screaming from the already captured seniors at the sight of another of their order being dragged in was like sweet music for Eric Saren. "Let's hope Raley and Jerry get Buttons back down here soon."

****

I really should quit smoking…

The thought was fresh on his mind with each stride he took down the suburban maze of residential housing on Croftlin Rise. How he managed to get back here while losing Raley and Jerry was nothing short of a miracle. *Those bastards are too fast.*

Jeff Chester slowed his pace to catch his breath, if even for a minute. He looked around to see just where the fuck he was. To his left were houses; on his right were the Northwest dorms. At the end of road was where the other interstate took over, but that was another few miles down. Unfortunately there were no good areas to lie low nearby.

As he continued looking around for any place to hide a car rounded the corner of University Grove and Croftlin. It was moving slowly in his direction. For a second Jeff couldn't figure out why. Then he saw them. Two figures were flanking the car.

Jeff quickly dove into the hedges of the closest house. Fortunately there didn't seem to be anybody home. *It'd be fucking awkward explaining why I'm hidden in the bushes.* In remarkably short time the figures closed in on where he was but they didn't know he was there.

"You really think Buttons would've gone this far off-campus?" Raley asked confusedly as they walked.

"He's a crazy motherfucker," J-Hood said from the driver's seat. He was driving slowly up the road while Jerry walked on the far side and Raley on the near.

"Believe me I know" Jake agreed immediately. "It just seems a little off."

"Yeah you're right" Jerry agreed as he walked over to the near side of the street. "If Buttons came this far then he can chill here for all I care. Biz just texted me, the rest of the seniors are all back down at the house. Four out of five aint bad."

At that point the two outside the car turned toward J-Hood and continued talking. They weren't facing him anymore so Jeff struggled to hear them. Jerry opened the passenger side door to get inside and in that instant he and Raley took off at Jeff in a dead-sprint.

Jeff dashed out from the hedges but tripped over one of the many roots. He landed on his stomach with a thud and nearly lost all the shots he'd taken earlier. *They're sure as hell not gonna take me sober.*

Before he could get back up the two actives were on him. In quick succession they had him up off the ground and in the backseat of the car on his stomach. Jerry and Raley were both sitting on top of him while J-Hood pulled away from the scene of the crime. For the life of him he couldn't figure out how they'd done it all so quickly.

Raley was laughing hysterically. Despite his dire situation, it was a welcome sound to hear. "You're right Jerry" the kid said. "This can be a lot of fun."

****

Somewhere between the Cradle and Thirst Point something happened. Riley went from only mildly sad about losing the seniors to the edge of flat out sobbing. She wasn't sure how it happened but it was a fair bet that the amount they'd all drank was at least partly to blame. It definitely hadn't helped that Riley had made it a priority to hang with as many seniors as possible. Each of them had the default setting of being utterly depressed even if they were trying their best to fight it by laughing and yelling.

Rachel Hager in particular was fighting a losing battle on that front and Riley had been front row center for most of it. "I'm gonna miss this all so much" she said as her eyes darted around the bar's familiar sights. Thirst Point was a dive in every sense of the word. To the less than clean bathrooms to the walls being covered in permanent marker with the scrawled drunken ramblings of a thousand college kids that rolled through every year, the bar had a lived-in feel.

"It definitely won't be the same without you Rach" Riley said in a moment of brutal honesty. She'd never really gone out of her way to hang out with the girl. They'd talk at parties and even play flip cup together but despite living in the house like so many of their other sisters, they'd just never connected. It might've had something to do with Felicia and Kayla's less than stellar thoughts about her election last year. Most days that wouldn't have even caused Riley to flinch since there were plenty of the forty-three actives that she was cordial with and yet not that close to. Today it was a huge problem, and one that she was coming to regret more and more as the minutes passed by, edging everyone closer to graduation.

"You mean that?" Rachel asked, apparently as shocked as Riley felt.

"We are sisters."

"Yes we are," the girl agreed as they lifted their gin and tonics to drink all over again. Once the burn from the disgustingly strong drink had fallen away Riley felt comfortable enough to talk again. "Don't forget that Rach...ever."

"It's gonna be the only thing keeping me sane when I'm dying in law school next year" she sulked. Riley felt powerless again. As she looked over at Danielle on the other side of their graduating sister she could tell she felt the same.

"I can't help with that," Riley admitted. "But I can tell you that right now, today, you don't have to worry about it."

"But tomorrow I will be."

"That's tomorrow."

"Not since I'm gonna pass out soon" Rachel confessed.

It hadn't been lost on anyone that the seniors were sloppier than the rest of them with the exception of Brynn and a few others but that's how it always was. "Hey, you have my guarantee that I won't let you fall asleep until you want to" Riley promised.

"What if I throw-up?"

"You know that's what the rest of the actives are here for. Seniors always cut a path of destruction through this town on Senior Day" Riley admitted proudly.

"No more than the frats do" Rachel exclaimed.

"Yeah and because of them we can sit here under the radar with nobody from the school ever noticing us throwing up in yards or hedges around the Grove." That got Rachel smiling, at least for a few seconds. Then the tears started flowing down her cheeks again. It was enough to melt Riley's heart. She had to fight hard to keep the same from happening to her.

"I don't want to leave," she admitted as the first sob rippled through her voice.

"I don't want you to leave either" Dani finally spoke from her place opposite Rachel. A lone tear rolled down her face. That got Rachel crying even more.

"Come on. We said no crying until at least eight" Riley joked in a futile attempt to stop any tears from leaving her eyes. Both Danielle and Rachel laughed through their tears. Riley could feel her eyes welling up. "Besides, just because you graduate doesn't mean you can't visit. What good is this place if you can't come back any time you need a break from real life?"

"Is that your plan?" Rachel asked, sniffling.

"Oh definitely. I've already called dibs on Danielle's couch for her entire senior year" she grinned back at her niece who nodded in agreement. "You can have it next year though" Riley offered a couch that wasn't even hers. Danielle didn't seem to mind.

Riley found herself actually hoping that today wouldn't be the last time she saw Rachel Hager wearing EIPi letters in Gladen Hills. She hadn't felt so depressed since Felicia's Senior Day. Fortunately she'd only have to endure one more of these...

****

No one could reach Jake or Jerry so Jared tried calling J-Hood. That was when they got the great news that the fifth and final senior had been captured.

"Come on Biz just untie me. I'm not going anywhere," Calvin promised.

Eric chuckled. "You tried running through the woods with your arms chained up so just chill Gretman" he patted him on the back in a patronizing way.

"Point taken" Calvin conceded. "How 'bout some more beer then?"

"That I can do."

With Calvin's arms tied to his sides with a truly large chain that Will had found somewhere Eric had to essentially force-feed the president. He didn't seem to mind as long as the beer was making it to his stomach.

It was at that moment that Jeff was led in by J-Hood, Jake and Jerry, with the latter two looking very pleased. J-Hood just looked content, nothing more. Buttons was tied up too, although Eric couldn't make out what it was with at first. "Hood didn't have any chains in the car and this fucker wasn't sitting still" Jake explained as Jerry led him to the wall that was currently occupied with the other four seniors. "But he did have twine in his trunk. That worked quite nicely."

"I like having it on hand for emergencies" J-Hood stated calmly while helping Jerry line Jeff up next to Calvin. He didn't look happy but Eric could tell he was playing it up; the guy might as well have been in heaven. *Another successful Senior Hazing.*

With the five seniors all lined up and their backs against the right wall, paddles could begin. Eric winced. *No way I get through this without a paddle.*

"It's time for paddles! Everyone shut-up!" J-Bro ordered as Jared and Dylan among others helped untie the seniors. Now that they were all here they couldn't run away. That was another of the unwritten rules of Senior Hazing.

"I'm glad you're here Brock because you might as well drop your pants. Game on!" Guapo shouted as soon as his hands were free. Summers handed him the Phi pledge paddle that had been made all those years ago when Guapo, Kevin and Buttons joined AZXi. It looked frayed and beat up just like all the rest. Today's events wouldn't help it look any better.

J-Bro didn't look happy but he did as commanded while the rest of the basement went up in cheers. The paddling of today was pretty much the exact same setup as it was when the pledges crossed each semester. Each of the new fucks or seniors as it was today could use their pledge paddle to hit the ass of any two brothers they wanted. Eric was quietly hoping that by standing off to the side and keeping away from the spotlight that he might be able to avoid getting hit, at least at first.

"There's just one thing I don't get" Jake began from beside him. Eric was so lost in thought that he hadn't noticed his cousin standing there.

"What?" he finally asked after the surprise subsided.

"When you were planning out where to look for the seniors how the fuck did you not think of checking the place the five of them pledged?"

Eric just smiled coolly. Considering no senior was driving when they'd left with the bottle that morning it was a fair bet they hadn't gone far. So where could they have gone that was nearby but still somehow 'a sick hiding spot' as Gretman had described. The answer was so simple he was actually surprised none of the other actives had thought of it. The barn behind the old AZXi house that was now being rented by the guy's soccer team was perfect. It had been deemed unsafe the semester before they'd moved to their current house and nobody had used it for anything other than storage since. It was secluded and out of the way but most importantly it actually meant something for each of the seniors. They'd earned their letters in that place so it only made sense for that to be the spot to say goodbye to them.

Eric made sure Jerry and his group stayed in midtown in case the seniors ran up that way, which they had. He also made sure that there were actives constantly looking around the barn, specifically back in the woods near the TAS. Once their alcohol ran dry the seniors made their way out and the actives were there to pounce.

"Who says I missed it?" Eric asked slyly while keeping his voice down.

****

"What do you mean?"

"I figured they were there. Especially when I remembered Buttons and Gretman bragging about how sweet their hiding place was." The look of shock on his face must've been obvious because Eric laughed before turning to watch Guapo's paddle stroke. It connected with J-Bro's ass in a hugely satisfying thwack. He curled back in pain while Guapo turned around and raised his hands like he was a boxer who'd just thrown a knockout punch. All the brothers laughed.

It felt good to laugh again. Jake hadn't had much cause to since things with Kelly had ended. "So why not check there when you figured it out?" Jake asked, still confused.

"For the same reason I let Gretman think I couldn't move when he had my arm twisted around. It's not always about winning. This is their day" he motioned to the five seniors. "*The* last day for some."

They were somber words that registered deeply for Jake considering the rest of the basement was in an uproar over the paddling. "I wanted them to have a crazy, wild day. They deserve it. So yeah I gave them enough time to finish their bottle and I kept everyone searching close to but not directly nearby. I wanted them to make the call to show themselves. I knew they would. No senior wants to stay hidden all day."

"That I wouldn't have guessed" Jake admitted although he should've seen what was happening from the start. His cousin had always been like that. Eric was usually the smartest person in the room while never flaunting it. He liked helping people whenever he could but didn't want to take credit for it. He probably wouldn't tell the seniors what he'd done either and the only reason he was saying it at all was because Jake was family.

"Today we still have these five guys here so we should enjoy it."

"Where's Biz!?" Calvin yelled through the crowd. It parted like the Red Sea and all eyes shifted to his cousin.

"How's that philosophy working for you?" Jake asked with an evil grin.

Eric looked terrified but not surprised. "I'll let you know" he replied as he began his march over to the spot J-Bro had just vacated.

Jake maintained his place near the crowd's rear. *Maybe there's actually something to this whole brotherhood thing...*

Chapter 37

Heavy breathing was the only sound ricocheting off the walls in the warm bedroom when only a few minutes ago the stifled moans from Jennifer were filling the place. The echoes of his girlfriend's pleasure were still as fresh as they'd been during the act. Thankfully Jen had come over last night at Eric's request to help take care of him once he got too drunk at the social following Senior Hazing. Calvin wasn't all that sure who their party had been with last night but he remembered having a great fuckin' time.

Jen had woken him up with purpose today and for some strange reason his hangover wasn't nearly as bad as he thought it would be. Jennifer must've sensed it because she took control and stayed on top until he finished inside her. *Thank God for the birth control pill.*

"Thanks Jen...I definitely needed that" he finally managed to speak. They were both lying on their backs, staring at the white ceiling. After her dismount she looked as light-headed as he felt.

"I could tell," she answered between breaths.

Calvin smirked. "Didn't realize I was so easy to read."

Jennifer turned his head to face her. She had a sly smile. "After three years it's kind of hard to keep that sorta thing secret. Although I don't get what you're so freaked out about."

"The elections are today" he replied, as if that would settle it. It didn't.

"And you're a senior" she pointed out. Calvin couldn't have forgotten that ugly fact if he wanted to, and he did. "So unless you're planning on failing your finals to stay another year then you aren't running for anything" she finished, not unkindly.

Now it was his turn to smile slyly. "Maybe that's *exactly* what I'm planning."

Jennifer wasn't impressed. "Please. You hate failing at anything, let alone school. It's a lot harder to explain that kind of thing to the parents."

Sometimes it sucked that she knew him as well as she did. But those times paled in comparison to ten minutes ago where her knowing him was nothing short of heavenly. "You're right...but I still have cause."

"Babe, it's not your problem anymore, enjoy it." The words stuck in his head. They seemed almost haunting. For all the bullshit he'd gone through recently with the pledges and Buttons there was something inherently worse about having no real stake in any future problems. Calvin had no idea how to let it all go.

"Well are you gonna stop worrying about everything Beta after you leave?"

"Probably not" she admitted. "But it's going to happen whether we want it to or not. We can't stay here forever. We aren't Guapo." Calvin felt the overwhelming urge to kiss Jennifer right then. Something about the way she casually threw Guapo under the bus was invigorating. He found it extremely funny and attractive that their circles of friends were so intertwined.

"You don't think Eric wants to be president do you?" she cut right from her joke to the meat of his anxiety. And he hated being anxious.

"I have absolutely no idea how it's gonna go down Jen" he confessed.

"James seems like a nice guy though."

"J-Bro is solid but Eric would be a much better fit…" his voice trailed off as the thoughts bubbled. "You'd think me telling him that would make a difference." The fact that it hadn't was enough to rip a hole in Calvin's ego although he'd never say that out loud. He'd always attributed his friendship with Eric to be of a kind where he could talk the guy into doing whatever Calvin thought was right. These days with him graduating and Biz going into senior year, he was becoming less and less sure of just how far his influence extended.

"Oh so you mean Eric is as stubborn as you?"

He frowned. Calvin couldn't remember the specifics about how Biz had been when he walked through those doors at Rush two years ago but he couldn't imagine him being so hell-bent on not doing what needed to be done for the frat.

"Let's just agree we're both presidential material and leave it at that" Calvin replied, getting weary from the implications. That was as close to an agreement as Jen was likely to get and she knew it.

"Whatever you say Cal." Even so early in the morning she looked beautiful. If he'd had any strength left he'd probably try to fuck her again. "You already talked to him though right?" she went on. He almost didn't hear the question since he was running through the repeat scenario in his mind.

"You know me and Buttons did already."

"Then you've already done all you could" she tried consoling him. He knew she was right but he didn't like feeling powerless either.

"It doesn't change the fact that I want to do more…I spent three years in this fraternity. I gave it everything…and now he won't do the same?" He turned to face his girlfriend again. She was blushing although he couldn't guess what for. *Is she embarrassed that I'm so obsessed?*

"I love you Cal," she finally offered with a loving smile.

"I love you too Jen."

They leaned in to kiss. The feel of her lips made him feel *a little* better about what was in store for the day…

****

The sight of the half-opened eyes of his cousin Eric was enough to throw a smile on Jake's face right away. He'd been knocking on his door without a sign of life for the better part of five minutes. It had only been after raising his voice that his cousin had found his way out of bed to unlock the door. The guy looked like shit, which Jake found funny. "I didn't think you were that drunk last night?"

"I wasn't really," Eric confirmed while slithering his way back to bed.

"Then what's with the zombie status? You don't even look this fucked up after a night at Raley's Ring."

Eric grimaced as he collapsed onto the bed. "I don't like waking up early unless I absolutely have to."

"Do elections not count as a necessity?"

It was at that point that Eric seemed to remember just what today was. It wasn't just any normal meeting although Jake had never actually gone to one since Crossing. There just never seemed to be a good time to go and fortunately despite what Eric and the others claimed, there were no fines in effect for ditching events like that. It made it all the easier to stay in bed with Kelly all those weeks after pledging ended. *And look where that got me.* Jake shook the uncomfortable thoughts about holding Kelly again from his mind. Those wouldn't do him any good now. He watched from the doorway as Eric got up from his slumped position to get to his desk. As soon as he sat down in the chair he shot back up. It was as fast as Jake had ever seen his cousin move.

"I'm guessing your ass still hurts?" Jake grinned.

"It's only been like twelve hours" Eric retorted, fighting through the pain he'd just experienced. It was no small wonder that he'd collapsed onto his bed via his stomach just seconds before.

"Jesus you make it sound like you've never been paddled before" Jake replied, mildly shocked. Eric had been an active brother through three pledge classes and one other Senior Hazing.

"When would I have been?" Eric said calmly. "The pledges never have any problem with me. I'm a saint compared to half the frat."

Jake took a second to *really* think about that. "Yeah I guess you're right...you never did haze us" he agreed while remembering some of the more colorful callouts.

"How am I gonna haze my own cousin? Or my Little? Or my friend from high school? Or J-Hood?" he replied sarcastically.

"I'm guessing you want a ride to the meeting?" Eric yawned and stretched out while being careful to remain standing. He may have looked and felt tired but his cousin's mind was still working perfectly.

"You're going up there anyways so I figured you wouldn't mind" Jake replied tentatively. He didn't like assuming his cousins would do things for him but that didn't stop him from sometimes doing it anyways.

Eric nodded. "Yeah that's a safe bet."

Jake took a look behind him and down the stairs that led to the right side of the house's kitchen. No one was coming up. He could've sworn he'd heard some girl moaning when he'd gotten there but it stopped shortly after. Once he realized no one else was around he knew he had to ask a serious question.

"So you figured out what you're gonna do Biz?"

His older cousin looked like a freight train was coming at him and there was nothing he could do to slow it down. Metaphorically that probably wasn't far from the truth. That freight train was the upcoming elections and the time between then and now was getting shorter by the second. "About the elections?" Eric asked hesitantly. He was careful not to meet Jake's eyes.

Jake's dormant sarcasm came roaring back at such an obvious opportunity. "No I meant about the weather. It's a little cold outside and I didn't know if you were gonna wear a sweatshirt or go full-on jacket."

Eric turned and grinned. "Gretman and Buttons want me to go for president," he blurted out with no pretext. It took Jake by surprise to say the least. "But I don't know man...it's gonna be a lot of work."

"You'd kick ass at it though. My cousin running everything...that'd be sweet."

"It's a lot of responsibility on top of all the shit I'm already dealing with."

"Well I know I'm a lot to deal with but I'd like to think I'm getting better."

"You know my classes make dealing with you seem like a party" Eric joked right back. Jake didn't know whether to take that as an insult or a compliment.

"That's just one more reason why I'm a business major pal."

They both chuckled while Eric paced. No doubt he was still afraid of sitting down but it was more than that. God only knew what the poor bastard was going to do when they got to Lenthan Hall.

Then the craziest thing happened. His older cousin and all-time advisor actually asked *him* for advice. Jake was so floored that he needed it repeated. When Eric asked why he just got an even more confused look. "I'm sorry I just need a second to get used to the role-reversal here," Jake stammered. Most of it was for show.

Eric just shot back a look of impatience. "Do you have anything useful?"

"Not really" Jake confessed. "This is above my pay-grade. That's probably why you've never asked me that question before."

His cousin rolled his eyes. "Figures."

"You know, as long as I've known you, you've always done what you thought you had to do...what you thought was right. It's worked out so far."

"Giving advice is so much easier than taking it." Jake smirked. Eric might as well have been reading from his mind like it was a physics textbook.

"If that wasn't true I would've ended things with Kelly the second you and Riley agreed that something was not right" Jake said confidently, even if he didn't really believe it. He'd like to think he'd learned enough about himself that he could make the right call in that situation if it ever came back around but he wasn't sure. "You two are my family. Sometimes you need an outside perspective to see the right choice."

"Where the hell was this Jake when we were trying to tell you all that?" Eric asked, only half kidding. It was a fair question.

"He was getting laid" Jake admitted. It was as much a mix of humor and seriousness as his cousin's previous comment although he didn't want to admit that, even to himself. "But as it turns out, so was some other guy" he finished bitterly. Eric looked uncomfortable at the direction the conversation was heading. "I know you'll make the right call Biz...I've never had to worry about you." He patted him on the back. Eric seemed to appreciate that as a slight smile crept onto his face.

"Go wake Jerry's ass up while I change" Eric ordered after a few seconds of letting his own thoughts settle. Jake was only too happy to oblige. He could only hope that Jerry was sound asleep so he could force him out of it. *Gotta enjoy the little things*.

****

You just gotta ask yourself...are you a Tory or are you a Jake?
The words of her Big circled Brynn's thoughts even as she attempted to shift in her warm bed. She wasn't ready to join the land of the conscious.

Madison was still fast asleep in the bed across from her. *Why can't I still be sleeping like that?* Her headache was raging even though she'd called it an early night after they'd left Thirst Point. Riley was busy talking to Rachel or Danielle all day so they hadn't hung out at all. That was almost a blessing since anything they could've talked about would've probably revolved around the elections and by extension Tory. That was the last thing Brynn wanted on her plate even as time ticked away. At the moment she couldn't have fallen back asleep without the help of some heavy drugs. And any she could get her hands on would definitely keep her from making the meeting today. *That wouldn't be so bad.* Missing it would keep her from doing anything she didn't want to do. The main problem was she wasn't even sure what she wanted to do.

Another minute passed by on the clock next to her bed.

Nothing about today had started bothering her until last weekend when she'd been carrying out her own patented walk of shame. It wasn't even a walk away from some frat boy's apartment or dorm. It was a long slow trudge from Tory Brye's room. She couldn't tell which of those scenarios was worse but she knew which one had actually happened. At first the events leading up to her getting to that place on Tory's couch were hazy at best, non-existent at worst. It was only on her walk back through the campus that flashes of the previous night started coming back. It had felt like staring out over an unsolved jigsaw puzzle without even having the cover to work off.

After talking with Madison and Angela and getting some details of their bottle binge earlier that night some of the pieces started fitting together. Brynn had flashes of being held up by Riley and then pounding beers with Felicia. She remembered screaming about how awesome they were and being looked at like she was crazy by some of the jackass Tau Chis. The thing that caught her completely off guard once the memories started flooding in was Tory actually *offering* to take Brynn home. What really boiled her blood was she couldn't tell if the girl had done that to allow Riley to stay at the party with Felicia or if she did it because she actually wanted to help. Or both. She knew she didn't like Tory during pledging. She knew she didn't like her at Crossing. Now she knew she wasn't sure about anything.

More memories came flooding back as the week wore on. Each flash from that night carried with it a new layer to the girl she'd swore only had the one. Brynn remembered confessing that Tory used to scare her. That mortified her as soon as it came back across her mind. Nothing she had said to or about her seemed to make the girl feel anything beyond mild amusement. She didn't get upset or bitchy the way Brynn would've guessed. Even after talking with her pledge sisters she was careful about not telling a single person that she remembered anything from that night. Fortunately things like that happened often enough in Gladen Hills that nobody questioned it. And since she'd done the drinking to corroborate that fact she was in the clear. Riley, Madison, Angela, Tory…none of them knew. She'd just as soon keep it that way. But even with Brynn concealing her own memories, Tory definitely still knew what happened that night though thankfully she hadn't pressed it. That too drove Brynn crazy.

You have someone like my cousin Jake who'd rather stay the hell away for a while after Crossing and then you have Tory who'd rather keep the past in the past and live for now. It was like Riley was standing right there saying it all over again.

Another minute passed.

Finally she gave in and just sat up in bed. There was no way she was going to get back to sleep. Today was going to be a long day…

****

Riley had to admit that not knowing why her best friend was so freaked out about elections was gnawing at her. The only thing she could say with absolute certainty was that Tory was losing her mind at the prospect of how today could go wrong for her. Not knowing the catalyst was annoying but the constant rundown of actives and which way they'd vote today was more so…and that was saying something. Tory was pacing in much the same way she'd made fun of Riley for doing when Felicia came back last weekend. *Is that really how it looks when I'm doing it?*

Thankfully a knock on the door came, which Riley was only too happy to hear. *Anything to stop all this bullshit.*

Dani came traipsing in looking as composed as ever. Clearly she wanted to appear her best today even if she'd drank almost as much as Riley had yesterday. Riley couldn't share that sentiment. She'd be wearing her most comfortable EIPi hoodie and that was that. No make-up, no hair straightening, no fuss, and zero fucks.

"We're over-thinking the election Dani. Won't you join us?" Riley asked sarcastically. Tory didn't notice.

Riley noticed something strange through Danielle's smile as she walked in. The girl looked almost disappointed to see Tory there. She wasn't sure why it was such a surprise. Where else was she going to be right now? If her constant stream of hook-ups meant anything it was that Tory Brye hated being alone in *any* fashion.

"Even if the Beta Thetas don't vote for me, based on what the rest of the girls do..." Tory paused to think. "It's gonna be tight." The girl was almost hyperventilating but Riley didn't know what to say.

"Come on T" she begged. "Why are we still doing this?"

"Because it's important to me" she lashed out, losing her cool in a rare display of emotion. Even Danielle looked concerned.

"You know there are a lot of things that are important to me that you don't do" Riley joked.

"Like what?" Tory asked immediately.

"Like *not* hitting on my cousins."

Both Tory and Danielle laughed. After that it was back to business. "That doesn't even remotely bother you Riles" Tory shrugged it off.

"No" Riley admitted. "But if it did I'd be so pissed." She started laughing at her own joke before realizing neither of her friends were. "Alright Dani please tell T there's nothing to worry about. You aren't worried are you?"

"No but then again I'm not running against any Beta Zetas" Dani replied. Riley winced. She was pretty sure the girl meant it as a joke but that was definitely not how Tory was going to take it. And she was right.

"Thanks again. That was real helpful" she threw a glare at their younger sister. She seemed to get the message because her posture shrank back.

"Alright Riles let's run through it again" Tory demanded as she continued her pacing. *That rug is getting a real workout between last weekend and now.*

"You'll be fine Tory" Danielle added calmly, trying to undo the damage she'd just done, accidentally or otherwise. That time Tory didn't even look like she registered that Danielle had said anything. *Of course she only registers the negative.*

"I'm gonna regret coming in here today aren't I?" Dani asked.

"I regret living here today...and have been all morning" Riley joked, hoping to snap Tory out of her insanity. It didn't work.

"Alright. Let's take it from the top" Tory said as she started listing off the sisters' names and which way they'd go in the event Amy ran against her. Riley wasn't even convinced it would come to that but something about the look Danielle had when she walked in gave her an unsettling feeling.

At least all the talk revolving on Tory had kept Riley from thinking about her own situation. Once her mind touched on it the dam that had been put up by her best friend came crashing down and all she could think about were her own choices.

Just what the fuck am I gonna do today?

****

There wasn't a single brother unaccounted for in the classroom stretching out in front of Calvin. They'd all packed in pretty comfortably too. Everyone was wearing some form of AZXi lettering. That just made him feel all the more nostalgic about today being the last batch of elections he'd probably ever see. He felt sadness creeping up from his stomach as he looked around the room. There sat the faces of the guys he'd come to call his brothers over the past three years. There wasn't a single one he wouldn't miss when the time came to leave.

Once he realized that everyone was actually sitting there waiting for him he cleared his throat to begin. "OK guys, chances are this is gonna take a while so let's do this. For the new guys around here" he said as his eyes tracked around the room to find the four Alpha Epsilons. At first he couldn't find Raley but when he actually did he found he was more surprised that the kid had shown up for the first time all semester. *Better late then never kid.* "The election process works like this: anyone can nominate any brother they want for the position in question. After that somebody else must second the nomination. Once we have all the nominees we go through the list and ask the people chosen if they accept or not. If they say yes they can give a quick speech about why they want it or think they'll be a good fit. Once everyone running has spoken they'll go out into the hallway so we can discuss the candidates without them hearing what's said so no one can get offended."

After Calvin finished he made a point to stare down each of the Alpha Epsilons to confirm they understood everything. He noticed a couple other actives looking decidedly bored at having to sit through the explanations...again. There was nothing to be done about that though. The explanations were needed. The new guys had never experienced elections. They'd have to get the same kind of speech explaining Bids and formal blackball next semester. Calvin was just sorry he wouldn't be around to teach them.

Calvin did his best to keep his eyes from wandering too far left where they'd undoubtedly rest on Eric if given the chance. It was difficult but he kept his gaze steadily forward. "Alright let's take it from the top. We'll hear the nominations for president."

****

Piling all forty good-standing actives into the chapter room for elections every semester was always a struggle. God only knew why the founders had mandated that elections be conducted in the house instead of Lenthan Hall where the rest of their meetings took place. Fortunately, Tory forced Riley to go with her early to get seats.

They'd been the first ones there, even ahead of Rachel who'd be running the whole thing as president. Tory was ashamed to admit that with everything going through her mind recently she had never really asked Riley what she was planning to do as far as the E-Board went. *She'll definitely go for president; it's who she is.*

As the room filled with sisters Tory was kicking herself for not finding a guy to fuck away her anxiety yesterday. Unfortunately she'd been too damn anxious throughout the day to focus on making that happen. *Would've, could've, should've.* She'd tried to size Amy up when she walked in but the girl's face didn't give anything away. She smiled back at Tory when she saw her looking in her direction. It drove her nuts trying to figure out what the smile meant.

Tory was still running through each girl's name in her head when Brynn strolled through the door. Tory was careful to throw a warm smile her way. *Why can't she remember anything from last weekend? Then I wouldn't have to freak out about her.* In response to Tory's smile Brynn just nodded. That made her feel incredibly uneasy whether that was the girl's intent or not. The thoughts were almost choking her in place when Rachel started talking.

"As we begin our meeting today on May 6, 2007 let us remember what it means to be a true and loyal EIPi sister." After a few moments of silence, Rachel went on. "The most important thing to remember today is not to hold any grudges after it's all done" she added cheerfully. Tory did her best to stay within herself. *Easy for you to say Rach. You waltzed into the presidency a month after getting letters.* She looked down so nobody could see her face and how disproving it probably was. She'd never felt bitter about last year's elections and Rachel's part in them until right now. "I know some people are going to be upset…that's always the case…but that doesn't change the fact that we are sisters."

It was a nice thought in theory but the fact that a sister who had never tasted the bitterness of defeat in an election was saying it lessened its effect. "For the Beta Thetas, this is your first election so this is how it works: we all can nominate girls for the position at hand. Then we hear their speeches. After that you will all close your eyes and Vicki and I will count the votes by a show of hands." Tory had almost forgotten Vicki was standing up there with Rachel. "We will then announce the winner after we get the totals. Is everybody clear on that?" Rachel asked calmly as she checked the room for the newest sisters and their reactions. Tory was so focused on Rachel that she didn't even pay attention to the other girls.

"Alright then, we will start with my position of President. I'll hear the nominations." At that point Tory couldn't help it. Between her anxiety and excitement she couldn't stop herself from turning left to look at Riley.

****

His heart was doing somersaults around his chest while Calvin went through the list of nominees for president. Even at this late hour Eric still hadn't made up his mind about what to do. There was a list of pros and cons going through his thoughts even now. The seconds were dwindling. Sweat started gathering along his brow and for the first time since he'd accepted the bid to AZXi Eric felt apprehension about his next choice.

"J-Bro, do you accept the nomination for president?" Calvin asked their brother who was sitting front and center before the E-Board table.

"I accept it, yeah," he said sternly. The guy was careful not to give eye contact to anyone but Calvin even while Eric was looking at him with equal parts jealousy and discerning. *How is he so sure?*

"OK Jerry, do you accept the nomination?" Calvin continued the list of names Buttons had written on the board behind the table. As secretary it was Jeff's job to list out the nominations the other brothers had made so that everyone could keep track of who was going for what position.

"I'm not gonna take this one guys" Jerry answered with a smile. To him it seemed to be all one big joke. He'd never had any intention of going for president, which Eric had always seen as an oversight from all involved. *Jerry would be just like me if he were president but Gretman and Buttons never harassed him.* It started angering him. Bitterness crept into the recesses of his thoughts as Calvin nodded at Jerry.

It was at that moment that time froze all around them. The only sound anyone heard was the whiteboard marker sliding over Jerry's name as Buttons crossed it out three feet behind where Eric was sitting. He didn't have to look to know what was happening. He'd heard that same sound multiple times over the semesters. Somehow this time echoed louder and deeper than any before. It sank into his soul, making him feel sick. Right then he felt Calvin's eyes on him. And not just his, the entire room seemed fixated. Except for James Brock. He was looking forward at the whiteboard. Ironically with everyone looking at Eric the only one he was looking to was the sole person who didn't seem interested in him but he saw through that façade. J-Bro was just as interested as the rest of the room. He was just fixated on Eric's name on the whiteboard, nothing else. *The only thing standing in your way is me.* It felt empowering and emasculating all at once. Eric didn't have the heart to look at Calvin so he turned to the clock in the back of the room where they'd all entered from not ten minutes before. *Do you accept the nomination?* He almost thought it was only in his head before he realized Calvin had already asked him once. It didn't register. Or maybe it did and that was why Eric was thinking it. The second time it came through clear as day. It sent a chill up his spine to rival the ones he got the second before he was handed exams in class.

"Do you accept the nomination Biz?" No one moved. There was complete silence. Eric didn't have the balls to look at Jeff even though he knew he was holding his breath, waiting for the response.

"I'm *not* going to accept" he finally let out. Only after his words left him did a collective sigh of relief filter through the room. Maybe that was how it felt to Eric but when he finally found the courage to look at Calvin it was clear he didn't feel relieved. On top of Gretman's look of disappointment there were looks of confusion spread throughout the brothers. Eric could feel the beating eyes of Jeff Chester boring through the back of his head as the marker slid across his name. Eric looked at James to give him a slight nod. His brother saw it but didn't nod back. It almost looked like he was expecting the response and as such, wasn't surprised when it inevitably became reality. *How was he so sure what I'd do?*

"Alright since there were no other nominations for president and two of the three have turned down the chance to run" Calvin began. Eric cringed in his seat as the current president spoke. He was hoping it went unnoticed by the majority of the room but he doubted his luck

would hold for that. *Just like getting fucked by a miracle river card.*
"The position goes to J-Bro. Snaps man." Calvin announced as he
started his fingers snapping. Clearly the guy was fighting some form of
depression but was trying to hide it, both from J-Bro and the rest of the
frat. *They don't need to know exactly what just happened.* Calvin
knew that much better than most. The rest of the guys in the room
started snapping to show their congratulations to J-Bro. Even Jake took
up the cause after a few seconds. He looked uncomfortable but settled
into the rhythm easy enough.

It was then that James finally stood up to speak. "Guys, I
know I can do really well as your president and I promise next year will
go smoothly. Thanks for the opportunity to lead you all." He sat back
down as soon as he was done. Eric didn't need to look behind him to
know that Buttons was rolling his eyes the whole time J-Bro spoke. It
was doubtful he was even trying to conceal his disdain.

"Well here's hoping the rest of the positions can be filled that
easily" Calvin joked to ease whatever tension there was. It did the job
well enough as mild chuckles filled the air. Sounds of agreement could
also be heard but Eric was zoning out. Second-guessing his decisions
wasn't something he was accustomed to.

Eric looked past Jared and Aaron to where Jake was sitting in
the middle section next to J-Hood. His cousin threw a nod in his
direction as if to ask if he was doing OK. Eric threw a half-hearted
smile back. When Jake turned his gaze to Calvin again Eric could've
sworn there was a look of confusion in the kid's eyes. *I've never had
to worry about you before Eric.* The words of his younger cousin
seemed more like a warning now. Even as Jeff wrote Jerry's and
Brent's names on the whiteboard for VP nominations the whole thing
felt unreal, almost like it hadn't really happened.

****

It had gone the only way Riley had pictured it going. She'd
given up the chance to be president. *Felicia is gonna kill me when she
hears this.* Riley shook her head. It just hadn't felt right. There were
times in her life when she'd had to go by her gut and today was one of
them. There'd been doubts creeping around her head about whether
she could've even won against Beta Zeta member Jessie Rander.
Those thoughts had only multiplied when Tory had insisted they get to
the chapter room early. Sitting in that chair and staring up at Rachel at
the pink and white podium gave her pause. *I can't picture myself there
next year.* A small part of her had actually wanted to go up against
Jessie just to see how things would shake out. Riley felt very secure in

her position within EIPi and frankly if anyone was going to beat a Beta Zeta, it was going to be her. By comparison though, that piece of her was small. It couldn't compete with the part of her that overwhelmingly favored sitting it out.

Once she'd turned down the nomination that Tory had started and Brynn had seconded the race was pretty much decided. Danielle had nominated Angela, which Riley had found partially funny considering how wasted an attempt it was. The other girls running didn't stand a chance once Riley backed out and Jessie accepted. With all twelve of the Alpha Chis voting for her along with a bunch of the remaining younger girls the course was clear: Jessie Rander was the next president of Epsilon Iota Pi.

Next up was treasurer and Brianna Paley took that position uncontested. That meant two E-Board positions were already filled with Beta Zetas. *A few more elections like that and they'll hold everything that matters*. The thought made Riley more than a little uneasy. Even with Rachel getting president immediately after Crossing Riley hadn't thrown a fit like Felicia because she didn't think it was that big of a deal to have her run things. Rachel had done a solid, if unremarkable job.

"We'll take nominations for VP next" Rachel announced.

Within seconds Tory spoke up just like Riley knew she would. "I nominate Riley," she said cordially, almost mimicking Rachel's official tone.

"I second that" Danielle agreed immediately after.

"Do you accept the nomination Riley?" Rachel asked.

"I do accept." After speaking her acceptance the room fell silent to Riley's ears. She knew there were still nominations being made but it was all white noise.

After what seemed like only a few seconds Rachel told her to give a speech. Riley nodded before standing up and looking around the room. The girls were all sitting intently, waiting for what they probably assumed would be a decent speech. For Riley, public speaking had never been a weakness or strength but the room of sisters in front of her made the task easier.

"I love EIPi. The things I've learned here and the friends I've made, I get to call my sisters. That's not something many people can say. We are all so lucky to have this chance and I'd like to be given the chance to work for this organization again, just like I did as pledge mom. During that time I worked with other active sisters to successfully put our pledges through EIPi traditions to get the most out of them." Out of the corner of her eye, she saw Brynn fidgeting. "It not only was a big responsibility, but it took a lot of time and dedication. I feel I did a good job maintaining the fundamentals of our sorority throughout those six weeks both semesters. I feel like I can really contribute in my senior year and leave a legacy after I graduate. It'd mean a lot to me if you guys could trust me enough to give me this chance one more time." Riley could feel the tears welling up around her eyes. All her words about it being the last time were saddening.

Once she sat back down the other girl that had accepted the nomination rose from a seat a few rows back. Riley was surprised to see it was one of her pledge sisters. She and Brittany were decently close so it shocked her all the more when she saw her stand. Adrenaline was still coursing through her veins so she found herself zoning out and missing whatever Brittany said.

"OK girls, eyes shut" Rachel ordered.

They all did as they were told. Normally it was a relatively easy battle to keep her eyes shut during elections. Even when she'd run for pledge mom she'd been able to force herself not to look out at who was voting for who. *This is the last election I'll run in. Fuck it.* Once Rachel asked who wanted to vote for her as VP Riley cracked open her left eye to gauge the room's response. She did so in a way that didn't attract the attention of Vicki or Rachel. It was only a centimeter open and it went by so quick that it took a second after she closed it to register what she'd seen. Granted she could only see the girls in front of her, which didn't amount to many but if that was a fair picture of how the ones behind her were voting then she'd be fine.

After Rachel asked for the show of hands of those voting for Brittany it was announced that Riley had won the election for vice president. She couldn't help but smile at the announcement even though it was a little ungracious. She made sure not to look in Brittany's direction. Adding the insult to losing the election wouldn't be right so she kept her gaze forward. Rachel smiled in her direction although it probably went unnoticed by most in the room. Riley nodded back. *Damn I'll miss her next year.*

****

"Thank you sisters" Riley said diplomatically while remaining in her seat. Tory couldn't fight the urge to check the look on their pledge sister's face to see how Brittany was taking the loss. Interestingly enough she didn't seem too hurt by it as the girl was clapping along with the rest.

Tory could almost feel the pressure surrounding her best friend when the presidential elections had come and gone. Part of her had expected Riley to go for it and run against Jessie and the others.

No doubt it would've made things more even than it had been given the landslide she'd witnessed it to be. She couldn't help but crack open an eye to see how people were voting. It didn't bode well if Amy chose to run against her given how Brianna and Jessie had already locked two other key positions.

"Congratulations to Riley" Rachel said casually. "Now moving to… nominations for house president."

Tory felt her throat tighten up at the mention of the title she'd been so intent on getting. A wave of silence sprouted up around her until Riley's voice cleared it all. "I nominate Tory," she announced with authority.

"I second that" Brittany's voice accompanied Riley's. Tory turned around to show a nod of approval for Brittany's support. They hadn't talked much since alumni weekend but it was hard not to know that Tory wanted the position. *I'll have to buy her a drink one of these days.*

"Do you accept the nomination Tory?" Rachel asked.

"Yes I do." That was the moment she felt her unease growing. The silence in between when she accepted the nomination to when the next one was spoken seemed to last hours.

A second or even an hour wouldn't have prepared her for hearing Amy's name nominated by Jessie. Hearing Danielle second it was what stung most. When Amy accepted the nomination Tory felt almost as bad as she had during her senior year of high school. It was a feeling she swore never to feel again and yet here it was, pulsing through her like cancer. The feeling of betrayal and loss was hitting her just like it had back then.

When she stood up to give her speech it felt like a lifetime in and of itself. Even before she started talking things felt hopeless…

****

Even though Jeff hadn't gotten a position on the E-Board, the most disappointing thing had to have been J-Bro's uncontested run for president. *Eric might as well have bent over so the guy could fuck him in the ass.*

Jeff had been mentally preparing for his brothers to be dumb enough not to elect him again for any position so that lessened the sting of it. Mostly. Add to that the fact that the election for secretary between him and AJ had gone on longer than the previous elections for VP and treasurer and he couldn't really feel all that bad about how things had gone down. *At least they talked about it before fucking me.* Maybe at some point he'd ask one of his brothers how things had shaken out when he and AJ had left the room so everyone could talk and vote. He might even get the truth if he was lucky enough, depending on which brother he asked.

Generally speaking, the guys running for positions weren't to be told anything about what was said or done once they left the room. It was part of the AZXi constitution to keep the affected brothers in the dark so that their feelings couldn't be hurt about who said what about being a position's better choice.

Unfortunately, he hadn't been able to devote too much thought to his own circumstances since he was continuously worried about *everyone's* next year. Every time he looked over to where he'd written J-Bro's name under the title of president a piece of him died. It had pained him enough to write it in the first place and now he was all but being forced to stare at it. *This must be what Hell feels like. No beer, no girls, just a bunch of idiots who don't see an issue with this ass-clown running AZXi next year.*

After the E-Board positions were done, the rest of the positions fell into place remarkably easy. There were no major squabbles or arguments regarding anything except for assistant pledge-master. Putting Gary in that position ahead of Jared was nothing short of a travesty. It damn near matched the level they'd sunk to by letting James Brock take the presidency. Gary Tonsic might be able to haze the pledges with ferocity but that didn't necessarily make him a good fit for leading a program. Nobody would know that better than Jeff, except maybe Petey or Kevin given that they'd all been pledge-masters. Neither of them had made much of a fuss about *anything* today though. That was probably because they were both graduating so they wouldn't be around to see any of these elections bear fruit or rain shit.

It was happening more and more with graduation getting so close. Jeff was having mental battles about whether or not it was a good thing he wasn't leaving Gladen Hills on time like Kev, Petey and Gretman. Today it seemed like a punishment since he'd be forced to witness J-Bro's tenure as president on top of Gary making an ass of himself trying to follow Jerry's lead next semester.

"Alright guys, snaps to everyone elected. It looks like you guys are pretty well stocked next year," Gretman stated cheerfully as he looked over the list of names Jeff had written on the whiteboard.

Just what the fuck is he so happy about? This isn't good news you dumbass. Jeff forced himself to look at the list he'd made one more time. He read over the names slowly while Calvin continued talking. *J-Bro is president, Jerry is his VP. What a fuckin' mismatch that is. Eric is treasurer...again. AJ is secretary. Dylan is social.*

The rest of the names filtered through his thoughts easily enough. It was only when he reached the end of the list that Gretman finally set them free. The brothers all got up to leave. Calvin stayed put and remarkably, so did Eric. It looked like he was expecting what was coming.

Once the room was clear, only leaving the three Jeff couldn't help himself. "What the fuck was that?" he practically shouted at their younger brother.

Eric didn't appear too affected. "That was a thankfully short election" he replied, trying to make a joke. Jeff wasn't laughing. Neither was Calvin.

"Come on Biz, what happened?" Gretman asked calmly.

Eric took a deep breath. "What happened is what I told you would happen," he answered sternly.

Jeff was shocked by Eric's tone. *I didn't think the kid had balls at all.* "You didn't tell us shit. All you said was that you'd think about it."

Eric sat up straight. "I did think about it…a lot…and I can't do it."

Jeff waved a hand in front of him. "Give me a fuckin' break."

"Because of your classes?" Calvin asked, again with diplomacy.

Eric nodded. "Just like I told you guys before. It's too much and I don't want to deal with all that during my last year. Being treasurer again is going to be more than enough on its own."

Calvin looked like he was going to say something but Jeff beat him to it. "And if the frat folds up during your precious senior year?" he asked with scorn.

"Oh come on Buttons. I kinda doubt it'll be that bad."

That wording gave Jeff the opening he wanted. "So you do think it'll be at least a little bad." *You knew Brock would fuck us all if given half the chance. Son of a bitch…*

"It's not ideal no…" Eric admitted. "But it'll work."

"I love how little you care" Jeff lashed out. *Unbelievable.*

"I do everything that I physically can for this frat" Eric defended himself vehemently. It almost made Jeff laugh when he heard the words.

"No pal. *I* did everything I could for this frat. There's a big difference between you and me." He felt like there was ice coursing through his veins as he talked down to his younger brother. That didn't stop it from feeling good in a way.

"This frat is still gonna be here after we're gone Jeff" Eric said blindly.

"Don't talk to me about down the line after we're gone. While we're here *this* is what matters. Here and now, it fucking matters."

"We were just hoping you would step up Biz" Calvin interrupted.

Jeff grimaced at Calvin's soft words. He didn't want any part of being delicate right now. "OK let's just say it. James Brock was given a bid during a time when we were handing the damn things out like fucking candy because we needed numbers. He doesn't give a fuck about the frat, never has."

The look on Calvin's face said it all. *He agrees but he'll never admit it. Fuckin' pussy.* Eric appeared to feel the same but was having a hard time putting those thoughts into words. "I know you care Biz but that's not good enough. You think it's not your problem but since you're still here, it is your problem." Jeff hadn't planned on it but his voice was coming across kinder.

"I'm still gonna be here and you will too. We can make this work," Eric replied.

"Come on, you saw the elections today. Fucking AJ beat me out of my old position. Nobody is going to expect a damn thing from me because of all that shit with the Alpha Epsilons. This is on you Biz." It hurt him to say it that plainly but it didn't make it any less true.

"The bottom line is that you both are going to have to help next year with *whatever* is needed. It's not something I'll be able to deal with anymore" Calvin stepped back in. If Jeff didn't know better he would've almost thought the guy was on the verge of sadness. *Now that'd be a sight.*

"We'll just have to wait and see who's right," Jeff stated ominously while staring directly at Eric. The guy chose that moment to leave.

"This is what's best for me. I'm sorry" Eric explained while gathering up his notebook and moving toward the back of the room.

Once the door swung closed Jeff nearly bit Calvin's head off just for still being there. "You know how incredibly fucked we are."

"I'm hoping it won't be as much of a train wreck as you're thinking." Jeff could see how unconvinced the guy looked. It was sad that one of the few things the two of them agreed on was the future of AZXi and how dim it now was.

****

She knew when she'd given her speech to the rest of the EIPi just how fucked she was. Amy had known it too. That was probably why she hadn't really tried all that hard with her own words or why she hadn't looked even slightly shocked when the election came back in her favor. Tory hadn't even had the heart to look out during the hand-raising sequence to see how badly she was losing.

"You know what this means right?"

They'd retreated from the chapter room as soon as the rest of the positions were filled. She'd been so depressed after the house president fiasco that she'd thrown a look to Riley letting her know she didn't want to be nominated for anything else. It was a split-second decision and one she was coming to regret. *Maybe I would've had a better shot at getting something...anything else.*

"It doesn't mean anything" Riley soothed. "Elections are tough every year."

"Says the girl that always gets a position" Tory answered bitterly. She immediately regretted saying it. Just like she was now regretting not opening her eyes to see how the girls had voted. *Had it been close? What had Brynn and her pledge sisters done? Why didn't I run for something else?* Her best friend looked hurt by Tory's comment, which she backtracked to instantly. "I'm sorry Riles."

"I know" she nodded. "But it's really not a big deal. We're still going to have a kick-ass senior year. You better not let this stop that."

"I won't," she promised. "I just...really wanted to do *something* next year..." her voice cracked and trailed off. Thankfully breaking down in front of Riley didn't frighten her the way it might've had it been anybody else.

"You can always help me," Riley offered genuinely. Tory shook her head on instinct. She knew her best friend well enough to know that she liked doing things herself whenever possible.

"VP doesn't have an assistant," she finally muttered while the thoughts rumbled around her mind.

Riley nodded. "True it won't be on the composite but if you just wanted to help out, this would definitely do that much at least."

"The title is important too" Tory replied honestly. When Riley looked back in mild shock she continued. "It isn't to you?"

"Of course it is...but I didn't think it'd matter for you."

"I don't know. It's because then people would actually know that I did something...it's hard to explain..." she trailed off again.

With senior year coming up the only thing she'd be listed on in EIPi's history was being the assistant pledge-mom to Riley Nichol. It wasn't exactly a glowing footnote. "You know I don't think Brynn voted for me," Tory confessed in another moment of weakness. Saying it out loud actually made it sting more. Riley didn't look all that shocked.

"Even if that's true it doesn't really matter" she tried glossing over the talk of her Little. "That's how elections work. Sisters are split. It's never straightforward."

Tory nodded. It was a little unfair that doing her previous job so well had cost her any chance of getting a future one. *This is why recently crossed pledges shouldn't be allowed to vote.* Tory had heard some of the older girls raise that point last year when Rachel had gotten the presidency but she hadn't paid much attention. Now it seemed like it was the only thing on Earth that mattered. *If we fixed that last year then it would've been six less votes going to Amy.* Tory still wasn't sure how close things were but that might've made a difference.

"You wanna watch a movie or something?"

"No I just want to relax by myself for a little while. Thanks though Riles."

"You know I'm right down the hall if you need somebody to stuff your face with" she grinned. Riley was trying her best to get a genuine smile from Tory. She almost felt compelled to throw her one for the effort but couldn't.

"Don't worry. You're on my speed dial."

Riley faked a look of scorn. "Are you calling me fat?"

"I'd never dream of it."

Tory turned and left the comfort of her best friend's room. The hallway seemed cold and empty. If it had been any other day then everything in the house would've appeared calm and inviting. Today wasn't that kind of day. And she didn't see any day like it on the horizon.

****

Even though the drive from Lenthan to Northeast was a little longer than the one he would've had back to the AZXi house it seemed like it was miles out of the way. Eric was relishing that extra time though, if it even existed, since it was keeping him from getting back. He wasn't sure he could stomach the looks of disappointment from Gretman as well as the murderous glares coming from Buttons.

"So you wanna talk about that?" his cousin finally asked as they traveled down University Grove. Jake had kept remarkably quiet since Eric had left Lenthan to join him in the parking lot. By that point the rest of the brothers had all gone their separate ways but his cousin had stayed by his car. At first Eric thought that was because he wanted a ride back to Northeast but now he wasn't so sure.

"Talk about what?"

"Oh I don't know Biz, maybe those elections. Maybe turning down that nomination everyone was expecting you to roll with or maybe that little meeting you had with Gretman and Buttons after the room cleared out." Jake sounded sarcastic but he was being equally as serious.

"No I don't think I want to talk about...any of that," Eric confessed.

"Come on man. After all the shit you put up with for me, let me help."

"Even if that were true, I don't know what to say."

"Why'd you turn it down?"

Eric couldn't tell whether he really cared or if he was just anxious to talk about a problem that didn't revolve around Kelly. To be fair, Eric would be content with either option even though he guessed it was a mix of both. "I don't know how to do both things J," he replied in a moment of brutal honesty.

Jake didn't look convinced. "Oh come on Biz. You're a kick-ass treasurer and that's coming from somebody who's barely been around to notice that." His cousin's words actually made Eric smirk for the first time since Lenthan Hall.

"Collecting money from people is different from handling *all* issues that may or may not spring up against the frat. The bottom line is I can't give one hundred percent to both things when that next big something, whatever it is, happens next year."

"What makes you think something big will come up?"

Eric nearly burst out laughing at the insane question. It could only have come from a new guy like Jake. It was especially ironic in Jake's case considering he'd been directly at the center of their most recent 'big' issue. "Trust me J. Something big *always* happens" he replied knowingly.

"I don't know Biz. I think you're selling yourself short" Jake brushed past his previous comment without so much as a second thought.

"School is gonna be insane next year. Like worse than it's ever been and I need to do well so I can go to grad school. I don't think the frat should take up that much time for me. As a matter of fact, it won't matter at all ten years from now" Eric said with authority. *If Jeff heard me say that he'd lose his mind...and then kill me.*

"Ten years from now aside" Jake began. "Now matters too. Now is when they need you."

"James is gonna do fine" Eric repeated for what felt like the hundredth time. He'd almost convinced himself that what he was saying would be true.

Jake didn't sound any more convinced than Eric felt. "But what if he doesn't?"

Chapter 38

Class registration was tomorrow. It chilled Jake's blood. It wasn't just that the idea of picking classes for the next semester was overwhelming although that was certainly true. The real reason for his fear reached deeper than that, to thoughts that had been all too prevalent recently.

Mere weeks ago the thought of registration would've been nothing more than a mild annoyance considering how early Jake would have to wake up for them. But today the world wasn't the same as it was three weeks ago. All Jake could do was stare blankly at the calendar he'd taped up on the wall the day he'd moved into the dorm. His own handwriting was covering tomorrow's date. He remembered when he wrote that note to his future self three months ago. The memory used to be a happy one but today it was just another in the long line of memories he'd happily forget. If only he could.

"You know we aren't even gonna have to choose classes 'til May anyways babe" Jake complained. He wasn't a fan of planning *that* far in advance. What to do tomorrow or a day from now was fine but not three months down the line.

Kelly wasn't like that; she wanted things laid out well ahead of their eventual arrival. Jake had learned to roll with that quirk of his girlfriend's. Registration would just be another test. She'd referenced some date in May as the day they'd need to have their specific class choices picked out by. The date had just sounded like white noise considering it was in May. *It's only February for Christ's sake. I still haven't even decided if I want to go to Rush this week.* The thought of that decision was far more pressing than the concept of picking classes he wouldn't even be sitting in until September.

Jake had never talked to Kelly about Rush considering she wasn't looking to join any organization. As the choices mounted he found himself warming up to the idea of talking things out with his girlfriend.

"And?" Kelly finally replied after looking up from the school's course catalogue. Thankfully his girlfriend had decided to switch majors a few weeks ago after sitting through a few lectures in the more advanced mathematics courses. As of now she was leaning toward accounting and that meant she'd have a ton of overlapping requirements with Jake's major.

"Well if my math is right, and I'd like to think that it is, that means we have three months left to worry about this" Jake declared with a grin.

Kelly wasn't amused. "We might as well deal with it now though babe" she patronized him.

Jake leaned in toward his girlfriend and kissed her lightly on the cheek. They both smiled. "Come on Kel, let's just watch the OC or something."

"Let's just get this done and then we can cuddle and watch TV" she compromised.

As long as he was going to get to hold her while they watched their favorite show at some point soon Jake was content. "OK fine babe you win" he agreed.

"I always do" she replied with a seductive look. Jake found himself getting lost in her dark blue eyes. All too quickly, she turned away to look back down to the catalogue in her lap. "OK so we need to take the lower level accounting stuff and stats" she began. Her eyes were darting up and down the pages but Jake's were still fixed on hers. Only after a few more seconds did he finally manage to break away.

He sat up and scrolled through the listings on the webpage he'd pulled up a few minutes earlier. "Rate my professor says Archer is better than Trineer for stats so if that works for you, that's the internet's recommendation. We all know the internet can't be wrong" he joked. Kelly didn't notice. She was too preoccupied reading the course descriptions. *Damn that book. I must be losing my touch.*

"That sounds fine babe. What about for accounting 105?" Kelly didn't even look up when she replied, instead remaining focused on whatever she was reading.

Jake smirked as he watched her. "I say we just have sex right this second" he said as seriously as he could.

At least that moved her. She winked at him playfully. "Maybe later."

That might as well have been a binding contract as far as Jake was concerned. Turning back to his laptop was a tough task considering how much he wanted her. He'd offered sex as a joke but there were very few instances, if any, when he'd turned it down outright. Tonight wouldn't be one of those times.

"Accounting 105's trickier. In the fall only one professor teaches it...why the fuck would only one professor teach a requirement? It's some guy named Sato." He read a little more on the next page. "And it says he absolutely sucks. We're better off waiting 'til spring to get a better professor" he finished confidently. It all sounded great to him. Procrastination was his best friend.

"Alright" Kelly agreed. "But we do need to take it eventually."

"I know babe. I'd just prefer to wait to take the class with a professor that I can actually stand." It sounded perfectly reasonable to him but he still wasn't sure if Kelly would buy that.

"Alright if that ones out then we need to take some more electives to get them out of the way before senior year." Kelly handed over a piece of loose-leaf paper that had a list of possible electives.

Jake glanced over it speedily and nodded. "Looks fine to me."

Kelly's clearly wasn't overjoyed about the fact that he'd only given a passing glance at the list she'd written out. "What?!" he said, faking confusion. "They're only electives. It really doesn't matter and as long as we're in them together, it'll be fine."

Finally she gave in and smiled while leaning in for another kiss. *Maybe now we can just relax and watch some TV.* There was nothing he liked doing more. That thought both comforted and frightened him.

As Jake prepared to get up out of his desk chair to join her on the bed she motioned for him to mark the day of class registration. He quickly grabbed a pen from his desk and marked it down for the first Monday in May. *Plenty of time to worry about that later.*

As long as we're in them together then everything will be fine.
On his desk sat the list of classes he and Kelly had picked out together. The only thing Jake knew for sure as of now was that he had no desire to spend an entire semester being in the same classrooms with *that* girl. *What if she signs up for her classes with that other guy she's been fucking?* Seeing her alone would probably suck the life out of him but seeing her with *him* day after day would be the very definition of torture. The question he had to ask himself was would Kelly go

through with registering for the classes they'd talked about? Or would she pick all new ones in an attempt to avoid seeing him? Either choice filled him with sickness. *What if she doesn't want to see me anymore? What if she doesn't care either way? Maybe I could just text her quick to see what she's taking.* Somehow that just seemed cleaner.

He reached over to the corner of his desk where his phone was charging and unplugged it. Jake scrolled through the contacts until he found Kelly's name, except it wasn't there. He'd deleted it the same day he'd taken her name off his Facebook page. Not that it mattered considering he had her number memorized even after he tried making himself forget it. Just like all their memories that seemed permanently seared into his brain, it wasn't going away. There were only a few numbers he'd ever fully memorized and Kelly's was one of them. Eric and Riley's were among the others as well as his parent's home numbers. He couldn't forget any of them any more than he could forget his ex's.

Just a quick message to see what she's taking and then I can work around that. Jake typed in her number and started writing up a message but he couldn't bring himself to hit send. *What if she doesn't respond? What if she does respond and just answers with her classes and nothing else?* He found himself actually wanting to talk to her again despite everything that had happened. They'd been together over a year and in one instant it had ended. It still didn't seem right.

Abruptly he cancelled the message, closed down his phone and hastily tossed it over onto his bed, out of reach. A cold feeling swept over him. Once again Jake felt utterly alone. He needed to talk to somebody, anybody. Eric was still reeling from the elections earlier today so Jake didn't want to continue to pile shit on him. Riley was dealing with some kind of bullshit over at the EIPi house, which he'd gathered only after he'd tried talking to her earlier about Eric's troubles. When she seemed distant Jake didn't push anything. Scribner and Dukes were getting dinner at the Blue Hold and he didn't feel like heading over there. He hadn't really had any appetite to speak of in the past couple weeks.

Jake got up from his desk chair after putting on his sneakers. He moved toward the common room, walked through the suite and out the main door. All his walking was done absent any thought or purpose. The need to feel the night's air and calm sounds of the campus was suddenly paramount. Anything was better than sitting around his room waiting for tomorrow morning.

****

It was nothing short of a miracle that Jennifer's parents had made her get a meal plan for the on-campus dining halls during her senior year. Calvin's parents had stopped pushing that particular issue once he became a junior. He hadn't had any real desire to have them waste money on it, not when it could be wasted on other things. Calvin would much rather have them just deposit straight into his account so he could buy food at the store and make it himself. Avoiding the chance to give Gladen Hills even more of his parent's money was a highlight for him. That was especially true as he'd gotten older and seen firsthand how the administration tended to shit on the Greek Circle. That aside, there were times when he missed some of the on-campus meals and it was at those points that he'd go to dinner with Jennifer. She usually only ate on campus with him or one of her sisters.

Even with the semester practically over she still had a fair amount of money left on the plan and they'd both be damned if it was never used. Almost every night last week she'd gone out to dinner with some of her sisters in a pursuit to deplete the funds before they expired. Tonight was just another in that line of attempts and Calvin was happy to be involved.

After the events of the weekend he wanted to get away from AZXi and its troubles, if only for a night. Senior Hazing had been a rousing success overall and paddling Eric was nothing short of euphoric. It was earlier today that he was coming to regret things even though he hadn't done anything wrong. That too went back to his brother Eric and his choice not to run for president. The whole thing felt wrong but there was nothing he could do. That would be even more true come next week when he'd officially be an alumnus with only a handful of brothers still around to chill with.

Calvin washed down a mouthful of his chicken with the water he'd gotten from the machine a few feet from their table. After he was finished he asked what Jennifer thought of the plan he'd just told her.

"You going to work for your dad?" she reiterated. "Wasn't that always the plan?"

"Yeah but it's different now" he explained. "In three months this plan is going to be on." Just having the words come out of his mouth somehow made them ring truer than they had before. The only things standing between him and his last summer vacation were three finals. Once he passed them all he'd be done with school in Gladen Hills. The real world would be the only thing in front of him.

"Three months" Jen said thoughtfully while eating her salad. "I can't believe you talked your parents into letting you stay here over the summer."

"It wasn't all that hard. They let Adam do it when he graduated." *Of course he'd spent the summer permanently hammered with his pledge brothers.* Convincing his mom and dad to let him continue renting a room in the AZXi house over the summer wasn't hard. His parents had always been all about treating their children equally. Sometimes it benefitted them but other times Calvin could twist it to his advantage and use the idea of them letting Adam do something previously to allow him the same leeway, whether they liked it or not.

"Of course they did" Jennifer smiled.

Thankfully Jen had always liked his parents, especially his mom. They meshed well together. Calvin's dad had always been a fan of pretty much any girl he and Adam had brought home over the years so long as they were nice and respectful. Unfortunately both he and his brother didn't have a perfect track record in that regard but Calvin had always felt different about Jen.

"Hey you should be nicer about this" he joked. "Driving from your place to Gladen is a lot quicker than going all the way to my parents' house. It'll be easier to see each other. Plus a couple brothers will still be around too" he added quickly. He'd be lying if he said the opportunity to live like a college kid for even a few more weeks wasn't incredibly enticing.

Not surprisingly, that caught Jennifer's attention. "Like who?" she asked quickly.

"I know Buttons wants to do some work around the house this summer and Biz, Jerry and a couple other guys only live like an hour away so they'll be down to visit." *It's not ideal but it'll work...*

Jennifer caught on immediately. Admittedly, the scheme wasn't well concealed. "Sounds like you'll all be partying a lot" she said with a hint of jealousy.

"I know you're jealous Jen but you know you can come visit anytime." That would be the icing on the cake of the awesome summer he'd envisioned when he'd asked his parents for the money to stay there through July.

"You know I would do that anyways, with or without your permission."

"I wouldn't have it any other way."

They continued eating before Jennifer asked another question. "You're gonna be getting an apartment when you move back home right?"

Calvin abruptly swallowed the food in his mouth when he heard the question. He understood full well how much of a minefield the subject was. "I love my parents but there's no way I could go back to living with them after four years here."

"Well I'm gonna spend the summer looking for a job near you so if I find one by then hopefully we can move in together" she replied, equally as confident. And that was the equivalent of Calvin stepping on one of the landmines. Talking about moving in together a few times previously was one thing, and nothing had been decided during those few times. Now it appeared a decision had been made without his knowledge. He'd known since the beginning of the year that it was always part of Jennifer's endgame; to have them get a place together. That didn't mean he'd fully wrapped his head around it, even now.

"Whoa now that's a lot of pressure" he replied sarcastically.

"You'd miss me Cal" she joked. "I'm doing you a favor." It was doubtful Jennifer knew just how true that was. It was going to be enough of a stretch living away from her over the summer. He finally started thinking about what it would really be like sharing a place with his girlfriend. He liked it.

"Three months" he thought out loud. "Just three months."

Jennifer smiled in the warmest way imaginable. Calvin found himself very much looking forward to spending more and more time with her when he finally moved away from Gladen Hills.

She finished eating first and asked if he wanted some ice cream from the next room over. He answered yes absently as she walked away to get it.

In the back of his mind there was a nagging feeling like he was forgetting something. He couldn't figure out what it was. Then it came back to him. Registration was tomorrow but for the first time in four years he didn't have to worry about waking up early to get into the best classes. *It's already all over no matter what day it is…*

****

Jake hadn't planned on it but somehow he found himself on the far corner of Northeast. He'd meant to head toward Northwest and by extension maybe swing by Riley's place but something kept him anchored on Northeast. He had to admit how nice everything looked in the sunset strewn courtyard he was walking through. Only a few kids were outside. None paid much attention to him.

It was still early enough in the night that his student ID card would work to get him into dorms that weren't his own. He made his way to the nearest building and swiped his way inside. He didn't know for sure where he was going until he hit the nearest stairwell. It was only then that he made up his mind on which way to go. Like Jake,

Jared McAlpin lived on the ground floor of his dorm in a suite with Gary, Dylan, Lenny, and a couple other non-AZXis. Everything had been so serious for Jake recently that he could probably use some of Jared's patented goofiness.

Once he reached the ground floor he found Jared's name listed on the wall by the left corner door. He knocked somewhat forcefully for a few seconds before Gary came to the door. He instantly laughed in his own unique way. Neither of them had said anything funny to warrant it though. That was just how the guy was. *It's gonna be interesting watching this guy handle a pledge class.*

Gary pointed Jake toward Jared's room that he shared with Dylan. As usual, Lenny was sacked out watching TV in their common room. According to Jared that was his usual pose throughout any given day of the week, Monday or Saturday it didn't matter. Jake hadn't been remotely shocked when he'd heard that considering that was how he always pictured Lenny. The guy looked permanently exhausted. Jake nodded at him; he did the same before returning his eyes to the TV.

After that he barged into Jared's room like he owned the place. What he found once he was inside the room was...weird. Jared was sitting at his desk watching porn, except he wasn't jerking off. It was almost like he was just soaking it all up. As Jake got closer it was clear why he wasn't jerking off. The website was full of massively obese women. Most people would've been mortified by being discovered viewing such things but Jared didn't even flinch. He looked at Jake and grinned. "Yo did you know there's entire websites devoted to banging fatties?" he announced gleefully. If Jake didn't know better, he'd swear the guy was overjoyed at the discovery. *If his internet search history could talk...*

"What the fuck?!" was all Jake could think to say.

"I'm not saying I'd watch them" Jared back-peddled. "I mean I would, but only to see what it's like."

Jake had to admit it was hard to tear his eyes away from the screen once he got to really looking but he finally did. "Well you think you could table that for a second and help me with something?"

Jared closed his laptop before turning his chair around to fully face Jake. "What's up bro?"

"Gotta plan for classes tomorrow."

"Right good call. I've gotta set my alarm for that" Jared interrupted. Just like that his focus shifted away so he could reach his alarm clock and set it. Only after he was done did his attention return. "So what's the deal? Don't know which classes to take?"

"Sort of" Jake admitted sadly. "Me and Kelly planned out which classes we'd take together next semester."

"Yikes."

"Exactly."

"You think it's gonna be a problem?"

"Only if you consider the fact that I never want to see her again, or at least I'm not sure if I do…" his voice trailed off.

Jared sat there intently while he gathered his likely scattered thoughts. Jake finally realized it wasn't Jared's decided lack of advice-giving ability that had drawn him here. It was his ability to listen and hold judgment at bay. He loved them but Eric and Riley wouldn't be able to do that for him. *That's what makes them family, pretenses be damned.* "So do you think I should just not give a fuck about her and take the pre-planned classes or just pick all new ones?"

Jared sat in his chair, rocking it back and forth in a pretty hazardous rhythm before finally stopping. "It's a lot of work just to avoid a girl you'll probably end up seeing anyways. This school isn't *that* big bro. Did you plan on taking every class together next semester?"

"Yeah" Jake shamefully admitted. Only now was that fact being seen for how insanely stupid it was. "A couple are electives though so I can swap them out if I wanted to…but I like the schedule I'd have. Plus one is a requirement so unless I wanted to put it off 'til spring I should take it now."

"I say you just do whatever you have to to give you the hottest schedule. It's all really up to you. I don't know bro. I guess I don't mind seeing my exes like you. Besides, you've got 'til tomorrow to make the call and even if you want to change it up after you can deal with that early next semester."

Jake nodded. "Yeah I know but changing things around during the semester is always such a pain in the ass." He'd only had to alter his schedule mid-semester one time before and it wasn't an experience he wanted to repeat. The constant webpage refreshing to check class capacities was about as nerve-wracking as waiting to get that fateful call leading to a callout.

"Well I think it's the best move."

"Yeah maybe you're right" Jake agreed.

They sat in silence for a few seconds before Jared spoke up again. The guy had yet to meet the uncomfortable silence he couldn't fill with uncomfortable words. "You want to watch some fatty porn? It'd be mad funny."

****

Jeff sat at his desk, staring sullenly at the screen. It was only minutes before his second to last class registration. It felt more final than it was. He couldn't sleep in as late as he wanted to, even today. His alarm had never gone off but he couldn't bring himself to stay in bed past six in the morning. He'd heard Eric leaving for the library around when he'd woken up so it seemed as good a time as any to get out of bed.

Once he made it to the desk his fingers had assumed a mind of their own. Before long he found himself looking at pictures of AZXi parties from the year he'd been suspended from school. There weren't many since whoever had been the historian that year had fucked things up eight ways from Sunday. Jeff couldn't tell if he was happy that there wasn't much photographic evidence or if he was pissed he couldn't live vicariously through those same pictures. The whole thing put his stomach in knots. *If that night never happened I'd be sleeping in my bed...just like Gretman is.* Sometimes he relived that night in his dreams and as fate would have it, he'd crossed paths with the memory again last night. It was fitting that the reason he'd have to wake up early today for registration was the very thing that woke him in a cold sweat.

Missing his planned junior year had felt like a knife carving through his body that day he'd met with Dean Standor to learn his fate. Even now, a year and a half later he was still letting the memory fuck him out of sleep. He wiped the latest lining of sweat from his forehead as he continued scrolling through the pictures. Kraylin's face whirled by as he clicked through the photos. He saw flashes of Petey, Gretman, Kevin, Guapo, Eric, Jerry and all the rest having the time of their lives without him. While they were drinking beer and dancing with chicks, Jeff was sifting through a long distance relationship with Dana and living at his parent's house. *How could they all be having so much fun while I was at home miserable... suffering for all of them?* Jeff slammed his fists on the desk. After recoiling he listened through the paper-thin walls to hear if anyone was awake now because of what he'd just been weak enough to do.

There wasn't a sound. Petey, Calvin and Kevin were all still asleep. Eric was gone, and it was likely Jerry was too. Guapo would need to register too but it was doubtful he'd get up right away. Being the night owl he was, the bastard was rarely awake before ten. In his case it wouldn't matter much since he'd fail whatever classes he took, willfully or otherwise.

After another couple minutes the time for registration was upon him. He opened up the school's webpage and logged in. Since he was going to be a senior computer science major he shouldn't have any trouble getting into the upper level classes he needed to graduate. Classes that high were rarely filled to capacity.

Sure enough, after a few more clicks of the mouse he found that each of the four core requirements he'd been planning to take were open. He signed up for each one without issue. The final elective he took was just a random one hundred level class he needed for the extra credit hours. *Next semester is going to suck...hard.* He wasn't all that upset though. He'd planned it out so that his second to last semester would be a pain in the ass, which left his final semester in the spring wide open to take a bunch of easy classes so he could sit on cruise control 'til graduation.

The final page of registration stopped him in his tracks just like it had since that same night sophomore year. *What semester do I plan to graduate in?* The school always wanted to know after each registration period so they could keep track of if a student was on schedule to have the needed credit hours by whatever date they chose. After waiting a few seconds he clicked on the spring of next year. It was later than the original plan but there was nothing to be done about it now.

Next spring it all ends.

Chapter 39

The morning whizzed by in a blur.

When he'd been with Gary, Lenny and Jared over at their dorm everything had seemed well enough but even Jake knew the feeling was temporary. As soon as he made it back to his dorm the thoughts of dread resurfaced. At the end of the day he'd come to the very realistic conclusion that Kelly was the kind of girl who wouldn't back down from what she'd previously decided on without good reason. Even though their relationship was in the past Jake didn't believe she'd actually go through with changing her schedule on the off chance that he'd be dumb enough to sign up for the classes they'd picked together. He'd had plenty of time to mull over all those thoughts and more while tossing and turning in bed last night.

Jake had picked all new courses while still managing to take the core classes required for his major. It wasn't a pretty schedule by any stretch of the imagination but it would definitely keep him away from Kelly and that was more important than sleeping in on Mondays, Wednesdays and Fridays.

After registering for the acceptable classes Jake tried going back to sleep but since his heart had been pounding all morning over whether he was making the right choice there was no chance in Hell he was gonna be sleeping anytime soon.

He'd slogged through the day's remaining classes, which thankfully ended around noon. Afterward, Jake found himself wandering around the campus once again. Today he'd gone downtown to Arkridge Avenue. It was all in some vague attempt to maybe catch Eric out of Cordan for once. Of course that definitely didn't happen as Eric, Jerry and Calvin's rooms were all locked signifying they were either not there or didn't want to be bothered. That only left the other side of the house, which Jake wasn't thrilled about even with recent events. Once there he wanted to use the bathroom but on his way down the hall he heard a voice call his name. He was in such a daze from lack of sleep and over-thinking that he barely registered the sound.

"Yo Raley!" it said again after he just stood there like a deer in the headlights. Amazingly he got his feet to move in the direction of the sound although he wasn't sure how that had happened. Jake stood in the doorway to Jeff's room and waited for him to turn around from his desk. "What're you doing?"

"Went for a walk after class...ended up here" Jake replied honestly.

"It's as good a place as any" Jeff answered with nonchalance while swiveling around in his chair. Jake hadn't yet looked in a mirror today but if he had it wouldn't have surprised him to see a reflection looking like the one staring back at him from that chair. Jeff Chester looked rundown, not unlike how Jake used to look during pledging. It brought a kind of sick satisfaction knowing his pledge-master was actually suffering.

"I figured..." Jake's voice trailed off. "Are you drinking?" he asked after noticing the open beer on the desk.

"Yup" Jeff answered quickly, channeling his best J-Hood impression. "Raley...somewhere there are people who aren't drunk...this is for them" he raised the bottle as if toasting some unseen person.

Jake looked back at him in mild shock. "My God you're breaking my heart."

"Hey I'm entitled to be depressing today so bite me" Jeff shot back. It wasn't in his usual venomous tone, it sounded almost sad. "Registration always brings up bad memories."

"Right there with you man" Jake agreed.

"By all means grab a beer then" Jeff ordered while motioning to the mini-fridge in the corner of the room opposite the door.

Jake absently walked toward it to pull out another bottle. Once he felt the cold glass in his hand he realized the implications of drinking so early but shrugged them off. *As long as I'm not drinking alone it's fine.* Taking a seat on Jeff's bed he turned his attention toward the open laptop Jeff was staring at.

"What're you working on?" Jake asked as he took the first sip from the freshly opened bottle. It had a tangy taste so he inspected the label. It didn't have any name he recognized but that didn't mean much since Keystone and Natural Ice were the only two beers he knew of.

"Working on some new features for the website" Jeff responded as if that wouldn't bring up entirely new questions.

"Wait...we have a website?"

"Ya know Raley, you really do suck" Jeff teased him.

Jake shrugged. "Just because I don't use a website I didn't know existed until now? That's fucked up. I'll get to it next semester" he assured an uninterested Jeff. "So what're you so pissed about today?" Jake was sure to add emphasis to the word 'today' since Jeff always seemed to be upset about something. The emphasis went unnoticed.

"Elections, choosing classes, graduation...take your pick Raley," Jeff said sourly while finishing off his own bottle. It looked to be his first of the day but Jake couldn't be sure. *If these walls could talk...*

"I wouldn't dream of stepping into that minefield" Jake replied dryly.

As expected Jeff wasn't looking for any particular response. "Your cousin made a fuckin' awful mistake yesterday."

"I didn't think it was that big a deal," Jake offered mildly. It was a veiled attempt at trying to defend his cousin.

Jeff wasn't buying it. "That's because you're a new fuck."

"So you guys keep saying," Jake said coolly. He was getting a little tired of being called a new fuck by anyone that had pledged before the Alpha Epsilons.

Jeff shook his head again. "You don't know any better," he added with unintended condescension.

"No but it doesn't stop you from trying."

"What are we without determination?"

Jake didn't know what to say. He took another sip of beer. The taste still made him shift in his seat even on the third try. As he sat there in the newly formed silence Jake started to feel apprehensive about entering Jeff's room.

****

Jeff Chester sat in his chair, cracking his knuckles before continuing the line of code he'd been trying to finish since Raley walked in but it was no use, he couldn't focus. That had been a problem all morning, Raley notwithstanding. "The best part about all this is that we had elections late this semester so that they fell right before registration which is always balls. I can't fucking believe it came to this."

"Biz told me you weren't graduating on time but he wouldn't tell me why."

"I'd need at least another beer before I'd even consider getting into that" Jeff responded with a slight smirk.

On cue the new fuck reached over to the mini-fridge to grab another bottle of the Killians he'd been drinking, handing it to Jeff along with a look that begged for a story. "It seems like these days are the ones we're all pissed about," Jake said while lowering his arm from the hand-off. "Shotty going next by the way."

Sophomore year was halfway over since spring finals were coming up in a month and a half. As usual Jeff felt pretty confident in his chances for acing them all just like he had the three semesters prior. Even the semester he'd pledged he'd thankfully been taking easy enough classes where the insomnia and absenteeism hadn't overtly affected his grades. With pledging so far in the past he'd made it to most classes so his notes were as good as they could get.

Standing there in the barn Jeff wanted to slap himself for even thinking about class right now. Even with finals coming up it was completely unacceptable to consider that kind of thing within these sacred AZXi walls.

Somehow he'd drawn the short straw to get the late shift of watching the door for their Open tonight. Jeff hadn't argued against it considering he was still relatively low on the frat's totem pole but standing here now with a solid buzz being forced to collect money from incoming students was less than ideal. With only two Psi pledges, they'd been relegated to tending the kegs and filling up the brother's cups. That left the doors to be covered by younger actives like himself, among others.

"You got the door 'til midnight right?" Calvin asked from beside him. The guy had only crossed last semester but he seemed to like taking on as much responsibility as humanly possible. He'd checked in with Jeff now twice during his half-hour shift just to make sure things were going well. Jeff didn't have the heart to tell him to just relax and enjoy the party. He doubted it would've made much difference. Calvin Gretman seemed like the kind of guy that could give advice better than taking it.

"Yeah. We should be good. We'll head to the bars after." Jeff checked the old clock that hung over the wooden bar one of the earlier pledge classes had made for their project. It said that there was about twenty minutes 'til midnight but the party was going well enough that it could easily go past then if the kegs held out.

With no one currently at the door Jeff took a second to check out the wooden bar the pledges were serving beer at. It wasn't pretty but it worked. Their own pledge class project had been a website, or at least a mildly functional one as of now. Jeff had practically built the damn thing himself with only minimal help from Kevin and zero from Guapo but that was expected. *It'll get done soon.* None of the brothers seemed overly concerned about its completion date. Before the website went up all AZXi had was a broken, outdated email system. That had been the sole electronic means of communication for their frat until the Phi class had come along.

While he and Gretman stood near the barn entrance surveying the party, a group of girls walked in with their money in hand. Jeff took five-dollar bills from each after checking their school ID's to prove they actually were students. They could never be too careful even though they'd never been bothered by the cops. Some of the other frats got hassled every now and then but AZXi had been fortunate. The girls walked past them, making their way to the keg. They were a little late considering how long the party had been raging but hot girls came and went as they pleased in Gladen Hills. Jeff checked each one out as they came through. They weren't bad to look at by any means but he had yet to meet any girl that made him want to give up the single life.

After prying his eyes away he folded up the recently gained bills into the wad of cash he was keeping in his pocket. He tried doing so in a way that wouldn't draw attention but there was zero chance that Calvin hadn't seen it all before he'd put it away. It was shameful to admit but he'd been focused on the third girl in the line. The name on her ID was Dana. She'd smiled at him while handing over her money. Jeff almost considered letting her in for free. She was really hot with a great ass and nice tits. With those things fresh on his mind he hadn't put the money away as quickly as he probably should have.

It was always good form to keep the regular partygoers from seeing the cash they were taking in on any given night. Gladen Hills didn't have much trouble with stealing but that was another of those things that they couldn't be too careful about. The only person he'd shown the money to once he'd gotten to his shift was the treasurer, Dave Kraylin. Since that's whom the money would be turned over to at nights end, keeping it hidden from him was pointless.

"Looks like the frat is doing well tonight" Calvin commented. He was almost trying to sound casual when it was clear he was happy with what he'd seen.

"We usually do with these Opens," Jeff agreed confidently. He'd worked the door enough times to know that AZXi was the place to be on a Friday night for the unaffiliated undergrads.

"Then why are we always so damn broke?" Gretman asked. Jeff smirked inadvertently. *That's a damn good question. I'd love to know where all the money ends up from these parties.* Obviously some of it went toward kegs and cups but it couldn't *all* go to that. "Doesn't it seem like every meeting we're told we need to save money and shit? Where do we piss it all away? Is the E-Board having steak dinners every Sunday?" Calvin asked, half-kidding. "I'm telling you man," he went on, unhindered by Jeff's lack of words. "One day when we're in charge we're gonna run the shit out of this place." The guy looked around the barn with eyes that screamed for conquest, just not with the females. *Where the fuck does he get all that motivation?*

"Jesus how much have you drank Gretman?" Jeff teased. "Sophomore year is a little early to be thinking about senior year."

"Well I did spend a little time on the ice luge," Calvin answered with a grin.

He motioned over to the huge block of ice set up diagonally on the end of the lone table on the other side of the barn. The idea behind it was to pour beer or usually Mad Dog 20/20's down the chiseled path in the block's center to make it to the person's mouth at the bottom. It was a disgustingly efficient way of getting hammered. During Opens they usually just used beer. Apparently Mad Dogs weren't a good use of frat funds, or so Kraylin had told them. He was only a junior but he'd made the E-Board as treasurer almost by default since no one else wanted it. Races like that with no contest had bothered Jeff ever since he'd witnessed the first elections after Crossing.

"I need to get laid tonight" Jeff announced, changing the subject as his eyes found their way back to the shorter girl who'd smiled at him. *Dana.*

Calvin patted him on the back easy enough. "Get a girlfriend pal. That'll help."

Jeff smiled absently. He'd heard enough stories about Calvin's impossibly hot chick Jennifer from the Rho Betas to last a lifetime. Fortunately he was one of the few brothers in AZXi with a girlfriend so most of the time they could all gang up on him for that questionable life choice.

"Guaranteed pussy isn't any fun" Jeff replied, half-serious. It'd be nice some nights when he didn't want to try for anything new but most of the time he enjoyed the pursuit.

"Not as fun as having to work for it every night with random chicks?"

"It just makes scoring that much better" Jeff responded haughtily. He'd be damned if he'd let this newer fuck lecture him about the joys of getting ass in Gladen Hills. *What the hell does he know about it anyway?* Before he could get into it with Gretman over the merits of being single versus tied up a loud knock came at the door that incidentally coincided with the music hitting a lull. With the amount he'd drank Jeff was too slow to stop the door from swinging open widely as four cops strolled inside.

Holy shit. Jeff felt himself paralyzed with surprise and anxiety.

Somehow during the shuffle of people walking out the side exits and even the ones the cops were coming in from Calvin got pushed away from the front door toward the back. That left Jeff alone with the lead officer. "What's your name kid?" the guy asked abruptly with all the condescension he believed his post afforded him.

"I don't suppose you guys have a warrant to be in here?" Jeff asked, sounding braver than he felt.

"Alright smartass. We don't need one since the door was open on top of the amount of noise complaints we've gotten for this property." The cop folded his arms around his lanky body, staring in Jeff's direction waiting for a response.

"Jeff Button Chester" he sighed finally.

"I don't suppose when we check everyone's ID's that we'll find any underage?" It was clear they both knew the answer to that question. As many people that had gotten out during the cops' initial entrance, there was still a good amount being corralled along the back wall. Jeff kept his mouth shut, trying to stand confidently.

"Empty your pockets" the cop ordered after he got a nod from another officer.

The wad of cash in his pocket was too big to pretend as though it wasn't there and the last thing he wanted to feel was the rough groping of a cop that had nothing better to do on a weekend. Reluctantly he pulled out his wallet and the stack of bills. The cop was doing his best to hide a self-satisfied grin. "Where's all that from kid?"

"It's mine. One of my friends owed me money," he answered casually.

It worked just as much as expected. "Selling alcohol to minors is a pretty big offense smartass. Come on, let's go for a walk" he motioned to the door so Jeff could exit first. Before he trudged outside he turned to look at the brothers who were standing along the back wall. A few were really drunk. Some were shaking their heads at just how fucked they all really were. Calvin in particular looked extremely depressed. Jeff couldn't understand why. At least he hadn't been caught at the door with a handful of cash.

"Damn that's crazy" Jake said sullenly as if to commiserate with Jeff over the depressing story. It had minimal effect. There were others who'd tried to do the same since that night but no one could really understand what that moment had felt like. Jeff just nodded while draining the beer he'd been handed not ten minutes ago.

"So what's your issue Raley?" Jeff asked, hastily changing the subject.

As expected, the kid was powerless not to talk about himself. "Just shit with my ex," he replied vaguely. It probably killed him not to dive right into exactly what was bothering him but Jeff admired the restraint, even if it was just for the moment.

"Like shit about who gets the kids when and the summer homes?"

Jake smiled although there was no happiness behind it. "We planned out our schedules for next semester…and I'd be happy never seeing her again so I changed everything around but there's still the chance we might be in *something* together."

Jeff smirked. *Yeah…something together like a bed. There's no chance you won't fuck her again, no matter how terrible an idea it is.* "That's not bad at all" Jeff replied, trying to lighten things up while keeping his predictions silent. He knew if he were Raley that he'd never want to see that cheating bitch again either. "Just keep drinking Raley. It'll numb the pain. Or at least it'll numb *you* enough where you don't give a fuck about the pain." Jeff doubted that was really the case but he didn't want to keep drinking alone like he had before the new fuck walked in. Raley finished his first beer and without prompting, reached into the fridge to grab two more, one for each brother.

****

"How long have you been in here?" Riley asked hesitantly as she set a smoothie down on Eric's table. He looked to be on the verge of passing out just like he sometimes did at Cordan. This was a different kind of exhaustion though, not one from partying too hard too fast. It was strictly academic fatigue. She wasn't worried since he always looked like that at the semester's end.

"Since it opened at six" Eric replied while eyeing the smoothie she'd bought for him. *The cold drink might actually wake him up for a second.*

"And you were up all night too I bet?" she asked rhetorically.

"No actually, I got like two hours but I'll get plenty of sleep after finals."

Riley felt sorry for her cousin. "Well how'd your weekend go?" It was a shameless way of turning things toward the topic she wanted to get to now that she'd been thoroughly depressed by Eric's near narcoleptic state.

"Not bad at all" Eric responded quickly, much too quickly for her to buy it.

"Jake mentioned something about an issue at the meeting?" she offered vaguely. Their younger cousin tried calling her about Eric but she was busy sorting through her own shit with Tory and Brynn. She'd only inferred the rest later in the night when she had time to actually sit and think about something not relating to EIPi.

"Yeah of course he did" Eric quipped, sounding a little annoyed. "They wanted me to be president and I didn't want it so I didn't run."

"I though you were at least thinking about it."

"I was."

"But you said no because of your classes right?"

"Exactly" Eric confirmed. "But Buttons and some others just don't get it. If you believe the guy, he thinks the frat is going to just up and die next year."

"So what do you think?" Riley asked unsurely.

"It'll be completely fine. Buttons is just being dramatic like Jake usually is because I'm not one hundred percent into the frat."

Riley nodded. "One hundred percent is a lot to ask for on anything." She suddenly felt better about her own decision when reflecting upon Eric's. *It won't help when I talk to Felicia but still...*

"I guess I can't really fault him given his track record" Eric said thoughtfully. He started guzzling the smoothie. If nothing else the brain freeze he'd likely get would definitely wake him up.

"Some people are like that though Eric."

He set the smoothie down after realizing the error of how fast he was downing it. "So how'd your elections go? I'm guessing you got VP since you haven't mentioned it."

Riley smirked. "Good guess."

"Not really" he admitted. "If you hadn't I doubt I would've gone this long not hearing about it."

"Yeah I got it...but there's still a problem."

"There always is" Eric answered somewhat sadly.

"Tory didn't get anything. She lost house president to one of the other girls. *Amy Brage and the Beta Zeta bloc is what she lost to actually, just like the rest of us.*

"It happens" Eric shrugged. Riley wasn't even sure why she expected that news to affect him any more than it had.

"I tried explaining that to her but something else is going on. My Little may have fucked some things up too." Riley was still trying to fight the idea in her head but it was a losing battle. The more she thought about it the more she believed that Brynn voted for Amy out of spite for Tory. It made complete sense in a warped way.

Eric shrugged again. He was clearly unimpressed with the line of conversation but didn't complain, knowing better than to bite the hand buying him smoothies. "Isn't she entitled to vote how she wants?" he put forth unsteadily. *Even with me right now, he doesn't wanna take sides...maybe that's why I couldn't do it. I can't stay impartial.*

Riley agreed begrudgingly while pushing her own thoughts aside. "Obviously she is. Tory usually doesn't take anything personally but she was really upset."

"I know the feeling" Eric admitted.

"Have you tried talking to Jeff at all?"

Eric immediately banned that idea. "I know better than to talk to him today. Class registration isn't a good time for him."

****

Eric Saren looked insanely hot in his profile picture. *The things I should do.* It wasn't the first time since elections that she found herself alone, scrolling through a friend's page on Facebook. The loss of house president was crushing, even more than Brian ignoring her during the core time of their hook-ups. It just tasted bitter from start to finish. Granted it had only been twenty-four hours but it was still hard to wrap her head around the feeling.

Fortunately she wasn't alone long. A knock on her door came within seconds of her clicking onto Eric's latest tagged photos. Once she announced to whoever was at the door that they could come in she quickly closed down the site and her laptop. *I don't need any more pity today but some sympathy might be nice.*

"Who are you Facebook stalking this time T?" Dani asked in an upbeat voice.

Ever since being elected pledge mom the threat of the world ending wouldn't have wiped the smile from her face. *Lucky her.*

"No one" Tory lied. "I'm just mad bored."

"No finals this week?" Danielle asked. It was clear that she came into Tory's room looking for Riley since she rarely visited. As the girl's eyes darted around the room quickly Tory knew she was right in her assumptions.

"Not 'til Thursday and there's no way I'm studying 'til at least tomorrow." Even that was a bit of a stretch considering how she was feeling. There wasn't much she felt inclined to do. And she doubted that would change with tomorrow's sunrise. "What about you?"

"I am studying actually," Danielle answered with a smirk.

Tory recognized the notebook she was holding immediately. It was the same one Riley had used to keep the pledge mom guidelines during the past year. Every spring the former pledge mom would hand the notes down.

"Yeah right. Studying notes for a pledge program that's over four months away. Come on Dani, there's gotta be *something* better to do" Tory teased. *But I don't have anything better to do so why should she?*

"No point in putting off the basics" Danielle chided her. "It's a good thing Riles remembered to give me these before she left for Cordan. I figured she'd be back by now." Dani's eyes surveyed the room again as if Riley would spontaneously appear.

"Yeah well…there's no room for another disappointed sister in the house today" Tory sighed. It wasn't the subtlest of ways to delve into her troubles but it would do.

Danielle closed the notebook she'd been looking at intently and shot a somewhat concerned look in Tory's direction. "How are you handling everything now?"

"It happened yesterday" Tory replied, almost angrily.

"Yeah but *any* time has to help."

In theory that sounded good but it didn't hold up in practice. If anything Tory might be even more depressed today since the whole thing had sunk in. Now that the whiplash had worn off all that was left was the knowledge that her sisters didn't think she could handle being house president over Amy. Waking up today had been cold and abrupt. It had taken a few seconds for her mind to remember the elections and the reality slap that accompanied the memory wasn't gentle.

"In any case it's done T."

They were harsh words but Tory knew they were correct. It was done. There'd be no changing things now. *Story of my fucking life.* Clearly she wasn't going to get much in the way of sympathy from Danielle like she originally thought but that wasn't surprising once she thought about it.

"So do you think Riles will mind if I don't follow her notes exactly next year?"

Tory wasn't sure how to respond. "Are you planning on blazing a brand new trail or something?" The question sounded crazy but the response might just be crazier still.

"I don't know." It almost sounded like Dani was backtracking. "I know Riles wants to stay involved in how things are run. I just think I might have some different ideas." Danielle was flipping through the pages in the notebook, looking disproving as she did. Tory would've given anything to see what pages Danielle was looking through at that moment but she was going too fast.

What the fuck is she thinking about changing? Can she really get away with changing things we've been doing for years? Pledging traditions and callouts have specific guidelines. Changing one thing would cause chaos. Damn…that's fucking dramatic. What's wrong with me?

All self-loathing aside, Danielle's plans were definitely something that would and should cause ripples in EIPi if she actually went through with anything like what Tory was picturing. *If Kayla and Felicia were still here to see this they'd go fucking nuts.*

****

"I just got the official word from the school boys" Will announced sullenly. It was one of the few times Jake had ever actually seen his pledge brother looking sad. His own buzzed stature disappeared as he sat up in his chair at the Lancaster dining hall to listen closer. "They're putting me on academic probation."

Jake found himself searching the faces of the other two at the table to gauge how they were handling the revelation. J-Hood and Summers looked to be in as much a state of shock as he was. There were times throughout the semester where the thought of William Anthony getting kicked out of Gladen Hills would've been nothing short of a gift from God. That time was gone. Will was still the same asshole Jake had come to hate during pledging but he was somehow able to deal with his shit better now.

"How the fuck did this happen?" Jake asked bluntly. No one could ever really brag about grades from the semester they pledged unless their name was Jerry or Eric but academic probation was something else entirely. "I mean how fucked did your GPA get this semester?" he corrected the question.

"It's below where it should be" Will answered while moving some of the mac and cheese around his plate. Being the bigger guy he was, Jake couldn't recall the last time Will hadn't picked his plate clean during a meal they shared, and they'd eaten together every weeknight for six weeks. The guy wasn't fat; he could just eat with purpose.

"How low is it?" J-Hood joined the conversation. That was a relief. He didn't want to seem like the only one concerned about their jackass pledge brother.

"It's a 1.2 right now, before finals. Even if I ace all of them it'll still be below the 2.5 it needs to be at."

"OK so what exactly does this academic probation shit mean?" Jake questioned further. The beers he'd shared with Jeff a few hours ago seemed like something much farther in the past considering what was on the table now.

"The only reason they let me pledge this semester is because I made a deal with the CGA supervisors. My GPA had to be above a 2.5 otherwise I'd go on probation. Now that means if my midterm grades next semester aren't above that same number, they'll kick me out of the school half-way through."

Jake stopped moving altogether. It didn't seem real. If Eric could be believed then Guapo failed almost every semester and yet his ass was going to be here for a fifth year starting next fall. How could Will only have one shot and then be fucked when he missed it? *That's not fucking fair.* His next words came to him in the heat of the moment. "Do you need help with anything?" The craziest thing was that he didn't regret making the offer even after it was made. The other three looked appropriately shocked.

"Now *that* I never thought I'd see" Summers finally chimed in.

"What?" Jake asked, having an idea of what the response would be.

"Probably you helping Will with anything other than his suicide" J-Hood said dryly. He looked back and forth between Will and Jake almost as if he was expecting someone to tell him he was the victim of a clever joke.

"I'll be fine" Will added casually. "This just means I won't be able to party *as much* next semester."

Jake sat there, equally stunned and skeptical. *We'll see if that actually holds up when we get back to school in the fall.*

****

The forecast of the day called for scattered showers. Jeff had almost been praying for that since it would've allowed him to avoid seeing what was currently happening on Northeast's athletic fields. As usual the forecast was completely fucked and not a single drop of rain had fallen on Gladen Hills since last night. Given how much he and the rest of the AZXis had drank at that point it stood to reason that they might've missed a few drops here or there. Eric in particular looked like he was hammered out of his mind but he'd somehow still left the bar with a chick who Jeff couldn't remember the name of.

As if the universe was taunting him, Jeff could clearly see past the trees between Arkridge Avenue and the track and field area of Northeast to the stage. It was being completed for the graduation ceremony today. He knew he shouldn't be torturing himself by looking that way but as hard as he tried he couldn't pry his eyes away. The only thing coming close to stopping him was the Rho Beta house at the end of the street but even that was providing a shallow block.

Calvin, Jennifer, Petey, Kevin and all the others would be waiting around nearby, ready to walk across the stage to get their diplomas. *That could've been me.* The worst thing about the past few days and weeks was that Jeff wasn't sure if he was pissed or relieved about not being at that stage right now. That caused him all kinds of anxiety and he wasn't used to feeling anything like it. Not since *that* day.

"Good morning Mr. Chester" Dean Standor greeted him kindly enough as Jeff took a seat on the opposite side of the man's desk. He'd only been waiting outside in the Dean's outer office a matter of minutes before his secretary had pointed him in.

Ever since the cops had busted their party two weeks ago Jeff had been living in almost perpetual fear about what might happen to him and AZXi at large. The school's first measure had been to step into their affairs and force the Phi class to cross immediately. They'd only had two pledges so it wasn't a large amount but cutting off the last two weeks of their program and crossing them on week four was a mistake that Jeff couldn't even begin to think about. It was a disservice to the pledges and the fraternity.

No one had been happy about that but there wasn't anything they could do. The school administration ran the CGA with a tight grip. The CGA controlled every organization's charters and without those a fraternity or sorority would lose the school's sanction. That in turn would kill Rush attendance and subsequently the organization altogether. So AZXi had to go along with the school's bullshit for fear of charter revocation. *Round and round we go, dancing to their fucking tune.*

The messed up part was that Dean Standor was relatively new in his position so no one in AZXi or anywhere else could tell Jeff what to expect from the guy before he had to meet with him. So far he seemed nice enough. *Maybe I could get out of this shit quick if he's a pushover.*

"Good morning sir" Jeff cleared his throat while straightening his posture in the uncomfortable chair.

"Well we have a bit of a problem here don't we?" Dean Standor asked abruptly after shifting his eyes quickly from papers on his desk to Jeff. A bead of sweat started forming on Jeff's forehead. He wasn't sure what to say. That indecision must've been visible because the Dean carried on. "The university police raided a party in the barn behind the Alpha Zeta Xi house. That fraternity is the one you are listed on the official chapter roster for correct?" It sounded rhetorical but Jeff nodded just in case. "Not only was there alcohol being served to minors who are also enrolled at this school, but they were being charged to drink illegally as well."

"Sir I'm not sure where you're getting your information but there was no one being charged to drink on that property. As I told the officer that money he saw was simply a debt I'd collected from another fraternity member" Jeff lied calmly. Calvin had gone along with his story after being convinced to do so by some of the older brothers. Gretman said he was the one to give Jeff all that money for a loan he'd borrowed earlier in the semester. Unfortunately he hadn't done so at the time of the raid so it didn't mean as much as it could have.

"Based on the official police report I received last week, you Mr. Chester, were the one caught by the door with the money so it can be safely assumed that you were the one doing the charging of minors to drink illegally." Dean Standor had made up his mind about what had happened that night already. It was just bad luck that he'd come to the correct conclusion.

Jeff fidgeted in his seat as he began to feel increasingly uncomfortable, and it wasn't just because of the chair.

"Let me be perfectly clear Mr. Chester, this is a very serious offense. Whether or not there was alcohol being sold or not may be hard to prove, but I am willing to bet it could be proven given adequate resources. Of course that'd require the courts and as you can imagine, our university wouldn't want any undue attention placed on the matter."

Jeff did his best not to smirk. *They don't want anything or anyone hurting their precious reputation about this school being anything other than a place of higher learning for the best and brightest. It's all about the money at the end of the day.* He found the very thought nothing short of sickening.

Gladen Hills was well known in the northern part of the country but any undergrad could tell you that the place was a party town as much as a learning institution. Ironically a good chunk of the people that applied and came to Gladen Hills were looking for a mix of both, not just one or the other. *That's what makes this place special you jackass: work hard, play hard.*

"I understand sir" Jeff replied cordially, keeping his composure.

"That being said" the Dean continued. "Alpha Zeta Xi is on very thin ice. This matter may shut down the entire organization. We'd revoke your charter. I imagine that'd make things a tad harder come Rush. The only ones around here to make it work without a charter are the SIMS but their time will come."

It was clear the Dean was plainly threatening AZXi as well as Jeff, maybe even the entire Greek Circle. It wasn't hard to see the guy was actually taking a kind of pleasure from it all. Anyone that knew about the significance of Rush numbers being related to having a charter knew how much of a death sentence it would be. Smiling about it just meant the bastard was enjoying himself.

Jeff nodded again, still finding it hard to speak.

"I want to know exactly what was going on at that party Mr. Chester. If you cooperate, given you were the one at the door and are the one most implicated in the matter, you and your fraternity may only be put on probation."

"So you're saying that the best that could happen to us is that we go on probation for a year or more?" Jeff asked, exasperated. He could feel frustration rising. *Who the fuck do you think you are?* Fraternities and bars got raided every few months in Gladen Hills and yet Jeff had never heard anything about probation or charter revocation. *If the AK's or Kappa Nus were in here right now they'd just get a slap on the wrist.* The older the organization was, the more influential their alumni were. The AK's had multiple alums that were professors at the school and they seemed to avoid trouble whenever it popped up. AZXi was still young and didn't have that kind of clout. That was the real problem here as far as Jeff could see.

"If you don't cooperate it's highly likely that myself and the administration would make an example of Alpha Zeta Xi and revoke the charter outright. I want details Mr. Chester…the truth, that's all." It was beginning to sound more and more like an order. "I'd suggest making it easier on yourself and your frat brothers by cooperating here today." There seemed to be extra venom in the Dean's use of the words 'frat brothers' almost like he was condescending to the entire concept. Jeff tried quelling his rage. *The school doesn't seem to mind our existence when it advertises this place.*

Scenarios started running through Jeff's mind faster and faster. *Even if I do tell him the truth there's no guarantee AZXi won't get fucked anyway. He wants me to tell him everything so he can go about it easier.*

"Yes sir you're right" Jeff finally admitted. He straightened up in the chair one more time while taking a deep breath. "I was the *only one* charging at the door. No one else in AZXi knew anything about it." Jeff said it with such conviction that it surprised even him. Dean Standor however, didn't look even remotely shaken.

They sat in silence for a while, simply sizing each other up.

"Mr. Chester, you frat boys really are all alike. All of you are so dedicated to making a mess of your own lives that the consequences never really sink in." The words set fire to Jeff's world. "I figured you might be in the mood for self-sacrifice so I spoke with the university's administration ahead of time. They agreed that if you went through with this…martyrdom that they'd have the punishment ready."

The time between the Dean's icy words and the actual punishment proclamation felt like years but it still wasn't long enough for Jeff to prepare for his fate. "Given that this illegal activity, whoever's fault it may be, was being conducted on property belonging to Alpha Zeta Xi, the university is placing your charter on a one year probationary period. During that time if *anything* else goes wrong, the charter will be revoked completely without the ability to appeal. I'll be meeting with the president of your fraternity later this week to discuss the situation in full. That way there will be no disconnect in the school's wishes regarding your fraternity."

Jeff steeled himself. *Or maybe you just want to see the look on another frat guy's face when you crush his soul.* Jeff stayed inside himself for what felt like another batch of years. He had to sit there and take what was coming next no matter what.

Given your predictable confession, the university and I have decided you will be suspended for a full year starting next fall. You will be able to rejoin the student community no earlier than the following fall of 2006. At that point it is highly recommended that you not re-enter the ranks of Alpha Zeta Xi for your own good. Of course that's only if the organization doesn't make any mistakes during its probation.

Almost two years after the meeting had taken place Jeff could still hear the words of the bastard Standor as though he were still sitting in that uncomfortable chair.

Jeff's forehead touched the window glass. It felt cool against his skin, which was beading in sweat while he remembered the end of sophomore year. He could see in the hollow reflection that his face was red, but not from anger, from something else.

He continued looking past where Arkridge Avenue ended and the interstate to where the athletic fields began. The vague outlines of students crossing the stage to get their diplomas were clear. The Dean was probably out there right now too, putting on a fake smile for the parents.

The images started to overwhelm him. Shame fell over him in a wave.

In the thankfully empty bedroom, a single tear rolled down Jeff's cheek.

Chapter 40

Tory always found it amusing when she witnessed one of her flings trying to get out of bed in the morning like a ninja. All guys thought they were so slick inching their way out from under the covers to find their clothes. Every one of them acted like that the morning after. Eric Saren was just like all the rest in that way. He'd struggled to open his eyes while lying next to her, each as naked as the day they were born. Once he'd finally gotten his bearings and figured out where the fuck he was he'd made moves to exit the warm bed they'd been sharing.

She knew she should probably feel some form of shame about being left here with him wanting to make a silent exit but he just looked a little pitiful while getting out of bed. Tory found it endearing.

After he stood up and got his boxers and pants back on it would've taken a deaf person not to hear all the noise. Eric didn't seem to think he was causing that much of a scene though because he never once looked back to see if Tory was awake. It was just as well since she didn't mind checking him out unnoticed.

"Where you headed?" she asked abruptly. She was going for maximum surprise and she achieved it. Eric had just finished putting his belt on from where Tory had flung it onto her couch the night before. He was still shirtless and it was clear the time he'd spent in the gym over the course of the previous semester hadn't yet faded entirely. *Next semester might be a different story though.*

"Whoa" he yelped while turning to face her. She was still doing a good job of concealing herself underneath the covers. That too was waiting to be shown at the moment that would promise maximum surprise.

"Good morning to you too" Tory offered with a smile. She lifted her arms out from under the covers into the crisp morning air of the EIPi house. Tory made sure that the quilt was still covering her chest as she stretched out. It wasn't cold but it was definitely warmer under the sheets. Goose bumps formed on her arms.

Eric looked positively uncomfortable as he stood shirtless mere feet away from where she was lying naked. The situation excited Tory. More often than not it would be the guy waking her up for another round in the morning. Most of the time she wouldn't even bat an eye at the idea of another go with a hot guy, even in the morning when she felt less than attractive. Sometimes though, she'd turn it down if the guy wasn't especially good in bed. She was sad to admit that it had happened more than a few times. *Some guys only want theirs*. Tory shook those thoughts away. Eric certainly didn't fall into that category.

"So where are you headed?" she repeated the question.

"Well once graduation is done I figure we'll all start drinking again."

That leaves plenty of free time. "True but that's still a ways away."

"Yeah…and it's not like I'll die without another drink but that's probably what the game plan is."

"Having another drink is the thing more likely to kill you actually Eric" she smiled with her best impression of a girl next door. *He needs to feel comfortable.* Tory couldn't say why but having him fuck her again now was something she wanted…a lot. There was something else driving her desires today but she couldn't say what it was.

"That's definitely fair" Eric chuckled unsurely.

Tory figured now would be beneficial to let her body out for some morning light. When she stretched out again she was sure to let the quilt slip down to her stomach so her chest was in plain view. Uncomfortable or not she'd yet to meet the frat guy that wouldn't jump at the chance for a morning session when she was lying naked in bed.

Eric sighed heavily, trying to keep his thoughts hidden. The way he was looking at Tory made her forget everything she'd gone through recently. Between the studying for finals and the elections shit, she felt warmth rush through her. It felt good to be wanted. "I guess I could hang out a little bit," he said with a shy smile.

Yeah you better. "That's good because you made me some promises last night" Tory smirked. Whether that was actually true or not was anybody's guess. She didn't remember it happening but that didn't matter, it was achieving the desired result.

"I guess I shouldn't go back on my word." Eric was still standing there as if he didn't know what to do next. *Does he still not get it? Come on Eric.*

Tory moved all the covers off her body and felt the goose bumps form on her legs as the morning air hit her skin. The look in her eyes should've been easy to read. It looked like Eric got the message loud and clear as he moved to rejoin her in bed. She kissed him as soon as he lied down next to her.

Tory usually woke up horny. Today she was just thankful she'd woken up next to a guy that would at least *try* to make her finish before he was done.

After their first kiss Eric moved his head over to her neck. It tickled at first but then she felt warmer and warmer. Her eyes moved up to the ceiling that she'd spent a lot of the year looking up at. Something about this time…about seeing the roof now made it seem like she was looking at it for the first time. It felt good to have someone next to her.

****

With the ceremony over Calvin could authoritatively say that the whole thing had been a huge waste of time. *Three fucking hours we were there just for two minutes to walk across the stage for a piece of paper.* Even though that piece of paper had been the culmination of four years it still seemed ridiculous that there wasn't an easier, less time-consuming way to have a ceremony for the graduates.

At its core, the whole thing was for the parents. And his had loved every second of the three plus hours they'd been out on that field. At least they'd said as much and to be fair, his mom probably *did* love it all. His dad had said the same but Calvin knew him better than that. He was definitely proud of his youngest son but Kenneth Gretman wasn't a fan of wasting time.

His poor mother had lived in a house with three men since Calvin was born. Due to that fact they'd all let her have whatever victories they could, in recent years at least. There was just no accounting for his or Adam's teenage years. Of course if it had been up to Calvin he would've had Jennifer record his walk across the stage so that his parents could still see it but avoid the two hours and fifty-eight minute downtime that had come along as a bonus. He'd be damned if he'd ever say that to his mother though. She'd been looking forward to today since he'd been accepted to Gladen Hills.

His parents wanted to take him to lunch on University Grove afterward, which Calvin had again agreed to reluctantly. As expected all the restaurants were packed with families looking to do the same.

Once they finished, they went back to AZXi.

All Calvin wanted to do was grab a beer and chill with his brothers. He'd had enough reminders today that he'd be leaving Gladen Hills soon. Thankfully his parents didn't want to come inside when they dropped him off. That was fine with him. It was always a little painful watching any of his brothers pretend to be upstanding individuals, even for a few minutes in the presence of anyone's parents.

He waved goodbye upon closing the car door. It was only a couple more steps from his dad's car to the house's front door but it felt longer. *I didn't think I was this tired; a nap might be good.* He tried shaking the thoughts from his head. *Sleeping now would just piss the other half of the day away.* That idea flew from his mind as soon as he got inside to find J-Hood, Jared and Jeff all sitting on the couches with beers in hand from the previous night's keg. They were all staring mindlessly at the TV. It was pretty clear that whatever was on wasn't even slightly important.

"Am I the first one back?" Calvin asked. He had to arch his head to see the screen that was facing the same direction as the front door. He didn't see what was on but the logo on the bottom right said it all. The 'VH1' network was playing and they rarely had on anything that required viewer attention in even the smallest degree.

"How'd it go?" Jeff asked, ignoring Calvin's question entirely.

"A pain in the ass like we always knew it would be."

It was good that it didn't taste like a lie either. Telling Jeff Chester that graduation was a great time would do nothing except rub more salt in the wound. That would be far from a good start to the two of them living together over the summer in the same house. *He's probably pissed off enough today already.*

"It was mad boring I bet" Jared laughed to himself while keeping his eyes locked on whatever reality garbage was playing.

"What time did you have to be there?" J-Hood asked firmly. He seemed almost too happy to turn his attention away from the TV.

"Around ten this morning."

"Jesus, you been there the whole time bro?" Jared chirped.

"No...I would've killed myself," Calvin said, only half-kidding. The clock on the cable box said it was past three, which sounded about right. "I went to lunch with my parents. I think Petey and Jen did too."

"Yeah that sounds awesome" Jeff added sullenly. He finished his beer and got up from the couch to look outside.

It was only within the past hour that the sky looked a little foreboding in terms of incoming rain. Calvin grinned at his luck. The ceremony had already been bad enough without being forced to remain inside all day.

"Well look at this" Jeff said while parting the window blinds. "It's Biz."

Jared and Calvin followed suit by looking out the other front window and the one on the door, respectively. "What do you guys think? Walk of shame?" Calvin asked, almost rhetorically. It was pretty clear from the shambling walk of their brother just what was going on. *Good for him. Maybe now he'll leave Jen alone.*

"Definitely" Jared exclaimed. Without a second's delay he opened the window and yelled outside for all of Arkridge to hear. "Yo Biz! Did you get it wet last night?!"

Calvin wouldn't have thought it possible given how slowly Eric was moving only seconds prior but with Jared's tactless yelling he veered toward them immediately with a good amount of speed.

Within seconds he was in the house, only slightly panting. "Chill son" Eric pleaded with Jared as if his brother's yelling would somehow diminish the fact that he'd gotten pussy last night. Maybe he was just afraid that announcing it would kill any chances with other girls or a repeat with the same one.

"When have you ever known Jared to be subtle about *anything?*" Calvin defended their brother. *He couldn't be serious if he had to.*

Eric immediately shook his head in agreement. "Are you trying to drink today?"

"Yeah, I just need a shower and nap first."

"That's ridiculous" Calvin replied in unison with Jared. He quickly smiled in response to having the same thought as his younger brother. *Guess there really is a first time for everything.*

"Who'd you bang last night cuz?" Jared asked, wanting details.

The fact that Eric tried playing it clueless at first was something he wouldn't be able to sell a blind man on. He looked uncomfortable but somehow also pleased. "Chill chill" was all he said.

"Taking a page from Jerry's book now?" Calvin asked, seeing right through the façade at once.

"It was one of the EIPis" Eric admitted. Calvin knew his brother enough to know that the guy probably wouldn't say much more, at least not at the moment.

"I hope you at least gave one hundred percent to whoever the chick was," Jeff slurred from his post at the window. He was looking unsteady, using the windowsill to remain upright. Calvin hadn't noticed it until now but Jeff was clearly the drunkest, by a wide margin. *He probably woke up and started slamming beers.*

Biz didn't acknowledge Jeff, he simply turned to Calvin with a curious look. It took him a second to figure out why because he'd forgotten that his parents had made him keep his graduation gown on even through their meal. His mother had wanted more pictures than she'd wanted during his entire life up until that point. It had just made more sense to keep the uncomfortable thing on rather than put it on anytime his mother wanted. Almost immediately upon his realization Calvin practically ripped the gown off and threw it over onto the couch Jeff had vacated. *Seriously...fuck that thing.*

"Congrats Gretman" Eric said warmly.

"Thanks Biz."

Eric made his way past Calvin and the others to the kitchen and by extension his bedroom. *He always tries to be a lot sneakier than he is.* "You are gonna be down to drink tonight right?"

"Dude obviously" Eric answered the only way he could. The look on his face almost looked like he was expecting no one else to notice his sly exit. *Even Jeff caught his escape and he's borderline hammered.*

"Is Raley still around?" Calvin asked just as Eric was clearing the doorway.

"Nah he went home after finals."

Calvin expected that. It would've been a miracle had that particular new fuck hung around with them at all during the last full weekend. "He didn't even say goodbye or anything. That kid needs to get it together Biz!" Calvin shouted to the footfalls making their way up the steps.

"What else is new!?" Eric shouted back once he reached the second floor.

After that they heard his door open and close. *That's the end of him 'til tonight.* Out of the corner of his eye Calvin saw J-Hood check the time on his phone before finishing his own beer. By now Jeff had found his way to the other couch Jared was on, probably because it was closer than the one he'd left behind.

"Gotta head out boys," J-Hood announced casually. When Jared and Calvin looked at him inquisitively he elaborated. "Apparently the girl from last night left her watch or something in my room. She wants me to let her in to get it."

"You trying to repeat bang?" Jared asked giddily, raising his cup in a toast.

J-Hood neither confirmed nor denied it. He just shrugged casually before nodding at each of them and heading out the front door. "I'll bet that kid gets anal sex on command" Jared exclaimed.

Calvin winced in jealousy and shame. "Thanks for that."

"What?! It looks mad hot in porn but God forbid I ever get any." The guy sounded far more disappointed than anyone had any right to be.

"I'm going to bed," Jeff mentioned on his way out.

And then there were two. "OK man I'm gonna change and then we can hit up the National" Calvin said to Jared once Jeff left.

"Sweet. I'll get a beer for the road" Jared answered happily.

****

Riley wasn't sure how she was feeling but she was pretty sure she wasn't mad. Truthfully she should've seen the whole thing coming but somehow she'd been so swept up in other thoughts that she couldn't see the obvious outcome.

She barged into Tory's bedroom as if it were her own much like Tory always did to her. She had to admit that it felt liberating. As soon as Riley saw Tory standing there she was reminded why she never just walked into a bedroom in EIPi. She could never be sure what she'd find.

Thankfully Tory was at least wrapped in a towel having just come out of the shower. It was clear by the amount of water dripping off her dark auburn hair that if Riley had been a minute earlier she might've seen more of her friend than she ever wanted to. *And that's why you always knock.*

"Riles?" Tory didn't even seem the slightest bit embarrassed by the clothing situation. It took a second for Riley to find her voice. *If she's OK with having only a towel on for this then whatever.*

"I just got an interesting text from Dani."

"Another of those chain texts that's supposed to be funny but really isn't?" Tory asked immediately. Riley smiled. Danielle had been attempting to start up a chain texting system for EIPi in the form of jokes similar to chain emails but unfortunately Danielle's sense of humor was a little too G-rated sometimes for any of the girls to find *really* funny. It was a good idea; it just needed refinement.

"No. She saw my cousin doing the walk of shame out of the house this morning." Riley was careful to monitor Tory's face when she was talking but as usual, it betrayed no emotions.

"Come on Riles. If I'd slept with Jake then that would've been *my* text you got, not Dani's" Tory replied with a grin. *Nice deflection T.* It was no secret that Tory thought her younger cousin was cute, and she loved reminding Riley of that. It was also true that Tory would've been the first to brag about hooking up with Jake *if* it happened.

"I'm pretty sure she meant Eric. She even sent a picture." Riley moved over beside her sister to allow her to see the picture Danielle had sent twenty minutes ago.

Tory once again played dumb. "How about that? I wonder who he fucked?"

Well that settles it. Even if Eric had the game to get with another EIPi, which was questionable, especially when he was hammered like last night, Tory wouldn't have been so easy-going about it. At the very least she'd be extremely curious. It was practically a guarantee that they'd been screwing in the bed that sat mere feet to her right. Riley threw the mental image from her mind before it even came close to materializing.

On the one hand she was happy for her friend since she'd gotten something she clearly needed, especially after elections but she found it was a hollow feeling considering she'd done so with a family member of hers. *Remember the pact girl.* "I only need one guess" Riley began, trying to hold back the confident smile for her deductions. Tory didn't look ready to admit anything. "Are you denying it was you T?"

"Of course not. I'm just messing with you."

"So you did sleep with my cousin...again?"

"Yes ma'am" Tory replied happily. "We both needed it. It was great!"

"OK *that* I didn't need to know" Riley put up her hand in protest.

"Hey you asked. I mean it wasn't like we were having board game night in here" Tory continued, still grinning.

"Fine" Riley admitted. "How're you feeling now?"

"Much better actually."

"Good because we're drinking right now so get dressed," Riley ordered. She felt like a pledge mother again with that firm feeling of command.

"You don't think I could go out like this?" Tory motioned to her lack of clothing.

"I didn't say that" Riley retorted. "I'd just prefer you didn't." *If anyone could pull off that look then it'd be you though T.*

"You never let me have any fun!"

I somehow think Eric would have something different to say about that. "I know. I'm such a bitch."

As she was turning to leave, her friend's phone went off. Out of the corner of her eye she saw it was a text from Eric. Immediately she turned away so that she didn't have to read whatever it said. It was probably something about last night...or today...or something else she didn't want to know any more about. Absently, she turned back around to tell her friend something she'd just remembered only to see her deleting the message without opening it.

Tory didn't notice that Riley saw it.

She closed the phone and tossed it over onto the still disastrous looking bed with its tangled sheets. Their eyes met and Riley started feeling uncomfortable once she realized she'd forgotten what she was about to say. Frantically she searched for something to say. "Twenty minutes good with you T?"

"Sounds good" Tory replied while taking a pair of jeans out of her dresser next to the bed. Riley nodded and left the room, still not knowing what to make of everything.

****

Jake could sense it. Something felt *wrong* about being back home in Reesewood. It was definitely great seeing his cat again but even Shelby was having a hard time lifting the weird feelings. Fortunately, his mother was once again out of the house for the day running errands. He really hadn't paid much attention to what she'd said on her way out that morning. Most adult chatter was just white noise.

He was just settling in to a comfortable spot on the couch with Shelby sleeping on his stomach when a knock on the door echoed through the living room. The cat jumped off him and ran to the basement in near record time. She always hated strangers. Jake couldn't really guess who could be at the door on a Saturday right now either so Shelby might've been on to something. Normally he made a point to check through the window to see who was at the door before opening it. That strategy had saved him a lot of headaches over the years but today he hadn't thought to do the same.

After opening the door the idea of using that precautionary step hit the front of his mind and lingered there. Even now he couldn't decide what he would've done had he seen who was at the door before opening it. *What the fuck do I even say?*

"Ummmmm" was all his brain would allow him to voice. He felt like someone awaiting a prison sentence while he stood there in the doorway, unable to move.

"Hey" Kelly said from her confident stance on the front steps.

All Jake wanted to do right now was be rude and unforgiving but his mind betrayed him and he couldn't let himself act that way. He hadn't talked to his ex-girlfriend since the day she'd told him she cheated.

Up until now Jake thought he was moving forward but seeing her standing in front of him in her make-up, short shorts and tank top it was clear he was still powerless.

"Hey" was all he could say back. *Maybe I'll actually be able to form a sentence soon.* He was mentally kicking himself for being so worthless at the moment.

"Can I come in?" Kelly asked hesitantly. Her hesitance was in words only because her stance screamed that she was waiting for him to move so she could.

"No...I don't think so" he responded firmly. *At least I said more than one fucking word that time.* He made a point to position himself to take up the center of the doorway so she couldn't pass.

"Can we talk outside then?" she asked, clearly disappointed that she'd been denied entry, not unlike Dracula. That gave Jake a slight sense of achievement.

"I don't know what you expect me to say that I haven't already said but fine."

He made sure the front door was unlocked before moving outside and shutting it behind him. They made their way over to the bench right in front of the window looking in on the living room he'd just been sitting in carefree with his cat. *If Shelby could talk, she'd be so pissed at me.* His cat had always hissed at Kelly whenever she came over. Jake always chalked that up to the cat not liking *anyone* that took attention away from her but these days he was starting to think she had a point.

"Is your mom home?" Kelly started in on small talk. Or maybe she just didn't want to be bothered in the middle of whatever she was about to say. Jake had to admit he was intrigued by what was on her mind.

"No, she's out shopping..." his voice trailed off, both because he didn't know for sure and he was feeling uncomfortable sitting outside with Kelly in front of God and the neighborhood. Not that anyone on the street knew anything about their issues but it was still unsettling.

"What do you want Kel?" Jake fought the urge to recoil. Calling her by that shortened name tasted bitter. *Fuck this. She doesn't get to make me feel this way.*

Kelly looked scared out of her mind. *She's probably never felt helpless in front of a guy before...well fuckin' tough.* "I wanted to say...I just miss you so much Jake" she finally let out.

A flood of feelings started washing over Jake but what they were, negative or positive, he couldn't say. Not yet.

"That's interesting," he replied in a deeply condescending tone, "since you were the one that caused all this. I mean I still don't know what I did wrong. What did I do?" his voice betrayed him and cracked slightly. He would've been much more content letting Kelly think he had no emotional stake in the conversation.

"You didn't do anything...I...I love you."

The words hit Jake like acid and burned just as much. Once again he couldn't tell if he was happy or angry. It was good to know she was suffering. And it definitely felt good that she still loved him, if only in her words. But that didn't shake the thought that it felt *wrong*. "What you did doesn't fit with what you're saying."

A tear rolled down Kelly's cheek. It took strength to just sit next to her without consoling. "I was so lonely when you were pledging Jake. I...I didn't know what to do. I was just alone and...he helped," she sounded ashamed admitting it. It made Jake feel powerful. *Good, I'm glad she's upset. I'm still fucking upset.*

"Yeah I'll bet he did." The comment was laced with equal parts contempt and sarcasm. Having the moral high ground never felt better. Kelly didn't look at all happy with his response to her honesty. "I'm sorry Kel but it's just hard to feel sorry for *you* and how *you're* feeling."

"Do you still love me?" she asked, tears now falling freely from her eyes. Even if he knew they were coming Jake would've been hard pressed to fully prepare.

Just how long the silence was between them Jake couldn't say.

"Yes...I still love you." The words betrayed him but he knew they were the truth. *I do still love her. God help me but I still do.*

"I ended things with the other guy. I'm not even talking to him anymore."

At the mere mention of the other guy Jake felt tears welling. He resolved to not let a single one fall. *She doesn't get to see me cry.* "Yeah but that's easy to do now that we're home. What happens when we get back to school?" Jake found himself waiting almost endlessly for her reply.

"I won't ever make this mistake again baby," she promised. She was trying to clear her eyes but to no avail. Her make-up was starting to run but she still looked amazing. Jake tried shunning his attraction for all the good it did.

"How could you do this to me...?" Jake voiced trailed off as the first tear came trickling down his face. *What's wrong with me? This needs to stop...*

Now they were both crying. Kelly leaned in to hug him softly. Jake was powerless to stop her. More than that he found himself wanting to hold her again. "I know Jake...I'm so sorry...I love you," she repeated while wrapping her arms around him. Having her body up against his made him feel good, too good. The whole thing was terrifying but the intoxication couldn't be ignored.

At first their embrace was soft and warm but then it got tighter and fiercer as they both latched on to the point where they couldn't be pried apart. Jake felt himself losing control. He tried pulling back but all he succeeded in doing was moving his head back.

In the briefest of instants his eyes locked with his ex-girlfriend's.

They just looked at each other, tears still slowly streaming down both their faces.

Jake didn't even know how it happened at first but somehow they were kissing. He didn't know who made the first move, him or Kelly but it didn't matter now. Their tongues were gliding along each other. Their hands were moving freely along their bodies. He couldn't say how long they sat on the bench or how they made it inside. The only thing to give that away was the front door slamming behind them.

They started kissing again in the front entrance hall with the stairs leading up to his bedroom in plain sight. Their eyes were closed as a result of the passion they were sharing but he knew full well they were there. The stairwell was almost daring him to make a move.

"I'm so glad your mom isn't home," Kelly mumbled in the fleeting moments when their lips weren't pressed together.

Jake felt terror...weakness and terror. *What am I doing? How did I get here?*

By the time they reached the bedroom his reservations were a memory.

Chapter 41

There wasn't a doubt in Brynn's mind. At the time she'd raised her hand to vote for Amy Brage as house president it felt right.

She'd even felt a rush, almost like the act itself was a source of happiness.

Today was a different story.

In the four weeks since Gladen Hills had cleared out the decision was weighing heavily. She didn't necessarily regret it but it didn't feel as overwhelmingly positive anymore. That rush was now a distant memory. That might've been due to the fact that she hadn't seen Tory at all in the past month and as such was having trouble retaining her again for the girl.

After all her conversations with Danielle and Amy about voting it felt right that day although her Big wouldn't agree. *She just might kill me for this one.* Amy seemed to really want the position and based on what she'd seen of the girl Brynn felt she'd do a good job. *She'll be better than Tory.* But what had once seemed like a sure thing was starting to waver.

Brynn had to admit she was shocked by how easily she'd been able to sway her pledge sisters into voting the way she was voting. Danielle had told her that sometimes with larger pledge classes a central figure united people. Brynn knew she was the most stubborn in her class. Convincing the other five girls hadn't been hard when she was in no way going to change to her own mind. Considering Madison was her best friend and Mary and Angela were the Little's of Amy and Danielle, respectively, it went smoothly. With four going one way, Jocelyn and Olivia followed suit.

The whole thing had almost given her pause about why recently crossed sisters could vote in such pivotal elections considering they didn't have much knowledge in how things were run. *Someone should really look into that.* The thought had been repeatedly circling her head before, during and after elections. She'd almost wished that someone would just take away the Beta Thetas ability to vote. Maybe then she could get out of the whirlpool she found herself in during those weeks leading up to it all. Of course if she hadn't been able to vote she wouldn't have been able to experience that sweet satisfaction in voting for Riley and Danielle...and Amy.

Brynn finished folding the laundry that had just come out of the dryer, which included the brand new EIPi tank top Riley had bought before she'd left Gladen Hills. It was bright pink just like everything else in the sorority. She couldn't decide whether she liked the color or not, even now. For what felt like the millionth time since she'd been home Brynn wondered about why she even pledged in the first place. *I needed something stable, that's all.* She kept reminding herself why she'd gone to Rush but it wasn't helping. She wasn't even sure why she cared so much. Joining EIPi had simply been a means to an end. It was a place to unwind and relax and drink.

Abruptly she fell onto her bed beside the folded clothes and let her eyes wander around her bedroom. As usual they found their way to the picture on the nightstand a few inches from her. It was an older photo of Brynn and her dad right after they'd finished her hometown's 5K marathon a few years ago. She'd always hated how she looked in that picture but her mom had insisted on taking one right after she crossed the finish line. She'd been almost ten minutes behind her dad but that was to be expected considering how experienced he was.

Brynn's mom had essentially given up running after having her. That meant her dad had been all about Brynn taking up the mantle once she turned thirteen. She didn't mind though. It kept her in shape, which she realized was more and more important once she hit junior high. Her dad's determination helped motivate her because she knew she sure as hell wasn't going to do alone. It made the whole concept of running around during pledging a little easier to grasp since her exercise had been severely cut in Gladen Hills. That wasn't a huge reason for why she'd wanted to join though. Brynn couldn't really decide what the number one reason for accepting the bid was but it couldn't hurt to define her motivation. It probably wouldn't hurt to know how she'd gotten into the sorority world since she'd be going back to it in ten short weeks.

That was when the fall semester would start back up but she wouldn't have to wait that long for a reminder. Brynn was planning a trip much earlier than that.

****

When he really thought about it, Jeff Chester had never really considered their current house as the *actual* AZXi house. That honor would always belong to the place past Arkridge Avenue further up Castle Lane near the corner of College Curve. That was Alpha Zeta Xi to Jeff. That was where he'd pledged. That was where he'd done countless push-ups and sit-ups, wall-sits, cherry pickers, monkey-fuckers and keg-lifts. *That* was his second home. It was no wonder why he and the other seniors had hid there for Senior Hazing. It was also a wonder as to how not a single one of the other actives could figure out that's where they'd go for their last hurrah. *Dumbasses.*

Now they lived on Arkridge with most of the other fraternities. While it was definitely nice being closer to the National for day-drinking affairs it still didn't *really* feel right to him, even now. That started to change recently though, just like so much else. The more time he spent here, the more time he had form new memories. The new ones overshadowed the older ones. Jeff wasn't a fan of it but try as he could; he couldn't stop it.

Had he not been suspended for that year he would've had one more in the new house. No doubt Gretman, Kev, Petey and Guapo all thought more of the Arkridge house than he did. Like most off-campus housing, their place was falling apart. Also like most others, the landlord didn't give a fuck. So long as everything was up to code and the rent money came in, the place could go to shit.

Since Jeff was knowledgeable about using tools he couldn't help but devote a lot of time into repairs. Where others saw an eyesore that was a room with fading, molded paint Jeff saw the hours it'd take to make it right. Where some saw an inconvenience like a leaky faucet Jeff saw the tools he'd need to fix it. That was partially why he wanted to stay there over the summer. On top of the fact that he'd gotten an internship at a decent sized firm about twenty minutes from Gladen Hills he wanted to help fix up the house. At least that had been the plan.

Gretman was the only other AZXi still there over the summer and the plan had been to straighten the place up during their downtime. Unfortunately between Jennifer's frequent visits and Dana's infrequent ones Jeff was stuck doing most of the repairs on his own. It was nice in a way since he liked doing things by himself but some tasks would've gone better with help. That had never been clearer than it was when he'd been stuck painting the entire common area on the opposite side of the house. Not only was it a pain in the ass painting the fifteen-foot room solo but he was also within earshot of Gretman's room and Jennifer was up visiting. That meant he was treated to the loud-ass sounds of the two of them fucking like rabbits the whole time. He'd tried combating the pornographic sounds with his laptop but even using the designated callout play-list with extremely loud heavy metal rock had a hard time competing.

The worst part was the jealousy. Dana hadn't been down in over two weeks and it was starting to wear on Jeff although he'd never admit it to Gretman or Jennifer. They were really the only two he'd talked to since everyone left four weeks ago. He'd text Kevin or Petey every few days but the conversations went nowhere fast. Thankfully, Jennifer would be heading back home soon. *Maybe then Gretman can get off his ass and help out.*

Now that the paint was dry after the second coat yesterday Jeff could start hanging the composite pictures of the full fraternity along the walls. He'd painted around the nails so they could be left in just to avoid the hassle later on. That decision was paying off right now. All he had to do was lift the marginally heavy wood-framed pictures up and set them down slowly along the nails. The metallic wire stretching across the back of each picture made the entire process very straightforward.

About halfway through his brother finally emerged from his monkey-cage of a bedroom. Calvin had the biggest smile on his face. Jeff couldn't really blame him for that but he was still annoyed.

Gretman strolled to the fridge in the kitchen and got out a carton of orange juice, which he promptly poured into two cups. *Good thing I didn't want any pal.*

"How's it going?" Calvin asked cheerfully.

"I could ask the same thing" Jeff replied coolly as he lined up the fourth composite to the wall. After it was set on the corresponding nails Jeff noticed that Calvin was chugging the orange juice with a confused look.

"It's been two days straight and around hour six today alone of you two fucking."

"Oh yeah…that" Calvin grinned. "It's going fucking amazing. It's the first time we've had the house to ourselves…except for you. No brothers saying shit outside the door or knocking just to be annoying."

Jeff could see where he was coming from. How many times had someone like Jared or Jerry or a drunken Biz come knocking during the worst time imaginable just to interrupt a sure thing. "Yeah that's a real pain in the ass."

"No kidding. And it really freaks Jen out when she knows people are listening."

I can't imagine that since she's usually so damn loud. "You'd think she'd be used to it by now" Jeff said dryly.

"So Dana would be cool with me and Petey saying shit outside your door?"

Jeff smiled. "Fuck no but I'd come out and beat your asses. That's for sure." Jeff paused mid-thought. "I can't wait 'til she comes back."

"How long has it been?"

"Two and a half long weeks" Jeff answered without pausing to think about it. *It's really been that long? Fuck.*

"You know there are kids back home at their parents places that aren't getting laid at all," Calvin stated diplomatically as if that would somehow make him feel better.

Jeff shrugged. "And when I start giving a fuck about any of them I'll be sure to let you know." He moved toward the fifth composite while looking at the front and the faces of the frat's older members. "Any chance you two are gonna finish up at some point today?"

"Why?"

"Oh no reason. You just said you'd help me with some of the house shit but I understand if you're too busy."

Of course Jeff knew Calvin didn't need to lift a finger to help with anything. For all intents and purposes he was no longer an active member of Alpha Zeta Xi. He'd graduated and joined the alumni ranks. Now he didn't need to worry about anything resembling frat house maintenance for the rest of his life but thankfully the guy didn't think that way. A wave of shame washed over his face as he finished his drink.

"Yeah my bad. Jen's leaving later today then we'll get to work."

****

Out of all the games in Raley's disgustingly large collection, Scribner liked playing the Wii ones the best if only because he had a better shot at winning.

"Fuck!" he nearly shouted after the game announcer stated their tennis match was over. Scribner had lost...again.

"You're too quick to rush and hit returns Scribbs. You gotta be patient."

"Let's play real tennis and then we'll see how it goes" Scribner retorted. His threat was as hollow as they came. Scribner had never picked up a tennis racket in his life but he was betting Raley didn't know that.

"Do you realize every time I beat you in anything you say something like that?" Jake asked with a grin. Once he thought about it he had to admit that his friend had a point...again. *Damn him.* "And you can't even play real tennis." *Damn him twice.*

"Maybe not but at least we'd both suck at it" Scribner shot back.

"Yeah, like I'd agree to that."

"Pussy."

"OK so what do you think?"

"I told you. You're a pussy," Scribner repeated, this time smiling.

Jake frowned. Clearly he didn't think that was an adequate response. "You know what I mean Scribbs. What do you think about me and Kelly?" he repeated the bombshell he'd dropped before their first game, one that he'd also been on the losing side of. *I should really get a Wii so I can beat this fucker…*

"Oh right right right…I think you're a pussy."

Putting his personal reservations about the girl aside, even Scribner had to admit his friend was a lot happier these days ever since they'd gotten home from Gladen Hills.

"Here I thought we might actually be getting serious for a second."

Now it was Scribner's turn to frown. "I am being serious. What the fuck are you thinking?" He wished for a second that he'd filtered his thoughts a little better but that idea vanished when he *really* thought about Raley's recent decisions.

"I'm not back together with her" Jake corrected him immediately. "I'm banging her whenever…and it's awesome."

"Can you really keep fucking this girl and not get caught up in all her bullshit again? I mean seriously Raley. You really think this is gonna end well?"

"It's not a big deal man. I'm just getting sex. That's it."

Scribner sat on the couch utterly unconvinced. He didn't care how much of that was showing on his face. "And this girl is OK with just fucking you, no strings attached?" He'd already formed an opinion before getting a reply. From everything Scribner had seen of Kelly Frazer she liked possessing her guys completely. Sex with no strings didn't seem to be her speed at all. *She can do whatever she wants but her boys need to be on a short leash.* "And you don't have any feelings for her at all?"

"Would you believe me if I said no?"

"No fucking way" Scribner grinned. *At least the kid's real brain does still work even if the other one is doing most of the thinking.*

"This is a stupid-ass idea Raley."

"It'll be fine" Jake assured him while loading up the next match. "I wouldn't be getting any over the summer anyways without this so I need it."

So the kid goes a month without pussy and the first girl that offers him up some just happens to be the only one he shouldn't go near even if his dick depended on it. Just fucking perfect. There's no way this will go wrong.

Dan Scribner could almost see the day when he'd have to help put the pieces of his friend's life back together. And it didn't look pretty. "What happens when we get back to school?" Scribner asked, already having a dark idea.

"We'll worry about that when we actually get back to school."

****

It had been four weeks of complete bliss as far as Jake was concerned. He was winning in the relationship or lack thereof with Kelly. She'd come back begging for another chance, which he'd been only too happy to keep at arm's length until he was ready to make a decision. In the mean time, he was content just fucking her whenever he wanted. She didn't seem to mind the extra attention either considering she'd 'ended' things with her other fling.

Jake knew deep down he was silently hoping all along for Kelly to come crawling back to him. It was just a miracle it actually happened. He'd rehearsed the idea in his head hundreds of times in the blind hope that she'd actually fold and run back to him. Of course in those fantasies he simply told her off, never to see her again. The reality had turned out quite differently. The more he found himself back in bed with her, the further into the whirlwind he sank. With each passing session he saw the way out getting further and further away. The worst part was that Jake didn't know if that was a bad thing.

The first time they'd had sex after their break-up had been painless enough. They both just really wanted each other and the session had gone only as deep as that. In the past four weeks since then it was getting murkier. They started kissing just to kiss, not for the endgame of sex. They started cuddling afterward and talking about their lives again. As much as Jake liked to think he was only in it physically, he couldn't keep lying to himself like he had to his friend Scribner and how he'd likely have to with his cousins Eric and Riley.

He didn't have to think too much about that since he was just relaxing on his day off from his summer job. Not only was it his day off, he was spending most of it with his Big Jared who lived twenty minutes away in Ridgewell. Jared had texted him yesterday asking him to chill when he'd been hanging out with Scribner, which Jake had only been too happy to agree to. On top of that Kelly was supposed to come over later and there was a Raley's Ring party on deck for the night. It was shaping up to be a great day, especially since Jake's mom was once again out.

"What'd you end up doing last night?" Jared asked while sipping on one of the canned beers Jake had brought home from Gladen Hills.

"After beating my friend eight ways from Sunday in Wii Tennis I just passed out early like a champ" Jake answered cheerfully. It was kind of difficult to make that statement sound like anything other than a lame cop-out but it was the truth.

"I didn't do much either, just chilled with my brother, played some basketball. Yo I can't believe your mom is cool with us having a couple beers" Jared announced.

They were sitting on the bench in front of his house, taking in the warm weather that came from a summer in the Northern U.S.

"Well, for one neither of us is drinking enough to be a huge issue. For another she isn't here to complain and lastly even if she was she'd probably be unhappy about it but there isn't much she can do to stop it. If there's one good thing about having divorced parents it's being on level footing with each one. As you get older they usually stop teaming up on you, then it's easy."

Jake's parents divorced when he was in the fifth grade and since then the fighting between them had essentially only flared up when they were actually together. Both his parents were smart enough to figure that out so they basically stopped talking altogether. That meant a unified front for disciplining him died on the spot.

"That's a little sick bro" Jared chuckled.

"I didn't say it was nice...but it works. Besides, like my dad always said: if I can join the army to kill then I damn sure better be able to drink."

"The worst thing that ever happened in this country was raising the drinking age," Jared agreed.

One of Jake's interview questions during week one of pledging had been about breaking any one law without a consequence. Jared in particular struggled with that. It came down to either speeding or drinking, both of which they all did anyways. Jared eventually came down on speeding, but not by much.

"I don't know man. I just feel like the whole reason we like drinking so much is because we shouldn't be. It's about rebelling. I feel like once we're twenty-one, drinking will become like anything else. It'll lose the rush."

While Jared pondered his words, Jake finished his beer. He still hadn't gotten accustomed to how alcohol tasted even though he'd been drinking for two years. He just couldn't shake the idea that he didn't like the taste in general.

"Hey man, I just wanted to tell you that I appreciate you chilling with me after Crossing as much as you did. I know I wasn't fun" Jake admitted solemnly.

Jared laughed. "Look bro, if there's one thing that town is good for it's the ability to hit the reset button. We'll never have that again." It was as serious and astute a comment as Jake had ever heard from the guy. It was refreshing.

"I don't really want to change."

"Who the fuck said anything about that? You don't need to change to fit in. You already fit in with Biz and me. That's a start. And there are worse things in the world than being used in a bad relationship."

"I'll bet pledging is one of those things" Jake joked. As terrible as pledging had been, Kelly's cheating had yet to be topped in terms of how terrible he could feel. If even for now, their current romance was taking away that past pain.

"That's for sure," Jared agreed. "But the good news is you never have to go through that shit again."

Jake smiled. It was always comforting to hear that pledging was over. That was probably just a testament to the huge mind-fuck Jeff had put the four of them through. *The sick bastard that he is.*

"I still don't know how I'm gonna handle being on the other side" Jake thought out loud. "I was a terrible pledge. What right do I have to tell other pledges what to do?"

"You're thinking about it too much" Jared assured him. "Have fun with it. The pledges are gonna be miserable regardless, if you treat them like shit or like kings. But which of those two options is going to make them feel like they earned their letters. There's a reason the Betas aren't that close bro…their pledging is a joke."

Jake sat there, lost among his own thoughts and Jared's words. The two continued drinking their beers in silence just taking in the sunlit front yard.

Living on a dead-end side street meant very little traffic. That left them almost in a vacuum. Not even the usual hum of a distant lawn mower was reaching them. Until Jared patted him on the back Jake zoned out completely. "Just get laid again man. It'll all come together."

Jake checked his phone and saw a message from Kelly confirming her plan to come over earlier before the party tonight. "Way ahead of you pal."

****

Calvin hadn't even felt so drained after Hell Night during week four when he was pledging. And that had been the night Brandon had made them run five miles for no reason. Normally the pledges were forced to run a mile, maybe two, and that was it. For whatever reason, Brandon Sarce thought it'd be a good idea to force him and Petey to go for a full five with no breaks. Even being in decent shape at the time Calvin was winded. Petey fared even worse considering he'd gotten a beer belly from freshman year.

Stumbling around in the kitchen, Calvin moved to the fridge once he'd gotten his bearings. The windows in his room had been opened when Jennifer left earlier but the air coming through the rest of the house seemed more refreshing somehow. It might've been the change of scenery since he and Jen had barely left his room since she'd come down Thursday. It seemed that the idea of graduating had kicked up their sex drives. He just found himself getting even more turned on at the thought of having her with their future so close. They'd be living together in a few months if everything went according to plan.

Realizing the fridge was now empty he reluctantly turned to the sink and found one of the few cups still in the house and filled it with water. Calvin proceeded to slam the entire cup right then and there. It helped, but only a little. Between sweating and finishing so many times his bodily fluids were running at an all time low.

"Well well well. I didn't think your ass would have the energy to get out of bed today after the shit you've been through" Jeff taunted him.

Calvin smirked. Even that felt like it took more energy than he had to spare. "Believe me I'm as surprised as you Buttons."

"You ready to help yet?"

"I'm good" Calvin answered, not believing it himself while he stood there haggardly with an empty cup. He was wearing mesh shorts and a white t-shirt with no socks or shoes. All he looked to be ready for was a return trip to bed.

"Are you sure you don't need to call Jennifer first to make sure she's OK with you helping out?"

"You really make me out to be a lot more whipped than I am."

"Oh that's not fair. You do most of the work for me" Jeff grinned. "But if you think you're good, you can help me bring the TV and its stand back up."

"Now that's a necessity," Calvin agreed. "I haven't had TV in a few days."

"What's wrong with the one in your room?"

"I don't know" he shrugged. "It's stuck on some weird mode."

Calvin wasn't sure how it had even gotten there but it probably had something to do with a random button he or Jen accidentally hit when they were rolling around in bed...or on the floor...or that time they'd gotten to his nightstand.

"And you didn't say anything to me about it?"

Calvin felt confused. It was more annoying to him than anyone else, having to resort to watching movies on his laptop over the TV. He'd meant to tell Buttons earlier but hadn't. *Why didn't I?* "I meant to" Calvin assured him. "I just didn't really need it all that much recently." He couldn't help but grin with the memories so fresh.

"Right right" Jeff replied sarcastically. "So when's the wedding?"

"Whoa wait what?"

"Relax. I was kidding Gretman. Unless of course it's actually happening in which case I am curious about the date." *More likely you're curious about whether or not you'd get an invite.* "You're not thinking about it are you?"

"Is that weird to you?"

"Not at all" Jeff shrugged it off. "A bunch of us are actually in a pool about when you'll actually make that move."

Calvin paused to think if that could actually be true. *It probably is.* It wasn't like the idea of ever getting married to Jennifer was foreign but it still seemed far away. *That was before though, when we were still in college. That's over; we're not in college anymore.* Cold chills started coursing through his blood. The future that he'd seen so clearly when he was in bed with his girlfriend started getting blurry. Having her in his arms felt right and perfect but standing here talking about it with a frat brother made it seem light-years away from possible. *What am I thinking? I'm only twenty-two years old. I can't get married. Not now.*

"Where'd you come out in this pool?" Calvin asked, trying to hide his terror.

"You'll wait until after you've got the job all set and you two are actually living together" Jeff replied without hesitating. He seemed much more sure than Calvin. *How does he know that? I can't even see that far ahead.* In college or not, he wasn't ready to make that kind of commitment to Jennifer…or anyone right now. "I gave it a year after graduation so the clock is ticking."

A year?! I'm not gonna be ready in one fucking year. No no no no no. His reservations had long been in the recesses of his mind. Now they were coming to the front with a fury he wasn't ready for. Just being with Jennifer in Gladen Hills had kept the concepts of the long-term on the fringes of his mind but now he found he couldn't stop them from being front and center. It was easy to forget forever when he was inside her, helping her finish. Now that she was gone and he'd be moving back home soon everything was changing. The apprehension must've been clear because Jeff caught on pretty quick.

"Relax…I'm kidding" Jeff said calmly. Calvin didn't hear him. *In this place, this town, it was all figured out. Away from AZXi and Rho Beta it's all different…and it's all gray. Out there we're not a college couple. Out there we're staring down the future.*

Calvin had met Jennifer inside a few months of being at Gladen Hills. They'd started dating at the end of freshman year. He'd picked his major before ever setting foot on campus. He knew which classes to take when. He even knew what he wanted to do after graduation. He'd go work for his Dad at his company and learn how to run it with Adam. Now that it was here the sure feelings he'd had all throughout his four years were evaporating. *I'm not ready to leave. I can't.* Fear had taken hold in a way it never really had since the day he'd moved into the dorms. It felt like he'd never be free of it.

Suddenly he felt Jeff's hand on his shoulder.

"You OK?" his brother asked sincerely. Calvin did a double take to make sure Jeff was the one who said it. *One hint of the guy talking like this and his pledges wouldn't have ever been intimidated.* Calvin wondered how much of his persona throughout the past year was devoted to keeping the pledges terrified. Probably more than he'd ever know.

Once he realized Jeff was waiting for a response he played it up like it was nothing. He was petrified about moving away but he wasn't sure he was ready to have such a serious talk about it with Jeff Chester. *Why couldn't Petey have been the one staying here this summer?*

"You really think I'd propose to my girlfriend based on your chances of winning a pool that I'm not even sure exists?"

Jeff smiled and removed his hand from Calvin's shoulder, almost in shame that it had ever been there. "Are you gonna let me fix your TV or not?" Jeff switched topics again. They were both anxious to move past whatever had just happened.

Calvin thought he could figure out the TV issue if he spent enough time screwing around with it. But on the other hand Jeff was more technically skilled. He felt the urge to say yes but had a nagging feeling that it would make him look weak.

Jeff took Calvin's silence for a yes though and walked off into his room without an invitation. His mind was still sprinting in a hundred directions on whether to stop him or not. He couldn't make a decision in time so he let it play out.

Within minutes Jeff had the remote and was fixing the screen settings to allow for cable television to continue filtering into the bedroom. Even though he'd watched the guy fix it he still wasn't sure what he'd done. It was humbling.

Jeff handed him the remote a little more forcefully than Calvin would've expected and then he nodded for him to follow to the basement. Calvin set the remote back down on his nightstand next to the picture of Jennifer and him from Bids last semester. Seeing her again, even in the picture, helped set his mind at ease.

****

His doubts and fears had withered away during the time Kelly had been on top working furiously. Any thing Scribner had said or his cousins could say wasn't even close to being relevant when Kelly was in control. There was a spark in her eyes that just screamed for more even before she'd actually screamed for more. Now that they were done, the thoughts were creeping back into his head. *Can't ever just enjoy a moment...*

"You know it's a damn good thing my mom's out of the house again."

"Oh yeah?"

"Definitely. I mean...you are really loud." He was talking in a way that suggested he didn't like how vocal Kelly could get but that was anything but the truth. Having her scream while he was inside her was the greatest thing he'd ever experienced.

"And?" she probed, continuing to pierce him with her dark blue eyes.

"And I think your loud moaning might very well freak my mother out."

Kelly smiled while sitting up and slipping on her jean shorts that barely covered her astonishing ass. "It's a good thing she loves me then."

Jake nodded. "Good point." Even though his cat Shelby didn't like Kelly it was clear his mother loved the idea of having another girl around him. It had never been lost on Jake that having a daughter was at the top of his mother's priority list but it had been enough of a struggle to have him that another seemed out of reach for his parents, even back when they got along. That was a fact his mother saw fit to constantly remind him of. "It took thirty hours of labor to bring you into this world" she'd often say without prompting. It drove him nuts. Until he'd introduced Kelly to her, Riley and her younger sister Nicki had taken the brunt of her motherly instincts. Jake had almost thought he could've brought *any* girl home and his mother would've still been overjoyed.

"I figured she wouldn't be home today since you're having your big party tonight" Kelly added. His mother's shopping sprees and subsequent errands tended to take up most of the day but she wouldn't be gone forever, maybe just until ten or eleven. And God willing by that point the party would be in full swing and even his loud, unhappy mother wouldn't be able to put a stop to it then. That was the hope at least. It had worked plenty of times in the past. "What time does it start?"

Jake arched his head to his nightstand so he could see what time it was. He'd pretty much lost all sense of it once Jared left and Kelly had come over. It was a little past five and Eric said he'd be heading over around seven, which was about when he'd told Scribner to get there. He said as much to Kelly, which immediately prompted a look of apprehension.

"You told them everything about us right?"

"Well I did tell Eric...*almost* several times" he said, somewhat ashamed. "I did tell Scribbs though."

"How did he take the news that we're back...together" Kelly managed to say while keeping her eyes averted.

Jake froze in place. "Are we? Back together I mean?" he somehow asked without seizing up. He hadn't wanted to have this conversation 'til at least much farther into the summer, if at all. And yet here it was in all the weirdness it was due.

"What do you call this babe?" Kelly asked, almost forcefully.

"I call this a damn good time" Jake smiled and moved closer to her so he could rub her shoulders and calm her down before anything snowballed beyond his control.

"Is that all this is to you?"

Even as his hands reached her skin he could see she looked offended and ashamed that she was seeing things differently. "I didn't think you wanted to go through this again since you said you wanted to be single." His heart was jumping from his chest. Remembering that day was painful. *I want to be single Jake.* It hurt as much now as it did then. *I'm the one in control, not her.*

"You're right," she agreed. A piece of Jake died when she agreed even though he should've been happy about being given an out of this 'relationship'. "I just don't want to lose you again" she corrected herself while turning to face him. Her eyes glistened with newly formed tears. He was ashamed to admit that he felt good about seeing her upset. It was only fair that she suffer like he'd suffered during the final month of school.

Kelly finished getting dressed even as Jake watched her skin disappear beneath the clothing. *I want her again right now.* He wasn't sure he could even go again so soon after their last session but he just wanted to have her to himself.

"I'll be back over around ten," she told him after leaning in for a kiss.

"Just give me some time to talk to Biz. It'll be fine."

Kelly smiled but it was only for show. Her eyes weren't smiling with her lips. *She knows Eric and Rye aren't gonna be happy.* Jake shook the thoughts from his mind. *What I want is all that matters. But what the fuck do I want?*

The rest of the evening flew by and before Jake could blink the time to throw it down at Raley's Ring was upon him. Can after can they loaded into the fridge down in the basement. A little cleaning here and there and the place looked just like it had during the hey-day before he'd ever left for Gladen Hills. Jake's sense of pride was palpable.

Bill-Butt and Scribner were off setting up cups for their preliminary round of beer pong so that left Eric and Jake off by themselves in the bar area. It was the spot that his dad had built a home-entertainment center into the wall before he'd moved out. It was a little nook among the rest of the basement, which served well as the area where all the drinks were stored and served. Even as they were finishing up the beer drop into the fridge Jake was waiting for the inevitable explosion.

"So you're banging her again?" Eric asked bluntly.

"Yeah."

"How long has it been going on?"

"I don't know" he lied. He knew full well how long he and Kelly had been fucking but he wanted to make it seem like it was less than it was. "Since we got back from school I guess."

"Huh" Eric said thoughtfully while continuing to avoid eye contact. "I'm guessing you didn't say anything because you're ashamed? Or is it because you knew she'd be here tonight and wanted to get this out of the way?"

"Ding ding ding!" Scribner interrupted from a few feet away. Clearly the two of them weren't as alone in their conversation as Jake thought.

"Oh bite me" Jake threw a look to his friend that urged to him to stay the fuck out of it. "I'm *not* ashamed," he stated while turning focus back to his cousin.

"Alright" Eric replied blankly. He was keeping every bit of his emotions and thoughts well covered behind that face. *No wonder he's so damn good at poker.*

"I'm not," Jake repeated, trying to make it sound truer somehow. It had always helped him in the past if he could believe the lie he was spinning.

"Except you are."

"Why would I be ashamed of just fucking this girl?"

Eric didn't flinch. "Because this girl clearly sucks and just because you're getting some doesn't mean it's a good idea...in fact I'd actually say that makes it a bad idea. Sex doesn't fix everything."

"Yeah come on Raley, there are easier ways of getting it wet" Will joined the conversation. He was just as unwelcome a presence as Scribner had been a moment before. *So now all three of them are against me.* "I'm just saying we go to school in Gladen Hills," his pledge brother continued. "The town is full of horny chicks. Trust me. Find a less painful way of getting laid."

If only wishing made it happen.

Jake didn't really believe he could get anywhere with girls even if he wanted to. Trying wouldn't make a difference. There was a kind of comfort with Kelly because he knew her and was experienced with her. He knew what she liked and she knew him. "This isn't painful" Jake assured all three. Each looked as unconvinced as the last.

"Yet" Eric answered forebodingly.

"We're just fucking. It's *not* a relationship."

"Please" Eric said, dripping condescension with every word. "I've never seen you find a gap between feelings and sex."

He doesn't know me as well as he thinks. "Well look no further Biz because here it is." Eric simply stared back at him as though he knew something Jake didn't.

Chapter 42

It was almost shameful that they'd gone through the past two years living at the new AZXi house without doing a full upgrade involving a better paint-job and organizing of the composite pictures. Now they were arranged so that the most recent year's picture was right next to the entrance. *The last one I'll ever be on.* From there the pictures went in backwards order. Calvin could trace his entire AZXi history by the last three composites. The one from the year he'd pledged looked appropriately dorky.

Even with everything nearly done Calvin found himself not wanting to overtly compliment the room's updated look for fear of the wrath of Buttons.

"Thanks again for fixing my TV Buttons" Calvin said genially.

"Thanks for finally asking me to help" Jeff answered quickly.

They were both a few beers deep already and inhibitions were disappearing. "I didn't realize it meant that much to you pal," Calvin said, trying to lighten the mood. With just the two of them living together for the past month he was amazed by how little they'd actually fought. The tension had been palpable since the rest of the frat had moved out but they'd never had an outright argument like they had frequently throughout the semester.

"Please. I could give a fuck if you actually watch your TV. I was just wondering if you'd ever ask anybody for help with *anything*. I had a bet going with myself."

With that, Buttons moved from the couch to get another beer. The orange juice may have been kicked but there was one thing the house was never missing and that was a spare beer…or thirty.

"Is it really that big of a problem for you?"

"Not really" Jeff said courteously enough while sipping from a freshly opened can. Calvin looked down at his own and felt the weight. He was running low. *It would've been nice if Jeff asked if I needed another.* "It's just good to know that even the almighty Calvin Gretman actually needs help sometimes. It hasn't happened since sophomore year." The bitterness in Jeff's tone was easy to read.

The idea that he hadn't asked for help on anything since sophomore year seemed entirely subjective. "You keeping track of that now?" Calvin asked quickly.

Almost immediately after he'd asked the question he regretted it. *Of course he doesn't have any memory past sophomore year, he was suspended through our regular junior year.* Calvin looked at his beer. *Maybe another one isn't a good idea.* Calvin sure hadn't overtly asked for assistance after becoming president. He'd always thought that it'd make him look like a puppet if he had.

"I'm thinking about making it a sub-section of the website actually."

"Right" Calvin sighed. "I look forward to that getting done" he eagerly changed the subject again. Even feeling mildly buzzed, he was in no mood for deep introspection.

"I didn't realize you were planning on visiting the AZXi website much."

"I gotta stay connected somehow. That seems like a good way to do it" Calvin responded. He didn't think it was *that* much of a stretch to assume that he, among other alums would want website access to keep up on what the actives were doing.

"Yeah you're right" Jeff began. "It's easier to hand out advice from a laptop."

"Is there something you want to say Buttons? I'm getting tired of the veiled shit."

"I don't have a damn thing to say."

Almost immediately Calvin reached for the remote on the central coffee table and turned off the TV. That got Jeff's attention.

"I don't buy that for a second" Calvin replied irritably.

"I can't say that I care."

"Let's go Buttons. It's only us in this house. I want you to say it. What the fuck is your issue with me?" Calvin continued standing there, near to letting his frustration boil over. After a few seconds he realized he didn't know for sure if he was ready to hear whatever Jeff had to say.

The guy looked at him closely, like he was appraising their standoff. After a second he took a few large gulps of beer before forcefully setting the can down on the table. "You know everyone around here kisses your ass right?"

"That's fucking ridiculous" Calvin replied angrily. He'd been preparing to say something defensive. He almost didn't hear what Jeff said at first. After the words settled, the thoughts began to swirl. *It's not my fault the brothers wanted me to be president over you. It's not my fault they like hanging out with me more than you.* Calvin had a strong urge to let his thoughts out but he fought against it. Throwing those things in Jeff's face wouldn't help, no matter how good it might feel in the moment.

"Is it really *that* insane?" Jeff patronized him, as if he wouldn't know the answer if it smacked him in the head.

"Well at the bare minimum it's dramatic as fuck" Calvin shot back.

Jeff rose to his feet, almost to challenge Calvin who was already standing. "It might be dramatic but that doesn't make it any less true. Nobody around here seems to notice and the ones that notice don't seem to care. You walk around here and do whatever the fuck you want, say whatever you want and nobody calls you on it. Except me. Everybody sucks your fuckin' dick."

Calvin almost felt sorry he escalated things. *No, this needs to be said. If I'm gonna leave, it's gonna be with everything out in the open.* "You sound jealous pal."

"Fuck yeah I am" Jeff surprisingly agreed. "I do just as much as you but the difference is either nobody notices or they give me shit for doing things my way...the right fucking way."

Calvin found that hard to believe and his face showed as much.

"That happened this fucking semester. I ran pledging *my* way and look what that fucking got me? I got shit all semester from everyone right down the line and then got fucked at elections for my trouble. You're telling me James Brock did more this year to prove he'd be a good president than me?"

Oh Jesus not this again...one problem at a time...

"What's that got to do with me?" Calvin asked. It sounded like Jeff was just venting for the sake of venting now. He wasn't sure why all his anger seemed to be focused on Calvin over anyone else.

"If you'd done what I did then it would've been accepted as the greatest thing to ever happen to this frat. And for the fucking life of me I can't figure out why. What the fuck makes Calvin Gretman so special!?"

By the time he finished ranting the veins in Jeff's neck and forehead were readily identifiable and he was breathing heavily on top of that. If Calvin didn't know better it would've looked like the guy was about to pass out. He wasn't quite sure if his actions would've been accepted in quite the fashion Jeff was suggesting but it was hard to deny that he probably wouldn't have been constantly second-guessed along the way. There was an easy reason to see why though, at least in Calvin's eyes. *If you'd been around junior year then people would've been more receptive to letting you do whatever. Instead you came back and did whatever you wanted because you thought it was your right after what happened. You did things free of anyone else and you got fucked because of it. And that's not my fault.*

He was just about to tell Jeff as much when more thoughts came pouring in. *He was only out junior year because he helped this fraternity. He took the fall when he didn't have to.* Calvin knew it didn't make sense for brothers to hold that against him but he wasn't around for a year. *He missed two pledge classes. That's eleven of the actives. Why should they let him ride rough-shot all year long without earning respect first?* It had been enough of a miracle when Jeff had gotten elected assistant pledge-master that year right before he was due back at school. Even then that was the result of the younger guys allowing the older guys who'd been around during Jeff's sacrifice to talk them into it. It felt like reparations for his past. In so many of their minds that election had been the closing of the tab for Jeff Chester.

The whole thing made Calvin's head spin. The one thing he couldn't quite decide on was if he would've done the same thing had he been in Jeff's position. The possibilities made him sick.

"You're giving me way too much credit man," Calvin finally confessed. The words tasted like ash, yet they were no less true.

"When have you known me to give credit easily, especially to you?" Jeff asked. "I just don't get what's so different about us..." his voice trailed off.

Guess it really never is too late to experience something new around here. The thought of doing new things turned sour in his mind when he remembered his capability for that was withering away week after week as they got further into summer. He was already living on borrowed time by staying in Gladen Hills. *Did Adam feel like this when he stayed?*

"I don't know Buttons" he lied. "But I'll tell you this much. I'd give anything to stay here another year with all of you."

The sudden burst of honesty was a lot to handle. Calvin had been active for all of his Little's time with AZXi. The same could be said for Eric, Jerry, Lenny, J-Bro, Jared, J-Hood, Raley and the rest. Next semester he wouldn't be sharing in their memories anymore. He wouldn't be talking about their weekend's bad decisions at Sunday meetings. *From now on I'll have to read about everything through a fucking website.* Losing his energy at the depression funneling through him, Calvin sat back down. Even the prospect of dealing with more of Jeff's outbursts seemed like a small price to pay for continuing to live carefree in Gladen Hills.

"I don't know if I buy that," Jeff admitted although it was clear he wanted to.

"You said you were jealous of me getting free run of this place? Well now it looks like we're even because I'd trade all that in a second to live here another year." Calvin was shocked at the truths he was sharing with a brother he didn't consider himself all that close to and yet he couldn't stop himself. He hadn't even said as much to Biz or Petey before they'd left. Jennifer knew on some level although he'd never said these exact words to her.

Some of the pain disappeared from Jeff's face at Calvin's honest words but it wasn't all gone. They both remained where they were, unmoving in the uneasy silence for a few seconds.

"Do you need another one?" Jeff finally asked him, pointing to his beer.

"Yeah actually" Calvin replied, feeling the weight of a half-full can.

Jeff moved away toward the kitchen. "I got you."

****

"So what's the plan tonight?" Tory asked again.

It hadn't been lost on Riley that her best friend had been on edge since Brynn was arriving soon. "Eric said there were a few AZXis still in town if we wanted to chill with them." Without her cousins around even Riley had to admit that idea sounded less appealing than usual and Tory reciprocated that thought. "There's a bunch of Lambdas in town too. I think they're having a party or something at their place."

"So that's where we're heading then?"

The only times Tory ever needed a solid idea of what the night would bring was when she was entirely unsure about what to expect. *Clearly she's freaking out about seeing Brynn again.* Not for the first time Riley started second-guessing putting the two of them together with no one else around but her. It felt daunting.

It was surreal. They'd be the only three EIPis in Gladen Hills tonight.

"Yeah if you want" Riley confirmed. If that's where Tory felt most comfortable tonight then she wasn't going to stop her. If they were lucky the guys down there would keep her and Brynn separate for most of the evening.

Tory nodded. Going downtown to the Lambda house on Arkridge would be their plan. It was as good an idea as any given the lack of undergrads left. The Lambdas weren't her favorite frat but even drinking with them was preferable to being alone with Tory and Brynn. And she loved both girls.

I am gonna get so drunk tonight.

Riley took a large sip of wine from one of the glasses they sometimes used to make themselves feel classier. Somehow it always felt better than drinking out of a plastic cup. Class could only be used to describe so much at the EIPi house and Gladen Hills in general so they took what they could get.

The sun was setting behind them and the landscape was blanketed in an orange hue. It was all so comfortable. *Feels like home to me.* Taking another large sip from the glass seemed like the thing to do. That only added to her good feelings, which were sure to be put to the test when her Little drove up.

There wasn't a single soul walking near the EIPi house. Even past that, there were no cars parked on the road further down by Cordan. That wasn't unexpected. Even with summer classes still technically in session the library didn't see much use. That was certainly true where she and Tory were concerned. They had Wi-Fi at the house and with only two of them living there it was quieter than Cordan anyways. Even though Riley sometimes preferred the quiet that came with an empty house on a Friday night after everyone went to the bars she still found it a little eerie.

She grew up in a house with two parents, an older brother and a younger sister. That meant there was always some crisis or argument happening, with or without her. That made living at EIPi an easy decision considering a chaotic environment was where she felt most like herself. Even loving Tory like she did Riley missed the other sisters.

"So everything is good between you and Brynn right?" she asked bluntly. They'd been outside a while doing damage on the first box of wine and it was clear Tory was feeling as affected as Riley.

"That depends on her I guess. We haven't talked since she went home."

"You said you're good though right?" Riley reiterated.

"I'm absolutely fine."

Guess we'll see T...

Riley returned her gaze to the setting sun. It was low enough that looking directly at it over the academic buildings didn't hurt her eyes. A ball of orange light was staring at her like it had so many times in the past; somehow it always made her forget whatever she was dealing with on any given night. Of course on the flip side, sometimes it made her very reflective. That was doubly true if she was drinking.

Being so caught up in watching the sun go down behind Lenthan and Cordan, she almost didn't notice the car pulling into the EIPi lot even if it was the first car they'd seen in hours. The one before that had been one of the five or so patrol cars of the university police that were tasked with watching the campus in the summer.

"Who's gonna help me unload all my shit?" Brynn yelled from the parking lot. Riley and Tory's cars took up the two places closest to the entrance so Brynn had taken up the third slot in the line facing the sorority house.

"Not me, not now" Riley announced happily. Only afterward did she realize how it sounded which immediately prompted her to turn to Tory. The girl looked incredibly amused as expected.

"Did you really just say that?" Brynn asked as she approached the picnic table the two of them were sitting at.

"Don't you dare judge me…I've been drinking" Riley retorted as if it wasn't painfully obvious. The boxes of wine were perched on the table with two near empty glasses outlined in red.

"I certainly hope so," Brynn said haughtily. It was as if she'd never done or said anything embarrassing after a few cups of wine. Riley had *several* memories that begged to differ with that claim.

Finally, she got up from her spot on the bench and gave Brynn the largest hug she'd given her Little to date. After a month of not seeing her it was completely acceptable in her mind to nearly squeeze the life out of her. Once Brynn was breathing normally again she turned to Tory. It was almost enough to kill Riley's buzz on sight.

"Hey Brynn" Tory said, upbeat yet unhappy.

"Hey T."

Jesus what have I done?

"Oh fuck that!" Riley bellowed. "There's no way my Little and my best friend are going to have issues. Get this shit sorted out right now."

"I'm good Riles" Tory said with conviction.

"Yeah me too. I'm fine" Brynn added.

Riley was unconvinced but at least the two of them had the common courtesy to lie about how they were feeling. *Maybe I should just stay the fuck out of this and let them handle it. Clearly they don't want my help.*

"Fine let's finish this wine and be done with it."

Oh yeah…I'm definitely getting drunk tonight.

****

As usual the place known as Raley's Ring had blown up within an hour or so of Scribner and Eric getting here. Will had tagged along with Eric so that made the idea of having pre-party beer pong matches all the easier considering four was a magic number. So much of the time it had just been Jake, Eric and Scribner starting the night alone. That meant one-on-one games and one person sitting out. They'd tried doing two-on-one games originally but after a few match-ups they'd all agreed that the one person team had too much of an advantage getting two shots per turn. Any novice beer pong player could agree that that was a sure-fire way to get into a deadly rhythm. Eric had been the first to openly protest the idea but he and Jake had followed suit not long after. With Will Anthony part of the pre-party mix it made the games much more balanced.

As of now Scribner could find no complaint. He'd only met Will a few times so their team chemistry was nowhere near the level that Raley and Biz were at across the table. Even so they'd managed to beat the set of cousins by one cup to win the ten-dollar bet on the table. That was why he and Will were enjoying a free round.

"This shot is on Biz" Will announced.

Raley and Eric had retreated from the central table shortly after their loss but he and Will stayed on another game as the reigning winners. Of course their lack of team chemistry came back to bite them square in the ass next game. Scribner was pretty sure that if Raley had actually been playing like he usually did then they would've lost the first game too but something had been on his mind ever since his earlier talk with Eric.

"It was awfully nice to give me this money Biz…and it was awfully nice of Raley to play so badly" Will said happily as he raised one of the ten shot-glasses the bar was equipped with.

Before Raley could make a comment defending himself or attacking Will, Eric chimed in with all the diplomacy Scribner expected. "Just shut up and take the damn shot," he ordered with a grin. That seemed to get Raley off any retaliation kick. They all drained their shots quickly and each of them made the same disgusted face once the liquid cleared their throats. *For ten dollars a handle it's no wonder it tastes like shit.*

"Oh yeah…never again" Raley voiced what they were all thinking.

Amen kid. If I'm gonna drink this shit again, it's gonna be in a mixed drink or not at all. All Scribner could do was nod since the vodka was still burning his throat. It had passed through a minute ago but it was still causing a horrible taste in his mouth.

"Son…what kind of shit did you get?" Eric asked as if he wasn't the one who supplied the place whenever Raley's older cousin Trevor wasn't around.

"You tell me, you bought this garbage" Jake replied playfully.

"I'd recommend drowning this paint thinner under a wave of sprite or something. Mixed drinks all day." Even though he'd said it, Scribner wasn't convinced all the sprite in the world would make that vodka go down any easier but that's all they had.

"Why'd you get such cheap shit Raley?" Will asked, almost sounding offended. *This guy is at a party in a basement…in suburbia. Does he expect top-shelf Grey-Goose and Jack Daniels for Christ's sake?* Just the thought made him chuckle.

"Cheaper shit means it's easier to break even. Besides, I'm not forcing anyone to buy from me, but it's there if you need it."

Scribner looked back fondly on that fateful night two years ago. Raley had just taken a loss on buying booze for about the third week straight and he wanted to change it up. He and Eric had tossed out the idea of running the place like an actual bar, albeit under the table. Now, Scribner would walk out with a cut from the night's sales. Shitty liquor or not, the underage among them didn't give a fuck. Those handles of vodka would be gone by the morning. *Just like clockwork.*

"Scribbs would you mind mixing us up a few drinks" Jake ordered gently.

He nodded. Technically speaking, Scribner did report to Raley but he was a firm second in command and could make decisions without him. He sometimes liked to flex that power by giving away shots to the hotter girls without having them pay for every one. Most of the time he was the one sitting behind the makeshift bar area.

Once the parties got crowded there was no better place to be. Raley had even learned that pretty quick so when he wasn't mingling, watching the door or running around outside to make sure the noise level was fine he was standing right next to Scribner. The two of them, among others like Eric, who came there to party had special agreements with Raley about how they'd be charged. Just five dollars would allow them all they could drink for the night. That way they wouldn't be charged per drink. It was ironic considering the people they had the deal with accounted for pretty much all the heavier drinkers but that didn't much matter to Raley. Making money was just a bonus to being the center of the underage drinking community in Reesewood. That was his real prize. Everyone knew who they were and what they could do. Reesewood was their playground. Scribner was just happy to be a part of it.

"Make mine strong please Scribbs" Jake requested while continuing to talk to Will. He thought he heard the word 'probation' but he couldn't be sure with all the noise surrounding them.

Scribner got to work mixing the drinks. Fortunately he was making Raley's drink last since his mixture tended to be a little different. He always said he made his friend's drink stronger but that was bullshit. If anything, he made them a little lighter if only to keep his friend from blacking out at his own parties. If Raley ever noticed he never said anything. It was a win-win for everyone: the kid got to think he was a heavier drinker while also staying decently coherent and the party could continue running smoothly with him still calling the shots. Drunk or not his friend generally knew what he was doing in terms of keeping the outside world from knowing what went on down here.

Scribner was still fairly certain that between himself and Biz they could handle things if Raley ever passed out early but he was in no hurry to test that theory. He doubted the guy's cousin was either. They both came down here to have a good time, not to run the place. "Drinks up boys" he announced while handing each of the three guys at the counter their respective drinks. They each took a sip and gave a thumbs up. Jake in particular made a face after his sip, which would've suggested it was a lot stronger than it was before smiling in approval. *Still got it.*

The three moved away and Scribner handled the next round of orders from the people behind Raley, Biz and Will. After they were all set, he took money from person before mixing a drink for himself. Looking around the basement, Scribner wanted to get a sense of who was around that he hadn't said hello to yet. He saw a few friends from high school that he wouldn't have minded shooting the shit with but he couldn't leave his spot. Raley would definitely not be happy about his sole bartender bouncing. That was fine though because one of the good things about running the bar every night was that by and large, *everyone* came to see him at some point so staying put wasn't really a sacrifice.

He took a sip of his drink and cringed. He tended to make his drinks stronger because he never had many. More often than not he never got *that* drunk down here if only so he could drive people home afterward. That kind of cab service came with tips from the more hammered party-goers and added up to a nice little side gig.

After taking another sip, Scribner noticed a new presence in the basement: Kelly Frazer. Instead of finding her way to where Raley was, Kelly hung around the group of people near the bottom of the stairs chatting. That didn't sit well with Scribner. *She should be thanking him everyday for giving her ass another chance. She shouldn't even be down here with the friends he introduced her to. What a bunch of bullshit.*

Finally Raley noticed her arrival and he was the one to go to her.

They kissed immediately. Between that visual and the terrible vodka he was drinking he felt the urge to throw-up but held it back considering he'd have to clean it up. That was an unwritten Raley's Ring rule. *If you're gonna throw-up, find a spare bucket or be ready to clean that shit up yourself.* Holding back the feelings of sickness at seeing his friend continue to make mistake after mistake with that girl Scribner took a giant gulp of his drink. It didn't taste as bad.

His eyes continued wandering until eventually settling on Eric who also looked sickened by his cousin even being next to Kelly again, let alone kissing her with everyone around them.

Once he turned away he saw Scribner looking at him. They both exchanged unhappy looks. There was no need for them to talk. They were both on the same page. *You know it pal...there's no way that's gonna end well.*

Chapter 43

Tory and Riley had already been halfway through the first box of wine when Brynn arrived in Gladen Hills so she had some catching up to do. Interestingly, it was Tory that seemed to slow her drinking while Riley went ahead and drank enough for both of them. Even after they'd helped Brynn empty her car's contents into the chapter room they were still clearly drunk. It had only taken them a half hour to finish moving everything but she was still surprised at how little that downtime affected the two girls. Now that they were on the second box of wine, Brynn was starting to feel the effects.

Before long it was dark outside. Brynn figured they'd probably head downtown to the Lambda house soon, or else risk passing out early. The problem was she wasn't sure Riley would be able to make that kind of walk. Not in her current condition at least.

"OK so here's what I don't get" Riley began abruptly while Tory and Brynn finished off their latest glasses of the wine. *Here we go again.* Humoring a sister when she was drunk might as well have been a national sport at the EIPi house.

"How are we even going to survive the mental picture I have in my head of senior year?" Riley asked casually while swaying back and forth on the bench she was sharing with Brynn. With how much she was moving it looked like a strong wind was blowing the girl back and forth.

"What exactly are you picturing Riles?" Brynn asked.

"We're gonna be drinking obscene amounts every night and getting crazy" Riley slurred. *Classic drunk status. You always think you can drink more.*

"Sounds like the same as every other year before it. I think we'll be fine" Tory assured her while rolling her eyes playfully. Clearly she'd seen the current version of Riley many times before. The thing throwing Brynn for a loop was how calm Tory was acting. Sure they'd both claimed they were fine earlier, but as far as she could tell that was just for Riley's benefit. It didn't *really* mean anything. That was why each passing drink that Riley had gave Brynn pause. *If she goes down early tonight then what the fuck am I gonna do?* Riley had promised Brynn that she'd be up the whole night but right now she wouldn't make it another hour, let alone five or six. *Just one more time she's not gonna be there for me...just like pledging.* Disgusted, Brynn refilled her glass and drank half on the spot.

"I don't know how much more my liver can take" Tory faked a look of pain while she continued drinking.

"Like seriously…it's gonna be so insane" Riley continued. *She's in her own world while I'm stuck here with a girl that hates me. Just perfect.*

"Are you sure you're gonna have free time with your VP stuff?" Brynn asked pointedly. That snapped her Big out of it, if only briefly.

"Please…I'll impeach myself before my drinking takes a hit" she said confidently while draining another cup. Brynn wished she'd been keeping track of how many glasses they'd each had. It would be nice to know how much they could handle before getting sloppy. *If only that were possible…*

"How did you get so hammered?" Brynn asked while checking the time on her phone. It wasn't even past ten yet. She'd only been there an hour and change.

"Well we did start before you got here," Tory reminded her coolly.

If that's true then what's your deal because you're nowhere near her. "Yeah but you're still fine" Brynn said directly to Tory. *I need to slow the fuck down right now.* The thoughts made complete sense but she couldn't bring herself to follow through. *If it's gonna be me and Tory I won't be sober for it.*

"I need to go swimming like right this second" Riley announced, still completely oblivious to whatever else was being said, even if it was about her.

With the shadows crossing Riley's face from the floodlights coming off the EIPi house, it was still clear she was struggling. With the sun having set a while ago the sole lights hitting them were coming from a story up on the house's corner. Two separate floodlights were attached to the bricks and the light was bright as Hell. *That's probably why they're attached so far up. I could use a pair of fuckin' sunglasses.*

"Wine is so sooooo good," Riley continued, jumping from one topic to the next without pause or regard. *Damn I wish I was her right now.*

"Yeah I just wish I'd had more of it" Tory grinned. She was on the opposite bench looking directly at Brynn and Riley so her face was visible. For all intents and purposes she looked buzzed at best. *If you didn't have enough that's your own fault.*

Out of nowhere Riley got up from the table while struggling as expected. It almost looked like she forgot where she was. The girl regained her footing and started to look around. Tory started giggling uncontrollably as she watched. It had Brynn very confused. *Maybe Tory's more hammered than I thought.*

"What's so funny?" Brynn finally asked, unable to control her curiosity.

"The family resemblance is ridiculous" she replied between bouts of laughter.

Brynn frowned. *Alumni weekend when I got fucked up and passed out early? There's no way I looked like that.* Brynn gave Riley another glance, if only to reassure herself that she'd never been *that* hammered before. "There's no way I was that bad." Even she had to admit the comment didn't carry much conviction.

"Right because I've never heard that before," Tory answered with mild condescension. She took another sip of wine in what looked like an attempt to conceal a knowing smile.

"Right…bathroom" Riley mumbled before setting off toward the side entrance.

"Bathroom Riles?"

"Mmmhmmm" Riley responded as she stumbled inside the house after fumbling with the door code. It looked like she'd tried and failed to enter it a few times.

Once the metal door closed behind their drunken sister everything felt different. The silence was deafening. Brynn took another large sip of wine with reckless abandon. *No one* was walking around Gladen Hills tonight. Not a single person. No cars were coming by the house. Even from here where they could see the edges of University Grove it didn't look like much was happening there either. *She could kill me right here and no one would know the difference.* Even with Tory sitting on the bench across from her bathed in the floodlights Brynn had never felt more alone. She would've been happy with a cop coming by to hassle them if only because it would take the focus off her.

Tory returned to her wine glass and proceeded to drink the rest of its contents. With each passing sip Brynn grew more restless. *What the fuck is going to happen when she finishes it?*

****

Jeff Chester definitely hadn't planned for it, but it happened. Somehow over the course of a Saturday night in the summer he'd finally gotten drunk with Calvin Gretman. It hadn't been a barrel of laughs but it wasn't painful either. The original plan had been to have a few beers and then get back to working on the website. The problem was a few beers turned into a few more. After most of the thirty had been drained he and Gretman had a completely honest talk for the first time, probably ever. Even now it hadn't seemed real. *He's terrified of leaving. I fucking knew it. Why wouldn't he be? He's got it all here. Out there he's gonna have to start again. Just like I did when I got back from my suspension.* Jeff was grinding his teeth as they walked back from the corner of Arkridge and Castle. As usual, his thoughts weren't calming. Jeff had seen something in Calvin's eyes the day before after Jennifer had left. It looked like *fear*. That same kind of fear Jeff had seen in the mirror that day he got back from his first visit to the Dean's office. The fear of what would come next.

Somehow they'd convinced themselves to go to the National. They'd already done decent damage to the beer at the house so a trip down the road sounded good. Getting to stretch their legs sounded great in fact. A change of scenery from the walls of the house sounded even better. When they'd walked to the bar on the corner from their house they heard music blasting from the backyard of the Lambdas next door. Between the two of them there was no love lost for that fraternity. That was saying something too since Jeff had always assumed everyone loved Gretman as much as the AZXi brothers.

These days he was kicking himself for getting so drunk during Calvin's Rush events nearly two years ago. Today he would've killed to see how many brothers were falling all over the guy even back then before he earned the letters. Gretman had always been a guaranteed bid because of his older brother Adam so Jeff never really made it his concern to talk to him. He figured he didn't need to since the guy's fate was already decided before he walked through the door. He regretted that choice now. Jeff would've liked to have some, *any* memory of how the guy acted at that point in time, knowing he didn't have to try. *Was he an ass or did I make it up in my head after that shit with the cops and Standor? What kind of guy was he before being king of the hill?*

It took a second for Jeff to remember just what they'd been talking about before his mind went off on its own. "So you're considering it then?" he asked hesitantly. *I think this is where we left off...maybe.*

"Yeah. The plan is to move in together after I get home" Calvin replied. His tone lacked the confidence Jeff expected. Either the alcohol was talking or he was legitimately terrified.

"So three months or some shit like that?"

"Nah I should be gone by next month."

Under normal circumstances that knowledge might've made Jeff extremely happy. Now the thought of continuing to live in that house over the summer without even the likes of Calvin Gretman and his concubine girlfriend for company made him feel hollow. "So you're gonna leave me here by myself?" Jeff asked incredulously, as if it was some great slight against him.

"You bet your ass I am" Calvin joked while patting him on the back.

They were still walking down Arkridge away from the National. No one was on the road other than them. The entire street felt bigger, like it stretched on for miles past its dead end. In reality Arkridge Avenue only extended a mile away from Castle Lane but tonight it seemed like it was double or triple that.

The National had also been appropriately empty even though they'd both been hoping otherwise. They only had a few shots with the owner before leaving. Without the music blaring from the Lambda backyard there wouldn't have been sound for a mile. Not even the hum of distant cars on the interstate. *This town really does live and die by the college. This is what I'm gonna have when he leaves. Nothing.*

"Well that fuckin' sucks. I'm not sure if you noticed but this place kind of blows when school's out."

There were only two streetlights on Arkridge, one on each end. The one in the middle had burned out and like so much on the campus fringes, it wasn't a priority. Now that they were walking through the center of the road, everything was dark. Usually there were tons of undergrads walking around looking for a party to offset the darkness. Tonight there was nothing.

"That all depends on who sticks around," Calvin said thoughtfully.

You have no idea how true that is pal. "We could've done worse," Jeff said quietly. He wasn't sure Calvin heard him. It was quite possible he hadn't but Jeff didn't feel compelled to voice those thoughts twice. It felt weird enough the first time.

"So what's good with Dana?" Calvin asked, changing topics.

"We're good I guess," Jeff answered quickly.

Even with the minimal amount of light hitting their position on the street Jeff's face was easy to read. Not even he believed what he'd just told Calvin. "Yeah I definitely bought that" he chided him. "You might be interested to know that nobody in their right mind throws out the words 'I guess' if they're sure."

Damn, that makes sense.

Even so, Jeff wasn't sure he was ready to talk to the guy about any relationship problems he might be having, real or imagined. *I don't even fucking know what's going on these days.* Jeff was content to let the conversation die right there but Calvin wasn't of the same mind. "Is everything cool man? I mean it's straight if you don't want to say anything but after putting you through listening to me and Jen the past few nights I think I owe you a favor."

Jeff's legs stopped working. *Talking about your issues is something chicks do. What are we? Are we chicks now?* Part of him wanted to keep walking but the bigger part of him was screaming to say something. "It's not the same as when we started dating," he nearly screamed in frustration. *Why the fuck would you say that? And to him of all people? Jesus I am a fucking chick.*

"Maybe it's the booze but I don't feel good about it...at all. It just feels like something's wrong. I haven't even said anything to Dana because I don't really want to know the answer. *Jesus get the sand out of your vagina and quit being a pussy. If any of the Lambdas hear this shit they'll think we're all gay.* "I have no idea how to even bring this up because who the fuck knows if it's just in my head. I mean, have you ever had any issues like this with Jen?" *Do I even really care?* He was almost ashamed to admit he wanted Calvin to answer, and quickly.

To Jeff's complete shock, all the guy did was laugh. *Oh I'm gonna fucking kill him if he ever says anything about this to anybody.* Jeff was just about to push the guy violently when Calvin noticed the angry look, even in the darkness.

"Oh my bad man, I thought you were kidding. *Obviously* we had our own shit to deal with. You can't go through college, especially in a town like this without hitting *some* problems. That's just the way it is."

Jeff found himself actually feeling surprised. "Damn. And here we all thought you two never fought...about anything."

"That's because you're all a bunch of idiots" Calvin slapped him on the back as they chuckled and resumed their walk.

Jeff actually went past chuckling to a full on laugh before he could say anything further. It felt good to laugh. It hadn't happened in a long time. "Now there's the high and mighty Calvin Gretman I know so damn well."

The look of happiness disappeared from Calvin's face with alarming speed. "When have we ever chilled like this to have a legit talk?" he asked, almost sullenly. The answer was obvious. It had *never* happened before and probably wouldn't happen again. "Look, either way Buttons...if you want to fix something with Dana then just fucking talk to her. I mean come on, it's obvious."

Jeff shook his head. "I don't know about that. I think the longer I do nothing the better I'll feel."

Calvin didn't even pretend to look convinced. "How's that working out for you so far? Well enough to bear your soul to a guy you don't even like?"

Jeff felt the sting off that comment, even with all the alcohol coursing through him. The more he thought about it though the more he decided that Gretman was no happier about that comment than he was. If he didn't know better than Jeff would've assumed Calvin's words came with a side of self-deprecation.

What the fuck does this guy even know about lacking confidence? Everything's been handed to him on a platter since he got here. Bids, girlfriends, respect...all of it. All his preconceptions about his brother came flooding back. "I'll let you know when I graduate...next year" he shrugged it off as though Calvin's thoughts weren't valid.

Calvin sighed. "Fair enough."

The last stretch of their walk back to AZXi was done in complete silence.

****

Thankfully it hadn't taken long for them to realize that Riley was not coming back outside again without some form of help.

Brynn had only been too happy to get up from the picnic table she'd been sharing solely with Tory. As expected, the climb up two flights of stairs to the third floor was done in silence save for their footfalls on the stone steps. Once they reached the top floor they made their way to the end of the hallway where Riley's new room was. Brynn hadn't even seen it yet. On top of that she'd never really gone through the EIPi house all that much even after Crossing. She supposed it was a testament to her pledge process that she still didn't feel all that comfortable walking through these halls unescorted. *If you aren't with a sister then stay the fuck out!* She heard the threats as though they'd just been yelled. Even now as she walking behind Tory, Brynn started getting uncomfortable flashes of Crossing and how she'd responded to the sisterly questioning. *I want to be your sister; do you want to be mine?* The words echoed across her head back and forth until they reached Riley's door.

It was shut but not locked. Tory twisted the knob and walked inside where they found Riley sprawled out on the floor. She was still moving, and pretty frequently at that. It took a second for Brynn to follow Tory inside to get a clearer picture. If she hadn't seen it with her own two eyes she doubted she could've imagined such a sight. By all accounts it looked like her Big was...swimming...on the carpet. The fact that there was no pool or water nearby didn't bother Riley in the slightest.

"Believe it or not, that's actually not the weirdest thing I've walked in on at this house" Tory announced proudly. At first Brynn frowned because she was hard pressed to recall any experience of her own that would match this one for sheer entertainment but then she started to think about the other girls who'd lived here.

The two of them just stood there watching their sister doing the backstroke across the carpet for a few minutes. She wasn't making any progress getting from point A to point B but that also didn't seem to bother her. Finally she noticed the two girls standing there and offered them to join her in the water because it was 'nice and warm'.

"OK seriously...what the fuck were you guys drinking before I got here?" Brynn asked. She couldn't fathom how wine could ever cause this kind of drunken stupidity but what she was seeing was countering that argument.

"Whatever she had, she sure as hell didn't share it with me."

"I love swimming so much. We should totally get a pool in the house!" Riley whisper-slurred from the floor.

"I know you love swimming sweetie but it looks like you're beating the shit out of the floor" Tory said in a cute, patronizing voice. Clearly she was trying to talk to the young child currently in control of Riley's actions.

"I don't think we could pry her away from whatever it is she's doing."

"Good point" Tory agreed. The older girl knelt on the ground next to Riley, being careful to avoid the swinging of her hands back and forth while she continued her backstroke. "I think it's time for bed girl" Tory said kindly while wrapping her arms around Riley. The words struck fear into Brynn's otherwise calm demeanor. She'd been so consumed by enjoying Riley's show that she hadn't taken into account what the end result would be. *Fuck...fuck...fuck.*

"No" Riley said, finally snapping back to reality. "I just need a nap and I'll be good." They both had to laugh at such a ridiculous promise. Once the girl's head hit the pillow there'd be no getting her back up tonight.

To Brynn's surprise Tory didn't argue with Riley's outrageous claim, she just agreed casually. "OK Riles, just come and get us when you're ready to go out" Tory urged while slowly moving the girl to her bed.

Brynn stood in shock, not moving, even to help Tory with Riley. She knew once her Big was asleep then they'd be well and truly alone together. Only after Tory gave her a beseeching look did she move to help. Together they lifted their sister into bed. It wasn't as gentle as it probably should've been but they couldn't help it, Riley was heavy dead weight heavy for the two of them to carry. Once they set her down on her stomach and untangled their arms from Riley's body Tory haphazardly moved a blanket over part of the girl. Each step they took to exit the room was brisk and swift but Brynn found wished the distance was longer.

They reached the hallway and Tory turned off the bedroom light before shutting Riley's door. The sound echoed through the empty house like nothing Brynn had ever heard before. "So do you want to head to the Lambda house and see what's going on?" she asked quickly.

"In a second" Tory replied before turning to face Brynn. "Why wait?"

Brynn didn't even wait for a response. She turned and started down the long hallway to the stairwell on the opposite end. She didn't get more than four steps away before hearing what she'd been dreading from the second she'd raised her hand during the house president elections.

"I wanna know why you didn't vote for me and I want to know before you go anywhere. For the love of God I want to know why you fucking hate me. If you can't tell me that then it's going to be a long year sis."

****

From where he was standing he would've been hard pressed to say that there was a party going on in the house twenty feet away. And it was a party with almost forty people drinking heavily no less. Jake would be happy to hear that much whenever he made his way back inside. His cousin liked to hear that the noise level from the basement hadn't permeated the outdoors for fear of the neighbors getting jumpy and calling the cops. Of course his cousin seemed to be happy enough already tonight with the arrival of his half-girlfriend or whatever she was going by these days. The thoughts made him feel sick, almost angry. *He can do whatever he wants.*

Eric Saren was standing far enough back that actually hearing anything from inside would've been a red flag to quiet things down but it was still good to be enveloped in silence, if only briefly. For so much of the night he'd been surrounded by conversations and loud music that he liked the quiet the backyard provided.

The row of bushes along the back hill of Jake's house served as a good spot for guys to piss whenever they had to. It saved them the trip upstairs to use that bathroom considering it was always in use by the girls. On top of that it would allow him to avoid having another drunken chat with his aunt who would be monitoring that area like she always did. Jake had often talked about just getting a porta-potty or two for the patio out back so that no one ever had to go upstairs but that sounded like a pipe dream to Eric.

After ceasing his stream behind the bushes Eric looked behind him to where the ravine began. Out in the distance he could see the headlights of the passing cars on the expressway about two miles down the hills through the trees. He found himself staring blankly into the distance before realizing he should go back inside. He'd only been down that ravine twice with Jake and Trevor. It wasn't something demanding a repeat.

Eric took off toward the surprisingly low-lit house. The brightest lights came from the nearly underground basement windows that allowed what little daylight was possible to enter. The windows were thick enough that even those lights didn't stand out much against a black night backdrop. Even with his aunt upstairs the light from the living room and the TV she was watching didn't even come through.

As he neared the house he noticed the people on the back patio were retreating inside, all except the farthest one to the left. Once he got closer he saw that the one person left outside was finishing up a phone call. They hung up and abruptly turned around. The figure reached the cellar door the same time as Eric. It didn't take him long to see who it was, even in the darkness.

"Hey Kelly" Eric said cordially enough. The alcohol in him was screaming for a more honest greeting but he couldn't bring himself to be mean. *Riley would rip this girl apart if she were here.* He found himself wishing his cousin was there.

"Hey Eric" Kelly replied uneasily.

"Jake didn't mention you were coming" he lied, if only to see how she'd react. Passive aggressive was the best he could do to match how Riley would act.

"Oh…did he talk to you at all about us?"

"He mentioned you two were back together or something" Eric replied, being as vague as he could, hoping she'd fill in the blanks.

"I'm…I'm not sure what it is yet."

It sounded honest enough so he couldn't say why that pissed him off. *She has no idea what she's doing to him but she knows she likes it, and that's all she cares about.* "OK well I'd appreciate it if you figured that out soon" he nearly ordered. *Let's see what cards you're holding when called.*

"And why's that?" she asked forcefully.

"Because that is *my* cousin down there," he pointed absently to the cellar door as if that would signify Jake. "And I haven't seen him this happy ever and..." he nearly lost his train of thought. "And I don't want him hurt like that again." Eric didn't even think about the words as he said them.

"I don't plan on hurting him" Kelly assured Eric.

"Just like you didn't last time?" he asked, trying hard to keep his real feelings at bay. *She'll fold first...just give it a second.*

Kelly turned away in shame. "That was a mistake," she said quietly while looking off in the distance.

Eric found himself smirking. *You're damn right it was.*

"Well that mistake cost him a lot. Please...don't do that to him again."

After a few seconds she turned back and they locked eyes. "I won't."

As if on cue his cousin came up through the double metallic cellar doors to greet them. He looked a little confused at seeing them alone outside. Eric couldn't blame him. It looked and felt weird enough to him, and he'd been part of it.

"I thought you got lost or something. I know how confusing it can get out here with all the bushes and grass," Jake announced sarcastically in Kelly's direction. Eric smiled without thinking. *He still loves her. It makes absolutely no sense but he does.*

"You are sooooo funny baby" Kelly replied, equally sarcastic.

"What do you say I buy the next round?" Eric joked. Both of the people he was offering that to never paid per drink at Raley's Ring. It was part of a special agreement they all had since they'd been there at the beginning. *At least Jake and I were.*

"What a guy" Jake replied cheerily as they moved back into the basement to rejoin the party.

After being outside in its serene surroundings, getting back downstairs was a shock to Eric's system. It wasn't unlike pissing outside at an AZXi party and then going back inside only to be bombarded with whatever music Guapo was playing. *God I miss that place.* It wasn't that Raley's Ring wasn't an adequate substitute. It was that the idea of living away from home with friends and cousins while being able to do whatever, whenever, wherever always won out in the end.

He wanted to go back more than anything. He just had to convince the others to go with him before summer ended. Eric would make the trip to Gladen Hills alone if he had to but he didn't much relish the idea of being stuck alone as the go-between for Gretman and Buttons. *God only knows how those two are doing.* He wouldn't be half surprised if they were barely talking.

As of now though all he could do was drink some more tonight with his friends and hope that Kelly kept her promise. No doubt Riley would kill him once she found out how easy he was on the girl but he just didn't have it in him to outright yell at her the way Riley claimed she would. Time would tell which course of action was better.

****

Tory meant for her words to sound forceful but they came off sounding like a far cry from her assistant pledge mom persona. They also had a slight hint of begging. She hoped it wasn't as apparent to Brynn but since she was facing the opposite direction it was hard to see just what the girl was feeling. Fortunately when she did turn around it was clear that she'd heard Tory's words in all the way she'd intended. *Did she think we'd just never speak about this? That I'd just let it all go?* It was obvious that it wasn't only Brynn's doing that cheated her out of that E-Board position but she'd never held out much hope for the Beta Zeta votes once Amy stepped in.

Brynn held her ground a few feet away. "As long as I've known you, you haven't given a fuck about anything."

Tory took a step toward her younger sister. "Good call. You know...since you've only known me for less than a fucking semester."

"It still doesn't make any sense."

Tory was fighting the urge to get in the girl's face and scream. She stayed where she was though, only because she didn't trust what her limbs would do if they did get *that* close. "Do you want to know why?"

Brynn didn't look impressed. "I'd love to know."

"Because when I do care *this* is what happens!" Her words bounced off the hallway walls. *Considering I might kill her Little it's good Riley's asleep.*

"Trying is failing...especially for me...that's why I act like nothing matters. And most of the time it really doesn't. This is college! But I wanted this. House president isn't central, but it's important. It's E-Board. It's involved, and I want to be involved...so I want you to tell me why!" Tory was near to tears now. Her thoughts were racing; going to places she didn't want. *You can't think about high school.*

"I...I...didn't know..." Brynn confessed.

No fucking shit you didn't know. Nobody knows. "Please just tell me why."

As Brynn moved toward her, Tory found she couldn't move away.

"…During and even after pledging…I hated you. I don't know why but I hated you. I thought I knew but now…I don't get it…and after it ended I hated you even more because you acted like none of it mattered…but it mattered to *me*."

Tory stood there motionless. "It was my job" she replied for what felt like the millionth time. How many times could she hide behind those words without feeling the sting of the truth behind them? "I'm sorry."

"It might've been your job but you enjoyed it didn't you?"

Tory blushed for the first time in years. Not much embarrassed her and she'd done plenty that would've weighed heavily on others but Brynn's words felt worthy of her shame. She had enjoyed hazing the pledges, always had, even before she'd gotten appointed assistant pledge mom. It was fun for her and the other sisters. *Why are you so different from the rest of us? It was only six fucking weeks.*

"My way of fixing all this was to make sure you didn't get another 'job' when I had the chance to stop it. I know it sounds fucked up…but that's how I feel."

"That doesn't make sense. House president isn't assistant pledge mom. Not even close" Tory stammered, still trying to wrap her head around it all. *If the rest of us could get past pledging then what makes you so fucking special to need revenge…on me? I did the same thing forty others have done before…*

"Maybe, but I had to do something…for how you were…smiling and having a good time while we suffered, running around like idiots…for you."

"If you didn't want that then why even join a fucking sorority? That's how they are here!" Tory fumed. *Was she expecting a free ride into letters like a Rho Beta?* "We earn our letters!"

"I did what I thought I had to. That's all I've got."

"And what if I decide this isn't the end" Tory threatened. *Let's see how she likes it if I want to fuck with her shit.* Brynn stood there shocked. It was like she'd never have guessed Tory was capable of that same kind of reasoning she'd used to vote for Amy in the first place. It was simultaneously a compliment and an insult.

"I guess I'm just hoping you're a better person. That you'll let it all go a lot easier than me" Brynn replied calmly.

Oh sure, be fuckin' rational when talking about how someone else feels.

Brynn turned and resumed her walk down the hallway. Tory wasn't sure where her younger sister was going but she didn't devote much thought to it.

It didn't make any sense. In the weeks and months after Crossing Tory hadn't ever seen Brynn so much as talk to Amy, let alone develop a relationship that would lend itself to blind loyalty.

So many times elections were decided based on popularity, very rarely were they decided on merit. And now she'd found out Brynn had raised her hand because of some revenge stunt. The whole thing made her head spin. Before she could do anything Tory felt a tear roll down her face. It felt warm and soothing even as shame washed over her.

Trying is failing. When are you gonna learn?

****

The harsh light of morning hadn't made the night's events any easier to think about but that was true of most mornings in Gladen Hills. And Brynn hadn't even lived here that long. *Just over one year and I'm already fucking shit up.* She almost took it as a compliment to herself before she remembered the crushed look on Tory's face. After walking away from her last night Brynn found herself walking around on University Grove. It had been just as empty then as it was on her drive in. Once that had gotten old she made her way back to the ElPi house and thankfully Tory was gone. Where she went and who she was with was anybody's guess since Riley was out cold.

Brynn entered her Big's bedroom only to find that she was in the exact same position she'd been left in.: on her chest with a garbage can right next to the bed for throwing up. Amazingly from the contents in the trash it looked like Riley never used it.

"Morning Riles!" Brynn shouted happily.

Riley moved ever so slightly, even at the sound of a loud voice. She shuffled around in bed. "Sweet Jesus don't yell," she said in a muffled voice while smacking her lips together.

"Got it!" Brynn continued yelling. "How are you feeling?"

Riley rolled over to inspect the garbage can where she too realized it hadn't been used. She smiled. "Go me…no wonder I feel fucking terrible."

"Well you were swimming last night."

Riley looked positively terrified. "You let me near the water?!"

"Of course we didn't…but that didn't stop you from showing off on the carpet."

"Oh no."

"It was pretty impressive considering the rug-burn looked painful."

"No no no" Riley continued shaking her head, wincing each time she did.

"The really interesting thing is Tory said it wasn't the weirdest thing she's ever walked in on at this house. And that's a story I'd love to hear."

Riley sat up, although it clearly pained her. "Ignorance is bliss Little. There's no need for you to get sucked in to the whirlpool of destruction around here. It's too late for me...clearly. What time did I go down?"

"Early. But I went to bed right after you." *And sleeping on the chapter room couch wasn't comfortable.*

"You two didn't go to the Lambda house? What happened?"

"She asked me about elections" Brynn confirmed what her Big was no doubt already thinking.

"And?"

"I didn't know what to say...so I told her the truth." Riley closed her eyes abruptly but whether it was due to what Brynn had said or in response to some wave of hangover pain she couldn't say. "She yelled at me...I didn't think she'd take it so personally."

"What did you say to her exactly?" Riley asked, finally opening her eyes and allowing them to adjust again.

"I just said it basically boiled down to revenge." Even as she said the words she was realizing how petty the whole thing was. *How could it be though? Danielle, Amy, Angela, Madison and the others had all gone along with it. Why should I feel guilty about going along with everyone else?*

"Revenge for pledging right?"

Even as the thoughts spun around her head she felt less and less conviction for them. What Danielle and Amy's motivations were was anybody's guess but Madison, Olivia and the rest of her pledge class were definitely following her lead. *Just how close were the numbers in that election? Did my class really matter?*

"Yeah it was. And you know what? It felt good...there I said it! It fucking helped!" She was almost yelling. Brynn hoped she wouldn't wake up Tory who was probably sleeping across the hall. The last thing she wanted was to face off against both Tory and her Big.

"I sure hope it helped" Riley replied coolly.

The sunlight streaming through the far window was hitting Brynn's back and causing sweat to form more quickly than it otherwise would have. The whole morning had gone from bad to worse. *I need to get back home...like now.*

"You know when I'd be willing to deal with all this drama shit?" Riley asked, clearly frustrated. "When we aren't all living in the same place enjoying what are supposed to be the best years. This is our time and we're fucking it up. Life is too short to be fucking over your friends or your sisters. You want to vote for anyone then you make sure it's because you think they're the best person for the job, not this kind of shit that makes you seem like a bitch. You just chose to tell that girl you fuckin' hate her and now we're all stuck dealing with it. There's only forty of us, there's nowhere to hide."

At first Brynn took offense to being called out in such a way. EIPi was clearly in the throes of all kinds of issues long before the Beta Theta class ever got their bids. But the same could be said for any organization in Gladen Hills. The ones she'd visited for Rush all seemed to have some kind of drama lying just below the surface. *Why the fuck did I even do this to myself?* "I'm sorry" was all she could say.

"Please tell me it's over now at least?" Riley asked unsteadily.

"It is for me. I just hope Tory can leave it alone."

That seemed to prompt an entirely new look from Riley that Brynn had never seen directed at her. It looked like a protective one. "Oh so you just want Tory to sit back and do what you couldn't?"

Brynn didn't know what to say. She'd never felt more speechless. *I'm just a fucking hypocrite now. What is wrong with me?*

"When September gets here, this better be over" Riley stated eerily. "We're gonna leave the fighting to the other sororities. That's not EIPi." *Spoken like a real president.* "You're my Little. She's my best friend. We need to make this work."

"I promise it's over Riles."

"Well…at least you two finally talked about everything."

"I didn't have much choice."

"Of course not. This is T we're talking about. She does what she wants, whenever she wants."

Brynn smirked before taking a step back to look out the window. In their haste to put Riley to bed last night they hadn't closed the shades so the view from the room was clear as the day. She looked out over the campus she'd spent the last year on, finding her bearings, tripping and struggling along. After all that she'd wound up here, at Epsilon Iota Pi.

"Do you really think Tory doesn't care about anything?"

"I think she thinks she doesn't care" Riley answered cryptically.

Brynn shook her head. "It's too early for something that complex."

"Don't talk to me about too early. I think I'm still drunk," Riley said as she tossed and turned in bed. All she seemed to be achieving was tangling herself up in the blanket but she didn't care.

"Now that all of my stuff is in the chapter room I don't think I'll need to come back up here again 'til August" Brynn announced casually.

"You aren't coming back this summer?"

"It's a six hour drive from home Riles. It's not exactly a good time. Besides..." she began hesitantly. "Being away from Tory for the next couple months couldn't hurt."

Riley nodded solemnly. "I guess that's true. But we will get this shit sorted out."

Brynn moved back over to the bed to give her Big a hug. Unlike the one she'd gotten last night, which had nearly caused respiratory arrest the one now was warm and gentle. For a few seconds Brynn forgot all the trouble. As soon as the hug ended it all came flooding back, just like she knew it would. Sometimes reality could be put off, but it always circled back around.

"You better text me...like daily" Riley warned her.

"Hourly" Brynn promised before leaving the room.

The walk down the hallway felt different somehow. Every step felt like a mile. The walls that once caused her so much apprehension and anger now looked warm and inviting. Brynn couldn't help but wonder if that would've happened regardless of what she'd done at elections. Even now she wasn't sure if Amy or Tory would do a better job. And yet she'd voted with such conviction that suggested she knew better than she really had. *I can't deny it was revenge.*

The thoughts pressed against her as she made it to the stairwell. The place she'd been yelled at without remorse by Tory and the others for a solid twenty minutes that felt like an hour and all the while there was no light to be seen and music had been blasting along with the screams already shattering their eardrums. It all seemed senseless in retrospect. All it had really done was force Brynn to be more annoyed with EIPi when it was all done. *I can't be the only person that's ever felt like this. One second this place is home, the next I can't stand it. Fuck my life.*

As she made her way down the stone steps the air from the outside started seeping into her skin. With each flight of stairs she felt freer. Finally she was out so the light of the sun could cascade over her.

The coded metallic door was quick to slam behind her. She'd heard far more nerve-wracking things in and around the house for the noise to cause any fear. *Welcome to Hell bitches.* The words were as fresh now as they'd been the night she'd heard them right before the window candles had been blown out. Now *that* had freaked her out. Just the fact that they'd all gone out in perfect sync was enough to give her pause about what else they could achieve. *As if the floor cleaning wasn't bad enough…*

Brynn made her way to the parking lot. Her car was right where she'd left it. Once she found the keys, she twisted them into the lock to get inside.

As soon as she caught motion in the corner of her eye she stopped.

Upon getting to Gladen Hills Brynn hadn't seen a single other person walking so close to the campus. In fact, outside of Riley and Tory she hadn't really seen anybody since she wasn't counting the sparse few on University Grove last night, all of which had been townies.

As the figure came into view she was sorry she hadn't just driven off when she had the chance. Tory continued to make her way to the sidewalk that crossed in front of the parking lot Brynn was in. Wearily, the girl locked eyes with Brynn and at first didn't seem to know how to react. *This would look so creepy if anyone's watching.*

After a few tense seconds of no movement Brynn finally nodded slightly in Tory's direction. At first she didn't respond but then the older girl actually went ahead and nodded back with what looked like a fraction of approval. With the sun hitting them so brutally it was hard to tell. Once that interaction was done Tory continued her trudge over to the entrance of EIPi and sauntered inside.

That's as warm a conversation as we've ever had. I guess it's a start.

Chapter 44

Riley had to admit that already being moved in five weeks before classes started in the fall took a huge weight off her shoulders. It hadn't been all that difficult to move her things from downstairs to her new room on the third floor. It probably would've gone a little faster with her cousins or brother and father to help out but she wasn't about to ask any of them to make a special trip down here just for that.

Trevor and her father had helped her move in freshman year. Sophomore year her brother had been away at the Air Force Academy, same as last year. Fortunately Eric and Nicki had helped during her junior year so her father hadn't had to make a separate trip. He was getting a little old to be lifting furniture up and down stairwells. Since it was just her and Tory in the house for the summer the moving process had taken about four or five days for both their rooms to get completed.

After their summer class session had ended Riley broached the idea of heading back home for a while to see her family. Tory on the other hand didn't have any desire to do the same. She kept saying that she could never dress how she wanted to back home. Since it was summer and hot outside she tended to short shorts and tank tops. Riley didn't have a problem with it but most of the time she wore Capri's and t-shirts. Occasionally she'd wear shorts but they were never at the length Tory's were.

Not wanting to leave her friend alone she decided against staying home all that long, instead she just made time to go back sparingly to visit Nicki when she was home from her summer job or have dinner with her parents or grandparents.

The further into summer they got though, the less Tory seemed to want Riley around. She had all the company she needed in the form of a Lambda brother. The night Brynn had visited was the night she'd started hooking up with Greg. They'd been texting non-stop since that point and screwing even more. Fortunately Tory would usually go down to do that at the Lambda house on Arkridge so Riley at least didn't have to hear it.

With the latest episode of Grey's Anatomy ending on her TV in the corner Riley looked over to her friend who'd crashed on the couch before the start of their marathon a few hours ago. As the day wore on Riley noticed more and more that she was texting constantly throughout each episode. It didn't much matter considering they'd seen all these episodes before, most multiple times but her lack of attention took something away from the whole experience.

"You still talking to Greg?" she asked with a subtle edge.

"Yeah" Tory answered plainly, not even looking up from her phone.

"What the hell have you guys been talking about?"

"Not much. He wants me to come down there."

Gee I wonder what activity he has planned. Riley had tried being a good sport about everything when Tory started her fling by going down to the Lambda house for their summer parties and little get-togethers. The problem was she didn't find any of the guys hot besides Greg and on top of that, none of them were very fun. Out of the five staying there over the summer, two were always high and the other two besides Greg didn't want to talk to her at all.

"Again?" Riley asked dryly.

"Again?!" Tory mocked her.

"I'm just saying you've been over there a lot since…" her voice trailed off, which caught Tory's attention. "Since Brynn was here."

"It's not like there's all that much to do around here in the summer except…him."

She's been like this ever since she talked to Brynn. "I don't know T. Greg seems like an ass." *Just like the rest of his brothers.*

"Relax Riles, it's not like I'm gonna date him."

Just the fact that she said that means she's considered it. That thought soured Riley immediately. If her best friend started dating a guy who couldn't even be troubled to come to their house to fuck her then he wasn't worth her time.

"You're coming out with me tonight right?"

"Are we going somewhere?"

"Probably onto University Grove. My cousins are on their way." *It would've been nice if they were here earlier to help move my shit but whatever.*

"Both of them?" Tory asked, closing down her phone and looking away.

Riley hadn't talked to her friend about Eric since she originally found out they slept together…again. For the first time Riley found herself actively wishing that the two of them would just do it, if only to move Greg out of the way.

"Yeah. Eric and Jake are driving up together with some of their brothers. Everything cool?"

"Yeah…what time did you want to meet up with them?"

Riley reached over to the nightstand to check her phone. She hadn't gotten any texts from either Jake or Eric in a while so she wasn't sure how far away they were. "Maybe an hour or two."

"OK good, that'll give me time to come back and shower" Tory said casually.

"So you're going to see Greg?"

"Yeah, why?"

"Nothing. Just call me when you get back."

****

"So how exactly did you get talked into buying all the liquor for tonight?" Jeff asked. His tone suggested he was astonished by the situation.

"I'll give you three guesses but you'll only need one" Calvin grinned as they made their way down the aisle of assorted rums.

"Biz?"

"Biz" Calvin confirmed.

Jeff looked confused even though that was really the only choice based on who was on the guest list tonight. One thing was for sure, it definitely wasn't Jerry or Jared that had convinced him to buy a few bottles, even if he was supposed to get paid back when the guys got here.

"You know the guy can be pretty persuasive."

Jeff looked pissed…again. Since he seemed to look that way so much of the time, especially in the last month, Calvin didn't really pay attention to it. "It's just too bad he doesn't use that gift when it could actually help" Jeff answered bitterly.

And there it is. Calvin prepared for an argument. Frankly he was tired of thinking about something he couldn't change. *Saying that will just piss him off more and we'll be fighting in the middle of the store. Fuck that.* "Wow that was crazy of me."

"What was?" Jeff asked, sounding confused as well as curious.

"Thinking you were over that by now" Calvin replied sarcastically.

Elections were over two months ago but Jeff had been suspended well over two years ago and he was still pissed about that too. Given the circumstances Calvin wasn't sure why he was surprised. Maybe he just kept hoping for the guy to lighten up.

"You're right, that was crazy," Jeff agreed coolly.

Calvin decided to ignore the subject in the hope that Jeff would do the same. Amazingly it seemed to work as the two continued to walk along the aisles, looking around without saying a word.

Gladen Hills was pretty small town, even *with* the college in play, so there were only two liquor stores to speak of. Most undergrads went to the one closest to campus if only because some didn't have cars or else when they needed the liquor for a date party or whatever they were in a hurry. The latter was usually the case where AZXis were concerned. *We're all huge fans of procrastination, even with alcohol.* The memories of how many times Calvin or another older AZXi had to rush to the store to get a new fuck some liquor for a predate party numbered beyond count. *Just another thing to miss when I leave tomorrow…*

"And the Ice 101 is for Biz" Calvin said to himself as he put the clear bottle with blue lettering into the basket. He was only getting three bottles but he didn't want to make Jeff feel inclined to help him carry them. It was enough of a shock that he'd wanted to leave his room at all. "That's everything."

"I hope they're paying you back for all that."

"After the tab I've been running up at the National this summer there's no way I could afford this otherwise" he exaggerated. His parents had already paid the three months rent to continue living at the house. And his expenses, even if they were a tad excessive at the National were far from being *that* pricey. He almost wished they were. At least then he'd have made a splash on his way out of Gladen Hills.

As they headed toward the counter Calvin walked past the lone mirror in the store to see just how haggard and run-down both he and Jeff looked. They both had untrimmed beards growing, sleeplessness in their eyes and three large liquor bottles in the basket to top it all off. Calvin grinned. *Always a good time confirming frat stereotypes.*

Neither Calvin nor Jeff said much on the drive back to Arkridge Avenue. It really wasn't all Jeff's fault either. Calvin was feeling very pensive recently. Everything he did seemed much sadder than it ever had before. Every action he took came with a question in his head. *Will this be the last time I ever play beer pong here? Will this be the last time I drive down to AZXi from the liquor store?* It was enough to depress him even before he drowned his system with actual depressants.

Fortunately, as soon as they got back to house there was a sight that lifted his spirits. It looked like Eric's car full of brothers had just pulled in a few minutes before they had. Calvin had to remind himself to park the car before greeting everyone.

It felt like Jeff had his own excitement building at actually getting a visitor he could talk to openly this summer. Dana still hadn't come down to see him once. *I can see why Buttons thinks they're having issues.* On the flip side, Calvin could barely keep Jennifer away. And there were times when he'd wanted just that, although they were few in number.

A few weeks ago she'd called to say she'd found a one-bedroom apartment they could rent about ten minutes from his parent's place. With that one phone call Jennifer managed to dredge up all the feelings he'd been trying to bury since that talk he'd had with Jeff. *Can I really be ready for all of this?* The question was like an incessant fly never far from his head.

"Perfect timing son" Eric said as Calvin and Jeff exited the car.

"It's the only way I roll Biz." The two shook hands the AZXi way before Eric moved over to greet Jeff in the same fashion. It felt good seeing his younger brothers again, even if it was for the last time in a while.

"You guys getting back from the liquor store?" Eric asked while staring down the brown bag the clerk had put their bottles into.

"Yes Biz we got your liquor" Jeff grinned.

"Dude we are getting hammered tonight!" Jared shouted.

"I'm not waiting until tonight," Jeff said with a knowing smirk.

"Now you're talking Buttons" Will agreed as he shook hands with both of them. Jared followed suit after he was done shouting. Jerry was close behind both of them. The fifth person in line wasn't somebody Calvin ever expected to see again. Even when he'd talked to Eric in the morning about them coming up it seemed like his cousin Raley was still a question mark and yet here he was.

"Well look who's here Buttons" Calvin nearly yelled, if only to make the kid feel special and a little uncomfortable right off the bat. Jeff had probably seen him before Calvin said anything but was likely waiting to see how he'd react. It had never been lost on Calvin that Raley and Buttons had a weird relationship.

Surprisingly, Jeff smiled at his former pledge as warmly as could be expected. "The kid can't be bothered to come to any socials while he actually lives here but drinking with six guys over the summer, he's in."

"Gotta have priorities man" Jake replied with a smirk.

Calvin smiled widely. He looked like Raley, sounded like Raley, but for all intents and purposes he seemed to be acting different from the Raley Calvin had briefly known throughout the past semester. And that wasn't necessarily a bad thing.

"Well at least it's good to know you actually have some now" Jeff retorted.

"Figured it was time."

Jake and Jeff shook hands in the AZXi fashion. It was nearly enough to get Calvin to smile like it was Christmas morning but he restrained himself. He likewise had to pause when he shook the kid's hand. *He just might be an AZXi after all.*

Once the greetings were done Calvin took the bag of liquor and set it down on the picnic table a few feet away by the back of their house. He lifted the bottles one by one.

"Thanks for getting these for us Gretman. It would've been a huge pain in the ass to get them after the drive in" Eric said warmly.

"It's straight. As long as I get at least one shot from each of the bottles" he replied. It was only half a joke and they both knew it.

"That's completely fair" Eric agreed. "I won't be able to finish that Ice without your help anyways." Like so much else in Gladen Hills, doing something stupid was better if others came along for the ride.

"Of course Gretman has to weasel some shots out for himself" Jerry said with a grin as he neared the table.

"Oh I'm sorry Jer-Bear. Did you go to the store to get these?"

Jerry laughed. That seemed to stop any further jokes on the subject, which was good since there was a lot of drinking to be done.

"Who's even still left in this town?" Will asked. "There was barely anybody on the Grove when we drove in. There are no cars on Arkridge either."

"Not really anybody" Jeff agreed. "Outside of a couple Lambdas there's nobody on Arkridge besides us. But I did see one of the EIPis leaving their house a few times."

Raley looked like he was about to have a seizure as he quickly turned to face Eric with an inquisitive stare. Eric looked as confused as Calvin felt. "Riley wouldn't fuck any of them right?" He asked in a way that sounded like it was the worst possible outcome imaginable. *The Lambdas suck but they aren't that bad kid.*

"No" Eric agreed. "Plus Buttons obviously knows what she looks like so he would've said so...right?" he turned to Jeff for confirmation which he got, albeit a few seconds after he let the two cousins sweat. *Some things never change.*

"That must mean it's the one Biz banged" Will chimed in without being prompted. Eric didn't look amused but everyone else definitely was.

"Well that'll complicate things" Raley perked up.

"Nah, she can obviously do what she wants."

I'll have to ask him about that later on...after a few drinks.

"Oh so you weren't trying to get it tonight?" Will asked with no tact.

"Obviously I am...just chill Bill-Butt" Eric ordered, not unkindly.

Biz's usually cool poker face was failing him. They all knew he wasn't happy with the news but there wasn't much they could do about it short of killing whoever that chick was fucking next door. *At least that'd be a crazy story to go out on top with.*

They cracked open each of the bottles and started pouring the drinks out into the plastic cups Raley had brought from some party at his house. The seven of them did their first shot together within seconds. Unlike it usually did, the opening Ice 101 shot didn't burn. It tasted a little sweeter.

"Well" Calvin began, surveying the brothers in front of him and lifting his second shot. "It looks like it's a real motley crew tonight." They all did the second shot quickly after his toast. The liquor didn't burn that time either. Maybe he was finally getting used to taking straight Ice 101 shots. *It only took four years.*

As Eric poured out the next round for himself and Calvin, he found himself just taking in the sparsely green backyard area of the AZXi house with its six other actives standing around the picnic table the Alpha Gammas built a year ago. *This is it. My last night living in Gladen Hills. One more night.*

Come tomorrow morning, Calvin was positive he wouldn't trade tonight's memories for anything.

The third shot went down easier than the first two.

****

Tory had only been down on Arkridge less than an hour before she made her way back up to the EIPi house. She'd only been fucking Greg for a month but whether he was sober or drunk he wasn't much for foreplay. That was all fine since these days she wasn't feeling particularly tied to that concept either. She was more than content riding him 'til she finished and then letting him do whatever he had to to get himself off. That usually amounted to him going behind and getting a few pumps in. It was a nice arrangement, all things considered.

"You got back pretty quick" Riley said casually. At least it might've sounded that way if Tory hadn't known her best friend well enough to see that it was bait. Tory shook her head. She wasn't going to deal with any of that kind of shit tonight.

"So now you don't even approve of the time involved?" she asked coolly. *Two can play it this game Riles.*

"Oh God no" Riley backtracked.

"Good."

They sat in silence for a few minutes just drinking some more of their latest box of wine. Riley was drinking out of one of her glasses but Tory was using a disposable plastic one. She just didn't feel like washing out her own glass and bringing it over to Riley's room so she took one out of the sleeve of cups in the chapter room.

"Do you think I'm mad or something?" Riley asked unsurely. It was almost enough to make Tory laugh. *It's always about her, all the time.*

"No Riles I don't. You aren't right?" she asked, only to cover her bases.

"You're my best friend T. I could never be mad at you."

I'd love to see that in writing one of these days.

"But that still doesn't explain why you've been a little…bitchy…since Brynn was here." The mention of her Little's name was enough to push away the last of the good feelings she'd had from her latest orgasm. Negative feelings started flooding her like she was no more than a sinking ship. "And I'm guessing that fucking Greg isn't helping your mood at all."

"What makes you so sure?" Tory asked abruptly.

"Because you're doing him daily and it's not helping."

There were few times since she'd moved to Gladen Hills where she'd found it annoying that Riley knew her so well. Now was one of those times. *Just leave me alone about it Riles…but that's probably asking too much.*

"Normally you don't get mad about anything, at least that I've ever seen. I was hoping you'd just let whatever this is go, or say something to me about what it is."

"Well this is different" Tory replied coolly while taking another sip of the wine. She was nearly squeezing the plastic cup to the point where the wine would overflow.

"There's one thing that's not different T…you've still got me to talk to, whenever you want" Riley offered warmly.

Tory just faked a smile and continued drinking.

I've heard that shit before, it's never fucking true.

****

Once the picnic table was set on the sparse front lawn they all took up spots at or around it. The table could only seat four comfortably so the remaining three were relegated to the lawn chairs that had been sitting out front since alumni weekend. *It's a miracle nobody's stolen them.*

As soon as Jake took a seat on one of the lawn chairs he realized why they had in fact not been touched by rival frats or drunk undergrads: they were old and very uncomfortable. The one he'd chosen felt as though it would fall apart any minute.

Not long after they'd all sat down a car came rolling down the street. A white university police cruiser was slowly making its way toward them. The officer within was likely trying to make sure nobody was doing anything too illegal. Given how few people were actually around during the summer Jake doubted there was anything worthy of the cop's attention. The cruiser slowed even more in front of AZXi. The officer inside took long looks at each of them as he went. If Jake didn't know better he would've thought the cop was taking even longer to look at him. The cruiser continued its leisurely stroll down the road before turning around in one of the driveways and leaving Arkridge.

He didn't even realize it until after the cruiser turned back onto Castle Lane that he hadn't taken so much as a sip from his drink in a while. Once he lost sight of the car he took a long deep gulp, not unlike the one he saw Jeff doing on the chair directly to his right. Eric was sitting directly to his left, which left Jared, Calvin, Jerry and Will sitting at the picnic table behind them.

"Fucking bastards," Jeff stated without a hint of remorse.

Jake found himself agreeing with his former pledge-master in another of the formerly rare instances. "Right there with you man."

"OK Raley, what could you possibly have against the Gladen Hills PD?" Calvin asked with immense curiosity.

Jake had to remind himself that outside of Jeff and Eric it was entirely likely that Calvin didn't have a damn clue about what really happened during pledging. Jake had been so pissed at the time he hadn't even wanted to say a word to Jeff but Eric convinced him to. It stood to reason that Jerry probably knew since he and Jeff were 'running' the pledge program but Jake doubted Calvin ever got the full story.

"Do you not remember the fact that we were under-grounded this semester?" Jake asked haughtily as he turned around in his chair to face Calvin. It felt good knowing something that the president of AZXi didn't.

Unfortunately for Jake's vanity, Calvin didn't look surprised or even slightly put off by his condescension. "How could I forget that? *I'm* the one that had to meet with the Dean about all of it."

It wasn't lost on Jake that Jeff flinched in the chair next to him when Calvin emphasized himself having to deal with the fallout.

Jake hadn't been given the full details about what the aftermath had been for the actives and quite frankly, now was the first time he'd ever wanted to know.

"I caught the cliff notes. Jeff never gave me the full story" Calvin went on.

"I didn't tell anybody what happened except Jerry, and even there I didn't say any more than I told you" Jeff said coolly. He'd since gotten up from his chair to pour more whiskey into his cup from one of the bottles sitting on the picnic table. "And I'm pretty sure Raley and Summers kept that shit to themselves."

"The only person I really gave any details to was Biz" Jake interrupted.

"Well it's my last night here Raley, humor me. I'd love to know how you two caused me that fuckin' headache" Calvin said with a smile.

"Yeah I'm definitely tryin' to hear this story too" Jared chimed in.

"What happened is that Raley and Summers both went fucking wild. Absolutely off the reservation" Will answered for him.

Jake turned back around to face Arkridge. Before he did he saw the looks of pure attentiveness from pretty much everyone sitting on the front lawn, all except Eric. He just sat in his chair with a smug smile, like he was enjoying the moment of knowing things few others did. *Must run in the family.* Taking another sip from his cup, Jake discovered he'd drained it all.

He'd never felt compelled to say anything to a single AZXi about the Triple-E incident but suddenly he wanted to tell them everything. *It is Gretman's last night.* He tried rationalizing the newfound desire for openness in his head. He raised his cup without getting up from his seat. "Well guys, fill me up another round and I'll tell you a story. It's probably *the* best story you'll ever hear" Jake said with confidence. *Over-selling is an art.* Somebody grabbed the cup from his hand quick enough and once he heard the liquid being poured he started talking. "We were all working on the scavenger hunt list Jeff gave us to finish by the end of week five…"

"This is the dumbest fuckin' thing I've ever done" Jake announced. *Having sex without a condom isn't smart either but fuck it.*

"Doesn't even crack my top ten" Will quipped from his spot in the driver's seat.

Easy for him to say, h*e's not going out there.* Jake handed back the seven-page list to J-Hood who was in the passenger's seat next to Will. Summers and he were in the back prepping for the next item.

It was agreed at the start that given the two hundred eighty-seven things on the list that they wouldn't be able to finish everything. Not with school and sleep also on the agenda. That meant they'd need to prioritize things based on what they thought would be more entertaining when the presentation came around.

Jake personally didn't give a fuck about what was entertaining, he was just biding time until week six came and went.

They all knew the pranks against the various sorority houses would likely be happily received so those were on the checklist tonight. They'd already tagged Alpha Zeta Xi letters in duct tape on the ABI house and taken a picture of it. They'd pissed on the Phi Theta house and documented that as well. Next up was the Trip-E's. He looked up past the seats to check the time on the car's clock again. It was past three in the morning.

All we need to do is light a bag of shit on fire on the porch, take a few pictures and put it out. No problem. J-Hood had already shit into a large paper bag from the local grocery store.

"It won't be that bad Raley" Summers reassured him. His pledge brother seemed remarkably calm about the situation given that they were the guinea pigs. *First the cow milking on that random farm with J-Hood and now this? Fuck me.*

It was deep into the fifth week of pledging and Jake was suffering from a severe lack of sleep…and just about anything else that was fun. His decision-making processes were completely fucked and he found himself either straight up volunteering for the dumb shit or somehow being talked into it by his pledge brothers. Even now, for the life of him, he couldn't remember which had happened to get him into this.

"I'll do it if you want" J-Hood offered, although even with his signature monotone voice, the offer didn't sound genuine.

Jake figured he'd take his place if called on but he didn't feel the need for that. "I said I'd do it and I will."

"Word."

Will started his dated SUV to get them moving toward Castle Lane. They'd been parked on Cadren Drive for ten minutes while they looked over the list.

"Just remember not to delete the pics this time Raley" Will teased him.

"I made one damn mistake, just let it go" Jake replied angrily. He'd heard enough about how his slip of the finger had deleted several pictures of tasks they'd already completed. It was getting more annoying with each passing reference, particularly when it came from Will. "We re-did them all anyways so it's not a big fucking deal."

"Yeah except for the cow milking" Will said coolly.

"Well considering me and Hood almost died, I'd say that's acceptable." *What the fuck does he know about that anyways? He wasn't with us. Running through that huge field at night nearly gave me a fuckin' heart attack.* Jake shook his head rapidly. Thinking about that night any more would only mess up his mindset for the here and now.

Will kept driving as Croftlin Rise turned into College Curve. The Triple-E house stood on the fringes of the hill that comprised all the campus buildings, right on the corner of Castle Lane and the residential areas. It was the last in a line of houses that stood against a thick wooded area whose other end held the campus. Unfortunately even at half past three in the morning the area was incredibly well lit. It was almost comical how many streetlights were in the area as opposed to Arkridge Avenue.

Once they pulled up outside the house Jake and Summers got out. They watched the truck drive away onto some road he didn't know the name of further away from campus. An ominous feeling settled over him as he turned on his digital camera. There wasn't a sound. The whole situation just served to make Jake feel more unsettled. Summers looked entirely calm in comparison.

They both looked around the immediate area and saw nothing. Summers moved up the first few steps of the porch and set the large brown paper bag upright next to the screen door. He took out the lighter Will had given him to set the bag on fire. It went up in flames exceedingly quick. The fast nature of the fire caught both of them off guard.

There was snow on the porch and all around them given that winter hadn't finished and yet Jake had never felt hotter. And it wasn't all because of the flames. The top of the bag had yet to catch fire but it was getting there. He immediately began snapping picture after picture, not caring about anything else. The only thing that mattered was that the pictures were being saved to the memory card within the camera. After five or six he stopped. *That better be enough for those assholes.* The unsatisfied look of Jeff Chester flashed into his mind.

"Good" Summers agreed as he reached out with his gloved hand to pick up the bag and move it off the porch. Jake put his camera away and they both proceeded to pour snow onto the bag until the flames died.

"It probably wasn't a good idea to spray the bag down with Lysol" Summers lamented quietly as they watched the snow melt before consuming the remnants of the fire. Jake immediately turned to his pledge brother.

Before he could ask him just what the fuck he meant by doing something so crazy a car appeared on Castle Lane directly in front of them. Summers was still facing the Triple-E house so he couldn't see the car but he could hear it was there. Jake was staring at the ground, being careful not to give the tinted windows eye contact. *That's not Will.*

"Is it the cops?" Summers whispered the question in Jake's direction.

Jake was still paralyzed with fear and unable to look directly at the SUV in front of him. Finally he pried his eyes off the snow-covered sidewalk they were on and saw the Gladen Hills police insignia on the vehicle's side. "Uh huh" was all he could say.

"Shit....run."

By the time the words registered in Jake's ears his pledge brother was already sprinting down the sidewalk back toward College Curve.

Somehow Jake felt his legs moving beneath him, probably as fast as they'd ever gone. He didn't care about the possibility of slipping and falling, he just wanted to get as far from where they were as humanly possible.

Summers was pulling further away. The guy ran right past College Curve and kept going. Jake heard the SUV's screeching tires behind him. *I'll never keep up with him.* Without thinking Jake took off to the left of the sidewalk and ran into the night surrounding the backyards of the houses on Castle Lane, praying he'd be safe. He nearly tumbled into the cars parked in the driveway of the house he was running past but thankfully regained his balance in time to push off one of them and resume his run. Jake couldn't even tell what color or kind of car he'd just touched everything was moving so fast. For all he knew there could be a cop right behind him but he was too afraid to turn around.

Once he reached the backyard he paused for a few seconds to let his eyes adjust to the darkness. The area was untouched by the various streetlights. As soon as his eyes settled he got his bearings and went further back.

There was far more space here than he'd ever pictured. The area was made up of a steep incline, which was to be expected considering how much of a hill there was to climb to get from Castle Lane up to the campus but the space wasn't filled with houses or even yards or sheds. It was essentially a miniature ravine not unlike the one behind Jake's own house in Reesewood.

After he realized there was no one nearby Jake moved as far back from the street as he could. That led him about a hundred or so feet into what could be classified as the house's backyard although he doubted the property lines extended so far. Quickly, he scanned the area and found a pile of branches and assorted sticks covered in snow on the ground to his left. Between the hills they were sitting on and the snow blanketing the area it made for a well-concealed nook.

Jake dove into the sticks, not even pausing to care. He moved some snow around and settled in between two large branches that looked to have fallen recently. He lied flat on his back and tucked his legs underneath some wet leaves. The ground was incredibly cold and uncomfortable but all the same he felt secure in how hidden he was.

Within a minute the cold from the ground started sinking into his uncovered skin, which included his face and hands. Suddenly all those times Kelly had told him to buy gloves when they were at the store didn't seem so annoying. His fingers were losing their feeling and he could sense his teeth starting to chatter. Realizing that such a thing would contribute to him being found he tried thinking about *anything* warm.

His thoughts immediately went to Kelly and how he always liked lying next to her in bed. Wrapping his arms around her while they slept or cuddled to watch a movie. Inevitably his thoughts turned to sex and how he wished they could do it more often, especially recently. But since he'd been pledging, his sex life had taken a noticeable turn for the worse. He could only imagine how Kelly was dealing with him being away for so much of the time. Knowing her, she was probably hanging with her roommates more and more just to find some kind of companionship while he was off doing crazy shit for AZXi. The mere fact that he was out here behind some random house in the dark, in the middle of the night when he could be in bed with Kelly only served to infuriate him. Up until now he hadn't had much time to be anything beyond terrified. *What the fuck am I even doing out here?*

Jake didn't have time to think further because something caught his eye. There were lights shining on the tree branches above him. Jake stayed perfectly still and watched the lights dart from one tree to the other, only stopping occasionally for an extended look. The paralyzing fear he'd felt when the cruiser had shown up on Castle Lane came back to him in a massive wave. Sweat was forming on his brow and back. Given that his back was up against a mound of snow and brush the sweat simply made him feel colder, but also somehow hotter simultaneously.

The urge to perk his head up to see where the lights were coming from started to overwhelm his need to stay still. After no more than a few seconds the urge won and he propped his head up from the ground slowly. He prayed with each inch that a twig or stick wouldn't crack around him with the added pressure his body was causing. Fortunately, he didn't make a sound and his head reached a point where he could see the sources of light. There were more beams surrounding him than he'd originally guessed. At least four separate locations were shining on the trees and the grounds around them. Three of them were a good distance away but the fourth was closer than Jake felt even remotely comfortable with. And it was getting closer still. He could hear voices shouting orders but he couldn't make anything out.

Did Summers come back here? No way. He was heading toward Arkridge, maybe even the interstate, no chance he'd double back. They're here looking for me. There were at least four cops around him that he could see and an unknown amount off in the shadows. *All this for a stupid fucking prank? Jesus, you'd think I killed someone.*

The fourth cop who was closest to Jake moved away. He looked to be heading back down toward where College Curve began. *Will and J-Hood better not have gone back there after they left Triple-E.* Even William Anthony would have a hard time talking his way out of just why he and another undergrad were sitting in a parked car on campus all dressed in their customary black callout gear so late at night. It wouldn't take a genius to figure out what was going on if and when the cops caught any of them. Given how fast Summers had been going and the likelihood that Will and J-Hood had gotten out of there as soon as the first cop appeared it was increasingly likely that Jake was the one they were after with purpose. *Lucky me.*

Once the fourth cop moved a safe distance away Jake sat up, probably quicker than he should have. His hands pressed down against the snowy ground and a new surge of cold went through them. He pushed through it to stand up. He looked directly to his right, back the way he'd come from. There didn't look to be any flashlights in that direction. *It looks safe enough.*

Jake started moving slowly back toward the house. The closer he got the more confident he became that there were no cops nearby. He reached the driveway he'd nearly fallen in during his initial run and found the two cars he'd collided with. Neither of them looked anything like the blur he'd zipped past earlier. They were parked one behind the other. One was an old two-door model and the other a larger boat of a car not dissimilar from the kind his grandmother drove.

Tentatively, Jake moved down the driveway, being careful to avoid the patch of ice that had threatened to kill him earlier. He finally got to the inner edge of the sidewalk and peered in either direction down Castle Lane. If he could get to the other side of the road then he could cut through the backyards and apartment complexes all the way back to Arkridge Avenue. From there he could call Kelly to get him back to Northeast. *Nobody will be looking for me that far from here.*

He reached into his inner jacket pocket only to come to the disturbing realization that his phone and wallet weren't there. Jake immediately thought he dropped them during his run. After taking a second to actually sift through his memories he came to the slightly less disturbing recollection that he'd left everything in Will's car. His wallet held his student ID and that was the only thing that would gain him access into his dorm considering he didn't have his cell to call any of his roommates. Dukes might've been awake but Jake wouldn't be able to make it all the way across town with what could very well be the entire university police force out looking for him. Making his way down to Arkridge seemed like the best option from the list of terrible choices.

Jake's mood plummeted again when he noticed a cruiser parked up the road toward the Triple-E house and another down the road past the corner of College Curve. Both cruisers were pointed inward watching the stretch of road he'd run down before darting into the backyards. *They're waiting for me. They want me to cross the road because they'll know exactly where I am.*

Jake felt apprehensive about returning to where he'd been hiding earlier. It was enough of a miracle that none of the cops had heard him leaving that spot. He didn't feel the need to tempt fate twice. Even so, he couldn't stay where he was. At the right angle, he was readily visible from several different directions.

Desperation set in. Jake could feel himself losing faith that he'd escape. *What the fuck am I gonna do?* He started feeling frantic. His head might as well have been on a swivel with the million different directions he was looking in.

Abruptly he moved backward to lie down on the ground. Once he was there he slid underneath the larger of the two cars in the driveway. The ground was just as cold as it had been in the backyard. His hands started shaking so he thrust them into his pants to press them against the warmer skin encased beneath. It was only a temporary solution though. He wouldn't be able to sleep here. Not when it was so frigid outside. *A jail cell would be just as cold you fucking idiot.*

After a few minutes of silence Jake's ears perked up at the sound of something moving toward him. *Great. Now I'm fucked for sure. What am I gonna say to my parents?* His thoughts were going a mile a minute. It almost got to the point where he didn't notice just how fast the footfalls were approaching. They were coming in quicker and quicker. *That's way too fast to be a person.*

Jake didn't have to wait long in his confusion. A German shepherd from the town's K-9 unit completed its run at Jake and stopped right outside his position under the old car. It lowered its head to start sniffing his body. He wanted to laugh at the absurdity of it all. *All this for a stupid fucking prank.* Something within him said to get move. The dog hadn't growled or even barked once. It was likely trying to figure out just what the hell was going on. *Join the fucking club pal.*

Upon standing upright Jake made sure to keep his movements slow and steady. He somehow knew that moving quickly would cause the dog to attack. Again he looked up and down the street to see the two cruisers exactly where they were the last time he'd looked. *They're still waiting for me.* If he was going to make that move he'd need to do it fast in the hopes of avoiding being seen. Of course if he moved as fast as he'd need to it was entirely likely that this dog would tackle him to the ground. *I can't go forward. I can't go back. Fuck.*

The consequences once again didn't even enter into Jake's mind as he calmly and coolly made his way to the chosen destination. The dog seemed utterly confused by Jake's slow movements and as such seemed content to simply follow along. Under normal circumstances it would've looked like the animal was his pet. Once Jake reached the porch of the house in front of him he quickened his pace. To his mild surprise the door handle twisted open easily and he darted inside. The dog took a quick bite of his ass as he went. A small, sharp pain stabbed through him. Jake made sure to securely lock the door after closing it. He stayed hovered over the door's window for a second to see how the dog would react. It stayed still for a second as if unsure what to do then it took off into the night without barking once.

Jake turned around to survey the house's surroundings. To his complete surprise he saw composite pictures hanging on the walls around the main room. They didn't look much different from the ones at the AZXi house. He moved in closer to the nearest one, which shared the same wall as the door he'd come through.

He'd never heard of the one displayed across the center of the picture. *Nu Rho Omicron? Who the fuck is that?* Jake had heard of the Alpha Kappa's or AK's. He'd heard about the Lambdas right next to AZXi. He'd heard about the Kappa Nus across the street. He'd even heard about the Phi Psis uptown past University Grove but never the Nu Rho Omicrons. He didn't even know this random house on Castle Lane was a fraternity. It didn't look like all the others he'd seen. It didn't look much like one on the inside either.

The feelings of apprehension dissipated slowly. It was definitely better to stumble into a fraternity house over a random undergrad's place considering other frat guys would likely be more forgiving. Some would probably find it downright hysterical.

What if the police come knocking at this door though? What the fuck is gonna happen then? Frantically Jake felt his pockets and again cursed the fact that he didn't have his wallet. A bribe to the frat guys living there couldn't hurt.

Jake peered out the front window again. There was no immediate movement outside but that didn't mean much. There was one lone light shining from the top of the staircase on the far side of the room. He stayed still but couldn't hear anyone moving upstairs. The doorway immediately to his left looked promising enough in that it was shrouded in darkness.

Upon entering the room it became clear it was a kitchen. And if nothing else, it looked like a typical frat house kitchen. At least it would've resembled AZXi's pretty well had he and his pledge brothers not been forced to clean it daily. The kitchen was littered with dirty plates and glasses. It looked like it hadn't been cleaned once all semester let alone in the weeks since pledging started. *Does this frat not have pledges? Where the fuck am I?*

Jake didn't stop long in the doorway before moving into the corner farthest from it. He settled into a crouched position to sit on the floor. As cool as it was it might as well have been a sandy beach in comparison to the snow he'd been wading through all night. He could hear heat coming from somewhere in the darkness.

Without his phone he had no idea what time it was or how long he'd been evading the cops. There was no sign of a clock anywhere in the kitchen save for the one on the microwave and that one just kept blinking midnight. It wouldn't surprise him if he learned it was well past four by now.

As he settled into a more comfortable stance he pulled out his digital camera from his jacket pocket and weighed the pros and cons of turning it on. It would cause a little light to filter into the room but he wanted to make sure he hadn't harmed it at all. He decided to risk it. Thankfully it wasn't damaged. *Thank fucking God.*

Within a few seconds of his nerves settling a light shone through the window upward to his right a foot away. The light jumped from place to place, surveying the kitchen from the outside. Jake slowly and carefully tucked his legs closer up into his body so they couldn't be visible from the angle of the window. The beam lingered there for a few more seconds, continuing to move around like a searchlight overlooking a prison yard. Then, abruptly it turned away and Jake was left with darkness again, the cool, comforting darkness. But then another light burst through the opposing window to his left. This window was closer to the corner of the room he was cowering in and it wouldn't take much for him to be seen if the cop outside looked in at the right angle.

The digital camera was still in Jake's hands. He was doing his best to keep them from shaking. If it dropped to the floor he doubted the cop outside would miss the sound. *If they catch me with this camera and all the stuff on it I am so fucked.* Immediately the most extreme measures he could think of started pouring in. *I could hide the memory card in this kitchen, there's no way they'd look around here for it. This isn't even my house for Christ's sake.* Even with that in mind he still couldn't shake the feeling that they just might find it if and when they conducted a search. Then he'd be fucked all over again. He couldn't bring himself to delete the pictures, if only because of that nagging voice inside his head that was chastising him for deleting the first batch. It sounded a lot like Will. *I could just swallow the damn thing couldn't I?* That'd probably fuck up the memory card beyond repair but there was still a chance it might not. That was better than outright deleting everything.

It took him a second to realize the flashlight that had been coming through the left window had gone. He could still hear movement outside but no beams came through.

After a while he couldn't hear anything. No footsteps, no cars, no dogs barking. There was no sound anywhere. *How the fuck did I get here?*

Jake had been so wrapped up in the retelling of his experience after Triple-E that he hadn't noticed he'd finished another drink. He also hadn't noticed how intently all the brothers were looking at him while he spoke. From Calvin on down to Jeff they all looked enthralled by every word. Eric looked more amused than anything else considering he'd heard it all before but he was the only outlier.

"What happened after that?" Jared asked giddily.

"After like an hour or so this kid makes his way out of the old N-Rho place and gets back down to Arkridge where he passes out on one of our couches. Lucky for him we don't lock our doors any better than the N-Rhos do" Jeff explained. "That was quite the surprise the next morning when I was going to class."

"Yeah my bad man. I didn't mean for your morning to be unpleasant at all" Jake joked. The memory of how pissed he'd been about the whole thing was still fresh enough in his head. Especially memorable was Jeff's reaction that morning as if he was the victim of the entire thing somehow and not Jake or Summers.

One thing he hadn't counted on during his re-telling was just how it would make him feel. In the past he'd simply bitched and bitched about how terrible the whole thing had been and how miserable he was the rest of that week. Now he felt something he had never expected to feel about it: pride. Pride and the exhilaration he'd felt but shuttered away during and after that night.

"So if you got away from the cops how'd you get caught?" Jared asked, switching from giddy to confused.

"Summers" Jake, Jeff and Will all answered in unison.

****

Calvin had sat patiently at the picnic table listening to Raley's story. He listened more intently to the kid than he had to probably *any* professor during his entire time at Gladen Hills. It was far more interesting than Econ101 had ever been. Not only could Raley tell a story well, even if he was slurring slightly because of his drinking speed but the story itself was memorable. *Lucky son of a bitch.*

"He sold you out right?" Calvin asked, almost unkindly.

"To be fair he didn't have much choice. The cops threatened to fuck him even more with charges if he didn't give them my name" Jake answered with a hint of sadness. "All I got was a fine for it."

"Yeah, that and a kick-ass story" Calvin added, happy and yet somehow saddened to admit it. *This one kid has been active a fraction of what I have and he's already done something crazier. How is that even possible?* It didn't seem fair. He tried remembering what Jennifer had told him about how some brothers were built for crazy adventures and others like him were made to keep shit from falling apart. It somehow didn't sit right with him like it once had.

Now that he'd heard the whole thing he started looking at the new fuck in a better light. The fact that he'd barely come around at all toward the end of the semester was fading from his mind and the idea that he'd thrown himself into doing just that one thing on the scav list was taking its place. *Well-done kid.* Calvin mentally slapped himself to contain the mounting jealousy. He knew he should be happy above all else that he was part of a frat that did crazy shit. But even then he couldn't shake the fact that he regretted never being directly involved.

"How'd Summers get caught?" Jerry asked between drinks.

"He ran all the way up the interstate past Northeast, through the woods on the other side of town before the dogs finally caught up with him. He must've thought he could outrun them because they bit his ass right off a fence he was climbing. After that he made his way onto some lady's porch and stayed there 'til the cops came, which blows. Since he was on private property the dogs didn't go after him but the police hit him with a trespassing charge" Will answered the question.

"Raley's just lucky no one was awake in the N-Rho house when he was there" Jeff announced casually.

"Fuckin-A" Jake agreed.

"It's obviously the most badass Raley's ever been" Will announced confidently.

"Stick around. You haven't seen anything yet" Raley replied coolly.

"What'd the judge say when you went to court?" Jared asked, happiness again fueling his words. He chuckled as if he'd already heard the response.

That guy is just as goofy today as he was when we gave him a bid. It always made Calvin proud when a new guy didn't change after a bid was accepted. The whole reason guys got a bid in the first place was because the current actives believed they were a good fit for Alpha Zeta Xi all on their own.

"I had to turn myself in the next day because otherwise the cops were apparently gonna come to my classes and announce my name…so fuck that. I went to the station in the morning. The deputy is writing something on a clipboard so he didn't see me come in. As soon as I say my name, it was like right out of a movie. He instantly stops writing and looks up at me slowly and starts grinning. The guy says tells me I'm a hard man to track down. Even I had to smile at that," Raley admitted happily. "I didn't even know what to say."

"You know if you had any game you could definitely get laid off that story" Will joked from his spot at the table.

Raley ignored Will's attempts at humor and continued talking. "So I go to court and the judge reads off the police report: 'Mr. Raley was caught lighting a bag of human feces on a private residential porch and then photographing said vandalism'. He looks up from the police report at me as the rest of the courtroom is staring me down with either smiles or just utter madness because of how stupid it sounds. And then the bastard goes on a rant saying how 'Gladen Hills is supposed to be for the best and the brightest and then I go and do something like this'. It was like getting a speech from a disappointed parent, fuckin' annoying."

They all either laughed.

Calvin could picture being in that courtroom. He was hard pressed to say what he would've done at any point had he been in Raley's position. *I probably would've been caught by the cops and begged for mercy in the courtroom.* As much as he admired the new fuck for what he did, he didn't know that he'd be able to do the same thing even now that he knew everything had worked out.

"Two hundred-fifty dollar fine" Raley added. "That's all it took."

The rest of his brothers sat there in various forms of surprise and awe at Raley's definitive version of what happened at Triple-E.

I'd say you had a better time than me and Buttons did at the Dean's office. You do all that shit, hide from the cops, turn yourself in and then I have to deal with the fallout. Unbelievable. It didn't seem fair. Raley could get away relatively unscathed from something so wild and somehow Calvin was one who had to deal with the aftermath. If he'd never gone to the Dean's office he would've been content but that was the second and far more uncomfortable time he'd been forced to sit with that condescending fucker.

One thing he knew in his heart even now. He'd gladly pay a two hundred-fifty dollar fine to be able to say he did something so crazy.

<u>Chapter 45</u>

The Cradle was appropriately deserted when Eric and the rest of his brothers walked through the front doors. Much like the rest of Gladen Hills, there was only a sparse few people sitting at the bar and surrounding tables. The total didn't number above fifteen. Something immediately caught his eye as they all showed their ID's to one of the two bartenders on the way in. Eric's cousin Riley and her friend Tory were two of ones inside. It looked like they were in the middle of draining a shot. *Not a bad idea.*

Normally on any given Saturday night during the school year this bar would be packed. The Cradle was a middle of the road bar in terms of the overall menu. It wasn't a hole in the wall like Thirst Point farther down University Grove, or even the National down near Arkridge. The Cradle was even probably more upscale than the Midway but that wasn't saying much. The only bar ahead in terms of sheer high class feeling was the Center. Eric was sure the latter was named as to remind people of just how upscale it really was as well as its position within the town. Ironically, that meant more often than not he and others tended to steer clear of it. Only the AK's and Phi Thetas populated the Center when there weren't rampant drink specials. 'Overpriced' wasn't a familiar term to most Gladen Hills students. That was especially true when it came to the alcohol supply. Sometimes a shot would be two or three dollars cheaper at the National than the Center.

Usually there was a bouncer at both the front and back doors but since it was summer only the bartenders checked the scant few ID's that even troubled to visit. Once they were all checked they took up residence at one of the many empty tables near the door. Even though Jake and Jared weren't twenty-one yet that didn't slow them down from getting OK'd all the same. That could've been the result of the bartenders simply not caring with so few customers around or they just didn't want to turn down some of the group and likely turn away the rest by extension.

Eric was already feeling pretty good considering how much of the Ice 101 he and Gretman had demolished before walking there. There were very few times when Eric generally wanted to have pledges around but every time he made that walk up the gigantic hills of the campus to get to University Grove he wished there were. Pledges always had to drive brothers around and basically act as their own personal shuttle service. That was by far his favorite part of the entire pledge process.

"You guys trying to do shots?" Eric asked as soon as everyone was situated.

"Whoa, is Biz trying to buy us a round?" Jeff asked slyly.

Eric hadn't wanted to foot the bill with the batch of alcoholics in front of him but he decided on the spot that he might as well. "Sure, why the hell not?!"

He got up from the table and was utterly unsurprised that his younger cousin Jake followed. Ordering a shot that everyone would like was a bit of challenge considering the diverse personalities in play. Finally he settled on just going with straight Jack. It wasn't the favorite of anyone but it would likewise not garner any complaints either. "You might as well keep the tab open too" Eric said as the bartender took his debit card. *Why not? I've been taking Jerry and Will's money all summer. I can afford it.*

"I love how generous Biz gets when he's drunk," Jake slurred slightly as he announced their presence to Riley. She must've seen them come in, or watched them come over to the bar because her reaction showed no surprise.

"It's one of those things I really wish you'd take after him on."

"Good Rye, I've never heard anything like that before."

Eric watched his two cousins hug amicably as the shots were filled. Truthfully he was just looking past Riley and Jake hoping that Tory would turn toward him and at least give eye contact. Unfortunately she didn't look away from her phone.

"Your mom was pissed you weren't home for last week's dinner" Jake announced, almost abrasively.

Riley rolled her eyes. It was her go-to response in most cases that involved her being told her mother was 'disappointed' in some fashion. *It's a wonder she ever goes back home.* "I'm sure she'll get over it."

"That's basically what I told her" Jake assured her.

It took Eric a second to realize that he forgot to ask for the shots on a tray so he could move them back to the table. He wasn't going to be an ass and ask for one now so instead he ordered two more for his cousin and Tory and called the guys over. Once everyone was assembled he made the first move to get everyone to raise their respective shot. No toast was needed. Eric moved to drain first and the other eight all followed suit rapidly. The looks on everyone's faces afterward ranged from expected to priceless in terms of how Jake and Riley were reacting. He'd forgotten until now that Riley hated drinking most straight liquors, with Jack Daniels at the top of that list. Jake on the other hand was just not seasoned enough so he often looked like he was dying after each straight drink.

"Alllllright" Eric began. "Who's trying to buy the next round?"

Not unexpectedly, nobody in the nearby area moved to answer his call. "Gee what a shock guys" he let his distaste be known. "Can I have an ice runoff please?"

"You gonna split that with somebody or take it all down on your own?" Will was quick to ask when he heard the order.

"Oh I'll split it...with Gretman."

The look in his friend's eyes conveyed a much unhappier look than Eric would've expected but what could he do? It was Gretman's last night in Gladen Hills. He and Will had another year to chill together. Once he conveyed that to Bill-Butt the feelings of being excluded disappeared.

"Jerry, why don't you get a runoff for you and Buttons?"

"Runoff race?"

"You know it."

Jerry smiled and agreed. "You're fucking welcome Buttons" he said to their brother as he handed his debit card to the nearest bartender. As Eric stood there waiting for Jerry's pitcher to be filled Jared, Calvin and Jeff all returned to the table to sit back down. That left Jake and Will up at the bar.

"So whatchu been up to Riley?" Will tried being smooth.

"You know it's really creepy when you do that stuff Will" Riley said remorse.

"What?" he asked, faking offense. "I'm just trying to chat with you."

"No. No you're not...and it's obvious" Jake interjected.

"Just chill Raley."

"You're just lucky I'm trying to play that hot Big Buck Hunter over there. As much as I'd love to stay and watch you work."

"You're gonna leave me alone with him?" Riley asked, perplexed.

"I'm just holding up my end of the pact," Jake answered with a smirk.

Riley looked mortified when she realized what their younger cousin was implying, then she switched to horrified. "No really, it's the least I can do." Jake took off like a rabbit toward the nearest video game machine. Eric continued smiling as he turned to walk away with Jerry once the second pitcher was filled.

"What'd Raley mean by that?" Eric heard Will ask as they walked away.

"Not a damn thing" Riley responded quickly.

The fact that Tory hadn't even turned to look at him the entire time they'd been at the bar was troubling. Not even the shots he bought for her and Riley seemed to make a dent. *So much for that brilliant idea.*

The other interesting thing was that Jerry and Riley pretended like they didn't know each other at all. As far as he could tell they hadn't even looked in the other's direction. Maybe he'd have to ask his pledge brother about that later. Eric was fairly confident that once they drank more the two would inevitably talk again. It might be best to wait it out and not ask too many questions. Hopefully the same could be said of him and Tory.

****

Runoff races at the Cradle were a common pastime for any AZXi uptown before heading to the MW. Most of them didn't go to the Cradle that often since it was out of the way but Calvin had definitely taken part in his share of runoff races all the same. If someone wasn't already drunk before racing, they'd be in a good spot after. For the most part he was feeling nicely buzzed, even after drinking at the house. Calvin had let Eric take down most of the Ice 101 if only because he'd paid for it and he didn't want to black out his last night in Gladen Hills. Waking up tomorrow was already going to be an assault on his system without adding a soul-sucking hangover.

As the four of them sat at the table draining the two pitchers between four straws the reality of the situation hit home. *This might be the last runoff race I ever do.*

The cold liquid went from the pitcher to the straw to his mouth down his throat. Calvin saw that he and Eric were winning. Even though the need to win was taking over, he found himself savoring every sip. He'd never counted a pitcher of ice runoff among his favorite drinks but that didn't mean he wouldn't miss it. It was just another piece of the puzzle that made the town something special. Calvin had seen bartenders at the Cradle mix up plenty runoff pitchers in his time but he still couldn't say for sure what was in it, only that it did its job.

Finally he and Eric claimed victory. Nothing had ever seemed as bittersweet even as Calvin was fighting a massive brain freeze. He'd heard many times from Eric and Jerry about how drinking through a straw somehow got a person drunker faster. If his current state of mind was anything to go by then they just *might* be onto something.

"Damn that was cold" Eric stated the obvious.

"Runoff races have gotta look mad gay to anyone watching" Jerry announced.

"Yeah but fuck it" Jeff said plainly.

Calvin patted Eric on the back before thanking him for the pitcher. Between the round of shots he'd bought to the pitcher and the Ice 101 bottle from earlier, Eric's tab was already well over fifty bucks. *How does he do it…and then not give a fuck?*

"I just wish we had some *real* competition around here" Calvin said casually as he allowed his eyes to wander around the room. Jared and Raley were over by the Buck Hunter game in the corner and Will was attempting to talk to one of the two girls sitting at the bar. *We already beat the two best in the room.*

"You wanna go again?" Jerry challenged.

"I thought it looked mad gay though?"

"I'm willing to risk it to redeem myself."

"It'd take a fuck ton more than a runoff race to do that much pal" Jeff interrupted.

"I need a second to breathe anyways guys," Eric added with a smirk.

"Don't be such a pussy" Jeff put in quickly.

Eric shrugged. He didn't seem to mind all that much that he was being called out. Unlike some or even most of their brothers, Biz couldn't be tricked into drinking obscene amounts solely for the purpose of making himself look manlier. Certainly he'd drink a lot, but on his own terms. Before Calvin could step in to the conversation he felt vibrations from his phone. He reached for it in his pocket after the surprise wore off. The caller ID wasn't surprising at all. *Jennifer.*

"My bad guys, I gotta talk to Jen," he said briskly before standing up.

"Oh weak son" Jerry said immediately.

Jeff was noticeably quiet although Calvin thought he saw the guy roll his eyes at the mere mention of Jen's name.

"You're not leaving are you?" Eric asked hesitantly.

"Relax, I'll be right back. I'm just gonna head outside for a second" Calvin promised. If the look on Eric's face was any indication, he didn't believe that any more than Calvin did.

****

"Hey there" a friendly voice forced Tory back to reality. She turned to face who was talking and saw Eric Saren. Smiling absently, she greeted him in return. Tory had been keeping a subtle eye on him and his brothers since they'd walked in.

"What's up?"

Most of the time it amused Tory to have 'small-talk' with her former flings but in Eric's case it rattled her. She wasn't a fan of that feeling.

"Not much" she responded quaintly.

Eric took a seat on the bar stool opposite where Riley was. It looked like her sister was on the verge of beating off the other guy she was talking to with a stick but it hadn't come to that…yet.

"So you never responded to any of my texts" Eric cut right through the tension. It caught Tory off guard. She was used to guys being forward with her in terms of wanting her to come to their rooms or cars but never like this.

"Yeah…I'm sorry Eric…I've been real busy." *My God girl is that the best you can come up with? What a terrible fucking excuse.*

"It's cool" he replied. "You want a drink?"

Tory turned away to check the contents of the mixed drink she still had in front of her. She'd been nursing it for the better part of twenty minutes. Riley hadn't been watching all that closely or she probably would've given her shit. Out of the corner of her eye she thought she saw her sister tilt her head to hear what she and Eric were saying. Tory smiled while looking straight ahead toward the rows upon rows of liquor behind the bar. "Sure."

"You OK with shots?"

"Ummmmm…are you OK with more shots?" Tory asked, only half-kidding. Considering that Eric was generally shy about what he wanted in bed even with the two of them naked and ready to go it stood to reason that the only way he'd been able to come talk to Tory in so abrupt a fashion was that he was already drunk. *They're all the same, only honest when they're hammered.*

"Oh I'm good" he assured her.

"Alright" she smiled. "I wouldn't say no to another drink."

Eric called over a bartender and ordered some SoCo-limes. While they waited for the shots Tory's mind started whirling. *He does look kinda hot tonight...but that's probably what he wants me to think...*

Greg and Eric were tied with how good they made her feel in bed. The difference was that Eric had potential to get better if she could coach him on just what she liked. On the other hand Greg was so locked in their rhythm that it was completely set. Before she could think any more Eric handed her one of the shots.

"What's the toast?" he asked.

"A great summer?"

"I could live with that."

The shot went down smooth enough. Eric had finished at the same time and now that they'd both set their respective cups down they locked eyes. For a second Tory felt herself getting warmer just looking into those green eyes...then Greg walked in.

****

"Hey" some guy said to Tory while Eric sat there impotently.

"Hey there" she smiled back. It was more emotion than she'd shown him in their entire exchange but he'd still felt he was making inroads...until that exact moment.

"I thought I said no shots without me," the guy continued. It might've been the alcohol but Eric couldn't tell for the life of him if the guy was kidding.

"I couldn't help it" Tory defended herself. "Eric was buying."

Well at least she remembers my name and that I'm still sitting here.

The guy had just walked into the Cradle with four others. The one talking to Tory had a Lambda hat on. Eric hadn't thought that Jeff was lying earlier about Tory leaving the Lambda house but it was still a little depressing seeing the guy standing there.

Realizing that Tory had just said something about him to the guy Eric just smiled absently. The Lambda looked more amused than anything else as he did a once over on Eric. He must've thought he wasn't a threat because he nodded in his direction before carrying on his conversation with Tory. "Come on, Ted's getting some drinks for our table" he motioned to one of the guys he'd walked in with who was now standing at the bar a few stools down.

"Alright" she agreed, to Eric's chagrin. It wasn't unexpected but it still cut like a knife. Tory got up from her stool and moved to follow the guy back to a table on the opposite side of the bar from where Jeff and Jerry were still sitting and talking. Calvin still wasn't back inside. The longer he stayed outside the less likely it was that he'd come back at all. *First Gretman, now Tory.*

He was about to turn his attention back to the bar to order another round for himself alone but he felt a nudge on his shoulder.

"Thanks for the drink" Tory said, kindly enough. She almost looked guilty, but only in her eyes. He didn't even get a chance to reply before she walked away. Not that he had anything in the pipeline. The whole encounter with that Lambda had thrown him into a loop of silence.

"Biz I need your help" his cousin stated frantically. Eric was about to get annoyed but then he realized he'd rather be with his cousin than alone at the bar.

"What's up?" Eric asked, already having an idea of what the latest crisis was.

"Jared is downright awful at that game. I need a seasoned veteran."

He shook his head. "Yeah I'm down."

As they went back to the game machine in the corner Eric once again caught bits and pieces of the conversation that Will was still trying to have with Riley. All he really heard was her say "it's never going to happen Will." That forced him to smile, even as he knew he'd lost his gamble with Tory.

****

The night air felt refreshing on his skin the further he walked inward through the campus. Even in the summer with no students to speak of, the outer lights still shined brightly. It only served to add to the melancholy feeling Calvin was already processing, and had been since he'd walked the stage nearly two months ago.

"No you aren't keeping me from anything Jen" he assured her again. It wasn't even really a lie. For as much as Calvin wanted to be sitting in the Cradle with the few brothers he still had he couldn't shake his depressing thoughts.

"You're sure?" she asked again from the other end of the phone. "I didn't want to interrupt your time with the guys. I just wanted to say goodnight."

"I know…and I appreciate that. I wasn't gonna stay out much longer, not really feeling it tonight." It felt like more of a half-truth. The more he drank, the worse he felt, not physically but emotionally. *Is this what it'll be like whenever I come back to visit? Just me trying to relive what happened before?* The thought curdled his blood.

"What's wrong Cal?"

Between the alcohol and his heightened emotions he was powerless to stay quiet. "I...don't want to leave," he blurted out. "I wish I was Jeff. And the fact that he's pissed about staying here only pisses me off. I don't want to feel this...but he gets to stay *here* while we leave." He hadn't even noticed until he was done that he was standing directly in the middle of the quad between four separate academic buildings. He'd been walking and talking for so long he was off University Grove and into the campus.

He was standing on a patch of grass in one of the four quads. The grass was so well kept that most students would just sit on the ground to read a textbook or type on their laptops and not bother using the few picnic tables sprinkled throughout.

How many times had he walked through here? Down these same paths, looking at kids, laughing or working? A couple hundred feet behind him was the college green, which stood directly in the middle of the biggest quad. How many times had he thrown around a Frisbee with Petey or Kevin over the years now past? *And it's all over.*

The memories that once comforted were doing nothing except haunting him. He felt powerless. Among all his swirling sadness he almost didn't hear what Jen was trying to say to him. "Yeah I'm still here" he answered her repeated questioning. He might've physically been on the line but he couldn't speak for mentally.

"It wasn't easy for me to leave either Cal" Jennifer explained. She sniffled slightly and he immediately felt ashamed. He'd been so caught up in how terrible he'd been feeling these past few months that they'd barely talked about how she was coping with being outside the bubble of Gladen Hills.

"You still have me," Calvin said softly.

"And you still have me."

He took a deep breath. "You know the one thing I keep thinking about? It's that when I drive out of here tomorrow...the one thing I still have to look forward to is being with you." It felt good to say it out loud.

"I love you Calvin. We'll get through this."

They just sat on the phone with neither speaking for a few seconds. It was soothing just to know she was there on the other end even if they weren't saying talking.

"Alright Cal, I just wanted to say goodnight but I'm glad I could give you someone to talk to. Let me know if you need anything."

"Thanks Jen. It means a lot...and I love you too." He smiled as he said it. *The guys would think I'm so whipped.*

"Good night baby" she said as the line disconnected.

Calvin stood still, just looking back down at the phone in his hand. The call he'd just ended with Jen was blinking on the screen signifying she'd hung up. It felt liberating but also hollow.

He suddenly felt the urge to walk to the dorms on Northwest even if they were completely out of the way. The last time he could remember being near a dorm was when he and Jeff had to deliver bids to the Alpha Epsilons in the middle of winter. It stood to reason now that he wasn't active anymore that he'd probably never have cause to go back into one of them again. *Going back will just depress me more.*

Once he made up his mind he went toward College Curve, winding his way through the rest of campus until hitting Castle Lane where a sickening sight greeted him. The flashing lights of a couple stopped police cruisers immediately caught his eye. *Raley must've done something crazy... again.* Even though he was past the legal age the cops would likely still want to question and hassle him so Calvin decided to avoid them altogether.

Cutting across the street, he headed down the long paved road that led to the off-campus apartments. Jennifer had lived there during her junior year before she'd essentially been forced to live in the Rho Beta house. From back here he could simply cut through the fields that lead into the TAS. After that it would be relatively easy to get onto the end of Arkridge opposite Castle Lane. It was a lot just to avoid the cops but Calvin was more than willing to go out of his way to cut that bullshit from his night.

Before going any further toward the TAS he stopped to consider going back to the bar and his brothers but couldn't make the move. He didn't feel any less depressed now that he'd talked to Jen. On top of not wanting to ruin the nights of the younger guys, he figured it'd be good to stay alone tonight.

Calvin found himself wishing that one of them; *any* of the guys in town tonight were also leaving with him. Maybe then he'd be able to sit and drink with them. As it stood, he couldn't help but feel like the odd man out even though he'd been drinking with a few of them for years. Unfortunately that didn't change the fact that tonight none of them could understand how he was feeling.

Entering the TAS was always weird. He hadn't really cut through that part of Gladen Hills since his junior year when Jennifer had lived on the other side of the road separating the two areas. He usually took those trips in the morning or early afternoon and he'd never gone through at night.

A space of light caught Calvin's eye as he walked through the darkness of the apartment complexes. Only a few streetlights lit up the vast area. The light in question was coming from a sizable shed off to the left. He wasn't even sure why but he wanted to get closer. Upon doing so, he noticed two larger guys moving around ladders and cinder blocks to create space within the shed. That wasn't what Calvin was focusing on though. Something along the back wall drew his gaze but he couldn't make it out yet, he was still standing too far away. The two guys didn't even notice he was around. Of course that was probably because the few lights in the TAS weren't anywhere near where he was standing.

Now they were unloading supplies off a nearby pickup truck, although they were moving slowly. Each one would carry an armful from the vehicle to the shed and set it down on the floor in the newly created space. On their third trip from the shed Calvin nearly sprinted from the sidewalk to the shed. Once he was inside he dove behind a large industrial riding mower. It gave him sufficient cover so the two guys wouldn't be able to see him, or so he hoped.

"Go ahead and close it down," one of them ordered gruffly. "We'll finish the rest in the morning." The other man grunted and the overheard lights that had drawn Calvin in shut off. Then the front garage door rolled down to seal him in.

His heart was racing at first before he realized that this wasn't as bad as he'd originally thought. The shed was big and it had windows. After a minute of waiting to make sure the two guys had left, Calvin moved to the nearest one and unlocked it. There was no screen on the outer sill so it led straight out into the night. Calvin was about to climb out when he remembered he'd ended up in here for a reason. Ashamed, he turned around and tried to feel his way around in the darkness. Finally he realized he had a light in the form of his cell phone so he flipped it open to gain his bearings. The farther back he went the closer together the supplies were packed in. It made getting by everything a pain in the ass but he finally reached the back wall. Carefully, he let his phone light guide his eyes along the wooden frame until he found what originally caught his eye.

He'd been right all along but seeing it there, mounted on the wall still threw his heart into a free-fall. *No...fucking...way.*

****

As had happened oh so many times before, Eric Saren woke up alone. The one good thing about that was he didn't have to endure any awkward small talk in the morning when his brain was still trying to function within the alcohol withdrawal. He'd always found it disconcerting having a girl in the same bed after the drinking had subsided. It just felt incredibly weird so the concept of morning sex was usually discarded quickly in favor of getting through the awkward situation as quickly as possible. Tory had been the lone exception.

After Calvin had left the Cradle Eric had stopped drinking as quickly as he had been up to that point. Between Gretman's exit and Tory's dismissal, Eric just hadn't had the stomach to go full-force in quite the same way that Jerry, Jeff and Will were.

The one good thing about the morning was that Eric was able to sleep in his own comfortable bed. Since he was going into senior year he hadn't had to move any of his things out of the house. It took a little getting used to the idea of leaving everything in a near-deserted Gladen Hills from May to August but Jerry was doing the same. Plus Calvin and Jeff were around for most of the summer.

Truthfully, Eric really hadn't wanted to live in the house again during his senior year. Considering how much his room had been used as a drug trafficking station on top of the little work he could get done in the confines of his room, he wanted out. The AZXi house was essentially a whirlpool of gateway behavior leading to poor grades and worse health. Even so, that sort of lifestyle was definitely fun to lead, if only on the weekends. What Eric wouldn't give to live like so many of his brothers during the weeknights if his class schedule could handle the strain.

Jerry was no doubt sleeping in his room right next to Eric's. That left Will, Jake and Jared all sleeping on the couches downstairs. Jeff would likewise be sleeping in his room on the other side of the house. Even with six of the seven all on one side Eric didn't hear any noise. Even though his head was pounding he decided to check out what was going on below.

He made his way down the steep stairwell from the second floor that housed his and Jerry's rooms and into the kitchen area. Calvin's door down the hall was closed and it looked like all three of his other brothers were sacked out on the couches in the adjacent common room. No movement or sounds outside of some breathing here or there. *Well at least they're all still alive.*

Eric used the bathroom right next to Calvin's room and it wasn't until after he flushed the toilet that he thought better of it. It tended to make a lot of noise and that tended to wake people up if they were in fact still sleeping.

Calvin was standing in his doorway when Eric exited the bathroom. The guy had a smile on his face that rivaled any he'd seen before. *I didn't think Jen was here last night but who the hell knows? Maybe that's what she was calling for?*

"Morning buddy!" Calvin said, not quietly.

Eric groaned slightly at how chipper his brother was acting. It was sort of annoying but it was definitely better than how depressed Gretman seemed last night.

"Morning" he choked out as he stood up a little straighter.

"You look like you're feeling absolutely amazing right now" Calvin teased him.

"Well that's weird because I feel absolutely atrocious."

Calvin chuckled. Even Eric didn't think it was that funny. Something clearly had to be up for him to be feeling so happy.

"What happened to you last night?" Eric couldn't contain his curiosity.

"Glad you asked" Calvin replied as if it'd been killing him before that point not being asked that very same question. "Where are the rest of the guys?"

****

It took a while to gather up all six of the other guys from their various sleeping states. Then a little longer to get them prepared to listen but finally they were ready.

"Where'd you bounce to last night cuz?" Jared asked. It was more upbeat than his eyes and stance would've suggested.

"I wasn't feeling that great. I talked to Jen and then just came back here." *They don't need to know the full details behind that shit.*

"That is so weak son" Jerry said, un-tempered by his hangover.

"You'd think it would be right?" Calvin asked cryptically.

"You sayin' it wasn't?" Jeff perked up.

"Definitely not."

"What happened?" Raley asked.

The excitement was building to the point where Calvin could barely contain it. It must've been showing on his face because all the brothers looked somewhat curious. He cleared his throat to tell them the story about the rest of his night. It felt extremely good to be sitting where he was, even now. He grinned. *This must be how Guapo and Dylan feel before a good and welfare story at our meetings.*

"So after I left the bar I was walking through campus 'til I got to Castle Lane. Of course some fucking cops had some roadblock in front of Arkridge and I didn't want anything to do with that shit."

Jeff shook his head. "Fucking bastards."

Calvin pressed on. "I went through the TAS. The back part that runs through across the other end of Arkridge."

"Yikes. That's rock bottom territory son," Jerry said confidently as he stretched out on the couch next to Raley.

Calvin smirked. "That's when shit got interesting though."

Before he could go on Jared interrupted. "You get a bite with one of the townie's bro?!" he asked giddily.

Calvin shook his head almost violently at the thought. "Come on Jared, that's fuckin' ridiculous," he said quickly. "So I'm walking through there and I see one of the maintenance sheds is open with the lights on. Those fuckers were bright too. There were some guys moving around between a truck and the shed but they didn't see me. It was after midnight so I didn't know what the fuck they were even doing" Calvin confessed.

"It's always so damn sketchy in the TAS" Eric admitted quietly.

"I banged out back there once" Will admitted happily.

Jeff and Raley both rolled their eyes.

"So I'm walking by on the far sidewalk and I'm a little drunk and I thought I saw something on the shed's back wall. I was still mad far away but I could've sworn it looked like something crazy. After a little while the two workers moved away from the shed to go on doing whatever the fuck it was they were doing so I went in closer. Somehow I got inside behind one of the mowers. Those things are huge so I chilled behind one of them." He couldn't help but let pride at the accomplishment seep into his voice. "Then the bastards closed down the shed. The lights were off and I couldn't see a fuckin' thing. I was so sketched out I nearly jumped out the nearest window. But I didn't. I got my cell and made my way to the back wall and what the hell do I find?" Calvin paused for a second to gauge the looks of his audience.

Calvin sat there confidently, letting the silence build. "It was one of our fuckin' paddles. The Rho paddle" he announced before anyone could ask.

That brought on looks of amazement from Eric and Jerry and even Jared to an extent. Jeff looked pissed. Raley and Will didn't know what the fuck he was talking about. That made sense considering they probably never knew the Rho paddle was missing. It'd been gone for the better part of two years and no one had any idea where the hell it went. The reigning theory was that one of the sororities had taken it years ago during a party. It never made the trip to their current house.

"Fuckers…" Jeff said angrily.

Eric immediately tried rationalizing the situation. "They probably just found it back there and were holding on to it for us."

"Wow. I really hope you don't fuckin' believe that" Jeff said, almost offended that he'd said anything like it.

"I thought that too Biz" Calvin admitted. "But the paddle was nailed to the back wall. They had it up like a damn trophy." That seemed to quiet Eric while angering Jeff even more.

"Damn, the townies around here are so ballsy" Jerry said thoughtfully.

"So what'd you do?" Raley asked.

"He better have ripped the damn thing off the wall or we're going there now to take it back," Jeff answered for Calvin. The anger in his voice was palpable. "They must've had tools back in that shed to get it down."

Calvin had been planning out how to tell his story during the rest of the walk back last night. Most of those thoughts had revolved around how to reveal what was going to come next. He reached over behind the couch he was sitting on next to Jeff and Eric. When he pulled out the Rho paddle the entire room went quiet. Then it erupted with cheers, mostly from Jared. Jeff looked like he'd just been told a bus hit Dean Standor. The entire scene was a thing of beauty to Calvin Gretman.

The paddle got passed around the room between the seven of them. Raley and Will didn't know what to make of it. They knew it was a big deal but they couldn't wrap their heads around it considering they were still new fucks. Jerry, Eric and Jared all looked content knowing that only one other paddle was missing from their collection as of now. Jeff looked the most satisfied by far. Calvin wished he could take a picture of that moment. It was a memory worth having. By missing out on the last night he'd have living in Gladen Hills with a few of his brothers he was able to do something he'd been wanting to do all year. Now he had a crazy memory worth bragging about.

"So did I earn the right to have you guys help me pack up my shit?" Calvin asked tentatively. The looks of approval he received were almost enough to take the sting out of just what he was asking them to help with. Almost.

****

Like so many mornings before, she'd gotten the call from her sister Tory about wanting a ride back from Arkridge.

A light rain started falling across the town right before her phone had gone off. The light tapping on her window had woken Riley up from an otherwise sound sleep. The lack of any sound that had actually begun as an eerie absence of life from the EIPi house had actually become a comfort as the summer went on.

Riley couldn't blame her best friend for not wanting to walk through campus in such weather. Light rain or not she'd likely be soaked by the time she reached EIPi from Arkridge Avenue.

The drive down had been pleasant enough. She'd been running on low fuel for a while now ever since she'd gotten back from her most recent trip home a few weeks ago but the near empty light had only come on yesterday. Even so, Riley decided to risk it. It was only a trip to Arkridge, not exactly a drive home to Harrisville.

Once she got into the Lambda driveway she called Tory and within a minute her friend came stumbling outside. Riley could've sworn she saw some movement through the hedges blocking the AZXi house but she wasn't all that motivated to check, especially with Tory now in the car. It had been awkward enough at the Cradle last night between her and Eric and that was *with* alcohol in the mix.

"I'm guessing you had a great night."

"I usually do" Tory grinned after buckling up. "Thanks for picking me up."

"It's more selfish of me than you think. I'm just hoping that I'll be given the same favor if I ever need it." Riley couldn't fathom the circumstances that would make her wake up in the Lambda house but one never knew what would happen over the course of a night in Gladen Hills so it was best to be prepared.

"Count on it" Tory agreed.

Once she backed out of the gravel driveway and turned onto Castle Lane there was an uncomfortable quiet settling in between them so Riley decided to make it more uncomfortable. "So why'd you cut Eric off?"

"I thought you'd be happy" Tory replied quickly and defensively.

"How could I be happy that you ditched my cousin in favor of a huge tool like Greg? That doesn't sound like me at all."

"I'm not fucking a bunch of guys. I'm only on one right now."

"Right and I can't figure that out either" Riley confessed. Her best friend's switch to monogamy had definitely been abrupt and surprising to say the least.

Tory shifted uncomfortably in the passenger's seat. "What's there to figure out? I like sex and now I'm only fucking one guy. It's done. I mean who knew fucking a bunch of them could screw you in the long run."

"You're serious?" she asked, almost laughing at how ridiculous it sounded.

"You saying I'm wrong Riles?"

"No, of course not...I'm saying you couldn't be any more wrong if you tried. Half our sorority does what you do. It's the flaunting of it that could probably use a rest T. The ones that sleep around at least *pretend* they're somewhat ashamed of doing the things they do. You don't even do that much."

"It's who I fucking am."

"I know that, and it doesn't bother me at all. You're my best friend...but I'd kinda like to know what's been going on with you all summer. Just talk to me T."

Tory sat in silence for a few seconds just watching the buildings on College Curve pass them by. They'd be back to EIPi soon and if she kept quiet Tory could just lock herself in her room and not have to say anymore on the subject.

"So I like having fun and not giving a fuck...I can't even get house president!"

So that's what this is all about. She thinks she didn't get elected because of how she is? Fuck me. She wanted to reach over and hug her friend but she was still driving.

"T that's not even close to being true. You know how the Beta Zetas are. With them and the Beta Thetas against you the odds were fucked. This had nothing to do with you really. Nobody would've been able to get through that. I'm...I'm sorry T. I'm sorry this happened."

****

"It's fine" Tory replied. "It's not like it matters now. We're seniors. Those were our last elections." Even as the words came out she couldn't bring herself to fully believe them. *If that's true then why do I still care so fucking much?* "You know this is your fucking fault right?"

Riley looked as stunned by the words as Tory felt saying them but she couldn't stop herself now.

"You just *had* to take a Little when you were pledge mom. You have any idea how much that sucked? Your Little couldn't hate you because you're her Big." Venom oozed from words as she threw that title back at Riley. *She just had to be a big sister when she wanted.* "You wanted a Little before your senior year so that you could have more time with her. Well guess what? That fucked me because instead of her hating you she started hating me. And for what? What exactly did I do that semester to that fucking girl that I hadn't done to all her pledge sisters too? That I didn't do to the Beta Etas in the fall? What exactly was different except you being selfish!?"

Riley looked beside herself as the accusations flew. Even then, Tory didn't stop.

"It's always gotta be your way though doesn't it Riley? You've always gotta do whatever you want. Well it must be great being you because nothing ever comes back to bite you in the ass. This time it hit me. I can only hope that one day you get shit for always getting things your way." Tory was close to tears by the time she was done. Riley looked to be on that same path. They both looked at each other but didn't speak.

"You know I love you right?" Riley finally choked out. "And you're right. Maybe I shouldn't have taken Brynn while I was her pledge mom. I figured I could handle it. I figured she could handle it…but I didn't know her that well. All I knew was that I wanted her to be my Little and that was all that mattered. I didn't think about you or anything else and I'm sorry. I'm so sorry Tory…"

Tory immediately felt awful about how she'd attacked her best friend. Who was to say that Brynn wouldn't have reacted the exact same way even if Riley hadn't been her big sister? They might never know for sure.

"No I'm sorry" she stuttered. "I just…" she struggled to find the right words. Suddenly she felt desperate to lighten the mood. Any more of their conversation and she might start crying. *Never again.* "You know…just once I wish you'd let me enjoy a hangover in peace."

Riley was unaffected. "No matter what happens T, you can't let anything like elections or how other people look at you affect how you live your life. Not even if it's me. Before you know it we are going to be out there…living apart. I don't want any bad memories from this place."

"What do you mean?"

"This is the best thing that's ever happened to any of us. I don't want to screw it up." Shame was creeping into her friend's voice in a way that she'd never really heard before. *I caused her to feel like this…me and my emotions…fuck me.*

"Do you really believe that?"

"I didn't even know you 'til freshman year and I can safely say I don't know how I survived without you before that" Riley replied confidently.

It caused Tory to smile. She hated feeling and acting in such a way. Being serious was something that made her feel terrible about everyone and everything. There was a reason she never liked taking things too much to heart. Even with that in mind she felt compelled to be honest a little longer. "I didn't shut Eric down because of Greg…"

"I know."

"I don't want anything serious right now and he's the kind of guy to date. *I could see myself with him…and I won't do it.* "I don't want to date anyone else for a long time." Immediately she regretted letting that bit of information slip but Riley didn't pursue it even if she looked curious for a moment.

"Just tell him that then. Otherwise you'll be stuck getting his drunken puppy-dog eyes every time you see him at the bars" Riley grinned.

At least I won't have to deal with that at all until next semester…

****

The euphoric feeling Calvin had felt during his story hadn't yet faded completely from his mind. He was thankful for that much at least. He knew he'd need all the good feelings he could get as they worked to pack up his room and systematically load it into the SUV that Jennifer had borrowed from his parents on her last visit down. She'd taken his car back with her when she'd left so that his dad would have something to drive while the SUV stayed to aid in the move.

Now that the truck was almost completely full, it looked like the task was about done. The trunk and backseat were crammed, almost to the point where the rearview mirror would be worthless.

He knew before they even started that he'd have to leave a few things here like his bed's box spring and the mattress. His dresser would be staying as well along with a box of assorted clothes and books. Calvin figured if he'd have to make at least one trip back here for the mattress and box spring that he might as well not completely overdo it now. That meant he'd have to convince his dad to let him have the SUV for a day at some point before the summer ended.

Once the last of his things had been moved to the car he examined the view from the mirrors in the driver seat just to make sure he could still use them all. Everything looked good.

Calvin could've definitely done it all on his own but it wasn't something he was relishing. Part of him wanted to prove Jeff wrong in that he could ask for help when needed. Still, even he couldn't deny that it felt…*weird.*

"Well thanks a lot guys," he said as the light rain continued falling around them.

"Like I'd have let you do it all on your own" Jeff cut in.
"It's no problem Gretman" Eric responded, ignoring Jeff.
"Speak for yourself Biz. I still feel fucked up" Will added.
"What the fuck else is new?" Jerry asked playfully.

Jared laughed at their bantering. "It's straight cuz. You've gotta come back next semester. It's not gonna be the same without you."

Calvin felt a twinge of regret knowing he wouldn't be around to go through whatever else would happen in the semesters to come. The headaches and the joys of AZXi's future were equally removed from his path now. There was never a more sobering thought in his head.

"How are you guys gonna survive here without me?"

"It'll be tough but we'll call if we need anything" Jeff replied sarcastically.

"I'm with Jared. You better get your ass back here as much as possible. The couches are damn comfortable in that house" Raley added as if he were the first person to ever sleep on one of them.

Before things could get too emotional Eric motioned for them all to get going. No doubt his younger brothers would want to get home and back to sleep as quickly as possible. It was actually a miracle they'd hung around for as long as they had today. Generally when anyone was visiting Gladen Hills and not planning to stay for more than a night they left as quickly as possible in the morning. *Is that how I'm gonna be?*

Each of the five visiting brothers shook his hand firmly in the AZXi way before retreating into Eric's car to drive home. It was all Calvin could do to stop himself from crying. He couldn't even watch them leave the driveway so he kept his eyes locked on the gravel-strewn ground that he'd walked over thousands of times.

"You handled that well," Jeff said once the car was gone. The rain was still falling all around them and it seemed to pick up in intensity the longer they stood there yet Calvin couldn't bring himself to move indoors.

"Well...I haven't left yet Buttons" he smiled half-heartedly.

Calvin was dreading the drive out of town. Not even when he'd walked across the stage months ago did he feel so anxious. Even at that point he knew he still had time to spare. Now, today he didn't have that same luxury. Every second he stood there he technically still lived in Gladen Hills. The rain started coming down harder but still he couldn't move. Jeff didn't either. Calvin felt warmth across his face and he realized he'd let a few tears fall to be camouflaged by the rain.

"You want to get some lunch at the National?" Jeff asked sincerely over the pattering of rain on the ground.

"Yeah actually...I do" Calvin answered, doing his best to hide the sadness.

This is it...it's really all ending...

Chapter 46

He knew he was already late but something just couldn't make him undo the plans. It wasn't the first time he felt powerless. In fact, that feeling was becoming increasingly common. Deeper and deeper he kept falling. Some days it felt good to have it all. Other days he felt like he was fighting addiction. Jake stood there, half in impotence, the other half in complete confidence. The two sides were at war, like they had been all summer. *What am I doing?*

At last, Kelly drove up in her car and parked in the otherwise empty driveway. Jake stared at the movement outside the living room window. He didn't move or even make a sound. All he could hear was his cat running off into the basement after noticing someone coming inside. Maybe the cat even noticed *who* was coming inside, adding fuel to her desire to get downstairs in a hurry.

Kelly saw Jake standing there on the other side of the window. She waved at him with her trademark smile. Half made it seem like she was an innocent girl next door with the other half alluding to more seductive thoughts. Only after melting at her smile did he actually find the strength to move his own limbs and wave back before going to the door.

The entryway had always been dim and dark since no windows besides the one at the top of the front door allowed any light through. Most times Jake considered that to be a pretty annoying trait but today he reveled in the shadows. It almost felt like he belonged there with how much shame he felt, especially now.

A millennium may well have come and gone before he actually opened the door.

Once Kelly came inside she smiled at him again. Jake felt the negative emotions bleeding away. All his thoughts and feelings culminated in one huge burst of energy that resulted in practically throwing himself at Kelly and kissing her as hard and passionately as they ever had. It hadn't felt that good since the first time they'd kissed freshman year. He missed that feeling.

Kelly didn't seem to mind his overture because she responded in kind and they practically fell over on to the carpeting in the adjacent dining room. Jake wrapped his arms around her tightly and continued kissing her as if he was about to lose it all.

****

Scribner was pleased with the fact that Raley hadn't made it to Eric's house before he had. *And I thought I was the one padding my time.*

Interestingly, today would mark the first time he was actually in Eric's house without having Raley in tow. At the same time he still couldn't shake the fact that Raley hadn't made it over here yet because he was busy making *another* huge mistake. That would account for yet another in a growing line.

Still, now was as good an opportunity as any to talk to Biz since there hadn't been much opportunity for that yet. So much of the time when they hung out it was either when they were both hammered in Gladen Hills or Raley's Ring. Scribner couldn't remember the last time he actually talked to Eric alone while they were fully sober. It was possible it might never have happened before now.

Eric Saren was sitting in the recliner opposite the TV in the basement playing Mario Golf. Raley had mentioned that it was one of his cousins' favorite games but Scribner had never really believed that until he saw it with his own eyes. He chuckled at the sight of Eric's deep focus. *Videogame obsession must run in the family...*

"What's up man?" Scribner asked cheerfully after the latest drive. Given how far and perfect the ball had gone on screen it was safe to assume that Biz *was* in fact a practiced veteran.

"Hey Scribbs. Just chilling" Biz replied genially while keeping his focus on the game for a few more seconds to check all the incoming stats.

"Raley's not here yet?" Scribner asked even though it was pretty obvious. He hadn't seen any other cars in the driveway besides Eric's. Where his parents or little brother were was anybody's guess.

"Nah. I thought you were him actually."

"Bet you five bucks he's fucking Kelly right now" Scribner said with zero tact. There was no point in sugarcoating anything with Eric. He generally wanted to hear the core of an issue as fast as possible. That was why Scribner immediately liked him when they met. A 'no bullshit' personality was always welcome.

"Yeah right, like I'd take that bet" Eric replied coolly.

Scribner figured Biz had already come to the same conclusion. It was good to get confirmation, even if it was a fucked up conclusion. "I really hope the sex is amazing for the shit that girl is pulling" Scribner stated in disgust.

His own thoughts shifted to just what exactly he'd do for a constant supply of sex but he was always stopped right before the point he'd need to be at to let a cheating ex back in. *There's just no fucking way.*

Eric waved him off between drives. "I don't want to hear any more about that man. It's already bad enough."

"Yeah it was rough enough last time," Scribner agreed thoughtfully.

"Who are you talking to Scribbs? Riley and I had front row seats."

Scribner nodded as he took up a seat on one of the foldout chairs next to the recliner. The metal was cold but as he surveyed the basement he found a startling lack of other places to sit. It wasn't anything like the setup down at Raley's Ring where there were more chairs around the walls and beer pong table than one person would ever need. Down in Eric's basement two metal foldout chairs were the only other places to sit besides the sparsely carpeted floor.

"That's what family's for right?"

"That's what I keep telling myself," Eric answered, almost sharply.

After watching a few more shots it was clear just how good Eric really was. *He might not admit it but he's pretty good at this kind of shit too, when he tries.*

"You getting pumped to go back to school?"

"Dude I can't wait. Living at home is awful after living there. We visited a couple weeks ago when one of the brothers was moving out. It's gonna feel so great being back" Eric answered without hesitation.

Once the silence between them started resurfacing Scribner realized why he'd never been over without Raley before. The conversation topics were already wearing thin. Scribner considered that a real shame since he liked Biz when they were all drinking. Making the friendship work sober shouldn't be difficult.

"So...I'm thinking I might want to go to Rush next semester" he announced tentatively. He didn't want to make it sound like a done deal without first seeing how Eric would react. He was by far the most mature undergrad Scribner knew so his opinion carried weight. To his surprise, Eric paused the game for the first time.

"I think that's a good call man," he said sincerely. "It was for me."

Relief shot through him. "After last semester I just felt like I was missing something. I saw Justin and Raley coming back mad late from callouts or whatever while I was busy doing nothing. I don't know…I can't really explain it."

Eric smirked knowingly. "Trust me, you'll be begging for nights when you're busy doing nothing if you end up pledging AZXi or anywhere else. Callouts are without a doubt the worst part …although waking up early every day sucks too."

"Did you ever think anything like that before you pledged?"

"I'm not sure if I was thinking quite along those same lines but I can tell you that after freshman year I was done with the random frat Opens and doing the same stuff all the time. For me especially, with my classes I needed *something* to look forward to on the weekends. AZXi gives me that."

If Scribner didn't know better he'd think there was more to AZXi besides the obvious partying that Eric wasn't mentioning. Something else was clearly on his mind, whether he said it or not, it was there. *Maybe Raley knows.*

"Why'd you choose AZXi?"

"You'll find out if you come to our Rush. I don't wanna spoil anything."

****

He probably didn't even notice Jeff looking at him through the window as he drove up onto the gravel driveway. It was just as well considering he couldn't help but crack a smile as the car pulled in. Whether it was just because he was happy to see him driving up or just happy that he'd have some form of company was undecided. Jeff would've been ashamed of either reason.

Calvin was driving the same SUV he'd left Gladen Hills in a few weeks ago when they'd all helped him pack up his shit.

All summer Jeff had just assumed Gretman would do it all on his own like he had all through college but he'd surprised Jeff at the end. He had just chalked that up to the guy getting soft in his old age. That was even before he thought he saw a tear come down the guy's face that same day. With the rain it was hard to tell the difference since they were standing a few feet apart. He never said anything about it, even after they went to the National for lunch.

Today Jennifer was in the passenger seat right next to him. *Right, because spending any time apart would just be fucking crazy.* Seeing Jennifer made him remember that Dana hadn't come down to visit once all summer. And classes were starting in three weeks so there was no point in making the drive now.

Jeff left the remote sanctuary of his bedroom once the SUV parked out front. His room was basically the one spot he'd been living in since the semester had ended. Besides a few trips to the bathroom every day there wasn't much else Jeff had to venture out of his room for. Not when he had a ridiculous amount of videogames to go through and nothing but time on his hands with his internship over. Most of the new website was done but he couldn't bring himself to work on it much after Gretman left. Even with how much he was enjoying the peace and quiet he was looking forward to having an actual conversation with someone standing in front of him. Equally nice was how good the outer air felt on his skin as he opened the front door to go outside.

"I didn't think I'd see your ass again so soon" Jeff broke into the relative silence outside. Jennifer and Calvin hadn't even noticed he was there until he spoke. Jen just smirked in his direction before greeting him. Gretman too let his face show some form of happiness. It took Jeff by surprise.

"Sorry to inconvenience you Buttons. I know you're probably *real* busy these days. I probably should've called first."

Smart-ass. "As a matter of fact I am pretty busy" Jeff lied. "What brings you back to the bubble? Came for the rest of your shit?"

Calvin nodded. "Jen left a bunch of shit here too so my dad let me have the truck for the day." He stopped and paused as if suddenly uncertain. "I didn't think you were staying here all the way through."

Jeff frowned. He could've sworn he told Gretman that much at least once over the course of the months they'd been living alone at the house.

"Damn, nothing gets by you pal."

"That's why I was president buddy." Calvin immediately looked like he regretted saying that in quite the way he had. Likewise, Jeff instinctively winced at the mention of Gretman's former position. He hadn't even meant to show any emotion but it couldn't be helped. *This is why I don't play poker.*

"My bad Buttons. I didn't mean it like that" he apologized. It was as quick an apology as he'd ever heard from Gretman. That too took Jeff by surprise. He tried his best to hide the shock, for all the good it would do.

"I'll let you have that one since you got the Rho paddle back" he joked.

As much as the mention of the presidency aggravated him he didn't want the first real conversation he'd had in weeks to be an argument, especially with someone he'd probably never really see again.

Jennifer seemed content to stand back and let them talk. That was probably for the best.

"You need help with anything?" Jeff asked sincerely.

"Actually yeah, that bed is gonna be a bitch to move...if you're cool with that" Calvin smiled as he gave an answer Jeff was in no way expecting. Jeff couldn't remember hearing Gretman stutter at all before now.

"Alright, if you two are gonna do that then I'm gonna go back to the house to move my stuff out by the door. Just come get me when you're done here" Jennifer said casually as she turned to walk down Arkridge to the Rho Beta house.

As usual, Gretman led the way inside and back to his former room. Just a couple boxes of clothes and DVD's were left besides the box spring and mattress. The same one he'd no doubt fucked Jen into oblivion on multiple times. It was at that point that Jeff regretted offering to help. *There's no chance this fuckin' thing has been sanitized since they banged on it.* The thought was ever present on his mind as he helped maneuver the mattress through doorways out to the truck.

"You really thought you were gonna do that on your own?" Jeff asked incredulously between pants. It hadn't looked all that heavy but the mattress was definitely a bitch to lift and maneuver.

"Give me a break" Calvin replied between stunted breathing. "I'm being exiled here." It was clearly meant as a joke but like the president comment it also hit a little close to home, even though it affected Calvin far more than Jeff.

Silence settled in between them as Gretman turned away from the car to face the battered AZXi house. It needed a new paint job at least and probably numerous other structural upgrades but it was still *theirs*.

"No such thing Gretman. At least not here" Jeff found himself saying, absent thought. The mere idea that he was trying to comfort Calvin Gretman left a bad taste in his mouth. He couldn't tell if it was just because it was him in particular or if he would've felt that way about anybody. Once again he didn't devote too much thought to it, mostly because he was afraid of the answer.

Calvin didn't look convinced and Jeff couldn't blame him. After all they'd been through in the past semester alone it was hard to remember how exactly they'd gotten to where they were.

They didn't say much during the moving of the box spring. While relocating the boxes they stayed similarly silent. The whole thing just felt wrong. Jeff felt compelled to say something, *anything* to his alumni brother. "You know..." he began before immediately second guessing himself. "For all the shit I gave you…there's really no doubt that I'd rather have you be president over the next one." Jeff couldn't even bring himself to say J-Bro's name out loud.

"You guys will be fine," Calvin promised.

Jeff was as unconvinced as he'd been at elections three months ago. "We'll see."

"Besides, you got my number Buttons. Unless I'm not the only one who has a hard time asking for help around here…"

"I'll have to get back to you on that" Jeff replied with a smirk.

Thankfully the conversation ended there as Calvin circled the SUV to close the doors and trunk they'd been using. Jeff found himself inexplicably making his way to the driver's side window as Calvin got in. The car door closed but the window was still down as it had been when they'd arrived.

"Take care of yourself" Jeff said once Calvin started the engine. Jeff was sounding less like himself the longer the day went on. *Jesus I'm getting soft too.*

"Likewise Buttons" Calvin smiled back.

To cap it all off Jeff reached out his arm and waited for Gretman to do the same. They shook hands one last time. *Index fingers to the wrist.* Jeff had to remind himself how AZXis shook hands because all his focus was somehow shifted to what exactly he was hoping to accomplish with the gesture.

The truck pulled out of the driveway shortly after. As it reached Arkridge Avenue Calvin made eye contact with Jeff again. They each gave the other a half nod before the SUV started down the road toward the Rho Beta house near the corner of Castle Lane.

Jeff stood there, frozen in time. He could barely see the outline of the truck through the hedges that separated AZXi from the Lambdas as it went down the road. The strangest sensation came over him as he waited for the truck to vanish into the Rho Beta parking lot. Was Jeff Chester going to miss Calvin Gretman?

****

Once the AZXi house was out of sight in the rear-view mirror Calvin found himself holding back tears in much the same way as the last time he'd driven away from the house. Today, he kept his emotions in check. Crying once about it had made him feel enough like a bitch to stop it from ever happening again. *Buttons was right. Even with Jen's help, moving that mattress and box spring would've been a huge pain in the ass.* It made no sense to him that even with that in mind he still was about to say he didn't need help. *Do I really like doing it all on my own that much?*

Calvin didn't have much time to ponder the implications because he saw Jennifer lugging a few smaller boxes through the side entrance of the Rho Beta house. He quickly unbuckled his seat belt to help his girlfriend. Thankfully, she'd already moved everything she planned to take with them to the steps. Calvin made quick work of getting everything from there to the truck.

"Is that everything then? You ready to go?" he asked, hoping there wasn't another stack of boxes hidden inside. *Please let this be it.*

"Yeah babe, what about you?"

"I think so yeah" he found himself answering. He knew there was nothing else of his in the house but couldn't answer so surely.

"Alright then let's get going. I told your parents we'd be back before dinner."

Calvin smiled. Ever since she'd moved into his hometown Jen and his mom had bonded in a way that had never really been possible before. Her latest comment only served to solidify that. That his mother and girlfriend could make plans like that without including him directly was equal parts scary and comforting.

"OK, let's go" he stated with as much confidence as he could. "You OK?"

"Yeah I'm good" he assured her.

"Then why aren't we moving babe?" Jen teased him.

Calvin had been so caught up in his own thoughts he hadn't the truck was still in 'park'. He would've felt some semblance of shame with anybody else but he knew Jen didn't mind.

"Maybe I should drive?" Jen offered soothingly as she rubbed his shoulder.

"I can handle it" Calvin promised her. It was as much a statement to convince her as it was for himself. *I better be able to handle it.*

Slowly he put the car in reverse and left the Rho Beta parking lot. If Jen was annoyed at how slow they were moving she didn't say anything.

Finally, between checking his rear-view and looking behind him he looked at her. To his surprise she wasn't looking back at him but rather at the house they were pulling away from. He found himself easing their exit all the more just so he too could take in the sight. It surprised him even now that he'd likely miss that house a lot too. Every Bids he'd ever spent with AZXi had been at Rho Beta. The last one had been capped off with some apparently insane shit from the

Alpha Epsilon class. *Just another story I wasn't part of. There'll be plenty of those next semester.*

After another minute passed he knew he couldn't stall their exit anymore so he returned his gaze behind them as he pulled back onto Arkridge Avenue. Jennifer's eyes were still locked on the sorority house. Calvin gave it one last glance before putting the truck in drive and pulling away down the road.

When they reached the corner of Arkridge and Castle, the National came into view and Calvin again slowed their advance. It took far longer to turn onto Castle than it rightfully should have since there were no cars going by but again Jen didn't say a word. *I can't go that slowly down every street in this town. We'll never get back.*

Calvin sighed and sped up.

There was going to be a cornerstone of their old lives wherever they went, whichever way they exited Gladen Hills. Every corner had a memory, every building had a story, and everywhere they went was a previous chapter in their lives. Everything looked and felt surreal.

Instead of feeling the awesome sadness and depression that had accompanied his last trip out of town weeks ago he felt something else. Calvin Gretman felt happy and thankful that he'd been a part of this world at all. To experience it all with the friends and brothers he'd come to know and respect was a gift he'd never let himself forget. He knew in that moment when everything was fading into the rearview mirror what he wished he could've seen all along: all of it was one big wild story worth telling…

****

Jake couldn't even take Kelly upstairs to his bedroom as soon as he'd attacked her with his lips. He honestly hadn't even thought about that until now when they were both lying half-naked on the carpeted floor of the dining room. Where they did it was irrelevant before this moment. Jake needed to feel Kelly's body again, to feel the inside of her, to feel connected. Even after dating for a year he was still craving her every day.

Once he caught his breath he finally found the words he was looking for. "You're amazing Kel."

"Is it just me or is it getting better and better?"

"Definitely it is. Every time is just fuckin' ridiculous."

It sounded like an exaggeration but it wasn't. Every time they had sex nothing else even came close to mattering. The two of them just lied there on the ground staring up at the white ceiling. Jake had wrapped his right arm around Kelly so that she was again resting her head on his chest as it went up and down heavily in the aftermath.

"Your birthday is coming up right baby?" Kelly asked, as if she didn't know the answer. She knew full well when his birthday was almost better than he did.

He smiled at the comment. "I believe it is."

"What do you want to do?"

"You."

Kelly leaned upright to look down into his eyes. She was smiling her classically seductive smile and Jake felt his blood rushing all over again. "I mean where do you want to go?"

"I hadn't really given it a lot of thought," he confessed. His mind had been so wrapped up in a hundred different things that his birthday plans hadn't really been important enough to consider. Even now there were more pressing matters. Like how he was going to explain how late he was in getting over to Eric's. With any luck, Scribbs wouldn't be getting there 'til around now so maybe his absence wouldn't be noticed.

"Do you want to spend it together?" Kelly asked tentatively.

Jake sat up while sliding his pants back up. "Of course I want to spend it with you Kel. I mean…we are…together…right?"

Kelly leaned it to kiss him as passionately as anything they'd experienced when she'd come into the house. It felt warm and comforting having their lips touch in such a loving way.

"Yes Jake. We're together" she smiled back at him after the kiss ended.

"Good" he smiled. "Then you're stuck with me for my birthday."

Kelly smiled warmly before lying back down on his chest. The carpet was far from comfortable but there was no other place Jake would rather be. Only the sounds of their breathing were echoing throughout the room. It was the most content Jake had felt in a long time.

After the return trip to Gladen Hills a few weeks back he'd started to feel more confident about his station at school. That in turn helped him whenever he hung out with Kelly. She seemed to be enjoying this newer, happier, more confident version of Jake. That made their conversations better and the sex hotter.

Everything seemed to be looking up the further into the summer he went.

Now that he and Kelly were officially back together he knew that her requesting a Facebook relationship update wasn't far off. That would likely set off a whole new chain of events for the upcoming semester. God only knew how Eric and Riley would react. Jake found himself not feeling all that apprehensive about everything, strange as that was. Now that he was starting to feel more comfortable with Alpha Zeta Xi he didn't think he'd rely as heavily on his two cousins going forward.

What excited Jake more than anything else was feeling like the next semester was going to be a whole lot different than what had come before...

47025614R00392

Made in the USA
Middletown, DE
15 August 2017